Your Face Tomorrow

3 Poison, Shadow and Farewell

JAVIER MARÍAS

Your Face Tomorrow

3 Poison, Shadow and Farewell

Translated from the Spanish by
Margaret Jull Costa

Chatto & Windus

LONDON

Published by Chatto & Windus 2009

2 4 6 8 10 9 7 5 3

Copyright © Javier Marías 2007
English translation © Margaret Jull Costa 2009

First published in Spain as *Tu rostro mañana, 3 Veneno y sombre y adiós* by Alfaguara,
Grupo Santillana de Ediciones, S.A.

Published by arrangement with Mercedes Casanovas Agencia Literaria, Barcelona,
and in association with New Directions, New York.

The publication of this book has been assisted with a translation subvention from the Director of
Books, Archives, and Libraries of the Cultural Ministry of Spain.

Javier Marías has asserted his right under the Copyright, Designs
and Patents Act 1988 to be identified as the author of this work

The publisher is grateful to Macmillan for permission to quote from 'Duino Elegy', *The Selected
Poetry of Rainer Maria Rilke*, ed. and trans. Stephen Mitchell, Picador, 1980. Extracts from
'The Love Song of J. Alfred Prufrock', *Collected Poems 1909–1962* and 'Little Gidding' taken from
Four Quartets © The Estate of T.S. Eliot and reproduced by permission of Faber and Faber Ltd.

First published in Great Britain in 2009 by
Chatto & Windus
Random House, 20 Vauxhall Bridge Road,
London SW1V 2SA
www.rbooks.co.uk

Addresses for companies within The Random House Group Limited can be found at: www.
randomhouse.co.uk/offices.htm

The Random House Group Limited Reg. No. 954009

A CIP catalogue record for this book
is available from the British Library

ISBN 9780701183424

The Random House Group Limited supports The Forest Stewardship
Council (FSC), the leading international forest certification organisation.
All our titles that are printed on Greenpeace approved FSC certified paper
carry the FSC logo. Our paper procurement policy can be found at:
www.rbooks.co.uk/environment

Printed and bound in Great Britain by
CPI Mackays, Chatham, ME5 8TD

For Carmen López M, who has been kind
enough to hear me out patiently until the end

And for my friend Sir Peter Russell and
my father, Julián Marías,
who generously lent me
a large part of their lives,
in memoriam

V

Poison

'While it isn't ever something we would wish for, we would all nonetheless always prefer it to be the person beside us who dies, whether on a mission or in battle, in an air squadron or under bombardment or in the trenches when there were trenches, in a mugging or a raid on a shop or when a group of tourists is kidnapped, in an earthquake, an explosion, a terrorist attack, in a fire, it doesn't matter: even if it's our colleague, brother, father or even our child, however young. Or even the person we most love, yes, even them, anyone but us. Whenever someone covers another person with his own body, or places himself in the path of a bullet or a knife, these are all extraordinary exceptions, which is why they stand out, and most are fictitious and only appear in novels and films. The few real-life instances are the result of unthinking reflexes or else dictated by a strong sense of decorum of a sort that is becoming ever rarer, there are some who couldn't bear for a child or a loved one to pass into the next world with, as their final thought, the knowledge that a parent or lover had done nothing to prevent their death, had not sacrificed themselves, had not given their own life to save them, it's as if such people had internalised a hierarchy of the living, which seems so quaint and antiquated now, whereby children have more right to live than women and women more than men and men more than the old, or something of the sort, at least that's how it used to be, and such old-fashioned chivalry still persists in a dwindling band of people, those who still believe in that decorum, which, when you think about it, is quite absurd, after all, what do such final thoughts, such transient feelings of

3

pique or disappointment matter when, a moment later, the person concerned will be dead and incapable of feeling either pique or disappointment, incapable, indeed, of thinking? It's true that there are still a few people who harbour this deep-seated belief and to whom it does matter, and they are, in fact, acting so that the person they are saving can bear witness, so that he or she will think well of them and remember them with eternal admiration and gratitude; what they don't realise at that decisive moment, or at least not fully, is that they will never enjoy that admiration or gratitude because they will be the ones who, a moment later, will be dead.'

And what came into my head while he was talking was an expression that was both difficult to grasp and possibly untranslatable, which is why, at first, I didn't mention it to Tupra, it would have taken me too long to explain. My initial thought was: 'It's what we call "*vergüenza torera*", literally "a bullfighter's sense of shame",' and then: 'Because bullfighters, of course, have loads of witnesses, a whole arena full, plus sometimes a TV audience of millions, so it's perfectly understandable that they should think: "I'd rather leave here with a ruptured femoral artery or dead than be thought a coward in the presence of all these people who will go on to talk about it endlessly and for ever." Bullfighters fear narrative horror like the plague, that final defining wrong move, they really care about how their lives end, it's the same with Dick Dearlove and almost any other public figure, I suppose, whose story is played out in full view of everyone at every stage or chapter, right up to the denouement that can mark a whole life and give it an entirely false and unfair meaning.' And then I couldn't help saying it out loud, even though it meant briefly interrupting Tupra. But it did, after all, add to what he was saying and was also a way of pretending that this was a dialogue:

'That's what we call "*vergüenza torera*".' And I said the two words in Spanish, then immediately translated them. 'I'll explain to you exactly what it means another day, since you don't have bullfighters here.' Although at that moment, I wasn't even sure there would be another day, another day at his side, not one.

'OK, but don't forget. And no, you're right, we don't have

bullfighters here.' Tupra was always curious to hear the turns of phrase in my own language about which I occasionally enlightened him, whenever they seemed relevant or were particularly striking. Now, however, he was enlightening me (I knew where he was heading, and both he and the path he was taking aroused my curiosity over and above the foreseeable revulsion I would feel at the end of the journey), and so he continued: 'From there to letting someone die in order to save yourself is only a step, and trying to ensure that someone else dies in your place or even bringing that about (you know the kind of thing, it's him or me) is just one more short step, and both steps are easily taken, especially the first, in fact, in an extreme situation, almost everyone takes that step. How else explain why it is that in a fire at a theatre or a disco more people are crushed or trampled to death than burned or asphyxiated, or why when a ship sinks there are people who don't even wait for the lifeboat to be full before lowering it into the water, just so that they can get away quickly and without being burdened by other passengers, or why the expression "Every man for himself" exists, which, after all, means discarding all consideration for others and reverting to the law of the jungle, which we all accept and to which we return without a second's thought, even though we've spent more than half our lives with that law in abeyance or under control. The reality is that we're doing violence to ourselves by not following and obeying it at all times and in all circumstances, but even so we apply that law far more often than we acknowledge, but surreptitiously, under cover of a thin veneer of civility or in the guise of other more respectful laws and regulations, more slowly and with numerous detours and stages along the way, it's all very laborious but, deep down, it's the law of the jungle that rules, that holds sway. It is, think about it. Among individuals and among nations.'

Tupra had used the English equivalent of '*Sálvese quien pueda*', which means literally 'Save yourself if you can', whereas 'Every man for himself' denotes perhaps even fewer scruples: let each man save his own skin and worry only about himself, save himself by whatever means are available to him, and let others look after themselves, the weaker, the slower, the more ingenuous and the more stupid (and the more protective, too, like my son Guillermo). At that moment, you can allow yourself to shove and trample and kick others out of the way, or use an oar to smash in the head of anyone trying to hold on to your boat and get into it when it's already sliding down into the water with you and yours inside it, and there's no room for anyone else, or you simply don't want to share it or run the risk of capsizing. The situations may be different, but that commanding voice belongs to the same family or type as three other voices: the voice that issues an instruction to fire at will, to slaughter, to beat a disorderly retreat or to flee en masse; the one that orders to shoot at close range and indiscriminately whoever you happen to see or catch, the voice urging us to bayonet or knife someone, to take no prisoners, to leave not a soul alive ('Give no quarter', is the command, or worse 'Show no mercy'); and the voice that tells us to fly, to withdraw and break ranks, *pêle-mêle* in French or pell-mell in its English form; soldiers fleeing en masse when there are not enough escape routes to flee alone, each listening only to his own survival instinct and therefore indifferent to the fate of his companions, who no longer count and who have, in fact, ceased to be companions, even though we're all still in uniform and feel, more or less, the same fear in that shared flight.

I sat looking at Tupra in the light of the lamps and in the light of the fire, the latter making his complexion more coppery than usual, as if he had Native American blood in his veins – it occurred to me then that his lips could perhaps be Sioux – his complexion now not so much the colour of beer as of whisky. He had not yet reached his destination, he had only begun his journey and would not be slow about it, and I was sure that sooner or later he would ask me that question again: 'Why can't one do that? Why can't one, according to you, go around beating people up and killing them?' And I still had no answers that would convince him, I had to keep thinking about something we never do think about because we take it as universally agreed, as immutable and normal and right. The answers going round in my head were fine for the majority, so much so that anyone could have given them, but not for Reresby, if he still was Reresby or perhaps he never ceased being him and was always all of them, simultaneously, Ure and Dundas and Reresby and Tupra, and who knows how many other names in the course of his turbulent life in all those different places, although now he did seem to have settled down. Doubtless his names were legion and he wouldn't be able to remember every last one or, indeed, every first one, people who accumulate many experiences tend to forget what they did at a particular time or at various times. There's not a trace in them of who they were then, and it's as if they had never been.

'But in those situations, there are always people willing to lend a hand,' I murmured feebly. 'People willing to help someone else into the boat or risk their own life by rescuing someone from the flames. Not everyone flees in terror or runs for cover. Not everyone simply abandons strangers to their fate.'

And my eyes remained fixed on the flames. When we'd arrived, there had still been the embers of a fire in the grate, and it had taken Tupra little effort to revive it, doubtless because he enjoyed an open fire or else to save on heating, which, I noticed, was turned down low – a lot of English people, even the filthy rich, like to economise on such things. This meant either that he must have servants or else didn't live alone, there in his three-storey house which was, as I'd speculated, in Hampstead, a very plush area, a place for the wealthy, perhaps he earned much more than I imagined (not that I'd given it much thought), he was, after all, only a functionary, however high up he was in the hierarchy, and I didn't think he was particularly high up. So perhaps it wasn't his house but Beryl's, and he was there thanks to their as yet unannulled marriage, or more likely thanks to his first marriage and to an advantageous divorce settlement, Wheeler had told me that Tupra had been married twice and that Beryl was considering trying to win him back because, since their separation, her life had signally failed to improve. Or perhaps Tupra enjoyed other sources of income apart from that of his known profession, or perhaps the extras that this brought him ('the frequent pleasant surprises, paid in kind', as Peter put it) far exceeded my imaginative capabilities. It seemed to me improbable that he would have inherited such a house from the first British Tupra or, indeed, from the second, one or the other must have been immigrants from some low-ranking country. Although who knows, perhaps his grandfather or father had been quick off the mark and swiftly amassed a fortune, anything's possible, by dirty dealings or through usury or banking, it comes to the same thing, such fortunes appear in a flash, like lightning, but with one difference, they persist and grow, or perhaps those first Tupras had married into money, unlikely, unless they already possessed the gift of making themselves irresistible to women and that gift was the legacy they bequeathed to Tupra, their descendant.

We were in a large sitting room, which was clearly not the

only one in the house (I'd glimpsed another from the corridor, unless it was just a billiards room, for it contained a green baize table), well furnished, well carpeted, with very expensive book-shelves (something I do know about) and on them some very fine and costly books (I can tell that, too, from afar, at a single glance), and I spotted on the walls what was certainly a Stubbs equine portrait and what looked to me like a Jean Béraud, a large-scale work depicting some elegant casino of the time, at Baden-Baden or Monte Carlo, and a possible De Nittis of rather more modest dimensions (I know about paintings as well), soci-ety people in a park with thoroughbreds in the background, and none of these pictures, it seemed to me, were copies. Someone in that house knew or had known a thing or two about art, someone keen on horse racing or on betting in general, and my host, of course, was keen on the former, as he was on soccer or at least on the Chelsea Blues. To acquire such works one doesn't necessarily have to be a pound or euro multimillionaire, but you do need either to have some surplus cash or to be absolutely sure that more money will be forthcoming after each extravagance. The place felt more like the home of a well-to-do diplomat or some eminent professor who doesn't depend on his salary – the kind who works not so much to earn a living as to gain recogni-tion – than the home of an army employee appointed to carry out certain obscure and indefinable civilian tasks, I couldn't for-get that the initials MI6 and MI5 meant Military Intelligence; and then it occurred to me that Tupra might be a high-ranking officer, a colonel, a major or perhaps the commander of a frig-ate, like Ian Fleming and his character James Bond, especially if he was from the navy, from the former OIC, the Operational Intelligence Centre, which, according to Wheeler, had provided the best men, or from the NID, the Naval Intelligence Divi-sion, of which it was part. I was gradually reading and learning about the organisation and distribution of these services from the books that Tupra kept in his office and which I sometimes leafed through when I was alone, working late at the building with no name, or arrived early to start or to finish some report, and when I might find the young Pérez Nuix drying her bare

9

torso with a towel because she'd spent the night there, or so she said.

I fixed my weary eyes on the fire that Reresby had lit and which contributed in no small part to transforming his sitting room into a story-book setting, a place of enchantment, and there came into my mind the image of a more welcoming and, in fact, unusual, but, how I can put it, not entirely non-existent London, the London of Wendy's parents in the Disney version of *Peter Pan*, with its square windowpanes framed by strips of white lacquered wood and its equally white bookshelves, its clusters of chimneys and its peaceful attic rooms, at least that's how I recalled the home I had seen in the dark in my childhood, cartoons so comforting that one wanted to live in them. Yes, Tupra's house was cosy and comfortable, the kind of house that helps you to forget about things and relax, it also had something about it of the house inhabited by Professor Higgins, as played by Rex Harrison in *My Fair Lady*, although his was in Maryle-bone and Wendy's in Bloomsbury, I think, and Tupra's was there in Hampstead, further to the north. Perhaps he needed these benign, tranquil surroundings in order to cancel out and isolate himself from his many intersecting, murky and even violent ac-tivities, perhaps his background as a low-born foreigner or his origins in Bethnal Green or in some other depressing area had made him aspire to a mode of decor so opposed to the sordid that it's almost only ever found in fiction, intended for children if they're by Barrie or for adults if they're by Dickens, he was bound to have seen that film based on the work of the former, the dramatist, when it came out, as did every child in our day in any country in this world of ours, I'd seen it dozens of times in my own childhood world.

He took out one of his Egyptian cigarettes and offered it to me, he was my host now and was mechanically aware of that, he'd also offered me a drink which, for the moment, I'd de-clined, he'd poured himself a port not from an ordinary bottle, but from one with a little medal about its neck, like those passed swiftly round in a clockwise direction by the guests (there were always several bottles, they never stopped coming) during the dessert course at the high tables to which I was occasionally invited by colleagues in my distant Oxford days, perhaps *his* Oxford colleagues still sent him some of that extraordinary port wine from the college cellars and which one can find nowhere else. I hadn't kept up with how much Tupra had drunk during that long, interminable evening which had still not yet ended, although he had, I imagined, drunk no less than I had, and I didn't want and couldn't hold another drop, he, however, seemed unaffected by the alcohol or else its ravages were not apparent. The quantity of alcohol consumed, however, had had nothing to do with his terrorising and punishing or beating or thrashing of De la Garza, for he had behaved throughout with precision and calculation. Who knows, though, perhaps it *had* influenced his decision to demonstrate to De la Garza his variant – varying – modes of death and to leave both De la Garza and me alive so that we would always remember them, it's rare for the resolve to do something and the actual execution of that act to coincide, even though the two things may follow on and appear to be simultaneous, perhaps he'd taken that decision when his head was still fuzzy, still hot, and his head had cleared and cooled during the few minutes I'd spent waiting for him in the Disabled toilet along with our trusting victim, for I'd tricked De la Garza into going there with the false promise of a line of cocaine, although I didn't know at the time why I was putting him, the victim, where I'd been asked to put him or that the promise was a mere pretext. I should have imagined it, I should have foreseen it. I should have refused to have anything to do with it. I'd prepared him for Tupra, served him up on a plate, I had, in the end, been a part of it all. I was about to ask him, out of curiosity: 'Was it real cocaine you gave the poor devil?' But, as often happens after long silences, we both spoke at once and he got in just a fraction of a second before me, in order to reply to the last thing I'd said:

'Yes, of course,' murmured Reresby almost lazily. 'You'll always get the kind of person who watches himself acting, who sees himself as if in some continuous performance. Who believes there'll be witnesses to report his generous or contemptible death and that this is what matters most. Or who, if there *are* no witnesses, invents them – the eye of God, the world stage, or whatever. Who believes that the world only exists to the extent that it's reported and events only to the extent that they're recounted, even though it's highly unlikely that anyone will bother to recount them, or to recount those particular facts, I mean, the facts relating to each individual. The vast majority of things simply happen and there neither is nor ever was any record of them, those we hear about are an infinitesimal fraction of what goes on. Most lives and, needless to say, most deaths, are forgotten as soon as they've occurred and leave not the slightest trace, or become unknown soon afterwards, after a few years, a few decades, a century, which, as you know, is, in reality, a very short time. Take battles, for example, think how important they were for those who took part in them and, sometimes, for their compatriots, think how many of those battles now mean nothing to us, not even their names, we don't even know which war they belonged to, more than that, we don't care. What do the names Ulundi and Beersheba, or Gravelotte and Rezonville, or Namur, or Maiwand, Paardeberg and Mafeking, or Mohacs, or Nájera, mean to anyone nowadays?' – He mispronounced that last name, Nájera. – 'But there are many others who resist, incapable of accepting their own insignificance or invisibility, I mean once they're dead and converted into past matter, once they're no longer present to defend their existence and to declare: "Hey, I'm here. I can intervene, I have influence, I can do good or cause harm, save or destroy, and even change the course of the world, because I haven't yet disappeared."' – 'I'm still here, therefore I must have been here before,' I thought or remembered having thought as I was cleaning up the red stain I found on Wheeler's stairs and the rim of which I had to work hard to erase (if, that is, there ever had been such a stain, I doubted it more and more), and the effort made by things and people to keep us from saying: 'No, this never happened, it never was, it neither strode the world nor trod the earth, it never existed and never occurred.' – 'Those individuals you mention,' continued Reresby, whose voice had gradually and unexpectedly taken on a more elevated tone, 'they're not so very different from Dick Dearlove, according to your interpretation of him. They suffer from narrative horror – isn't that what you called it – or narrative disgust. They fear that the manner in which they end their life will blot and taint everything, that some belated or final episode will cast its shadow over what came before, covering and cancelling it: don't let it be said that I didn't help, that I didn't risk my life for the sake of others, that I didn't sacrifice myself for my loved ones, they think at the most absurd moments, when there's no one there to see them or when those who can see them, principally themselves, are about to die. Don't let anyone say I was a coward, a callous swine, a vulture, a murderer, they think, feeling the glare of the spotlight, when no one is shining a light on them at all or ever going to talk about them because they're too insignificant. They'll be as anonymous when dead as they were alive. It will be as if they had never existed.' He fell silent for a moment, took a sip of his port and added: 'You and I will be like them, the kind who leave no mark, so it won't matter what we've done, no one will bother to recount or even to investigate it. I don't know about you, but I don't belong to that type, the ones you mean, the people who are like Dick Dearlove even though they're not celebrities, quite the contrary. The ones who, in our jargon, suffer from some form of K–M complex.' He stopped, gave a sideways glance at the fire and added: 'I know that I'm invisible and will be more so when I'm dead, when I'm nothing but past matter. Dumb matter.'

'K–M?' I asked, ignoring his final prophetic, oracular words. 'What's that? Killing–Murdering?'

'No, it doesn't mean that, although it could, it had never occurred to me,' replied Tupra, smiling slightly through the smoke. 'It means Kennedy–Mansfield. Mulryan insisted on the second name because he's always been fascinated by the actress Jayne Mansfield, a favourite of his since childhood, and he bet us that she would linger in everyone's memory and not just because of the singular way in which she died; he was quite wrong of course. The truth is that she was the dream of every boy or adolescent. And of every truck driver. Do you remember her?

13

No, probably not,' he went on, without giving me time to reply, 'which is yet further proof of how inappropriate and gratuitous and exaggerated that "M" was when it came to giving a name to the complex. Anyway, we've called it that for quite some time now, it's become the custom, and it's used almost exclusively in-house. Although, believe it or not,' he said, correcting himself, 'I've known some high officials use it too, having picked it up from us presumably, and the term has even appeared in the odd book.'

'I believe I do remember Jayne Mansfield,' I said, taking advantage of that minimal pause.

'Really?' Tupra seemed surprised. 'Well, you're certainly old enough, but I wasn't sure if such frivolous films would have made it into your country. During the dictatorship, I mean.'

'The only thing we weren't cut off from was the movies. Franco loved films and had his own projection room in the palace of El Pardo. We saw almost everything, apart from a few things that the censor strictly forbade (they weren't forbidden to Franco, of course: he enjoyed being shocked, the way priests do, at the vile deeds committed in the outside world from which he was protecting us). Others were cut or had the dialogue changed in the dubbing process, but most movies got shown. Yes, I think I do remember Jayne Mansfield. I can't quite recollect her face, but I can recall her general appearance. She was a voluptuous platinum blonde, wasn't she, very curvaceous. She made comedies in the '50s and possibly the '60s. And she had fairly big boobs.'

'Fairly big? Good grief, you clearly don't remember her at all, Jack. Wait, I'm going to show you a funny photo, I have it here.' Tupra had little difficulty in finding it. He got up, went over to one of the shelves, wiggled his fingers about as if he were trying the combination of a safe and then took from the shelf what seemed to be a hefty volume but which turned out to be a wooden rather than a metal box, disguised as a book. He took it down, opened it there and then, and rummaged for a couple of minutes among the letters kept inside, heaven knows who they were from, given that he knew exactly where to locate them and kept them so easily to hand. While he was doing this, he tapped the holder of his Rameses II cigarette and nonchalantly tipped ash onto the carpet, as if it didn't matter. He must have had servants. Permanent staff. Finally, he carefully removed a postcard from an envelope, using his index and middle fingers as tweezers, then held it out to me. 'Here it is. Take a look. You'll remember her clearly now, as clear as clear. In a sense, she's unforgettable, especially if you discovered her as a boy. You can understand Mulryan's fascination. Our friend must be more lecherous than he seems. Doubtless in private. Or in his day perhaps,' he added.

I took the black-and-white photo from Tupra – like him with index and middle fingers – and it immediately made me smile, even while he was commenting on it in words very similar to those going through my own head. Seated at a table, elbow to elbow, in the middle of supper or before or possibly afterwards (there are a few disorienting bowls), are two actresses famous at the time, to the left of the image Sophia Loren and to the right Jayne Mansfield, whose face ceased to be vague the moment I saw it again. The Italian, who was herself far from flat-chested – she had been another dream for many men, a long-lasting one too – is wearing a dress with a very modest neckline and she's giving Mansfield a sideways look, but making no attempt to conceal the fact, her eyes drawn irresistibly, with a mixture of envy, perplexity and fright, or perhaps incredulous alarm, to the far more abundant and far barer breasts of her American colleague, which really are very eye-catching and prominent (they make Loren's bust seem positively paltry in comparison), and even more so in an age when augmentative surgery was unlikely or certainly infrequent. Mansfield's breasts, as far as one can judge, are natural, not stiff and hard, but endowed with a pleasant, mobile softness – or so one would imagine ('If only I'd encountered breasts like that tonight and not Flavia's rock-hard pair,' I thought fleetingly), and must have caused a tremendous stir in that restaurant – whether in Rome or America who knows – the waiter who can be seen in the background, between the two women, maintains a praiseworthy impassivity, although we can only see his body, his face is in shadow, and one does wonder if he isn't

perhaps using his white napkin as a shield or screen. To the left of Mansfield is a male guest of whom one can see only a hand holding a spoon, but his eyes must be turned as sharply to the right as Loren's are to the left, although probably somewhat more avidly. Unlike Loren, the platinum blonde is looking straight at the camera with a cordial but slightly frozen smile, and although not totally unconcerned – she's perfectly aware of what she has on show – she's quite at ease: she is the novelty in Rome (if they are in Rome) and she has put the local beauty in the shade, made her look almost prim. A childhood memory of that pretty woman, Jayne Mansfield, came to me then and with it a title, *The Sheriff of Fractured Jaw* (or *La rubia y el sheriff* – *The Blonde and the Sheriff* – as it was known in Spain): a large mouth and large eyes, she was all large, vulgar beauty. To a boy at any rate, and to many grown men too, like me.

This was what Tupra was saying and what I was thinking, while he continued to enlighten me. He gave occasional short laughs, he found both the photo and the situation amusing, and they were.

'May I look to see what caption they gave it? May I turn it over?' I asked, for I wasn't going to read, without permission, what had been written on the back by the person who had originally sent it.

'Yes, please do,' Tupra replied with a generous gesture.

There was no noteworthy or imaginative or saucy caption, only 'Loren and Mansfield, The Ludlow Collection', that much I saw, I didn't bother trying to read the message someone had scrawled for him in felt-tip years ago, two or three sentences, punctuated by the odd jokey exclamation mark, in a possibly feminine hand, large and rather round, my eye caught the signature for a second, just an initial, 'B', perhaps for Beryl, and the word 'fear'. A woman with a sense of humour, if it was a woman who had sent it to him. A very unusual sense of humour, out of the ordinary, because a photo like that mainly causes amusement among men, which is why I laughed out loud at Sophia Loren's apprehensive sideways look, at the way she distrustfully shrinks back from that triumphant, intimidating, transatlantic décolletage, Reresby and I laughed in unison with the kind of laughter that creates a disinterested bond between people, as had happened once before in his office, when I was telling him about the hypothetical clogs worn by some minor tyrant – albeit elected, voted in – and about the patriotically starry print on the shirt I saw him wearing once on television, and when I said 'liki-liki', that comical word which it's impossible to hear or read without immediately wanting to repeat it: *liki-liki*, like that. I had asked myself then, apropos of that disarming laughter, his and mine united, whether, in the future, he or I would be the one to be disarmed, or if, perhaps, both of us would.

'He's got some balls,' I thought crudely, in De la Garza style, feeling irritated, 'he's managed to make me laugh out loud. Only a while ago I was furious with him and still am, those feelings won't just go away; a while ago I was witness to his brutality, afraid he was going to kill a poor wretch with methodical coldness, that he was going to cut his throat for no real reason, if there ever can be a reason for doing so; that he was going to strangle De la Garza with his own ridiculous hairnet and drown him in the blue water; and I saw from up close the beating he gave him without ever using his own hands to deal a single blow, despite the threatening gloves he was wearing.' Tupra hadn't forgotten about those gloves: the first thing he'd done after getting the fire going again was to take them out of his overcoat pocket and throw them on the flames along with the pieces of toilet paper he'd wrapped them in. The smell of burning leather and wool was finally fading and what predominated was that of burning wood, the gloves must have dried off considerably since we left the Disabled toilet, 'The smell won't last,' he'd said as he threw them onto the fire with an almost mechanical gesture, like someone putting down his keys or loose change when he arrives home. He had kept them with him until he had the opportunity to destroy them, I noticed, and in his own house too. He was cautious even when he had no need to be. 'And now there he is, perfectly at ease, showing me a funny photo and cheerily commenting on it. (The sword is still in his overcoat, when will he take it out, when will he put it away?) And I'm equally at ease, seeing the funny side of the scene in the photo and laughing with him – oh, he's a pleasant fellow all right, in the first and the next-to-last instance, we can't help it, we get on well, we like each other.' (He wasn't so pleasant in the *last* instance, but that didn't usually occur, although that night it had.) I quickly traced back in my mind (it did little for my recovered anger, but it was better than nothing) why he had shown me the postcard in the first place. For a few moments, I'd forgotten what that photo was doing there, and what he and I were doing there. It was no night for laughter, and yet we'd laughed together only a short time after his transformation into Sir Punishment. Or Sir Revenge perhaps. But if the latter, what had he been avenging? It had been so over-the-top, so excessive, and for what? A trifle, a nothing.

I returned the postcard to him, he was standing next to my armchair, looking over my shoulder at me looking at the two actresses or bygone sex symbols – one far more remote than the other – sharing or rather studying my unexpected amusement.

'Why Jayne Mansfield?' I asked. 'What's she got to do with Kennedy? I presume you mean President Kennedy? Was he her lover too? Isn't it Marilyn Monroe who was supposed to have had an affair with him – didn't she sing him some sexy version of "Happy Birthday" at a party? Mansfield must have been an imitation of her.'

'Oh, well, there were several of them,' said Tupra, while he was returning the photo to its envelope, the envelope to the box and the box to the shelf, all in order. 'We even had one in England, Diana Dors. You probably don't remember her. She was pretty much for national consumption only. She was coarser, not bad-looking or a bad actress, but with a rather stupid face and eyebrows too dark for her platinum blonde locks, I don't know why she didn't have them dyed as well. In fact, I met her when she was in her forties, we went to some of the same places in Soho that were fashionable then, in the late '60s and early '70s, she was already beginning to get a bit matronly, but she'd always been drawn to the bohemian lifestyle, she thought it made her more youthful, more modern. Yes, she was coarser than Mansfield, and somehow darker too, not so jolly,' he added, as if this were something he had pondered for a moment. 'But if *she'd* been sitting at the table in that postcard, I don't know who would have been most startled. In her youth, Diana Dors had a real hourglass figure.' And he made the familiar movement with his hands that many men make to indicate a woman with a lot of curves, I think the Coca-Cola bottle imitated that gesture and not the other way round. I hadn't seen anyone do that for a long time, well, gestures, like words, fall into disuse, because they're nearly always substitutes for words and therefore share the same fate: they're a way of saying something without using words, sometimes very serious things, which, in the past, might have proved the motive for a duel, and even nowadays can provoke violence and death. And so even when nothing is said, one can still speak and signify and tell, what a curse; if I'd patted myself under my chin two or three times with the back of my hand in Manoia's presence, he would have understood me to be making the Italian gesture indicating scornful dismissal of one's companion and would have unsheathed his sword against me, if he, too, had one hidden about his person, who knows, compared with him, Reresby seemed reasonable and mild.

Yes, Tupra was distracting me with his anecdotes, his conversation – or was it merely chatter? I was still furious, even though I sometimes forgot to be, and I wanted to show him that I was, to call him to account for his savage behaviour, properly and more thoroughly than I had during our false farewell opposite the door to my house in the square, but he kept leading me from one thing to another, never getting to the point of what he had announced or almost demanded that I should hear, and I doubted if he would ever tell me anything about Constantinople or Tangiers, places he had mentioned while sitting at the wheel of his car, he'd specialised in Medieval History at Oxford, although you'd never know it, and in that field he might well have been an unofficial disciple of Toby Rylands, who, to his regret, had very briefly been Toby Wheeler, in that distant, forgotten New Zealand, just like his brother Peter. Tupra had also promised to show me some videos which he kept at home and not at the office, 'They're not for just anyone's eyes,' he had said, and yet he was going to show them to me, what could they possibly be about and why did I have to see them, I might wish I never had; I could always close my eyes, although whenever you decide to do that, you inevitably close them just a little too late not to catch a glimpse of something and to get a horrible idea of what's going on, too late not to understand. Or else, with your eyes screwed tight shut, once you think that the vision or scene has finished – sound deceives, and silence more so – you open them too soon.

'What happened to Jayne Mansfield, then? What did she have to do with Kennedy?' I asked again. I wasn't going to allow him to continue wandering and digressing, not on a night prolonged at his insistence; nor was I prepared to allow him to drift from an important matter to a secondary one and from there to a paren-thesis, and from a parenthesis to some interpolated fact, and, as occasionally happened, never to return from his endless bifurca-tions, for when he started doing that, there almost always came a point when his detours ran out of road and there was only brush or sand or marsh ahead. Tupra was capable of keeping you distracted indefinitely, of arousing your interest in a subject totally lacking in interest and entirely incidental, for he belonged to that rare class of individuals who seem themselves to be the embodiment of interest or else have the ability to generate it, they somehow carry it around inside them, it resides on their lips. They are the most slippery characters of all and the most persuasive.

He eyed me ironically, and I know he gave in only because he wanted to, he would have been perfectly capable of sustain-ing a protracted silence, withstanding it long enough for my two questions to dissolve in the air and thus be erased, letting them vanish as if no one had ever asked them and as if I were not there. But I was.

'Nothing. They're just two people marked by the final episode of their life. Exaggeratedly so, to the point that it defines or configures both of them and almost cancels out everything they did before, even if they had done important things, which

Mansfield clearly hadn't. If they'd known what the end had in store for them, those two people would have had good reason to suffer from narrative horror, as you said of Dick Dearlove. Both Jack Kennedy and Jayne Mansfield would have suffered from their own complex, K–M as we call it, if they'd guessed or feared how they would die. There are, naturally, many more such examples, from, say, James Dean to Abraham Lincoln, from Keats to Jesus Christ. The first and almost only thing anyone remembers about them is the way – shocking or unusual, premature or bizarre – their lives ended. Dean dead at twenty-four in a car crash, with an extraordinary career as a movie star still before him and the whole world at his feet; Lincoln assassinated by John Wilkes Booth, highly theatrically, in a box at the theatre, shortly after winning the War of Secession and having been re-elected; Keats dead in Rome from tuberculosis, at twenty-five, such a loss to literature; Christ on the cross at thirty-three, a mature adult in the eyes of the age he lived in, even a little slow off the mark in carrying out his work, but young, if not in years, and gone to an early grave according to our idle, long-lived times. As I said, it was at Mulryan's insistence that we called it the K–M complex, but any of those other names would have done, or many more, quite a few people owe their great celebrity or the fact of not being forgotten to the manner of their death or its timing, when it might be said that they weren't ready or that it was unfair. As if death knew anything about fairness or was concerned with meting it out, or could even understand the concept, quite absurd. At most, death is arbitrary, capricious, by which I mean that it establishes an order it doesn't always follow, one that it chooses either to follow or discard: sometimes it approaches filled with resolve and, as if intent on its business, draws near, flies over us, looks down, and then suddenly decides to leave it for another day. It must have a very good memory to be able to recall every living being and not miss a single one. Death's task is infinite, and yet it's been carrying it out with exemplary thoroughness for centuries. What an efficient slave, one that never stands idle and never wearies. Or forgets.'

His way of referring to death, of personalising it, again made me think that he must have had more dealings with it than most, that he must have seen it in action many times and had perhaps, on a few occasions, himself taken on the role of death. That very night he had approached De la Garza filled with resolve, he had drawn near, flown over him wielding his Landsknecht sword just like the helicopter with its whirling blades that had so frightened Wheeler and me in his garden by the river: in the end, it had merely ruffled our hair, and Tupra had merely cut off De la Garza's fake ponytail and plunged his head into the water and beaten him, and left him for another day, as if he really were Sir Death on a night when he had decided not to follow his own established order of things. Or perhaps Tupra, as a medievalist, albeit non-practising, was accustomed to the anthropomorphic vision of past centuries: the decrepit old woman with her scythe or Sir Death in full armour and bearing a sword and a lance; but just whose 'efficient slave' did he think death was: God's, the Devil's, mankind's, or life's, even though life only has this one method of proceeding?

'I know what happened, I mean I know, as does everyone else, how President Kennedy died,' I replied. 'But I don't know what happened to Jayne Mansfield. In fact, I know almost nothing about her and her extraordinary hourglass figure.' And after humorously quoting his own words back at him, I added a Spanish note to what I had said: 'I suppose García Lorca would fit that complex too. We wouldn't evoke him so frequently, he wouldn't be remembered or read in the same way if he hadn't died the way he did, shot and thrown into a common grave by the Francoists, before he was even forty. However good a poet he was, he wouldn't be missed or praised half as much.'

'Exactly, that's another clear example of a death defining a life, of ever-present death enfolding and sweeping someone along,' replied Tupra, not really listening to what I'd said; I wondered how much he knew about the circumstances of Lorca's murder. 'Throughout her brief and brilliant career and her almost equally brief decline, Jayne Mansfield was always ready to turn her hand – and certainly her bust – to doing whatever was necessary to attract the attention of the press and to publicise herself. She always kept her door open to reporters, wherever she was, in motels when she was on the road, in the suites she stayed in and even in hotel bathrooms; she loved them to come and photograph her in her pink Spanish-style mansion on Sunset Boulevard in Beverly Hills, full of dogs and cats, and she would wear provocative outfits and strike suggestive poses, and nothing was ever too ridiculous or too trifling, she would welcome anyone, however stupid or malicious, from even the most mediocre of publications. She posed nude for *Playboy* a couple of times, married a muscle-bound Hungarian, and would happily show off her swimming pool and her bed, both of which were heart-shaped, to the least significant of provincial hacks. She divorced the strong man and the odd subsequent husband, went to Vietnam to cheer up the troops with her saucy remarks and her tight sweaters, and when even Las Vegas would no longer have her, she toured Europe appearing in tacky shows and Italian films about Hercules. She took to drinking, she picked fights and worked very hard at creating scandals, but as her career declined, she found this increasingly difficult because no one took much notice and, besides, she wasn't very talented. It was said that she converted to the Church of Satan, a nonsense invented by one Anton LaVey, its High Priest, a bald fellow sporting a puerile diabolical goatee and fake horns on his bald head, who claimed, falsely, to be of Hungarian or Transylvanian origin, and was just as publicity-hungry as she was, as well as being a compulsive con artist: he claimed to be the author of *The Satanic Bible*, which was blatantly plagiarised from four or five different writers, among them the famous Renaissance alchemist John Dee and the novelist H. G. Wells; he claimed, also, to have had an affair with Marilyn Monroe and, needless to say, with Mansfield too. This was all complete fantasy, of course, but then, as you know, people will believe all manner of vile and despicable things about celebrities. He was mad for her and she would sometimes phone him from Beverly Hills, surrounded by her friends, so that she could laugh at and make fun of his demoniacal ardour, filling his shaven head with titillating thoughts from afar. Later, it was rumoured that a vengeful LaVey put a curse on Mansfield's then lover, a lawyer named Brody, and there begins the legend of her death. In June 1967, she was driving in the early hours from a place called Biloxi in Mississippi, where she'd been standing in at a club for her friend and rival Mamie Van Doren, en route to New Orleans, where she was going to be interviewed the next day on a local TV programme, as you see, nothing was ever too much trouble or too trivial. The Buick she was travelling in was crammed with people: the young man who was driving, namely Brody, Mansfield and three of her five children, the ones from her marriage to the muscle-bound Hungarian, plus four chihuahuas; really it's hardly surprising that they had a crash. About twenty miles from their destination, the car slammed into the back of a truck that had braked suddenly when it came upon a slow-moving municipal vehicle spraying a swamp for mosquitoes, Mulryan always emphasised that sordid, boggy, Southern detail. The impact was such that the roof of the Buick was sliced clean off. Mansfield and Brody – her driver and lover – died instantly and their bodies were hurled out onto the road. The three children, asleep in the back, only suffered bruises, and there's no news of the chihuahuas, probably because they were unharmed and perhaps escaped.' Tupra paused, threw something onto the fire, I didn't see what, perhaps a speck of fluff from his jacket or a match I hadn't seen him light and which he had been holding between his fingers. He told the story as if it were a report he had in his head, memorised. It occurred to me that, given his profession, he might have hundreds and thousands of such reports stored away, reports on both real events and possibilities, on proven facts and speculation, written not only by him, but by me and by Pérez Nuix, Mulryan, Rendel and others; and by other people in the past such as Peter Wheeler and, who knows, Peter's wife Valerie and Toby Rylands and even Mrs Berry. Perhaps Tupra was a walking archive. 'Jayne Mansfield's ostentatious blonde wig fell onto the bumper,' he went on, 'which gave rise to two rumours, both equally unpleasant, which is probably why they became so fixed in people's imaginations: according to one rumour, the actress had been scalped in the accident, her scalp torn off as if by an

Indian from the Wild West; according to the other, she had been decapitated along with the roof of the Buick, and her head had rolled across the asphalt into the swampy mosquito-infested area by the side of the road. Both ideas proved irresistible to popular malice: it wasn't enough that the woman whose opulent curves had for a decade adorned the walls of garages, workshops and dives, as well as trucks and the lockers of students and soldiers, should suffer an extremely violent death at the age of thirty-four, when she was still desirable despite her rapid decline and when she might still have profited from her physical splendours; it was much more satisfying to know that death had also left her bald and ugly, or grotesquely decapitated and with her head in the mud. People like cruel punishments and the sarcastic turns that fortune takes, they like it when someone who had it all is suddenly dispossessed of everything, not to mention the ultimate dispossession of sudden death, especially a bloody death.'

'Why is he talking to me about heads being cut off,' I thought, 'when only a short while ago, he was about to cut one off himself, right before my eyes?' And it seemed to me that Tupra was using this gruesome story in order to drive me to some destination much closer than either New Orleans or Biloxi. However, I didn't interrupt him with questions, I merely quoted back to him the words he'd said to me at our first meeting:

'And besides, everything has its moment to be believed, isn't that what you think?'

'You don't know how true that is, Jack,' he replied, then immediately took up his story again. 'It was then, after her death, that LaVey started to boast in public about his affair with her (as you know, the dead are very quiet and never raise any objections) and to put it about in the press that the spectacular accident had been the result of a curse he'd put on her lover Brody, a curse so powerful that it had blithely carried her off too, since she was seated beside him, in the place of highest risk. And people love conspiracies and settlings of scores, the weird and the wonderful and the dangers that come to pass. Most people deny the existence of chance, they loathe it, but then most people are stupid.' I remembered hearing him say

27

the same thing or something similar to Wheeler, perhaps it was one of the beliefs on which our group had always based itself, as does every government. 'If Jayne Mansfield had been attracted by or flirted with the Church of Satan, no less, it was hardly odd that her pretty face should have ended up like that, in a swamp, being nibbled by animals until it was picked up; or with her celebrated platinum blonde hair snatched from her skull, for it had always been her second most striking feature, the first being the one on such conspicuous display in the postcard I showed you. The rabble demands explanations for everything' – Tupra used that word 'rabble', which is so frowned upon now – 'but it wants explanations that are ridiculous, improbable, complicated and conspiratorial, and the more those explanations are all those things, the more easily it accepts and swallows them, the happier it is. Incomprehensible as it may be, that's the way of the world. And so that bald, horned grotesque LaVey was listened to and believed, so much so that those who still remember Mansfield and worship her (and there are plenty of them, just take a look on the Internet, you'll be surprised), what survives of Jayne Mansfield are not the four or five amusing Hollywood comedies she made, nor her two flamboyant *Playboy* covers, nor the wilful, dissolute scandals she was involved in, nor her crazy pink mansion on Sunset Boulevard, nor even the bold fact that she was the first star of the modern era to show her tits in a conventional American film, but the dismal legend of her death, so humiliating for a sex symbol like her and created perhaps by a satanist, a pervert, a wizard. This, ironically, caused more of a sensation and brought her more publicity than anything she ever did during a lifetime spent pursuing the limelight, daily renouncing all privacy and what the overwhelming mass of people would call dignity. What a shame she couldn't enjoy the thousands of reports about her and the accident, and see whole pages devoted to her horrible death, like something out of a novel. It made no odds that the coffin in which she was buried was pink: her name was for ever swathed in black, the blackness of a fatal, diabolical curse and a sinful life crowned by punishment, a dark road surrounded by mud, and a lovely head separated from its voluptuous body until the end of time. If she hadn't died in that way, with the possibly invented details that so fire the rabble's imagination, she would have been almost completely forgotten. Kennedy wouldn't, obviously, if he'd simply suffered a heart attack in Dallas, but you can be quite sure that he would be remembered infinitely less and with only slight emotion if his name were not immediately associated with being gunned down and with various convoluted, unresolved conspiracy theories. That, in essence, is the Kennedy–Mansfield complex, the fear of having one's life for ever marked and distorted by the manner of one's death, the fear that one's whole life will come to be viewed as merely an intermediary stage, a pretext, on the way to the lurid end that will eternally identify us. Mind you, we all run the same risk, even if we're not public figures, but obscure, anonymous, secondary individuals. We are all witnesses to our own story, Jack. You to yours and I to mine.'

'But not everyone fears such an ending,' I said. 'There are those who desire and seek out theatrical, spectacular deaths, even if, lacking any other recourse, they can only achieve this with words. You have no idea the care many writers have taken to utter a few memorable last words. Although, of course, it's hard to know which will truly be your last word, and more than one writer has blown the opportunity, by being over-hasty and speaking too soon. Then, at the final moment, nothing suitable has come to mind and they've spouted some utter nonsense instead.'

'Yes, I agree, but it's still a response based on fear. Anyone who yearns to die a memorable death does so because he fears not living up to his reputation or his greatness, whether assigned to him by others or by himself in private – it makes no difference. The person who feels, to use your term, narrative horror, as you believe Dick Dearlove does, is as afraid of someone spoiling his image or the story he's been telling as someone might be who's planning his own brilliant or theatrical and eccentric denouement, it depends on the character of the individual and on the nature of the blot, which some will confuse with a flourish, but death is always a blot. Killing and being killed and committing suicide are not the same thing. Nor is being an executioner, or being mad with despair, or a victim, or being a heroic victim or a foolish one. Obviously, it's never good to die before one's time – and, still worse, foolishly – but the living Jayne Mansfield wouldn't have disapproved of the legend of her death, although she might well have wished she hadn't worn a wig on that particular car journey. And I don't think your Lorca or that rebellious, provocative Italian film-maker, Pasolini, would have been entirely displeased with the kind of blot that fell on them, from an aesthetic or, if you like, narrative point of view. They were both of them somewhat exhibitionist, and their memories have benefited from their unjust, violent deaths, both of which have shades of martyrdom about them, don't you think? In the minds of yokels, that is. You and I know that neither one nor the other consciously sacrificed himself for anything, they were just unlucky.'

Tupra had used the word 'rabble' twice and now he was using the word 'yokel' (or was it 'fool', I can't quite remember now). 'He can't think much of people,' I thought, 'to use such words so easily and so casually, and with a kind of natural, unaffected scorn. However, in the latter category he's including both the cultivated and the common, from biographers to journalists and sociologists, from men and women of letters to historians, all those people, in short, who view those two famous murder victims – made even more famous by their murders – as martyrs to a political or even a sexual cause. Reresby clearly doesn't think much of death either, he doesn't see it as anything extraordinary; perhaps that's the reason he asked me why it was that one couldn't go around dealing it out, or maybe he thinks it's just another instance of chance, and he neither denies nor loathes chance, nor does he require explanations for everything, unlike stupid people who need to see signs and connections and links everywhere. It could be that he loathes chance so little that he doesn't mind joining forces with it now and then, and setting himself up as Sir Death with his sword and playing serf to that efficient slave. He must have been a yokel himself once, possibly even for quite a long time.'

'You don't think much of people, do you?' I said. 'You don't think much of death either, of other people's deaths.'

Tupra moistened his lips, not with his tongue but with his lips themselves, as if pressing them together would be enough – they were, after all, very large and fleshy and would always have a little saliva on them. Then he took a sip from his glass, and I had the disquieting sense that he was licking his lips. He again offered me some port, and this time I accepted, my palate felt as if it were covered by a communion wafer or a veil, he poured from the bottle until I raised my hand to say 'Enough'.

'Now you're beginning to get there,' he replied, which again made me think that he was driving or leading me; yes, as long as I was the one demanding an explanation, he was the person doing the leading. A bad defendant and a bad witness. He looked at me smugly from his blue or grey eyes, from his eyelashes shaped like half-moons, which gleamed in the firelight. 'Now you're going to start criticising me again, asking why I did what I did and all that. You're too much a man of your time, Jack, and that's the worst thing to be, because it's hard if you always feel other people's suffering, there's no room for manoeuvre when everyone agrees and sees things the same way and gives importance to the same things, and the same things are deemed serious or insignificant. There's no light, no breathing space, no ventilation in unanimity, nor in shared commonplaces. You have to escape from that in order to live better, more comfortably. More honestly too, without feeling trapped in the time in which you were born and in which you'll die, there's nothing more oppressive, nothing so clouds the issue as that particular stamp. Nowadays, enormous importance is given to individual deaths, people make such a drama out of each person who dies, especially if they die a violent death or are murdered; although the subsequent grief or curse doesn't last very long: no one wears mourning any more and there's a reason for that, we're quick to weep but quicker still to forget. I'm talking about our countries, of course, it's not like that in other parts of the world, but what else can they do in a place where death is an everyday occurrence. Here, though, it's a big deal, at least at the moment it happens. So-and-so has died, how dreadful; such-and-such a number of people have been killed in a crash or blown to pieces, how terrible, how vile. The politicians have to rush around attending funerals and burials, taking care not to miss any – intense grief, or is it pride, requires them as ornaments, because they give no consolation nor can they, it's all to do with show, fuss, vanity and rank. The rank of the self-important, super-sensitive living. And yet, when you think about it, what right do we have, what is the point of complaining and making a tragedy out of something that happens to every living creature in order for it to become a dead creature? What is so terrible about something so supremely natural and ordinary? It happens in the best families, as you know, and has for centuries, and in the worst too, of course, at far more frequent intervals. What's more, it happens all the time and we know that perfectly well, even though we pretend to be surprised and frightened: count the dead who are mentioned on any TV news report, read the birth and death announcements in any newspaper, in a single city, Madrid, London, each list is a long one every day of the year; look at the obituaries, and although you'll find far fewer of them, because an infinitesimal minority are deemed to merit one, they're nevertheless there every morning. How many people die every weekend on the roads and how many have died in the innumerable battles that have been waged? The losses haven't always been published throughout history, in fact, almost never. People were more familiar with and more accepting of death, they accepted chance and luck, be it good or bad, they knew they were vulnerable to it at every moment; people came into the world and sometimes disappeared at once, that was normal, the infant mortality rate was extraordinarily high until eighty or even seventy years ago, as was death in childbirth, a woman might bid farewell to her child as soon as she saw its face, always assuming she had the will or the time to do so. Plagues were common and almost any illness could kill, illnesses we know nothing about now and whose names are unfamiliar; there were famines, endless wars, real wars that involved daily fighting, not sporadic engagements like now, and the generals didn't care about the losses, soldiers fell and that was that, they were only individuals to themselves, not even to their families, no family was spared the premature death of at least some of its members, that was the norm; those in power would look grim-faced, then carry out another levy, recruit more troops and send them to the front to continue dying in battle, and almost no one complained. People expected death, Jack, there wasn't so much panic about it, it was neither an insuperable calamity nor a terrible injustice; it was something that could happen and often did. We've become very soft, very thin-skinned, we think we should last for ever. We ought to be accustomed to the temporary nature of things, but we're not. We insist on not being temporary, which is why it's so easy to frighten us, as you've seen, all one has to do is unsheathe a sword. And we're bound to be cowed when confronted by those who still see death, their own or other people's, as part and parcel of their job, as all in a day's work. When confronted by terrorists, for example, or by drug barons or multinational mafia men. And so it's true, Iago.' I didn't like it when he called me by the name of that troublemaker; it sounded grubby to me, it wasn't a name I wanted to answer to (I, who answered to so many). 'It's important that some of us don't think much of death. Of other people's deaths, as you said, outraged, oh, I noticed despite your neutral tone, it was a good try, but not enough. It's lucky that some of us can step out of our own era and look at things as they used to in more robust times, past and future (because those times will return, I assure you, although I don't know whether you and I will live to see them), so that we don't collectively suffer the fate described by a French poet: *Par délicatesse j'ai perdu ma vie.'* And he took the trouble to translate these words for me, and in that I saw a remnant of the yokel he had left behind: 'Out of delicacy I lost my life.'

I glanced down at his feet, his shoes, as I had during one of our first meetings, fearing that he might be wearing some abomination, short green boots in alligator skin, like Marshal Bonanza, or even clogs. This wasn't the case, he always wore elegant brown or black lace-ups, they were certainly not the shoes of a yokel; only the waistcoats he was rarely seen without were questionable, although now they looked more old-fashioned and dated than ever, like a leftover from the '70s, at the time when he would have been starting to take life more seriously, I mean, to be fully aware of his responsibilities and the consequences of his actions, or with a proper sense of the options available to him. Nevertheless, there was something about him that did not quite ring true: his work, his gestures, his surroundings, his accent, even that very comfortable English house, so textbook perfect, like something out of an expensive film, or a picture in a story book. Perhaps it was the abundant curls on his bulging cranium, or the apparently dyed ringlets at his temples, perhaps the soft mouth seemingly lacking consistency, a piece of chewing gum before it goes hard. Many people doubtless found him attractive, despite that slightly repellent element I could never entirely identify or isolate or pin down with any exactitude, perhaps it didn't depend on just one characteristic, but on the whole. Perhaps I was the only person to see it, women clearly didn't pick it up. Not even perceptive women like Pérez Nuix, accustomed to noticing and intuiting everything, and with whom he had probably been to bed. That's something we would have in common, Tupra and I, or should that be I and Reresby. Or Ure or Dundas.

'And because of that you allow yourself to beat up and scare to death a poor inoffensive fool, and with my help too; except, of course, I had no idea what you were planning to do to him. And for no reason, just because, because one shouldn't take death too seriously. Well, I couldn't disagree with you more. By the way, I believe that line is from Rimbaud,' I added to make him feel inadequate, he'd already gained far too much ground. I was taking a risk, though, because I wasn't sure at all.

He paid no attention; I was cultured, I knew other languages, I had taught at Oxford in the past, and so he didn't give me any credit for knowing that. He would expect me to recognise the quotation. He gave a wry laugh, just one, a mere simulacrum of bitterness.

'There are no inoffensive people, Jack. None,' he said. 'And you don't seem to take into account that it was all your fault. Think about it.'

'What do you mean? Because I introduced him to the lady and they hit it off? She was longing to be courted by the first mameluke who appeared, whoever he was. Just think back a bit. You yourself warned me about it.' The word '*mameluco*' had been going round and round in my head ever since Manoia confirmed to me that it was the same word in Italian, and words don't go away until you've used them, possibly several times. Of course, 'mameluke' sounded more recherché in English, and inappropriate too, it doesn't even have the same principal meaning as in Spanish, namely 'numbskull'.

'That wasn't the only reason. I asked you to find them and to bring Flavia back, I told you not to take too long and to remove that De la Garza fellow from the scene. You failed. So I had to go after you and sort things out. And still you complain. By the time I found them, Mrs Manoia already had a great welt on her face. If I hadn't stepped in, it would have been far worse, you don't know her husband, I do. I couldn't just have that useless Spaniard thrown out.' It occurred to me that he sometimes forgot that I, too, was a Spaniard, and possibly a useless one as well. 'Given that Flavia had a mark, a wound on her face, that wouldn't have been enough for him. He would have gone up to your friend and, if your friend was lucky, torn off his arm, if not his head. You criticise me for some trifling, unimportant thing that I did, but you live in a tiny world that barely exists, sheltered from the violence that has always been the norm and still is in most parts of the world, it's like mistaking the interlude for the whole performance, you haven't a clue, you people who never step outside of your own time or travel beyond countries like ours in which, up until the day before yesterday, violence also ruled. What I did was nothing. The lesser of two evils. And it was your fault.'

The lesser of two evils. So Tupra belonged to that all-too-familiar group of men who have always existed and of whom I've known a few myself, there are always so many of them. The sort who justify themselves by saying: 'I had to do it in order to avoid a greater evil, or so I believed; others would have done the same, only they would have behaved more cruelly and caused more harm. I killed one so that ten would not be killed, and ten so that a hundred would not die, I don't deserve to be punished, I deserve a prize.' Or those who answer: 'I had to do it, I was defending my God, my king, my country, my culture, my race; my flag, my legend, my language, my class, my space; my honour, my family, my strongbox, my purse and my socks. And in short, I was afraid.' Fear, which exonerates as much as love, and of which it's so easy to say and to believe 'It's stronger than I am, it's not in my power to stop it' or that allows one to resort to the words 'But I love you so much' as an explanation for one's actions, as an alibi or an excuse or as a mitigating factor. Perhaps he even belonged to those who would claim: 'It was the times we lived in, and unless you were there, you couldn't possibly understand. It was the place, it was unhealthy, oppressive; unless you were there, you couldn't possibly imagine our feelings of alienation, the spell we were under.' On the other hand, at least he would not be one of those who dodged the issue altogether, he would never pronounce those other words: 'I didn't intend to do it, I knew nothing about it, it happened against my will, as if befuddled by the tortuous smokescreen of dreams, it was part of my theoretical, parenthetical life, the life that doesn't really count, it only half-happened and without my full consent.' No, Tupra would never stoop to the sort of pathetic excuses even I have used to justify to myself certain episodes in my own life. Just then, however, I preferred not to go into that aspect of things, and so I replied to the last thing he'd said to me:

'I work for you, Bertram, I do my job. Don't ask me to do any more than that. I'm here to interpret and to write reports, not to deal with drunken boors. Nor even to entertain ladies in their declining years, clasping them to me, sternum to breast.'

Tupra couldn't help being amused despite himself. Up until then we hadn't had the chance to talk about my torment, still less to laugh about it, or for him to laugh at me, at my bad luck and my imperfect stoicism.

'Rocky peaks, eh?' And he let out a genuine guffaw. 'There's no way I would have accepted her invitation to dance, not with those bulwarks of hers.' He used the word 'bulwarks', which might best be rendered in Spanish as 'baluartes'.

36

He'd done it again. I myself sometimes laugh at things despite myself. I couldn't suppress my own laughter, my anger vanished for a moment, or was postponed because it was no longer relevant. For a few seconds, we both laughed together, simultaneously, with neither of us hanging back or pre-empting the other, the laughter that creates a kind of disinterested bond between men and that suspends or dissolves their differences. This meant that, for all my irritation and my growing feelings of apprehension – or was it perhaps unease, aversion, repugnance – I hadn't entirely withdrawn my laughter from him. I might have been on the way to rationing it out, but I hadn't removed or denied him my laughter. Not altogether, not yet.

Yes, we would have that in common, our having slept with young Pérez Nuix, I was almost sure of it, although it had never occurred to me to ask him, still less her, even though sharing a bed while awake arbitrarily marks the frontier between discretion and trust, between secrecy and revelation, between deferential silence and questions with their respective answers or, perhaps, evasions, as if briefly entering another's body broke down not only physical barriers but others too: biographical, sentimental, certainly the barriers of pretence, caution or reserve, it's absurd really that two people, having once entwined, feel that they can, with authority and impunity, probe the life and thoughts of whoever was above or below, or standing up facing forwards or backwards if no bed was needed, or else describe both life and thoughts at length, in the most verbose and even abstracted fashion, there are people who only screw someone so that they can then rabbit on at them to their heart's content, as if that intertwining had given them a licence to do so. This is something that has often bothered me following one of my occasional flings, one that lasted a night or a morning or an afternoon, and, in the first instance, all such encounters are just that – flings – as long as they're not repeated, and all encounters start out the same with neither party knowing if it will end right there, or, rather, one of the parties knows, knows at once, but politely says nothing and thus gives rise to a misunderstanding (politeness is a poison, our undoing); they pretend that this relationship isn't going to come to an immediate halt, but that something really has opened up and there's no reason why it should ever be closed again; the most terrible mess and confusion ensues. And sometimes you know this before you've even entered that new body, you know you only want to do it that one time, just to find out, or perhaps to brag about it to yourself or to shock yourself, or you might even make a mental note of the occasion so that you can recall or remember it or, even more tenuously, have it on record, so that you'll be able to say to yourself: 'This happened in my life', especially in old age or in one's maturer years when the past often invades the present and when the present, grown bored or sceptical, rarely looks ahead.

Yes, it's often bothered me that the other person involved has then gone on to describe to me her characteristics, her inner world, painted me a portrait of herself, not, of course, entirely true-to-life, or has tried to make out that with me it's different ('This has never happened to me with any other man'), partly to flatter me and partly to save a reputation upon which no one had cast a doubt. I've found it irritating when she's started moving about my house or apartment – if that's where we were – with excessive familiarity and nonchalance and with an appropriative attitude (asking, for example, 'Where do you keep the coffee?' taking it for granted that I do keep coffee and that she can make some herself; or else announcing 'I'm just nipping to the bathroom', instead of asking if she can, as she would have done a little while before, when she was still dressed and as yet unskewered; although that verb is too extreme). It has infuriated me when one of them has settled down to spend the whole night in my bed without even consulting me, taking it for granted that she has an open invitation to linger in my sheets just because she's lain on the mattress for a while or rested her hands on it to keep her balance while bending over, her back to me, *more ferarum*, with her skirt hitched up and the heels of her shoes firmly planted on the floor. It has angered me when, a day or so later, that same woman has turned up at my door, to say a fond and spontaneous hello, but really in order deliberately to repeat what happened before and to make herself more at home, on the baseless assumption that I will let her in and devote time to her at any hour or in any circumstances, whether I'm busy or not, whether I have other visitors or not, whether I feel pleased or regretful (though I've more than likely forgotten) that I allowed her to set foot on my territory the day before. When I want to be alone or I'm missing Luisa. And it's really riled me when one such woman has phoned up later saying 'Hi, it's me', as if yesterday's bit of carnal knowledge had conferred on her exclusivity or uniqueness, or made her instantly identifiable, or guaranteed her a prominent place in my thoughts, or obliged me to recognise a voice that possibly – if I was lucky – uttered only a single groan or a few, purely out of politeness.

However, what has most enraged me has been the feeling that I was somehow in her debt (absurd in this day and age) for allowing me to sleep with her. This is probably a hangover from the era into which I was born, when it was still considered that all the interest and insistence came from the man and that the woman merely gave in or, more than that, conceded or assented, and that she was the one making a valuable gift or granting a large favour. Not always, but all too frequently, I have judged myself to be the architect or the person ultimately responsible for what has happened between us, even if I hadn't sought or anticipated it – although I've seen it coming on most occasions, suspected it – and assumed that they would regret it as soon as it was over and I'd withdrawn or moved away, or while they were getting dressed again or smoothing or adjusting their clothes (there was even a married woman once who asked to borrow my iron: her tight skirt, by then, looked like a concertina, and she was going straight on to a dinner party with some very proper married couples and didn't have time to go home first; I lent her my iron and she left looking very pleased with herself, her skirt silent and showing no trace of its recent ups and downs), or perhaps later on, when they were alone and in pensive or reflective mood, gazing up at the same moon – to which I would be oblivious – through windows that, for them, had suddenly taken on a nuptial feel, as they dozed in the early hours.

And so I have often felt an impulse to repay them at once, by being sensitive, patient or prepared to hear them out; by attending meekly to their woes or engaging with their chatter;

by watching over their unfamiliar sleep or bestowing on them inappropriate caresses that certainly didn't come from the heart, but which I dredged up from somewhere; by thinking up complicated excuses so that I could leave their house before dawn, like a vampire, or leave my own house in the early hours, thus letting it be understood that they couldn't stay overnight and that they had to get dressed and go downstairs with me and pick up their car or get a taxi (with me having paid the driver in advance), instead of admitting to them that I could no longer stand seeing them, listening to them or even lying breathing sleepily by their side. And sometimes my impulse has been to reward them, symbolically and ridiculously, and then I've improvised a gift or prepared them a good breakfast if it was that time of the morning and we were still together, or I've bowed to some wish that it was within my power to grant and which they had expressed not to me but to the air, or agreed to some implicit and unformulated request, made long enough ago for the two things not to be connected or only if there was a stubborn insistence on bringing together word and flesh. Not, on the other hand, if the request was made explicitly and immediately after the event, because then I've never been able to shake off the unpleasant feeling that some sort of transaction or exchange has taken place, which falsifies what has happened and makes it seem somehow sordid or, indeed, glossed over, as if it had never happened.

Perhaps that's why Pérez Nuix asked me for the favour early on, when it still hadn't even occurred to me that by the end of the night we would get so close and even reach the morning without entirely letting go of each other. Well, actually the idea had crossed my mind, not as a possible possibility but as a hypothetical improbability (a strange idea in the back of the mind, acknowledging to yourself that you would accept something that is clearly never going to happen), and the first time had been while she was repeatedly zipping and unzipping her boots and drying herself on my towel and there was a snag in one of her tights that degenerated into a long, wide run, and she had blithely revealed her thighs to me and thus indicated that she did not exclude me. 'She doesn't rule me out, but that's as far as it goes,' I had thought. 'Nothing more, that's all, I am the one who notices and bears it in mind. In reality, though, it's nothing.' And: 'There's a great gulf between feeling desire and not entirely rejecting someone, between affirmation and the unknown, between willingness and the simple absence of any plan, between a "Yes" and a "Possibly", between a "Fine" and a "We'll see" or even less than that, an "Anyway" or an "Hmm, right" or something which doesn't even formulate itself as a thought, a limbo, a space, a void, it's not something I've ever considered, it hadn't even occurred to me, it hadn't even crossed my mind.' I was still invisible to her when she asked me the favour, and perhaps I remained so throughout the night and even into the morning. Except perhaps for that brief moment when she cupped my face with her open hands as if professing some affection for me, the two of us, by then, lying in my bed ready to go to sleep, her soft hands; when she looked into my eyes and smiled at me and laughed and delicately held my face, just as Luisa sometimes used to do when her bed was still mine and we were not yet sleepy, or not enough to say goodnight and turn our backs on each other until the morning.

But that came later. And as almost always happens when you ask a string of questions one after the other, young Pérez Nuix began by answering the last one. 'You still haven't asked me the favour, what is it exactly, I still don't know. And which private private individuals do you mean?' had been my two questions, repeating the expression she had used 'private private individuals'.

'Strange though it may seem to us today, Jaime, with our nerves constantly on edge and with everyone in a permanent state of panic over terrorism,' she said, 'there was a period of a few years, quite recently in fact, although it seems a long time ago to us now, when MI5 and MI6, shall we say, lacked work. After the fall of the Berlin Wall, their duties diminished as did their concerns, and the budgets they had at their disposal collapsed, which, as we now know, was a great mistake. For example, the budget for MI5 went from £900 million in 1994 to less than £700 million in 1998. Then it gradually started creeping up again, but until the attack on the Twin Towers in

2001, which set all the alarm bells ringing and provoked much breast-beating and many dismissals from the ranks of middle management, there were about seven or eight years when a large part of the world's Intelligence Service, and, of course, our own, felt almost useless and superfluous, how can I put it, unoccupied, unnecessary, idle and, worse, bored. Many of the people who had spent decades studying the Soviet Union found themselves not unemployed exactly, but surplus to requirements, with a sense that they had not only wasted their time, but also a large portion of their lives, which were abruptly coming to an end. A sense that they had become the past. Those who knew German, Bulgarian, Hungarian, Polish and Czech were called on less frequently, and even Russian experts lost prominence and work. Suddenly, there was a kind of unacknowledged superfluity, suddenly, people who had been of fundamental importance were no longer needed, or only for minor matters. The situation was so depressing that even the department heads realised how demoralising it was, and I can assure you that in any job anywhere, they are always the least likely to notice their subordinates' problems. Anyway, the fact is that they did finally cotton on, incredibly late – and only a few days before 11 September, if I remember rightly, the press, *The Independent*, I believe, reported that MI5, through the then Director General, Sir Stephen Lander, was preparing to offer its espionage services to the major companies of the land, like British Telecom, Allied Domecq, Cadbury Schweppes and others, whom it could provide with very useful information about their foreign competitors. Apparently, it was the agency that approached the companies, and not the other way round, in the course of a seminar held at their headquarters in Millbank, the very first time, if I'm not mistaken, that representatives from industry and the financial world, both from the public and the private sectors, had been invited there. The reason given was that it was just as important and as patriotic to help the British economy and make it more competitive in the world, as well as shielding our large companies from the foreign spies who doubtless exist, as it was to protect the nation from dangers and threats to its security, be they internal or external, political, military or terrorist. The idea was basically to commercialise the activities of the SIS' – I remembered this acronym, I'd heard Tupra and Wheeler use it: the Secret Intelligence Service, she said the acronym in English, *s, i, s,* or to Spanish ears, *es, ai, es,* even though we were speaking Spanish – 'to win lucrative contracts, which was tantamount to a partial privatisation of the agency, to reap immediate large rewards and rescue from boredom a good number of the idle and depressed by sending them to work more or less directly for these companies. And that, of course, brought with it a real risk of dividing their loyalties. Lander roundly denied this through a spokesman, who stated that offering to spy for private companies in exchange for remuneration would go beyond the competence of MI5 and that such a proposal would be illegal. He admitted that MI5 had, for some time, been mounting operations with a view to uncovering foreign spies in British companies, and that they provided free advice mainly to the defence industry and to those developing new technologies when they were preparing to sign large contracts or if there was any suspicion of computer fraud. The spokesman added, however, that Lander's controversial paper at the seminar, whose theme had been "Secret Work in an Open Society", had dealt only with the growing threat from hackers, and that he had offered advice, with no mention of money, to public and private companies on the best ways of guarding against hackers and of combating software piracy. Several of the invited guests, however, acknowledged in private that Lander's initiative had been quite different, and that he had promised to aid them in their business dealings with a constant stream of privileged information about companies and individuals, "if they asked for it".'

Young Pérez Nuix paused and now she did accept my offer of a drink, her mouth must have been getting dry after her long speech, a mouth with attractive firm red lips, like Capitán Trueno's Viking lady-love, Sigrid, or some other character out of a children's comic, one always looks at the lips of anyone who talks for any length of time, students look at their teachers' lips, audiences look at actors' lips, spectators at the lips of speakers and politicians (the latter always make a bad impression). I got up, went into the kitchen, and from there (not very far away, my apartment was not that big) I called out to her what I had in the house, only Coca-Cola, beer, wine and water, I was perhaps a less than perfect host because in London I wasn't in the habit of being one, almost everyone who came to see me, and they were very few, came to do just that, to be only briefly occupied with me. I also offered her a black coffee, perhaps a glass of milk, or a white coffee if she preferred something warm and comforting, and she replied that she'd like wine as long as it was white and chilled. I remembered that I had six unopened bottles of Sangre y Trabajadero sent to me by a kind, long-standing friend from Cádiz, but I couldn't be bothered to set about opening a crate at that hour.

'Here you are. It's cold enough for me, but it may not be for you,' I said, placing before her knees, on two coasters (I'm a clean fellow) the bottle of Ruländer that I opened there and then (I don't know much about wine) and a not entirely suitable glass, which she allowed me to fill almost to the brim. 'If she's drinking because she's thirsty, she'll be drunk in no time,' I thought when she didn't raise her hand to stop me. The run in her tights kept growing each time she made a movement, however slight or delicate, or when she crossed her legs, and she crossed and uncrossed them often, with the consequent upward movement of her skirt, this was only minimal with each crossing and uncrossing, but her skirt was gradually creeping up (until she tugged it down again). She still hadn't noticed the damage being wrought, when perhaps she should have. Given the nature of runs, it didn't look out of place on her leg, although it did seem destined to reduce her tights to tatters if our conversation lasted long enough, and she had, it seemed, completely forgotten that, in her words, 'it'll only take a moment', and, in part, forgotten about me too. I realised that, after the initial surprise and my sense that the visit would only be a brief one, I was in fact enjoying her prolonged presence there, especially with the dog at her feet, for dogs, when they are still, do make one feel calmer, even comfortable. The creature, which had apparently dried off considerably, was still dozing with one eye open, lying close to his mistress. ('Sleep with one eye open, when you slumber,' I sometimes sing or repeat to myself.) He seemed kindly and ingenuous and honest, the very opposite of a joker or a trickster.

'Aren't you having anything?' Pérez Nuix asked. 'Don't tell me you're not going to join me. It's embarrassing drinking alone.' And she immediately overcame any embarrassment by emptying the glass as if she were Lord Rymer the Flask in one of his greedier moments. She was probably thirsty, which was perfectly normal after that walk in the rain, what was odd was that she hadn't asked me for a drink earlier. I refilled her glass, not quite to the top this time.

'Later, in a few minutes,' I replied. 'Go on.' And so that this did not sound like an order, I leaned down and again stroked the dog's head and back, felt his thin bones. This time he didn't even lift his neck, he must have got used to my presence and simply took no notice of me, he was very dignified that pointer. Everyone thinks it makes you look a nicer person if you behave affectionately towards animals, and that was the effect I wanted then. (If there's one thing I can't stand it's writers, and there are hundreds of them, who have themselves photographed with their dogs or cats in order to project a more amiable image when, in fact, they just come across as affected and twee.) I took advantage of my friendly bowed position to take a long look at Pérez Nuix's thighs from close up, I will not deny that they continued to attract me. I suppose she pretended not to notice, she certainly didn't cover them up or move them a fraction of an inch. At that point, I did feel as puerile as De la Garza, but then the sexual admiration that precedes sex is always puerile, and there's nothing to be done about it.

'I don't know what happened to those measures, they may have gone ahead, but under cover and with much less fuss than planned,' she went on, having, without a pause, downed half of her second glass of wine: I hoped that her speech wouldn't start to become slurred. 'Because shortly after came September 11th and from that day on no one was entirely superfluous. However, those measures, especially if they were genuine, came too late and were, anyway, hardly original, they simply made offi-

46

cial what had been going on for years without the intervention and almost without the knowledge of the high-ranking officers in the service, well, they half-knew about it, but that knowledge was accompanied by a degree of passivity, a lot of turning a blind eye, little curiosity and a desire not to cramp anyone's style. The agents with least to do, once they'd got over the long period of confusion that followed the fall of the Berlin Wall, had started looking for external clients, both occasional and otherwise, according to their respective fields and possibilities. Some, who felt sidelined, actually resigned, those who could simply left (depending on how much responsibility you've been given, that isn't easy and sometimes impossible). The majority, though, didn't manage to do so or simply didn't want to, and although still employed by the state, started getting other work here and there, which meant they were serving different masters. They offered their skills to the highest bidder or accepted the best-paid commissions. And what kind of people or private institutions were or are interested in employing agents? Well, some were given work more suited to private detectives, confirming an infidelity, investigating cases of embezzlement or misappropriation of funds, collecting money from debtors in arrears; or working as bodyguards to protect show-business types or tycoons at public events, things like that. Others gave a hand or two to those ex-colleagues of theirs who had become mercenaries, of whom there were quite a few, and there's never any shortage of that kind of work in Africa. The range of jobs kept widening, and eventually the lower-ranking field agents began to suggest and supply such work to the middle-ranking officials and I imagine that, by 2001, the latter had convinced the higher-ranking officials of the advantages of not working solely for the state. The fact is that during those seven or eight years, during that long interval without a principal enemy, a parallel network of diverse clients of every kind was created. More than once, members of MI5 and MI6, whether knowingly or not, or preferring not to know but sensing it, would doubtless have worked for criminals or even criminal organisations, and perhaps, at the darker, more remote end of the chain, for foreign governments.

It's possible, no one knows and no one's going to try to find out, for at this point in time nothing's very clear and everything's very muddled. You get used to not asking who is paying the bill, and besides, almost everything is dealt with and discussed by intermediaries and front men. If you first had to carry out an investigation to discover who was behind each commission, you'd never finish and never start, and any deal would be worthless.'

Young Pérez Nuix paused and finished off the second half of her second glass of wine. I hesitated, but, out of courtesy, made a very slight move as if to refill it, without actually touching the bottle. Up until then, I had noticed no hesitancy or difficulty in speaking on her part, but if she carried on at the same rate, this might well happen at any moment, or if not that, incoherence or somnolence, and now I wanted to hear everything she had to say. There were, however, no signs of any such symptoms, she must have been accustomed to drinking wine. Even her vocabulary was select and precise, that of a well-read person, she used unusual words, such as '*arrumbados*' for 'sidelined', '*encomienda*' for 'commission', '*rasos*' for 'lower-ranking'. Perhaps, despite her ancestry on her father's side, she was like certain English people who have learned my language more from books than from speaking it, and whose Spanish therefore seems rather bookish. And so I got up and, before she could say 'Yes' or 'No' to my hint of an interrogative gesture, announced:

'I'm going to get a glass for myself, I'm ready for a drink now too.' And I then ventured the following warning or caution: 'Do you think it's wise to drink three glasses one after the other like that? That's drinking English-fashion, not like a Spaniard. Anyway, I'll bring a few nibbles just in case.'

When I came back with my glass and a few olives and crisps in their respective bowls, I caught her inspecting the run in her tights. In the corridor, before going into the room and almost hidden from view – I stopped and spied on her for a few seconds: one, two, three; and four – I saw her looking at it and carefully running her index finger over it (a finger moistened with saliva perhaps or a drop of nail varnish, which is what women used to apply to a catch in their tights in order to stop a run, to

48

see if it would stay decent at least until they got home; although it was too late now to stop anything). When I rejoined her, she, with arms and legs crossed now, made no reference to this imperfection in her apparel, which was odd: it would have been the moment to express surprise and regret and, if she so chose, to apologise for the theoretically scruffy appearance the run conferred upon her, although it didn't displease me in the least or trouble me, I found it rather entertaining being able discreetly to observe its progress. I wondered how much longer she would keep up the fiction that she hadn't yet noticed, and why, since it was beyond concealment now. And for the first time that evening – for the first time ever – it occurred to me that not only did she not exclude me, but that, without a word or a touch or a look – although she looked straight at me when she spoke, as if there were nothing more to that look than her explanatory, neutral remarks – she was telling me that what did finally occur could occur, quite a lot later and when I was no longer expecting it, despite our insistent nearness in my bed, which was not that big: the opening of silk or nylon as a simile or promise or sign, its steadily growing length and width, the fact that she did not try to stop or remedy it by going to the bathroom and taking off her tights and even changing them (I know women who always carry a spare pair in their bag, Luisa is one of them), allowing the run to continue to grow and expose an ever larger expanse of thigh and soon, possibly, the front part of the calf, for which I've never known the name, if it has one, perhaps shank or shinbone, but neither word seems quite right; that area, of course, was covered by her boots, although her boots had opened fleetingly too, been unzipped, as soon as their drenched owner had arrived and sat down; yes, the run in her tights was like a zip without teeth, uncivilised and autonomous and uncontrollable, with the added rogue element of being a thing that can be torn, except that this was a tear in which neither my hand nor anyone else's was intervening, the cloth was coming apart of its own accord, while still clinging to the leg, covering and uncovering at the same time and pointing up the contrast, the unveiled flesh advancing in both directions, down and up, and we men know what lies hidden at the top of a long female thigh. (I would accidentally see it myself – a dark triangle – in the Ladies' toilet of a disco, where a woman would say to me with great self-confidence: 'You come and see.')

I felt slightly ashamed, almost embarrassed, when I realised I was having these thoughts, that I was thinking them. They were entirely inappropriate, they had taken me pretty much by surprise, and the worst thing is that once an idea gets into your head, it's impossible not to have had it and very hard to drive it out or erase it, whatever it might be: anyone plotting an act of revenge is very likely to attempt to carry it out, and if he can't, out of cowardice or vassalage, or if he has to wait a long time for the right circumstances, then it's probable that he nevertheless already lives with the act and that it sours his light sleep with its nocturnal beating; if one feels a sudden hostility towards someone, it would be odd if that were not translated into machinations and defamations and acts of bad faith, of the sort that seek to cause harm, or lie there watching, in the rearguard, oozing resentment until the long-awaited morning comes; if the temptation to make some amorous conquest arises, the normal thing would be for the *conquistador* to get straight down to work, with infinite patience and intrigue if necessary, but if he lacks the courage, he will be unable fully to abandon the project until the far-off day when he finally grows bored with so much uncertainty, with such theoretical, future-oriented and therefore imaginary activities, and only then does the condensation that hangs over his misty wakenings dissipate; if what lies ahead is the possibility of killing someone – or, as is more frequent, of having someone killed – it will be easy enough at least to ascertain the current rates charged by hit men and tell yourself they'll always be there or, if not, their sons will, so that you can approach them once you've overcome your vacillations and your anticipated remorse; and if it's a case of sudden sexual desire, as unexpected as the desire that erupts in our dreams, and as involuntary perhaps, it will be difficult then not to feel it at every moment, for as long as that desire remains unsatisfied and the person inflaming it is still there before us, even though we're not prepared to take a single step towards satisfying it and cannot imagine doing so at any point in what remains of our existence. What remains of the past no longer counts, as regards yearnings or fantasies, or even avarice. Or regret. Although it does as regards speculations.

When I recalled this in Tupra's house, in his comfortable living room that invited a sense of confidence bordering on easeful calm, I wondered if I had spied on Pérez Nuix's run and thighs with the same apprehensive, unguarded look Sophia Loren had turned on the white breasts of Jayne Mansfield floating above the tablecloth in a restaurant, although my gaze would have been filled with admiration and desire rather than envy and suspicion. If I had, she would have noticed and very quickly too (the person being observed can sense such looks). I filled my glass and Pérez Nuix moved hers a little closer, and I couldn't not fill it without appearing paternalistic or stingy when it came to wine, both of which are extremely unattractive qualities; and so she immediately started on her third glass, taking only a small sip, and at least she ate a couple of olives and a potato crisp. My thoughts were, I felt, vain and idiotic, but I was nonetheless convinced that they were right, sometimes idiotic things are. 'It could be', I thought, 'that she's allowing that run to grow so as to show me the way to unexpected lust, to guide me, but be careful: she *is* about to ask me a favour, she hasn't done so yet in any detail, we're still at the stage when she can't afford to annoy me and when offering me something, or who knows, even giving it to me, must seem to her advisable even though I've made no demands or dropped any hints, a stage that will last at least until I answer "Yes" or "No", or "I'll see what I can do, I'll do my best", or "But I'll want this in exchange". And it would be only natural if this stage were to last still longer, for several days, until I had done what I said I would do, with irreversible words or deeds, beyond the promise or announcement or the half-open possibility of a "Let me think about it" or a "We'll see" or an "It all depends". However, she hasn't yet formulated her petition to me, not entirely, and therefore the moment hasn't yet come for me to speak, to concede or deny, to put off, to play hard to get or to be ambivalent.'

'Anyway,' she went on, holding another of my Karelias cigarettes from the Peloponnese, 'once a field has been opened up, it's very hard to set bounds on it again, especially if there's no real will to do so. What do you want me to say?' – Yes, Pérez Nuix spoke both languages very well (the expression 'to set bounds on something' is not that common), but now and then she came out with some strange anglicisms – for example '*¿Cómo me quieres que diga?*' – when she spoke my language, or, rather, ours. 'You open a crack, and if there's a storm blowing outside, there's no way you'll close it. Something growing isn't programmed to shrink but to expand, and almost no one is willing to give up a ready income, still less if he's already started earning it and has grown used to it. The field agents were pioneers in accepting external commissions during the period when there was a gap in activities, let's call it that anyway, although it's not quite accurate, and don't go thinking that even now, when they're working at full capacity again, they earn high salaries, most earn no more than you and I, and that's not much, or so they feel, given the risks they sometimes have to run and the time involved in finding out some trivial piece of information. Many of them have families, many get into debt, they spend long periods travelling and not always at someone else's expense. They're asked to justify their expenses and sometimes that's not possible: you're hardly likely to get a signed receipt from the person you're bribing or paying for a tip-off, or from traitors, informers or moles, or from someone who does the occasional job for you or covers for you or hides you, not to mention the thugs you sometimes have to hire to get out of a tight corner or remove obstacles, or the person you have to pay to spare your life, because the only way to do that is to give him more money than he was given to kill you, a form of auction really. How are people like that going to give you receipts? The financial bureaucracy is irrational, counterproductive, absurd, and deeply unhelpful, a burden really, and discontent is always rife among the agents, they have a sense that they do more than they're given credit for, that they're soiling their hands and having a lousy time in order to protect a society that not only knows nothing about their sacrifices and their acts of bravery and occasional acts of barbarism, but one that also, by definition and on principle, doesn't even know their names. They don't know them even when they die in service, it's forbidden to reveal them, you see, however many decades they've been pushing up daisies. They get depressed and ask themselves every day why they're doing what they're doing. They're not selfless individuals or simple patriots, satisfied to think that they're doing their best for their country without anyone ever knowing, not their friends or their neighbours or, for the most part, their families. That attitude belongs to another era or to the kind of innocent era that soon gets left behind. Some might have been like that to begin with, when they joined, but, I can assure you, any feeling of personal satisfaction doesn't last, there comes a point when everyone wants to do well and get some thanks, a pat on the back, a little flattery, to see their name mentioned and their good works, even if it's only in an internal memo from the firm they work for. And since they're not going to get that, they at least want money, ease, a little luxury, to enjoy themselves when they're not working, to give their children the best, to buy their wives or husbands nice presents, to be able to afford lovers and keep them, and since agents are often absent or unavailable, they have to recompense said children or spouses or lovers, and that costs money, having fun is expensive, pleasing people is expensive, showing off is expensive, making others love you is expensive. They want what everyone else wants in a world in which there's no longer any discipline, and so they don't look too closely at the people who come to them with extra work. And since their bosses don't want to upset the agents on whom they depend, they ignore these other missions when they hear about them and, later, some even go on to travel the same path. Why do you think you and I earn so much, relatively speaking, that is? It's not much for a field agent, who might be away from home for long periods, endure certain hardships or even risk his own life, and who probably, in the most extreme cases, will have to decide whether or not to take another man's life. Nevertheless, it's a lot of money for what we do and for where and how we do it, with fairly relaxed working hours and no danger involved, in considerable comfort, with a glass screen between us and them and without exactly working our arses off.' – Again I thought how rich her vocabulary was compared with the norm in Spain, she was clearly a person well-read in superior literature, not like the low-grade stuff you get now, any ignoramus can publish a novel and be praised to the skies for it: most of my compatriots would barely know how to use words like '*cundir*' – to be rife – '*holgura*' – ease – '*transitar*' – to travel – '*deslomarse*' – to work one's arse off. I had never heard Pérez Nuix talk so much or for so long, it was as if I were meeting her for the first time, and this second impression was as unusual as the first. She stopped for a moment, took another meagre sip of wine and concluded: 'How do you think Bertie manages to live so well and to have so much? Of course we all work for private private individuals now and then, knowingly or not, possibly more often than we think, as I've said, it's not our responsibility, we just take orders. And besides, why shouldn't we do that work, why not make use of our abilities? So what if we do, Jaime? It's been going on at all levels for years now and it really doesn't matter very much. You can be quite sure that nothing very essential changes because of it, it doesn't make the lives of citizens more dangerous. On the contrary. Well, perhaps, but the more avenues we explore, the more fingers we'll have in more pies, and the better equipped we'll be to protect them.'

I remained silent for a moment, I couldn't help shooting another surreptitious, Lorenesque glance at the run, which was still following its course. It wouldn't be long before her tights split apart, and then she'd have to take them off, and what would happen then?

'Wasn't James Bond supposed to be a field agent?' I asked unexpectedly, unexpectedly to her at least, because she gave a startled laugh and answered, still laughing:

'Yes, of course. But what's that got to do with anything?'

'I don't know, but he spends money like water, and it's never seemed to me that he has any problems with budget restraints.'

Young Pérez Nuix laughed again, and perhaps not only out of politeness, but because my facile joke had genuinely amused her. It may have been the wine or her growing sense of ease and confidence, but her laughter, I noticed, bubbled up unaffectedly and unimpeded, just like Luisa's laughter when she was in a good mood or caught off guard. This wasn't to me an entirely new facet of her personality. I had seen it in the building with no name and on the occasional night out with Tupra and the others, but, at work, people's qualities and characteristics seem muffled: feelings of annoyance are contained and amusement postponed, there's not enough room or time. Her laughter also contributed to the further destruction of her already injured tights.

'Bear in mind,' she replied, 'that real-life agents have never enjoyed Fleming's fortune nor the financial backing of the Broccolis. And without them, everything is harder, meaner and more prosaic.'

She said this as if I should know who the last rather comically named people were, if, that is, it was a real name ('*broccoli*' in Italian is the plural of '*broccolo*' which has the unfortunate secondary meaning of 'idiot'). And I had no idea who they were.

'I don't know who they are,' I confessed, not bothering to pretend I knew more than I did. They were obviously well-known in England, despite their evident Italian origins, but I'd never heard of them.

'For decades Albert Broccoli was the producer of the Bond films, along with a guy named Saltzman. In the more recent movies, his name has been replaced by those of a Barbara Broccoli and a Tom Pevsner. I suppose she must be the daughter and that her father is now dead, in fact, I seem to recall reading an obituary a few years ago. The family must have made a fortune, because the films, can you believe it, have been going since 1962, and they're still making them I think – anyway, I always go and see a Bond movie when I can.'

'I must ask Peter about it,' I thought, 'before he dies,' and it seemed odd to me that such a fear and such an idea should occur to me: despite his advanced age I never imagined the world without him or him without the world. He wasn't one of those old people who wear their imminent disappearance on their face or in the way they speak or walk. On the contrary. Both the adult and the young man he had been were still so present in him that it seemed impossible that they would cease to exist merely because of something as absurd as accumulated time, it doesn't make any sense at all that it should be time that determines and dictates, that it should prevail over free will. Or perhaps, as his brother, Toby Rylands, had said many, many years before, 'When one is ill, just as when one is old or troubled, things are done half with one's own will and half with someone else's in exactly equal measure. What isn't always clear is who the part of the will that isn't ours belongs to. To the illness, to the doctors, to the medicine, to the sense of unease, to the passing years, to times long dead? To the person we no longer are and who carried off our will when he left?' 'To the face we wore yesterday,' I could have added, 'we'll always have that as long as we're remembered or some curious person pauses to look at old photographs of us, and, on the other hand, there will come a day when all faces will be skulls or ashes, and then it won't matter, we'll all be the same, us and our enemies, the people we loved most and the people we loathed.' Yes, I would have to ask Wheeler about those dedications from the fortunate and ill-fated Ian Fleming, who had known great success but few years in which to enjoy it, how they had met and how well they had known each other, 'who may know better. *Salud!*' – that is what Fleming had written in Wheeler's copy in 1957. Since starting work with Tupra I'd had less time to go and visit Peter in Oxford, or perhaps it was rather that I had too much time and my spirits were heavier, but then again my visits to him always helped fill up the former and somewhat lift the latter. However, we never let more than two weeks go by without talking for a while on the phone. He would ask how I was getting on with my new boss and with my colleagues and in my new and imprecise trade, but without demanding any details or enquiring into the present-day activities of the group, that is, into our translations of people or interpretations of lives. Perhaps he knew better than anyone how fundamentally reserved I was, or perhaps he didn't need to ask, perhaps he had a direct line to Tupra and knew all about my main activities, my advances and retreats. Sometimes I thought I sensed in him, however, a desire not to meddle, not to draw me out and even not to hear me if I began telling some story related to my work, as if he didn't want to know, or as if being on the outside made him jealous – that was possible, when someone like me was on the inside, and I was, after all, a foreigner, an upstart – or as if he felt slightly hurt to have lost, in part, my company and to have brought about that loss himself in his role as intermediary, through his intrigues and his influence. I never noticed in him a hint of spite, nor of self-reproach, nor resentment at my absence, but something resembling the mixture of grief and pride, or unspoken regret and suppressed satisfaction, that sometimes assails patrons when their protégés break free, or teachers when they see themselves outstripped by their students in audacity, talent or fame, even though both parties pretend that this hasn't happened and won't happen in their lifetimes.

The person he was most interested in was Pérez Nuix, despite his growing distance from that group to which he had belonged in another age, so remote and so different. I wasn't sure whether this was because he had heard so much from Tupra about her qualities ('That very competent half-Spanish girl of his,' he had said of her when I had still not met her, 'I can never remember her name, but he says that, with time, she'll be the best of the group, if he can hold on to her for long enough.' And he had added as if remembering another such case: 'That's one of the difficulties, most of them get fed up and leave') or because he occasionally thought I might get together with her and thus leave behind me my sentimental daze and my occasional sexual toings and froings, far less frequent than he imagined, the old tend to deem anyone whom they believe to be still virile, and therefore still young, as promiscuous – I mean truly and successfully so. Wheeler could see that the months were passing and that the situation with Luisa had still not been sorted out, as he would have preferred – there wasn't so much as a flicker, not even a tremor, even of the kind that leaves the doors more firmly shut than before; because even if they only open a crack, there is still a slight fluster of agitation – and so from his distance, fumblingly, not to say blindly, with a touch of ingenuousness and respectful paternalism, he would act as a very tentative matchmaker whenever a female name cropped up in our conversations, and that of Patricia Pérez Nuix was, inevitably, the most persistent and enduring.

'Do you get on well with her? Are you, would you say, comrades?' he asked me once. 'Contrary to what is generally believed, the best relationship you can have with the opposite sex is one of comradeship, it's the best way to make conquests and it lasts longer too.' On another occasion, he questioned me about her abilities: 'Do you find her talk interesting, her view of things, the details she picks up on? Is she as good as Tupra says she is? Do you have fun with her?' And on a third occasion, he was even more direct or more curious: 'Is the girl pretty? Apart from her youth, I mean. Do you find her attractive?'

And I had answered every time, without alacrity but with due deference: 'Yes, the beginnings of comradeship, I mean it could happen. But it's early days for that, we haven't found ourselves yet in a situation where we could unequivocally help each other, get each other out of a difficulty or a dilemma, because those are the kinds of things that create comradeship. Or long habit, and the unremarked passage of time.' And then: 'Yes, she is good, she's sharp and perceptive; she's subtle too, but never overembellishes, she doesn't invent or show off; and she's certainly fun, I don't get irritated or bored when I have to interpret alongside her, I'm always glad and willing to listen to her.' And later: 'Yes, she is rather pretty, but not too pretty. And she's funny and physical and she laughs easily, which is so often the most attractive thing about women. I don't know that I find her so attractive that I'd go to the kind of bother I might have once or actually take a step in that direction, but I certainly wouldn't turn up my nose if the opportunity happened to arise.' I remember that I resorted to Spanish for the whole of that last sentence, well, there isn't any real equivalent in other languages for '*no hacer ascos*', although 'to turn up your nose at something' comes close, and I added: 'It's just a hypothesis: it's not something I think about, not something I'm considering doing. Besides, it would be inappropriate, she's much younger than me. In theory, she's not someone I could ever aspire to.'

Wheeler responded with genuine bemusement:

'Really? Since when have you set such limits on yourself? Or put obstacles in your way? I think I'm right in saying that you're younger than Tupra, and as far as I know, he doesn't set limits on himself or put obstacles in his way in that or any other field.'

He could have been speaking in general or making a specific reference to the liaison between Tupra and Pérez Nuix about which I had so many suspicions. This was another piece of information to back up those suspicions.

'We're not all alike, Peter,' I replied. 'And the older men get, the more unalike we become, don't you think? You should know. Tupra and I are very different. We probably always were, right from childhood.'

He paid no attention to this remark, however, or else took it as a joke.

'Oh, come now. You're not going to persuade me that you've suddenly gone all shy, Jacobo. Or that you've developed a complex about your age and with it all kinds of scruples. What do ten or twenty years matter? Once someone becomes an adult, that's it, and things even out very quickly from then on. It's a point from which there's no return, I'm pleased to say, although there are some people who never achieve adulthood, not in how they live their lives or intellectually – in fact, there are more and more such people, they're a real pest, I can't abide them, and yet shops, hotels and offices, even hospitals and banks, are full of them. It's a deliberate ploy, fostered by the societies we live in. For reasons I can't understand, they choose to create irresponsible people. It's incomprehensible. It's as if they set out to create people with a handicap. How old is this bright young thing?'

'Twenty-seven at most, I would say. Certainly not much less.'

'She's a grown woman, then, she'll already have crossed Conrad's shadow line, or will be about to do so. It's the age at which life takes charge of you, if you haven't already taken charge of it yourself. The line that separates the closed from the open, the written from the blank page: it's when possibilities begin to run out, because the ones you discard become ever more irrecoverable, and more so with each day you live through. Each date a shadow, or a memory, which comes to the same thing.'

'Yes, that would be so in Conrad's day, Peter. Now, at twenty-seven, most people feel as if they're only just starting, with the doors of life flung open and real life as yet unbegun and eternally waiting. People graduate from the school of irresponsibility at a much later age now. If, as you say, they ever do.'

'Be that as it may, your age will be a matter of indifference to that girl, if you interest her or she takes a liking to you. And if she has such a keen eye as you and Tupra say, she won't have fallen asleep in puberty or childhood, she won't have dug herself in, but will be fully incorporated into the world, she'll have scrambled aboard as quickly as she could, perhaps obliged by circumstance. And if she's as acute as all that, she won't be the kind of girl who likes very young men. They'll seem too transparent, overly decipherable, she'll have read their whole story even with the book closed.' Wheeler paused for a long time, the kind of pause that announced he was weary of talking, he tired very quickly on the phone, in the hand of an old man even a phone weighs heavy, and his arm would find it tiring to hold. Before saying goodbye, he added: 'You and Tupra are not so very different, Jacobo. Well, you *are* different, but not as much as you think, or as you would like. And you ought not to spend so much time alone there in London, I've told you before, even though you have more to do now and are busier. It's not the same thing.'

And there she was before me, that bright and not-too-pretty young woman, in my apartment, at night, on my sofa, with her dog, a run in her tights, and drinking too much wine, all in order to ask me a favour, and outside I could see the steady, comfortable rain, so strong and sustained that it alone seemed to light up the night with its continuous threads like flexible metal bars or endless spears, it was as if it were excluding clear skies for good and discounting the possibility of any other weather ever appearing in the sky – or even the idea of its own absence, just like embraces when they are given willingly and with feeling and just like repugnance when repugnance is the only thing that still exists between those same two people who once embraced; the one before and the other afterwards, things almost always happen in that order and not the other way round. There was young Pérez Nuix, probably the best of us – there was no need to allow any more time to pass before saying so – the one who saw most and the most gifted of our group in the building with no name, the one who took the biggest risks and saw most deeply, more than Tupra and more than me and much more than Mulryan and Rendel, I wondered if she would guess or know what my reactions and my response would be when she finally asked me straight out what she had come to ask me after her long walk, drenched despite her umbrella. And I thought she would doubtless have made her measurements, her calculations and her prognostications, and that she would probably know what I still did not know about myself – perhaps she had her own kind of prescience; I must tread very carefully and sidestep her predictions, or deliberately prove them wrong, but that would be difficult, because she was also capable of foreseeing when and how I would intentionally and far-sightedly sidestep the predictions I had foreseen. We could end up cancelling each other out and our conversation would then lack both truth and meaning, as was the case with everything we did. When two equal forces meet, that is the time to lay down one's weapons: when the spear is thrown to one side and the shield is lowered and laid on the grass, the sword is stuck into the ground and the helmet hung on its hilt. I should just relax and try not to get ahead of myself or act against my own best interests; I should try not to be artificial, but drink a little more of my wine calmly and unconcernedly, knowing that in the end I could answer either 'Yes' or 'No' and still direct the conversation.

'Broccoli, Saltzman, Pevsner, they're all foreign names, I mean non-British. It's striking, isn't it, a little odd, that the producers of Bond should be German or Italian in origin.' That is what I in turn replied, taking a sip of my drink and at the same time giving in to my onomastic-geographical curiosity and not urging her to get to the point. They must have been false Englishmen and women too, the members of those wealthy families. For one reason or another, there really were quite a lot of them. 'Even if they had British nationality or were born here, they still sound false.'

'Well, it seems perfectly normal to me, I don't know what you mean by "false". People have the mistaken idea that there isn't much of a racial mix here or that any foreign presence is very recent, like that Abramovich man who's taken over Chelsea or Al Fayed or other millionaire Arabs. Great Britain has been full of non-English surnames for centuries. Look at Tupra, look at me, look at Rendel, look at you. The only one of us whose name doesn't come from elsewhere is Mulryan, and he, I bet, is really an Irishman.'

'But I'm not English, I don't count,' I said. 'I'm to all intents and purposes a Spaniard, and I'm only here temporarily. At least I think I am, that's my feeling, although, who knows, I might end up staying. And you're only half-British, aren't you? Your father is Spanish. Nuix, I assume, is a Catalan name.' I pronounced it as it should be pronounced, not as a Castilian would, but as if it were written 'Nush'. I had noticed that the English, on the other hand, called her 'Niux', as if her name were written 'Nukes'.

'He was Spanish, yes, but he isn't any more,' replied young Nukes. 'Anyway, I'm not half anything, I'm English. As English as Michael Portillo, the politician, you know who I mean, at one point it looked as if he might be the next Tory Prime Minister, his father, though, was an exile from the Spanish Civil War. The next leader of the Tories was that fellow Howard, he

62

may have changed his surname, but he's Romanian originally. And many years ago in Ireland, there was that President with the unequivocally Spanish name De Valera, as nationalistic as any O'Reilly, and who, incredibly enough, emerged out of Sinn Fein. Then you have the Korda brothers, who for decades dominated this country's film industry and the painter Freud, and the composer Finzi, and the conductor Sir John Barbirolli, and that director who made *The Full Monty*, Cattaneo or Cataldi, I can't quite remember. There's Cyril Tourneur, a contemporary of Shakespeare, and the poets Dante and Christina Rossetti, and Byron's lugubrious friend, Dr John Polidori, and Conrad's real name was Korzeniowski. Gielgud is a Lithuanian or Polish name, and yet no one spoke better English on the stage; Bogarde was Dutch, and then there was that old actor Robert Donat, who played Mr Chips, his name was an abbreviation of Donatello, I believe. There were prestigious publishers like Chatto and Victor Gollancz, and the bookseller Rota. Then you have Lord Mountbatten, who started off as Battenberg, and even the Rothschilds. Not to mention the Hanoverians, who have reigned here for centuries now, however they may conceal the fact by calling their dynasty Windsor, a name-change that only occurred thanks to George V. There have always been loads of such examples, and most are or were as British as Churchill or Blair or Thatcher. Or as Disraeli, for that matter, Prime Minister during Queen Victoria's reign, and there's very little that's English about his name.' She paused for a moment. She was better informed and more cultivated than I had thought, she had probably studied at Oxford, like so many civil servants; or perhaps because she herself had a foreign surname she had learned all these antecedents by heart and identified with them. She felt entirely English, which was interesting, she would never suffer any conflicts of loyalty; it seemed to me that her reaction betrayed even a certain patriotism, which was more worrying, as is anyone's patriotism. She finished off her third glass of wine, lit another of my Peloponnese cigarettes and took two puffs, one after the other, as if she had finally decided to get to grips with her subject and these were her final preparations, the equivalent to the little mental run-up she often took at work before she came over to talk to me, beyond I mean just greeting me or asking me some isolated question; taking a drink and smoking a cigarette marked a new paragraph. All this movement (she had been gesticulating during her proclamation of Britishness and her assurance that she was no compatriot of mine, contrary to my belief or, rather, feeling) had caused the run in her tights to advance downwards and it was getting close to the top of her boot now; on its upward path it had already reached the edge of her skirt, and so I would not see it grow further in that direction unless her skirt inched up a little or she hitched it up herself, but why would she do that, though it wasn't impossible that she would do so distractedly, or perhaps that was just wishful thinking on my part. The paragraph, however, turned out to be a full stop: 'Oddly enough,' she said in another tone, 'the favour I want to ask you has to do with English people with foreign surnames, and with a daughter and a father, I'm the daughter, and the father is my own, which is why this is such a big favour. We're not as rich as the Broccoli family, of course, and that's part of the problem.' She stopped, as if unsure whether it was appropriate to slip in the odd joke, hesitating between solemnity and frivolity, almost everyone who ends up asking for something opts for the former, fearing that otherwise their plea will lack force. And exaggeration is obligatory, it's up to the person listening to water down the gravity of the request. Lying and fantasy are less obligatory, but it's still as well to assume their presence – absolute credulity when given an account of some drama or danger can prove disastrous to the person hearing it. And so while I did not prepare myself to suspend belief, I did prepare to combat or undermine it because I am, by nature, credulous until, that is, I hear a false note.

'Tell me what it's about. Tell me and I'll see what I can do, if I can do anything. What's happened to Mr Pérez Nuix, both names are his, are they not?' I couldn't help saying this in the patronising tone of someone preparing to listen, consider, think it over, be a momentary enigma, keep the other person dangling and then concede or deny or be merely ambiguous. It always makes you feel rather important, knowing that you'll take equal pleasure in saying a 'Yes' and a 'No' and a 'Possibly' ('I'm being so good,' you say to yourself; or 'I'm so hard, so implacable, I wasn't born yesterday and no one's putting anything over on me'; or 'If I don't give a decision right now, I will be the lord of uncertainty'), and so you magnanimously, patiently draw the other person out: 'What is it?' or 'Tell me' or 'Explain what you mean'; or else speak threateningly and urgently: 'Come on, spit it out' or 'You've got two minutes, make the most of them and get straight to the point' (or 'Make it short') – I was giving that young woman all the time in the world that night, the rain outside removed all sense of haste.

'Yes, my mother's maiden name was Waller. He hyphenates his two names,' she said, and she drew the hyphen in the air, 'but I don't. I'm like Conan Doyle.' She smiled, and that, I thought, would be the last smile for quite some time, for as long as it took her to present her case. 'My father's getting on a bit now, he had me quite late, from his second marriage, I've got a half-sister and half-brother somewhere who are much older than me, but I've never had much to do with them. Even though my mother was considerably younger than him, she died six years ago from galloping cancer. He was already retired by then; well, insofar as anyone can retire from doing far too many things, most of them unproductive and vague and never entirely abandoned. He was always a womaniser, and still is within his limitations, but he was quite lost or perhaps disconcerted when my mother died: he even lost interest in other women. Naturally, this didn't last very long, just a few months of playing the part of the suddenly aged widower, but he soon recovered his youth. He'd had a terrible time as a child in Spain, during the War and afterwards, until his father managed to get him out and bring him to England, my grandfather had left in 1939 and couldn't send for him until '45, when the war against Germany ended; my father was fifteen when he arrived and was always torn between the two countries, he'd left some older brothers behind in Barcelona, who, when they had the chance, chose not to change countries. And he didn't have an easy time in London at first either, until he started to make his own way. He married well, both times; not that it was hard for him, he was a charming man and very handsome. It was a great error and injustice, to use his words, that he'd had such a difficult start in life, but he, of course, forgot about the difficulties and soon made up for them. And he'd laugh when he said this. He maintains, and always has, that we come into this world in order to have a good time, and anyone who doesn't see it like that is in the wrong place, that's what he says. He was a very good-humoured man, and still is, he's one of those people who avoids sadness and is bored by suffering; even if he has real reason to suffer, he'll shake it off eventually, it just seems to him like a stupid waste of time, like a period of involuntary, enforced tedium that interrupts the party and may even ruin it. He was terribly shaken by my mother's death, I could see that, his grief was very real, some days it bordered on despair, he was almost mad with it, shut up at home, which was unheard of for a man who has spent his entire life going to sociable places in search of diversion. However, he was incapable of remaining anchored in sorrow for more than a few months. He can only cope with pain, his own or other people's, as if it were a brief performance in need of encouragement and compliments, and he would have seen wallowing in grief as not making the most of life, as a waste.'

That was the word both Wheeler and my father had used to refer to a very different thing, to the war dead, especially once the fighting's over and it becomes clear that everything has remained more or less the same, more or less as it probably would have been without all the bloodshed. That, with few exceptions, is how we all feel about wars, when we become distanced from them by passing time, and people don't even know about the crucial battles without which they might not have been born. According to young Pérez Nuix's father, time spent on heartbreak and mourning was also a waste. And it occurred to me that perhaps his idea was not so very different from that of my two old men, simply more categorical: not only were deaths a waste, whether in wartime or peacetime, it was just as much a waste to allow ourselves to be saddened or dragged down by them and not recover or be happy again. Like a knee pressing into our chest, like lead upon our soul.

'What was your father's name, I mean, what *is* his name?' I asked, correcting myself at once. I had been influenced by her temporal oscillations, 'He maintains, and always has', 'He said, he says', 'He was, he is', I imagined that she kept slipping into the wrong tense because her father was old, and she would find it harder and harder to see in him the father of her childhood; it happens to all of us, we take the fathers and mothers of our childhood to be the real, essential and almost only ones, and later, even though we still recognise and respect and support them, we see them slightly as impostors. Perhaps they, in turn, see us like that, in youth and adulthood. (I was absenting myself from my children's childhood, who knows for how much longer; the only advantage, if that banishment were to prove prolonged, would be that, later, we would not see each other as impostors, they would not see me that way, nor I them. More like uncle and nephews, something strange like that.)

'Alberto. Albert. Or Albert.' The second time, she said the name as it would be pronounced in Catalan, with the stress on the second syllable, and the third time as it is in English, with the stress on the first. I deduced from this that she must have ended up pronouncing her father's name in that third way in his adopted country, and that this is what friends and acquaintances would call him, and his second wife when they were at home, and how the child Pérez Nuix would have heard him addressed before she relinquished that pretentious hyphen. 'Why do you ask?'

'Oh, no reason. When someone is talking to me about a person I don't know, I always get a clearer idea of them if I know their first name. Names can be very influential sometimes. For example, it's not insignificant that Tupra is called Bertram.' And with my next words, I took advantage of my temporary position in the control seat, it was an attempt to make her feel insecure, or to instil in her a sense of now unnecessary haste, I was used to the situation now and to her agreeable presence, my living room was infinitely more welcoming with her inside it, and more entertaining. 'I still don't know why you're telling me all this about your father. Not that I don't find it interesting, mind. Plus, of course, I'm interested in you.'

'Don't worry, I haven't really been beating about the bush, or not entirely, I'm getting to the point now,' she replied, slightly embarrassed. My words had had an effect, sometimes it's very easy to make someone feel nervous, even people who are not the nervous type. She was one such person, as were Tupra, Mulryan and Rendel. And presumably I was as well, given that they'd made me a member of the group, although I didn't believe that to be a virtue I possessed, not at least that I was aware of, I often feel like a real bundle of nerves. Of course it might be that we were all pretending or that we simply kept our cool at work, but were less successful at doing so outside. 'Anyway, since my mother died, my father has spent the last six years more out of control than ever, more desperate for activity and company. And after a certain age, however sociable and charming you might be, getting both those things can cost money, and without my mother there to keep a check on him, he's been spending it hand over fist.'

'You mean he let her manage his affairs?'

'Not exactly. It's just that the money was largely hers, she was the one with the income, from her family, and all more or less in order and assured. Not that she was rich, she didn't own a fortune or anything, but she had enough not to suffer any financial difficulties and to spend a life, or even a life and a half, in comfort. His earnings were sporadic. He would plunge optimistically into various risky businesses, film and television production, publishing houses, fashionable bars, would-be auction houses that never got off the ground. One or two went well and brought him large profits for a year or two, but they were never very stable. Others went disastrously wrong, or else he was cheated and lost everything he'd invested. Either way, he never changed his lifestyle, or went without his usual entertainments and celebrations. My mother did try to curb his excesses and ensure that he didn't squander so much money that it constituted a danger to her finances. But that ended six years ago. And about a month ago now, I found out that he's incurred enormous gambling debts. He's always loved the races and betting on his beloved horses; but now he bets on anything, whatever it might be – and he's widened the field to the Internet where the possibilities are endless; he frequents gambling dens and casinos, places where there's never any shortage of overexcited people, which for as long as I can remember is what has always attracted him, and so those places have become his principal way of keeping the party going, given that for him, the world is one long party; and to go to those places, he doesn't have to charm anyone or wait to be invited, which is a great advantage for a man getting on in years. Then he took to disappearing from home for long periods, and I'd hear nothing from him until it occurred to him to call me up one night from Bath or Brighton or Paris or Barcelona or from here in London, where he'd taken it into his head to book into a hotel, in the city where he has his own house, and a very nice house too, simply in order to feel more a part of the hustle and bustle, to wander through the foyer and strike up conversations in the various reception rooms, usually with absurd American tourists, who are always the keenest to chat with the natives. I also learned that, up until only a few months ago and for decades now, he'd been renting a little suite in a family-run hotel, the Basil Street Hotel, which isn't luxurious and a bit old-fashioned, but, still, imagine the expense, and imagine what he must have used it for, and hospitality is the thing that always costs most. At least that debt has been paid, the people at the hotel were very understanding and I came to an agreement with them. That isn't the case with the gambling debts, of course, which have got completely out of hand, as tends to happen to innocent aficionados, especially those who like to ingratiate themselves with their new acquaintances, and my father loves to keep refreshing his circle of friends.' Young Pérez Nuix paused for breath (albeit unostentatiously), she uncrossed and crossed her legs, inverting their position (the one beneath on top, and the one on top beneath, I thought I heard the run advance still further, I was keeping my eye on it), and she pushed her glass towards me an inch, propelling it forward by its base. I would have preferred her not to drink so much, although she seemed to hold her drink well. I pretended not to notice, I would wait until she insisted, or until she pushed it a little closer. 'Fortunately, the debts aren't too widely spread, which is something. So he doesn't entirely lack sense, and he borrowed money from a bank, well, from a banker friend, on a semi-personal basis, the banker was really a friend of my mother's and only my father's friend by proximity and association. However, this gentleman, Mr Vickers, brought in a front man, in order, I understand, not to involve his bank in any way: he's a man with very varied business dealings, he's into lotteries and betting and a thousand other things, including acting as an occasional moneylender. The sums always came from the banker in this case, but the front man was charged with delivering the money and recovering it, along, shall we say, with the bank's interest. And if he can't recover the money, then he'll have to answer to Vickers and pay him the money out of his own pocket, now are you beginning to get some idea of the mess my father is in?'

'I'm not sure; they'd report him, wouldn't they? Or how does it work? Can't you come to some arrangement with this man Vickers, if he was a friend of your mother's?'

'No, that isn't how it works at all, you don't understand,' said Pérez Nuix, and in those last few words there was, for the first time, a hint of desperation. 'The money is originally his, but to all practical effects it's as if it wasn't. It's as if he had given the order: "Lend this gentleman up to this amount and have him return it to you with this much interest and by this deadline, and if he doesn't return it, bring me the money anyway." Officially, he doesn't even touch it, when it comes to handing it over or to recovering it. It's not up to him to worry about the transactions, these are the responsibility of the front man from start to finish, and the banker exercises no control over them whatsoever; and that is precisely how he wants it; consequently, he refuses to intervene, nor would he wish to. He doesn't even want to know if the money he receives on a certain date comes from the debtor or not; he will receive it from the person who received it from him in the first place, which is how it should be. That's all. The rest is not his responsibility. And so my father doesn't have a problem with Vickers, but with this other man, and he's not the sort to go to the police to make some pointless formal complaint. It isn't like it was in Dickens' day when people went to prison for the most paltry debts. What would he gain by that anyway, putting a seventy-five-year-old man behind bars? Assuming that were a possibility.'

'Wouldn't they first impound your father's goods or something?'

'Forget about all those slow, legal routes, Jaime, this man would never resort to anything like that in order to settle an outstanding debt, and I assume that's why Vickers and other people use him, so that no one has to waste time and so that everything turns out as planned.'

'Couldn't your father sell something, his house or whatever else he has left?' Pérez Nuix's look, a flicker of impatience despite her inferior or disadvantageous position (she had now started asking me the favour), made me realise that such a solution was impossible, either because the house had been sold already or because she wasn't prepared to leave her father without his own home, which is the one thing that consoles and calms the old and the sick when the time comes to rest, however fond they've been of wandering. I didn't insist, I changed tack at once. 'Well, if what you're saying is that you're afraid they'll beat him up or knife him, I don't see what they'd gain from that, the banker or his front man. The corpse of an elderly man turning up in the river.' – 'I've seen too many old films,' I thought then. 'I always imagine the Thames giving back swollen, ashen bodies, rocked by the waters.'

'The front man would pay the banker, so the banker's no longer involved, you can forget about him; he merely triggered the whole thing, and although the money comes from him, it doesn't any more.' – 'According to that theory,' I thought, 'matters are not triggered by the person doing the asking, but by the person who grants the request; I'd better take note' – 'As for the front man, he might suffer a loss on this occasion, but on others, he'll have made a profit and will continue to do so. What he can't allow is for there to be a precedent, for someone not to keep their word and for nothing to happen to him. Nothing bad I mean. Do you understand?' And again there was that note in her voice, perhaps it was more incipient exasperation than anything else. 'Not that they'll necessarily inflict physical harm on my father, although that can't be ruled out at all. One thing is sure, though, they will seriously harm him in some way. Possibly through me, if they can find no better way of teaching him a lesson, or, from their point of view, of applying the rules, penalising non-payment and seeing justice done. They couldn't let a bold seafarer who has failed to pay the toll go unreprimanded. Besides, that isn't what most worries me, what might happen to me I mean, and it's unlikely they would turn on me, they know that I know some influential people, that on some flanks I'm protected and can look after myself; I'm not protected against a beating or a knife attack, obviously, but they wouldn't take that route with me, they'd try instead to discredit me, to make sure I didn't get to work again in any of the fields that interest me, to ruin my future, and doing that to a young person isn't at all easy, the world keeps turning and sometimes, inevitably, things right themselves again. What I most fear is what they might do to him, physically or morally, or biographically. He walks so proudly through life that he wouldn't understand what was happening to him. That would be the worst thing, his confusion, he would never recover. I don't know, they would spoil what remains of his life, or else shorten it. Always assuming, of course, touch wood, fingers crossed, that they don't decide simply to take his life.' And she touched wood and crossed her fingers. 'It's very easy to ruin an old man, or indeed, heaven forbid, to kill him.' And she again crossed her fingers. 'He'd fall over if you pushed him.'

She fell silent for a moment and sat looking at her empty glass, but this time she preferred not to or didn't even think to push it closer to me. She used the same two fingers to stroke the base of the glass. It was as if she could see her blithe, frivolous, fragile father in that glass, and you would only need to tip it over to shatter it.

'But what can I do about it? Where do I come into all this?'

She glanced up at once and looked at me with her bright, quick eyes, they were brown and young and not yet overburdened with tenacious visions that refuse to go away.

'The man you're due to interpret the day after tomorrow or the next, or at the latest next week,' she replied, barely letting me finish my second question, like someone who has spent a long time in the fog waiting for the lighthouse to appear and who cries out when she does finally spot it. 'Well, he's the front man, our problem, *the* problem. And he's another Englishman with a strange surname. He's called Vanni Incompara.'

Vanni or Vanny Incompara, that, she said, was how he was known, although his official name was John, and he was presumably English, but she wasn't sure whether he was so by birth – she was currently trying to put together facts about his past, but the search kept throwing up unexpected lacunae, and he was turning out to be a most elusive man – or by virtue of a very rapidly acquired citizenship, thanks to influential contacts or to some strange secret subterfuge, and so she didn't know whether he was a first- or second-generation immigrant, like her and Tupra, who had both been born in London, although for all she knew, Bertram might be third- or fourth- or nth-generation, perhaps his family had been settled on the island for centuries. She had never asked him about that, nor about the origin of his strange surname, she didn't know if it was Finnish, Russian, Czech, or Armenian – or Turkish as I guessed and as Wheeler had suggested to me the first time he mentioned the person who would later become my boss, slightly mocking his name before I had even met Tupra – or, as she suddenly suggested, Indian; the fact is she had no idea, perhaps she would ask him one day, he never mentioned his roots, nor any relatives alive or dead or distant or close, that is, blood relatives – she must have been thinking about Beryl when she added this, and I, of course, thought of her too – as if he had sprung into being by spontaneous generation; although there was no reason why he should mention his roots, in England people tended to be reserved if not opaque when it came to personal matters, he sometimes talked about himself and his experiences, but always in vague terms, never giving a place or a date to his exploits, recalling each one with almost no context, isolated from the others, as if he were showing us only tiny fragments of shattered tombstones.

It was possible that this John Incompara had arrived in England not that many years ago, which might explain why he still liked to be called by the diminutive form of his Italian name, Giovanni, she explained, didactic and helpful, just in case I hadn't picked up on that. Anyway, his activities had only come to light fairly recently, and he was clearly an able fellow: he had quickly made himself some money – or perhaps he had brought it with him – and some relatively important friendships, and if, as was likely, he was breaking the law, he was careful to disguise or camouflage any illegalities with other entirely legitimate deals and to leave no proof or evidence of the more drastic, more brutal actions he was suspected of carrying out. She could find nothing incriminating, or, rather, nothing she could use as a negotiating tool to persuade him to write off the paternal debt. The only thing she had now was me. Vanni Incompara was going to be examined, studied and interpreted by the group and I had been assigned to do this work alongside Tupra. As far as she knew, this report had been commissioned by a third party, by some private private individual who was doubtless considering doing business with Incompara and wanted to be extra careful and find out more – to what extent he could be trusted and to what extent he would deceive, to what extent he was constant and to what extent resentful or patient or dangerous or resolute, and so on, the usual thing. In turn, should the opportunity arise during this probable encounter with Tupra, Incompara wanted to try and establish the beginnings of a relationship or even friendship with him, for he knew that Tupra had excellent contacts in almost every sphere and could prove a fruitful introduction to many celebrities and other wealthy people. What Pérez Nuix was asking of me was no big deal really, she said. It would be a huge favour to her but would not require much effort from me, she said again, despite my earlier protests, now that she was explaining what would be required. I merely had to help Incompara – insofar as this was possible and prudent – to emerge

75

from this scrutiny with a Good or a Pass; to give a favourable opinion about his trustworthiness, his attitude towards associates and allies – could he prove dangerous, did he hold a grudge – his ability to resolve problems and overcome difficulties, his personal courage; but neither must I exaggerate or diverge too much from what Tupra saw in him or from what I believed Tupra saw (he didn't tend to give his own opinion in our presence, instead he would ask us and urge us on, and that way we would guess where he was leading us and where he was heading), but introduce shades and nuances – which would be easy enough – so that I would not present our boss with a picture lit by only one light or painted all one colour, which he would be inclined to distrust on principle because it was far too simple; I must, in short, in no way prejudice Incompara's chances. And if I happened to notice the slightest hint of affinity or sympathy between the two men, I should foment and encourage this later, although again unemphatically, discreetly, even indifferently; just a quiet echo, a whisper, a murmur. 'The tranquil and patient or reluctant and languid murmur,' I thought, 'of words that slip by gently or indolently, without the obstacle of the alert reader, or of vehemence, and which are then absorbed passively, as if they were a gift, and which resemble something easy and incalculable that brings no advantage. Like the words carried along or left behind by rivers in the middle of a feverish night, when the fever has abated; and that is one of the times when anything can be believed, even the craziest, most unlikely things, even a non-existent drop of blood, just as one believes in the books that speak to you then, to your weariness and your somnambulism, to your fever, to your dreams, even if you are or believe yourself to be wide awake, and books can persuade us of anything then, even that they're a connecting thread between the living and the dead, that they are in us and we are in them, and that they understand us.' And immediately I remembered more or less what Tupra had said at Sir Peter Wheeler's buffet supper by the River Cherwell in Oxford: 'Sometimes that moment lasts only a matter of days, but sometimes it lasts for ever.'

'But if this man won't even write off the debt of a defenceless old man,' I said to Pérez Nuix after we had both fallen silent for a few seconds; I had rested my right cheek on my fist while I listened to her, and I was still in that same position; and I realised that she had done the same while she was talking to me, both of us in that identical posture, like an old married couple who unconsciously imitate each other's gestures, 'and if you believe him capable of brutal acts and if that's what you most fear about him in your father's case; and if he's not the dissembling type, as you said a little while ago ("I know this, I know him," you said), then I don't see how I could possibly persuade Tupra not to see what is glaringly obvious. Maybe you're attributing to me gifts I don't possess, or too much influence, or else you take Bertram for a scatterbrain and a greenhorn, which I find hard to believe. He's far more experienced than I am, not to mention more know-ledgeable and more perceptive. Probably even more than you, more experienced, I mean.' I made this unnecessary clarification, thinking of Tupra's own views on her abilities, at least according to Wheeler, and also because I didn't want to downgrade her. She didn't, however, pick up the indirect compliment.

'No, you haven't fully understood me, Jaime,' she replied, again with that instantly suppressed note of desperation or exasperation. 'I didn't explain myself properly when I said that. I've been with Incompara, I've met him a couple of times now, to see what I could get out of him or what could be done for my father, to try and calm him down and gain time, to see what he's interested in and to see if I have some bargaining chip in my hand I wasn't aware of, and it turns out I do have one. If you will help me. It's true, he's not the dissembling type. By which I mean that you can tell at once that he'll have no scruples he can't set aside if he needs to. And that he's probably brutal about it. Not personally perhaps (I can't imagine him beating anyone up himself), but in the orders he might give and the decisions he might take. There's his rigidity about any agreements he makes, the obsessive importance he gives to obligations being met, in a way he's a stickler for the rules, although that might just be an act he's putting on for my benefit to justify his intransigence in my affair. He only cares about other people meeting their obligations, of course, not about meeting his own. A characteristic he shares with far too many people nowadays, never have so many eyes been so contented to wear their beams with pride.' She didn't use the Spanish word '*vigas*' here, but the English 'beams'; this happened very rarely, but it did happen now and then; as she herself said, she was, after all, English. 'But none of these things is necessarily bad or negative or off-putting in a prospective colleague. On the contrary, and that's precisely why he's used by people like Mr Vickers, an honourable man who simply doesn't want to bother with or know anything about the confusing or unpleasant details. Bertie will, of course, see all of that in Incompara, and you won't say anything to contradict it, because you'll observe that too and there would no point in arguing over something so obvious. No doubt about it, Incompara is a frightening guy (if he wasn't, my situation wouldn't be so serious), and in that respect it's not a matter of him dissembling, that would be extremely hard for him to do. I'm not really asking you to lie about anything very much, Jaime, especially when there would be no point. There's no point to any lie unless it's believable. Well, unless it's believed. Forgive me for insisting so much on this, but while I'm really not asking you for very much, *I* would gain enormously.'

'What would you gain exactly?'

'Vanni Incompara would be willing to write off the entire debt in exchange for this.'

'In exchange for what exactly?' I asked, repeating the word 'exactly'. 'What would satisfy this man? What would the consequences be? What would your part in all this be? And do you believe him?'

'Yes, I do in this case. He wouldn't hesitate to teach my father a lesson or anyone else who didn't keep his word, but I'm also sure that he would always rather save himself the bother. He won't mind not getting the money back if he's compensated for it with something worthwhile; he's got plenty of money. He knows that someone has asked our group to assess him, I mean, that they've asked Bertie, since he's the one who receives instructions from above as well as most of the private commissions, those of any substance. I don't know who has asked for the report, Incompara hasn't told me, but that doesn't matter to us, does it? We don't usually know anyway. Whoever they are, it's important to him that he wins their approval and that they don't reject him, or that he reaches an agreement with them or strikes a deal or gets to participate in their projects. He'd consider the debt paid off entirely if I made all or any of those things happen – if he's accepted by the people who are submitting him to this examination, that's all he needs. He would, he says, put it down to my intervention, to my collaboration, however partial, as long as it did the trick; he's obviously not a hundred per cent sure of himself, he must know what his weak points are and will imagine a trained eye would detect them, well, we all feel that way under scrutiny. It would take a few days to know the result, perhaps a week or more, but meanwhile . . . well, at the worst, we would have bought my father a deferment.' Yes, her Spanish was decidedly bookish: she didn't manage '*vigas*', but she did use '*escarmentar*' – to teach someone a lesson – '*entablar negocios*' – to strike a deal – and '*enjundia*' – substance. She had made the matter her own, she wanted to leave her father out of it as much as possible, to spare him even the negotiations, she had taken on his debt, which is why she had said 'He'd consider the debt paid off entirely' and 'my situation' and 'my affair'. No 'we' or 'our'.

'Why are you so sure that I'll be the one chosen to interpret this fellow Incompara? It could be you, and then you'd have no problem and wouldn't have to ask anyone for a favour.'

'I've worked with Bertie for several years now,' she replied. 'I usually know who's going to be assigned to whom, when it's not routine work and I'm told about it beforehand. When there's a lot of money involved or if, for whatever reason, special tact is required – for example, if we had to make a study of the Prince's current girlfriend (and it will happen, we'll be asked to do that sooner or later) – he would use me for the task. To help him out, shall we say, for a second opinion, as a contrast, because he wouldn't delegate such a task to just anyone. Other- wise, he follows a complex system of turn-taking, depending on our individual characteristics. He doesn't stick to it rigidly, but according to that system and to my calculations, it's your turn. I'd love it if he chose me to interpret Incompara. If only . . . And if I'm wrong and that's what happens, I can assure you I'll be the first to celebrate, more than you or him, more than anyone. That would make things much easier for me, I'd prefer not to have to depend on you. Not to have to bother you with this or get you mixed up in it all. I gave all this a lot of thought before asking you. I've been thinking about it for the last few days, and just now, during the walk over here, more than once I was on the verge of turning around and going home. What I can't do is offer myself for the job, or show a particular interest in taking it on, because Bertie would immediately wonder why and ask me questions and get suspicious; he never shies away from suspicions or brushes them under the carpet, he never thinks anyone is above suspicion. Not even his own mother, if she's still alive, although, as I said, I've never heard him mention his family. And there's another element too: from what I know, Incompara must have a finger in a lot of pies. Bertie will probably think that, among other factors, you are the least exposed to previous chance contaminations because you've not been in London all that long.'

I sat looking at her and then poured her the glass of wine I'd denied her before, the fourth. I could see that she was tired, or perhaps beginning to feel the effort of having to persuade and to ask, which takes a lot of energy, and that she was tense too, which is exhausting, and there's always a moment when, however enthusiastically we might have begun an assault, we doubt that we'll get what we want, that we'll succeed. The whole thing suddenly seems pointless, we're convinced people will say 'No' or even take pleasure in saying 'No' and refuse, and that they'll be able to come up with cast-iron reasons for doing so: 'I'm a bit hard up at the moment', 'I don't want to get involved', 'Sorry, you're asking too much of me', 'It won't work, I'm no good at that kind of thing', 'I have my loyalties', 'It's too big a risk', 'If it was up to me, I'd do it, but there are other people involved'; or more clearly, 'What's in it for me?' Perhaps young Pérez Nuix, in a sudden loss of faith, was already asking herself which of these formulae I would opt for. Yes, what *was* in it for me? I could see no benefit at all, and she would know that I couldn't, because there was none. She hadn't even tried that route, at least not yet, and hadn't even attempted to invent some benefit. During those moments when she seemed distracted, almost resigned, I again glanced at the run in her tights, at her ever more naked leg. I hoped she would do something before her tights exploded (that would be a shock) or went all baggy and loose (that would be repellent) or suddenly dropped to the floor (that would be humiliating), none of these three possibilities appealed to me, but they would break the spell of that torn but still taut fabric. And so I indicated her thighs with a lift of my chin and said (the words just came out, my will did not intervene, or appeared not to):

'I don't know if you've noticed, but you've got an enormous run in your tights. It must have happened while you were walking. Or perhaps the dog did it.'

'Yes,' she replied easily, unsurprised, 'I noticed it a while ago, but didn't want to interrupt you. I'd better just nip to the bathroom and take them off. How embarrassing.' She stood up (farewell, vision) and picked up her bag, the dog got to his feet as well, ready to follow her, but she stopped him with two words in English (he was, of course, a native English dog), persuaded him to lie down again, and disappeared. 'How embarrassing,' she said again when she was already in the corridor, out of my field of vision. But she didn't seem in the least embarrassed. 'She isn't really that tired or discouraged or depressed,' I thought. 'Interrupt *me*? That can't have been a mistake or a slip. Not even after all the wine she's drunk. She's the one doing the talking, the telling, the one who came here to plead with me, although she hasn't really done that yet, neither by her tone of voice or her choice of vocabulary nor by being tedious or insistent. Yet she is, nevertheless, pleading, only without actually running the risk of provoking a flat refusal, which would be counterproductive. She's asking me something, but without a hint of pathos and without humiliating herself, almost as if she weren't asking for anything, but she isn't doing so out of pride. She's simply setting out the information.' When she returned, she was no longer wearing any tights, so she wasn't one of those far-sighted women who always carry a spare pair; or perhaps she was, but had decided not to put them on, preferring boots against her bare skin, and it wasn't cold in the apartment. She crossed her legs as if nothing had happened (the vision returned, rather improved in fact), she picked up two olives, nibbled a crisp and took a timid sip of her wine, perhaps she was watching what she was drinking more closely than I thought. 'So, Jaime, what do you say? Can I count on your help? It's a big favour I'm asking you.'

I had been sitting down for too long. I got up and went over to the window, I opened it for a few seconds and put my head out and looked up at the sky, at the street, my cheeks and the back of my neck got slightly wet, the rain wouldn't stop for several days and nights, it looked as if it were going to hang over the city for some time, or over the country which for her was '*país*' or perhaps also '*patria*', the dangerous, empty concept and the dangerous, inflammatory word, which would allow a mother to say in justification of her son's actions: '*La patria es la patria*' – one's country is one's country – and when it comes to defending one's country, lies are no longer lies. Poor trapped mother, the mother of the man who betrayed not his country, but his former friend, it's always safer to betray an individual, however close to them we might be, than some vague, abstract idea that anyone can claim to represent, for then, at every step, we might find ourselves accused by strangers, by standard-bearers we have never seen before, who will feel betrayed by our actions or lack of action; that's the bad thing about ideas, their self-declared representatives keep crawling out of the woodwork, and anyone can take up an idea to suit their needs or interests and proclaim that they'll defend it by whatever means necessary, bayonet or betrayal, persecution or tank, mortar or defamation, brutality or dagger, anything goes. Perhaps it would be easier for me than for Pérez Nuix to try and betray Tupra. For me he was a single individual and nothing more, while for her, he might, in some measure, represent her country or at least embody an idea. The deception would come from her, but via an intermediary, namely me, and such intermediaries help enormously to diffuse blame, it's as if one were less involved or, once the thing is done, almost not involved at all, in the eyes of others, but also in one's own eyes, which is why people so often resort to front men, hired assassins, soldiers, thugs, straw men, paid killers and the police, and even the courts, which often serve as the executive branch of our passions, if we first manage to draw them in and later convince them. It's easier to do away with someone or bring about their ruin if you only give the order or set the appropriate mechanisms going, or pay the money or hatch a plot or approach the appropriate person with a tip-off, or if you merely make a formal complaint and conspire and have other people lead your victim to the cell, not to mention execute him once he has passed through the hands of innumerable intermediaries, all of them legal, who share the blame out among themselves as they follow that long road and return to us only the lukewarm leftovers, a few insubstantial crumbs, and all we receive at the end of the process that we originated are a few terse words, a mere communiqué and sometimes only an enigmatic phrase: 'Sentence has been passed', or 'It's done', or 'Problem solved', or 'No need to worry any more', or 'The torment's over' or 'You can sleep easy now'. Or even 'I have done the deed' (in the words of that ancient Scotsman). It would be less sinister in my case, merely a matter of phoning Patricia one day or not even that, of whispering to her in the office, when we met or passed: 'He fell for it.' The first traitor's name, Del Real it was, had also used intermediaries against my father: first, he recruited the second traitor, that Professor Santa Olalla who lent his signature to back up a complaint against someone he didn't even know, and then . . . Those two men did not go in person to get Juan Deza on the feast day of San Isidro in 1939, they sent Franco's police to arrest him and put him in prison, and then others intervened, witnesses, a prosecutor, a sham lawyer and judge, almost nothing is ever done directly or face to face, we don't even see the face of the person bringing about our ruin, there is almost always someone in the middle, between you and me, or between me and the dead man, between him and her.

'Why haven't you gone straight to Tupra and asked him? Surely if you explained, as you have to me, about your father he'd understand and grant you this one favour? He'll be sure to make an exception. You know him better than you know me, you seem quite close, you share a kind of ironic affection, if I can put it like that, as if you had an out-of-office relationship too.' I didn't want to continue along that route, I didn't want to insinuate what I suspected existed between them; although I didn't believe that it still existed, I imagined it to be more a thing of the past, and possibly only a very transient thing, or only half-voluntary. I was speaking to her now from more of a distance, with my back against the open window, I could feel the air through my shirt, fortunately it wasn't raining hard, I would have to shut the window as soon as the smoke cleared. 'In fact, you hardly know me at all. What made you think I would be more accessible than him, readier to agree to what you're asking, more helpful? I'm sure he must owe you some debt of gratitude, even if only for the years of collaboration and the good work you've done. I, on the other hand,' I hesitated for a moment, did a swift recap and found nothing, 'I as yet have no reason to be grateful to you, as far as I know or can recall.'

'You're Spanish,' she said, 'and therefore less rigid when it comes to principles. You're new to the job, you might leave soon and you're on a salary. Not that Bertram has that many principles – in the usual understanding of the term – nor are they of the noblest kind; obviously he's capable of making exceptions, he has no alternative in his job, or indeed in most jobs. But the principles he has, he holds to, and one of them is not to mess around in any way with his work. If a mistake occurs, he'll accept that, but not if it's due to negligence or if it's a deliberate, a false mistake. He only accepts unavoidable errors, when we really are misled or are wrong or we miss something, it happens to us all from time to time, not seeing clearly and getting things totally wrong. No, this is one favour he wouldn't grant. He'd urge me to find other solutions, he'd think that there must be some other way, but I know there isn't, I've gone over and over it in my head. More than that, if he knew about the situation, he'd take it as just another bit of information on Incompara, he'd use it in the report and possibly to Incompara's disadvantage, I would run the risk of everything turning out exactly as I don't want it to, and it would be all my fault. He cares about his own prestige and fancies himself as an expert. He doesn't think he's infallible, but he does believe he renders a real service to the state and to our clients, I mean, the people who come to him aren't just anybody. He also believes he has a very good eye when it comes to choosing the staff he works with. He doesn't take on just anyone, in case you hadn't noticed. You started as an interpreter of languages. The fact that you've gone on to other things is because he saw that you had real ability and because he trusts you. You've risen really fast. The last thing he would expect would be for one of us to deliberately distort an interpretation or ask him to do so. I get the impression with you, though, that none of this really matters. I have the feeling you're just waiting and meantime earning some money, doing something that you find fairly easy, and more fun than working for the radio. Waiting to know what to do, to see what to do, or to be summoned to Madrid, waiting for someone to say "Come back". Don't take this the wrong way, but I don't think your heart is really in this job. That's why I'm asking you and not Bertie. What does it matter to you? And it really is a big favour.'

'Come, come, I was so wrong about you before,' I thought. 'Sit down here beside me, somehow I just couldn't see you clearly before. Come here. Come with me. Come back and stay here for ever.' The nights continued to pass and I heard no such words, nothing like them, not even a contradictory murmur or a false echo. Perhaps Pérez Nuix was right, perhaps I was just there waiting, 'waiting without hope', in the words of an English poet whom so many have copied since. But if the voice never came, over the phone or in some unexpected letter, or in person when I finally went to see my children, there would come a day when I would wake up with the feeling that I was no longer waiting. ('Last night I was still all right, but today? I'm another day older, that's the only difference and yet my existence has changed. I'm no longer waiting.') On that morning, I would discover that I had become used to London, to Tupra and to Pérez Nuix, to Mulryan and to Rendel, to the office with no name and to my day-to-day work and, from time to time, to Wheeler, who had known Luisa and would soon become a link with my forgetting. I would discover that I had got used to everything – I mean to the point of not feeling surprised when I opened my eyes or not even thinking about any of them. These others would become my everyday and my world, the thing that requires no reason to exist, my air, and I would no longer miss Luisa, or my former city and life. Only my children.

I closed the window, I was starting to feel a little chilly and, more to the point, I noticed that she was too: she was no longer wearing tights, and I saw that she was tempted to pull her skirt down over her thighs, thus depriving me of that pleasant view. However, I stayed where I was, with my back to the street, the sky and the rain. And I thought: 'As she doubtless foresaw, this woman is well on the way to persuading me. But it's still up to me to answer "Yes" or "No" or "Maybe".'

'Before, you said that I wouldn't really have to lie about anything very much,' I said. 'What exactly is that "nothing very much"? What should I tell Tupra that I see or don't see in Incompara and that I probably will or won't see? In any case, won't he also see or not see the same thing?'

Young Pérez Nuix was hardly drinking at all now. Either her furious thirst had passed or she knew exactly how much she could drink and how fast. She was, however, smoking. She lit another Karelias cigarette, she must have liked the slightly spicy taste. With the lighter still in her hand, she uncrossed her legs and left them slightly apart, and from where I was, I thought I could see as far as her crotch, a flash of white panties. I was careful not to let my eyes remain fixed on that point, she would have noticed at once. I merely allowed myself the occasional fleeting glance.

'There are some fundamental things that are not at all easy to pick up on at a meeting, during a conversation or on a video, and I don't know if there is a video of Incompara that Bertie could show you. It's unlikely, but possible – he can get hold of video footage of almost anyone. It isn't easy to see, for example, that a person is a coward, and that in a moment of great danger he'll leave you in the lurch, especially if there's some physical danger or, let's say, a risk of prison. But that's certainly been my impression on the couple of occasions I've met Incompara. I may be wrong, however, and it would be inadvisable for the report to reflect that; it would cause him irreparable harm. The people who have commissioned the report would want nothing to do with Incompara if such a characteristic were attributed to him, that's for sure. Well, it's not a characteristic anyone likes, it makes you feel vulnerable, unsafe. In fact, it's everyone's worst nightmare, thinking that if things were to take an unexpected turn or if a situation got nasty, the person who should be helping would simply take off, duck out and leave us high and dry or, worse, pin the blame on us in order to save himself. If you get that feeling too, you mustn't mention it to Bertie, that's where you would have to lie, or, rather, say nothing. And if Bertie also picks up on it, you'll have to try, very carefully, to persuade him that it isn't so.' She paused very briefly and her gaze grew abstracted, as if she really were thinking or puzzling something out even as she was speaking, and people rarely do that. 'It's one of the hardest things to identify, as is its opposite. It's where we're most likely to slip up, and even when we think we know, there's always a nagging doubt that won't go away until we've had a chance to put it to the test. Not that one has to try very hard to sow that seed of doubt. People's forecasts or declarations on the matter, regarding their valiant or pusillanimous character, are almost no use at all. It's the thing they hide best, although the verb "hide" is inappropriate really: most of the time, they conceal it so well because they themselves have no idea how they'd react, just as a new recruit doesn't know how he'll react to his baptism of fire. People tend to imagine what they would do in accordance with their hopes or fears; but almost none of us knows just how we'd respond if placed in a dangerous situation. At most, we find out when we're put to the test, but that doesn't happen very often in our normal lives and might never happen, we usually get through the day with no major upsets or dangers. Not that the discovery that we behaved with valour or cowardice in a particular circumstance proves anything anyway, because the next time we might behave quite differently, possibly in exactly the opposite way. We can never guarantee either boldness or panic, and if we ourselves know nothing about this facet of our character, it would take enormous skill on the part of an observer, an interpreter, to discern it in someone else, that is, to manage to foresee a response about which even the person in question has his doubts, and to which he is, indeed, half-blind. That, among other reasons, is why you're here: you have a good eye for that characteristic, better even than Rendel, and that's not just my opinion, I've heard Bertie say so and he's not exactly lavish with compliments. He clearly trusts you in that field more than anyone, including himself. So it wouldn't be hard for you to make him waver, anything you said certainly wouldn't go unheeded. You would have more difficulty when it came to other aspects, for example, Incompara's relative lack of scruples, his harshness towards those over whom he has power, the brutality by proxy that I mentioned before. You wouldn't have to lie about those things, though, nor even keep quiet about them; as I said, they wouldn't prevent the people who've asked for this investigation from taking him on or letting him in or whatever, such qualities would be seen, rather, as advantages and virtues. Cowardice, on the other hand, brings no benefits at all. No one thinks of it as a desirable quality. I mean other people's cowardice, of course, not our own. We all have to come to terms with our own.' She didn't use the normal Spanish expression here either, but translated it literally as '*llegar a términos*'. Maybe, although it didn't show, she *was* a bit tired or slightly drunk, which is when language tends to falter.

It's true, almost no one knows, not even when put to the test. If that night someone had asked me how I would react when confronted by a man who suddenly produced a sword in a public toilet and threatened to cut off another man's head in my presence, I wouldn't have had the slightest idea or, if I had ventured an opinion, I would have been quite wrong. It would have seemed to me so improbable, so anachronistic, so unlikely that I might perhaps have dared to respond, with the optimism that always accompanies our imaginings of something that isn't going to happen, or which is purely hypothetical and therefore impossible: 'I'd stop him, I'd grab his arm and block the blow, I'd force him to drop the sword, I'd disarm him.' Or else, if the image had seemed real and I had believed it or, for a moment, fully accepted it, I would have been able to reply: 'God, what a nightmare, how dreadful. I'd run away, without a backward glance, take to my heels so that no two-edged sword fell on me, so that I wouldn't be the one for the chop.' The incident in the toilet had happened not long after that night of rain, and I had, so to speak, been caught between those two extremes. I had neither confronted him nor fled. I didn't move and didn't close my eyes as De la Garza had closed his and as I closed mine later on at Tupra's house, where I was not so much in real or physical danger, but perhaps in moral danger, or perhaps my conscience was; I had stood there astonished and terrified and had shouted at him, I had resorted to words, which are sometimes more effective than the hand and quicker and sometimes quite useless and go entirely unheeded, and I had also looked on impotently, or perhaps prudently, more concerned about saving my own as yet unscathed skin than about the already condemned man, who couldn't be rescued from his fate. I don't know if such a reaction is natural or pure cowardice.

Yes, Pérez Nuix was right: you can almost never precisely pin down the nature of such a reaction or what it consists of because it wears an infinite number of masks and disguises, and never appears in its pure state. Most of the time, you don't even recognise it, because there's no way of separating it from everything else that makes up our personality, of splitting it off from the nucleus that is us, nor of isolating or defining it. We don't recognise the reaction in ourselves and yet, oddly enough, we do in others. I wasn't at all convinced by what she and apparently Tupra believed, that I had a particular ability to spot and predict this in a person before it even revealed itself. What I knew for sure was that I couldn't see it in myself, any more than I could see courage, before or after either had shown its face. It's burdensome having to live with such ignorance, knowing, too, that we will never learn, but that is how we live.

'I think you overestimate my influence,' I said, 'the influence I can bring to bear on Tupra and his opinions, in that particularly tricky area or in any other. I don't believe that any view I took of a person would make Tupra abandon or modify his own, I mean assuming he'd already formulated his own, had noticed something, and he always notices lots of things. The very first time I met him, I was struck by his gaze, so warm and all-embracing and appreciative. Those flattering and at the same time fearsome eyes are never indifferent to what is there before them, eyes whose very liveliness gives the immediate impression that they're going to get to the bottom of whatever being or object or gesture or scene they alight upon. As if they absorbed and captured any image set before them. However elusive a quality cowardice may be, it wouldn't escape him. And if I do notice it in your friend, as you suggest, Tupra will notice it too and form his own idea. And I won't be able to shift him from that view, even if I try. Even if I get him drunk.'

Young Pérez Nuix burst out laughing, a pleasant, slightly maternal laugh, with no mockery in it or, if so, only the kind of mockery with which one might greet a child's naïve response or angry retort, and I took advantage of that momentary lowering of her guard to direct my eyes to the place at which I'd been trying not to look, at least not fixedly – she had not yet re-crossed her legs.

'I'm sorry,' she said, 'it just amuses me that even an intelligent man like you should suffer from the same inability. It's astonishing how wrong our perception of ourselves always is, how hopeless we are at gauging and weighing up our strengths and weaknesses. Even people like us – gifted and highly trained in examining and deciphering our fellow man – become one-eyed idiots when we make ourselves the object of our studies. It's probably the lack of perspective and the impossibility of observing yourself without knowing that you're doing so. Whenever we become spectators of ourselves that's when we're most likely to play a role, distort the truth, clean up our act.' She paused and looked at me with a mixture of jovial stupefaction and unwitting pity. She'd described me as 'intelligent' and had done so quite spontaneously; if this was flattery, she had disguised it very well. 'Don't you realise, Jaime, how much Bertie likes you? How stimulating and amusing he finds you? That he's so fond of you that he'll make a genuine effort to accept your view of things, as long, of course, as it's not arrant nonsense, and to believe what you tell him you can see, even if only to confirm to himself that you are his most magnificent acquisition, his most successful hire? Remember, too, that you came to him recommended not only by Wheeler, but by his teacher Rylands, from beyond the grave. Not that this situation will necessarily last; he'll grow tired of it one day, or get used to your presence; he'll even disapprove of you sometimes or scorn you, Bertie is not the most constant of people and he quickly tires of almost everything, or his enthusiasms come and go. Now, though, you're the latest novelty and, besides, you really do seem to have hit it off, in that sober, masculine, unspoken way of yours – or whatever it is – but I know what I'm talking about. At the moment, you have far more influence over him than you think, and yet it seems to me you haven't even noticed. It's a rather temporary state of affairs, and partial too, because Bertie never entirely trusts anyone and he's not a man to be manipulated or led and certainly not deflected. But there are a few areas where he can be made to entertain doubts, and you're in a position to sow a few doubts now. I know because I've been through the same process and can recognise it. I recognise his pleasure and enjoyment, how being with you amuses and stimulates him, just as he used to find my company enlivening too. We really hit it off as well, and that lasted a long time. Not in the same masculine way in which you and he get on. And it's not as if we don't any more, I have no complaints about the high esteem in which he holds me or his professional respect for me. But I no longer represent for him the small daily celebration that I did at first and even later on too, that's what he felt about me for quite a while, and I know I shouldn't say so, but it's true, ask Mulryan or Rendel, or Jane Treves, who, being a woman, naturally suffered more from jealousy, I'm sure you'll meet her one day, she felt positively neglected when she and I were both there with Tupra. You can persuade him, Jaime. Not about just anything, that won't happen either today or indeed ever, but if it's about some area he's unsure of and in which he believes you to be an expert, as with cowardice and bravery; there, as I said, he's convinced of your expertise. I am too, by the way, you're really very good. Anyway, that's what I'm asking you, Jaime. The man will then cancel the debt and my father will be safe. As you see, it's a big favour to ask.'

She had used the word 'favour' several times, it was a way of saying 'please' or '*por favor*' without actually saying it or not in so many words – words that denote pleading or begging, especially when repeated, 'Please, please, please' – '*Por favor, por favor, por favor*'. She crossed her legs, blocking my view, but I could instead direct my gaze anywhere with impunity, I could still see her bare thighs for example. She took a small sip of wine and put another Karelias cigarette to her red lips – again that flashback to childhood cartoons – without lighting it. The dog was fast asleep, as if he had got used to the idea that he might be staying there all night, and lying down like that, he seemed even whiter. I glanced out of the window, then moved away, nothing had changed, the flexible metal bars or endless spears of the ever more dominant rain continued to fall, as if excluding the possibility of clear skies for good. I took a few steps and then sat down where I had been sitting before. I had the feeling that the silence was not a pause this time, but that Pérez Nuix had finished her presentation; that she considered her plea to be over and done with: her few timid attempts at flattery, her various lines of argument and her deployment of prudent powers of persuasion. I felt that I now had to give an answer, that she was not going to add anything more. To answer 'Yes' or 'No' or 'Possibly' or 'We'll see'. To give her a little more hope without actually committing myself to anything: 'I'll see what I can do, I'll do my best.' 'It depends' would not, of course, put an end to the conversation or the visit. And I wasn't sure I wanted either to end, and so I didn't give her an answer, but asked her another question:

'How much is the debt exactly?'

She lit the cigarette and I thought I saw her blush for a moment, or perhaps it was just the glow from the match, or a lurking embarrassment, as when in the office with no name, I would sense in her a brief gathering of energy before she came over to talk to me, that is, beyond greeting me or asking me some isolated question, as if she had to gather momentum or take a run-up, and that was what gave me the idea that she didn't rule me out, although probably without knowing that she didn't, nor having even considered the possibility. I thought: 'She's embarrassed to tell me how much. Either because it's so low, and then I'll know that she can't afford to pay even that, or because it's so high, and then I'll find out what an enormous sum it is, or how crazy her father is, and perhaps how crazy she is as well.'

'Nearly two hundred thousand pounds,' she said after a few seconds, and she raised her eyebrows in a gesture that was not, of course, English, as if she were adding: 'You see the fix I'm in.' Though what she did, in fact, say was not so very different. 'What do you think?'

I made a rapid calculation. It was nearly three hundred thousand euros or fifty million pesetas, I had still not quite reaccustomed myself to the pound and will perhaps never get used to the euro when it comes to the kind of large quantities one does not deal with every day.

'I think that, considering his defects, Incompara is very generous,' I replied. 'Or else that report is worth an awful lot to him.' And then I asked another question, perhaps the one I least expected to ask, although I don't know if she was quite as surprised as I was, that depended on how well she knew me, on how much more she knew of me than I did of myself, on how much and in what depth she had translated or interpreted me – to employ the terminology we sometimes used to describe our indefinable work – during those months of working together. It occurred to me as a joke really and I saw no reason to resist. Besides, it would force her to put something on the table, to put a value on my participation, to consider me and the risk I was taking, to consider the possible damage to me and the unlikely benefits. Asking a favour is easy, even comfortable, the difficult,

disquieting thing is hearing the request and then having to decide whether to grant or deny it. A transaction involves more
work and more care and calculation for both parties. With a favour, only one of the parties has to decide and calculate, the one
who is or isn't going to agree to it, because no one is obliged to
return a favour or even be grateful. You ask, wait and receive a
'Yes' or a 'No'; then, in either case, you can calmly leave, having
offloaded a problem or created a conflict. No, favours granted
are not binding, they carry with them no contract, no debt, or
only moral ones, and that's nothing, mere air, nothing practical.
So, to my surprise, what I said was: 'And what's in it for me?'

Pérez Nuix, however, had not fallen into my trap, into my improvised and semi-unintentional trap. She didn't immediately go on to offer me something, a reward, a sum of money, a percentage, a gift, not even the promise of her eternal gratitude. She doubtless knew that the latter has no tangible or even symbolic meaning. People say it far too much, 'I'll be eternally grateful' is one of the most vacuous statements ever uttered and yet one hears it often, always with that unvarying epithet, always that same irresponsible 'eternally', another clue to its absolute lack of reality, or truth or meaning, and sometimes the person saying it will add: 'If there's ever anything I can do for you, now or later on, you only have to ask', when the fact is that almost no one immediately asks a favour in return, that would seem exploitative – a case of *do ut des* – and if, in the future, one does ask for something, the empty words will have been long forgotten and, besides, no one resorts to that, rarely does anyone remind the other person: 'Some time ago, you said . . .'; and if they do, they're likely to meet with this response: 'Did I say that? How very odd. Did I really? I don't remember that', or else 'No, ask anything but that, that's the one thing I can't grant you, the very worst thing, please, don't ask me' or else 'I'm so sorry, I'd love to help, but it's simply not in my power, if only you'd come to me a few years ago, but things have changed'. And so the person who was only seeking the return of an old favour ends up asking a new favour, as if nothing had happened before, and is reduced almost to begging ('Please, please, please'). She was intelligent enough not to promise me chimeras or outlandish rewards in kind, nothing graspable or ungraspable, present or future.

'Nothing,' she said. 'For the moment, nothing, Jaime. It's simply a favour I'm asking and you can say "No" if you want to, you're not going to get anything out of it, you'll get nothing in return, although I really don't think it will be all that hard for you or that you'll be running any risk. If things don't work out, if he doesn't take the bait, you can always tell Bertie you made a mistake, it happens to us all, even to him, he knows perfectly well that no one's infallible. His hero Rylands wasn't, nor was Wheeler, something Wheeler, later on, had great cause to regret, apparently. Vivian wasn't either, nor were Cowgill, Sinclair or Menzies, people from another age, some of the best and most renowned, both in our field and beyond.' She knew how to pronounce that last name like a good Englishwoman or like a good spy, she too said 'Mingiss'. 'Nor were the big names of more recent times, Dearlove, Scarlett, Manningham-Buller and Remington, they all blundered at some point, in some way. Even Montagu wasn't infallible, nor were Duff Cooper or Churchill. That's why I said earlier that while this was a big favour for me, it wasn't such a big deal for you. That bothered you at the time, but it's true nonetheless. No, I don't think you'll get anything in return or profit in any way. But you won't suffer any misfortunes or any losses either. Anyway, Jaime, it's entirely up to you whether you say "Yes" or "No". You're under no obligation. And I can't think of any way I could tempt you.'

'"Dearlove" did you say? Who? Richard Dearlove?' I recalled that this was one of the unlikely and to me unfamiliar names I'd stumbled across while rifling through some old restricted files one day at the office. It had struck me as a name more suited to some idol of the masses than to a high-ranking official or civil servant, which is why I used it for the singer-celebrity whom here I call Dick Dearlove to protect his real identity, a vain endeavour. My immediate curiosity proved too much for me and so I put off giving my answer a little longer. And there was something else I was curious about, a curiosity that demanded satisfaction, less immediately perhaps but more insistently.

'Yes,' she said. 'Sir Richard Dearlove. For several years, until not long ago in fact, he was our invisible leader, didn't you know? The head of MI6, "C" or "Mr C".' She pronounced this initial English-fashion, 'Mr Si', we Spaniards would say. 'No one has published a recent photograph of him, it's forbidden, no one has seen him or knows what he looks like; not even now, when he's no longer in that post. And so none of us could identify him; no one would recognise him if he walked by in the street. That's a great advantage, don't you think? I wish I had the same advantage.'

'And have we never done a report on him? I mean a video interview, although I can't imagine he would have been taken up to Tupra's office so that we could spy on him from our hiding-place in the train carriage, from our cabin.' I realised at once that I had said 'we' and 'our' as if I already considered myself part of the group and had since even before my arrival. I was developing a strange and entirely involuntary sense of belonging. But I preferred not to think about that just then.

'I don't know,' she said half-heartedly. 'Ask Bertie. As I said, he has videos of everyone.' I had the feeling she was growing impatient with my delay, or with my waffling around, I still hadn't heard that order, or was it a kind of motto, 'Don't linger or delay', not that I've ever taken any notice of it, either before or since. She must simply have wanted to know where she stood and then she could leave. Certainly if my final answer was 'No', she would leave there and then and not waste any more of the night on me, but set off with her gentle dog, doubtless feeling rather ridiculous and perhaps filled as well with a sense of instant rancour or even lasting grievance. If the answer was 'Yes', on the other hand, perhaps she would stay longer, to celebrate her relief or to issue new instructions, now that what she had come for was in the bag. She must have found it irritating that I should bother her now with questions about Sir Richard Dearlove, the real Dearlove this time, or about any other person or subject. That I should, at this point, open a parenthesis or invent tangents. She would just have to put up with it, I was still the one guiding the conversation and determining its course, and she could not afford to upset me – yet. That, when you think about it, is the only calculation anyone asking a favour must make really, once they've taken the first step and made their request (before that, it's different, they have to be more cautious, estimating whether it's worthwhile or even advisable for them to reveal their deficiencies and inabilities): they have to be pleasant and patient and even unctuous, to keep to the tempo being set for them, to consider their steps and their words and the degree to which they can insist, until they get what they've asked for. Unless, that is, they're someone so important that doing them a favour is in itself an honour for the person granting it, a privilege. This was not the case here, and so she added in another tone of voice: 'No, I don't think so, but anything's possible. I suppose photos of him must exist, nowadays you can track down pictures of anyone; and if only very few have access to his photos, it wouldn't surprise me at all if Bertie was one of them.'

'Why did you say that Wheeler regretted not being infallible? What happened? What happened to him? What did you mean?' That was the deeper, more insistent curiosity demanding satisfaction.

Again I noticed her annoyance, her frayed nerves, her mutable state of exhaustion, which came and went. I was probably annoying her or driving her mad. But she once more suppressed her feelings or pulled herself together, she had still not lost heart.

'I don't know what happened to him, Jaime, it was a long time ago, during or after World War II, and I don't know him personally. People say that he made an interpretative error that cost him dear. He failed to foresee something and that left him feeling dreadfully guilty, useless, destroyed, I don't know exactly. I've heard it mentioned in passing as an example of great misfortune, but I've never asked or no one's ever given me an answer, most of our work is still secret even after sixty or more years, it may remain so for ever, at least officially. Any leaks usually come from outside and are often pure speculation, not to be trusted. Or they come from people with an axe to grind, who either resigned or were sacked, and who distort the facts. It's difficult to know anything very precise about our past, especially about us insiders, who tend to be the most discreet and the least curious, it's as if we had no history. We're the most keenly aware of what should not be told, because we live with that all the time. So, I'm sorry, but I can't help. You'll have to ask Wheeler himself. You know him well, he was your champion, your sponsor, the one who introduced you to the group.'

She, I noticed, used 'we' and 'our' without even thinking, naturally and frequently – she had been part of the group for much longer than me and felt herself to be an heir to the original group, the one that had been created by Menzies or Ve-Ve Vivian or Cowgill or Hollis or even Philby or Churchill himself to fight the Nazis, Wheeler thought Churchill had been the one who sparked the idea, being the brightest and boldest of the lot, and the least afraid of ridicule.

'Who have you heard mention it? Tupra? Can you remember if what happened involved Wheeler's wife? Her name was Valerie. Does that ring any bells?'

'I don't know who I heard it from, Jaime. It could have been Bertie, it probably was, or Rendel, or Mulryan, or perhaps some other person in some other place, I don't recall now. But that's all I know, nothing more – that something bad happened, that he failed in some way, or at least he thought so, and I believe he came close to withdrawing from the group altogether, to giving it up. It was all a very long time ago.'

I didn't know if she was telling me the truth or if she didn't feel authorised to tell me the story or if she simply wanted to get away from my endless questions and not – at this late hour of the night – get into some obscure, possibly long tale about someone else, which she would, at best, know only at second hand and which bore no relation to her current problems, the problems that had brought her to my house after much thought and much trudging through the rain: her father and that man Vanni Incompara and the banker Vickers and that leap-frogging debt of two hundred thousand pounds, I'm amazed at some people's ability to accumulate sums of money they don't have, and in a way I envy them – it's quite a talent, if not a gift; it requires a cheerful mindset – although any envy I might feel is purely theoretical or fictional, literary and cinematographic, Pérez Nuix's vicarious position at that point was not in the least enviable. For the first time, I felt sorry for her (pity always intervenes), perhaps because tiredness made her seem more childlike, or perhaps it was the suppressed anxiety that surfaced now and then in her bright darting eyes and at the corners of her mouth, which kept trying to form brief, fearful smiles, to please me. I decided that it was time to put her out of her misery: she had expended a lot of effort, she had followed me for a long time through that half-deserted city, getting drenched in the process, she had pondered what to do, she had put her case and she had expended on me, first, her indecision and her time and then her resolve and still more time.

'All right, Patricia,' I said, bringing to an end my session of interrogations and postponements. 'I'll try, although I still think Tupra will see whatever there is to see, and more than me. But I'll do what I can, I'll try my best.'

This was the lowest level of commitment I could give. I might fail and make a mistake and not do as well as I had hoped, she herself had said as much and so she wouldn't be able to reproach me with failure. Nor be disappointed, for I had given her due warning. This left me much freer than if my answer had been 'I want this in return', mainly because now I ran no risk of beginning to desire or to hope for what I had demanded from her, and thus to fear my own defeat. More than that, if you're not afraid, your chances of success will probably increase, and there'll still be time later on to raise your hand and demand a prize and say: 'I want this as a reward.' Naturally, this could be denied to us outright, with no explanation or excuse: there's no moral obligation then, no link, no agreement, nothing explicit, and there may very soon be no trace left of the immense favour we granted, just like the drop of blood or its rim that one looks for after it has disappeared, having been scrubbed and rubbed away, or the infinite crimes and noble acts not known about since their commission or which the slow centuries amuse themselves by very slowly diluting until they're completely erased and then by pretending that they've never been. As if everything always fell like snow on our shoulders, slippery and docile, even things that make a great din and spread fires. (And from our shoulders it vanishes into the air or else melts or falls to the ground. And the snow always stops, eventually.)

Almost no trace remains of what happened next or only the faintest of vestiges in my more languid memory and perhaps in hers too, but we will never find out – I mean she and I, face to face, through an exchange of words. It happened as if in the very moment it was occurring we both wanted to pretend that it wasn't happening, or preferred not to notice, not to register it, to pretend it didn't matter, or to keep it so hushed up that later on we could deny it to each other, or to others if one of us let the cat out of the bag or started boasting about it, even if each of us only did so to ourselves, as if we both knew that something of which there is no record or no explicit recognition and which is never mentioned simply doesn't exist; something which, in a way, is committed secretly or behind the backs of its perpetrators and without their full consent or with only a drowsing aware-ness: something we do while telling ourselves we're not doing it, something that occurs even as we're persuading ourselves that it isn't happening, something not as strange as it sounds or seems, indeed, it happens all the time and causes us almost no alarm or doubts about our own judgement. We convince ourselves that we never had that unworthy or evil thought, that we never de-sired that woman or that death – the death of an enemy, husband or friend – that we never felt even momentary scorn or hostility towards the person we most respected or to whom we owed the greatest debt of gratitude, nor envied our irksome children who will go on living when we're no longer here and who will ap-propriate everything and quickly take our place; that we never intrigued or betrayed or plotted, never sought the ruin of any-one when in fact we diligently sought that of several people, that we were never tempted to do anything we might feel ashamed of; that we never acted in bad faith when we recounted some malicious gossip to someone so that he could defend himself – or so we argued, thus becoming instantly virtuous and charitable – and so that he would stop being so naïve and realise just who he was dealing with; and – even more extraordinary, because it affects actual events and not just the easily deceived mind – that we didn't flee when in fact we ran away for all we were worth and left all regrets behind us, that we didn't push or shove a child out of the way to make room for ourselves in the life-boat when the ship was sinking, that we didn't shield ourselves behind someone else when things were at their worst, so that the blows or the knife-thrusts or the bullets hit the person next to us who was, perhaps, expecting our protection: who knows, perhaps the person we loved most in the world, to whom we declared a thousand times that we would unhesitatingly give up our life for him or her, and it turns out that we did hesitate and didn't and haven't given up our life, nor would we if a second opportunity were to arise; that we didn't lay the blame for something we did on someone else nor make a false accusation in order to save ourselves, that we never acted out of the most terrible egotism and fear. We really believe that we weren't born when and where we came into the world, that we're younger than we are and from some nobler, less obscure place, that our parents aren't our parents and bear a much less vulgar surname; that we earned by our own merit what we stole or was given to us, that we fairly inherited some sceptre or throne or mere stick or chair without using guile and without usurping them, that we came up with witticisms and ideas written or spoken by other wiser and more thoughtful men, whose dread names we never mention and whom we loathe for having 'got in' before us, al-though deep down we know, in some small surviving corner of our consciousness, that there was no question of their 'getting in before us' and that if they hadn't 'preceded' us, those ideas so personal to them would be even less our ideas, indeed could never be ours; we believe ourselves to be the person we most admire, and to make this come true, we set out to destroy him, believing we can supplant and obliterate him with our achievements which we owe entirely to him and drive him from the world's fickle memory, reassuring ourselves with the thought that he was only a pioneer whom we have exceeded and absorbed, and thus made highly dispensable; we persuade ourselves that the past does not weigh on us because we have never traversed it

('It wasn't me, it didn't happen to me, I never lived through that, I didn't see anything, I know nothing about it, it's the fruit of someone else's imaginings, someone else's memory that has somehow or other been transplanted into mine or else infected it') and that we never said what we said or stole what we stole, that we never cheered the dictator or betrayed our best friend who was so unbearably much better than us from the first day to the last ('He brought it on himself, I had nothing to do with it, I kept my mouth shut, he was a hothead, he made his own fate, he stood out when he shouldn't have and didn't change sides in time, didn't even want to'); and we don't even call ourselves by our real name, but only by a false one or by whichever of the ever-changing names that keep coming along and being added, be it Rylands or Wheeler, or Ure or Reresby or Tupra or Dundas, or Jacques the Fatalist or Jacobo or Jaime.

People believe what they want to believe, and that's why it's only logical – and so easy – that everything should have its time to be believed. We'll believe anything: even something that's manifestly untrue and contradicts what we can see with our own eyes, yes, even that has its time to be believed, each separate event in its own time and, in the fullness of time, everything. Everyone is prepared to look away and turn a deaf ear, to deny what's there before them and not to hear the shouting, and to maintain that there are no screams only a vast peaceful silence; to modify events and what has happened as much as they need to – the one-legged man still able to feel his leg and the one-armed man his arm and the decapitated man staggering three steps forward as if he hadn't yet lost both will and consciousness – but above all their own thoughts, feelings, memories and their anticipated future, which is sometimes mistaken for prescience. 'It wasn't like that. This isn't going to happen or won't have happened. This isn't happening' is the constant litany that distorts the past, the future and the present, and thus nothing is ever fixed or intact, neither safe nor certain. Everything that exists also doesn't exist or carries within itself its own past and future non-existence, it doesn't last or endure, and even the gravest of events run that same risk and will end up visiting and travelling through one-eyed oblivion, which is no steadier or more stable or more capable of giving shelter. That's why all things seem to say 'I'm still here, therefore I must have been here before' while they are still alive and well and growing and have not yet ceased. Perhaps that's their way of clinging grimly to the present, a resistance to disappearing put up by the inanimate, by objects too, not only by people, who hang on and grow desperate and almost never give in ('But it's not time yet, not yet,' they mutter in their panic, with their dwindling strength), perhaps it's an attempt to leave their mark on everything, to make it harder for them to be denied or erased or forgotten, their way of saying 'I have been' and to stop other people saying 'No, this was never here, no one saw it or remembers it or ever touched it, it simply never was, it neither strode the world nor trod the earth, it didn't exist and never happened'.

It was nothing very grave, almost insignificant given the times we live in, and pleasurable too, the thing that happened without happening between young Pérez Nuix and me late that night, perhaps at the hour the Romans called the *conticinio* and which doesn't really exist in our cities now, for there is no time when everything is still and silent. She gave a sigh of satisfaction or relief and thanked me for my promise that was not a promise, for my declaration that I would do my best, which is hardly a major commitment. She seemed suddenly very tired, but this lasted only a moment, she immediately sprang to her feet, went over to the window and looked more closely at the tireless rain. She stretched discreetly – just her hands and wrists, not her arms; and her thighs, but without standing on tiptoe or rocking back on her heels – and then she asked me if she could stay. She couldn't face going home at that hour, she said, and I needn't worry, she'd get up very early to take the dog out, she'd leave in time to go back to her place and shower and change ('And put on a new pair of tights,' I thought at once), and we wouldn't have to go together to the building with no name, like some strange married couple who, when they set off to work, don't go their separate ways. No one there would guess that we had met outside work to conspire nor that we had said goodbye only a short time before. I agreed, how could I refuse such a minor request after granting the major one (well, at least its attempt), even though they were quite different in nature; it was a filthy night to be heading off out into the street again and who knew how long it would take for a taxi to come, and I'd have to phone for one first, if, that is, anyone answered the phone. Besides, I would prefer, for reasons of dramatic delicacy, that she didn't just leave as soon as she'd got what she wanted (or at least a declaration of intent), which would have made her visit exclusively utilitarian. It was, of course, utilitarian, as we both knew, but it would be best not to draw attention to that, nor was it appropriate given how much remained to be done in the next days, especially by me, for I would have to interpret and perhaps meet Incompara. I offered to sleep on the sofa and let her have the bed; she, however, wouldn't allow this; she, after all, was the intruder, the unexpected guest, she couldn't possibly deprive me of my mattress and my sheets.

'No, I'll take the sofa,' she said. But when she looked at it properly and saw how uncomfortable it was, and possibly still wet from her and the rain she'd brought in, she made the only suggestion someone of her age and self-assurance could make: 'I don't see what's wrong with us sharing the bed, as long as you don't mind, that is. I don't. Is it fairly wide?'

Of course I didn't mind, I had been young during an age when you were happy to sleep in any bed and alongside new acquaintances wherever you happened to find yourself after a night of wild excess or induced ecstasy or supposed spirituality or partying – the '70s, so effortfully spontaneous and so unhygienic, not to say downright grubby at times, and part of the '80s, which continued in the same vein. And of course I did mind, I no longer was that young man nor was I accustomed to sleeping anywhere but in my own bed, and I had spent too many years getting used to sleeping only beside Luisa, not even by the side of that stupid short-lived lover who ruined much of what I had, or what I treasured, even though Luisa never knew for certain about her existence; and later, in London, only by the sides of a few sporadic women – three, to be exact – with whom the unhygienic or, if you like, grubby part had happened earlier and with whom, therefore, there was no danger that I'd want to grope them for the first time in dreams or while half-asleep, nor that I'd try to brush up against them, holding my breath and pretending to have done so purely by chance, nor that I'd want to observe them in the dark with my five senses alert and my eyes wide open, and with pointless intensity.

So it was that I found myself in bed with young Pérez Nuix, so aware of her warmth and her presence that I couldn't really get to sleep, and what made it even more difficult was the question that kept going round and round in my head as to whether the same thing was happening to her, if she was waiting or fearing that I would move closer, a slow, stealthy approach, so gradual at first that she would doubt it was happening, just like those men who used to feel women up on buses or trams or on the underground, using as their excuse the crush of people and the swaying motion, and who would rub and even press them- selves against the uncomplaining bosom of the chosen woman, but never using their hands – so 'feeling up' is perhaps not quite the right phrase – and always with the excuse that any contact was entirely involuntary and attributable to the overwhelming pressure of the crowd and the bends in the road and the jolting. I speak of this in the past, because it's been ages since I saw this embarrassing spectacle on any form of public transportation and I don't know if it still happens in this day and age, which is more respectful at least in that one area; I often saw it during my child- hood and adolescence, and I can't rule out having timidly done the same myself when I was thirteen or fourteen, when, in the minds of we fledgling men, everything is imaginary or frustrated sex. And I suppose it's because I associate such scenes with the remote past that I mention trams, which have been ghosts for decades now, as are those nice Madrid double-deckers that they withdrew only a short while ago, and which were identical to the London ones, except that they were blue not red, and had the same doorless entrance, just an open platform at the rear with a vertical bar to grab hold of and haul yourself aboard – on the right rather than the left, in keeping with the side of the road we drive on in my country.

Genitalia, women's that is, are also like entrances with no doors, I mean that if they're unobstructed by clothes there's no need to open them in order to enter. I let her get into bed first, alone, I waited in the living room for a while so that she could get ready and get undressed as she wished, and so when I eventually went into the bedroom, after those few minutes, young Pérez Nuix was already in bed and I had no way of knowing which clothes or how many she had removed before lying down. I had lent her a clean T-shirt, short-sleeved, because that's what I wear when it looks like it might be cold, I don't own any proper pyjamas. 'That'll do fine, thank you,' she had said, which meant that this was probably all she was wearing and that her legs were bare, although I was almost sure she would have kept her knickers on out of modesty, or out of consideration, or out of cleanliness, so as not to stain someone else's sheets, just as I kept on my boxer shorts and also donned a T-shirt, less because it was cold that night than to avoid any chance contact with her, skin on skin, flesh on flesh, such contact would happen only with our legs, my hairy ones against her smooth ones, for she was a hundred per cent Spanish as regards waxing her legs. However, before turning out the light – the bedside lamp – which she had left on so that I wouldn't have to enter the room in the dark, I pretended I was making sure my clothes weren't mixed up with hers, for we had both placed them on the same armchair, and then I could see and count the items of clothing she had taken off, and I counted not only her bra, as I had imagined, but also her other underwear, as I hadn't imagined at all, for there, neatly folded, were her white knickers, they were tiny, which is to say normal, and I thought at once: 'I'm taller than she is, so the T-shirt will probably be long enough for her to feel covered.' This thought, though, was of no use to me, and from the moment the room was in darkness and I had slipped in between the sheets, I realised that I would spend the whole night unable to forget that strange and unexpected fact and that it would be almost impossible for me to go to sleep, as I lay agonising over it and looking for some meaning: what did she mean by taking off her knickers and leaving her genitalia – how can I put it – exposed, so close to me and to mine, we were separated by only a few inches and two bits of flimsy cloth or not even that, by the cloth of my boxer shorts with their ready-made opening and that of her borrowed T-shirt, if, of course, it hadn't ridden up when she was getting into bed and she hadn't bothered to pull it down, for then it was possible that her bottom – she had lain down on the other side of the bed and so had her back to me – was bare and very close to my irremediably aroused member, it was hopeless, I wouldn't get a wink of sleep in that state of physical alertness and repetitive mental activity, thinking and thinking about the singular fact, about my member, about her buttocks and below, about the nearness of everything and the absence of doors and of any barrier, even a barrier of cloth, wondering whether to approach surreptitiously and alight tentatively, making it look as if it were unconscious, something done in dreams, something merely instinctive, involuntary, animal almost, all the time wait-ing tensely, wide awake, to see if she would escape at once, if she would shy away at the first contact or accept it and stay where she was and not flee, neither surrender nor let me fall into the air, into the void, into emptiness; I didn't dare expect any pres-sure or stimulus from her, all of this was going on in my mind, which, in such circumstances, immediately becomes obsessed, it's the kind of doubt or idea which, once started, won't dissolve or withdraw, still less if the blood has gathered and impedes all abatement and all breathing, all appeasement or distraction or truce, and the temptation then becomes fixed. After a while spent listening to her breathing – it didn't sound to me like that of someone sleeping – and holding in, almost stopping my own, it occurred to me that I should get up and go and sleep on the sofa, with a blanket, but the truth was I didn't want to leave the bed or lose the unlikely proximity thus far achieved, it was a kind of promise that was its own satisfaction and which allowed me to remain in that state of mortifying, hopeful ignorance, to fantasise about what might happen at any moment if we did touch and neither of us avoided it or started away, we were only a little way apart and it's all a question of time and space and of coinciding in those two dimensions, we had the time and, very nearly, the space as well, all that was needed was a slight slippage, a minimal shift, for things to be completely in our favour, it was so easy that it seemed impossible it would not occur, one first tentative caress perhaps and my member would slip inside her and then both would be in the same place, one inside the other almost without our realising, we could even pretend not to know and to be asleep even though we were both fully awake, I knew I was and thought the same was true of her; I was pretty convinced but not certain, of course, and that was what held me back or one of the things.

This situation of sexual imminence was not new to me, that is, it was new with young Pérez Nuix, but not in my previous existence, it had happened more than once with Luisa, silently and peacefully at first, after the initial tentative caress and the minimal shift that had caused us to coincide in both space and time, that's what matters, that's what determines important events, which is why it's so vital sometimes not to linger or delay, although it can also be what saves us, we never know what would be for the best and what is the right thing to do; if bullet and head or knife and chest or sword-blade and neck do not coincide in the same place and moment, no one dies, and that's why De la Garza was still alive, because his neck and Reresby's Landsknecht sword, or his *Katzbalger*, had not coincided exactly, despite having been on the point of doing so several times. However, with Luisa, her acquiescence was almost certain, and from her I could expect both pressure and stimulus, after all, we got into the same bed each night, she earlier and I later, as if I were coming to visit her in her dreams and I were her ghost, and the rest formed part of the foreseeable and the probable, or at least the possible. And if one of us said 'No', either her or even me, it was a chance rejection, reasoned and momentary ('I'm exhausted', or 'I'm too preoccupied today, my mind's on other things' or even more trivial 'I have to get up really early tomorrow'), not essential either to the totality or to the act itself, as young Pérez Nuix's refusal might be, expressed in unequivocal and crushing terms:

'What the hell are you are up to? Who do you think you are?' or perhaps gentler and more diplomatic, 'I wouldn't continue down that road if I were you, you won't get anywhere', or more humiliating: 'Huh, I thought you'd have more self-control, more maturity, I didn't have you down as your average Spanish sex maniac, or an old-fashioned Spanish macho-man.'

None of these wounding words was spoken, indeed no words of any sort were uttered when I finally dared to make that tentative approach and lightly rested my member against her buttocks and was immediately aware that I was touching not T-shirt but firm, warm flesh, she was probably one of those women who are really sensitive to the cold, but who give off the heat they themselves don't feel, they're like a warm oven to the person who touches them, even though they themselves may be shivering, like someone with a fever. Nothing was said, there was no reaction, no movement either towards me or away, no discouragement and no encouragement, it really was as if she were deep asleep, I wondered if she really could be sleeping so profoundly that she wouldn't notice the touch of skin on skin with nothing in between, I thought not and that she must be pretending, but when it comes to other people, and possibly even when it comes to yourself, you can never be absolutely sure about anything, or almost anything. I got a little closer, pressed a little harder, but so very little that I wasn't even sure of having done so, sometimes you think you've moved or shifted, or pushed or caressed, but your approach is so timid and terrified that you can sometimes deceive yourself, and your advance or even your touch may prove imperceptible to the other person. And that was where I was, caught between a yes and a no, between irresistible desire and fearful or perhaps civilised restraint, applying such minute pressure that it might not have been pressure at all, when a thought suddenly, ridiculously, occurred to me: 'A condom,' I thought. 'I can't do anything without a condom on, and for that I need a minimum of consent, permission, agreement. If I get up now and fetch one and then come back to bed with it, I'll have lost my position, lost this closeness, I'd have to start all over again, she might move away or perhaps prove less accessible. And with a condom on I would no longer have an alibi, I would no longer be able to say to her, if she told me off or pulled me up short: "Oh, sorry, I didn't mean to, I was fast asleep and didn't realise I was touching you. It wasn't intentional, I'm sorry, I'll keep to my side of the bed," because the ridiculous sheath would be irrefutable proof that it *was* intentional and premeditated as well.'

This thought immediately made me draw back a little, enough to lose contact, and that reaffirmed me in my uncertain belief that there had been contact and that the ghostly pressure had been neither avoided nor rejected; and after a few seconds, I abandoned my position ('Bloody condoms,' I thought, 'in my youth, we despised them, it never even occurred to me to buy them, now, though, we always have to use them') and no longer lay behind her, in that privileged place, but on my back, wondering what to do or how to do it or whether I should give up despite my growing hopes and try to go to sleep and do nothing. I put my arm under the pillow the better to rest my head, an involuntary gesture of deliberation, and in doing so I uncovered my chest, almost as far as my waist, and uncovered her shoulders. And that was enough – or a pretext – for young Pérez Nuix to wake up or pretend she did. And for the first and only time in the whole of that night we spent together I was not invisible to her, despite our being in darkness: she turned over and placed the open palms of her hands on my cheeks as if to show her fondness for me, they were very soft palms; she looked into my eyes for a few seconds (one, two, three, four; and five; or six, seven, eight; and nine; or ten, eleven, twelve; and thirteen) and smiled at me or laughed as she delicately cupped or held my face, as Luisa sometimes used to do when her bed was still mine and we weren't yet sleepy or not sleepy enough to say goodnight and turn our backs on each other until the next day, or when I came to her late like a ghost she'd arranged to meet and for whom she was waiting, and welcomed me. Only then was I not invisible to Pérez Nuix, when there was no light. My eyes were accustomed to seeing in the half-dark of my room without blinds or shutters, like almost all bedrooms on that large island whose inhabitants sleep with one eye open; but not her eyes, which were unfamiliar with the space. Nevertheless, she looked at me and smiled and laughed, it was very brief. Then she turned over again and offered me her back, adopting the same position as before, as if that gazing at each other in the dark hadn't taken place and she were ready to continue sleeping. But it had taken place, and that for me was the necessary sign of consent, permission, agreement I needed, it made me get out of bed for a moment and rapidly search out a condom, put it on and return with much more confidence and aplomb to my previous position, and to the rubbing and touching and gentle pushing, not against her buttocks now but slightly lower down, towards the dampness and the passage, the passageway, *more ferarum*, in the manner of the beasts, that's the Latin tag for it. She didn't move, at least not as I began to slide in, easily now ('I'm screwing her,' I thought as I entered her, I couldn't help it), she just let me, she didn't participate if one can say that or if that's possible, at any rate, we didn't speak, there was no indication on either side that what was happening was happening, how can I put it, we pretended to pretend to be asleep, to be unaware, to recognise nothing of what was going on as if it were taking place in our absence or without our knowledge, although occasionally she did utter a few sounds and perhaps I did too when I came, I conscientiously repressed them though, telling myself I had merely breathed more deeply, at most sighed, but who knows, one hears oneself so little, and anyway sounds and even groans are permissible during sleep, some people even deliver whole speeches while asleep, but they're never accused of being awake. Almost nothing was heard or seen, I could see only the back of her neck in the darkness and from far too close, and that's doubtless why I kept picturing things, the same things I had just spent a long time contemplating in the living room ('It'll only take a moment,' she had announced from the street, I wondered if she knew just how wrong she would be), the zippers on her boots going up and down, the run in her tights advancing in all directions along her thigh, but especially upwards, as if pointing the way, and another older vision, that of her naked breast, a tight skirt, and in her hand a towel and a raised arm that added an additional nakedness to the image by unembarrassedly revealing her clean, smooth, newly washed and, needless to say, shaven armpit, early one morning in the building with no name, that time when she did not blush, making me think that young Pérez Nuix did not rule me out, or did not entirely exclude me, although she didn't necessarily feel attracted to me either, having been seen by me and having decided not to cover herself up, or perhaps no decision was involved. It was all very silent and timid, ghostly really, and it remained so, except that, after a while, I noticed that she was pushing too, it wasn't just me now and neither of us was pretending not to push or else pushing only gently, it was as if we were locked in a tight embrace, but without making use of our arms, she was pressed against me and I against her, but with just one part of our body, the same part, as if we were only those parts or as if we consisted solely of that, it was as if we had been forbidden to entwine in any other way, with our arms or our legs or round the waist or by way of kisses. I don't think we even held hands.

Yes, we almost certainly shared that in common, Tupra and I, or Ure or Reresby or Dundas, or who knows how many other names he would have used in other countries and which he perhaps now never used in this more sedentary stage of his life, safe and settled in London, where it was possible that he felt slightly bored, although he did go off now and then on short trips, or perhaps not, maybe he had already grown weary of all that gadding about, and of spreading outbreaks of cholera and malaria and plague and of igniting fires in far-off countries. His house was not that of a man who felt either temporary or in a hurry, that of someone who goes out and comes in, takes a quick look around, then leaves and returns and smokes a cigarette and never lingers anywhere. Perhaps the thing we shared in common was, nonetheless, very limited: I had slept with Pérez Nuix in a manner that was utterly tacit and clandestine, not only as regards other people, but as regards ourselves as well. On the other hand (and this was only a suspicion, but a strong one), he would have known her intimately over perhaps a long or at least a not insignificant period of time, perhaps when she was still a novelty and the person who most stimulated and amused him and was an important element in creating for him that sense of a small, or large, daily celebration. They would, at any rate, have seen each other's faces when they slept together, they would have talked afterwards, they would have told each other something of their lives and their opinions (although Tupra would have done so only in his usual fragmentary way, that is, very little), and when they were together in a room, they would have known for certain that what was happening was really happening, unlike me, for I felt certain of nothing – even less certain, given that what happened immediately became the past – when I withdrew from that passage, the end of which one never reaches, and emerged from it as carefully and tentatively as I had approached and entered; when I moved away and turned over onto my side and for the first time presented my back to that young woman just as she had presented hers to me for almost the whole time – except when she looked at me and cupped my face in her hands – and I slipped one arm under the pillow, not this time in order to think or to curse, but in order to summon sleep.

Perhaps the only thing Tupra and I would have in common was a pale, vague relationship of which most men know nothing and which languages fail to include, although they recognise the sentiment and, on occasion, the feelings of jealousy or even of camaraderie; apart, that is, from the Anglo-Saxon language as I read once in a book, not by an Englishman, but by a compatriot of mine, and not in an essay or a book on linguistics, but in a fiction, a novel, whose narrator recalled the existence of a word in that ancient language which described the relationship or kinship acquired by two or more men who had lain or slept with the same woman, even if this had happened at different times and with the different faces worn by that woman in her lifetime, her face of yesterday or today or tomorrow. That curious notion remained fixed in my mind, although the narrator wasn't sure if it was a verb, whose non-existent modern equivalent would be 'co-fornicate' (or 'co-fuck' in coarse, contemporary parlance), or a noun, which would denote the 'co-fornicators' (or 'co-fuckers') or the action itself (let's call it 'co-fornication'). One of the possible forms of the words, I don't know which, was *ġe-brȳd-guma*, I had remembered it without trying to and without effort, and sometimes it was there on the tip of my tongue, or the tip of my thoughts: 'Good God, that's what I am, I've become this man's *ġe-brȳd-guma*, how degrading, how horrible, how cheap, how dreadful', whenever I saw or heard that an old lover or girlfriend of mine was pairing up or spending too much time with some despicable, odious man, with an imbecile or an *Untermensch*; it happens all too often or so it seems, and besides we're constantly exposed to it and can do nothing about it. (I had decided that the word was pronounced 'gebrithgoomer', although, naturally, I had no idea.)

When I first met Tupra, I had thought or feared that I might acquire that relationship with him through Luisa, in some bizarre, unreal way – or, rather, I had been glad that she was in Madrid and that they would never meet and that this would never happen – when I saw that almost no woman could resist him and that I wouldn't stand a chance against him if I ever had to compete with him in that field, regardless of whether I got there first, or second, or at the same time. And now it seemed that I had probably acquired such a relationship through another unexpected and more frivolous activity, one that made me the person who came *afterwards* not the person who was or had been there *before*: the former is in a slightly more advantageous position, because he can hear and find out things from the latter, but he is also the one most at risk of contagion if there's any disease involved, and that – a disease if there is one – is the only tangible manifestation of that strange, weak link to which no one gives a thought any more, even though it exists without being named and hovers unnoticed above the relations between men and between women, and between men and women. No one speaks that medieval language any more and hardly anyone knows it. And when you think about it, there is, in some cases, something else that is transmitted by the person in the middle, from the one who was with her *before* to the one who was with her *afterwards*, but which is neither tangible nor visible: influence. Throughout my conversation that night with young Pérez Nuix, I had now and then had the feeling that Tupra was speaking through her, but this could also have been because they had worked and been in continual contact for several years, not necessarily because they were ex-lovers. The truth is that we never know from whom we originally get the ideas and beliefs that shape us, those that make a deep impression on us and which we adopt as a guide, those we retain without intending to and make our own. From a great-grandparent, a grandparent, a parent, not necessarily ours?

From a distant teacher we never knew and who taught the one we did know? From a mother, from a nursemaid who looked after her as a child? From the ex-husband of our beloved, from a *ǧe-brȳd-guma* we never met? From a few books we never read and from an age through which we never lived? Yes, it's incredible how much people say, how much they discuss and recount and write down, this is a wearisome world of ceaseless transmission, and thus we are born with the work already far advanced but condemned to the knowledge that nothing is ever entirely finished, and thus we carry – like a faint booming in our heads – the exhausting accumulated voices of the countless centuries, believing naïvely that some of those thoughts and stories are new, never before heard or read, but how could that be, when ever since they acquired the gift of speech people have never stopped endlessly telling stories and, sooner or later, everything is told, the interesting and the trivial, the private and the public, the intimate and the superfluous, what should remain hidden and what will one day inevitably be broadcast, sorrows and joys and resentments, certainties and conjectures, the imagined and the factual, persuasions and suspicions, grievances and flattery and plans for revenge, great feats and humiliations, what fills us with pride and what shames us utterly, what appeared to be a secret and what begged to remain so, the normal and the unconfessable and the horrific and the obvious, the substantial – falling in love – and the insignificant – falling in love. Without even giving it a second thought, we go and we tell.

'Believe me, I wouldn't have either, if I'd had the choice,' I said to Tupra when we'd finished our shared, disinterested laughter, with me laughing despite myself, about the 'bulwarks' onto which he had thrown me. 'But you made me do it, just as you've made me do everything else tonight, including still being here at this unearthly hour,' I said in my sometimes rather bookish English, literally '*a una hora no terrenal*' in Spanish. 'I don't know if you realise, but you've done nothing all day but give me orders, most of them after hours. It's time I left. I need to sleep, I'm tired.' And so I shifted again from brief treacherous laughter to a more enduring seriousness, if not annoyance. And

I made a movement as if to suggest that I was thinking about getting up, but no more than that, because he wouldn't let me leave just yet: he wanted to talk to me about Constantinople and Tangiers in centuries past, there are always more exhausting voices and stories that we have not yet heard. However, he didn't start again and probably wasn't going to, there are some things that are mentioned but never returned to, that are sown and then abandoned, like verbal decoys; and he was supposed to be showing me his private tapes, or perhaps DVDs. That didn't happen either. 'If you don't tell me about Tangiers and Constantinople right now, Bertram, I'm leaving. I've had enough. I'm dog tired and I'm in no mood to go on chatting.'

Tupra emitted a kind of dull roar, halfway between a brief guffaw and a stifled snort of scorn. He stood up and said:

'Don't be impatient, Jack, this is no time to be in a hurry. I'm going to show you the videos I told you about, you'll learn a lot from them and it will be useful for you to see them. Not immediately useful, they're not at all pleasant and they may well drive away any current desire for sleep that you feel, at least for the next few hours, but I've already given you permission not to come to work tomorrow, or rather today, so let's waste no more time.' He glanced rapidly at his watch; so did I: it was an unearthly hour for London, but not for Madrid. The children would be asleep, but I had no idea what Luisa would be up to, she might still be awake, with someone else or with no one. 'But it'll be useful to you later on to have seen them. In a matter of days really, and they'll always come in handy. It may be that you are already someone who gives no importance to the unimportant, because that's the first thing everyone should be taught and yet everyone behaves as if exactly the opposite were true: people are brought up nowadays to think that any idiot can make a great drama out of any kind of nonsense. People are brought up to suffer for no reason, and you get nowhere suffering over everything or tormenting yourself. It paralyses, overwhelms, stops growth and movement. As you see, though, people nowadays beat their breast over harming a plant, and if it's an animal, what a crime, what a scandal! They live in an unreal, delicate, soft, twee world.' – 'Cursi,' I thought, 'English doesn't have that useful, wide-ranging word' – 'Their minds are permanently wrapped in cotton wool.' And he briefly made that strange roaring noise again; it sounded this time like a short sarcastic cough. 'In *our* countries, that is. And when something happens here that's perfectly normal in other places, common currency, we find ourselves vulnerable, at a loss what to do, helpless, easy prey, and it takes us a while to react, and we do so disproportionately and blindly, missing the target. And with too much retrospective fear as well, as happened with the attacks here and in your own city of Madrid, not to mention the attacks on New York and Washington.'

'Nothing much has changed in Madrid,' I said. 'It's almost as if it had never happened.'

But he wasn't listening, he had his own agenda. His deep voice had grown mournful. It always did sound slightly mournful, like the sound made by a bow moving over the strings of a cello. Sometimes, though, that tonality was more marked and it produced in the person hearing it a gentle, almost pleasant feeling that eased all affliction; at least in me it did.

'I'm not saying there's nothing to be afraid of, you understand. It's just that we should have been frightened before and to have taken fear as much for granted as the air we breathe, and to have instilled fear too. Instilling and feeling fear, all the time, that's the unchanging way of the world, which we've forgotten. It's normal in other countries that are more alert to these things. But no one here realises it and we fall asleep without keeping one eye open, we get caught unawares and then we can't believe it's happened. Retrospective fear is useless, even more so than anticipatory fear. That's not much good either, but at least it puts one, if not on one's guard, at least in a state of expectancy. It's always best to be in a position to instil fear in others. Anyway, let me show you these scenes, they're not long. Some I'll fast-forward for you.'

He poured me some port without first consulting me, thinking perhaps that I would need it in order to face these unpleasant but instructive scenes, then he picked up his own glass and, at his urging, I picked up mine; he beckoned to me with a motion of his head and one finger and led me to a smaller room which he unlocked with a key from his keyring. Given that Tupra clearly didn't want anyone to enter that room without his permission or alone, I wondered who else lived in the house, or perhaps it was just the domestic staff who were barred. He turned on a couple of lights. It was a kind of study which immediately reminded me of his office in the building with no name, it was full of books as costly as those in the living room or possibly more so – perhaps they were his bibliophile's jewels; on the other hand, there were no paintings, only the framed drawing of a soldier, just head and shoulders, with a slightly curled moustache, perhaps some idol of his from MI6 or whatever it used to be called; it appeared at first sight to date from the First World War or, at the latest, from the 1920s, I didn't think it was an ancestor, a Tupra, for he was wearing the uniform of a British officer, though what rank I couldn't say. There was a desk with a computer on it; a chair on casters behind the desk, which must be where Reresby worked when he was at home; and two pouffes. He manoeuvred these with his foot so that they were in front of a low cabinet whose wooden doors he opened to reveal a television inside, an absurd piece of camouflage, like the minibars you get in certain posh hotels, ashamed of having them in their rooms. He indicated that I should sit down on one of the pouffes and I did so. He went over to the desk, walked round it and removed a DVD from a drawer, which, again, he opened with a key, he obviously kept a few DVDs in there, well, more than one and probably more than two. He turned on the television, the DVD player was underneath and he put the disc in. He sat down on the other pouffe, to my left, almost next to me and a little behind, both of us were very close to the now blue screen, but I was closest, he picked up the remote control, I had to look at him out of the corner of my eye and turn my neck if I wanted to see the expression on his face. We were each holding a glass, he did everything with one hand or else, as I said, with his foot.

'So what are we going to watch, what are you going to show me?' I asked with a mixture of impatience and self-assurance. 'It's not a film, is it? It's hardly the right time for that.'

I still felt no fear, I was prevented from doing so by irritation and tiredness, it seemed unlikely to me that anything could wake me up. Besides, I'd seen quite enough unpleasant and painfully instructive things for one night, and not on a video but in palpable, breathable reality, right next to me, I could still feel in my body, albeit less keenly, the shock of that sword being brought down on the numbskull's neck, and in my head was the echo of the useless thoughts that had assailed me then: 'He's going to kill him, no, he can't, he won't, yes, he is, he's going to decapitate him right here, separate his head from his trunk, this man full of rage, and I can do nothing about it because the blade is going to come down and it's a two-edged sword, it's like thunderless lightning that strikes in silence, and he's going to cut right through him.' I didn't believe there could be anything worse, and whatever Tupra showed me would, moreover, belong to the past, it would be something that had already happened, that was over and had been filmed, and in which I would not be expected to intervene. There would be nothing to be done about it; with every viewing, the same thing would be repeated identically. But I must have felt it, the dread, the apprehension, the cringing, the shrinking back in fear, from the moment when Tupra's voice had suddenly grown more mournful than usual and awoken in me a suggestion of motiveless, meaningless anguish, the way mournful music does, for no reason – yes just a few notes on a cello or violin or viola da gamba, or on a piano – as if he knew all there was to know about those retrospective disasters which could, nevertheless, be reproduced and made present again an infinite number of times, because they had been recorded or registered, the kind of disaster of which I had no knowledge or even the tiniest suspicion.

'What you're going to see is secret. Never talk about it or mention it, not even to me after tonight, because tomorrow I will never have shown it to you. These are recordings we keep just in case we need them one day.' – 'Just in case,' I thought, 'that, it seems, is our motto.' – 'They contain shameful or embarrassing things, as well as crimes that have never been reported or pursued, committed by individuals of some consequence but

121

against whom no steps have been taken or charges made because it wasn't or isn't worth it or because it's still not the moment or because little would be gained. It makes much more sense to hang on to them, to keep them, in case there's ever a use for them in the future, with some of them we could obtain a great deal in exchange. In exchange for them staying buried here, never seen by anyone, you understand, only us. With others we've already obtained a lot, made good use of them and, besides, their possible benefits are never exhausted, because we never destroy anything or hand it over, we just show them occasionally to the people who appear in them, to the interested parties, if they don't trust us or don't believe that such recordings exist and want to see them to make quite sure. Don't worry, they don't come here (very few people ever have), well, it's so easy now to make copies and you can even show them on your mobile phone or send them. So these videos are a real treasure: they can persuade, dissuade, bring in large sums of money, force some insalubrious candidate to stand down, they can seal lips, obtain concessions and agreements, foil manoeuvres and conspiracies, put off or mitigate conflicts, provoke fires, save lives. You're not going to like the content, but don't scorn or condemn them. Bear in mind their value and the uses they can be put to. And the service they render, the good they sometimes do for our country.' – He had used a similar expression the first time we met at Wheeler's buffet supper in Oxford, when I had asked him what he did and he had been evasive in his reply: 'My real talent has always been for negotiating, in different fields and circumstances. Even serving my country, one should if one can, don't you think, even if the service one does is indirect and done mainly to benefit oneself.' He had repeated the word 'country' which can be translated as '*patria*' in my language, a word which, given our history and our past, has become a disagreeable and dangerous term that reveals a great deal, all of it negative, about those who use it; its imperfect English equivalent lacks that emotive, pompous quality. 'Our country,' he had said. How odd. Tupra had again forgotten that his country and mine were not the same, that I wasn't an Englishman but a Spaniard, probably, like De la Garza, a useless Spaniard. That was the moment when I came closest to believing that I had gained his trust without his noticing, that is, without his having decided to give it to me: when, late that night, in his house that almost no one ever visited, before the as yet blank screen, when he was about to show me those confidential images, he lost sight of the fact that as long as I was working for him, I was serving him, for a salary, and not working for his country. Nor, of course, mine. As for him, it was impossible to guess what services, indirect or otherwise, he rendered to his country, or if he always acted mainly to benefit himself. Perhaps, in his mind, the two things were now indistinguishable. He added: 'Prepare yourself. We're going to start. And not a word to anyone, is that clear?'

And he pressed Play.

What I saw thereafter should not be told, and I should do so only in short bursts. Partly because some scenes were shown in fast-forward mode, as Tupra had promised, and so fortunately I just caught glimpses of them, but always enough and more than I would have wanted; partly because for a few seconds – one, two, three, four; and five – I turned away or closed my eyes, and on a couple of occasions I held my hand like a visor at eyebrow height, with my fingers ready, so that I could choose to see or not see what I was seeing. But I saw or half-saw enough of each film or episode, because Reresby urged me to keep looking ('Don't turn away, resist the desire not to look, I'm not showing you this so that you can cover your eyes, don't hide,' he ordered me when, in one way or another, I tried to avoid the screen, 'and tell me now if what you witnessed earlier was so very terrible, tell me now that I went too far, tell me now that it was of any importance at all'; and by 'earlier' he was referring to what had happened or to what he had made happen in the Disabled toilet, in my presence and in the face of my impotence, my passivity and fear, my cowardice pure and simple). And partly, last of all, because I dare not describe it or I'm not capable of doing so, not fully.

As I looked and half-looked and saw, a poison was entering me, and when I use that word 'poison', I'm not doing so lightly or purely metaphorically, but because something entered my consciousness that had not been there before and provoked in me an immediate feeling of creeping sickness, of something alien to my body and to my sight and to my mind, like an inoculation, and that last term is spot on etymologically, for it contains at its root the Latin 'oculus', from which it comes, and it was through my eyes that this new and unexpected illness entered, through my eyes which were absorbing images and registering them and retaining them, and which could no longer erase them as one might erase a bloodstain on the floor, still less not have seen them. (Perhaps only when my eyes had recovered could I begin to doubt those images: when the time that levels and dissolves and mingles had passed.) And thus they entered, as if through a slow needle, things that were quite external to me and of which I was entirely ignorant, things I had never foreseen or conceived or even dreamed of, things so beyond my experience that it was of no use to me having read about similar cases in the press, for there they always seem remote and exaggerated, or in novels, or indeed in films, which we never quite believe because, deep down, we know it's all fake, however much we care about the characters or identify with them. Nevertheless, the first scenes Tupra showed me on the screen contained, relatively speaking, a deceptively comic element, which is why I could still make jokes and ask him about it (had he begun with what followed, I would probably have been struck dumb from the start):

'What's this? Porn?'

And this was tantamount to giving Reresby permission to enlighten me as much as he wanted – never very much, always concisely – about that initial recording and about others or most of them, although about two or three he kept a strange and total – or perhaps significant – silence, as if there were no need to say anything.

'That was neither the intention nor the result,' he replied very coldly; my comment had clearly not amused him. 'That woman is a very influential figure in the Conservative Party, one of the old school, and currently has high hopes of being promoted, as a reassuring counterweight for the more hard-line Tory voters; and since she usually gives fiery speeches about the decline in society's morals and habits, and about unbridled sex and all that, it's interesting to see what she gets up to in this video, and one day it might be useful to show it to her. Her husband, of course, is not present.'

There were no preliminaries, by which I mean that it had probably been cut to show only the basics, or the nitty-gritty, which I rather regretted because I would have liked to know where they had come from, or what they had proposed to her, or how they had reached that situation, the two guys who – the scene began, as I say, *in medias res* – were already enjoying a sex sandwich, the three of them writhing about on a rather faded green carpet, or perhaps it was the film quality, which was only fair, but clear enough for me to recognise the woman, that is, I remembered having seen her before on television, in Parliament or on the news. I even remembered her rather gruff voice, a voice like a hairdryer, she was one of those people who, even if they try, cannot or don't know how to speak softly or even to pause for a moment, which must be a torment for her nearest and dearest. Fortunately, there was no sound, if there had been, judging by the look of double ecstasy on her face at being impaled simultaneously by the two men, one from in front, one from behind – or intermittently, they were not very well synchronised or not always a very good fit, they came apart – her howls would have sounded to us like a gale or else a handsaw. As far as one could tell from their scant clothing, the two men might have been civil servants and neither was very young or very svelte, and one of them – with only his fly open, a sign of laziness rather than urgency – was wearing a pair of very bracing braces over his bare torso, which gave him an incongruous air, as if he were an impossible blend of office worker and butcher. As for the woman, she was about forty years old and, in turn, had not bothered to remove her skirt, which was transformed now into a crumpled belt, nor was she particularly attractive despite her bare and ample bosom, clearly unaugmented by surgery. They could have been in a hotel room or in an office, the narrow field of vision did little to clarify this, the camera being focused only on the fornicators, the two jerks in question were both fully paid-up *ġe-brȳd-guma*, indeed, they were being so there and then. It really did look like a low-budget or amateur porn movie made with understudies. Just who had filmed the scene and how was, needless to say, a mystery, but nowadays anyone would be able to do it, by using their mobile phone or even from a distance, without being present at all, and so no one is safe from being caught on camera in the most intimate or the most outrageous situations.

After about a minute or less, Tupra pressed the fast-forward button, for which I was grateful, there was no point in watching all that effort in order to reach an ending that would be of no surprise to anyone. I got as far as glimpsing a look on the Conservative lady's face at the conclusion of her double-decker experience, a look of pleased surprise, as if she were saying: 'How amazing. How could I have done such a thing? I'll have to try it again just to see if it really was as good as I think it was.' Perhaps it was her first act of daring duplicity. My boss returned the tape to its normal speed then, and we moved on at once to the second episode, with sound this time, which showed two famous actors and a third individual, unknown to me, spouting nonsense and falling about laughing while snorting cocaine in a living room, on a sofa, with the large, not to say enormous, lines of cocaine set out on the coffee table, which they were gradually snuffling up like someone taking sips from a glass.

'I don't know who he is,' I said, pointing to the man on the right and making it clear to Tupra that I had recognised the two juvenile leads.

'He's a member of the royal family. A long way down the line of succession, very secondary. It would have suited us perfectly if it had been someone more prominent, someone closer to the throne.' And he again pressed the fast-forward button, it was very dull footage, nothing but moronic laughter and that banquet of cocaine.

His remark momentarily gave me food for thought, I wondered why it would have suited them perfectly (I took 'us' to mean MI6, or the Secret Services as a whole, rather than our group) for anyone to take drugs, commit adultery, engage in corruption or break the law. They should have been glad that the Queen's closest relatives were not, like that trio, up to their eyeballs in cocaine.

'I don't understand,' I said, bewildered. 'Why would that have suited you?' And I made a point of not including myself.

Tupra froze the image in order to answer me.

'That's a very naïve question, Jack, you disappoint me sometimes. Anything like that suits us, with anyone of any importance, weight, decision-making ability, fame or influence. The more blots and the higher up the person, the better it suits us. Just as it suits everyone everywhere with those close to them. It's in your interests that your neighbour should be in your debt or that you should have caught him out in some way and be in a position to hurt him by reporting him or doing him the favour of keeping quiet about it. If people didn't infringe the law or try to get round the rules or if they never made mistakes or committed base acts, we would never get anything, it would be very hard for us to have any bargaining power and almost impossible to bend their wills or oblige them to. We'd have to resort to force and physical threats, and we tend not to use that much any more, we've been trying to give it up for some time now, because you never know if you'll emerge from that kind of thing unscathed or if they'll end up taking you to court and ruining you. Truly powerful people can do that, they can make your life very difficult and have you dismissed, they can pull strings and make you the scapegoat. We still use force on insignificant people like your friend Garza. There's no more effective method, I can assure you. With people who won't utter so much as a murmur of complaint. But with other people, it's always a risk. You can't influence them with money either, because they have so much. On the other hand, almost all are capable of weighing things up and making a judgement, of listening to reason, of seeing what's in their best interests. Everyone has something to hide, as you know; I've never known anyone who wasn't prepared to give in, either a little or a lot, in order to keep something quiet, so that it didn't get around or, at least, didn't reach the ears of one particular person. How could it possibly not suit us that people should be weak or base or greedy or cowardly, that they should fall into temptation and drop the occasional very large gaffe, or even be party to or commit misdemeanours? That's the basis of our work, the very substance. More than that, it's the bedrock of the state. The state needs treachery, venality, deceit, crime, illegal acts, conspiracy, dirty tricks (on the other hand, it needs very few acts of heroism, or only now and then, to provide a contrast). If those things didn't exist, or not enough, the state would have to invent them. It already does. Why do you think new offences are constantly being created? What wasn't an offence becomes one, so that no one is ever entirely clean. Why do you think we intervene in and regulate everything, even where it's unnecessary or where it doesn't concern us? We need laws to be violated and broken. What would be the point of having laws if everyone obeyed them? We'd never get anywhere. We couldn't exist. The state needs infractions, even children know that, although they don't know that they know. They're the first to commit them. We're brought up to join in the game and to collaborate right from the start, and we keep playing the game until the very last, even when we're dead. The debt is never settled.'

I kept occasionally turning my head a little to look at him out of the corner of my eye, but Tupra, who was behind me in relation to my position on the pouffe, was mainly addressing my back. His voice sounded very close and very gentle, almost a whisper, he had no reason to speak more loudly, there was nothing but silence all around. That last 'us' ('where it doesn't concern us') had been even more comprehensive than the previous one, he felt himself to be part of the state, its representative, possibly its guardian, possibly a servant of the nation, despite his tendency to consider his own benefit before all else. I imagined that he, too, would be capable of treachery, even if only to keep the country's supplies topped up, to satisfy its needs.

'The state *needs* treachery?' I asked, somewhat puzzled (although only slightly, for I was beginning to see what he meant).

'Of course, Jack. Especially in time of siege or invasion or war. That is what we most commemorate, what most unites people, what nations most remember over the centuries. Where would we be without it?'

It occurred to me that when I betrayed him with my interpretation of Incompara, I had perhaps been inadvertently useful to him in his role as man of the state, but this in no way helped me to feel that my debt had been paid off. This was doubtless partly why I put up with him – I could always leave – why I showed him such consideration, such leniency, or so I believed, because of that enduring sense of unease and because of that deliberate mistake of mine, I was still not sure if he had realised just how deliberate it had been. It was also because we liked each other, much to my regret sometimes and perhaps to his as well, young Pérez Nuix was far too optimistic in that regard. That night Tupra had put my liking for him to the test, and was still doing so with this film-show.

He stopped talking and immediately pressed the play button again. The previous scene ended abruptly and a new one appeared on the screen, and that was when the poison began to enter me. Two men in T-shirts and camouflage trousers and short boots, soldiers presumably, were standing over a third man, who was wearing a hood and sitting on a stool, his hands and feet shackled. There was sound this time, but all I could hear was a desperate panting coming from the prisoner, as if he had just run five hundred yards or were having a panic or anxiety attack. It was distressing, that loud, fast, somehow unquenchable breathing, it was quite possible that it was brought on by fear, being tied up and unable to see must make you dread every next second, and the seconds pass relentlessly. The room was lit from above, although the source of that light was off-screen, probably a lamp with a shade hanging from the ceiling, which revealed all three men or, rather, lit the two in camouflage trousers only intermittently because they kept prowling round the hooded man and, as they did so, were plunged every now and then into shadow. Beyond the circle of light, at the back, there were two or three other people, sitting in a row against the wall, arms folded, but in the darkness I couldn't make out their faces and only barely their shapes. The soldiers stopped their pacing and roughly hauled the prisoner to his feet and made him stand on the stool, helping him up. I saw them grab a rope, and although the hooded man's head was out of the frame now – the shot was fixed, the camera static – everything led me to believe that they had put the rope around his neck and that the rope was tied to a beam or some other high, horizontal bar, because one of the T-shirted men suddenly kicked away the stool and the victim was left dangling, unable to touch the floor, even though it was very near; this was a hanging.

I started, perhaps gasped or panted unexpectedly, I turned to Tupra and said in alarm:

'What's this?'

As he fell, the prisoner must have struck or perhaps brushed against the invisible lamp, because for a few seconds the light swayed gently back and forth.

'Don't turn away, keep looking, it isn't finished yet,' Tupra said imperiously. And he tapped my elbow with his stiff fingers, as if I were a disobedient child.

When I again fixed my eyes on the screen, I saw the feet of the hanged man still flailing around for support, while his panting gave way to a kind of guttural groan, a choking sound that never became more than that – it couldn't. The feet, however, suddenly found some support: one of the men in camouflage trousers grabbed the man's two legs and lifted them up as high as he could while the other man retrieved the stool and placed it once again beneath the hanged man's feet. Once he was firmly installed, they removed the rope and lowered him to ground level. Then they gave him a shove and he sat down again on the stool, and the two soldiers recommenced their prowling round the prisoner, who was now coughing, his lungs must have been bursting. The short boots made more noise this time, as if their owners were marching in unison and deliberately bringing their feet down hard in order to make that threatening noise, evocative of a roll on the drums at the circus announcing some still more dangerous feat or in public squares just before a much-anticipated execution. And after about thirty seconds – or perhaps ninety – they repeated the whole operation, that is, they made the hooded man stand on the stool and again pretended to hang him, or, to be more exact, they started to hang him – the stool kicked away as before – and then, soon afterwards, stopped. On that occasion, the prisoner lost a shoe during his desperate kicking, perhaps this time the hanging went on slightly longer than before. He was wearing very ordinary shoes, old lace-ups without the laces. He wasn't wearing socks. 'This is just like Tupra in the Disabled toilet,' I managed to think confusedly, 'when he raised and lowered the sword and then raised and lowered it again. Each time I thought he was going to cut the moron's head off, and now, although what he's showing me is over and done with and although he can freeze the action on the video, or even leave it for another day as if it really didn't matter (the scene will still be there unchanged), right now, I've no idea if those guys will end up hanging the poor devil on one of these dummy runs or not, and I want to know, even though the man's a stranger and I can't even see his face. He wouldn't have known how it would end either, when it was still not yet the past. He can't be a young man, not with those old battered brown shoes.' Before sitting the man down again, they put his shoe back on, as if driven by some mysterious impulse to maintain tidiness and good order. One of the soldiers started waving his hand about in front of his nose, as if some terrible smell were suddenly emanating from the man. They still said nothing, no one spoke, not even the obscure spectators, and that's bound to fill anyone unable to see or move with even more fear, more than surly voices or insults, unless they're asked something in an unfamiliar language, and that's the most frightening thing, I think, not understanding what is being said to you in a life-or-death situation.

They went on to repeat the whole operation a third time,

exactly the same, with the prisoner's head at first out of the frame only to reappear later along with the already taut rope, the body dropping straight down, albeit only a short way, so that nothing irreparable happened during the fall, the light swaying briefly either because he had brushed against it or perhaps from the sudden jolting, the second or third time they may have left him hanging there for fewer seconds, although, in my distress, it seemed much longer. The victim would be getting weaker with each cruel attempt, he had probably dislocated something and his heart would be racing. Obviously his neck hadn't been broken, that would have been the end, the men in the camouflage trousers didn't leave him long enough for that to happen, they were well trained, they must have known at what point it would be too late, not, I imagined, that it would matter very much if they got it wrong and the man snuffed it, perhaps no one in the world knew of his fate, nor even where he was. Everyone seemed relatively relaxed, both executioners and witnesses, diligent or alert but without malice, as if they were carrying out or watching some unpleasant procedure, but which was nothing more than that, a procedure.

Tupra froze the image when the prisoner had again been taken down and was coughing, his legs very weak and uncooperative, and on that occasion they did not sit him back on the chair. He still had on the black hood, with a single opening for mouth and nose (with adhesive tape covering the mouth), but none for the eyes. They seemed about to take him away, perhaps back to a cell, perhaps to the infirmary. His breathing was once more gradually slowing to a pant.

'Did you see?' Tupra asked. And in his voice I heard a note of almost amused excitement, to me inexplicable, for I was already aware of the poison entering me.

'What are you doing?' I replied. 'I want to know how it ends, to know if they finish off the poor guy.'

'That's where it ends, there isn't any more, it moves on to something else. But did you see him?' he said, referring clearly now to a man, not to an object or a particular detail or to the episode itself, in that case, he would have said 'it' not 'him'.

'Whom?' I asked, falling perhaps into hypercorrection, another example of that mysterious impulse to impose excessive good order and tidiness in the midst of the shock I was feeling.

Tupra tut-tutted in spontaneous scorn.

'You're being very slow on the uptake, Jack. Come on, what are your eyes for? The eye is quick and catches everything. You've done better than this in the past, you're losing your powers, or perhaps you're just tired.' Then he rewound the images with the remote control, found a particular point in the recording and froze it again, he did this quickly and skilfully, he was obviously very practised. It was one of the moments in which the prisoner was falling, the rope tightening, the stool kicked away, and the light swaying very briefly and gently, hardly at all and less and less with each movement, and covering a shorter distance. Two, at most three movements back and forth, but in that moment, just for a fraction of a second, the three men in the background were suddenly lit up by the shifting light. I looked at them, I couldn't quite make them out, but there was something familiar about them. 'What do you see now?'

'Wait,' I said, still uncertain, screwing up my eyes to see more clearly. 'Wait.'

Tupra did not wait, he activated the zoom and framed their faces in enlarged form, he had a DVD player with far more features than I had on mine in Madrid, I still hadn't bought one for myself in London. And then I clearly saw the familiar square, lined face, known to half of humanity, the half that watches television and reads the newspapers, with his unmistakable glasses and his look of some German doctor or chemist, or rather some Nazi doctor or chemist or scientist, whenever I'd seen him on-screen or in a photo, I'd had no difficulty at all in imagining him wearing a white coat over his tie, more than that, his face almost cried out for, no, demanded that white coat, it seemed strange that he didn't wear one. He, like all democratic world leaders and politicians, had repeatedly and publicly denied having anything to do with such things, or having given orders, approved or consented or even known about such practices, even ones that were less brutal and merely humiliating. No one in the outside world knew what I knew now: that, far from not knowing, he had been present, at least once, at the triple half-hanging of a man chained hand and foot, and that he had literally sat idly by, arms folded, impassive, the highest authority there, as he would have been almost anywhere. As Tupra had said, those videos could not be seen by just anyone (a journalist would have been jumping up and down). And the reason they were treasured as if they were gold dust was because each of them contained the fixed image – indefinitely repeatable – of someone famous or powerful or wealthy or someone with prestige and influence. After a while, I had forgotten all about that and focused only on the main action, how could I not? Perhaps for Tupra, on the other hand, the only thing that counted was the dark backdrop, or that one illuminated moment. Obviously, he had seen it before, it didn't take him by surprise. His attitude confirmed to me, at any rate, that he gave little importance to someone's possible death, but that neither was he a sadist. At least he took no pleasure in the suffering of another, those dummy hangings were not an object of fascination, they were merely the necessary framework for what really interested him.

'Yes, I can see him now,' I said. 'But why do you keep this? He's an American, an ally, one of yours.' And I realised at once that I hadn't said 'one of ours', as would perhaps have seemed logical to Tupra and as would have been logical at that point; it seemed to me that, without even realising it, I had entered some very murky territory. Yes, I was inside and I knew it, I really did belong to one particular side, despite feeling that I belonged to none. And what was even more unexpected and would have seemed unthinkable a year or even six months ago: I had seen something that was forbidden to almost all other eyes in the world, or, rather, had seen only the half of it.

'So what if he is? You never know.' He took a sip of port, I no longer felt much like drinking mine. He took out and lit a Rameses II. He only offered me one afterwards, when his cigarette was already smoking, and that I did accept. 'We don't even know who is "one of ours", or if they'll still be one of ours tomorrow, it's best not to worry too much about that aspect of things. That's something I can't know about you or you about me. Anyway, let's continue.'

And he resumed the session, the injection of poison, and, at my side and slightly behind me, occasionally spoke to make some brief point or comment, almost as used to happen at slide-shows, with a projector and a screen, given after a journey con-sidered unusual for the times – in my childhood, for example – with the travellers, the ones showing the slides to relatives or friends, placing each one in its context and giving an explana-tion: 'Here we are on top of the Empire State Building, the tallest skyscraper in the world,' when it still was, 'it's enough to give you vertigo, isn't it?' And vertigo, yes, vertigo was exactly what I felt with each new scene. Some were innocuous, people caught performing perfectly normal sexual acts, but which if made public or seen by others become strangely anomalous, es-pecially if performed by famous people or very serious people or people of a certain age or respectable people, there's always something laborious and ridiculous about objectified sex, and it's hard to understand why, today, there are so many people who film themselves for pleasure, to bask later on in the semi-embarrassment of it all. There were also individuals offering and accepting bribes, some in cash, some whose faces I knew, the occasional Spaniard or, rather, one particular Spanish woman, the blonde hypocrite, but Tupra fast-forwarded over all of these and only returned to normal speed when the scene involved violence or something bizarre. Bizarre to me, that is; not to him, of course; who knows, perhaps they would have seemed so to Pérez Nuix and Mulryan and Rendel, they might never have seen such images either or perhaps they were fully aware of them and knew every detail; perhaps, who knows, such images would have struck Wheeler as bizarre too, or maybe he would have seen more than enough of such things during his youth, and not on-screen. But I had not, I had never seen an execution before, except in films, or more recently on television, where the news they show always seems as unreal as the cinema; three men and a woman standing quite still on the seashore, waiting, their hands untied, they're helpless, so why tie them up, a dawn light, it reminded me at once of that painting in the Prado, by Gisbert, at least that's the name that came to me, the shooting of Torrijos and his liberal companions in Málaga, you can see the sand and the waves, perhaps a little of the countryside behind and, in the centre, a large group of condemned men, and when I looked it up on the Internet later that morning, I counted sixteen if you include the wife and child to whom one of them is clinging, but doubtless wife and child were merely saying goodbye to their soon-to-be-dead husband and father and would not meet the same fate, so there were fourteen and four more already fallen, with their eyes blindfolded, and nearby, on the ground, there's a top hat that one of the corpses must have tenaciously kept on his head until the moment he became a corpse, they would have killed them in batches to make things manageable, fifty or so men fell there in 1831 ('Late at night they killed him, along with all his company,' I recalled Lorca's great ballad on the subject and quoted it to myself), the six most smartly dressed are grouped on the right, the troops are bunched together in the rear and the man in the Phrygian hat looks disdainful and proud (social class matters even in a shared death), more so than the bespectacled fellow who forms part of the gentlemen's group, Torrijos must be the one with fairish hair ('the noble general, with the clear brow'), or perhaps not, he must be the one wearing boots and holding the hands of two of his comrades ('A gentleman among the dukes, a heart of finest silver'), betrayed on his return to the country by the Governor of Málaga ('they drew him there with deceitful words, which he, alas, believed'), he, too, had sought refuge in England for several years, it's always dangerous return- ing to Spain, where faces change so much between today and tomorrow, even if you were a hero of the Peninsular War or the War of Independence ('The Vizconde de La Barthe, who com- manded the militias, should have cut off his own hand rather than commit such villainy'), and there were the friars who are always present at our most sombre events (and if not them, priests and if not priests, then nuns), one reading or praying and two applying blindfolds, all three are ominous figures, and behind stand the blurred and waiting shapes of the firing squad ('Great clouds are

building above the Mijas mountains'), it's possible that the man commanding them let fall the white handkerchief he's holding in his left hand, or attached it perhaps to the point of his sabre, at the same time shouting 'Fire!' ('Amongst the sound of the waves the rifle shots rang out, and he lay dead upon the sand, bleeding from three wounds . . . Death, being death, did not wither his smile'); and I remembered, too, those who were executed without trial or given, at most, a sham version of justice, on those same Málaga beaches by the man who took the city more than a century later with his Francoist and Moorish hordes and with the Blackshirts of Roatta or 'Mancini': the Duque de Sevilla was his untimely title, the man who strewed with corpses the shore and the water and the barracks and the prisons and the hotels and the walls, about four thousand, it was claimed, and so what if it was fewer; and in front of the condemned men and woman stood two men with machine guns or something similar, I don't know much about these things, two men wearing ties and with their hair neatly combed, I bet they always carried a comb in their pocket as I do, as do most southerners, and when one of them said '*Dai*', they both unleashed interminable bursts of gunfire, they fired and fired, squandering bullets as if they had to get rid of them all, while the bodies were falling and once they had fallen too, the woman and one man face upwards and the other two on their sides, the gunmen moved closer, still firing, holding their weapons almost vertically now, the sand jumped and it seemed as if the flesh and the modest clothes of the already very dead dead, bleeding from twenty wounds, also jumped at every gratuitous shot. 'This is a settling of accounts on some secluded beach on the Golfo di Taranto, probably not far from Crotone in Calabria, a few years ago now,' murmured Reresby, correctly stressing the first syllable of Taranto, and he spoke so very softly now, it was as if his voice were emerging from inside a helmet. 'It's interesting. One of the executioners has since carved out a career for himself, first in the construction industry, then in politics, and he now has an excellent post in the current government. The other man, however is dead, he was bumped off straight away, in reprisal for this. It's useful for us to have this video, don't you think?' And I sensed in that question a kind of collector's pride, and maybe he was right to feel proud.

Nor had I ever seen, or even conceived of, an arranged bestial rape, with spectators as if they were at a tryout for young fighting bulls, a small arena, or perhaps the central courtyard of a group of houses, well-dressed men sitting beneath white, red and green awnings, a vicious sun, thick moustaches and Texan hats and not a few Havana cigars clenched between teeth, there was the festive sound of a brass band in the background, encouraging shouts in Spanish and in English, and in the arena, a woman, a horse, a few *mamporreros* – men employed to help stallions mate with mares – and something tearing, I couldn't bear it, I closed my eyes, 'Don't close your eyes!' and so I looked away, 'Don't look away!' But I did, except for the odd moment, this I really couldn't stand because I couldn't believe it, I'd never imagined such a thing were possible in the world, purely as a form of entertainment, and it really was a mortal poison, the images – what I glimpsed of them, for my eyelids and my turned-away face were quick to save me – entered my mind as if they were an ugly reptile or a kind of serpent, or perhaps an eel, or leeches under the skin, how can I put it, internal leeches, the images slipped inside me like a foreign body that caused me immediate pain and a sense of oppression and suffocation and the urgent need for someone to remove it ('Let me sit heavy on thy soul'), but you cannot root out what enters through the eyes, nor what enters through the ears, it installs itself inside you and there's nothing to be done about it, or else you have to wait some time in order to be able to persuade yourself that you did not see or hear what you did see or hear – there's always a doubt or the trace of a doubt – that it was imagination or a misunderstanding or a mirage or a hallucination or a malicious misinterpretation, we are none of us immune from them when our thoughts and our perceptions become twisted and we judge everything in the same slanted sinister light. 'This is Ciudad Juárez, in the state of Chihuahua, in Mexico,' murmured Tupra in his ever more sunken voice and in a tone that wasn't in the least indifferent, but almost sorrowful, grave, and it didn't sound to me as if he were putting it on, 'and there you have one of the thousand women who have disappeared and about whom so much has been written in the press. That, however, is not what matters to us, important though it is, but, rather, that man there, to the right in the second row, the one all in white and wearing a red tie.' This forced me to look for a moment, reluctantly and out of the corner of my eye – how hard it is to resist curiosity when someone points a finger at something – I saw a man in the audience, a fat, smiling, middle-aged man with shiny skin and thick hair, though I couldn't help but see, as well, the terrible irrationality and more tearing and some blood now – like a sword or a spear – and I turned away again, towards where Reresby was sitting, his eyes fixed on the screen, but screwed up now, as if he needed glasses or were preparing to close them at any moment, perhaps that episode, even though he had seen it before and knew how it would end, really set his teeth on edge or provoked anguish or even repugnance ('Bloody and guilty, guiltily awake'), no one can bear everything and, as I said, he was not a sadist. 'At the time, and this is a few years ago now, he was a very rich businessman, not yet a tycoon. Now he is, though, and he's standing for the post of mayor in an important town, in another region, in another state on the border with the United States, Coahuila. And he'll get it too. It will be useful for us to have this film of him enjoying the show.' He mispronounced Coahuila, saying it as if it were an English word – it's less well known than Chihuahua – something like 'koh-hoo-why-lah'. The worst thing was that the event seemed not to be a single episode, I certainly didn't get the impression that everything had been arranged for this one occasion, the band, the awnings, the horse and its experienced handlers, the invitation, doubtless made over the Internet and in code, or through messages left on mobile phones, doubtless in a whisper. What I glimpsed had probably happened before, perhaps with minor variations, with a different animal perhaps, but I didn't want to go down that road and I tore out all further imaginings by the roots.

'It's pronounced koh-ah-wee-lah,' I said, unable to resist the desire to correct him, a further example of that mysterious impulse to impose good order and unnecessary precision at all costs. I said this while looking at him. But he wasn't looking at me, he still kept his eyes glued to the screen for a few more seconds, almost half-closed now, his expression one of scorn and disgust for what he was seeing, his wasn't the face of a man unmoved by cruelty and by the suffering of others, he was judging them severely; then he fast-forwarded again and, after a while, froze the image.

'It's all right, you can look now. I've stopped at another scene, the next one. But Jack,' he added with barely suppressed irritation, yet almost kindly, 'I'm not showing you all this in order for you not to look at it, quite the opposite. Otherwise, what's the point?'

'I don't want to see any more, Bertie,' I said. 'If it's all like that, I don't want to see anything. I think I understand where you're going with this, and I don't need to know any more; besides, why don't you use these images to do something about it? You could use them to find out, through that fat man you appear to know so well and who's been so very successful, just what's going on in that place and to stop it. I don't understand your passivity, the organisation's passivity.'

'Do you really think that the Mexicans and the Americans don't already have a copy of this tape? If *they* don't intervene in the matter, there's not much we can do at our end; and it's not always easy to take action; in some countries, such a video would be unacceptable as proof, the way it was obtained would invalidate it. And what would we accuse our fat friend of? Attending an illegal event? Doing nothing? Refusing to help? Bah. I can understand why they might simply keep it filed away for a better occasion, just in case. I can't criticise them for that, we do the same with most of the footage that concerns us and our territories. You might save more lives by forcing one individual to do something later on than by immediately coming down hard on the less important people. And we're always interested in saving lives. We're always making calculations, weighing up whether it's worth letting one person die now if that will mean many others will live. Our priority, understandably enough, is saving British lives. As it would be in time of war. We have to get the most benefit out of everything, even if that means waiting a few years. It's the same with the day-to-day work in the office, sometimes you have to wait until someone is in a position to carry out what we have predicted that he or she is capable of doing. Including the things you predict, Jack, the things you tell us about. Everything you tell me counts, nothing is wasted. And it's the same with this.' He did finally look at me as he spoke these last few sentences, his eyes – grey in the gloom – no longer half-closed, his now wide-open, absorbent eyes that made anyone they alighted on feel worthy of attention and of interpretation; and it seemed to me that his words had been intended to increase that feeling in me. I had still not yet turned back to the screen again, despite his reassuring words. 'Go on, look. You must see at least one more recording. I'll fast-forward more quickly, I'll jump over a few, since you find them so upsetting.' Here he did not spare me his sarcasm.

I didn't care. I held up my hand to indicate that it was not yet the moment, that there was something I wanted to clear up first. Perhaps I needed a minute to recover from what I had seen and another to get myself used to the idea that there were doubtless still more unpleasant things to see, more poison. However, I disguised this by asking, as if my curiosity needed to be urgently assuaged:

'Where do you get them from? How do you find them? The things you've shown me up until now, I mean. None of them is a situation where cameras would be permitted.'

'From anywhere, from all kinds of places and in all kinds of ways, the opportunities are endless nowadays. On the one hand, we have our own traditional means: our installers and our infiltrators and other people we bribe to do the filming. But people sell images too, there's a whole floating market out there and we just buy whatever might be of interest to us, we get them cheap when the seller doesn't know the identity of the people who appear in them. We usually *do* know or we can find out, whether they're mere minions or obscure hired assassins or people of a certain importance. It's the same as in the art market: if the buyer knows the true value and the seller doesn't, then the result is a bargain. Now every fool owns and carries a mini-camera in his pocket or has one on his mobile phone, and if a tourist chances to capture some serious incident, even a crime, he's more likely to try and make some money out of it than take it to the police. The police don't pay, but we do, as do others, through inter-mediaries. It's the same if they catch some celebrity naked or screwing someone, they'll put it up for sale to the sensationalist magazines and TV shows, it's good to have someone keeping an eye on such things. At other times, our colleagues in other countries send us videos, and we reciprocate with anything that might be of use to them, satellites pick up a lot too. Nowadays, it's the easiest thing in the world, there are recordings of every-thing. People no longer have any idea where cameras might be hidden or still don't believe that there are quite that many, the most sensible thing is to assume that they're everywhere all the time, even in hotel rooms and in brothels and in saunas and in public toilets (not in the Disabled toilets, though, they don't tend to put them there), and even in private houses. No one is safe any more from being filmed doing anything and in any circumstances, whether committing a crime or indulging in de-praved sexual acts, always good possibilities. We aren't always so lucky, of course, and what we get hold of and watch is a tiny fraction of what's available. We can make immediate use, I mean legal use, of very little. But our archive is pretty good for future or hypothetical use, with a view to reaching private agreements. People really care about their image and can always be persuaded to withdraw or to make some kind of pact. You'd be surprised how much they care, even the non-famous, even businessmen who are unknown to most people, I mean, to those who watch television and read newspapers, because they know they would immediately cease to be unknown. It's very wide-spread that panic of yours, that narrative panic or horror, as you called it, everyone is convinced that they could have a story or could provide the material for a story, they just need someone to tell it, to decide to tell it. And there's nothing easier than rescuing someone from anonymity. Many people struggle and do their utmost to drag themselves out of anonymity, you know the kind of thing, they offer up their daily life on the Internet, twenty-four hours a day, they plan scandals or notorious frauds, they try to launch themselves into celebrity even of the ugliest kind, they invent some ridiculous piece of tittle-tattle in order to be invited to talk about it on the most obscure and paltry of programmes in the small hours, they seek out the indirect contagion of someone else's fame, however vile, or they pick a fight in the TV studio and trade insults, and try to have stupid, inane photos taken of themselves with an actor, a soccer star, a singer, a millionaire, a politician, a member of the royal family, a model. They'll even murder an acquaintance or a stranger in the most gruesome, complicated way, in a particularly cruel or striking or spine-chilling fashion, a child killing a much younger child, an adolescent killing his parents, a young woman killing a weaker colleague, an adult staging a massacre in a public place or secretly doing in seven people, one after the other, hoping to be discovered at last and to amaze the world. Because anyone – even the most stupid person – can kill someone. And they don't know that all they have to do is carry on with their lives until someone finds them interesting and adopts the appropriate point of view and decides to tell their story, or at least takes an interest and pays them some attention. As long as there is in that life some shameful, untold episode, a stain or an anomaly. And that's not so very difficult, Jack, because we all have something of the sort in our past, possibly without even knowing that we do or without being able to put our finger on it. It depends on who's looking at us. And the worst that can happen to anyone is for no one to look at them. People can't bear it and go into a decline. Some people die of it or kill.'

And he paused long enough for me to think: 'Tupra has adopted my theory, or snippets of it. He has the delicacy not to use my exact words or, when he does, to acknowledge that he has done so, "as you called it" or "to use your term", he says when he's quoting me verbatim. He has the good taste not to appropriate, at least not in my presence, the idea that people hate being left out or passed over and prefer always to be seen and judged, for good or ill or even for worse, and even need this and yearn for it; the idea that they still cannot do without the supposed eye of God that observed and watched us for centuries, without that companionable belief that some being is aware of us at all times and knows everything about us and follows every detail of our trajectory like someone following a story of which we are the protagonist; what they can't bear and won't allow is to remain unobserved by anyone, to be neither approved nor disapproved of, neither rewarded nor punished nor threatened, to be unable to count on any spectator or witness regardless of whether they are for us or against us; and they seek out or invent substitutes for that eye, which is now closed or wounded, or weary or inert, or bored or blind, or which has simply looked away from what I am doing; perhaps that's why people today care so little about being spied on and filmed, and often even provoke it, through exhibitionism, although that can prove detrimental and draw down upon them precisely the thing they most dread, the conversion of their story into a disaster. It's a contradictory double need: I want it to be known that I exist and have existed, and I want my deeds to be known, but that frightens me too, because it might ruin for ever the picture I'm painting of myself. And so when I'm not there, Tupra will probably have no qualms about appropriating wholesale everything I said to him when I talked about Dick Dearlove or indeed on other occasions, and he'll think he thought of it himself (in that regard he'll be like any other boss). Perhaps Pérez Nuix was right and I do have more influence over him than I think, perhaps I do stimulate and amuse him. Maybe that's why he has a soft spot for me and invites or drags me to his house and shows me this collection of horrible videos, and is so patient with me, and lets me get away with so many things, even letting me cover my eyes and not look at what he's generous enough to show me, in an act of great trust, or to watch it with only one eye open.'

146

And I immediately went on to think: 'But everything has its end, and banks will only honour your cheques while there's still cash in your account, so I mustn't take anything for granted.' And then I said:

'All right, show me what you've got to show me and let's get it over with. It's very late and I want to go home.'

'Ah, of course,' he replied ironically. 'Those lights. Do you think she'll still be waiting for you? If so, it won't be easy for you to get away afterwards, she'll be very insistent.' He glanced at his watch and added: 'You've certainly kept her hanging around. Do give her my deepest apologies.'

He was the kind of man who feels excited by the mere thought of women, by the idea of them, whoever they may be, and still more by the thought of his friends' wives or girlfriends and of sending messages to those female strangers through their husbands or boyfriends. That way, he thinks, they'll find out about him, they'll at least know of his existence and perhaps feel curious and imagine what he might be like, and thus indulge in a form of aimless, imaginary flirtation.

'I've told you already, Bertram, no one is waiting for me and no one has my keys.' I downed my drink in one, as if to show that at least something had been concluded. 'Come on, get on with it, what else do you want me to see?' And I indicated the TV with a lift of my chin.

He pressed Play again and then the fast-forward button, although he put it on at its second fastest speed, not at maximum, so that I could still see the images fairly clearly, albeit without sound, and they were all of them unpleasant to a greater or lesser degree, the worst kept feeding the poison into me, while others were, at best, boring or sordid, two guys with grey hair and reddish skin lying on a bed in their underpants, sniffing cocaine (drugs really provide a lot of material, perhaps that's why no government wants to legalise them, it would mean reducing the number of possible offences), people who were of no interest to me and made no impression whatsoever, so I abstained from asking who they were, they were probably well-known or important folk, perhaps British or Canadian or Australian, perhaps police officers, one of them had on an incongruous navy-blue peaked cap worn at a jaunty angle; I very nearly went back on my resolve and came close to giving in to jocular curiosity when there appeared on the screen a Spanish politician, a nationalist, whom we're all heartily sick of seeing (he, of course, would have objected to being described as Spanish), standing before a full-length mirror in the process of meticulously disguising himself as a lady or, rather, as an old-fashioned whore, it took him ages to get his tights on straight, every time they became twisted or wrinkled he had to take them off and start again, he tore two pairs in the process and glumly flung them down, he was also wrestling with a kind of girdle, it was a half-comic, half-pathetic sight, for which someone in my country would have paid good money; anyway, as I say, I was tempted, but I stopped myself in time and succeeded in not asking Tupra to play it at its proper speed, I wanted to finish as quickly as possible; in a billiard hall, four sinister-looking men were beating up some poor man of advancing years and distinguished appearance, they flung him face down on the green baize and beat him with billiard cues, holding the thin ends and thrashing him with the thick ends, then they rolled him over and immediately set to smashing his glasses and continued hitting him in the face – with glass flying everywhere and doubtless embedding itself in his skin with each new blow – and then they beat him all over his body, his ribs and his hips and his legs and his testicles, yes, they even beat him there, with the cues held upright, they must have broken his kneecaps and his tibia, the man didn't know how best to protect himself, they must have broken his hands too as he tried in vain to cover himself, four billiard cues are a lot when they're raised and lowered and raised and lowered, again and again, like swords. Here, I couldn't help commenting:

'You're not going to tell me that one of these savages is now a prominent figure in some lofty position. I can hardly believe it of thugs like them.'

Tupra stopped the film for a moment, he wasn't going to let me miss any of those barbaric acts, even in fast-forward. The image remained frozen on the poor man, his castigators already withdrawn, lying motionless on the table, bleeding from his nose and eyebrows, possibly from his cheekbones and from other cuts, a swollen, wounded heap.

'That wouldn't be impossible, not at all. But no,' he replied from behind me, this time I hadn't turned round to look at him, just as well, I thought afterwards. 'The important figure here is the old man, who would feel deeply ashamed of this scene. Bear in mind that some people want to hide the fact that they have been the victim as much as or more than if they'd been the executioner. There are people who would do almost anything to keep people from knowing what happened to them, what barbarous, humiliating things have been done to them, and who would go to still greater lengths to prevent that being seen. So that their loved ones, for example, never see or know about it, because they would suffer and be heartbroken and be unable to ever forget it, I mean, imagine if this man were your father. But he's important in a different way from the others you've seen, he's another type altogether. He has little power or influence, at least not directly. Don't you know who he is? Really?' And without even giving me time to answer 'No', he told me. 'It's Mr Pérez Nuix, our Patricia's father.' And he pronounced that double-barrelled surname English-style, so that it sounded as if he'd said something like 'Pears-Nukes'.

It was then that I thought how glad I was he couldn't see my face. I felt a sudden wave of heat spreading over both face and neck and then throughout my body, just like when I'd been caught red-handed at school, with no possibility of arguing or lying my way out of the situation. 'I obviously didn't deceive him,' I thought at once, 'and he doubtless knows that I tried to do so deliberately. That I lied to him about Incompara, perhaps he realised this at once and so it was all pointless, useless, because he didn't take the bait, and Incompara didn't get what he wanted, and so the debt wasn't cancelled, or the man paid off his debt with this brutal beating, but filmed by whom, they must have arranged to meet the father at that billiard hall to sort things out, they set a trap, and probably Reresby knew about it beforehand, knew what was really awaiting the old man, ordered a hidden camera to be installed there or else paid the manager or a fifth thug who doesn't appear in the frame because he wasn't taking part in the thrashing and was only directing it or witnessing it so that he could report back afterwards that the deed was done, meanwhile filming it on his mobile phone or on his miniature camera. Thoughts crowded into my mind and also a feeling of intense shame that took various forms, or perhaps they were all different, simultaneous shames. But I couldn't give myself away so easily, silence was hardly the normal response after such a revelation, that would have been tantamount to acknowledging that I knew everything or at least a part of it.

'But why?' I asked nervously. Such a question wasn't suspicious, any nervousness on my part could be attributed to the vicious attack I had just witnessed, fortunately with the sound off. 'Why? Why him? What did he do to those guys?'

'He had a lot of gambling debts, and you know what happens with things like that. It depends who you owe the money to, but they never let you off.'

'He's pretending,' I thought, 'he's telling me this as if I didn't already know, when he must be aware that I know a lot. He's testing me. He wants to see if I'll cave in and confess or if I'll play the innocent until the end, without giving anything away. He wants to see how I handle being found out.'

'When does this video date from, when did it happen?'

'Relatively recently,' he replied. 'A couple of months ago or less.'

'Does Patricia know? I mean, has she seen this?'

She had said nothing to me, perhaps because my favour or my pretence had failed so completely: why give me the bad news which, after all, did not concern me, why make me feel responsible, why get me any more involved than I already was? She hadn't told me the opposite either, that everything had turned out well and the debt had been settled, thanks, in part, to my good offices. Then again, it had never occurred to me that she would and I hadn't asked her about it, she had only asked me that one favour, after all, and that ought to be respected; contrary to popular belief, the first occasion doesn't necessarily give rise to a second, whatever it might be.

Tupra gave that same laugh, like a short cough, which indicated sarcasm or incredulity at what he was hearing.

'No, of course she hasn't seen it. What do you take me for? It was bad enough for her seeing him in the hospital. Her father spent a long time there, in fact he may only have been sent home a short time ago, I'm not sure, and it's still unclear whether he'll recover, and well, he's getting on a bit now, he'll never completely get over something like that, they gave the poor devil a real going-over.'

Yes, there was young Pérez Nuix's poor father, whom she loved so much, frozen before my eyes at his saddest moment, his eyes were half-closed, and what little expression could be read in them bespoke disappointment, as if he had never expected the world to inflict such cruelty or that he would experience it in his own flesh, that frivolous man who found suffering tedious; I felt guilty for what they had done to him and that was one of the various shames I felt, perhaps I hadn't been convincing enough when I gave my views on Incompara, it's hard to lie when one doesn't oneself believe the lie, I should have tried harder, have been more insistent and underwritten my words with my thoughts thus making them true, or perhaps it wasn't a failure on my part at all and Tupra had merely seen what he had seen, which was, moreover, as clear as day: that Vanni Incompara was not to be trusted in any way and that he was also utterly ruthless, Pérez Nuix would have picked that up, but would have had to deceive herself, which is what we all do, even those who have the gift, even the most gifted, when what we see affects us and proves unbearable. Perhaps it had been an impossible undertaking, that of persuading my boss that things were otherwise, the same boss who was now showing me this video for who knows what reason, or was it pure coincidence and he had no ulterior motive, after all, I could have said nothing, and then he wouldn't have paused the tape, but let it run without making any further reference to it and without telling me who the victim was. 'And yet he seems to be saying to me: "Take a good look, you didn't deceive me, just see where your attempt at deceit has led, Iago, your cunning plan didn't work, and I paid no attention to your treachery, I wasn't taken in by your recommendations and so I rejected him, and then, of course, he flew into a rage because of the false expectations you had aroused in him; it would have been so much better if you hadn't bothered, he might have been more magnanimous with that cheerful and distinguished old man, your compatriot, and sent him only one thug instead of four, armed perhaps with a blackjack, not a long hard billiard cue, or else he would have found another way to settle the matter, without anger or violence. You really made a blunder there and underestimated me too, thinking you could pull the wool over my eyes, but you've a long way to go before you'll manage that. A whole lifetime." It could also be that he's not saying anything to me.'

'But why didn't you stop it, when you knew he was Patricia's father?' I continued to act dumb; once you set off along a path you have to follow it until it's cut off by the sea, a precipice, a wall, the desert, or the jungle. 'You're not telling me you knew nothing about this, or that the camera filming it was there by chance, that you had nothing to do with it and bought the video on the market. That would be a coincidence, don't you think, the father of a colleague being beaten up?'

Tupra remained impassive, or so I imagined. I still had my back to him, preferring not to see his expression and for him not to see mine. His voice sounded calm:

'Of course it wasn't a coincidence. It was precisely because it involved a colleague that they brought it to us, offered it to us. They thought it might be of interest, either by revealing where her weaknesses might lie, or to help us carry out reprisals against the aggressors. You know, in our group, we don't talk much about our personal problems – Pat says almost nothing. If it hadn't been for this tape, I would hardly have known a thing. All she told me was that her father had had an accident and was in the hospital. We don't tend to mix socially, as you know.'

'And didn't you take reprisals? Not even in a case like this? Then why keep the tape?'

'As I told you, nothing here gets thrown away or given away or destroyed, and this beating is perfectly safe here, it's not going to be shown to anyone. Although, who knows, it might be necessary to show it to Pat one day, to convince her of something, perhaps to stay, not to leave us, you never can tell. For the moment, though, there's no point in taking reprisals, those four men are rank nobodies, they do things like that – a hundred similar things for a hundred different masters – and they're sure to get caught now and then with no need for us to go after them, they're used to prison. As for the men behind it, as I've explained, it's best to wait, as we so often do, to make some better future use of it.'

'Is that what you wanted me to see?' I knew it wasn't, if it had been, he wouldn't have been fast-forwarding over it, risking me not saying anything and depriving him of the opportunity to enlighten me. He had still more poison with which to inoculate me, or more torment to put me through.

'No, that's not it. Let's get on.'

And more scenes, albeit fewer, sped silently by, I could still see most of them, I saw a man screaming at another man who was sitting in a car in an underground car park, I mean a private not a public one, he was leaning against the car and screaming at him, resting one elbow on the open window so that the other man couldn't wind it up, their two faces so close that he must have been spraying him with spit, I saw how with a rapid movement he took a pistol from his jacket pocket and placed the barrel beneath the ear lobe of his adversary or victim, I saw how he took not even three seconds to squeeze the trigger and shoot him right there, beneath the ear lobe, at point-blank range. I put my hand to my eyes, so that I could see only through the chinks between my fingers, ridiculous I know, I saw blood spurt out and tiny bits of bone, but that way you somehow feel that you're seeing less or could at least stop seeing it at any moment, although that moment never arrives because you never draw your fingers together. The blood spattered the murderer too, not that this appeared to bother him, there must be a shower nearby or else he has a fresh shirt in his car, another suit, or perhaps this was the underground car park for his own apartment building, he turned and disappeared, returning the pistol to his pocket, it was a very brief sequence, but judging by the cut of his trousers – rather short and narrow and made of shiny grey fabric – I would have said he was American, and the fact that Tupra kept the video must mean that the man belonged to the CIA or something similar, the army perhaps, I refrained from asking questions, perhaps he was now one of its highest-ranking officers, who knows, well, Reresby would.

Immediately after this, I saw someone being beaten to death with a hammer, at least I assume he was killed, a woman of about thirty was wielding the weapon, she was wearing a skirt and high heels and a pearl necklace over her tight V-necked sweater – the clothing and shoes in the same matching green, she looked like someone out of the 1950s or the early '60s, a secretary or an executive or a bank clerk, certainly an office worker – she felled a man considerably taller than herself with a savage hammer blow to the forehead, he was my age or Tupra's, but heavier and broader than either of us, this was probably taking place in a hotel room, the burly man fell backwards and she sat astride him hitting him with the hammer, smashing his skull, which is why I assume that he died, she must have feared or hated him intensely, her necklace jiggled up and down, her skirt was all rucked up; strangely enough, despite her autumnal outfit, she wasn't wearing tights, perhaps she'd taken them off before and perhaps her panties too, in order to have sex fully clothed, or perhaps she didn't have to take off her panties, or he took them off so as to rape her and would have liked to have her like that, on top of him, or underneath with her legs spread, what would that have made her then, what was she now and who was the victim, I still said nothing, the recording ended abruptly, the woman poised with her hammer in the air, like Tupra with his sword, she had not yet finished delivering her blows, I couldn't help remembering that rather odd actress Constance Towers in that old movie, *The Naked Kiss*, in Spain it was called *Una luz en el hampa – A Light in the Underworld* – a slightly ridiculous title – in which she did something similar in the first scene, not with a hammer but with the sharp heel of her shoe, or was it a telephone, and while she was committing this crime her hair fell off, it turned out she was wearing a blonde wig and was revealed to the viewers as completely bald, and maybe that's what was most shocking, like those false stories about Jayne Mansfield; and the image of Luisa also crossed my mind, the dread image I had fantasised about in my darkest or maddest moments, attacked by the man who would replace me, a devious sort who wouldn't give her so much as a moment's breathing space and would isolate her totally, and who, one rainy night, when they were stuck at home, would close his large hands around her throat while the children – my children – watched from a corner, pressing themselves into the wall as if wishing the wall would give way and disappear and, with it, that awful sight, and the choked-back tears that longed to burst forth, but could not, the bad dream, and the strange, long-drawn-out noise their mother made as she died, I just hoped she had a hammer at hand so that she wouldn't be the one to die, but the devious man, the despotic possessive man who wasn't like that in the early stages, on their first dates, but deferential, respectful, even cautious, who, like me, didn't stay the night, even if begged to do so, but put all his clothes back on despite the lateness of the hour, the exhaustion and the cold, and when he went out into the street once again put his gloves on, that man so similar to Tupra.

It's also possible that I was too tired to say a word, as scene succeeded scene, I felt more and more shrivelled, diminished, atrophied ('Dream on, dream on, of bloody deeds and death'), as if that one facet of the world I was being shown were driving out all the other more usual ones, not just the happy smiling ones, but also the anodyne and the neutral, the indifferent, the routine, which – especially the latter – are our salvation and essence. That is what poison does, it infiltrates and contaminates everything. The tiredness, however, must have been cumulative because, at the same time, I realised that, despite all I had seen, nothing being paraded before me made such a painful impact on me as the incident I had witnessed with my own eyes, unmediated by a screen, in the Disabled toilet. Violence that happens right next to you and that breathes and stains is not the same as violence projected onto a screen, even if you know it's real and not fictitious, television doesn't spatter us, it only frightens us. And now and then, Tupra's question would resurface in my mind, the question he had asked me in the car before setting off and that had made him decide to drive us both to his house, 'Why can't one go around beating up people and killing them? That's what you said.' What nonsense, everyone knows why, anyone could have given him the answer. But in the light of what he was showing me ('Let these visions sit heavy on thy soul; and lay down thy edgeless sword and let thy shield roll away; take off thy helmet and let fall thy lance'), I could still find only idiotic puerile answers, inherited but never thought through, the usual trite and vacuous ones that everyone has learned by rote and is ready to trot out without ever having given them a thought, however paltry or vague, without ever having questioned them: why is it wrong, because it's immoral, because it's against the law, because you can get sent to prison or to the gallows in some countries, because you shouldn't do unto others what you wouldn't want done unto you, because it's a crime, because there is such a thing as pity, because it's a sin, because it's bad, because life is sacred, because once it's done it's done and cannot be undone. Tupra was clearly asking me something that went beyond all that.

I saw more flurries of activity, perhaps I shouldn't describe them, I saw worse things, more confused, almost run together. Reresby had increased the speed, he needed to sleep too, yes, maybe he was growing sleepy, although he sounded wide awake, perhaps he was at last in sympathy with my desire to get it over with as quickly as possible, I wanted an end to the fever, my pain, the word, the dance, the image, the poison, the dream, at least for that day and for that very long night, the things that compromise or accuse are not very varied – weird sex, violent sex, adulterous or merely laughable sex, beatings, drug consumption, a bit of torture, cruelty and sadism, corruption, bribes, con tricks and betrayals and debts, failed conspiracies and treacheries exposed, improvised homicides and planned murders, and not much else really, almost everything can be reduced to that, but then there are the massacres, I saw another machine-gunning, on a larger scale this time, of civilians in some African country, twenty or so women and men and children and old people, they fell in quick succession, like dominoes, and thus it seemed less grave or even less true, executed by black soldiers or marksmen under orders from a white officer in uniform, whether regulation or half-invented I don't know, perhaps he was a mercenary who later rejoined his army, there are Englishmen and South Africans and Belgians who have made that return journey, and Frenchmen too, I believe. If that were the case, Tupra had that European soldier exactly where he wanted him, he would have allowed him to rise, make a career for himself, he certainly wouldn't have warned him of the existence of that film nor would he have denounced him, he would be waiting until the man reached some lofty position, in his own country, in NATO, so that he could then ask him an enormous favour, or, rather, in the light of that video, force him to grant the favour.

And finally he stopped, I mean that he resumed normal speed for one particular sequence and with it restored the sound, he had to rewind a little to catch the beginning.

'Here it is,' he said. 'This is what I want you to see before you go home. Take a good look, and when you're lying in bed think about me and think about this.'

It was, like all the others, a short scene, he hadn't lied about that, even though I seemed to have been there for ever, almost all the episodes had been edited together onto that one DVD with barely any preamble, what mattered was the brutality, the crime or the farce, not what came before or afterwards, but what could be used to blackmail the subject of the film. Three men were in a kind of hut, in the background I could make out the tail of an animal whisking back and forth, probably a cow or an ox, there was straw scattered about the floor, I could imagine how it must have smelled in there. Two of the men were standing and they had tied up the third man, who was sitting on a wicker chair, his hands behind his back and each foot tied to a chair leg, to the front legs, of course. There was a cassette or a radio playing, I could hear a tune that I half-recognised, with my reliable memory for music: Comendador had taken a liking to the local songs during his prison stay in Palermo after being arrested by customs because of a drop of blood that trickled from his nose at an inopportune or perhaps opportune moment and aroused the suspicions of a border guard with a very sharp or deductive eye, and who literally set the drug-sniffing dogs on him. He had sent me a couple of CDs as a present, one by Modugno and the other by someone called Zappulla, and I was almost sure that it was the latter's voice I could hear at full volume in the cowshed, singing a song that appeared on my CD, I could remember some of the titles: 'I puvireddi', 'Suspirannu', 'Luntanu', 'Bidduzza', or 'Moro pe ttia', pretty, pleasant songs, slightly tacky in their melancholy, and I had enjoyed listening to them, over and over, during a melancholy and rather tacky period of my own life, that cowshed must then be in Sicily, an idea confirmed by the presence of the weapon one of the men standing guard wore slung over his shoulder on a chain, a *lupara*, the sawn-off shotgun once used there for hunting and for settling scores, and perhaps still used for both, the other man had a large pistol in a holster under his arm, his jacket draped elegantly over his shoulders, the sleeves hanging empty, and his shirtsleeves rolled up, a large square watch on his wrist, his hand resting on the back of the chair in which sat the prisoner, stouter and older than the two younger and thinner men, and all three were mouthing the words of the song, they all knew it by heart and were singing along with Zappulla, and although each was doing this of his own accord, so to speak, absorbed and isolated, as if to himself and not in unison, there was nonetheless something very odd about them all momentarily sharing that melody, as if they weren't two guards and their captive or two executioners and their victim, and as if nothing bad awaited the latter, and the tails of the animals in the background seemed to move to the same rhythm, all the living beings in that out-of-the-way place were strangely and incongruously in tune, the man carrying the *lupara* was even swaying slightly, not lifting his feet, but just moving his legs and his torso and the twin-barrelled shotgun, dancing to the lilting melody of '*I puvireddi*' or '*Moro pe ttia*', which mean, in dialect, 'The poor devils' or 'I'm dying for you'.

This lasted only a few seconds, then the door was flung open – a glimpse of grass, a pleasant field – and three other men came in, closing the door behind them, and the first man, the man in charge, was Arturo Manoia. There he was with his glasses – the glasses of a rapist or of a civil servant – which he kept pushing up with his thumb even when they had not slipped down, I noticed that he was doing the same thing there, while standing up and active and occupied, and his gaze, almost invisible due to the reflected light and to his incessantly shifting, lustreless eyes (the colour of milky coffee), as if he found it hard to keep them still for more than a few seconds, or else could not stand for people to be able to examine them. I recognised him at once, I had just spent a whole unforgettable evening with him and he didn't look very much younger, so it must have been a recent video or else he was one of those men who don't age and who, unlike his wife, don't change either, there he was with his invasive, too-long chin, perhaps not long enough to be termed prognathous, but still meriting the word *bazzone*. And there he was, with his evident readiness to take revenge. The moment I met him, I thought he would be likely to lash out without the slightest provocation or on the slightest pretext or even with no need for either, that he was an irascible man, although he would doubtless be considered, instead, as measured, because he would almost never give vent to that anger. But I had also thought that on the few occasions when his rage did surface, it would doubtless be terrifying and best not witnessed. And now, having said goodbye to him and seen the last of him in person, there, unexpectedly, at the end of the night, I was about to witness one of his attacks of rage on-screen. It was almost, it seemed to me, a curse and I knew this as soon as I saw him, in suit and tie, come in through the door of the cowshed. I prepared myself, I told myself that, whatever happened, I would not look away or cover my eyes. I wanted to show Tupra that I had toughened up during our late-night session or had created inside myself an antidote to his poison, or at least some resistance.

The music didn't stop when the three newcomers arrived, they didn't even turn down the volume, and so I heard little of what Manoia was saying to the bound man and understood still less, he seemed to me to be speaking with an exaggerated southern accent or else mixing dialect and Italian. I could tell, though, that he was speaking to him proudly, indignantly, scornfully – his wounding voice raised in anger now – waving his hands around and giving the man the occasional smack across the face as if this were simply another gesture made in passing, a way of underlining each reproof, almost involuntary or as if he were barely aware of what he was doing, which is a sure sign that the person being slapped is now worthless and has become a mere thing. The other man answered as best he could, and *he* was definitely speaking in dialect, because I couldn't understand a word, he managed only truncated sentences, constantly interrupted by the swift cease-less flow of words from Manoia, I tried not to look too much at the prisoner, the less I perceived him as an individual, the less it would matter to me what happened to him in the end, because something horrible was about to happen, that much was certain, the situation demanded it and, besides, the scene was part of that specially chosen and edited DVD of embarrassing or downright vile episodes, but I did look at him despite myself, out of habit, he was a plump man, with a small mouth and a large head, short, curly, straw-coloured hair, bulging eyes, and the weather-beaten skin of a small landowner who still walks his own fields, well-dressed in a country way, and about forty or so years old. Finally, Manoia's cascade of words ceased – but not his rage – or else he made a brief pause, and then I did understand what he said: '*Tap-pategli la bocca*,' he ordered his henchmen, although it sounded more like '*Dabbadegli la bogga*', with unvoiced consonants converted into voiced, or perhaps I understood this a posteriori from the images, when I saw how the man with the pistol and the man with the shotgun stuffed two wads of cloth into the man's mouth, one after the other, I don't know how there was room, and on top of that placed a large strip of adhesive tape, from ear to ear, so that he couldn't cough freely as he needed to, his face grew red and inflamed, his eyes seemed, for a moment, about to pop out of their sockets, his cheeks puffed up like boils, the henchmen used red-and-white checked cloths, perhaps napkins from a *trattoria*, and the ends stuck out above and below the tape, what could he have done that was so very terrible or so grave, had he been an informer like Del Real, had he betrayed someone, lost his nerve, failed, fled, fallen asleep, he did not seem like a mere enemy, although he could well have been, perhaps someone had died because of him, some agent from the Sismi who wasn't due to die, always assuming Manoia belonged to the Sismi. Manoia then took an object out of his jacket pocket, I couldn't see what it was, something short, a small penknife, a teaspoon, a sharp metal file, a pencil. '*Adesso vedrai*,' he said, 'Now you'll see,' and those words I did hear clearly despite the music. The seated man's head was at the same height as Manoia's chest and arms. Manoia moved closer, only a couple of steps, and with whatever he was holding in his hand he made two rapid movements over the man's face, the gesture of an old-fashioned dentist preparing to pull out a tooth by main force, first one, then the other, and he did pull them out, he really did, by the roots, but not the man's teeth, he sliced them out the way someone uses a dessert knife to cut out the stone from a peach half, or the seeds from a watermelon, or walnuts from their shells after the initial struggle to open them, and then I had to close mine, despite my earlier resolution, what else could I do, but I tried not to cover them with my hand so that Tupra might think that I had kept them open, while Zappulla kept singing and I caught only the occasional word, '*sfortunate*', '*mangiare*', '*cerco*', '*sofro*', '*senza capire*', '*malate*', 'unhappy', 'eat', 'I seek', 'I suffer', 'without understanding', 'sick', not enough to make any sense of them, although one can always give meaning to anything, unhappy the empty sockets of my eyes, they force me to eat napkins or cloths, I seek to save myself and I suffer mutilations, without understanding the cruelty of these sick beasts . . . '*E quando son le feste di Natale*', that didn't help in the least even though it was the longest phrase my ears had caught, because I could still hear the inhuman snorts of incredulity and despair and pain, but no screams, there could be no shouts with those checked cloths stuffed in his mouth, but at least I couldn't see, which was something, even though I was trying to make Reresby believe the opposite and possibly succeeding.

And in short, I was afraid ('O that I could forget what I have been or not remember what I must be now'). Afraid of Manoia and afraid of Tupra and also vaguely afraid of myself, because I was mixed up with them ('Yes, O that I could not remember what I must be now'). Tupra used the remote control to freeze the image, he had inoculated me with the last drop of his poison and through the eyes too, as indicated by its etymology. I knew he had stopped the film because I could no longer hear the sound. I opened my eyes, I dared to look, fortunately the film was frozen at a moment when Manoia's back was covering the face of the now blind man.

'You've seen enough,' said Tupra, 'although the scene isn't over yet: our friend heaps further insults on his victim and then slits his throat, but I'll spare you that – there's a lot of blood – just as he could have spared that man, I mean, why make someone suffer like that when you're going to kill him anyway, and only a few seconds later?' He said this in a tone of genuine perplexity and horror, and as if he had given much thought to that 'why' but never managed to get beyond it. 'I don't understand it, do you, Jack? Do you understand it, Jack?'

I had fallen silent, I preferred not to say a word for a few moments because I was afraid that if I spoke, I would crumble and my voice would shake, and I might even cry, and I couldn't let that happen under any circumstances, I wouldn't allow myself to do so in that place and at that time. I clenched my jaw and kept it clenched, and finally I felt sufficiently composed to respond with what I intended to be an imitation of sarcasm:

'You should have asked him. You missed an opportunity there. You had all night to find out.' This seemed to disconcert him slightly, he obviously hadn't been expecting such a response. I went on: 'Perhaps when he did that first thing he didn't know he was going to kill him. Maybe he hadn't yet decided. Sometimes a first punishment isn't enough to satisfy one's fury and you have to go still further. Perhaps he had no option but to kill him. For some people even that isn't enough, and they try to kill the person twice, to vainly try and kill the already dead. They mutilate the corpse or profane the tomb – they even regret having killed him because they can't now kill him again. It happened a lot during our Civil War. It happens now with ETA, for whom once isn't enough.' Then I went back to my first question: 'But why ask me, he's your friend, you should have asked him.'

Tupra lit another cigarette, I heard the sound of the lighter, I had still not turned round to face him. He stopped the DVD, got up, removed the disc, stood in front of me, holding it delicately between his fingers, and said:

'Certainly not, Manoia doesn't even know I have this video, he hasn't a clue. Well, he'll assume I have something on him, but he won't know what. And it would never occur to him that it would be this. Anyway, as you can see, I very likely saved that imbecile Garza's life. Instead of getting angry with me, you should be grateful that I took charge of his punishment, to use your word. He would never have got away scot-free, that's for sure.'

I had known for some time now where he was heading. 'I had to do it in order to avoid a greater evil, or so I believed; I killed one so that ten would not be killed, ten so that a hundred would not fall, a hundred in order to save a thousand', and so on, ad infinitum, the old excuse that so many would spend centuries preparing and elaborating in their Christian and non-Christian tombs, waiting for the Judgement that never comes, and many still believe in that Judgement at the hour of their departing, certainly almost all murderers and instigators of murder throughout history. However, I wasn't concerned so much with heaping more blame on him as with holding myself together, which I was managing only with difficulty, how I would love to have appeared completely indifferent. And so I asked him a genuine question, that is, one I would have wanted to ask him anyway, when I was more myself.

'If he assumes you have something on him and you've got something like that, how come you were pussyfooting around him all evening? It looked like you were trying to placate him, not making any demands. According to what you've just told me, these videos are used above all to make it easier to wheedle concessions out of people, to blackmail them, but my impression was that you were having a hard time persuading him to do whatever it was you were trying to persuade him to do, or getting out of him what you wanted.'

Tupra looked at me in a slightly amused, slightly irritated way. I had still not moved from the pouffe, and so he was looking down on me.

'How do you know he doesn't have some footage of *us*? We could lose our advantage or it could be cancelled out.' He said 'of us', not 'of me', I thought that it could be footage of Rendel or Mulryan, although the latter seemed a very cautious type, and I couldn't imagine Pérez Nuix behaving like Manoia in that cowshed. Or it could be Tupra, of course, or someone above him or, rather, above us, for I, too, was 'us'. Or a compromising video of another sort, not equivalent, not comparable, not as vile, or so at least I hoped. What I had seen in that film from Sicily was utterly repellent, as were the scenes shot in Ciudad Juárez and other places, I would never be able to forget them or, better still, erase them: as if they had never existed or trod the earth or strode the world, or passed before my eyes.

'That was in Sicily, wasn't it?' I asked then, adopting a technical tone of voice, which is the most helpful when one is on the verge of collapse.

'Very good, Jack, you get better and better,' he replied and made as if to applaud me, although he couldn't do so while holding the disc in one hand and his cigarette in the other. 'How did you glean that, from the song, the language or both things?'

'Three things – there was the guy with the *lupara* as well. It wasn't that hard.' I assumed he would know that word, even if he didn't know Italian. I was wrong, and this surprised me.

'The what?'

'The *lupara*.' And I spelled it out for him. 'That's what they call that kind of double-barrelled shotgun in Sicily.'

'Well, you do know a lot.' Perhaps he was bothered because I was managing to put on a semblance of composure; after spending so much time covering my eyes, he must have felt sure that I would completely fall apart when I saw the man with whom I had shared both supper and drinks, whose hand I had shaken, with whose wife I had danced, gouging out a person's eyes. And of course I had fallen apart, I was trembling inside and I wanted to get out of that room as quickly as possible, but I wasn't going to let Tupra see that, he had tormented me quite enough for one night and I wasn't prepared to give him still more pleasure. Flavia would have no inkling of her husband's sadistic side, it's astonishing how little we know the faces of those we love, today or yesterday, let alone tomorrow.

'What I'd like to know is how come there was a camera in what I assume to be a remote cowshed somewhere in the back of beyond? Isn't that rather strange?' I tried to maintain that technical tone of voice, and I was doing quite well with my efforts to pull myself together.

Tupra again looked down at me from above, more amused now than irritated.

'Yes, it would have been very strange, Jack, if the fellow with the *lupara*, you see what a quick learner I am' – he pronounced the word as if it were English, 'looparrah', he didn't have a very good ear – 'hadn't hidden it there beforehand. If they'd discovered it, he might have ended up just like the man in the chair.'

I didn't really want an answer to my next question, but I asked it purely in order to shore myself up, until the moment when I could leave, and I asked it in that same technical tone:

'You're not telling me that guy's English, are you, looking like that? You're not telling me he's our agent?' I almost said 'your', but I corrected myself or changed my mind in time, possibly ironically, possibly because in some way it suited me.

The answer was obvious, 'What else do you think we spend our money on?' or 'Why else do we have contacts?' or 'Why else do we resort to blackmail?' but Tupra, at that late hour, wanted to draw the attention back to himself. The fact is he had been doing this intermittently all night.

'That's a big question, Jack.' He moved away from me, went to the desk from which he had taken the disc, carefully put the disc back inside, and locked the drawer with the key, the key to his treasures. Then he turned to ask me the question again, from the other side of the desk, in the near-darkness. He said it with his large mouth – with his overly soft and fleshy mouth, as lacking in consistency as it was over-endowed in breadth – at the same time blowing out smoke: 'You've had plenty of time to think about it, so answer the question I asked you in the car. Now that you've seen things you'd never seen before and, I hope, never will again. Tell me now, why, according to you, one can't go around beating people up and killing them? You've seen how much of it goes on, everywhere, and sometimes with an utter lack of concern. So explain to me why one can't.'

None of the classic responses would work with him, I had known that from the start. I hadn't expected Reresby to come back to it, although I don't know why, given that like me and like Wheeler, he never lost the thread or forgot any unresolved matter or let go of his prey if he didn't want to. I looked stupidly around me, as if I might find an answer on the walls; the room lay in semi-darkness, the lights down low. For a moment, my eyes rested on the one image, perhaps as a respite from all the others, from those I had seen on that wretched television screen and from Tupra's living image: the portrait of a British officer wearing a tie and curled moustache and a Military Cross, his hair grown into a widow's peak, his eyebrows thick and an elegiac look no doubt like mine in his eyes, and in that mournful look I saw a reflection of my own exhaustion, a look that might give me away to Tupra, despite my artificial tone of voice. I could just make out the signature on the drawing, 'E. Kennington. 17',

a name I had heard in Wheeler's mouth when he spoke to me about the Careless Talk Campaign of 1917, during World War One, the war that both he and my father had experienced as children, it seemed incredible that the two of them had still not been erased from the world, that they were not safe more or less in one-eyed, uncertain oblivion as the officer in the portrait would certainly be, unless Tupra knew his identity, the killing in that conflict had been worse than in any other, I mean people were killed in the very worst of ways, with new techniques but also in hand-to-hand combat and with bayonets, and those who had fallen at the front were uncountable, or no one had dared to count them. I tried a slight diversionary tactic, playing for time:

'Who's that military gentleman?' And I pointed to the drawing.

Reresby's answer was contradictory, as if he simply wanted to get rid of the question:

'I don't know. My grandfather. I like his face.' Then he immediately returned to the matter at hand. 'Tell me why one can't.'

I didn't know what to reply, I was still very shaken, still dismayed and upset. I nevertheless said something, almost without intending to and certainly without thinking, purely in order not to remain silent:

'Because then it would be impossible for anyone to live.'

I couldn't judge the effect of these words or indeed if they had one, I never found out if he would have laughed or not, if he would have mocked them, if he would have refuted them or scornfully allowed them to fall without even bothering to pick them up, because just then, the moment after I had spoken them, I heard a woman's voice behind me:

'Who are you with, Bertie, and what are you doing? You're keeping me awake, do you know what time it is, aren't you coming to bed?'

This was said in a domestic tone of voice. I turned round. The woman had switched on the light in the corridor and her shadowy figure on the threshold was silhouetted against the brightness, she had opened the door but her face was invisible. She was wearing a transparent, ankle-length dressing gown,

made of gauze or something similar, tied with a belt or else in
another way caught in around the waist and the rest was loose
and flimsy, at least that was my impression, her apparently naked
figure could be clearly seen through the gauze, although it was
unlikely she would be naked, if she had heard my voice, or our
voices; she had on slippers with high slender heels, as if she were
an old-fashioned model of lingerie or negligees or nightdresses,
a pin-up girl from the 1950s or the early '60s, a woman from
my childhood. She looked like a calendar girl. She smelled good
too, a sexual smell that wafted into the room from the doorway,
creating the illusion of dissipating its horrors. She didn't have an
hourglass figure nor that of a Coca-Cola bottle, but very nearly,
it was outlined perfectly and very attractively against the bright
light behind her; she was tall and had long legs, a toboggan down
which to slide, so she could have been his ex-wife Beryl, who
had so inflamed and aroused De la Garza. I suddenly thought of
him perhaps still lying on the floor of the Disabled toilet – less
clean now – badly injured and unable to move. I felt a twinge
of conscience, but I would not be the one, that night, to go and
find him and see how he was, I felt shattered, drained. I'd phone
the embassy another day, someone, sooner or later, was bound to
pick him up and call an ambulance. The Manoias, on the other
hand, would have long since been sleeping in their beds in the
Ritz, placid and reconciled, and Flavia would be satisfied and
content to have enjoyed a nocturnal triumph and to have provoked an incident, although she would also have asked herself
as she closed her eyes: 'Tonight, I was all right, but will I be all
right tomorrow? I'll be another day older.' Whoever the woman
on the threshold was, her appearance there obliged me to leave,
or finally allowed me to – it didn't seem to me that Tupra was
about to introduce me to her.

'Just working late with a colleague. I'll be right with you, my
dear,' he said from behind the desk, and he used that rather old-
fashioned term 'my dear'.

'So there was someone waiting for him, and he doesn't live
alone, or at least on some nights he doesn't lack for loving company,' I thought, standing up. 'So he does have a weak point,

someone at his side. And he likes the old ways, which isn't quite the same as what he calls the way of the world. Perhaps the way of the world was there in what I had seen on the screen, and in the Disabled toilet, and that's what he's just poisoned me with.'

VI

Shadow

I didn't hurry, I lingered and delayed, and allowed a few months to pass before that 'other day' came when I finally decided to go in person to the embassy to see how De la Garza was. Not that I wasn't concerned about his fate, I often pondered it with unease and sorrow, and in the days that followed that long unpleasant night, I kept an attentive eye on the London papers to see if they carried any report of the incident, but none of them picked it up, probably because Rafita hadn't reported the assault to the police. Tupra's intimidation, or mine when I translated Tupra's words giving those very precise instructions, had clearly had its effect. I also bought *El País* and *Abc* each day (the latter because it took more interest than most in the vicissitudes of diplomats, as well as those of bishops), but during the first few days nothing appeared in those either. Only after about ten days, in an article on the comparative dangers of European capitals, did *El País*'s London correspondent mention in passing: 'There was some alarm among the Spanish colony in London a week or so ago when an embassy employee was admitted to a hospital after being beaten up one night by complete strangers, for no apparent reason and in the middle of the street, according to his initial version of events. Later, he admitted that the brutal attack (which left him with many bruises and several broken ribs) had taken place in a fashionable disco and had been the result of a fight. This somewhat reassured people, since it was clearly a chance, isolated event that he possibly brought on himself and that was, at least, directed at him personally.'

It would have been impossible for De la Garza to conceal his state from superiors and colleagues, and so in order to justify being away on sick leave, he would have told that story, saying, perhaps, that some brutish louts had provoked him, or that he had acted in defence of a lady (offenders of ladies like to pass themselves off as the exact opposite: I could still remember his words 'Women are all sluts, but for looks you can't beat the Spanish'), or that someone had insulted Spain and he'd had no alternative but to get rough and come to blows, I was curious to know what fantasy he would have invented in order to emerge from the episode relatively unscathed (well, unscathed from his point of view and according to his account of things, because whoever it was had clearly thrashed him): 'Oh, they gave me a thorough pummelling, true enough, but I gave as good as I got and beat the shit out of them,' he would have crowed, still mingling coarseness with pedantry, like so many Spanish writers past and present, a veritable plague. Only the antipathy felt for him among his own circle could explain the words: 'that he possibly brought on himself', it was a little uncalled-for, and the correspondent would doubtless have received a reprimand for his lack of objectivity. It amused me to imagine myself as a hard Mafia type, and at least I learned that Tupra had been spot on, he had diagnosed it right there, in the toilet, two broken ribs, maybe three, at most four, perhaps he was one of those men who could estimate the effect of each blow and each cut, depending on the part of the body and the force with which the blow was dealt, like surgeons or hit men, perhaps he was experienced in this and had learned to gauge the intensity and depth and never went too far, but knew exactly how much damage he was inflicting and tried not to get carried away, unless, of course, he intended to. It would clearly be best not to get into a fight with him, a physical fight I mean.

And so I let time pass, telling myself that it would be better to phone De la Garza or to go and see him when he was more recovered and the anger and shock had subsided a little; and the fear, of course, which would be the feeling that had gone deepest. As far as I knew, he had obeyed us, Tupra and me, he had done as we said; he hadn't even gone telling tales to Wheeler or to his father, Don Pablo, with his now waning influence. I hadn't visited Wheeler for some time, but I still spoke to him on the phone every week or every two weeks, and while these were, as almost always, delightful stimulating conversations, they were, nonetheless, fairly routine. One day, I casually mentioned Rafita and he interrupted me at once: 'Oh, haven't you heard? It was terrible, he got beaten up good and proper and is still in the hospital, I believe. I haven't heard anything from him directly, he's not yet in a state to speak to anyone, only from people at the embassy and from his father, who flew over to London to be with him and look after him during the first few days, and since he didn't leave Rafa's bedside for a moment, he had no time to come up to Oxford, and since I never go anywhere now, we didn't see each other.' 'Good heavens, what happened?' I asked hypocritically. 'I don't know exactly,' he said. 'He must have been drunk and he has, apparently, changed his story several times, contradicting himself, he probably doesn't know what happened either or doesn't remember because he was too far gone, you've seen how fond he is of the bottle, do you remember when he was here, how he immediately bonded with Lord Rymer? He went too far with his impertinence, I imagine, with that crude and to me incomprehensible lexicon he occasionally adopts, apparently it was some compatriots of his, of yours, that is, who beat the living daylights out of him in a toilet in a disco, as if they'd been waiting there to pounce on him, it sounds like something schoolboys would do, which fits of course. But the fact is they beat him to a pulp, and there's nothing schoolboyish about that, they broke several major bones. And in a Disabled toilet of all places; that doesn't bode very well, does it?' Wheeler couldn't help seeing the comical side of almost everything and he added slightly mischievously (I could imagine the twinkle in his eyes): 'Apparently he's completely encased in plaster. When the other patients catch a glimpse of him from the corridor, they mistake him for The Mummy.' And he immediately moved on to another subject, to do with the peculiar Spanish expression he had used – *zurrarle la badana a alguien* – to beat the living daylights out of someone: 'Do you still say that in Spanish or is it very old hat now? By the way, I've never known what "*ba-dana*" means, do you?' I realised that I hadn't the faintest idea and felt the same embarrassment I used to feel years ago when my Oxford students would confront me with their malicious questions, and I would find myself having to lie to them in class and to improvise ridiculous, false etymologies which they diligently noted down. 'It's quite common in Spanish not to know the actual meaning of what you're saying, far more so than in English or in other languages,' Sir Peter went on, 'and yet you Spaniards come out with those phrases with such pride and aplomb: for example, what the devil does "*joder la marrana*" mean? Literally. Or "*a pie juntillas*" (I've noticed that some ignorant authors write "*a pies juntillas*", and I don't know about now, but that used to be considered unacceptable)? Or "*a pie enjuto*" or "*a dos velas*" or "*caérsele los anillos*"? Why have an idiom about rings falling off when rings, if they do anything, tend, on the contrary, to get stuck. And why do you call street blocks "*manzanas*"? Apparently no one knows, I've even asked members of the Real Academia Española, but they just shrug unconcernedly and with not a flicker of embarrassment. I mean, why "apples"? It's absurd. Street blocks don't look anything like apples, even from above. And why do you make that odd gesture signifying "*a dos velas*" where you place the index and middle fingers of your right hand on either side of your nose and draw them down towards your upper lip, it's very strange, I can't see any connection at all with being down to your last two candles, which is presumably what it means. You use gestures a lot when you talk, but most of them make no sense at all, they're virtually opaque and often seem to have nothing to do with their meaning – like that one where you rest the fingers of one hand on the upright palm of the other, do you know the one I mean, I'd demonstrate it for you if you could see me, but I never see you, you hardly ever come now, is Tupra exploiting you or have you got a girlfriend? Anyway, I think it's used to indicate "Stop, don't go on" or perhaps "Let's go".'

Wheeler was tireless when it came to discussing linguistic matters and idioms, he paused and lingered over them and momentarily forgot about everything else, and, as I knew, from the days when I first taught translation and Spanish at Oxford, I was profoundly ignorant of my own language, not that it mattered much, for it's an ignorance I share with almost all my compatriots and they couldn't care less. I was beginning to think that sometimes his mind wavered slightly, rather as he occasionally lost the ability to speak. Not in the same way, he didn't go blank, not at all, and he didn't talk nonsense or get confused, but he strayed from the subject more than usual and didn't listen with his usual alacrity and attention, as if he were less interested in the external, and as if the internal were gaining ground – his disquisitions, his deliberations, his insistent thoughts – and, as is often the case with the old, perhaps his memories too, although he didn't care to tell or share these, but maybe he did go over them in his mind, put them in order, unfold them to himself, and explain and weigh them up, or perhaps it was simply a matter of putting them straight and contemplating them, like someone taking a few steps back and surveying his library or his paintings or his rows of tin soldiers if he collects them, everything he has accumulated and arranged over a lifetime, probably with no other objective – this does happen – than that of stepping back and looking at them.

This form of loquacious introspection, which I noticed when we spoke on the phone, occasionally made me fear that I didn't have much time left in which to ask him all the things I'd always wanted to ask him and which I kept postponing for reasons of discretion, respect and a dislike of worming things out of people and stealing from them what they are keeping in reserve or storing away, or of seeming overly curious or even impertinent, together with a natural tendency to wait for people to tell me only what they really want to and not what they are tempted to tell me because of a particular conversational thread or the direction a conversation is taking or because they feel flattered or moved – the temptation to tell is as strong as it is transient, and it soon vanishes if you resist it or, indeed, give in to it, except that in the latter case, there's no remedy but regret or, as the Italians put it, *rimpianto*, a kind of sorrowful regret to be ruminated upon in private. And the truth is that I wanted to ask him those things before it became problematic or impossible, I wanted to know, however briefly and anecdotally, about his involvement in the Spanish Civil War – a war that had so marked my parents – and about which I had known nothing until recently; about his adventures with MI6, his special missions in the Caribbean, West Africa, and South-East Asia between 1942 and 1946, according to *Who's Who*, in Havana and in Kingston and in other unknown places, although he was still not allowed to talk about them even after sixty years nor, doubtless, after however many years of life remained to him; he would take his story to the grave if I didn't get it out of him, that Acting Lieutenant-Colonel Peter Wheeler, born in the antipodes as Rylands; about his unspoken relationship with his brother Toby, whom I had known first and admired and mourned, with no idea that they were related; as well as about his activities with the group that had no name when it was created and still has none now, nor any 'interpreters of people', 'translators of lives' or 'anticipators of stories', indeed, he had criticised Tupra for employing such terms in private: 'Names, nicknames, sobriquets, aliases, euphemisms are quickly taken up and, before you know it, they've stuck,' he had said, 'you find yourself always referring to things or people in the same way, and that soon becomes the name they're known by. And then there's no getting rid of it, or forgetting it'; and it was true, I couldn't forget those terms now, because I was part of that group and those were the terms I'd learned from Wheeler's diminished contemporary heirs; and I wanted to know, too, about the death of his young wife Val or Valerie, although he always preferred to leave that for another day and, besides, he believed, deep down, that one should never tell anything.

It even seemed to me – I had no proof of this, it was only a suspicion – that Wheeler might be loosening the grip of that hand that never let go of its prey, as was not yet the case with Tupra or with me or, probably, with young Pérez Nuix, all three of us were still at the restless or at least vigilant age, how long do those energetic years last, the years of anxiety and quickened pulses, the years of movement, unexpected reversals, and vertigo, the years when all of that and so much more occurs, so many doubts and torments, in which we struggle and plot and fight and try to inflict scratches on others and avoid getting scratched ourselves and to turn things to our own advantage, and when all of those activities are sometimes so very skilfully disguised as noble causes that even we, the creators of those disguises, are fooled. I mean that Wheeler was distancing himself from his machinations and his plans, at least that was the impression he gave me, as if his will and determination were finally on the wane or as if he suddenly scorned them and saw them as pointless and futile, after decades of building and cultivating and feeding them and, of course, of applying them. He was focused entirely on himself, and little else interested him. But then he was over ninety, and so this was hardly surprising or deserving of reproach, it was high time really.

And despite these warnings and my growing fear that I didn't have, as I'd always felt I had, unlimited time with him, I continued putting off my visits and my questions and still did not go and see him. I would also have liked him to tell me more about Tupra, about his antecedents, his history, his potential dangerousness, his character, the 'probabilities that ran in his veins' – he would know more about those, he had known him for longer – especially after that night of the sword and the videos, the memory of which had been bothering me for weeks and would do so indefinitely; but given that I'd decided not to leave or decamp, not yet to abandon my post and with it my work, salary and general state of confusion, perhaps I was avoiding the possibility of really finding out and – if Wheeler did as I asked him and deciphered Tupra fully – of having to stop what I had, for the moment, not without some violence to myself, determined to continue. I realised that I had reached a point when each passing day made it harder and harder for me to go back, let alone just to pack it all in and return to Madrid – doing what exactly, living how, just to be closer to Luisa as she moved further away from me? – a place which, nevertheless, I had still not entirely left. My mind was largely there, but not my body, and the latter was growing accustomed to strolling about London and breathing in its smells on waking and on going to sleep (always with one eye open, because of the lack of shutters, and like just one more inhabitant of that large island), to spending part of the day in the company of Tupra and Pérez Nuix and Mulryan and Rendel and, on occasions, Jane Treves or Branshaw, to the initially saving grace of certain routines in which, unexpectedly, you suddenly find yourself caught as in a spider's web, unable to imagine any other way of life, even if it isn't any great shakes and happened purely by chance and without your asking. No, it was no longer easy for me to think of myself taking another less comfortable and less well-paid job, less attractive and less varied, after all, each morning I was confronted by new faces or else went deeper into familiar ones, and it was a real challenge to decipher them. To guess at their probabilities, to predict their future behaviour, it was almost like writing novels, or at least biographical sketches. And sometimes there were outings, on-the-spot translations and the occasional trip out of London.

And so I also kept delaying my return to Madrid, I mean, to see my children and my father and my siblings and my friends, too many months had passed without my setting foot in my own city and, therefore, without seeing or hearing Luisa, which was what most attracted and frightened me. I had told her, two days after that night when I'd phoned to consult her about Botox and the bloodstains left by women, that I would not be back for a while. 'The kids have been asking when you'll be coming to see them,' she had said, taking great care not to include herself and making it plain that she wasn't the one doing the asking. 'Not in the immediate future I shouldn't think,' I had replied and mentioned that I had a trip with my boss coming up, I didn't know exactly when yet, but it could be any time, so I was busy until then. And it was true, Tupra had told me this, although, in the end, he dragged me off, instead, on several different trips during that month, short hops lasting only a couple of days, three within the large island itself and one to Berlin, to the Continent. We went to Bath with Mulryan, to Edinburgh on our own and to York with Jane Treves, who, it seems, was from Yorkshire and knew the terrain, although it didn't seem to me that you needed to be an expert to find your way around those very human-sized cities. He didn't take Pérez Nuix with him, perhaps to punish her for trying to deceive him in the matter of Incompara and her poor beaten father, in which he must have considered me to be merely a naïve and secondary accomplice, or perhaps, it occurred to me, so that she and I did not end up in the same hotel: sometimes I had the feeling that there was nothing he didn't know about, and that he was therefore sure to know what had happened in my apartment, in my bed, in silence and as if it hadn't happened, on that night of constant rain.

In each of those cities we only ever had one meeting at which I could prove useful as an interpreter, of languages or people, and if Tupra saw more people, as I imagined he did, he did so on his own and never invited me to join him. In Bath, he stayed at a very fine hotel, the Royal Crescent if I remember rightly (Mulryan and I stayed in another which was pleasant rather than fine – we, after all, occupied a different place in the hierarchy), in which there lived 'on an almost permanent basis', according to my boss, a Mexican millionaire, 'officially retired but still very active from a distance and from the shadows', with whom he wished to come to some agreement. This elderly man – with white hair and moustache, the vestiges of what was, by then, a very precarious elegance and a resemblance to the old actor César Romero, and whose two surnames were Esperón Quigley – spoke impeccable English with a thick Spanish accent (it happens to many Latins on both sides of the Atlantic), and my help was only necessary on a few occasions, when the gentleman's diction proved so opaque to the purely English ear of Tupra and to the half-Irish ear of Mulryan that perfectly correct words became completely unrecognisable in Esperón Quigley's eccentric pronunciation. As usual, I paid no attention to what they were discussing, it was no business of mine, I was bored by it a priori and preferred not to know. The rest of the time I was free, and I spent it walking, looking at the River Avon, visiting the Roman baths and a few antique shops, and rereading Jane Austen in a place where she had spent a few years of scant literary productivity, as well as the odd page by William Beckford, who'd shut himself away there for a long time and where he reluctantly lived and died, far from his beloved Fonthill Abbey, which had led him to his ruin. On one of my strolls about the city, I was amazed to come across a shop, a rather average jeweller's, which, implausibly, bore the name of Tupra. It wasn't far from another shop with larger pretensions and which, if memory serves me right, declared itself in its window to be a supplier to the Admiralty (I imagine this referred only to watches, and not to precious stones and glass beads for the navy). When I mentioned this coincidence to Tupra, he replied tartly:

'Oh, yes, I know. Nothing to do with my family though. No relation at all. None.' This might have been true or totally false, and the watchmaker might have been his father. However, I didn't dare press the matter further.

Even so, I couldn't resist making a private joke:

'Nevertheless, it would be more appropriate for Tupra's jeweller's shop to be made supplier to the Admiralty rather than that other shop nearby which, I noticed, lays claim to just that. Even if only because of your connections, or, rather, our connections with the former OIC, don't you think?' I remembered what Wheeler had said that Sunday before lunch, in Oxford, when he spoke to me about the difficulties they'd had recruiting the first members of the group, just after it had been formed: 'It was necessary to comb the country for recruits as quickly as possible. Most were from the Secret Services, from the army, a few from the former OIC, which you've probably never heard of, the navy's Operational Intelligence Centre, there weren't many of them, but they were very good, possibly the best; and, of course, from our universities.' And I saw a look of surprise and slight suspicion appear on Tupra's face (as if hearing that old acronym in my mouth – an odd thing for a twenty-first- or even late-twentieth-century Spaniard to know – made him wonder what else I knew and if he had underestimated how much I had learned).

He also allowed me some free time during the two days we spent in Edinburgh, and there, too, I walked and reread the work of two of that city's finest sons, Conan Doyle and Stevenson, just a few of their stories, and climbed up Calton Hill to see the view which so enthused the latter, and which is still astonishing even after all the time that has passed. I also took away with me a few poems by Stevenson and a little book about the city, subtitled *Picturesque Notes* and published in 1879 no less. In it he talks about Greyfriars, telling of how, close to this verdant cemetery, from the window of a house since demolished, but whose site was pointed out to him by a grave-digger, the body-snatcher Burke used to keep watch, for he and his mate Hare would disinter the still-fresh bodies from their graves in order to sell them to scientists and anatomists, and had eventually taken to murdering people so as to speed up the process and to prevent business from falling off: 'Burke, the resurrection man,' as Stevenson noted with irony, 'infamous for so many murders at five shillings a head, used to sit thereat, with pipe and nightcap, to watch burials going forward on the green.' Now there, I thought, was a man who lacked the patience to wait for tomorrow's faces to be revealed to him, no, he preferred to sit, smoking, and watch them file past, as they had been yesterday and would be always.

And on the train journey up to Edinburgh, the two of us alone, I read out to Tupra some lines that Stevenson had written towards the end of his life in the South Seas, in Apemama, lines filled by a strange and yet very real nostalgia for 'our scowling town': 'The belching winter wind, the missile rain, The rare and welcome silence of the snows, The laggard morn, the haggard day, the night, The grimy spell of the nocturnal town, do you remember? Ah, could one forget!' he wrote, genuinely nostalgic for that desolate scene. And further on, he added: 'When the lamp from my expiring eyes shall dwindle and recede, the voice of love fall insignificant on my closing ears, what sound shall come but the old cry of the wind in our inclement city? What return but the image of the emptiness of youth, filled with the sound of footsteps and that voice of discontent and rapture and despair?' Another poem is infused with the same spirit, scorning the warm distant seas he had so diligently sought out and yearning terribly for the 'inclement city' of Edinburgh: 'A sea uncharted, on a lampless isle, environs and confines their wandering child in vain. The voice of generations dead summons me, sitting distant, to arise, my numerous footsteps nimbly to retrace, and all mutation over, stretch me down in that denoted city of the dead.' And so I read him those lines, in his language of course, in the language of Tupra and of the lines themselves: 'The belching winter wind, the missile rain, The rare and welcome silence of the snows, The laggard morn, the haggard day, the night . . .'

'Do you think that always happens, Bertram?' I asked; he was sitting opposite me, with him facing the engine and me with my back to it. 'You know a lot about deaths,' I added somewhat cruelly, 'do you think that, in the end, we all turn to that first place, however humble or depressing or gloomy it was, however much our life has changed and our affections have been transformed, however many unimaginable fortunes and achievements we have amassed along the way? Do you think that we always look back at our earlier poverty, at the impoverished quarter we grew up in, at the small provincial town or dying village from which we peered out at the rest of the world, and which for so many years it seemed impossible to leave, and that we miss it? They say that the very old remember their childhood most clearly of all and almost shut themselves away in it, mentally I mean, and that they have a sense that everything that happened between that distant time and their present decline, their greeds and their passions, their battles and their setbacks, was all false, an accumulation of distractions and mistakes and of tremendous efforts to achieve things that really weren't important; and they wonder then if everything hasn't been an interminable detour, a pointless voyage, all merely to return to the essence, to the origin, to the only thing that truly counts at the end of the day.' – And I thought then: 'Why all that conflict and struggle, why did they fight instead of just looking and staying still, why were they unable to meet or to go on seeing each other, and why so much sleep, so many dreams, and why that scratch, my pain, my word, your fever, and all those doubts, all that torment?' – 'You must know a lot about that, you must have seen many people die. And you can see how it was with Stevenson: he travelled halfway round the world and yet in the end, in Polynesia, there he was thinking only of the city where he was born. Look how this one begins: 'The tropics vanish, and meseems that I, from Halkerside, from topmost Allermuir, or steep Caerketton, dreaming gaze again . . . '

'Those are hills close to Edinburgh,' Tupra said, interrupting me as if he were a footnote, and then fell silent again. I waited for him to reply to my questions and for him to add something more. I hadn't read those lines to him purely for pleasure or to pass the time. I had mentioned impoverished quarters and provincial towns trusting that he might take the hint and think of Bethnal Green, if that's where he came from, or of the watchmaker of Bath, if he had spent part of his childhood with him, for example, and that he might tell me a little about them. Tupra, however, as I should have known, only answered the questions he wanted to answer. 'As I remember,' he said after a few seconds, 'Stevenson went to Samoa chiefly for his health's sake, not in search of adventures. Besides, he wasn't old. He died when he was forty-four.'

'That doesn't matter,' I said. 'When he wrote those poems, he must have known that the end was not far off, and all he could think about, with enormous nostalgia, was the inhospitable city of his childhood. Listen to what he says: "When . . . the voice of love fall insignificant on my closing ears . . ." You see, not even having his wife near will count for much, or so he imagines, in his final consciousness of the world, in his final seconds, only those momentary pictures from the past that "gleam and fade and perish". He set this out clearly in the closing lines: "These shall I remember, and then all forget", that's what he says.'

Tupra remained thoughtful for a while. I know from experience that no one can resist analysing texts.

'How can that be? Read me the bit about insignificant love again.'

And I did:

'When . . . the voice of love fall insignificant on my closing ears . . .'

'Nonsense,' said Tupra, again cutting me off. 'Nonsense. That's not Stevenson at his best. Poetry wasn't his forte really.' He fell silent again, as if to underline his verdict, and then, to my surprise, added: 'Read me a bit more, go on.'

Almost everyone likes being read to. And so I did:

'Far set in fields and woods, the town I see spring gallant from the shallows of her smoke, cragg'd, spired, and turreted, her virgin fort beflagg'd.' And as I read I stole occasional glances at Tupra and saw that he was enjoying it, even though he didn't like Stevenson's poetry. 'There, on the sunny frontage of a hill, hard by the house of kings, repose the dead, my dead, the ready and the strong of word. Their works, the salt-encrusted, still survive; the sea bombards their founded towers; the night thrills pierced with their strong lamps. The artificers, one after one, here in this grated cell, where the rain erases and the rust consumes, fell upon lasting silence.'

Who knows, perhaps no one had read to him since he was a child.

There in Edinburgh, on the Firth of Forth and opposite Fife, Tupra only required my services on one night, for another supper-cum-celebrities or -cum-buffoons, which was also a supper-cum-Dick Dearlove, that is, the global singer to whom I've chosen to give that name. Fortunately, Tupra did not also oblige me to go to the concert Dearlove was giving at the Festival beforehand, although he did force me to pretend that I'd watched the concert from the first chord to the last with indescribable enthusiasm: 'Remember to mention his fantastic renditions of "Peanuts from Heaven" and the miraculous "Bouncing Bowels", he always comes up with strange new versions, and they sound different every time, even though they're two of his all-time classics,' he warned me, just in case anyone or even Dearlove himself should ask, for Tupra had engineered things so that I would be sitting near the singer. 'On the pretext of entertaining those two compatriots of yours who are often in his entourage now, try to get him talking, even at the risk of appearing nosy and boring, the worst that can happen is that he'll ignore you or change places to avoid you. Talk to him about the tremendous success he enjoys in Spain, but, whatever you do, don't say "especially in the Basque country": even though that's true, it might offend him, as being too local, too limited. Get his attention, charm him, encourage him to confide in you, draw him out as much as you can on his supposed role as a universal sex symbol wherever he goes, or so he believes. Make him feel flattered and in the mood to boast, invent Spanish people you know who've got the hots for him, who would love to get their hands on his basket, acquaintances of yours, real people, anything to inflame his imagination, any young things you happen to know, your own children perhaps, how old *are* they, oh no, they're far too young, well, then, your nephews and nieces, whoever, but probe him to see what you can get out of him, he's always exhausted after a performance, but euphoric too, his guard's down, and he's eager to talk, what with all the excitement and the acclaim plus whatever he took before the concert to cope with the whole insane affair, I'm surprised he's lasted this long really, after all these years of supercharged love-fests. He knows me too well, but with a stranger he'll never see again (I don't think he remembers you from last time), with someone like you, he might reveal much more than he would to me or to some other Englishman, he'll feel less vulnerable, besides, stars love to show off to newcomers, they're always in need of a fresh influx of the easily impressed. With luck he'll describe an affair he's had, some striking sexual triumph, some exploit, anyway, that's the route you need to pursue, even if it seems impertinent – as I say, the worst that can happen is that he'll turn his back on you and refuse to take the bait. Let's see if we can get some confirmation, a clearer idea, of just how capable he is or would be of endangering the way people see him and his life, to what extent he would risk exposing himself to that narrative horror of yours and end up swelling the ranks of the Kennedy–Mansfield fraternity, from which there is no possible escape.' That's how Tupra often spoke, especially when he was giving us instructions or asking us to do something, with that mixture of colloquialisms and old-fashioned turns of phrase, some peculiar to him alone, as if he brought together in his speech his probable origins in some slum and his undoubted Oxford education as a medievalist under the tutelage of Toby Rylands, of which I frequently had to remind myself, or was it just that the figure of Toby was gradually fading from my mind, absorbed by that of his brother Peter, sometimes the living do incorporate or embrace or superimpose themselves on the dead to whom they were close, and even cancel them out.

· I felt that what Tupra was asking was an impossible enterprise: to get Dick Dearlove to talk to me in those terms, and about such things, much less with other people around, at a supper for twenty or more guests, all gazing at him reverently. Nevertheless, I had a go; Tupra was determined that I should get results. He placed me almost opposite the idol, and while the people on either side tried to capture his attention through flattery, I managed to slip in a few remarks that aroused his curiosity, more because of their peculiarly Spanish nature than because of me.

'Why are the Spanish so sexually permissive?' he asked after a brief exchange of comments on customs and laws. 'For a long time we always had exactly the opposite impression.'

'And your impression was correct,' I replied, and in order to see if I could get anything more out of him, I refrained from saying that his current impression was also correct, and said instead: 'Why do *you* think we're so permissive now, Mr Dearlove?'

'Oh, please, call me Dick,' he said at once. 'Everyone does, and with good reason too.' And he gave a rather weary laugh, which his neighbours echoed. I assumed this was a joke he had made thousands of times during a lifetime of being lauded and idolised (but there's always someone who hasn't heard it, and he was aware of this, that nothing has ever been entirely wrung dry, however hard you squeeze it), punning crudely on one of the meanings of the word 'dick', which is, of course, '*polla*'. He was, after all, famous for his hypersexuality or pansexuality or heptasexuality or whatever it was, although he never acknowledged this in public, that is, in the press. 'Well, I don't know what kind of life you lead in your country,' he said paternalistically, 'but you're obviously missing out. Whenever I've been on tour there, I haven't had the energy or the time to meet the enormous demand. Everyone seems to be up for a roll in the hay, women, men, even children it seems.' And he gave a slightly less time-worn guffaw. 'With the exception of the Basque country, where they don't seem to know about sex or else restrict themselves to performing only a pale imitation of it because they've heard about it in other places, but in the rest of Spain, I've had to hold auditions to choose who to invite into my bed, or my bathroom if it's just for a quickie, because there's so much on offer after each concert, and beforehand too: lines have formed in hotel lobbies for a chance to come up to my room for a while, and I've nearly always found it worth interrupting my well-earned rest. They're much more ardent than they are here, and much easier too; incredible though it may seem, people are more chaste in Great Britain, though the Irish are as prim as the Basques.'

Suddenly, it bothered me that he should speak of my compatriots in these terms, in that offhand manner, like sex-mad hordes. It bothered me to think that this famous fool should take young women and young men to his bed – through no merit of his own and with no effort – in Barcelona, Gijón, Madrid or Seville or wherever, each time he set foot in Spain, and he'd given quite a few concerts there over the years. I was even glad to hear that he'd had a harder time of it in San Sebastián and Bilbao, that was some consolation; and when I noticed this puerile idiotic reaction of mine, I realised that we never entirely free ourselves from patriotism, it all depends on the circumstances and where we're from and who's speaking to us, for some vestige, some remnant, to burst to the surface. I can think and say dreadful things about my country, which, personally, I consider now completely debased and coarsened in far too many respects, but if I hear those criticisms in the mouth of a despicable fatuous foreigner, I feel a strange, almost inexplicable pang, something similar to what that primitive creature De la Garza must have felt when he saw that I was not prepared to defend him from the sword-wielding Englishman who was about to decapitate him, and he perhaps considered squealing on me to the Judge later on 'when all those legs and arms and heads, chopped off in battle, shall join together at the latter day, and cry all, "We died at such a place"', at the end of the uncountable centuries: 'This man killed me with a sword and cut me in two, and this other man was there, he saw it all and didn't lift a finger; and the man who watched and did nothing spoke my language and we were both from the same land, further south, not so very far away, albeit separated by the sea; he just stood there like a statue, his face frozen in horror, a guy from Madrid, can you believe it, a fellow Spaniard, one of us, and he didn't even try to grab the other guy's arm.' It does make it worse being from the same country, and that's how I always felt when my father told me terrible tales from our own War: they were both from the same country, the militiawoman and the child whose head she smashed against the wall of a fourth-floor apartment on the corner of Alcalá and Velázquez, so were Emilio Marés and the men who baited him like a bull in Ronda, and even more so the man from Málaga in the red beret who killed him, gave him the *coup de grâce*, and then couldn't resist castrating him too. Del Real the traitor and my father were, as was Santa Olalla, the professor who contributed his weightier and more authoritative signature to the formal complaint, and even that novelist who enjoyed a certain degree of tawdry commercial success, Darío Flórez, who appeared as witness for the prosecution and delivered that sinister warning to the betrayed man via my mother, when she wasn't yet my or anyone else's mother: 'If Deza forgets that he ever had a career, he'll live; otherwise, we'll destroy him.' For me they had always been the names of treachery, which should never be protected, and they were traitors because they all came from the same country, my father and them and, in two of the cases, because they had been friends before and he had never given them any reason to withdraw or cancel their friendship, on the contrary.

I brushed aside my absurd feelings of bruised patriotism. I had to – not only to carry out my assignment from Tupra (broaching the subject had been much easier than expected; and I could see my boss's grey eyes in the distance, near the head of the table, observing me, intrigued, wondering how I was getting on), but also because there was no sense in clinging on to bruises. Dearlove's comments could have been made by a compatriot of mine, De la Garza to look no further, had he been a pop idol and able to choose on tour from among dozens of girls to sleep with, and I would have been equally put out by such arrogant and disrespectful comments. And yet, and yet . . . there was an added bitterness, I could not deny it, something irrational, disquieting, disagreeable, atavistic. Perhaps Tupra felt the same when, in his presence, people spoke scornfully of Great Britain or of the British, especially when those people were from the Continent or from across the Atlantic or from the green isle of Erin, where such talk is almost the norm. And perhaps for that reason, which would be logical, he had no hesitation in doing what he did, possibly with more dedication and diligence than I thought, and perhaps it was true what he had said to me shortly after we met, albeit tempered with a touch of cynicism: 'Even serving my country, one should if one can, don't you think, even if the service one does is indirect . . .' I understood then, rather late, that he probably served his country ceaselessly as long as it was in his own best interests, and that in time of need, in time of war, or when the moment came, I would be no more to him than another useless Spaniard whom he wouldn't hesitate to have shot, just as, during my burst of patriotic feeling, Dearlove had been for me merely a conceited English bastard I'd happily have slapped.

One of the other guests nearby, a designer of extravagant clothes who was getting on in years (she herself was wearing an incomprehensible jumble of petticoats, feathers and rags) unwittingly gave me a helping hand in keeping that conversation going along the path that most suited me:

'Really?' she said. 'And there I was thinking that it was only in Britain that everyone found you irresistible, Dickie, but it turns out that it's Spain where you've got both bed and bathroom jam-packed.' She used that expression 'jam-packed' – '*de bote en bote*' or '*a reventar*' in Spanish.

It was clear that they were friends and knew each other well, or perhaps Dick Dearlove (as also seemed to be the case) spoke openly to almost anyone about even the most intimate things, to me for example; this often happens with the very famous and the constantly praised, they end up thinking that anything they say or do will be well received because it's all part of their ongoing performance, and there comes a point when they can no longer distinguish between public and private (unless there's a photographer or a journalist around, and then they're either more discreet or more exhibitionist depending on the circumstances): if they're so warmly applauded in the first sphere, and so spoiled, why shouldn't they be equally so in the second, given that in both spheres they are the undisputed protagonists every day of their life until the end?

'As you know better than I do, Viva, even though you're a woman,' replied Dick Dearlove, in a tone that was half-ironic and half-regretful, 'at our age, however famous we might be, and I'm much more famous than you are, there are occasions when we have no option but to pay, cash or in kind. There's a certain kind of particularly tasty morsel that I almost always have to pay for here in Britain, I hardly ever get it for free now, although just a few years ago I still did, half the nation has turned into a load of tight-arses; whereas in Spain, you see, I've never had to spend a euro, it's as if the young people in Spain aren't really so interested in the act itself – at my age I'm hardly going to boast about my performance, I mean, my body can no longer keep up with my imagination – that's indefatigable, in fact I rather wish my mind would slow down a bit, oh, if only the two things were more compatible, it's all very badly thought out, at least in my view – no, people are more interested in being able to tell their friends afterwards, or spill the beans on some TV programme. It's extraordinary how much people there experience things not because they really want to, it seems, but simply in order to talk about it afterwards, it's a country that really revels in gossip and boasting, isn't it, a country very given to tattle-tales – and absolutely shameless about it.' – These rhetorical questions were directed at me, as someone who knew the territory. – 'Everyone tells everything and asks everything, it cracks me up at press conferences and interviews, dodging questions, they're so coarse and brazen and have no sense of shame at all, which is unheard of in a European country. I've fucked a few Spaniards who I could see were simply desperate to get it over with, not because they weren't having a reasonably good time – I haven't entirely lost my touch, you know – but because they couldn't wait to leave and spread the news, I can imagine them striding proudly into their local bar or into school the next day: "I bet you can't guess who's just had me good and hard and every which way too."' He paused for a moment and smiled rather dreamily, as if he had found the situation so amusing that he was able to retrieve it intact years later, in the middle of a post-concert supper in Edinburgh. But also as if he were recalling something from the past, something lost that might never return. 'I don't know if their friends will believe them, they might not prove that easy to convince, and that could become a problem, because some of them come along now armed with their digital camera or their mobile phone, I'm sure they want photographic evidence, although they all say it's because they don't go anywhere without them, so they have to be frisked before I let them in, it would be no joke being photographed in the act. Anyway, now I routinely check them out, I've got one of those gadgets they have at airports, you know a sort of wand-like thing – I touch them up with it in the process, which they love and which makes them laugh like crazy, and you get an idea of what to expect too, although they're all usually pretty well-endowed. And they let you do this, meek as lambs, just to get into your bedroom. In Britain, though, they're much less compliant and less fun too, they don't try to sneak in cameras or anything, but that's the downside: it's not that big a deal, going and telling someone else and boasting about it, though maybe people here have just grown tired of me. That's partly why I have to pay probably, you know how word gets around, and they know I'm a soft touch and that they'll be able to get some money out of me. But sometimes you don't get much even when you pay, we're easy prey – eh, Viva? – in our beloved England, Scotland and Wales. Now don't go depressing me by telling me that you're doing just fine.'

I was the one who was getting depressed. Dick Dearlove was over fifty now, and although he was still extremely famous, he wasn't as famous as he had been at the peak of his career. His concerts were still packed and wildly successful, but perhaps more because of his name and his history than because of his present-day powers, the common fate of most of the enduring British singers from the 1970s and 1980s who continue to perform, from Elton John to Rod Stewart and the Rolling Stones. Dearlove wore his hair pathetically long for a man his age, very blond and curly, he looked like a former member of Led Zeppelin or King Crimson or Emerson, Lake & Palmer who, thirty years on, was trying to preserve, unchanged, his perennially youthful appearance. From behind, with that almost frizzy mop of hair, he could easily be mistaken for Olivia Newton-John at the end of *Grease*, except that if he turned round or offered his profile, his features were the very opposite of that sweet young Australian or New Zealander or whatever she was: his nose, while still aquiline, had become sharper and more prominent rather than more hooked, growing along the horizontal plane only; his eyes, which had always been small, seemed much bigger, but in a rather strange and creepy way, as if he had managed to emphasise them by resorting to the drastic method of shaving off his eyelashes or having his eyelids surgically reduced or some such barbarity; and his evident efforts not to put on weight had had the unfortunate consequence of leaving him with a scraggy neck and deep lines on cheeks, chin and forehead (perhaps his most recent dose of Botox had worn off), and yet these efforts had not, on the other hand, prevented a slight paunch developing in the middle of an otherwise thin and toned body. None of this was apparent from a distance, when he was writhing around on stage, but it became so as soon as he stepped off the stage or in the close-ups on the giant screens, of which there were not that many. He had moved his chair away from the table and was now sitting sideways on so as to be face to face with the designer Genevieve Seabrook and had crossed his extremely long legs, so that I could see with surprise and dismay that he had, at some point, beslippered himself, that is, on the way to the restaurant, he had discarded his trademark musketeer boots – he wore them at every performance and had done so for three decades or more, even in hot weather – and had put on a pair of ridiculous gold and black slippers with a curved pointed toe (his bare heels, I observed queasily, were tattooed), which lent him a domestic or almost summery air that only added to my depression. He seemed as much of a buffoon as the first time I met him and even more repellent, but I also felt very slightly sorry for him because of the candour with which he acknowledged his current amatorial difficulties, having no option now but to chip in some money, at least when it came to his British encounters with those 'tasty morsels'. I hoped not to find out just how tasty they could be during what remained of that aberrant conversation, I certainly didn't intend to investigate further despite being charged by Tupra with that depressing mission. Indeed, I decided not to ask or enquire anything further of Dearlove (after all, I had little opportunity with so many other guests around, admiring, sycophantic and even extremely famous in their own right), what I had heard would be quite enough for me to write a brief report, and I could always invent the rest if Ure insisted or demanded more of me (it occurred to me that Tupra would tend to call himself Ure in Scotland, or perhaps he would prefer to be known as Dundas in Edinburgh).

'No, I won't do that, dear Dickie,' replied Viva Seabrook with a smile that was as affectionate as it was mischievous, at least insofar as I could ascertain, the layers of lurid make-up she applied must have been as thick as an Egyptian, by which I mean a Pharaoh's, death mask. 'You must bear in mind that very young boys will do almost anything as long as they get to dip their wick in some woman. So I'm lucky that way, although they do sometimes cover my face with the sheet or even with my own skirt and that does make me feel pretty bad. Well, not so much now, but the first time one of them stuck a pillow over my face, I hit the roof, and the boy fled, terrified by my insults and cursing. I consider myself rather attractive, but naturally they might associate me with their mothers or their aunts, and that could be a bit of a turn-off and, generally speaking, they're so primitive, so utterly heartless and brutal . . . Well, you know what I mean.'

I found it odd that she, too, should speak so bluntly in front of a complete stranger like me. Perhaps the milieu and their vanity spurred them on; perhaps they didn't notice the people around them, as if only the very famous really connected with each other, and the rest of the world was just a mist that didn't matter or counted only as an audience or a claque who might cheer and applaud, or, in the worst case, maintain a respectful or constrained silence and, as if sitting in the dark of a theatre, merely listen to this celebrity dialogue. In a sense, it was as if they were there all alone, just the two of them. And what Dearlove said in reply, having first rested his curls for a few moments on Seabrook's vast décolletage, as if seeking consolation or refuge in the bosom of an old friend, confirmed me in that impression:

'Oh, Viva, how much longer have we got, how much longer have I got? A day will come when I'll be nothing but a memory for the elderly, and that memory will gradually fade as those who keep it alive all die, one after the other – with the number of those who remember me steadily decreasing, with no chance of it ever increasing – after it had been constantly growing for years and years, that's what I can't bear. It's not just that I will grow old and disappear, it's that everyone who might talk about me will gradually disappear too, those who have seen me and heard me and those who have slept with me, however youthful they were at the time, they'll become old and fat and will die too, as if they're all under some kind of curse. It's unlikely that my songs will survive and that future generations will continue to hear them – what will become of my songs when I'm no longer here to defend and repeat them, when I'm no longer up to performing concerts like tonight's? They'll never be played again. I've hardly written a thing in the last fifteen years, great tunes that others might rediscover and sing tomorrow, even if they're in ghastly new versions; I no longer have the energy to sit down and write new ones. Besides, I doubt I could come up with anything very memorable.' And he added disconcertingly, 'I mean if not even Lennon and McCartney have managed to write anything for ages and ages now, how could I? I'll be entirely forgotten, Viva. Not a trace of me will be left.'

There was something rather theatrical about his tone of voice and about the gestures that accompanied these laments, but it was clear that they contained some truth as well. He again stretched his legs, and I leaned forward a little to get a better look at those hideous ink-daubed heels of his, I felt curious to know what design or motto he'd had tattooed on his skin.

'But John Lennon has been dead for thirty years,' I couldn't help saying. 'How the hell *could* he compose anything?'

'That doesn't matter,' Dearlove responded sharply. 'He wasn't much good anyway. If someone hadn't shot him, his songs would probably make people nowadays throw up.' – 'Another candidate for the Kennedy–Mansfield brotherhood,' I thought. – 'Such a wet, pretentious git, and he couldn't sing either.' – And he shot me a fulminating glance with his once small and now unnaturally large eyes with their cropped lids, as if I were a staunch defender of Lennon, which I never have been and never will be. I rather agreed with former dentist Dearlove's diagnosis, but telling him so would have seemed like the lowest form of sycophancy.

At least my imprudent intervention had the virtue of briefly angering him, that is, of enlivening and rescuing him from the melancholy state into which he had subsided, and during the rest of supper he was once again a jolly man making rather inopportune jokes that verged on the tedious. I spent most of the time in silence, now and then attempting to lean over discreetly and crane my neck so as to read his heels, but without success.

Later on, thoroughly fed up, I gave Ure or Dundas the shortest possible report:

'I can confirm everything I told you before, but with this one amendment: he is so concerned about his posterity that, who knows, he might one day commit some atrocity in order to be remembered just for that. He doesn't believe that his music will last any longer than he will. So, in a moment of desperation, far from avoiding such a blot at all costs, he might very well blot his own life and thus deliberately enter the ranks of the Kennedy–Mansfield clan, as you call them. However, this would have to be while he was in the grip of a deep depression or else confused, or in a few years' time when he's retired and no longer gives concerts or enjoys the protective adoration of the crowd. He's so focused on himself that he sees it as some kind of unfair curse that those who admire him and have met him should die, as if this were something that didn't touch and wasn't shared by all those who have trod the earth or strode the world.' And I added at once: 'Listen, you know him better than I do, what is it he has tattooed on the heels of his feet?' I thought it best to formulate the question in this rather absurd way, because, in English, 'heel' can also mean the heel of a shoe.

Tupra, however, ignored me. He wasn't satisfied and I had to recount every last sentence exchanged over supper, by Dearlove, by Viva Seabrook, by my show-business compatriot who had been sitting near us and by anyone else who had made a contribution, however minimal, to the conversation. I loathed having scrupulously to reproduce these dialogues and being forced to relive them. I felt like those vacuous diary writers recording their mean little lives in great detail and then publishing them, to the tedium of unwary readers or perhaps readers who are equally mean and vacuous.

Why he took me with him to York, I don't know. We walked a long way around the very long wall surrounding the city, as if we were two sentinels or two princes. He wanted us to drive out to the neighbouring village of Coxwold, where, two and a half centuries before, the writer Laurence Sterne had his home in Shandy Hall, named in honour of his most important novel, *Tristram Shandy*. I attributed Tupra's interest to the influence of Toby Rylands, who, when I knew him, had already spent years working on 'the best book ever written', as Rylands told me once – not so much immodestly as with conviction – about Sterne's other major work, *A Sentimental Journey*; as if Tupra wanted in this way to pay homage to his former teacher at Oxford or at MI6 or both, and I had nothing against the idea, on the contrary, and besides who was I to object? Nevertheless, as soon as we arrived, he sought out the man in charge of that house-cum-museum, a man younger than either of us, and whom he introduced to me with the unlikely name of Mr Wildgust before shutting himself up with him in his office, having first urged me to have a look around the house and garden on my own. In each room of that pleasant, peaceful, two-storey mansion was an elderly man or woman – volunteers, doubtless retired people – who, whether you wanted them to or not, provided you, the visitor, with extensive information about the life and habits of its eighteenth -century owner and about the renovation work carried out on the mansion, both in the days of a certain Mr Monkman, revered founder of the Laurence Sterne Trust (I gladly made a small contribution to the cause), and now. In the spacious garden I did something that is probably punishable by law: I uprooted a tiny plant, which I concealed and kept moist for the rest of the trip, and later, in London, with barely any care or effort on my part, it grew into a plant of extraordinary lushness and vigour, although I never discovered its name, in English or in Spanish (I was thrilled to have carried off and preserved some living thing from the garden of the Shandy family). Tupra didn't bother to visit the house, he had done so before, he said, and this was doubtless true. After an hour, he reappeared with Wildgust, a semi-youth of an affable, innocent, jolly appearance, with glasses and rather long fair hair, and we returned to York, where Tupra may have met up with someone else, but I did not. He didn't ask me to provide him with an interpretation of anyone or an opinion on anything, not even on Sterne or York's endless city wall or Shandy Hall.

It was hard to believe that such a practical man as Tupra would have anything but a professional relationship with Coxwold or with Mr Wildgust, and it was equally hard to imagine why he would go and see the latter in person or of what possible use he could be to him, a mere employee leading an apparently contemplative life – he obviously didn't have much to do: when we arrived, he was immersed in reading a novel at the stall selling souvenirs and postcards, with not a customer in sight – stranded in a Yorkshire village where, in his day, the worldly, irreverent and not very vocational Reverend Sterne had been appointed curate. Nor was it easy to comprehend what business he might have with the Berlin shoemaker whom we visited in a tiny elegant shop called Von T (bespoke shoes for gentlemen), on the one occasion when we travelled to the Continent, shortly after these other trips on the large island. To be sure, Reresby did try on and buy some shoes, and it was at Tupra's urging that Herr von Truschinsky of Bleibtreustrasse, using beautiful hand-crafted wooden tools the like of which I had never seen before, took the exact and complete measurements of my two feet – length and width, height, instep and tattooable heel – in the confident belief, he said with modesty and tact and in excellent English, that I would be pleased and inspired enough to follow my boss's example and order more pairs in future, from England or from Spain, and the truth is that, despite the high prices, I bought two pairs, with excellent results and a consequent improvement to my appearance at ground level. (And to think that I had once feared that Tupra might wear boots or clogs or worse, if there is anything worse.) The odd thing is that the shoes bought by Reresby and myself were both English brands I had never heard of before – perhaps because they were so exquisite – Edward Green of Northampton, established 1890, and Grenson, from I don't know where, established 1866. It seemed somewhat extravagant to travel to Berlin in order to get them – Tupra chose two models, one called Hythe and the other Elmsley, the first in 'Chestnut Antique' and the second in 'Burnt Pine Antique', and I chose Windermere in 'Black' and Berkeley in 'Tobacco Suede' – instead of buying them in our own country, that is, in Tupra's country in which I was living at the time. After the measuring ceremony, carried out with extreme delicacy and care by the owner and sole employee, Tupra went into the back of the shop with von Truschinsky and they conversed behind the curtain for about fifteen minutes, while I amused myself looking through catalogues of fine shoes, which is why I know so much about the actual names of the colours and why some of the shoes I wear now were created by the superlative John Hlustik, which did not mean much to me at the time, but sounded important and Czech. The murmur that reached me was not English, but neither did I have the impression that it was German.

As in York, Tupra didn't require me to interpret anyone in Berlin or to meet anyone else. He left me free to do as I pleased and did not invite me to a supper he attended with people from the city. On the flight back, I thought he would at least ask me for my necessarily superficial opinion of the shoemaker and, perhaps belatedly, of Mr Wildgust, even though I hadn't been present for a substantial part of either conversation. But since, after an hour of discomfort in the air, Tupra was still talking to me only about horse racing and soccer (he was infuriated by the unnatural Russian wealth and Lusitanian antipathy of the soccer team he had supported all his life, Chelsea), I couldn't resist asking him:

'Just out of curiosity, what language were you and Mr von Truschinsky speaking when you and he were alone?'

He looked at me with such an accomplished show of surprise that I even thought it might be real.

'What language would we be speaking? English, of course. The same language in which I was speaking to you. Why would I change? Besides, I hardly know any German.'

It wasn't true that they had been speaking in English, but I didn't want to argue. So I changed the subject, or perhaps not that much:

'Listen, Bertram, I can understand why you asked me to accompany you to Bath and Edinburgh, and I hope I proved useful to you there. But I can't understand why you wanted me to go with you to York nor why I came to Berlin. You didn't set me any task, and I can't see what use I was. And don't tell me that it was to keep you company, that you don't like travelling alone. In York, you had the company of Jane, although in the end we hardly made use of her at all.' Jane Treves hadn't been part of the excursion to Coxwold nor had she walked for a long time around the medieval city wall. We had merely had supper with her. It could be, why not, that he had made use of her and that she had slept in his room.

'She was very busy seeing relatives. I included her in the trip more than anything so that she would have the chance to see them. She hasn't visited them for ages. I'm very pleased with her work. She's hardly stopped lately.'

'And yet, on the other hand, with all these short trips, you're forcing me to postpone my journey to Madrid. You may not realise it, but it's been ages since I saw my kids; I'll hardly recognise them. Or my father. My father's very old, you know, he's only a year younger than Peter. Sometimes I'm afraid I won't see him again.' And here I did insist. 'Why did you ask me to come with you to Berlin? To buy shoes? To renew my footwear?'

Tupra smiled with his thick lips that hardly grew any thinner when stretched.

202

'I wanted to introduce you to Clemens von T., he's an old friend of mine now and provides a magnificent service, you can trust him absolutely. I'm sure that, from now on, you'll be much better shod. And you'll be able to deal with him direct. Anyway, I have no trips planned for next month, so if you want to spend a few weeks in Madrid – two or three if you like – that will be fine.'

Such a generous amount of leave. I was taken aback. I thanked him. But there was no way he was going to reply to a question to which he was determined not to reply, I knew that all too well, nor would he explain something he either shouldn't or couldn't explain. I gave up. I assumed that when he mentioned my being able to deal direct with Clemens von T., he was not referring to shoes, and that in future he would ask me to consult him about something other than footwear. Nevertheless, the truth is that even now, when that time of fever and dream has long passed, I continue to order my handsome long-lasting pairs of shoes from that tiny shop in Berlin.

Tupra meant what he said on the plane, and so I arranged my trip to Madrid for the following month, a stay of two weeks, I realised this would be quite long enough, possibly even too long, I mean, once I had seen everyone, I wouldn't know what to do with my time.

Nostalgia, or missing some place or person, regardless of whether for reasons of absence or abandonment or death, is a very strange and contradictory business. At first, you think you can't live without someone or far from someone, the initial grief is so intense and so constant that you experience it as a kind of endless sinking or an interminably advancing spear, because each moment of privation counts and weighs, you feel it and it chokes you, and all you want is for the hours of the day to pass, knowing that their passing will lead to nothing new, only to more waiting for more waiting. Each morning you open your eyes – if you've had the benefit of sleep which, while it doesn't allow you to forget everything, does at least numb and confuse – thinking the same thought that oppressed you just before you closed them, for example, 'She's not here and she won't be coming back' (whether that means her coming back to you or back from death), and you prepare yourself not to trudge through the day, because you're not even capable of looking that far ahead or of differentiating one day from another, but through the next five minutes and then the next, and so you'll continue from five minutes to five minutes, if not from minute to minute, becoming entangled in them all and, at most, trying to distract yourself for just two or three minutes from your consciousness, or from your ponderous paralysis. If that happens, it has nothing to do with your will, but with some form of blessed chance: a curious item on the television news, the time it takes to complete or begin a crossword, an irritating or solicitous phone call from someone you can't stand, the bottle that falls to the floor and obliges you to gather up the fragments so that you don't cut yourself when out of laziness you wander about barefoot, or the dire TV series that nonetheless amuses you – or that you simply took to straight away – and to which you surrender yourself with inexplicable relief until the final credits roll, wishing another episode would start immediately and allow you to keep clinging on to that stupid thread of continuity. These are the found routines that sustain us, what remains of life, the foolish and the innocuous, that neither enthuses nor demands participation or effort, the padding that we despise when everything is fine and we're busy and have no time to miss anyone, not even the dead (in fact, we use those busy times to shrug them off, although this only works for a short while, because the dead insist on staying dead and always come back later on, the pinprick pressing into our chest and the lead upon our souls).

Time passes, and at some ill-defined point, we go back to being able to sleep without suddenly starting awake and without remembering what has happened in our dreams, and to shaving not at chance moments or at odd times, but each morning; no bottles are broken and we remain unirritated by any phone call, we can make do without the TV soap opera, the crossword, the random soothing routines that we look at oddly as we bid farewell to them because now we can scarcely understand why we ever needed them, and we can even make do without the patient people who entertained us and listened to us during our monotonous, obsessive period of mourning. We raise our head and once more look around us, and although we see nothing particularly promising or attractive, nothing that can replace the person we long for and have lost, we begin to find it hard to sustain that longing and wonder if it was really such a loss. We're filled by a kind of retrospective laziness regarding the time when we loved or were devoted or got overexcited or anxious, and feel incapable of ever giving so much attention to anyone again, of trying to please them, of watching over their sleep and concealing from them what can be concealed or what might hurt them, and one finds enormous relief in that deep-rooted absence of alertness. 'I was abandoned,' we think, 'by my lover, by my friend, by my dead, so what, they all left, and the result was the same, I just had to get on with my own life. They'll regret it in the end, because it's nice to know that one is loved and sad to know one's been forgotten, and now I'm forgetting them, and anyone who dies knows more or less what fate awaits him or her. I did what I could, I held firm, and still they drifted away.' Then you quote these words to yourself: 'Memory is a tremulous finger.' And add in your own words: 'And it doesn't always succeed when it tries to point at us.' We discover that our finger can no longer be trusted, or less and less often, and that those who absorbed our thoughts night and day and day and night, and were fixed there like a nail hammered firmly in, gradually work loose and become of no importance to us; they grow blurred and, yes, tremulous, and one can even begin to doubt their existence as if they were a bloodstain rubbed and scrubbed and cleaned, or of which only the rim remains, which is the part that takes longest to remove, and then that rim, too, finally submits.

More time passes, and there comes a day, just before the last trace vanishes, when the mere idea of seeing the lost person suddenly seems burdensome to us. Even though we may not be happy and may still miss them, even though their remoteness and loss still occasionally wounds us – one night, lying in bed, we look at our shoes alone by the leg of a chair, and we're filled with grief when we remember that her high heels once stood right next to them, year after year, telling us that we were two even in sleep, even in absence – it turns out that the people we most loved, and still love, have become people from another era, or have been lost along the way – along our way, for we each have our own – have become almost preterite beings to whom we do not want to return because we know them too well and the thread of continuity has been broken. We always view the past with a feeling of proud superiority, both it and its contents, even if our present is worse or less fortunate or sick and the future promises no improvement of any kind. However brilliant and happy our past was, to us it seems contaminated with ingenuousness, ignorance and, in part, silliness: in the past we never knew what would come after and now we do, and in that sense the past is inferior, in objective, practical terms; that's why it always carries within it an element of hopeless foolishness and makes us feel ashamed that we lived for so long in a fantasy world, believing what we now know to be false, or perhaps it wasn't false then, but which has, anyway, ceased to be true by not resisting or persevering. The love that seemed rock solid, the friendship we never doubted, the living person whom we always relied upon to live for ever because without him the world was inconceivable or it was inconceivable that the world would still be the world and not some other place. We cannot help looking down slightly at our most beloved dead, the more so as more time passes and in passing wastes them, not just with sadness but with pity too, knowing, as we do, that they know nothing – how naïve they were – of what happened after their departure, whereas we do. We went to the funeral and listened to what was said there, as well as to what people muttered under their breath, as if afraid the departed might still be able to hear them, and we saw those who had harmed him boasting that they had been his closest friends and pretending to mourn him. He neither saw nor heard anything. He died deceived, like everyone else, without ever knowing enough, and that's precisely what makes us pity them and consider them all to be poor men and poor women, poor grown-up children, poor devils.

Those whom we left behind or who left our side know nothing about us either, as far as we're concerned they've become as fixed and immovable as the dead, and the mere prospect of meeting again and having to talk to them and hear them seems to us like hard work, partly because we feel that neither they nor we would want to talk about or hear anything. 'I can't be bothered,' we think, 'it's been far too long since she was a witness to my days. She used to know almost everything about me, or at least the most important things, and now a gap has opened up that could never be filled, even if I were to tell her in great detail all that has happened, everything of which she did not have immediate knowledge. I can't be bothered with having to get to know each other again and explain ourselves, how upsetting to recognise at once the old reactions and the old vices and the old anxieties and the old tones of voice in which I addressed her and she me; and even the same suppressed jealousies and the same passions, albeit unspoken now. I'll never be able to see her as someone new, nor as part of my daily existence, she'll seem simultaneously stale and alien. I'll go home to see Luisa and the children, and once I've spent a good long time with them and they're starting to get used to me, I'll sit down beside her for a rather shorter time, perhaps before going out to supper at a restaurant, while we wait for the babysitter who's late arriving, on the sofa we shared for so many years, but where I sit now like a visiting stranger, dependable or otherwise, and we won't know how to behave. There'll be pauses and clearings of the throat and, given that we're face to face, extraordinarily inane remarks such as "So, how are things with you?" or "You're looking really good". And then we'll realise that we can't be together without really being together, and that we don't want that. We will be neither completely natural nor completely artificial, it's not possible to be superficial with someone we've known deeply and since for ever, nor deep with someone who has lost all track of us and covered her own tracks completely, for both of us there is so much that is now unknown. And after half an hour, perhaps one, two at the most, over dessert, we'll consider that there's nothing more to be said and, even stranger, that once is quite enough, and then I'll have thirteen days' holiday left to kill. And even if the unthinkable happened and we fell into each other's arms and she said the words I've been wanting to hear for so long now: "Come, come, I was so wrong about you before. Sit down here beside me again. I haven't yet shooed away your ghost, this pillow is still yours, I just couldn't see you clearly before. Come and embrace me. Come to me. Come back. And stay here for ever"; even if that happened and I gave up my London apartment and said farewell to Tupra and Pérez Nuix, to Mulryan and Rendel and even to Wheeler, and began the swift task of transforming them into a long parenthesis – even seemingly interminable parentheses close eventually and then they can be jumped over – and returned to Madrid to be with her – and I'm not saying that I wouldn't, given the opportunity, if that happened – I would do so knowing that what has been interrupted cannot be resumed, that the gap would remain there always, hidden perhaps but constant, and knowing that a before and an after can never be knit together.'

And so, despite my genuine desire to return to my city and to see my family again, even the one person who no longer considered herself mine, to see yesterday's faces, having absented myself from today and from their today, and to find myself, without preparation or warning, confronted by tomorrow's faces, I not only planned a stay of two weeks rather than the three my boss had offered me, I also postponed my departure for a little longer on our return from Berlin, in order to find out first what had happened to De la Garza.

I thought of simply phoning him out of the blue and enquiring after his health, but it occurred to me that if I gave my name, he might not even want to speak to me, and that if I gave a false name or invented an excuse or some fabricated query, it would be difficult then to move the conversation on and ask about his physical state, suddenly and for no reason, given that I was supposedly a stranger. So I decided instead to pay him a surprise visit, that is, without making a prior appointment. However, since nowadays no official organisation will allow in anyone unless they have first specified the purpose of their visit or proved that they have some legitimate business there, I phoned an ex- colleague at the BBC with whom I had worked on various tedious programmes about terrorism and tourism at the start of my life in London – before I was recruited by Tupra or, rather, by Wheeler – and who, like me, had managed to escape his boring post and had doubtless improved his lot by taking on a vague although not entirely insignificant job with the Spanish embassy at the Court of my patron saint St James, or San Jacobo.

The name of this unctuous, treacherous individual, part-despot, part-serf (despite the apparent contradiction, the two often go together), was Garralde and when it came to ensuring his own well-being he lacked all scruples; he was always ready to be servile, not just with the powerful and the famous, but also with those he reckoned would one day enjoy a little power and fame, however minimal, enough, at any rate, to do him some future favour or for him to feel able to ask for one; in just the same way, he was scornful of those who, in his view, would never be of any use to him, although he had no qualms about suddenly and cynically turning on the charm if he discovered later on that he had been wrong. He had a broad face, like an almost full moon, small eyes, very porous skin, like pulp, and rather widely spaced teeth, the latter giving him a highly salacious appearance which, as far as I know, accorded only with his greedy mentality – he looked as if he were constantly secreting juices – but not with his activities: he was the kind of man who laughingly pays everyone amorous compliments – probably both women and men, although he would do so only implicitly and, how can I put it, interrogatively with the latter, by taking a great interest in them – but on the rare occasions when one of his flatterees responded in kind, he would, equally laughingly, make his escape, fearful that he would not be able to oblige. He had the strangest hair too, it looked just like Davy Crockett's hat (without the beaver or racoon tail or whatever it was, there were quite enough dangly bits in that embassy with De la Garza; although the latter didn't wear his hairnet to work), and I always wondered if that hairstyle-cum-cap wasn't in fact a wig, so thick and flamboyant that no one dared suspect it was false. Whenever I saw him, I felt like giving it a good tug, under the guise of masculine affection or in manly, boorish jest, just to see if it came off in my hand and, in passing, to find out what it felt like (it bore a creepy resemblance to velvet).

He had never paid me much attention – poor radio hack that I was – when we first knew each other – he always thought he was better than that, even though he was a hack too at the time – but now he had me down as someone with influence and a touch of mystery. He didn't know exactly what I did or who I worked for, but he knew something about my occasional appearances at chic discos, expensive restaurants, racecourses, celebrity suppers, Stamford Bridge, as well as ghastly dives no Spaniard would ever venture into (Tupra's sociable spells sometimes went on for weeks), and all of this in the company of the natives, which is rare in England for almost any foreigner, even diplomats. (On this occasion, moreover, he would have noticed me wearing those extraordinary shoes made by Hlustik and von Truschinsky, and Garralde had a keen eye for such things and an infuriating tendency to copy them.) He felt what it best behoves acquaintances to feel about oneself: confusion and curiosity. This led him to imagine that I had all kinds of contacts and powers, which meant that he would do anything I asked. And so, offering no explanation, I asked if I could come and see him at the embassy and, once I was there at his desk, immediately clarified the situation (in a prudently low voice, for Garralde shared a room with three other functionaries; if he was thinking of staying there, he still had quite some way to go before he made it to the top).

'I haven't actually come to see you, Garralde. I made the appointment so that I wouldn't have any problems getting in. I'll just spend a couple of minutes with you, if that's all right. We can have a proper chat over lunch another day, I've just discovered this fantastic new place, you'll love it, you see lots of people there, fresh out of bed. They skip breakfast, you see.' – For him 'people' meant 'important people', the only kind he was interested in. He spattered his Spanish with really ghastly foreign expressions like 'the cream of society' or even worse '*la crème de la crème*', 'the *haut monde*' and 'the jet set'; he talked about 'big names' and people being 'top-notch', and said that at weekends he was 'unplugged'. He might climb quite high with his blend of grovelling and abuse, but he would never be anything more than a social yokel. He would also exclaim '*Oro!*' whenever he thought something particularly wonderful or remarkable, having heard an Italian friend use the expression and finding it highly original. 'As soon as we finish here (it will only take two minutes), I want you to tell me where I can find the office of a colleague of yours, Rafael de la Garza. He's the person I really want to see, but I don't want him to know I'm coming.'

'But why didn't you ask him for an appointment?' asked the vile Garralde, more out of nosiness than to make any difficulties. 'I'm sure he'd have said "Yes".'

'I don't think so. He's upset with me over some nonsense or other. I want to make it up with him, it was all a misunderstanding. But he mustn't know that I'm here. Just show me where his office is and I'll turn up there on my own.'

'But wouldn't it be best if I told him you were here? He's a higher rank than me.'

It was as if he hadn't heard what I'd said. He may have been clever when it came to manipulating friends and acquaintances, but he was basically an oaf. He irritated me, and I was on the point of hurling myself on his abundant hair, its similarity to the legendary hat of Davy Crockett, king of the wild frontier, was really quite incredible (although it looked more matted than on other occasions, perhaps it was beginning to bear more of a resemblance to a Russian fur hat). I once again restrained myself, after all, he *was* about to do me a small favour that he would soon ask me to pay back, he was not the sort to wait.

'What did I just say, Garralde? If you announce me, he'll refuse to see me, and besides, it might get you into trouble.'

Since he was a base creature, this last argument sharpened his wits a little. He would never want to make an enemy of a superior, or to annoy him, even if that person wasn't his direct superior. For a moment, I felt sorry for him: how could he possibly consider Rafita de la Garza his superior? Our world is very badly ordered and unfair and corrupt if it allows other people to be at the orders of that prize dickhead. It was just pathetic. Of course, it was equally shocking to think that someone might have Garralde as their superior and have to obey him.

'Fine, if that's what you want,' he said. 'Let me just check if he's on his own. It wouldn't do you much good to burst in on him if he's in a meeting. You wouldn't be able to undo the misunderstanding with witnesses present, now would you?'

'I'll go with you. You can show me the way and the right

door. Don't worry, I'll wait outside and before I go in, I'll give you plenty of time to clear off. He'll never know you had anything to do with my visit.'

'And what about lunch?' he asked before we even set off. He had to make sure he got his reward, at least the minimum and immediate one. He would try to get something better out of me later, that was his way of charging interest. But I didn't care a fig about that or indeed about our lunch date, which I probably wouldn't keep. He'd be momentarily angry, but it would only increase his respect for me and his curiosity when he saw how little care I took over my social commitments. 'I'd love to go to that restaurant you mentioned.'

'What about Saturday? I have to fly over to Madrid for a few days after that. I'll phone you tomorrow and we'll arrange a time. I'll reserve a table.'

'*Oro!*'

I couldn't bear him saying that. Well, I couldn't bear anything about him. I decided there and then that I would not damn well reserve a table nor would I damn well phone him, I'd invent some convincing excuse later on.

He led me down carpeted and slightly labyrinthine corridors, we changed direction at least six times. Finally, he stopped at a prudent distance from a door that stood ajar or almost open, we could hear declamatory voices, or rather one voice, barely audible, which sounded as if it were reciting poetry in a strange, insistent rhythm, or perhaps it was a litany.

'Is he alone?' I whispered.

'I'm not sure. He might be, although, of course, he is speaking. No, wait, now I remember: Professor Rico is here today. He's giving a lecture this evening at the Cervantes Institute. They're probably rehearsing.' And then he felt it necessary to enlighten me: 'Yes, Professor Francisco Rico, no less. You may not know it, but he's a great expert, really top-notch, and very stern. Apparently he treats anyone he deems stupid or importunate like dirt. He's much feared, very disrespectful and has a caustic wit. There's absolutely no way we can interrupt them, Deza. He's a member of the Spanish Academy.'

'It would be best if the Professor didn't see you, then. I'll wait here until they've finished. You'd better go, you don't want to get a dressing down. Thanks for everything and, don't worry, I'll be all right.'

Garralde hesitated for a moment. He didn't trust me. Quite right too. However, he must have thought that whatever happened next and whatever I did, it would be best if he wasn't there. He set off back down those corridors, turning round every now and then and repeating noiselessly to me until he had disappeared from view (it was easy enough to read his lips):

'Don't go in. Don't even think of interrupting them. He's a member of the Academy.'

I had learned from Tupra and Rendel how to move almost silently, and to silently open closed doors, if there were no complications, and how to jam them shut, as with the door of the Disabled toilet. And so I made my way over to De la Garza's office, keeping close to the farther side of the corridor. From there I could see practically the whole room, I could certainly see both men, the numbskull and Rico, whose face I was familiar with from television and the newspapers and which was, besides, pretty much unmistakable, he was a bald man who, curiously and audaciously, did not behave like a bald man, he had a disdainful or sometimes even weary look in his eye, he must get very tired of the ignorance surrounding him, he must constantly curse having been born into an illiterate age for which he would feel nothing but scorn; in his statements to the press and in his writings (I had read the occasional article) he gave the impression that he was addressing himself not to a few cultivated people in the future, in whose existence he doubtless did not trust, but to readers from the past, all good and dead, as if he believed that in books – on both sides of the divide: for books speak in the middle of the night just as the river speaks, quietly and reluctantly, and their murmur, too, is tranquil or patient or languid – being alive or dead was merely a secondary matter, a matter of chance. He perhaps thought, like his compatriot and mine, that 'time is the only dimension in which the living and the dead can talk to each other and communicate, the only dimension they have in common and that unites them', and that all time is therefore inevitably indifferent and shared (we all existed and will exist in time), and the fact that we coincide in it physically is purely incidental, like arriving late or early for an appointment. I saw his characteristically large mouth, well-formed and rather soft, slightly reminiscent of Tupra's mouth, but less moist, less cruel. His mouth was closed, his lips almost pressed together, so the primitive rhythms I could hear were emanating not from there, but from Rafita, who, it seems, not only considered himself to be a black rapper by night, in chic and idiotic clubs, but a white hip-hopper in the broad light of day and in his office at the embassy, although he was dressed perfectly conventionally now and wasn't wearing a stiff, over-large jacket, or a gypsy earring in one ear, or some faux matador's hairnet or a hat or a bandana or a Phrygian cap, or anything else on his empty head. His recitation droned to a halt, and he said with satisfaction to Francisco Rico, that man of great learning:

'So what did you think, Professor?'

The Professor was wearing a pair of large spectacles with thick frames and lenses possibly made of anti-glare glass, but even so I could see his icy gaze, his look of sad stupefaction, as if he were not so much angry as unable to believe De la Garza's pretentiousness or presumptuousness.

'It doesn't thrill me. *Ps. Tah.* Not in the least.' – That's what he said, '*Ps.*' Not even the more traditional '*Pse*', which means 'So-so' or 'No great shakes' (or '*Ni fu ni fa*', which Spaniards use all the time, even though no one really knows what it means). '*Ps*', especially when followed by '*Tah*', was far more discouraging, in fact it was deeply disheartening.

'Let me lay another one on you, Professor. This one's more elaborate, has more arse to it, it's more, like, kickin'.'

There he was again with his semi-crude, semi-youth slang; no one could dishearten or discourage Rafita. I felt relieved to see that he was little changed since the last time I had seen him, beaten and lying on the floor, literally with the fear of death in his shaking, silently supplicant body, his eyes dull and his gaze averted, not even daring to look at us, at his punisher and at me, his punisher's companion by association. I saw that he had recovered, his injuries couldn't have been so very grave if he were still prepared to importune anyone anywhere with his nonsense. He must be the kind of man who never learned, a hopeless case. It was, of course, unlikely that Professor Rico would draw a sword or a dagger on him, or grab him by the neck and bang his head on the table several times. At most, he would give a loud, dismissive snort, or bluntly tell him what he thought of him, because, as the vile Garralde had said, he did have a reputation for being caustic and wounding and for not keeping to himself his harsh opinions or his insults when he considered them to be justified. He was seated indolently in an armchair, his head thrown back like a disinterested, sceptical judge, his legs elegantly crossed, his right forearm resting on the back of the chair and in his hand a cigarette whose ash he was allowing to fall onto the floor, helped by an occasional light tap on the filter with his thumbnail. It was clear that unless someone placed an ashtray immediately underneath his cigarette, he was not going to bother looking for one. He sometimes blew the smoke out through his nose, a somewhat old-fashioned thing to do nowadays, and for that reason still stylish. He probably couldn't care less about the ban on smoking in offices. He was well dressed and well shod, his shirt and suit looked to me as if they were by Zegna or Corneliani or someone similar, but his shoes were definitely not by Hlustik, that much was sure, they, too, must have come from the South. Rafita was standing in front of him, clearly rather worked up, as if he genuinely wanted to know Rico's opinion, to which, however, he paid no attention because that opinion was not, for the moment, benevolent. There are more and more such people in the world, who only hear what pleases and flatters them, as if anything else simply passes them by. It started off as a phenomenon among politicians and mediocre artists hungry for success, but now it has infected whole populations. I was watching the two of them as if from the fifth row in a theatre, and if I centred myself opposite the half-open door, both appeared in my field of vision uncut.

'Look here, young De la Garza,' Rico said in an offensively

paternalistic tone, 'it's as plain as day that God has not called you to follow the path of foolish nonsensical verse. You're light years away from *Struwwelpeter*, and Edward Lear could run rings round you.' The Professor was being deliberately pedantic, that is, he was having fun at Rafita's expense, because he probably knew that Rafita wouldn't have heard of either name, I knew of Edward Lear purely by chance, from my pedantic years in Oxford, the other name meant nothing to me, although I've found out more since. 'And I feel you should not oppose His wishes, *derr*, and that way you won't waste any more time. He obviously hasn't called you to the higher path either, why, you wouldn't even be capable of writing something like "*Una alta ricca rocca*", even though you have six long centuries of progress on your side.' He spoke this line in an immaculate Italian accent, and so I assumed it was not Spanish but Italian, despite the similarity of vocabulary; perhaps it was from Petrarch, on whom he was an expert, as he was on so many other world authors and doubtless on *Struwwelpeter*, too, his knowledge was immeasurable. 'There are some things, *ets*, that simply cannot be. So give up now, *pf*.' I was struck by the fact that, despite his role as member of the Spanish Academy, he used so much onomatopoeia that was strange to our language and initially indecipherable, although, at the same time, I found it all perfectly comprehensible and clear, perhaps he had a special gift for it and was a master of onomatopoeia, an inventor, a creator even. '*Derr*' obviously indicated some sort of prohibition. '*Ets*' sounded to me like a very serious warning. '*Pf*' seemed to me to indicate a lost cause.

But Rafita was very much a man of his age and preferred not to hear or perhaps did not hear, and maybe the plethora of other people like him nowadays are just the same. And so he continued unabashed:

'No, you'll really like this one, Professor, it'll blow your mind. Here goes.' Then I saw him doing ridiculous things with his hands and arms just like a rapper (I'm applying the word 'ridiculous' not to him, although he was ridiculous, but to all those who devote themselves to gesticulating and mumbling that witless, worthless drivel, as if the religious doggerel we had to chorus when we were kids, God help us, was making a comeback after all these years), he flailed about, making undulating movements in an attempt to emulate the angry gestures of some low-life black man, although every now and then his Spanish roots would reveal themselves and he'd end up striking poses more like those of a flamenco dancer in full flow. It was truly pathetic, as were his awful so-called verses, a ghastly dirge accompanied by a constant bending of the knees in time to the supposed rhythm of some thin, imaginary tune: 'I'm gonna turn you baby into my ukelele', was how it began, with that so-called rhyme, 'I'm food for the snakes, like a fine beefsteak, I'll fill you up with venom just for wearin' denim, don't go stepping on my toes if you want to keep your nose, hoo-yoo, yoo-hoo.' – And then, without even pausing to take a breath, he attacked another strophe or section or whatever it was: 'My bullets want some fun, no point in trying to run, and they're looking for your brain and are out to cause you pain, to burn up your grey matter, send it pouring down the gutter, flushing down the can, you'll be shit down the pan, hoo-yoo, yoo-hoo.'

'Enough!' – The very eminent Professor Rico had looked him straight in the eye ('*de hito en hito*', another phrase that everyone understands without knowing quite what it means); and I suppose he had listened to him '*de hito en hito*' as well, if that's possible, which I doubt, although I really don't know. He had, at any rate, turned pale on hearing those defiling dactyls, as must I, I imagine, although there were no mirrors to confirm this. Immediately afterwards, however, I felt a wave of heat to my face and I must have blushed, out of a mixture of fury and embarrassment (not for myself but for De la Garza): how did that great nincompoop dare to waste the admirable Francisco Rico's time and bother him with such out-and-out bunkum and baloney? How could he possibly think that his crude ditty had any poetic value whatsoever, not even as a kind of pseudo-limerick, and how could he expect to receive the approval of one of Spain's leading literary authorities, a great expert, on a visit to London, perhaps still tired from his journey, perhaps needing time to put the finishing touches to his magisterial lecture that evening? I felt as indignant as when I saw De la Garza on the fast dance floor at the disco, flailing the imprudent Flavia's face with his ludicrous hairnet. My one brief, simple thought then had been: 'I'd like to smash his face in', and at the time I knew nothing of the imminent traumatic consequences of that incident. I had remembered that thought much later, with sadness, with a kind of vicarious regret (on my own behalf, but also, vaguely, on behalf of Tupra, who seemed to regret nothing, as was only natural in someone so single-minded and conscientious; he had no regrets, at least about work-related matters), both during and after the thrashing – and, of course, before – each time that Reresby's Landsknecht sword rose and fell. How could De la Garza not have learned his lesson, how could he not have grown more discreet? How could he have composed anything, however incoherent and grotesque, that contained elements of violence, when he himself, courtesy of us, had such painful first-hand experience of it? How could he even mention the words 'pan' and 'can', when he had nearly been drowned in the blue water of a toilet? 'Perhaps that's why,' I thought to myself as I stood in the corridor, still unnoticed, invisible, a voyeur and an eavesdropper. 'Perhaps he's obsessed with what happened to him, and this is his one (idiotic) way of coming to terms with it or overcoming it, by believing (in his clumsy, puerile way) that he could be Reresby and fill someone with bullets or at least with fear, or poison them, or blow their brains out, or do all those things to Tupra himself, of whom he must be scared witless and whom he doubtless prayed each day never to meet again – in this city that they shared. Fantasising is free, we know this from childhood on; we continue to know it as we grow older, but we learn to fantasise very little, and less and less as the years pass, when we realise that there's no point.' I immediately felt rather sorry for him and that feeling tempered my indignation, although this was not the case with the illustrious Professor, of course, who shared neither my thoughts nor my outstanding debts: 'Enough!' he cried, without actually raising his voice, but the way he projected his voice it sounded like a shout, rather in the way that waiters in Madrid bars can bawl out orders to the people in the kitchen or at the bar, above or below the hubbub from the customers. 'Are you out of your tiny mind, De la Garza? Just what *has* got into you? Do you really think I could possibly be interested in hearing that string of inanities,' he paused, 'that tom-tom-like tosh you were spouting? What filth! *Regh*. What dross!' – Many of the expressions he used were old-fashioned or perhaps it was simply that the lexicon used by Spaniards nowadays has become so reduced that almost all expressions seem old-fashioned, things like '*¿qué ventolera te ha dado?*' – 'What *has* got into you?' or '*sarta de necedades*' – 'string of inanities' or '*tabarra*' – 'dross', as well as '*no estar en sus cabales*' – 'to be out of your mind', and I was pleased to see that I was not the only one to use them; for a second, I identified with Rico, a self-identification I found flattering, unexpectedly or perhaps not (he *is* a very eminent man). His latest onomatopoeia, '*Regh*', seemed to me as transparent and eloquent as the previous ones, conveying disgust, both moral and aesthetic.

The Professor did not move, did not get up, he was clearly capable of controlling his body, it was enough for him occasionally to unleash his tongue, however briefly. He merely deposited his cigarette end in a handy pencil-holder and touched the bridge of his glasses, first with his index finger and then with his middle finger, twice, as if he wanted to make sure they hadn't flown off his nose when he erupted. De la Garza stood paralysed, knees momentarily bent, not the most graceful of poses, as if he were about to crouch down. Then he straightened up. And since he'd had nothing to drink, he might well have felt alarmed.

'Oh, forgive me, Professor, I'm so sorry, I don't understand, I'd read somewhere that you were interested in hip-hop, that you saw a connection with certain archaic forms of poetry, with doggerel, you know, chapbooks, songbooks, ballads, and all that . . .'

'You're confusing me with Villena,' Rico cut in, referring to a very well-known Spanish poet with a sharp eye (a sharp eye for all the latest trends). He didn't say this in an offended tone, but in a purely professorial and explanatory one.

'. . . that you'd said you found it very medieval . . .'

And then it happened. He stopped speaking because that was when it happened. As he was shaking his head to express his incomprehension and his contrition, shocked by Rico's blunt or rough reaction (which he'd brought on himself), he saw me and immediately recognised me, as if he had been fearing just such an encounter for some time or had often dreamed of me or as if, in his nightmares, I was a crushing weight on his chest. When he glanced to the right, he saw me there, straight ahead of him, standing on the other side of the corridor like a spectre at the feast, and instantly recognised me. And I saw the effect of that surprise and that recognition. De la Garza shrank back, every bit of him, the way an insect sensing danger contracts, curls up, rolls into a ball, tries to disappear and erase itself so that death will not touch it, so as not to be picked out or seen, to cease to exist and thus deny its own existence ('No, really, I'm not what you see, I'm not here'), because the only sure way of avoiding death is no longer to be, or perhaps even better, never to have been at all. He clamped his arms to his sides, not like a boxer about to defend or cover himself, but as if he'd suddenly been seized with cold and were shivering. He drew in his head too, much as he had done in the Disabled toilet, when he turned his head and for the first time spotted the blurred gleam of metal overhead and saw, at the very periphery of his vision, the double-edged sword about to swoop down on him: he instinctively hunched up his shoulders as if in a spasm of pain, the deliberate or unwitting gesture made by all the victims of the guillotine over two hundred years or of the axe over hundreds of centuries, even chickens and turkeys must have made that gesture from the moment it occurred to the first bored or hungry man to decapitate one. As happened then, too, his top lip lifted, almost folded back on itself in a rictus, revealing dry gums on which the inner part of his lip got stuck for lack of saliva. And in his eyes I saw an irrational, overwhelming, all-excluding fear, as if my mere presence had plucked him from reality and as if, in a matter of seconds, he had forgotten where he was, in the Spanish embassy in the Court of St James or San Jacobo or San Jaime, where he worked or spent time every day surrounded by guards and colleagues who would protect him, they were only a step away; he had forgotten that before him sat the prestigious and very irritated Professor Rico and that, given the situation, I could do nothing to him. What I found most disquieting, what left me troubled and transfixed, was that I didn't want to do anything to him, quite the contrary, I wanted to ask if he'd recovered, enquire after his health, make sure that nothing irreparable had happened, and, if the opportunity arose, and even though I couldn't stand the man, to say how sorry I was. How sorry I was that I hadn't done more, that I hadn't stopped it, that I hadn't helped him to flee, that I hadn't defended him or made Tupra see reason (although with Tupra everything was always calculated and he never rushed into anything or lost his reason). And I would even have liked to convince the dickhead that, all in all, he'd been lucky and got off lightly, and that my colleague Reresby, despite his brutality and incredible though it might seem, had done him an enormous favour by stepping in and thus preventing the bloodthirsty Manoia (whom I had seen and not seen in action on that video, now *he* really was Sir Cruelty, I'd closed my eyes, I hadn't wanted to cover them, but that scene really cried out for a blindfold) from taking charge of the punishment himself. But I neither could nor should tell him any of that, still less in front of Rico, who, on seeing Rafita's transformation, glanced with disdainful curiosity in my direction (he must have despised everything about De la Garza and considered him a peabrain and a madman).

It was a very disagreeable feeling, more than that, it was incomprehensible, to discover that I could provoke such fear in someone. It was doubtless by association, by assimilation, after all, I hadn't even touched him, perhaps De la Garza assumed that we always went around together and was afraid that Tupra might suddenly hove into view behind me. I was, however, alone and had gone there without the knowledge of my boss, who would not have been in the least amused by my visit. 'Tell him not to phone you to demand an explanation, but to leave you alone, to forget he ever knew you,' Tupra had told me to tell him, to translate those words to the fallen man, before he abandoned De la Garza, brushing his face with the tail of his armed coat as he left. 'Tell him to accept that there's no reason to demand an explanation, that there are no grounds for complaints or protest. Tell him not to talk to anyone, to keep quiet, not even to recount it later as some kind of adventure. But tell him always to remember.' And Rafita had followed those instructions to the letter, he had invented some tall story to explain his battered state to friends and colleagues. And, of course, he would have remembered, indeed, he would have done little else since then, a bundle of nerves day and night, awake and asleep, night and day, even though he later had the cheek to sing a rap song to Rico and commit other unimaginable acts of nincompoopery. When he saw me there, so close, in the corridor, perhaps, from his point of view, stalking him, he might have been panicked into thinking that I was the one who would never leave him in peace or forget him. 'He could have been left with no head, he came very close,' Reresby had added. 'But since he didn't lose it, tell him there's still time, another day, any day, we know where to find him. Tell him never to forget that, tell him the sword will always be there.' I had omitted those last few words, I hadn't translated them, I had refused to endorse them, but I had translated the rest. Everything would have remained engraved on De la Garza's memory, despite his diminished consciousness after the shock of the sharp steel and being hurled against the blunt cylindrical bars: 'We know where to find you.' Nothing could be truer, and now I had found him and I was his terror, his threat.

'He's absolutely terrified of me,' I thought fleetingly. 'But how can that be, I can't recall having terrified anyone very much before, and yet here's this man, frozen to the spot and consumed with the horror he feels on seeing me, even though he's here in his inviolable office, in the embassy, along with a member of the Spanish Academy, objectively speaking safe and sound, why, all he'd have to do is shout and fellow diplomats and the odd vigilante or guard would be here in a trice. However, his feeling is that they would arrive too late if I had a gun or a sword or a knife and used them on him right away, with no thought for my own fate and without saying a word, that is what he knows intuitively, or perhaps the memory is still all too vivid of that moment when he first glimpsed the double-edged sword and knew there was nothing he could do to save himself:

death comes in a second, one moment you're alive and the next, without realising it, you're dead, that's how it is sometimes and, of course, all the time during wars and bombardments from on high, that widespread practice, which, however customary and accepted it may have become, is always illegitimate and always dishonourable, far more so than the crossbow in the days of Richard Yea and Nay, that changeable *Coeur de Lion* who was slain by an arrow from a dishonourable crossbow at the end of the twelfth century: you hear the bang and see and hear nothing more, and it won't be you, but possibly someone else who's still alive, who will hear the whistle of the bullet that embeds itself in your forehead. Yes, right now, this man would do anything I ordered him to do, his dread of me – or rather of Tupra, whose representative or henchman or symbol I am – is something he not only experienced in reality for a few minutes that would have seemed to him, as they had to me, an eternity, he would also often have anticipated it, asleep and awake: perhaps he saw us striding towards him like two hired assassins come to slice him up, perhaps we had appeared in his nightmares of being chased and caught, then chased and caught again, and perhaps we have sat heavy on his soul since then.' Because 'even dreams know that your pursuer usually catches up with you, and they've known it since the *Iliad*', as Tupra had said to me that night, somewhat later, the two of us sitting in his car outside the door to my apartment, where he believed someone was waiting for me, but where there was no one, only the lights still on and possibly the dancer opposite.

Then I strode quickly into the room and spoke. I walked into the office and said confidently, almost jovially:

'So, how are you doing, Rafita? I can see you've made an excellent recovery.' And I added at once, so that he would see I was keen to keep up appearances and that my intentions were not violent or aggressive, 'Forgive me bursting in like this. Won't you introduce me?' And I went straight over to Professor Rico, who made not the slightest effort to get up, but merely held out one hand to me, the way grand ladies used to do, reaching out as far as he could without actually moving, he had a most distinguished hand and a most elegant shirt-cuff, by Cuprì or Sensatini at the very least, excellent brands, I shook it warmly (his hand that is). And since De la Garza still did not respond or utter a word (he just stared at me, terrified, so afraid that he didn't even stop me approaching Rico, in fact, he wouldn't have stopped me doing anything, I could, I realised, do what I liked), I introduced myself: 'Jacques Deza, Jacobo Deza. You're Don Francisco Rico, aren't you? The celebrated scholar.'

It pleased him to be recognised and he deigned to answer, doubtless for that reason alone, for his general attitude revealed no actual interest (whoever I might be, I was, after all, already stigmatised as someone he associated with that rapper-attaché).

'Deza, Deza . . . Aren't you a friend or acquaintance or student . . . or, er, whatever . . . of Sir Peter Wheeler? Your name rings a bell.' Both men were great scholarly figures, and I was aware that they knew and admired each other.

'Yes, I'm a very good friend of his, Professor.'

'I knew the name rang a bell. I recognised it. He must have mentioned you to me once, although I've no idea why. But it definitely rang a bell,' he said, pleased with his own retentive memory.

De la Garza wasn't listening to this superficial exchange. He had moved away from me and was now standing behind his desk as if his desk would protect him and so that he could run away if necessary.

'What the fuck do you want?' he asked suddenly, but despite the expletive, his tone was neither hostile nor ill-tempered, but imploring, as if all he wanted was for me to magically disappear (for the terrible vision, the bad dream to go away) and wishing with all his might that I would reply: 'I'm off now. I don't want anything. I was never here.'

'Nothing, Rafita, I just wanted to reassure myself that you'd recovered from your accident, that there weren't any after-effects. I happened to be passing and it occurred to me to pop in and ask you, I've been worried. It's a purely friendly visit, I won't stay long, so don't get uptight about it. So, are you all right? Completely better? I'm really sorry about what happened, I mean it.'

'What happened? What accident?' asked Rico sceptically.

'Having seen what I've seen and heard what I've heard, no accident could possibly be serious enough,' he added under his breath, but perfectly audibly.

Rafita, however, paid no attention to this harsh comment, he had relegated the Professor and his annoyance to the background, he was too preoccupied with me, alert and tense, as if he feared that at any moment, I would leap at his throat like a tiger. This was an odd sensation for me, almost amusing at first, because I knew myself to be incapable of harming him and had no wish to do so. *I* knew that, but he did not and contrary to what teachers believe, knowledge is not transmissible; one can only persuade. I found the gulf between his perception and my knowledge almost funny, and yet, at the same time, it was distressing to have someone see me that way, as a danger, as someone threatening and violent. De la Garza was almost beside himself, on tenterhooks.

'Believe me, I just wanted to find out how you are,' I said, trying to calm him, convince him. 'I know you made a real nuisance of yourself and really put your foot in it, but I certainly didn't expect my boss to react like that, and I'm sorry. It took me completely by surprise and was totally disproportionate. I had no idea what he was planning and could do nothing to avoid it.'

'What boss? Sir Peter, you mean? I'm completely lost, what *are* you talking about, *élgar*. If he did turn nasty, I'm not surprised, Sir Peter's far too old for such imbecilities.' Rico returned to the charge, not so much because the matter interested him, but because he was bored. He appeared to be the sort of man who cannot bear his brain to be inactive for a moment, because if you don't understand something immediately, you soon will if you wait, but such waiting is unbearable for people who are constantly thinking. That '*élgar*' denoted a need to know.

'Look, go away, just go away,' said the nincompoop childishly. He took no notice of what I was saying, he wouldn't listen to reason, he probably hadn't even heard me. He'd lost his nerve completely and so very quickly that it reaffirmed me in my view that Tupra and I must often have strolled through his nightmares, in which we were probably inseparable. 'Please leave, I beg you, leave me alone, shit, what more do you want, I haven't said anything, I haven't told anyone the truth, surely that's enough.'

Rico lit another cigarette, having realised that this obscure conflict was a matter exclusively and perhaps pathologically between De la Garza and me, and that he was not going to glean anything more. He made a dismissive gesture, indicating that he was happy to abandon any further attempts at clarification, and he gave vent to one more of his varied repertoire of onomatopoeia.

'*Esh*,' he said. It sounded to me exactly like: 'To hell with these two idiots, I'm going to think my own thoughts and not waste any more time on them.'

I saw how shaken Rafita was – his clenched fists still held close to his body (not as a weapon, but as a shield), his eyes wild, his breathing agitated – gripped by a panic that he was now reliving and which he had perhaps been dreading for months, he had also developed an intermittent cough, which, when the fit took him, proved uncontrollable. That cloud of perpetual fear would last for some time yet, it wouldn't be quick to clear. He must have suffered greatly that night, because one is always instantly aware when there is any real danger of death, even if, in the end, it turns out to be something that merely frightened one half to death. It was pointless trying to talk to him. I wondered what state he would have been in if it had been Reresby and not me who had appeared unexpectedly at the door of his office. He would have fainted, had a seizure, a heart attack. I had gone there out of consideration for him (insofar as that were possible), and there was no sense in making him suffer further with my continued presence. On the other hand, I could leave with a clear conscience. He looked fine physically. He might still suffer some pain or other damage, but he had, on the whole, fully recovered. His present and future feelings of insecurity were, however, quite another thing, and they would stay with him for a long time. He would feel uncomfortable in the world, with the added inconvenience of fear and a permanent sense of unease. Not that this would prevent his spouting nonsense, but it would have dealt a fatal blow to his sense of pride at its deepest level.

'Anyway, I'll go now, so don't upset yourself. I can see that you're fine, although not perhaps at this precise moment. It's my fault, I suppose. You seemed in pretty good form while you were singing your rhyming couplets. I'll come and see you again some other time.' I realised that these last innocent words had terrified him still more. From his point of view it was the equivalent of a threat. I let it go, however, I didn't try to put him right, he wouldn't have listened, and I didn't really care. In a moment of weakness and guilt I had chosen to visit him and had paid the price for both weakness and guilt. 'Goodbye, Professor. It's been an honour to meet you. I'm only sorry it was so brief and so . . . odd.'

'Everything about young De la Garza is odd,' he said scornfully, playing down the importance of the episode, he had probably seen worse; and he stood up, not in order to shake my hand, but to leave. His anger had passed, the situation had nothing to do with him, and his mind was already wandering pastures new. 'Wait, I'm leaving too. I'll see you this evening, Rafita. I doubt I'll have the good fortune of you missing my lecture.'

And there we left De la Garza, still barricaded behind his desk, not daring even to sit down. He didn't say goodbye, he obviously still wasn't capable of articulating any civilised words. And while we, the Professor and I, walked back along those slightly labyrinthine corridors towards the exit, I couldn't help at least attempting an apology:

'You see we had a bit of a falling-out and he still hasn't got over it.'

'No,' he said. 'You should feel very pleased with yourself: you had him scared shitless. You're lucky you can keep him at arm's length like that. He's terribly clinging. I'm vaguely friendly with his father, which is why I put up with the son. Only from time to time, fortunately, and only when I come to London for one of these dull official dos.'

Once we were out in the street and we went our separate ways, I noticed (strangely enough, I hadn't noticed before) that

Rafita's fear had cast me in a rather flattering light. Imposing respect, instilling fear, seeing oneself as a danger had its pleasurable side. It made one feel more confident, more optimistic, stronger. It made one feel important and – how can I put it – masterful. But before I hailed a taxi, there was time for me to find this unexpected vanity repugnant too. Not that the latter feeling drove out conceit, they lived alongside each other. The two things were mingled, until they dissipated and were forgotten.

When you haven't been back for some time to a place you know well, even if it's the city you were born in, the city to which you're most accustomed, where you've lived for the longest time and which is still home to your children and your father and your siblings and home even to the love that stood firm for many years (even if that place is as familiar to you as the air you breathe), there comes a moment when it begins to fade and your recollection of it dims, as if your memory were suddenly afflicted by myopia and – how can I put it – by cinematography: the different eras become juxtaposed and you start to feel unsure as to which of those cities you left or departed from when you last set off, the city of your childhood or your youth or the city of your manhood or maturity, when where you live dwindles in importance, and, hard though it is to admit, the truth is you'd be happy enough with your own little corner almost anywhere in the world.

That's how I'd come to see Madrid during my now prolonged absence: faded and dim, accumulative, oscillating, a stage-set that concerned me very little despite having invested so much in it – so much of my past and so much of my present, albeit at a distance – and, more to the point, one that could get along without me quite happily (it had, after all, dismissed me, expelled me from its modest production). Of course any city can do without anyone, we're not essential anywhere, not even to the few people who say they miss our presence or claim they couldn't live without us, because everyone seeks substitutes and, sooner or later, finds them, or else ends up resigned to our absence and feels so comfortable in that mood of resignation that they no longer wish to introduce any changes, not even to allow the lost or much-mourned person to return, not even to take us in again . . . Who knows who will replace us, we know only that we will be replaced, on all occasions and in all circumstances and in every role, and the void or gap we believed we left or really did leave is of no importance, regardless of how we disappeared or died, whether far too young or after a long life, whether violently or peacefully: it's the same with love and friendship, with work and influence, with machinations and with fear, with domination and even longing itself, with hatred, which also wearies of us in the end, and with the desire for vengeance, which darkens and changes its objective when it lingers and delays, as Tupra had urged me not to do; with the houses we inhabit, with the rooms we grew up in and the cities that accept us, with the corridors we raced madly along as children and the windows we gazed dreamily out of as adolescents, with the telephones that persuade and patiently listen to us and laugh in our ear or murmur agreement, at work and at play, in shops and in offices, at our counters and our desks, playing card games or chess, with the childhood landscape we thought was ours alone and with the streets that grow exhausted from seeing so many fade away, generation after generation, all meeting the same sad end; with restaurants and walks and pleasant parks and fields, on balconies and belvederes from which we watched the passing of so many moons they grew bored with looking at us, and with our armchairs and chairs and sheets, until not a trace, not a vestige of our smell remains and they're torn up to make rags or cloths, and even our kisses are replaced and the person left behind closes her eyes when she kisses the easier to forget us (if the pillow is still the same, or so that we don't reappear in some sudden, treacherous, irrepressible mental vision); with memories and thoughts and daydreams and with everything, and so we are all of us like snow on shoulders, slippery and docile, and the snow always stops . . .

It had been some time since I visited Madrid, from which I, too, had evaporated or faded, leaving not a trace behind or so it seemed, or perhaps all that remained of me was the rim, (which is the part that takes longest to remove), and also my own first name, which I had not yet left behind me, not having yet reached that state of strangeness. I hadn't ceased to exist, of course, in my father's house, not there, but I wasn't referring to his home, but to the home that was once mine. And now I would perhaps find out who had replaced me, even if he was only temporary and had no intention of staying, the permanent replacement takes his time or patiently awaits his turn, the one who will truly replace us always hangs back and lets others go ahead to be burned on the pyre that Luisa one day lit for us and which continues to burn, consuming all who come near, and which does not automatically extinguish itself once we've been burned to a cinder. I wouldn't need to worry that much about whoever happened to be by her side now, or only a little, just a touch, because of the mere fact that he *was* by her side and by the side of my children too.

I had decided not to give them prior warning from London, but to wait until I arrived, so that my phone call could be followed immediately by a semi-surprise visit. I wanted to make sure they were home – I knew the hours they kept, but there are always exceptions and emergencies – and then turn up a few minutes later, full of smiles and laden with presents. To see the children's excitement and, out of the corner of my eye, Luisa's amused, perhaps briefly nostalgic expression, that would allow me a simulacrum of triumph and a flicker of illusory hope, enough perhaps to sustain me during that artificial two-week sojourn, which seemed to me far too long the moment the plane touched down.

I stayed at a hotel and not at my father's house, for I had learned from my brothers and my sister – rather than from him, for he never spoke about his problems – that his health had deteriorated badly over the last two months, after the doctors discovered that he'd had three mini-strokes – as they called them – of which he had been entirely unaware, not even knowing when they'd occurred; and although my brothers, my sister, some of his granddaughters and my sisters-in-law often dropped in to

233

see him, there had, in the end, been no alternative but to provide him with a live-in carer, a rather nice Colombian lady, who
slept in the bedroom I would have occupied, and who relieved
his maid, who was getting on in years now, of some of her tasks.
I didn't want to upset the new order with my presence. With
my current salary, I could easily afford the Palace Hotel, and so I
booked a suite there. It was easier for me to stay at a hotel than
in someone else's house, even that of my father or of my best
friends, male and female, the women being rather more hospi-
table: with them I would not only have felt like an intruder but
also an exile from my own home, whereas in a hotel, I could
pretend I was a visiting foreigner, although not a tourist, and feel
less acutely that unpleasant sense of having been repudiated and
then offered shelter.

I spoke to my father on the phone, as usual a brief conversation, although now he didn't have the excuse that I was calling
him from England, which he assumed must be a very expensive thing to do (he belonged to a thrifty generation who only
used the phone to give or receive messages, although Wheeler
wasn't like that, so perhaps it was a generation that existed only
in Spain), and I arranged to see him the next day. His voice
sounded normal, just as it had on the last few occasions when
I had called from London, I phoned him every week or even
more frequently sometimes; he sounded slightly tired, but no
more than that, and disliked having to hold the phone to his
ear for too long. The strange thing was, though, that he made
no fuss about the prospect of seeing me and expressed no excitement, as if we had seen each other only a couple of days
before, if not yesterday. It was as if he suddenly had little sense of
time or its passing, and kept those people closest to him, those
he knew best, always in his thoughts, either so as not to miss
them quite so much, their palpable presence I mean, or so as not
really to notice their absence. I was simply me, one of his children,
and therefore unchanging and sufficiently established in his mind
for him not to feel my physical absence or my distance or the
unusually long gaps between visits or, rather, the non-existence
of those visits. He hardly went out now. 'I've flown over from

London, Papa,' I said, 'I'll be here for a couple of weeks.' 'Good. And how are things?' he asked, showing no particular surprise. 'Oh, not too bad. But we'll have a proper talk tomorrow when I come and see you. Today, I want to go and see the kids. I probably won't even recognise them.' 'They were here a few days ago with their mother. She doesn't visit that often, but she comes when she can. And she phones me.' Luisa was not as fixed and stable as I was, which is why he could remember when she came to see him and when she didn't – she was, up to a point, still new to him. 'She must be incredibly busy,' I said as if she were still part of my life and I had to apologise for her. I knew there was no need, she was very fond of my father, and, besides, her own father had died a few years before, and she had, insofar as such a thing is possible, replaced that lost figure with *my* father. If she didn't go and see him more often, it must be because she really couldn't find the time. 'Was she looking pretty?' I asked stupidly. 'Luisa is always pretty. Why do you ask? You must see her more than I do.' He knew about our separation, I hadn't hidden it from him, as one does occasionally hide potentially upsetting news from the elderly. 'I'm living in England now, Papa,' I reminded him, 'and I haven't seen her for a while.' He said nothing for a moment, then: 'I know you're living in England. Well, if that's what you want. I hope your stay in Oxford is proving fruitful.' It wasn't that he didn't know I was living in London, but now and then he got the different times confused, which isn't that surprising really, since time is a continuum in which we are all caught up until we apparently cease to be.

I had to phone Luisa before going to her house, not only to make sure the children would be there, but out of respect for her. I still had the keys to the apartment and she wouldn't necessarily have changed the locks; I could probably just walk in, without warning, causing first shock and then surprise; but that seemed an abuse to me, she wouldn't like it at all, and besides I risked bumping into my temporary replacement, whoever he was, assuming she had granted him habitual access. It was unlikely, but when in doubt, it's best to do nothing: it would have been embarrassing and I would have liked it even less than she. It turned my stomach, the mere idea of finding a complete stranger sitting in my place on the sofa or preparing a quick supper in the kitchen or watching television with the children in order to appear all fatherly and friendly, or making out he was Guillermo's best friend. I was prepared to be told this as a fact, but not actually to see it and then, unable to forget it, have that picture in my mind once I was back in London.

I dialled her number, it was mid-afternoon, the children would be back from school. She picked up the phone, and when I told her I was in Madrid, she was really shocked and took a while to respond, as if she were rapidly taking stock of the situation in the light of this unforeseen event, and then: why didn't you warn me, how could you, it's not fair; I wanted to give you all a surprise, well, the kids mostly, and I'd still like it to be a surprise, so don't tell them I'm here, just let me walk through the door without them knowing a thing, they're not going out this evening, I assume, can I come over now?

'They're not going out, but I am,' she replied hastily and somewhat flustered, so much so that I even wondered – I couldn't help it – if it was true or if she had just made a last-minute decision to leave the house, I mean, to skedaddle, so as not to be there when I arrived, so that she wouldn't have to see me or meet me.

'You've got to go out now?' I had counted on her presence, on her benevolent gaze when the four of us met once more, it wouldn't be the same without her as witness.

'Yes, any moment actually, I'm just waiting for the babysitter,' she said. 'In fact, let me phone her right now, before she sets off, to warn her that you're coming. She doesn't know you, and she might not want to let you in unless she's forewarned, I've told her not to open the door to strangers under any circumstances, and you, I'm afraid, would be a stranger to her. Hang up now so that I can call her, and I'll call you right back. Where are you?'

I gave her the numbers of the hotel and my room. It was as if she were in the most terrific hurry, besides, nowadays you can track down a babysitter anywhere and at any time even if they're not at home, they all have mobile phones. It occurred to me that

236

she had not in fact yet spoken to the babysitter and was phoning her now so that the babysitter could race over to deal with this unexpected situation – hence the urgency – and have time to arrive, and give Luisa time to leave, before I appeared. Even if this was a genuine spur-of-the-moment decision to go out, she would never just assume that my key would still work and thus leave the children alone, not even for a minute, to wait for me there unaware they were waiting. I had the awful feeling she was trying to avoid me. But I couldn't be sure, perhaps I'd grown too used to interpreting people, those I came across at work and outside as well, to analysing every inflection of voice and every gesture and to seeing something hidden behind any show of haste or delay. This was no way to go about the world, all it did was feed my imaginings.

She took what seemed an age to call back, long enough for me to grow impatient, to rekindle my suspicions, and to hope she would dispel them by telling me she'd cancelled her date. And to think, too, that she was playing for time, I mean, allowing time for the babysitter to get there and so delay my setting off in the same direction, towards our apartment which was no longer mine. I sat motionless on the bed, which is what you do when you're expecting something to happen from one moment to the next, a wretched expression that makes every second seem an eternity and leaves us dangling. More than a quarter of an hour had passed when the phone finally rang.

'Hi, it's me,' said Luisa, as young Pérez Nuix had done when she rang my doorbell on that night of heavy, sustained rain, but with much more justification, after all, as far as I was concerned she had been an unequivocal 'me' for many years – that's usually taken for granted in marriages, that there is only one 'me' – and, by then, I had been waiting for her call for some time. She was also within her rights to assume that I would recognise her without any need for further identification – who else would it be, who else but me, but her – from the first word and the first instant, and she could be almost sure of occupying most or many of my thoughts, although that wouldn't be high on her agenda just then, her mind was elsewhere, or she was trying to combine that elsewhere with my unwanted presence, for I couldn't shake off the feeling that I was just that, a nuisance. 'Sorry, the babysitter's phone was busy, and I've only just managed to get through to her. Anyway, she knows you'll be coming and that she's not to spoil your surprise, so she won't say anything to the children. How long will it take you to get here?'

'I don't know, about twenty minutes I should think, I'll take a cab.'

'Then would you mind not leaving for another fifteen or twenty minutes, that will give her time to settle in and sort the kids out. And please try not to keep them up too long past their bedtime, otherwise they'll be worn out tomorrow and they've got school in the morning. If possible, make sure they're in bed by eleven at the latest, which is already much later than usual. You'll have other opportunities to see them. How long are you staying?'

'Two weeks,' I said, and again it seemed to me that this created another unforeseen problem for her, that it was even an annoyance, a bother, something she would have to wrestle with.

'That long?' She couldn't suppress her feelings, she sounded more alarmed than glad. 'How come?'

'As I think I told you, I had to accompany my boss on a trip. In the end, it turned out to be four trips, one after the other. Anyway, he's rewarded me, I suppose, with a longer trip just for me.' And I added: 'So I won't see you tonight, then?'

'No, I don't think so, by the time I get back the children will be in bed. The babysitter will stay as long as she needs to, so don't worry about that; as soon as they're in bed, you can leave, don't wait up for me. If you'd warned me you were coming, I'd have arranged things differently. We'll talk later, when we've got more time.'

The same city, which, just the day before, was faded and dim, becomes suddenly crystal-clear as soon as you set foot in it again; time condenses, yesterday disappears – or becomes just an interval – and it's as if you had never left. You suddenly know once more which streets to take, and in which order, to get from one place to another, wherever they may be, and how much time to allow. I had reckoned on twenty minutes by taxi to my apartment through the abominable traffic, and I was almost exactly right. And instead of thinking excitedly about my children, whom I would be seeing at last after a long absence, I couldn't help worrying about Luisa instead during the whole disenchanted journey. It wasn't that I had expected her to give me a wonderful reception, but I'd thought at least she'd show a little curiosity and sympathy, as she had on the phone whenever I'd spoken to her from London, what had changed, why had she turned against me, was it because I was now breathing the same air as her? Perhaps she had only felt that sympathy and that vague curiosity about me from a distance, as long as I was far away, as long as I was just a voice in her ear, a voice with no face, no body, no eyes, no arms; then she could allow herself those feelings, but not here, not where we had lived happily together and where, later on, we had wounded each other. This was where she had survived without me, become unaccustomed to me, and so she didn't quite know what to do with me any more: I hadn't been around for quite some time. She said not a word about her date, which had arisen, or so it seemed to me, as soon as she learned that I was there in the flesh. She was under no obligation to tell me, of course, and I hadn't asked, nor had I suggested that she cancel, which is easy enough and perfectly free and something that people do on the slightest pretext, simply because they feel like it ('Oh, please, please, today's a really special day, I would so love to see all of you together, surely you can change it, go on, why don't you try?'); and people usually do give explanations even if they're not asked, and provide needless excuses, and tell you about their inane life and speak at length and babble on, out of the sheer pleasure of using language, or so as to provide superfluous information or to avoid silences, or to provoke jealousy or envy or so as not to arouse suspicions by being enigmatic. 'The fatal word', Wheeler had called it. 'The curse of the word. Talking and talking, without stopping, that is the one thing for which no one ever lacks ammunition. That is the wheel that moves the world, Jacobo, more than anything else; that is the engine of life, the one that never becomes exhausted and never stops, that is its life's breath.' Luisa had held in that breath and said only: 'They're not going out, but I am,' without even adding the minimal excuses usual in such cases, 'It's an appointment I can't break, I made it weeks ago,' or 'It's too late to cancel,' or 'I can't postpone it because the people I'm meeting are visiting Madrid and they're leaving tomorrow.' Nor had she expressed polite regret at the clash, even if that regret was false (it still gives some small consolation to the jilted person and makes him feel better): 'Oh, how annoying, what bad luck, what a shame, I would love to have seen the children's reaction when they saw it was you. If only I'd known about it beforehand. Are you sure you can't wait until tomorrow? It's been such a long time.' She had kept her mouth shut, just as if she didn't know who her date was or where she was going, more as if she had just made it up than as if she wanted to keep it secret. That was my suspicion, an occupational hazard perhaps, acquired in England. She must have somewhere to go, somewhere to spend a few hours, the hours I would spend in her apartment. She was sure by now to have a boyfriend, a lover, however transient. It would just be a matter of finding him, or probably not even that if he'd already given her the keys to his place. 'It's as if she doesn't want to see me,' I thought in the taxi. 'But she's going to, that's for sure. I didn't come here to spend yet another day without seeing her, without once more seeing her face.'

The children were hugely surprised. At first, Marina gave me a hard, distrustful stare, then she got used to me, but more in the way that small children get used to strangers – it takes only a matter of minutes if the adult in question has a way with kids – than as if she really remembered me clearly and in detail. It also helped that her brother filled her in right from the start ('It's Papa, silly, don't you see?'). The presents helped to ease matters too, and the babysitter's approving, almost beatific smile, she was a very able young woman who came to open the door to me: I didn't dare try my key in the lock, in case it had been changed, I rang the bell like any other visitor. Marina asked me absurd questions ('Where do you live?' 'Have you got a dog?' 'Does it always rain there?' 'Are there any bears?'), while Guillermo was in charge of asking questions of a more reproachful kind ('Why don't we ever see you?' 'Do you like it better there than here?' 'Have you met any English children?') as well as of the bookish-adventure film variety, he read quite a lot and watched films all the time ('Have you visited Harry Potter's school?' 'And what about Sherlock Holmes' house?' 'Aren't you afraid to go out at night with all that fog and with Jack the Rippers about, or aren't there any Jack the Rippers in London now?' 'Is it true that if the real person stands next to his wax figure at Madame Tussaud's, you can't tell which is which?'). I hadn't visited Harry Potter's school, but I had been to 221B Baker Street, because I lived nearby and often popped in; and in York, I had discovered the dark, neglected grave of Dick Turpin, the highwayman in the red jacket, mask, three-cornered hat and thigh-high boots, and next to him was buried his faithful horse, or rather mare, *Black Bess*, and I had seen the place where, still elegantly dressed, he had been hanged at the Tyburn, just outside York. One night, a white dog had followed me, tis tis tis, through the streets and squares and parks to my house, he was all alone in the heavy rain, for children it would be much more mysterious if I didn't mention his mistress; I let him dry himself and sleep in my apartment, and yes, I would have kept him, but he left the following morning when I took him out for a walk, and I've never seen him since, perhaps he didn't like my human food, well, I didn't have any dog food. On another night, I saw a man take out a sword in a disco, a two-edged sword, he produced it from inside his coat and threatened people, who drew back in terror; he sliced through several things with great skill and mastery, a table, a couple of chairs, some curtains, he shattered a few bottles and ripped the skirts of two women without causing them the slightest harm, he judged things perfectly, he was a real artist; then he put the sword back in the sheath inside his long coat, put the coat on – this made him walk very stiffly, like a ghost – and he left just like that, and no one dared to stop him; I didn't either, what do you mean, are you mad, he would have made mincemeat of me in seconds, he was so fast with that sword (like thunderless lightning that kills silently). I was about to tell them that I had spent a third night at the house of Wendy, Peter Pan's girlfriend, but I held back: Marina was young enough to believe it, but not Guillermo, and I didn't want to recall the videos I had been shown there, in fact, I didn't want ever to remember them and yet I thought of them constantly ('The wind moves the sea and the boats withdraw, with hurrying oars and full sails. Amongst the sound of the waves the rifle shots rang out . . . Cursèd be the noble heart that puts its trust in evil men! . . . Aboard the boats, all the sailors were crying, and the most beautiful women, all in black and distraught, walk, crying, through the lemon groves.' That poem about Torrijos would always be associated in my mind with that string of evil scenes). And I realised – I had forgotten, it was such a long time since I'd spoken to Guillermo and Marina – that almost everything that happens to one, can, with very few changes, easily be converted into a story for children. Intriguing or sinister tales, the kind that protect and prepare them and make them resourceful.

Once they had gone to bed, I was sure for the first time in many months that they were safe and sound; time again condensed or concertinaed, and for a few seconds I felt as if I had never left their side and never known Tupra or Pérez Nuix, Mulryan or Rendel; when, shortly afterwards, I tiptoed into their respective rooms, to turn out the lights and to check if they were all right, the Tintin book the boy must have been reading just before he fell asleep had slipped to the floor without waking him, and the girl was embracing a little bear destined once more to be smothered by the diminutive arm of her simple dreams. Almost nothing had changed in my absence. Only Luisa, who wasn't there, and although I was, I still hadn't seen her. In her place was a discreet babysitter, and she had kept out of the way, hadn't interfered in the reunion at all, she had merely helped with the children when it was time for supper and bed. She said her name was Mercedes, even though she was Polish: perhaps it was an adopted name, to hispanicise herself more quickly. She spoke good Spanish, she had learned it during the three years she had been there, before that, she hadn't known a word, she said, but her boyfriend was from Madrid, and she was thinking of getting married and settling there (I noticed she wore a little crucifix around her neck), she told me all this while I was playing for time. 'Don't wait up for me,' Luisa had warned, well, it had sounded to me rather like a warning. She was perfectly within her rights not to want me there while she was not, I might have started snooping, looking for anything that might have changed and poking around in her mail, opening her wardrobes and sniffing her clothes, going into her bathroom and smelling her shampoo and her cologne, checking to see if she still kept a photo of me in her bedroom (unlikely), although in the living room there were still a few family snapshots in which I appeared, the four of us together, she wouldn't want the children to forget me completely, at least not my face.

'Do you often come here?' I asked Mercedes. 'The children seem to know you well and they do as they're told.' This wasn't an entirely innocent question.

'Yes, sometimes, but not that often. Luisa doesn't go out much at night. Although she has gone out more lately, usually in the evening.' And then she betrayed Luisa, although she certainly didn't intend to, but she did, without lingering or delaying – people just have to start speaking in order to tell too much, even when they don't seem to be telling anything; they supply the listener with information as soon as they open their mouth, without being asked and without realising that it *is* information, and so they give someone away without intending to, or they betray themselves, and no sooner are the words out than it's too late: 'Oh, I didn't realise, how stupid of me, I didn't mean to' – 'She was lucky to find me in. She doesn't normally leave it so late to call me, she always phones at least the day before. I might have been booked somewhere else, because I babysit for four different families. Four, excluding Luisa.'

'She was lucky then. How much notice did she give you?'

'None. Just enough time for me to get here. I normally have to catch a bus and a metro, but tonight she said she'd pay for my taxi. The thing is, there aren't that many taxis where I live, which is why it took me so long. "Come as soon as you can," she said, "something urgent's cropped up." She told me about your visit and that I should let you in. But I would have looked through the peephole and let you in anyway, because I know you from the photographs.' And she gestured shyly towards them, as if she were embarrassed to have noticed.

So my suspicions had been right, perhaps all that practice in the office with no name had not been in vain. Luisa hadn't intended to go out, she'd done so in order not to see me. She hadn't dared make me postpone my meeting with the kids, she would have found it far harder to come up with a credible excuse ('That long,' she had said, aware that it really was a long time). Where would she have gone, it isn't easy to spend hours away from home if you've nothing planned, when evening starts to come on, at twilight. She could have gone to the cinema, any film would do, or gone shopping downtown, although she really hated that; she could have sought refuge with her lover, or gone to see a friend or her sister. She would have to kill an awful lot of time until I left, until she reckoned that I would have left the apartment and the coast would be clear, and she would know, too, how hard I'd find it to drag myself away, I felt very comfortable there, almost nothing had changed.

It was past eleven o'clock, which was the very latest the children were allowed to stay up on special occasions, we'd had a very entertaining few hours, but I could see they were tired too, it hadn't been particularly hard to persuade them that it was high time they went to bed, and Mercedes was in equal parts persuasive and firm. It wouldn't be long before Luisa was back. If I hung on for another half an hour, we'd almost certainly meet. I could at least say hello, give her a kiss on the cheek, perhaps a hug if that seemed appropriate, hear her voice, no longer disembodied, see how she had changed, whether she had grown slightly faded or was perhaps more beautiful now that I was far away and she had someone more flattering closer to hand; I could at least see her face. I wanted no more than that, so very little, but I was filled with impatience, an unbearable impatience. Added to that were feelings of insecurity, intrigue, possibly rancour, or perhaps wounded pride: she didn't even share my elementary curiosities, but how could that be after we had been each other's main motive for so many years, it seemed positively insulting that nothing should remain, that she was quite happy to wait another whole day and not even necessarily see me tomorrow – there was no guarantee that, on various pretexts, she wouldn't also avoid me tomorrow and the day after and the day after that, and so on, during the whole of my stay; she might even suggest I pick up the kids downstairs at the entry door on my next visit and take them out somewhere or arrange it so that when I arrived, she'd always be out, or else she might drop them off at my father's apartment so that I could spend time with them there and they'd get to see their grandfather as well. Yes, it was rude of her to be in so little hurry to recognise me in the changed man, the absent man, the solitary man, the foreigner returned; not to immediately want to find out what I was like without her, or who I had become. ('What a disgrace it is to me to remember thy name, or to know thy face tomorrow,' I thought.)

'Do you mind if I stay a bit, until Luisa comes?' I asked the false Mercedes. 'I'd like to see her, just for a moment. She won't be much longer, I shouldn't think.' – 'What a painful irony,' I thought, 'here I am asking the permission of a young Polish babysitter whom I've never seen in my life to stay a little longer in my own apartment or what was my apartment, and which I chose and set up and furnished and decorated along with Luisa, in which we lived together for a long time, and which I still pay for, indirectly. Once you abandon a place you can never go back, not in the same way, any gap you leave is instantly filled or else your things are thrown away or dumped, and if you do reappear it's only as an incorporeal ghost, with no rights, no key, no claims and no future. With nothing but a past, which is why we can be shooed away.'

'Luisa said I should stay until she got back,' she said. 'She's going to pay for my taxi home as well, if she's very late. So that I don't have to wait to catch a *buho*, there aren't many during the week.' – The word *buho* rang a bell in that context, they were, I seemed to recall, the late-night buses or metros, I'd forgotten all about them. – 'There's really no point in waiting,' she added. 'She's likely to be some time yet. I'll be here if the children should wake up, if they need anything.'

She was very discreet, but her words sounded discouraging, almost like orders. As if Luisa had briefed her when she phoned and what she was really saying to me was: 'No, the best thing would be if you left, because Luisa doesn't want to see you. And she doesn't want you hanging around when she's not here, unchecked and unwatched – my presence isn't enough; I don't have any authority – she doesn't trust you any more, she stopped trusting you some time ago.' Or else: 'She's erased you, all these months she's been scrubbing away at the stain you left and now she's struggling to remove the rim, the final remnant. She doesn't want you to leave any more stains and to see all her hard work ruined. So please be so kind as to go, if not, you'll be considered an intruder.' And these last two interpretations of her words were what made me decide once and for all to stay.

'No, I think I'll wait for her anyway,' I said and sat down on the sofa, after first having taken a book from the shelves. The books hadn't changed, they were in the same arrangement and order in which I had left them, there was my entire library, I mean, our library, we hadn't divided the books up, and I had nowhere to put mine, everything in England was provisional and, besides, I had no space, and I wasn't going to start moving things if I didn't know where I was going to live, either in the short term or the long. Mercedes wouldn't dare oppose me, she wouldn't dare throw me out if I sat down and read and said nothing, if I asked her no more questions and didn't bother her or try to worm things out of her. She hadn't realised that was what I was doing, or perhaps only when it was too late. 'I'm in no hurry,' I added, 'I've just arrived from London. This way I'll be able to say hello to her – in Madrid and in person.'

I waited and waited, reading in silence, listening to the small noises that seemed either eerily familiar or instantly recognisable: the fridge with its changing moods, occasional distant footfalls in the apartment above and a sound like drawers being opened and closed – the upstairs neighbours obviously hadn't moved and kept up their nocturnal customs; there were also the faint notes of a cello coming from the boy who lived with his widowed mother across the landing and who always practised before he went to bed, he might well be almost an adolescent by now, his playing had improved a lot, he got stuck or stopped less often from what I could hear, which wasn't much, the boy always tried not to play too loudly, he was well-brought-up and used to say 'Good afternoon' to us even when he was only small, but in a friendly not a cloying way, I tried to work out if he was playing something by Purcell or by Dowland, but I couldn't, the chords were very tenuous and my musical memory was out of training, in London I listened to music at home and rarely went to concerts, not that I spent much time at home, where I couldn't rely on the consoling daze that sustained me daily and liberated me from the curse of having to make plans. The only thing I knew for sure was that the music being played wasn't Bach.

The Polish babysitter got out her mobile phone and made a call, retreating into the kitchen so that she could talk to her boyfriend where I wouldn't hear her, perhaps out of modesty, perhaps in order not to bother me with a schmaltzy or perhaps obscene conversation (however Catholic she was, you never can tell). It occurred to me that if I hadn't been there, she would have used Luisa's landline, on which she could talk at greater length because she would be saving herself the expense, for that reason alone it must have really irritated her that I hadn't left when I should have. I had taken *Henry V* down from the shelves, because Wheeler had quoted from it and referred to it in his house by the River Cherwell, and since then I had kept it handy and dipped into it or leafed through it now and then, even though I had long since found the fragments he'd alluded to. Or, rather, what I picked up was *King Henry V*, to give it its full title, a copy of the old Arden edition, bought in 1977 in Madrid according to a note I had written on the first page, and at some point I had written in it, although I couldn't remember when – but before I would have met Luisa – and my mind was in no fit state to pay due attention to the text or to trawl back through the past, I merely glanced through it, looking at the underlinings left by the young reader I had been on some distant day, so long forgotten that it no longer existed. My mind was concentrating on one noise only, which is why I heard all the other noises too, my ear cocked and waiting for the sound that mattered to me, that of the lift coming up, followed by the key in the door. I heard the first several times, but it always stopped at other floors and only once at ours, and on that occasion it was not accompanied by the second sound and wasn't Luisa returning.

Mercedes returned to the living room, looking happier and more relaxed. She was an attractive girl, but so excessively blonde and pale and cold that she appeared not to be. She asked if I would mind if she turned on the TV, and I said I didn't, although that was a lie, because the sound of the television would wipe out all other sounds; but I was there as a mere unexpected visitor, if not an out-and-out intruder, which I was more and more becoming with each minute I lingered there. The young woman used the remote control to flip through the channels and finally opted for a film with real animals in the main roles, it was as I realised at once, *Babe*, I recalled taking Guillermo to see it at the cinema a few years before, it was mystifying why the moronic programmers should put it on at that hour, when most

248

children would be asleep. I was happy to watch it for a while, it was less demanding than Shakespeare and the little pig was a great actor, I wondered if perhaps he had been nominated for an Oscar that year, but I doubt he would have won; I would buy it on DVD for Marina, who, having been born later, might not have seen it. I was just considering the sad fate of actors – anyone can do their job, children and dogs, elephants, monkeys and pigs, but, so far, no one has found an animal capable of composing music or writing a book; although, of course, that depends on how strict you are with your definition of animal – when I saw Mercedes spring to her feet, scoop up her things in a matter of seconds and, after addressing an abrupt 'Goodbye' to me, race to the front door. Only when Mercedes was already there did I hear the key in the lock and the door opening, it was as if she was endowed with extraordinarily acute hearing and had picked up the exact moment when Luisa arrived at the street door in a car or taxi. She, the babysitter, must have been in a tremendous hurry to leave, she clearly didn't want to stay any longer than it took for her to be paid and provided with her promised expensive transportation home, for it was nearly midnight, Luisa had been out for a little over four hours. Or perhaps it wasn't just that, perhaps she wanted to warn Luisa immediately that, contrary to her expectations, she wouldn't find herself alone: that I had insisted on waiting for her, against her wishes, or perhaps in disobedience to the orders that Mercedes had received and failed to enforce.

I heard them whispering for a few moments, I got up from the sofa, but didn't dare to join them; then I heard the door close, the Polish babysitter had gone. After that came the sound of Luisa's footsteps in the corridor – she was wearing high heels, I recognised the click-clack on the wooden floor – she always wore them to go out – heading towards the bathroom and her bedroom, she didn't even look in at me, she must be desperate for a pee, I assumed, as one so often is on arriving home; that seemed quite normal really, if she'd been with other people and not wanted to get up, for example, during a meal, either at someone's table or in a restaurant. Or perhaps she wanted to tidy up before showing herself to me, assuming she had spent the evening with my ephemeral replacement and was returning as women sometimes do return from such prolonged encounters, with her skirt all wrinkled and slightly askew, her hair dishevelled, her lipstick erased by kisses, a run in her tights and the signs of all that impetuosity still in her eyes. Or perhaps she was so angry with me that she had decided to go to bed without even saying hello and to leave me in the living room until I got fed up or until I understood that when she had said she wasn't going to see me that night, she had meant it. She'd probably decided to shut herself in the bedroom and not come out, to get undressed, turn off the light and climb into bed, pretending that I wasn't there, that I was still in London and did not exist in Madrid, or that I was a mere ghost. She was perfectly capable of that and more – I knew what she was like – whenever anyone tried to impose something on her that she didn't want. But she would have to leave the bedroom before she closed her eyes, at least once, and if the worst came to the worst, I could intercept her then, for it would be quite beyond her powers not to go in and see the children and make sure they were safe and sleeping peacefully.

I continued to wait, I didn't want to rush anything, still less go and pound on her door, beg her to let me see her, bombard her with awkward questions through that barrier, and demand explanations I had no right to demand. That would have been a bad start, after such a long separation, it would be best to avoid anything that smacked of confrontation or reproach, unnecessary and absurd and not at all what I wanted. From now on, the initiative lay with her, I had already made things awkward for her by refusing to leave, once the excuse of enjoying spending time with my children had lapsed. On hearing the key in the door, I had muted the TV, but could still see the antics of that porcine emulator of De Niro and John Wayne – he was an extremely polite little pig – and his co-stars: a few dogs, some sheep, a horse, a bad-tempered duck, all of them superb actors.

After a few minutes, I heard the door of her bedroom open and a few footsteps, she was still wearing her high heels, so she obviously hadn't changed her clothes, but she walked more quietly, trying not to make any noise: she peered into Marina's room and then into Guillermo's, she didn't go right in or only a little way, just far enough to see that everything was in order. I still didn't want to get up and go and find her, I preferred for her to come into the living room, if she did, and when at last she did – her footsteps firmer, normal, now that she had breathed in the sound of the children's deep sleep, which had been enough to reassure her that she ran no risk of waking them – I thought I understood, despite any efforts at concealment she may have made in the bathroom that had once been mine, why she had wanted to avoid me, and that it hadn't been because she didn't want to see me, but because she didn't want me to see her.

At first sight, she looked very good, well-dressed, well-shod, although rather less well-coiffed, and yet wearing her long locks caught back in a ponytail suited her, gave her a youthful, naïve air, almost that of a young girl caught in flagrante on returning home late, but who was I to say anything, or even to feel surprised. Before I noticed anything was wrong, she had time to say a few words, with an expression on her face of mingled pleasure to see me and annoyance at finding me there, but also of fear that I had caught her out or perhaps it was embarrassment doing battle with defiance, as if I had surprised her doing something I wouldn't like or that would seem to me reprehensible, and, realising that, she didn't know whether to strike her flag or to run it up the flagpole and stand and fight, it's odd how former couples, long after they have ceased being a couple, still feel mutually responsible, as if they owed each other a certain loyalty, even if that amounts only to knowing how they're coping on their own and what's going on in their life, especially if something strange or bad is happening. Things were happening to me about which I, being far away, had said nothing: I had clearly lost my footing or lost both grip and judgement, employed as I was in a job about whose consequences I knew nothing, not even if it *had* any consequences, and being paid a suspiciously large salary too; I had, by then, been injected with strange poisons and was leading an existence that grew ghostlier by the day, immersed in the

dream-like state of one who lives in another country and is starting not always to think in his own language, I was very alone
there in London, even though I was surrounded by people all day,
they were just work colleagues and never really developed into
pure friendships, even Pérez Nuix had turned out to be no different – not even my lover, which she wasn't, since there had been
no repetition and no laughter – after that one night I had shared
with her carnally, a fact we had kept concealed and excessively silent, from others and from ourselves, and when one pretends that
something hasn't happened and it's never spoken of, it ends up
not having happened, even though we know the opposite to be
the case; what Jorge Manrique wrote in his 'Lines on the Death
of His Father' some five hundred and thirty years ago, and only
two years before his own early death when he was not yet forty,
wounded during an attack on a castle by a shot from a harquebus
(even worse and more dishonourable than that of Richard Yea
and Nay, felled by an arrow from a crossbow), 'If we judge wisely,
we will count what has not happened as the past' is as true as the
contrary position which allows us to count the past, along with
everything else we have experienced, our entire life, as also not
having happened. Then what does it matter what we do in our
lives, or why it does it matter so very much to us?

'You just *had* to stay, didn't you, Jaime?' Luisa said before I
could say anything. 'You just had to wait up to see me.'

Now, though, after that initial glance, I spotted what was wrong
at once, it was impossible not to, at least for me. She had tried
to cover it with make-up, to conceal it, hide it, perhaps in the
same way that Flavia would have tried unsuccessfully, with the
unlikely help of Tupra in the Ladies toilet, to make the wound
on her face invisible, the mark of the rope, the weal left by the
whip, the welt caused by De la Garza's clumsy lashings during
his wild gyrations on the fast dance floor. That wasn't what
Luisa had on her face, it wasn't *uno sfregio*, not a gash or a cut or
a scratch, but what has always been known in my language as '*un
ojo morado*' – literally 'a purple eye' – and in English as 'a black
eye', although since the impact or cause was not recent, the skin
was already growing yellow, the colours that appear after such a

blow are always mixed, there's never a single colour, but several, which combine at every phase and keep changing, perhaps the disagreement between the two languages stems from that (although mine does lean more to English when it refers to such an eye as '*un ojo a la funerala*' – more or less 'an eye in mourning'), they always take a long time to fade, it was just our bad luck that not enough time had yet passed. When I saw it, I no longer had to respond to her words, nor to apologise. Unfortunately, I couldn't greet her either or give her a kiss or embrace her, I had waited so long for this meeting and now I couldn't even manage a smile or an '*Hola, niña*' – 'Hello, love' – as I used to when we were still together and on good terms. I immediately went over to her and the first thing I said was:

'What's that? Let me see? What happened? Who did it?'

I took her face in my hands, taking care not to touch the affected area, she had clearly just been in the bathroom applying various creams, to no avail. Her eyelid was no longer puffy or only a little, but it obviously had been. I calculated that the injury must have occurred about a week or perhaps ten days ago, and it was the result of a blow, I was sure of that, dealt by a fist or a blunt instrument like a bat or a blackjack, I had seen such bruised eyes and cheekbones and chins years before, under the Franco regime, when students who had been arrested and beaten up would emerge from the police station, from the headquarters of the security forces in Puerta del Sol or from Carabanchel prison, my fellow university students who'd had much worse luck than I did during the small semi-spontaneous street demonstrations that we called '*saltos*' and at illegal rallies that were broken up with the aid of very long, flexible truncheons, which really hurt because the truncheon flexed on impact, they were used by the police or '*grises*' who charged on horseback, sometimes it seems incredible to me that it was only in the mid-1970s that we used to flee their hooves every few days or weeks, as we left our classes. Although, of course, everything can come back.

She moved away, avoided me, retreating two steps in order to re-establish the distance between us, smiling as if my questions amused her, but I could see that they didn't.

'What do you mean? No one did anything to me. I collided with the garage door about a week ago. It was my wretched mobile phone's fault. Someone called me, I got distracted and misjudged the distance when the door was closing. It hit me full on, it's really heavy, it must be made of solid iron. It's nearly better now, it looked worse than it was. It doesn't hurt.'

'Your mobile phone? So you've got a mobile phone now? Why didn't you tell me? Why didn't you give me the number?' And while, in my surprise, I was asking her all this, I thought or remembered: 'Reresby made me say the same thing to De la Garza, I had to translate it for him while he was lying motionless on the floor, bruised and beaten: "Tell him that if he has to go to hospital, then he should give them the same line drunks and debtors do – that the garage door fell on him." Luisa has become neither of those things, neither a drunk nor a debtor, as far as I know. But Tupra was obviously aware that blows from garage doors are almost always inventions.' And thanks to him I was even more convinced that she was lying to me. She lacked the kind of imagination that a habitual liar develops, and so she had resorted to cliché, like any inexperienced liar who avoids the implausible, which is precisely the thing most likely to be believed.

'It's because of the kids,' she said. 'I realised that, however much we might hate mobile phones, there's no sense in a babysitter or my sister, for example, or the school, not being able to locate me immediately if anything should happen to them.' – So the Polish babysitter could have called Luisa's mobile phone from the kitchen and warned her that I was refusing to shift from the apartment, and also found out with some degree of accuracy when she would arrive. – 'Especially since you're not here. I bought it for my own peace of mind. Now that I'm alone with them, now that I'm the only person anyone can contact in an emergency. And anyway why would you need the number in London? It's not as if we still spoke every day . . .' – Unfortunately, I sensed no reproach in these last words, I wished I had. I couldn't stop looking at her purple, yellowish, bluish black eye, the white of which was still slightly red, it would have been criss-crossed with red veins during the first few days after the blow. She was pretending that she wasn't even aware of it, but she could see me staring at it and this made her slightly nervous, as became apparent when she turned to look at the television so that she was in profile, to escape my scrutiny. And she tried to change the subject too. 'What were you watching, a film about pigs? Is this some new interest of yours?' she added with the amiable irony that was so familiar to me and so attractive. She must have seen my fleeting smile. 'I'm sure the children would enjoy it. How did you think they looked, by the way? Have they grown a lot? Do they seem very different?'

While I did want to talk to her about the children, to tell her what impression they'd made on me after such a long time, I wasn't going to let myself be diverted so easily. I was the way I was, and now I had the examples of Tupra and Wheeler, who never let go of their prey as long as there was something to be got out of him or her, after all the digressions and evasions and detours.

'Don't lie to me, Luisa, you and I haven't changed that much. That business about the garage door is so old hat, they're always rebelling and hitting people,' I said, and again I noticed that I only called her by name when we were arguing or when I was angry, rather as she only called me Deza in similar situations, as well as in other very different ones. 'Tell me who did this to you. I hope it's not the guy you're going out with, because if it is, we've got a problem on our hands.'

'*Our* hands? Just supposing I was going out with someone, what's that got to do with you?' she said at once, parrying my remark not sharply, but firmly; and she had enough spirit to recover her irony and immediately soften the blow: 'If you're going to continue down that road, you'd better go back to watching your little animal friends while I tidy up, but once it's over, you leave; the children have to get up early, and it's already very late. We'll talk another day when we're both a bit fresher, but not about this. I told you what happened, so don't insist on seeing phantoms. And if that was just a way of asking me if I'm going out with someone, that's none of your business, Deza. Go on, finish watching your pig, and then go back to the hotel and sleep, you must be tired from your trip and from the children. They're exhausting, and you're out of practice being with them.'

She could always make me laugh and could always win me over. I still had a soft spot for her, and that hadn't changed during my time spent in London. This was hardly news – it was something that would probably never change – but being there with her only confirmed and made still plainer to me that I should, at all times, be careful not to allow myself unwittingly to be charmed, while she bustled around and took no notice of me. Quite apart from our conjugal life and our unforgotten love, Luisa was for me one of those people whose company you seek out and are grateful for and which, almost in itself, makes up for all the heartaches, and which you look forward to all day – it's our salvation – when you know you'll be seeing her later that evening like a prize won with very little effort; one of those people you feel at ease with even when times are bad and about whom you have the sense that wherever they are, that's where the party is, which is why it's so hard to give them up or to be expelled from their society, because you feel then that you're always missing out on something or – how can I put it – living on the margins. Thinking that such people could die is unbearable to us: even if we're far from them and never see them any more, we know they're still alive and that their world exists, the world that they themselves create merely by being and breathing; that the earth still shelters them and that they therefore retain their space and their sense of time, both of which one can imagine from a distance: 'There's the house,' we think, 'there's the atmosphere filled by her steps, by the rhythm of her day, the music of her voice, the smell of the plants she tends and the pause of her night; I no longer play any part in it, but there is the laughter, the wit and charm and the dear departed friends to whom Cervantes bade farewell when he was dying, "hoping to see you soon, happily installed in the other life". And knowing that therein lies all help, that we possess a memory not shared by everyone, which, as far as I'm concerned is the past, but not truly so, not in the absolute sense – that it's only by accident, or bad luck, or my own fault that I daily perceive it as the past – a place where others come and go and enjoy themselves without ever giving it much thought, just like us when we were part of that atmosphere and that rhythm, that wit and charm, part of the music of that house and even the pause of its quiet night. Knowing that it was not just a pleasant dream or something that existed in another imagined life.' And there I was, a witness to its permanence and not wanting to leave. There stood the person who was, for me, where the party was happening, with her good humour and her steadfastness and her frequent smiles, and even her high heels. That was enough, up to a point, knowing that she had not ceased to be, that she still trod the earth and still traversed the world, that she was not safe more or less in one-eyed, uncertain oblivion or already on the side of time where the dead converse.

And yet now there was a threat, or worse still there was an already visible wound that someone had inflicted and that might be repeated, possibly something worse next time, who knew (who knows when anything will stop once it's begun). What I did know was that nagging would get me nowhere: if she had decided not to tell me something or talk about it, there was no way I could twist her arm, I would have to find out by other means, but by what means, just then I could think of none apart from the kids, but I didn't want to use them, and then I was surprised to find myself thinking: 'I could always ask Tupra for help.' If, as I assumed, he had found out about the night Pérez Nuix had spent at my apartment and about the agreement we had reached behind his back; if, therefore, my favour to her had proved useless and Incompara had gained nothing from it, and young Pérez Nuix's father had received the inevitable beating for his recurring debts, a beating that Reresby had made me watch (the billiard cues – doubtless to inform me of my failure and to teach me a lesson), he would have no difficulty in finding out the name of the man Luisa was going out with, even though it was in another country and the wench, fortunately, was not yet dead. That had been one of my fears during my time in London, since my departure, when I thought about who would, sooner or later, replace me, and of the various possibilities that had always terrified me, the figure of the despotic possessive man, who subjugates and isolates and, little by little, quietly insinuates his demands and prohibitions, disguised as infatuation and weakness and jealousy and flattery and supplication, a devious sort who declines her first invitations to share her pillow in order not to appear intrusive and who reveals not a trace of any invasive or expansionist tendencies, and who initially appears always deferential, respectful, even cautious; until one day after some time has passed – or perhaps on a rainy night, when they're stuck at home – when he has conquered the entire territory and doesn't allow Luisa a moment's peace, he closes his large hands around her throat while the children – my children – watch from a corner, pressing themselves into the wall as if wishing the wall would give way and disappear and, with it, this awful sight, and the choked-back tears that long to burst forth, but cannot, the bad dream, and the strange, long-drawn-out noise their mother makes as she dies. In the face of that nightmarish scene, I had always thought, in order to dispel it: 'But no, that won't happen, that isn't happening, I won't have that luck or that misfortune (luck as long as it remains in the imagination, misfortune were it to become reality) . . .' Now I was faced by a real mark left by that imagined horror, in the form of a black eye or an eye of changing colours, and by the knowledge that in this area of reality there wasn't a single drop of luck, only a vast sea of misfortune drowning everything and driving out all trace of the imaginary, such a sphere would no longer exist, or is it just that it can never coexist with real danger: there are far too many poisonous cowards in Spain who, each year, kill their wives or the women who were their wives or whom they wanted to be their wives, and sometimes they kill their own children as well in order to inflict more pain on the women, it's a plague that remains unquelled by persuasions, threats, laws, or even the most severe prison sentences, because such men take no notice of the outside world and they get carried away because they love these women so much or hate them so deeply that they cannot, like me, simply live without them, content in the knowledge that cheers me in my sadness (that consoles me as regards Luisa), that they continue to exist in the world and will be or are the past only for us, but not for everyone else. 'I can't take any risks in a country like this,' I thought. 'I can't take any risks with a black eye inflicted by a punch, I can't just leave the matter entirely in her hands and to her possibly weakened will and not get involved, it's enough that I know she's put herself in danger and therefore the children too, even if only because they might lose her, and they've already suffered a semi-loss with me leaving home.'

And so I took two steps back and decided not to ask her any more questions, I would ask elsewhere, I had two weeks, that should be time enough to investigate and to convince her, and perhaps, during my stay, she would receive another blow and then she wouldn't want to keep quiet and close her mind to my words ('Keep quiet and don't say a word, not even to save yourself. Put your tongue away, hide it, swallow it even if it chokes you, pretend the cat's got your tongue. Keep quiet, and save yourself.' But perhaps we shouldn't always do that, however much, in the gravest of situations, we are advised and urged to do precisely that).

'All right, I'll go,' I said. 'I won't take up any more of your time, you're right, it's late, I'll phone you tomorrow or the day after and we can meet whenever it suits you. And don't worry about the pig, it was your Polish babysitter who started watching him, although, it has to be said, he is a wonderful actor, up there with the greats.' And at the front door, to which she accompanied me, smiling ever more brightly, as if the imminent absence of my gaze were already a source of relief, I added: 'But *te conosco, mascherina.*' – This was an expression I had learned a long time before from my distant Italian girlfriend, who had taught me her language, more or less; and that carnivalesque expression, known to Luisa as well, was tantamount to saying: 'You don't fool me.'

I wasted no time. The following day, I went to see my father, as I'd said I would; I had lunch with him and, while we were eating dessert, my sister arrived, she dropped in on him most days and since she knew nothing of my visit (my father had forgotten to mention it, 'Oh, I thought you all knew'), finding me there was a cause of great surprise and pleasure. And when my father went to lie down for a while, at the request of his carer, and left us alone, Cecilia brought me up to date on the medical situation, providing me with more details (the outlook wasn't good, either in the medium or more likely short term), and once she, in turn, had told me about her and her husband and I'd done my best not to tell her anything about myself beyond the innocuously vague, I finally got up the nerve to ask if she knew anything about Luisa: what kind of life she was leading, if they ever got together socially, if she knew whether or not she was going out with anyone yet. She knew almost nothing, she told me: they talked on the phone now and then, especially about practical matters involving their respective children, and they occasionally met up there, at my father's apartment, but generally only for a matter of minutes because Luisa was usually in a hurry, they would exchange a few friendly words and then Luisa would leave the children to spend some time with their grandfather or with their cousins, my sister's children or my brothers', one or another of whom would usually be there on a Saturday or a Sunday; then, after a couple of hours, Luisa would return to pick up Guillermo and Marina, but, again, she was always in a rush. My sister understood, though, that Luisa sometimes visited my father on her own, on a weekday, to chat and keep him company, they had always got on well together. So it might be that she talked more with him, or about more personal matters, than with any other member of the family, even if only once in a blue moon. No, she had no idea what kind of life Luisa was leading in her spare time, not that she would have a great deal of that. There was no reason why Luisa would keep her up to date on her comings and goings, least of all the romantic kind. Her husband had bumped into Luisa one evening, about two or three months ago, coming out of an art gallery or an exhibition, she couldn't quite remember which, accompanied by a man he didn't know, which was hardly surprising really, it would have been far stranger if he *had* known him; they had seemed to him like friends or colleagues, by which he meant that they hadn't been walking along arm in arm or anything. The only thing he did say was that the man looked to him like an arty type. At that point, I interrupted her (my reflexes in my own language were beginning to go).

'You mean he's an artist? Why? Did Federico say what he looked like?'

'No, by "arty" he meant one of those people who like to look the part of the artist, the eccentric. They may or may not be artists, it doesn't matter. They dress in a way that gives that impression, it's a deliberate ploy, to fool people into thinking that they're very intense and, well, arty, it could be a black polo neck or a fancy walking stick with a ghastly greyhound head on the handle, or an anachronistic hat they never take off, or long wavy musician's hair, you know the sort I mean.' – And she made a corresponding gesture with her hands around her head, rather as if she were washing her hair without touching her scalp. – 'Or a ridiculous Goyaesque hairnet,' I had time to think fleetingly. 'Or tattoos anywhere, especially on their heels' – 'Or', she went on, 'women who wear caps, or those baggy tights that reach just above the knee, or a sailor's hat or the kind of hat some smug sassy black woman would wear or else some ghastly rasta braids.'

It amused me to know that she hated that particular kind of

tights. I had no idea, on the other hand, what she meant by 'the kind of hat some smug sassy black woman would wear' and I was curious enough to be tempted to ask. However, I couldn't afford to waste any time, my other curiosity was more urgent. 'I see. So what was the guy wearing? Or did he have the whole caboodle, polo neck, walking stick *and* hat?'

'He had a ponytail. Federico noticed this because he wasn't a particularly young man, your age or thereabouts. Our age.'

'Yes, in certain places, it's quite a common sight now. You get grown men wearing a ponytail, in the belief that it makes them look like a pirate or a bandit; or else it's a goatee, and then they think they're Cardinal Richelieu or a psychiatrist or someone's clichéd idea of a sage – there's a positive epidemic of them among professors; or they grow a moustache and an imperial and think they're musketeers. They're complete frauds, the lot of them.' With my sister I could allow myself to be as arbitrary and cranky and over-the-top as she herself tended to be, it was a comical family trait, shared by all of us except my father, whom we did not greatly resemble in terms of equanimity or good temper. I, for example, never trust men who wear those rather monk-like sandals, I figure they're all impostors and traitors; or anyone in bermudas or short trousers (men, I mean), which nowadays means that in summer I trust almost no one, especially in Spain, that paradise of shameless ignominious get-ups. It may be that those intuitions–made-rules, those radical prejudices or defining superficialities, which are based solely on limited personal experience (as are all such intuitions), had helped me with Tupra in my now not-so-new job, even if only in the categorical way I sometimes pronounced on the individuals presented to me for interpretation and conjecture, once, that is, I'd acquired both the confidence to issue judgements out loud and the irresponsibility one always needs when handing down any verdict. Nevertheless, those generalisations are based on something, even if that something belongs only to the realm of perceptions: each person carries echoes of other people within them and we cannot ignore them, there are what I call 'affinities' between individuals who may be utterly different or even polar opposites, but which, on occasion, lead us to see or intuit the shadows of physical resemblances which seem, at first, quite crazy. 'Objectively speaking, this beautiful woman and my grandfather have absolutely nothing in common,' we think, 'and yet something about her makes me think of him and reminds me of him,' and then we tend to attribute to her the character and reactions, the irascibility and opportunism of that despotic ancestor of ours. And the surprising thing is, we're often right – if enough time passes for us to find that out – as if life were full of inexplicable non-blood relationships, or as if each being that exists and treads the earth and traverses the world left hanging in the air invisible intangible particles of their personality, loose threads from their actions and tenuous resonances from their words, which later alight by chance on others like snow on shoulders, and thus are perpetuated from generation to generation, like a curse or a legend, or like a painful memory belonging to someone else, thus creating the infinite, exhausting and eternal combination of those same elements. 'What else did he tell you? What was the guy like, apart from the ponytail? How was he dressed? Didn't Luisa introduce him? What was his name? What does he do?'

'How should I know? I've no idea. Federico didn't notice and anyway he only saw him for a moment. They just walked past each other and said "Hello", that's all, but they didn't stop. Besides, Federico and Luisa don't really know each other that well.'

'So the lovely couple were in a hurry, were they?'

'They all were, Jacobo, Federico didn't stop and neither did they. Now don't start going around giving funny looks to every guy with a ponytail you happen to meet. Besides, whoever he was, they've probably split up since then. And don't go calling them "the lovely couple" either, because there's no basis for that, not the slightest indication, I've told you what happened, but I obviously can't tell you anything much at all. You're just getting yourself all worked up about nothing.'

I preferred not to tell her about the punch, the unbearable blow, about the shiner, the black eye, it was best if I continued investigating on my own without alarming her, if Cecilia knew no more than she had told me, she wasn't going to be able to provide me with any further information, I didn't mind if she attributed my disquiet exclusively to feelings of jealousy, those were enough to justify my insistent curiosity and, after all, they did exist, perhaps as much as my concern that some poseur, some wretch, with ponytail or without, it didn't matter, was abusing Luisa: someone who was trying to take my place but who would have difficulty keeping it, because it wasn't his turn. Even so he must be got rid of. If he was violent, if he was dangerous, if he raised his hand to her, he must be ejected without delay, before he had a chance to settle in, because life is full of surprises and there's always the risk that something that seems to have no future at all could go on for ever. And if she lacked the will, the strength, the resolve or the courage, I was the only one capable of attempting it, or so, at least, I told myself.

And so I waited for my father to get up (or for him to be helped out of bed and brought to the living room, to the armchair where he had always done his reading, beneath the pleasant light of the lampstand) and for my sister to leave, and then I could continue my investigations, or my soundings. I didn't really expect that he would know very much, possibly nothing, but if, of all the people I had to hand, he was, according to what Cecilia had said, the one who perhaps talked most to Luisa about her personal life – even if only now and then and given the natural constraints felt by a daughter-in-law and a father-in-law, or rather by two people with such a great age difference between them – I might be able to find out, if not about the man who aspired to my position – she wouldn't tell him anything about that; and there might well be several aspirants – at least about what most concerned me: how she saw me, now that I had abandoned the field and gently removed myself from her existence – and even from her practical life – and detached myself, unprotesting, from her time and from that of our children. I asked my father about her and again he said that she didn't often come to see him, although I was gradually discovering or realising that he had grown rather bad at gauging the presences or absences of certain people, as if it seemed to him that his most pleasant or enjoyable visitors always visited him far too infrequently, although I knew that some of those people visited almost every day, as was the case with my sister and my older nieces; he had always enjoyed the company of women and now that he was so weak and in need of gentleness, this liking had become even more marked. I guessed that something similar was happening with Luisa, who would certainly not have been able to visit him quite that often, but who, given the familiarity with which he referred to her and the odd telling comment, clearly did so more often than he imagined or felt that she did. I pressed him ('What does she say, what does she talk about when she comes? Does she talk about me or does she try not to mention me? Do you think she has doubts, might she have regrets, or does my name on her lips sound always as if she had found a place for me from which I don't and won't move, a place that is far too calm and stable?'), and suddenly he looked at me with his pale eyes, without answering, resting his forehead on one hand, his elbow on the arm of the chair, his usual pose when he was thinking and preparing to say something, I had the impression sometimes that he mentally constructed his sentences before uttering them, the first few at least (but not the subsequent ones). He sat looking at me with a mixture of interest, slight impatience and slight pity, as if I were not his son exactly, but a troubled young friend, of whom he was very fond and in whom he found two things strange or perhaps disappointing: one, that I should take such pains over a matter involving the extent of someone else's feelings or, indeed, self-interest, neither of which one can do anything about; and the other, that, despite being a grown man, a father, and despite my years and experience, I had still failed to grasp the insuperable nature of such griefs, or are they perhaps merely disquiets, and their laments.

'You don't seem at all resigned to the situation, Jacobo,' he said at last, after studying me for a while, 'and you have to resign yourself. If someone no longer wants to be with you, then you have to accept it. On your own, and without always watching to see how that person is changing or always looking out for signs and hoping for some drastic change. If such a change occurs, it won't be because you're watching or asking me questions or sounding out someone else. You can't keep on at someone all the time, you can't apply a magnifying glass or a telescope or resort to spies, nor, of course, must you pester them or impose yourself on them. Pretending doesn't help either, there's no point in feigning indifference or politeness when you feel neither polite nor indifferent, and I don't think you feel either of those things – yet. She'll know that you're pretending. Remember, transparency is one of the characteristics of being in love and other related states, in all their many guises (love can often be confused with stubbornness in its first stages and its last, when one thinks that the love of the other person has not yet put down deep roots or is slipping away). It's very difficult to deceive the person you love, or who feels or has felt loved (who has known love), unless, of course, that person prefers to be deceived, which, I must admit, is not uncommon. But you always know when you're no longer loved, if you're open to finding that out: when everything has become mere habit or a lack of courage to bring things to a close, or a desire not to make a fuss and not to hurt anyone, or a fear for your life or your purse, or a mere lack of imagination, most people are incapable of imagining a different life from the one they're living and they won't change it for that reason alone, they won't move, won't even consider it; they patch things up, postpone, seek distractions, take a lover, go gambling, convince themselves that what they have is bearable, allow time to do its work; but it won't occur to them to try something else. Only self-interest can defeat feelings, and then only sometimes. And in the same way, you always know when you're still loved, especially when you would like that love to abate or to stop altogether, which is usually the case with a couple in the process of splitting up. The one who made the decision, if he or she isn't an egotist or a sadist, longs for the other person to leave, to disentangle themselves from the web, to stop loving them and oppressing them with that love. To move on to someone else or, indeed, to no one, but to wash their hands of the whole business once and for all.' – My father paused for a moment and again looked at me hard, the way one sometimes looks before saying goodbye. He seemed to be scrutinising me, which was unlikely because his sight had deteriorated greatly and he found it hard to read or even to watch television, I think he listened to it rather than watched. And yet that look had exactly the opposite effect, those ever paler blue eyes fixed on my face seemed to see right through me and to know more about me than I did myself. – 'I think you need to let Luisa go, Jacobo. You haven't done so, even though you've respectfully and courteously taken yourself off to another country and so on. But you still haven't let her go. And now you have no option, you have to do it whether you like it or not. Let her breathe freely, give her some air, don't stand in her way. Let her take the initiative. It's not in your hands to do anything. If, one day, she discovers she's unhappy without you, if she realises that she misses you so much that it's making her miserable, I don't think she would hesitate to tell you so and to ask you to come back, if I know her as I think I do. She's capable of admitting she was wrong, she's not proud. If she doesn't do so, it's because she doesn't want to, and she won't change whatever you do or say or however you behave, here or at a distance; as far as she's concerned, you're transparent, as she will be for you if you're prepared really to see her and to recognise what you see. If you're not, then that's another matter, and I understand that. Just don't ask me something I don't know, but *you* do; she isn't transparent to me.' And he added at once: 'Do you have a girlfriend at all in London?'

Now it was my turn to sit thinking for a moment, but not because I wasn't sure. No, I didn't have anything remotely like a girlfriend; I'd merely had a few fleeting encounters, especially in the first few months of settling in and reconnoitring and weighing things up, but they had all lacked either continuity or enthusiasm: of the three women who had slept at my apartment during that period, only one had returned with my consent (another had tried but without success), and that relationship had soon foundered, after our third or fourth date. Subsequently, another woman had passed through, but without any consequences. Then there was young Pérez Nuix who, I could not deny it, had meandered through my imagination, and after

267

the one night we spent together, she still did occasionally, but that strange encounter had become tinged with vague ideas of favours and payments, and such things quickly douse the imagination; and although ideas of secrecy and silence ignite it, they are perhaps not enough to counteract the former, which have more weight and force.

'No,' I replied. 'Just the odd fling, but at my age such things are no longer stimulating or particularly diverting. Or only to those who are easily flattered. Which is not my case.'

My father smiled, he was sometimes amused by the things I said.

'No, maybe not now. It was in the past though, when you were younger, so don't be so superior. It's not the case with Luisa either, of that I'm sure. I have no idea whether she's seeing anyone else. Needless to say, she doesn't talk to me about such things, although she will one day, if I live that long. She trusts me, and I think she would tell me about any serious relationship. What I do see is that she doesn't discount the possibility and might even be in a hurry for such a relationship to appear. She's in a hurry to get back on her feet or to remake her life, or however people put it nowadays, you'll know, I'm sure. I mean that I don't think she yet has doubts about her attractiveness, that's not the problem, although neither of you is as young as you were. It's more that she's afraid of starting "the definitive relationship" too late. For many years, she clearly thought you were that – "definitive" I mean – but realising that you weren't hasn't made her think that such a thing doesn't exist, rather that you both made a mistake and that she has wasted a great deal of precious time. So much so that she must now make haste to find that definitive relationship, which she hasn't given up on, she hasn't yet had time to adapt her expectations, or her illusions, she must still feel quite bewildered.' – Now the look of pity on his face grew more marked, similar to the look one sees on the face of many a mother as she watches her small children and sees how ignorant they still are and how slow they are to learn (and therefore how vulnerable). Naïveté does, more often than not, provoke pity. My father seemed to see that quality in

Luisa, of whom he was speaking, but he may have seen it in me too, for asking him about her when he couldn't help me. All he could do was distract me and listen to me, that, after all, is what it means to take on another person's anxieties. – 'It's rather childish, I suppose. As if she'd always had a particular model of life in her head and as if the enormous upset with you hasn't made her abandon that, not yet at least, and as if she were thinking: "If he wasn't the person I thought he was, there must be another one. But where is he, I must find him, I must see him." That's all I can tell you. She's not in need of flattery, nor, of course, of ephemeral conquests in order to bolster her confidence. Whenever she goes out with someone, if she does, she'll be looking at him as if he might be the definitive one, as a future husband, and she'll make every effort to make things turn out right, she'll treat him with infinite goodwill and patience, wanting to love him, determinedly desiring him.' – He paused and looked up at the ceiling, the better perhaps to imagine her at the side of some permanent imbecile, practising her patience upon him. Then he added sadly: 'It doesn't look good for her. I'd say that such an attitude tends to frighten men off or else attract the pusillanimous. It would certainly scare *you* off, Jacobo. You're not the marrying kind, even though you were married for several years and miss being married now. What you really miss is Luisa, not matrimony. I was always surprised that it suited you so well. I was surprised, too, that it lasted so long, I never thought it would.'

I didn't want to go down that road, I certainly didn't feel any curiosity about myself or, as that anonymous report in the files at the office had put it, I just took myself for granted, or assumed I knew myself, or considered myself a lost cause upon whom it would be pointless to squander thought. And so I insisted on talking about someone I knew much better or, who knows, perhaps not that well:

'Do you think that in her haste she might end up with the wrong kind of man, with someone dangerous?'

'No, I wouldn't go that far,' he said. 'Luisa's an intelligent woman, and when faced with disappointment, she'll accept it, however reluctantly, however much she resists and however hard it is to do so . . . She might end up with someone merely average or with whom she feels only partially satisfied, or even someone who has qualities she dislikes, that's possible. What I do think is that whatever he's like, she'll give innumerable opportunities to that potential husband, to that project, to the person upon whom she's fixed her gaze, she'll do more than her share, she'll try to be as understanding as she can, as she no doubt tried to be with you until, I suppose, you overstepped the mark, although I've never asked you what exactly happened . . . She won't hand this man any blank cheques, but rather than get rid of him, she'll use up almost the whole chequebook, little by little. Nevertheless, as far as I know, no such person exists as yet, or he's still not important enough for her to talk to me about him or to consult me. Bear in mind that I am now the closest thing Luisa has to a father, and that she still preserves a childlike attitude that makes her such a delightful person and leads her to ask the advice of her elders. Well, in some respects, but not, of course, in others. When did you say you were going back to Oxford?'

I could see that he was tired. He had made an effort, yes, an effort of translation or interpretation, as if he were me and I were Tupra in our office, and Tupra was putting pressure on him to talk about Luisa, I just hoped they never put her under scrutiny, there was no reason why they should, but the mere thought made me shudder. My poor father had done as I asked, he had tried to help me, as a favour to his son, he had told me what he thought, how he saw Luisa, what, it seemed to him, could be expected from her immediate future. Perhaps he was right in his estimations, and if Luisa *was* going out with someone who, at one fateful moment, on one fateful day, had gone too far, it might be that she was trying to excuse him or change him or understand him instead of distancing herself or running away, which is what you have to do while there's still time, that is, when you're not tied to someone, but only involved. It might be that she wanted to ignore or erase that moment, that she was seeking to relegate the fact to the sphere of bad dreams or to toss it into the bag of imaginings, as most of us do when we don't want that other face to fail us so soon, not today, without them even being considerate enough to wait until tomorrow to disappoint us. Many women have almost infinite powers of endurance, especially when they feel themselves to be saviours or healers or redeemers, when they believe that they will be able to rescue the man they love, or whom they have decided to love at all costs, from apathy or disease or vice. They think he'll be different with them, that he'll mend his ways or improve or change and that they will, therefore, become indispensable to him, sometimes it seems to me that for such women redeeming someone is a form – foolish and naïve – of ensuring the unconditional love of that person: 'He can't live without me,' they think without entirely thinking that or without quite formulating the thought. 'He knows that without me he would revert to his former self, disastrous, incompetent, sick, depressed, an addict, a drunk, a failure, a mere shadow, a condemned man, a loser. He'll never leave me, nor will he endanger our relationship, he won't play dirty tricks on me, he won't run the risk that I might leave him. Not only will he be for ever grateful to me, he'll realise that with me he can stay afloat and even swim on ahead, whereas without me he would sink and drown.' Yes, that is what many women seem to think when some difficult or calamitous or hopeless or violent man crosses their path, they see a challenge, a problem, a task, someone they can put right or rescue from a little hell. And it's quite incomprehensible that after centuries of hearing about other women's experiences and of reading stories, they still don't know that as soon as such men feel sober and optimistic and healthy again – as soon as they feel real rather than mere spectres – they will believe that they got back on their feet all by themselves and will very likely see the women as mere obstacles who keep them from running freely or from continuing their upward climb. It seems equally incomprehensible that the women don't realise that it is they who will be the most entangled or the most tightly bound and who will never be prepared to abandon those dependent, disoriented, irascible, defective men, because they will have made them neither more nor less than their mission, and if you have or believe you have a mission, you never give up on it, if you have finally found a mission and believe it to be an endless lifelong commitment and the daily justification for your gratuitous existence or for the countless steps taken upon the earth and for your slow, slow journey through the shrunken world . . .

I got up and placed my hand on his shoulder, it was a gesture that, in recent years, had always calmed my father, whenever he felt frightened or weak or confused, when he opened his eyes very wide as if seeing the world for the first time, with a gaze as inscrutable as that of a child born only weeks or days before, and who, I imagine, observes this new place into which he has been hurled and tries perhaps to decipher our customs and to discover which of those customs will be his. My father's sight must have been as limited as the sight of such newborn babies is sometimes said to be, he may have been able to make out only shadows, blotches, the familiar light and the blur of colours, it was impossible to know, he always claimed to see much more than we thought he could, possibly out of a kind of pride that prevented him from recognising how physically diminished he had become. He knew who I was, and his hearing was as acute as ever, and so perhaps, more than anything, he saw with his memory. And that is why, in part, he accordingly located me in Oxford, where I had in fact lived, albeit many years before and from where I had, moreover, returned. As regards London, on the other hand, he didn't yet know for sure that I would return from there (I had returned now, but not for good). During my two-week stay I would, at some point during my visits to him, place my hand on his shoulder: I would leave it there for a while, exerting enough pressure for him to be able to feel it and know that I was near and in touch, to make him feel safe and to soothe him. I could feel his slightly prominent bones, his collarbone too, he had grown thinner since I left, and when I touched them they gave an impression of fragility, not as if they might break, but as if they might easily become dislocated, by a clumsy gesture or excessive effort; when his carer helped him up, she did so with great delicacy. On one occasion, however, he turned to look curiously at my hand on his shoulder, although in no way rejecting my touch. It occurred to me that he perhaps found it odd to be the object of a gesture that he had possibly often made when I was a child, when he was tall and I was growing only very slowly, the father bending down and placing his hand on his son's shoulder in order to tell him off or to instil him with confidence or to offer him some symbolic protection, or to pacify him. He looked at my hand as if at an innocuous fly that had alighted there, or perhaps something larger, a lizard momentarily pausing in its scurryings, as if hearing approaching footsteps. 'Why do you put your hand on my shoulder like that?' he asked, half-smiling, as if amused. 'Don't you like me to?' I asked in turn, and he replied: 'Well, if you want to, it certainly doesn't bother me.' However, on that first visit, he didn't really notice, as was usually the case, but was merely silently aware of that gentle, guiding, soothing pressure. I said:

'I don't live in Oxford any more, Papa. I only go there occasionally to visit Wheeler, I've mentioned him to you before, do you remember? Sir Peter Wheeler, the Hispanist. He's about your age, well, a year older. I live in London now. I'll be going back in a couple of weeks.'

Perhaps his wise interpretation of Luisa had taken its toll, he had made a great effort for me and now he was paying the price. It was as if he had grown suddenly tired of his own perspicacity and had again become confused about time, as he had the previous day on the phone. Perhaps he could no longer stand being himself for very long, I mean being his old self, his alert intellectually demanding self, the one who urged his children always to go on, to go on thinking, the one who used to say 'And what else?' just when we felt that an exposition or argument was over, the one who made us keep on looking at things and at people, beyond what seemed necessary, at the point when we had the feeling that there was no more to see and that continuing would be a waste of time. 'At the point,' in his words, 'where you might say to yourself there can't be anything else.' Yes, as I get older, I know how that wearies and wears one out, and sometimes I wonder why I should and why, to a greater or lesser degree, we *do* pay so much attention to our fellow men and women or to the world, and why we don't just ignore them, I'm not even sure that it isn't yet one more source of conflict, even if what we see meets with our approval. He was ninety years old. It was hardly to be wondered at that he should want to take a rest from himself. And from everything else too.

'Oh, honestly,' he said somewhat irritably, as if I had deceived him on purpose and for my own pleasure. 'You've always told me you were in Oxford. That you'd been offered a job there, teaching. And there was a man called Kavanagh, who writes horror novels and is a medievalist, isn't that right? And of course I know who your friend Wheeler is, I've even read a couple of his books. But didn't he used to be called Rylands? You always used to call him Rylands.' I didn't tell him they were brothers, that would have led to still more confusion. 'So which university are you teaching at in London?'

That is how the memory of the old works. He remembered Aidan Kavanagh or his name, and even the successful novels he used to publish under a pseudonym, a pleasant and deliberately frivolous man, the head of the Spanish department during my time in Oxford, but long since retired; he remembered Rylands too, although he confused him with Wheeler; and yet he didn't remember that I had gone to work for the BBC during my second English sojourn, so recent that it was still going on. There was no reason why he should remember what had happened subsequently: as with Luisa, I had told him very little – only a few vague, possibly evasive remarks – about my new job. It's strange how one instinctively hides, or, which is somewhat different, keeps quiet about anything that immediately strikes one as murky: just as I would say nothing to Luisa about meeting a woman with whom I had barely exchanged a word at a meeting or a party and with whom nothing could or indeed would happen, but to whom I had felt instantly attracted. I had possibly never even mentioned Tupra to my father or to Luisa, or only in passing, and yet he was, without a doubt, the dominant figure in my life in London (and after a few days I realised just how dominant a figure he was). It didn't seem to me, at that moment, worth disillusioning my father and telling him that I no longer did any teaching anywhere.

'I've got to go now, Papa,' I said. 'I'll pop in now and then, when I've got time. Do you want me to warn you? Shall I phone before I drop by?'

My prolonged absence made me feel rather like an intruder and as if I needed to ask such a question, which was perhaps inappropriate in a son with respect to his father's home, a home that had for many years been mine too. I was still standing, still with my hand on his shoulder. He looked up at me, whether seeing me or guessing at my face or remembering me, I don't know. His gaze was, at any rate, very clear, surprised and slightly helpless, as if he had not quite grasped that I was leaving. His eyes were now very blue, bluer than they had ever been, perhaps because he no longer wore glasses.

'No, there's no need. As far as I'm concerned, you all still live here, even if you left a long time ago.' He fell silent, then added: 'Your mother too.'

I wasn't sure whether he meant that she still lived there as well or if he was reproaching her as well for having left, when she died, longer ago than anyone else. He probably meant both.

And I continued to waste no time. I didn't linger or delay or loi-
ter or dally. I was longing to see my children again, not to mention Luisa and my sister, and, for the first time since my return,
my brothers and a few friends, and to stroll around the city like
a foreigner, but I felt I had something concrete and urgent to
do, something to investigate and resolve and remedy. That was
something I *had* learned from Tupra, at least in theory: Luisa was
clearly in danger, and now I understood that sometimes one has
no option but to do what has to be done and at once, without
waiting or hesitating or delaying: I had to do this unthinkingly,
like some very distracted, busy person, as if it were merely my
job. Yes, there are occasions when one knows precisely what
would happen in the world if no pressure or brake was imposed on what one perceives to be people's certain capabilities,
and that if those capabilities were to remain undeployed, it was
necessary for someone – me, for example, who else in this case?
– to dissuade or impede them. In order for Tupra to adopt the
punitive measures which he deemed necessary and appropriate,
he simply had to convince himself of what would happen in
each case if he or another sentinel – the authorities or the law,
instinct, the moon, the storm, fear, the hovering sword, the invisible watchers – did not put a stop to it. 'It's the way of the world,'
he would say, and he would say this about so many things and
situations; he applied those words to betrayals and acts of loyalty, to anxieties and quickened pulses, to unexpected reversals
and vertigo, to vacillations and torments and to the involuntary
harm we cause, to the scratch and the pain and the fever and the

276

festering wound, to griefs and the infinite steps we all take in the belief that we are being guided by our will, or that our will does at least play a part in them. To him all this seemed perfectly normal and even, sometimes, routine – prevention or punishment and never running too grave a risk – he knew too well that the Earth is full of passions and affections and of ill will and malice, and that sometimes individuals can avoid neither and, indeed, choose not to, because they are the fuse and the fuel for their own combustion, as well as their reason and their igniting spark. And they don't even require a motive or a goal for any of this, neither aim nor cause, gratitude nor insult, or at least not always, or as Wheeler said: 'they carry their probabilities in their veins, and so time, temptation and circumstance will lead them at last to their fulfilment.' And for Tupra this very radical and sometimes ruthless attitude – or perhaps it was simply a very practical one – was just another characteristic of the way of the world to which he conformed or adhered; and that unreflecting, inclement, resolute stance (or one based perhaps on a single thought, the first), also formed part of that way of the world which remained unchanged throughout time and regardless of space, and so there was, therefore, no reason to question it, just as there's no need to question wakefulness and sleep, or hearing and sight, or breathing and walking and speech, or any of the other things about which one knows 'that's how it is and always will be'.

I was feeling now as he did, that is, like someone who didn't bother to issue any prior warning, at least not always, someone who makes decisions at a distance and for barely identifiable reasons, or without the actions appearing to have any connection of cause and effect with those reasons, still less with the proof that such acts have been committed. Nor did I need proof of that arbitrary or justifiable occasion – who could tell which it was and what did it matter? – nor did I intend sending any warning or notice before unleashing my sabre blow, I didn't even require any evidence of actions committed or proven, of events or deeds, or even certainty in order to set to and remove from Luisa's existence the man marring and threatening her life and, therefore, the lives of my children. First, I had to find out more about the man and then track him down. She wouldn't say a word to me about him, especially now that I had voiced my immediate suspicion that this as yet nameless, faceless man was the person responsible for her multicoloured black eye. After my father's conjectures and his belief that my wife would be inclined to humour or encourage whoever she was attracted to or whoever she was focused on now ('Yes,' I thought, 'strictly speaking, she *is* still my wife. We're not divorced and neither of us seems in a hurry to get a divorce or has even suggested it,' and this confirmed me in my determination or in my first thought that admitted of no second thought), my next step was to go and see her sister or talk to her on the phone; and even though she and I had never got on particularly well or had much to do with each other and even though she led a very independent life with few family ties and saw myself and the children only infrequently, as mere extensions of Luisa, she did meet up with Luisa once or twice a month; Luisa would either go to her place without the kids and without me, her husband, or they would lunch together in a restaurant and tell each other about their respective lives, just how much I didn't know, but probably almost everything. If anyone knew what was going on, if anyone knew the identity of that man with violent tendencies, his face and name, that person was Cristina, Luisa's somewhat surly younger sister. And although her first loyalty was to Luisa and even though she considered me to be a mere dispensable appendage, I was sure that if something was worrying her – and if my deductions were correct, and even if they weren't, this guy was very worrying indeed – she would tell me and welcome hearing the views of someone who felt the same way about the matter.

I phoned her that evening, much to her surprise, for she didn't even know I was in Madrid, but then how could she unless she had spoken to Luisa during the day and Luisa had told her, she asked me how things were going in London, and I was amazed that she actually knew where I was currently living, 'Fine,' I said, without going into detail, after all, it was just a reflex question, and then I asked if we could meet up as soon as possible, 'No,' she said, 'impossible, I'm off on a trip tomorrow and I've got loads of things to do before I go.' 'How long are you away for?' 'A week.' 'It will be too late when you get back, I need to see you before you leave, I'm only here for two weeks, well, less than that now, what time are you leaving?' I asked. 'At lunchtime, but I'm really tied up until then, can't you tell me over the phone? Is it about Luisa?' 'Yes, it's about Luisa.' Then she fell silent for a few seconds and it seemed to me that she had sat herself down on a chair in readiness. 'What have you got to say, then? Come on, tell me.' 'What? Now?' 'Yes, now. If it's what I think it is, it won't take much time and I imagine we'll be pretty much in agreement on the subject. It's about Custardoy, isn't it?'

'Who?'

'Custardoy, the guy she's going out with. Or didn't you know? Oh, Jaime, don't tell me you didn't know.' She said this not as if she were afraid she had put her foot in it, but as if she couldn't believe I wouldn't know. Perhaps she had always thought of me as rather absent-minded, or worse, a fool.

'I've only just got back. I didn't know his name.' Now, however, I did and knew of his existence in Luisa's life, so it wasn't all conjecture on my part. All I needed now was to know what he looked like and find out where he lived. Custardoy. It was an unusual surname, odd, there wouldn't be many in Madrid. 'I've been away for ages, and when you only talk on the phone, it's hard to know what's really going on. Who is he? What does he do?'

'He's a painter, a copyist, or both of those things. Some people say he's a forger too, but at any rate, he's in the art world. I'm glad you phoned actually, I've been really worried – although I'm not sure anything can be done, in this kind of situation there's rarely much you can do.'

'Worried? Why? What situation?'

'Tell me first why you phoned. Has Luisa told you anything?'

I wondered if I should pretend to know more than I did, but that seemed unwise, Cristina could be very touchy and, if she caught on to what I was doing, she might refuse to say another word. And that was the last thing I wanted, I was entirely dependent on her for help, and she had, inadvertently, already told me a lot, with no need for me to worm it out of her.

'No, not really,' I said at last. 'According to Luisa, what she does is no longer any of my business, and she's right of course. The thing is, I saw her briefly last night, I'd gone over there to see the kids, and she avoided me and left before I arrived, but I waited until she got back, she was away for several hours, I've no idea where she went, she left me with the babysitter, and I think the reason she was avoiding me was because when I did see her, her face was a real mess, and that was obviously the reason she hadn't wanted to be there. She claims she collided with the garage door, but she's got a black eye and it looks to me as if someone punched her, and I don't just find that worrying, I find it downright alarming, and it *is* my business, how could it not be? It would be the same if someone had hit you or any female friend. Do you know anything about it?'

'It wouldn't be the same if someone had hit me, Jaime, because you don't give a damn about me.' My sister-in-law's sharp tongue could not resist getting this comment in first. Then her tone changed and she said almost as if to herself: 'Not again. That's dreadful.'

'Again? You mean it's happened before?'

Cristina didn't respond at first. She paused as if she were biting her lip and weighing something up, but her hesitation lasted only a moment.

'According to her, no, nothing has ever happened, not what you suspect now nor what I've suspected in the past. Look, I'm telling you this because I'm worried, and even more so after what you've just told me, I didn't know anything about that, I haven't seen her for a couple of weeks, and she hasn't put any pressure on me to meet up before this trip of mine, presumably because she thinks the mark will have faded by the time I get back and then I won't ask any awkward questions. But I don't think she would be at all pleased if she knew I was talking about this to you. The only reason she hasn't told me not to talk to you is because it would never occur to her that you and I would be in touch. It wouldn't have occurred to me either, to be honest. Did she know you were coming to Madrid?'

'No, I phoned her when I arrived yesterday. I wanted it to be a surprise for the children.'

'She won't have had time to prepare herself,' she said, 'nor to worry about you finding out. She probably doesn't even want you to know she's going out with the guy.'

'What is it that you suspected?'

'Well, according to her, a couple of months ago or so she fell over in the street and hit her face on one of those metal posts the council have put up everywhere, which is perfectly possible, because the city's full of the things, bollards I think they call them, you have to make a real point of avoiding them if you don't want to fracture your kneecap. Did she mention anything to you about falling over?'

'No, nothing. And we talk at least once a week.'

'Well, I'm surprised she didn't. It was a really nasty cut, a su-perficial one, but it went from one side of her nose to halfway across her cheek, you couldn't miss it.' – '*Uno sfregio*', I thought, that recently learned word sprang immediately into my mind, 'a gash'. – 'And she had a graze on her chin. From the way she talked about it, I just didn't believe her, and it looked more like a scratch or a welt or as if someone had slapped her, I know a bit about these things because a woman I was vaguely friendly with some years ago used to get beaten up by her husband; in fact, he killed her in the end, after I'd stopped seeing her luck-ily, which is something.' I instinctively knocked on wood. 'So I asked her straight out if Custardoy had hit her, if he'd beaten her up. She denied it, of course, and said I must be mad, how could I even think such a thing. But she blushed when she said it, and I can tell when my sister is lying from years of watching her face whenever she lied as a child. And I've heard other things since.'

'What things? Do you know the guy?'

I realised that I preferred not to mention his name, although I had it stored away in my memory, as if it were a find, a treasure. It was a valuable piece of information.

'Yes, by sight. And by hearsay too. A few years ago, he was often to be seen drinking in smart bars like the Chicote, the Cock, or the Del Diego, or in others, he's an arty type, a nocturnal womaniser, although apparently he didn't restrict his activities to the night-time only, he's the kind of man who can tell at once who wants to be chatted up and for what purpose, the kind who's capable of creating the necessary willingness and purpose in someone else, that is, in women. At least so I've heard. I don't know if he still goes to those places, because I don't go any more myself. You probably saw him once or twice there yourself, in the '80s or '90s.'

'What does he look like? Has he got a ponytail?' I asked, I couldn't help myself. I was burning to know this.

'Yes, how did you guess?'

'Oh, it was just something someone said. But in that case, no, I've never seen him. I mean, I can't remember anyone in particular with a ponytail. Then again, I pretty much stopped going out at night when Guillermo was born, and the guy probably didn't have a ponytail before that. And of course the surname doesn't mean anything to me either. What things have you heard?'

'Well, after seeing that cut on Luisa's face – which left me with a really bad feeling – I asked an acquaintance of mine, Juan Ranz, about Custardoy, who he's known since they were children. They never got on well and have had hardly any contact for years, but their parents were friends and used to leave them together to play and entertain each other, so he had to put up with his company quite often. He says Custardoy was one of those very grown-up kids, impatient to enter the adult world, as if he wanted to climb out of his as yet unformed body. Then, when he was older, Custardoy used to make copies of paintings for Ranz's father, who's an art expert (apparently, Custardoy's a brilliant copyist and can make a perfect copy of anything from any period, in fact, it's hard to tell them from the originals, which, of course, is where his reputation as a forger comes in), and so he still used to see him from time to time, through his father. Juan is an interpreter at the United Nations, and, as a matter of fact, his wife's name is Luisa too.'

'What else did he tell you?'

'The most notable or perhaps the most troubling fact, and

the one that most concerns us, is that, although he's a great success with the ladies, there's obviously something slightly sinister about the way he treats them because Ranz knows of some women who've emerged from a night with Custardoy feeling really scared, after having sex I mean (some of them were prostitutes, and so it was purely sexual). And afterwards, they didn't even want to talk about it, as if they needed to forget it as quickly as possible and shake off the whole experience. As if the experience, or even the mere memory of it, had burned itself into them and didn't lend itself to being turned into a story. And even when there were two prostitutes involved at the same time (apparently he's into threesomes, although always with women), both had emerged feeling equally scared and refusing to say anything about it. And inevitably, there are lots of other women, prostitutes or not, who feel an irresistible desire to know just what it is he does or doesn't do. There's no shortage of stupid women out there as you know.'

This was the worst possible news. A ladies' man who was also into whores, and who left his mark on women, even if that mark was only a mark of terror. 'A man like that won't even have to bury me or dig my grave still deeper, the grave in which I'm already buried,' I thought, 'because he will have erased my memory at a stroke, with the first terror and the first entreaty and the first fascination and the first command, and Luisa could already be under his thumb.'

'But Luisa isn't stupid, at least she didn't used to be, no, she's never been stupid,' I said. 'Perhaps he's different with women who aren't whores. Perhaps when he has more than one night at his disposal his behaviour changes to the exact opposite, purely in order to ensure that there will be more nights to come. Or do you think that's precisely what is so sinister about him, that he beats up all the women he goes out with? I can't believe that. Someone would have said something, someone would have found out, the women he'd been with would have warned each other. You women talk about such things, don't you, I mean details? Spanish women do. In what sort of terms has she spoken to you about him? Is she in love or infatuated? Desperate, mad, distracted, flattered? Just how serious is she? She can't be in love. And how did she meet him? Where did he spring from?' The information provided by this Ranz fellow had perhaps made me even more uneasy than Luisa's now yellowing black eye. 'What else did this friend of yours say?'

'Nothing very good, except that he's brilliant at his job. According to Ranz, though, he's a slippery customer, not to be trusted under any circumstances. And he's not the sort to fall in love, or didn't use to be, he said. But who knows, love is an area in which people can change at any moment. When I told him that my sister was going out with him, he said: "Oh God" like someone heralding a disaster. That's why I was trying to find out more, well, because of that and her supposed collision with a bollard and that worrying cut. In fact, I asked him outright if he thought Custardoy would be capable of hitting a woman.' And Cristina paused, as if she'd completed that particular sequence of sentences.

'And what did he say? Tell me.'

'He wasn't categorical about it, but nevertheless . . . He thought about it for a moment and then said: "I suppose so. I don't know that he has, no one's ever told me he has and he wouldn't tell me so himself. It's not the kind of thing you boast about. But I suppose that, yes, he would be perfectly capable of doing so." You see what I mean. (Of course, Ranz doesn't like the man and so can't be taken as the oracle.) That was when he told me about the prostitutes and, well, I assumed it wasn't only prostitutes. Now you tell me that Luisa has another injury, one she hasn't even mentioned to me. If she'd bumped into a door and given herself a black eye, the normal thing would be for her to tell me about it, we may not have seen each other lately, but we've spoken on the phone. And she didn't tell you about the incident with the bollard. Yes, now I really am very worried. And Jaime, Luisa may not be stupid, but you've only known her in a stable situation, when she was with you. Apart from the last few months before you left, of course, but there was still a remnant of stability while you were at home, a kind of postponement, an inertia. But how long have you been away now? Nine months, twelve, fifteen?

That's a long time for the person left behind, longer than for the one who leaves. Neither you nor I know what she's like in that situation, and she was still very young when she met you. People are unpredictable when they've just split up with someone. Some might closet themselves at home and not want to see anyone, others might hit the streets and climb into the first bed that's offered. Some might do first one thing and then the other, or the other way round, I mean, who knows what foolishness *you've* been getting up to in London, fancy-free and with no family obligations. There are half-measures too, of course. Luisa won't have hit the streets because, to start with, there are the children to consider. But she won't simply have wept into her pillow. She must feel slightly impatient, excited, curious to meet another man and see how it works out, and curiosity leads to all kinds of silliness and to persisting in that silliness until the curiosity wears off. She hasn't told me a great deal, about her feelings, I mean, or her expectations; she probably doesn't have any great expectations and is simply letting time pass until she can see more clearly what she wants or, indeed, if she wants anything. From what Ranz told me, and given Custardoy's reputation, it's highly unlikely that he'll put any pressure on her to move in with him or to get divorced or whatever, if he isn't the sort to fall in love. Not that I've asked her much about it either, I suppose: you know what I'm like, I'll listen to what others tell me, but I'm not that interested really, unless things get serious. All I know is that she's going out with this guy, has a good time with him and obviously likes him. How much she likes him I don't know, possibly a lot, she might be crazy about him, which is why she's being discreet and keeping quiet about it. She doesn't try and hide their relationship, but she's not shouting it from the rooftops either. Not with me, I mean, and I would think with other people she says even less. She didn't announce it to me with a great fanfare, as if it were headline news. And I've only seen them together once, very briefly and from the car, so I haven't spent time with them or anything. I get a sense of reserve, modesty almost, as if after all those years as a married woman, she was embarrassed to have a boyfriend.'

285

'How did you happen to see them?' Even if it was as brief as she said, that would provide me with the only image I had of the two of them together, apart from the indirect and imprecise one provided by my brother-in-law via my sister. And I needed to be able to imagine them. It was odd to imagine Luisa being with anyone other than me. It seemed not so much repugnant or offensive as unreal, like a performance, a farce. Yes, it was more unreal than painful. Separations like ours make no sense, however commonplace they have become in the world and have been for a long time now. You spend years orbiting round a particular person, depending on her at every turn, seeing her every day as if she were a natural prolongation of yourself, including her in all your comings and goings, in your aimless thoughts and even in your dreams. Thinking of telling her the slightest thing seen or experienced, for example, a Romanian mother asking for a packet of baby wipes for her children. You are *with that person*, just as the Hungarian gypsy was *with her children* or Alan Marriott's dog was *without a leg*. You have a detailed, constant and permanently refreshed knowledge of her thoughts and preoccupations and activities; you know her timetable and her habits, whom she sees and how often; and when you join her each evening you tell each other what has happened and what you've been up to during the day, during which neither of you has ever entirely left the consciousness of the other for a single moment, and sometimes those reports are quite elaborate; then you go to bed with her and she's the last thing you see that day and – even more extraordinary – you get up with her too, for she's there in the morning, after those hours of absence, as if she were you, someone who never goes away or disappears and of whom we never lose sight; and so on, day after day over many years. Then suddenly – although it isn't sudden, it just seems like that once the process is over and distance has been established: in fact it happens very gradually and both parties know when it began, even though they prefer not to – you cease to have any notion of what that person's daily thoughts, feelings or actions are; whole days and weeks go by with almost no news of her, and you have to resort to third parties – who used to know much less than you, well, nothing really, in comparison – to find out the most basic things: what kind of life she's leading, who she sees, how the kids are taking it, who she's going out with, if she's in pain or ill, if she's in good or low spirits, if she's still looking after her diabetes and taking her long prescribed walks, if anyone has upset or hurt her, if she's finding work exhausting, if it's getting her down or is a real source of satisfaction, if she's afraid of growing old, how she sees her future and how she views the past, how she thinks of me now; and who she loves. It makes no sense that it should go from all to almost nothing, even though we never cease to remember and are basically the same person. It's all so unbearably ridiculous and subjective, because everything contains its opposite: the same people in the same place love each other and cannot stand each other; what was once long-established habit becomes slowly or suddenly unacceptable and inadmissible – whether slowly or suddenly it doesn't matter, that's the least of it, someone who helped set up a home finds he's forbidden from entering it, the merest contact, a touch, once so taken for granted that it was barely conscious becomes an affront or an insult, it's almost as if you were having to ask permission to touch yourself, what once gave pleasure or amusement becomes hateful, repellent, accursed and vile, words once longed for would now poison the air or provoke nausea and must on no account be heard, and those spoken a thousand times before seem unimportant. Erase, suppress, take back, cancel, better never to have said anything, that is the world's ambition, that way nothing exists, nothing is anything, the same things and the same facts and the same beings are both themselves and their reverse, today and yesterday, tomorrow, afterwards and in the long-distant past. And in between there is only time that does its best to dazzle us, the only thing with purpose and aims, which means that those of us who are still travelling through time are not to be trusted, for we are all foolish and insubstantial and unfinished, with no idea of what we might be capable nor of what end awaits us, foolish, insubstantial, unfinished me, no, no one should trust me either . . .'

'We'd arranged to have lunch one day,' Cristina said. 'This

287

was a few months ago now, before the business with the bollard and that ugly cut, I had no anxieties or concerns at the time, in fact, I really didn't care what she did or who with as long as it cheered her up a bit, she *is* the older sister, don't forget, and I've never tended to be very protective of her, although she is of me, which is only normal. Luisa had arranged to meet him afterwards, at his apartment or studio, I don't remember which now. Anyway, lunch went on longer than expected, and it got a bit late and she was really alarmed when she saw the time, because they hadn't arranged to meet actually in his apartment or studio or whatever, but outside in the street and they would then go up together or perhaps go on somewhere else, I don't know, but she was horrified at the thought of keeping him waiting. So I gave her a lift in my car, because she hadn't brought hers; she'd planned to take the metro, she said, which, normally, would have been quicker, but it was quite a way from the nearest station to his place and so would have taken too long, anyway, I dropped her off at the door. It's impossible to park in that part of town, I could barely stop, just long enough to let her out, I dropped her almost on the corner. She didn't introduce him or anything, although, as I say, I knew him by sight already from seeing him out and about in bars at night. I only saw them together from the car, for a matter of seconds, while I waited for the lights to change, from the corner.'

'What part of town was it? What corner?'

'At the end of Calle Mayor, just past Bailén, next to the viaduct. Just before you reach Cuesta de la Vega.'

'Can you remember which number?'

'No, I didn't notice. Why do you want to know?'

'Which side of the road?'

'The only one with houses. The eyesore's on the other side, if you remember. But why do you want to know?'

The 'eyesore' was the Almudena or museum of ecumenical horrors, the ghastly modern cathedral, largely the work of Opus Dei or so it seems, with a statue of the Polish Pope outside, *totus tuus*, with a bulging forehead, worthy almost of Frankenstein's monster, and arms flung wide as if he were about to dance a *jota*;

and this, though hideous, is perhaps the least of the uglinesses, because there are, among other monstrosities, some monstrous stained-glass windows made by an unimaginable artist called Kiko (Kiko something-or-other), well, nothing good can come from a man with a name like that.

'Oh, no reason. Just so that I can imagine them there. What did you see?'

'Well, not much really. Nothing. She leaped out of the car with the lights on red at the junction with Calle Mayor, she was in such a hurry, about ten minutes late. The one thing I did notice was that it had started to rain, and he, instead of taking shelter in the doorway (he only needed to step back two paces), was waiting for her on the pavement, getting drenched. Perhaps he was there so that he would be sure to see her arrive, out of impatience.'

'Or perhaps to have one more reason to reproach her for being late,' I said, wilfully misinterpreting the facts. 'That way he could make her feel even guiltier, by saying it was her fault he had got soaked or even caught a cold. How did he greet her? Did they embrace, did he kiss her, put his arm about her waist?'

'I don't think so, I don't think they actually touched. From her attitude and certain gestures, it seemed to me that she was apologising profusely, she pointed to my car, to explain why she was late. What does it matter?'

'Did you see them go in?'

'Yes, just before the lights changed. Now that you ask, he might have been a bit annoyed, because he went in ahead of her rather than giving way to her, and Luisa followed behind, placing one hand on his shoulder, as if to soothe or placate him, as if she were still apologising.'

'Ah, I see. A quick-tempered, artsy-fartsy, hysterical type. Well, certainly not a gentleman anyway.'

'I wouldn't go that far, I only saw them together for a moment, but he's definitely not the gentlemanly sort. He's well-dressed, mind, always wears a tie, very traditional. But his success, I suppose, comes from the roguish air he has about him and which lots of women find attractive. I don't myself, not at all, but maybe I'm odd or maybe I've met a few rogues already and know they're not worth the bother. That day, with his hair scraped back and all wet, he did look slightly menacing. He gives the impression of being a tense, self-contained, nervy sort, I mean, someone under constant tension. He's always seemed to me a rather sombre figure. Friendly and seductive, but somehow sombre too.'

'How old is he?'

'I don't know, he must be around fifty now, I should think. Although he looks younger.'

'Ten or twelve years older than Luisa. That's not good; he'll have authority over her, influence. Do you know his first name?'

'Esteban, I think. Wait. Yes, Esteban. Luisa has called him that occasionally, although she tends to refer to him more by his surname, as if she wanted to distance herself from him and make it seem as if they weren't that close.' – 'I call young Pérez Nuix by her surname too,' I thought, 'but that's not the same thing at all.' – 'As I said, sometimes it's as if she were embarrassed to have a boyfriend. Because of the kids and you and all that.'

'Esteban Custardoy. Are you sure? He's not known as a painter, then? I mean, his name doesn't appear in the papers, he doesn't hold exhibitions and so on?'

'Not that I know of, no; but I don't take much notice, to be honest; the last thing I would be interested in is modern art. I think he's more of a copyist. Luisa mentioned that sometimes he's commissioned to copy paintings from the Prado and that he spends hours there studying and copying. Or he gets commissions to copy paintings in museums abroad, in Europe, and then he goes away for a few days to study those paintings. Ranz told me that he learned the trade from his father, Custardoy the Elder as he used to be called, who made copies for his father, Ranz's father that is. And at first the son was known as Custardoy the Younger, but I don't know if he still is.'

I fell silent for a moment. I lit a Karelias cigarette, of which I had brought ten packs with me, knowing that I wouldn't be able to find them in Madrid.

'There's something that doesn't quite make sense, Cristina. I just can't believe that Luisa would put up with someone mis-treating her, still less if she's only known him for a short time, a matter of months. If our suspicions are right, he hasn't hit her once, but twice. I don't understand why she would go on seeing him and going to bed with him as if nothing had happened, why she didn't break it off the first time, let alone the second. Only yesterday she denied anything was wrong; in a way she was pro-tecting him or protecting herself, I mean her relationship with him, to make sure no one meddles or gets involved or sticks their nose in where it isn't wanted. It's understandable that I'd be the last person she'd want to talk to about her boyfriend, especially if relations with him are problematic, and even if he represents a danger to her. But she doesn't even talk to you! How would you explain such forbearance? And she's hardly the submissive type.' I suddenly realised that this was the first time I had spoken about or thought about or really imagined their relationship as some-thing real and regular and ongoing; the words that came out of my mouth were: '. . . and going to bed with him as if nothing had happened.' Of course they went to bed together, that's one of the benefits of going out with someone, it's the norm. 'But that doesn't necessarily mean very much,' I thought at once in order to mitigate that fleeting image and those words. 'I've slept with Pérez Nuix and with others too and it's almost as if it never happened. They don't occupy my thoughts, I don't remember them, or only very occasionally and without any feeling. Well, it's a bit different with Pérez Nuix because I see her every day and each time I see her, I do remember or, rather, know, even though screwing her was an extraordinarily impersonal expe-rience, performed, how can I put it, almost with eyes closed, almost anonymously, in silence. I've slept with other women in the past on a regular or continuous basis, Clare Bayes in England was a case in point, or my girlfriend in Tuscany to whom I owe my Italian. But so what, they're just data in an archive, recorded facts that have long since ceased to affect or influence me. No, those things don't really mean very much once they're over. The problem is that Luisa's affair is happening now and isn't yet over, and it's harming her and threatens us all, all four of us.'

Now it was Cristina's turn to pause and think for a few seconds. I heard her sigh at the other end of the line, perhaps she was weary of our conversation or felt she should be getting on with preparations for her trip.

'I don't know, Jaime. Perhaps we're wrong, and he hasn't done anything to her, maybe she did collide with a bollard and with the garage door, and is just having a run of bad luck. The trouble is that neither of us believes that. My feeling is that she's determined to stick to him, however much she may pretend not to know or care, and in that case anything is possible – when a person's set on loving someone then nothing circumstantial or external will dissuade them. People are much more long-suffering than we think. Once involved, they'll tolerate almost anything, at least for a time. I should know. They believe they can change the bad things or that the bad things won't last. And Luisa is patient, she'll put up with a lot, after all, look how long it took her to break up with you. I don't really know why we're talking about it. For the moment, as we've seen, she's not going to tell us anything, and even if she did, we wouldn't be able to persuade her. I don't see what we can do. Anyway, Jaime, I have things to do, I'm leaving tomorrow and this conversation is getting us nowhere, apart from feeding our mutual anxieties.' I said nothing, I was pondering what she had said: 'Once involved, they'll tolerate almost anything, at least for a time.' 'It's all a matter of involving the other person, of intervening, making a request, a demand, asking a question. Of speaking to him and interfering,' I was thinking, still saying nothing.

'Jaime, are you there?'

'We could try persuading him,' I said at last.

'Him? We don't know him, least of all you. What an idea! You can count me out. Besides, I'm off tomorrow. Anyway, if you did go and talk to him, he'd probably laugh in your face or punch you, don't you see, if he really is a violent man. Or were you thinking of offering him money to go away, like an old-fashioned father? Huh. For all I know, he may not even need the money, the art collectors he works for must be rolling in it. Then he'd go straight to Luisa and tell her, and exactly how would you justify such interference in her life? You are, after all, separated. She would never speak to you again, you know that, don't you? You're aware of that?'

But perhaps none of those things would happen after my attempt to persuade him. And so I ignored her objections and merely asked, as if I hadn't heard what she had said:

'Apart from the ponytail, what does he look like?'

I had learned a few things from Reresby and Ure and Dundas and even from Tupra, but I still wasn't like him, nor did I wish to be, except on the odd occasion, and this was just such an odd occasion. Perhaps it's not possible to imitate someone else only now and then and when you choose, and perhaps in order to act like your chosen model – even just once – you have to resemble him all the time and in all circumstances, that is, when you're alone and when there's no need, and for that to happen you must have more than just accidental reasons, reasons that come upon you suddenly and from without. You have to have a deep need, a profound desire to change, which was not my case. Initially, I behaved as I thought he would have behaved, but there came a point when I wasn't sure, or couldn't imagine exactly, how he would have behaved, or perhaps I preferred not to, or else couldn't imagine myself behaving like that, and I was filled with doubt, which he never would be; and so I went back to the idea that he might be able to help me, or at least give me advice and reassure me, or at least not dissuade me. I didn't phone Tupra until a few days into my stay and after my first visit to the children, my stolen glimpse of Luisa, my meeting with my sister and my father, my phone conversation with my sister-in-law Cristina Juárez, and after I had already taken a few steps in his imaginary wake.

I began by consulting the phone book and looking for that unusual surname, Custardoy. I discovered that I had been way off in my calculations, because there weren't a few Custardoys in Madrid, there was only one, who lived in Calle de

Embajadores and whose initial, alas, wasn't E for Esteban, but a wretched R for Roberto, Ricardo, Raúl, Ramón or Ramiro and what use were they? His number must be under another name, possibly his landlord's if he was renting, although it seemed to me likely that he would own his apartment or studio or whatever it was, if those art collectors really did pay him well, doubtless for forgeries that could later be switched for the real thing in some ill-supervised church or sold as authentic to naïve, provincial museums, for I had already decided to myself that the man was a fraud, a con man. It might also be that he was listed under his second surname, some people do that to avoid being pestered, the ringing of the phone would disturb him when he was work- ing, he would lose precision, concentration, he would jump and make the wrong brushstroke or put a hole through the canvas, the paint would run, he was, after all, an 'arty type', but I couldn't think who would be likely to know that second surname, prob- ably not even Luisa. I called directory enquiries just in case, and asked for the number of someone called Custardoy living in Calle Mayor, but they had no one of that name, only the Cus- tardoy in Calle de Embajadores. So I set off to the short stretch of Calle Mayor beyond Bailén and just before Cuesta de la Vega and the nearby park called Atenas, which I knew only from hav- ing driven through it once a long time ago, and I was in luck, because there were just two doors, and since one belonged to the offices of the nearby town hall, I deduced that it must be the other door, number 81. There were no names on the intercom – or *portero automático* as we call it in Spanish – only the numbers of the apartments, of which there were four and one on the ground floor. It was almost lunchtime – bad planning on my part – and the vast ornate carved door was closed, so there was no way of knowing if there was an actual flesh-and-blood door- man whom I could approach on another occasion. I thought of ringing a couple of the bells and enquiring after Custardoy, but if, by chance, I pressed the right bell and he answered in person, furious at this unexpected interruption to his fraudulent activi- ties, I would have to invent some pretext, saying, perhaps, that I had a telegram for him and then not going up when he opened the street door for me, well, postmen are so often unreliable and incomprehensible, he would wait for a while, mutter a few curses and then forget all about it, summoned back to work by his false art. I pressed a bell at random and no one answered. I tried a second one and, after a while, I heard a woman's voice.

'Is Don Esteban Custardoy there, please?' I asked.

'Who?' The woman was doubtless elderly.

'Cus-tar-doy,' I said slowly and clearly. 'Don Esteban.'

'No, he doesn't live here.'

'I must have the wrong apartment. Would you be so kind as to tell me which apartment he lives in? I have a telegram for him.'

'A telegram for me? Who from? We never get telegrams.'

'No, not for you, Madam.' I realised that I would get nowhere with her. 'It's for your neighbour, Señor Custardoy. Would you mind telling me which floor he's on?'

'Which floor? This is the second floor,' she said. 'But there's no Bujaraloz living here. You've got the wrong address.'

The sound on those tinny intercoms is always dreadful, but the lady in question must, like Goya, have been both Aragonese and deaf for her to be able to trot out so blithely and so fluently the name of that rather obscure town in the province of Zaragoza. I apologised and thanked her, then left her in peace.

I decided to press a third bell, but there was no response, so many people have lunch out in Madrid. I tried a fourth bell and immediately heard another female voice, younger and more encouraging.

'Esteban Buscató?' the voice asked. That was the surname of a former basketball player, she must be a fan, I thought. 'No, I don't know the name. I don't think he lives here.' There was some creaking and the sound of the sea in the background, it was like having a seashell pressed to my ear and as if a ship somewhere out there was about to be wrecked.

'The name's Custardoy,' I said again. 'Cus-tar-doy. He's a painter. Perhaps you could tell me which floor he lives on or where he has his studio. He's a painter, Custardoy the painter.'

'We're not expecting any painter here.'

'No, *I'm* not a painter, Madam,' I said, fast losing hope. 'I have a telegram for Señor Custardoy. *He's* the painter. Don't you know of a painter living in this building? A painter, not a house painter, but a painter like Goya, do you know him?'

'Of course I know Goya. He's the one who painted *La Maja*.' And she sounded rather offended. 'But as I'm sure you can imagine, he doesn't live here, or anywhere else for that matter. You may not know this, but he's dead.'

I silently cursed the forger's outlandish surname and gave up. I couldn't stay there much longer, ringing every bell, or I could do so on another occasion (ringing two was enough at any one time, I shouldn't overstep the mark), or return at a different hour when the real-life doorman would be in, if there was one. Besides, it occurred to me that Custardoy might have rented or bought his apartment or studio under a false name, as befitted a criminal, or maybe under his own name, Custardoy being a pseudonym. In either case, no one in that building would be able to tell me where to find him.

I was almost certain I had the right place, which was promising, but I had to make sure and find out what floor he lived on and in which apartment; Tupra, I knew, would have had no qualms about stationing himself outside my house from early on – that is, outside Luisa's house – waiting for her to come out and following her as often as proved necessary, knowing that on one such sortie she was sure to head for that area near the Royal Palace and the cathedral-cum-eyesore, near Cuesta de la Vega and Atenas Park and the various other local parks and gardens, Sabatini, Campo del Moro, Viaducto and Vistillas or what remained of them (I had read that the Council and the Church were plotting to do away with them and use the land to build episcopal offices or semi-clerical housing or a car park or something), where the Madrid of the Habsburgs mingled with that of Carlos III, until she arrived at that or another door. I, however, did have qualms. It wasn't just that it seemed wrong and contemptible of me to shadow her like that, I feared, above all, that she might spot me and then all my plans would be ruined: she'd be on the alert, she'd be sure to get angry and forbid me from interfering in any aspect or area of her life, and then I would be unable to talk to Custardoy or influence him without her attributing to me any resulting change, and blaming me for any rupture with the con man or, indeed, his withdrawal, the thing I so desired, and then, as her sister had predicted, she would never speak to me again; well, perhaps not never, but certainly not for a long time. I had to save Luisa without her suspecting my intervention, or as little as possible. She would always have an inkling that there was some connection, because of my presence in Madrid: her boyfriend vanishing just when I appeared or shortly afterwards would be too much of a coincidence, and she'd be left with the conviction that I'd had something to do with it. However, if I performed my task well and kept out of the way as much as possible, that conviction would have no grounds, no proof, and, as such, would soon fade and end up tossed into the bag of suspicions and imaginings.

During the days that followed, I visited my children and took them out as often as I could, occasionally meeting Luisa when I picked them up or dropped them off, but usually encountering only the Polish babysitter. I avoided hanging around, as I had on the first night; I avoided asking Luisa anything more about her black eye, or, at most, ventured some neutral, indirect comment: 'I see it's getting better – but try to be more careful in future.' Nor did I insist we meet on our own one day, to go out to supper and talk in peace, it was best to see very little of her during that stay and concentrate on trying to extricate her from the unhealthy relationship she had got herself into, even if she didn't see the relationship like that or, worse, was drawn to it. And if she was bemused by my lack of insistence, I could always say chivalrously: 'You've got too much to do. I'm just passing through, almost like a tourist really. And it seems more appropriate to let you take the initiative. Besides, I need to spend time with my father, who's not at all well. He sends his love by the way, and always asks after you.' And so I tried to remove myself and not to coincide with her except where the coincidence was genuine, not to make myself too visible or to be always bumping into her, as would have been tempting, and as I might have tended to do had I not immediately taken on that unexpected, specific, urgent, vital task as soon as I arrived in Madrid. Not that I found it easy to maintain a discreet pose, especially when the first week had passed and Luisa showed no sign of regret at not being able to spend time with me nor – most woundingly of all – did she show any curiosity about my life in London, about the kind of person I was when I was there, about whom I hung around with, nor if I had become someone else, even if only superficially, nor about my current job of which I had spoken so little over the phone, almost avoiding her occasional questions, perhaps asked only perfunctorily and out of politeness, but at least they were questions. Now there were no questions of any kind, nor did she seek the opportunity to ask them: during that first week she never made a single proposal to meet or get together, to go out to lunch, to linger a while in the apartment or have supper or a drink with her when I returned with Guillermo and Marina in the evening, having taken them to the cinema or the Retiro or wherever. It was as if she had no mental space to think of anything apart from her relationship with Custardoy, or at least that was what I assumed must be filling it entirely, for what else could it have been? She seemed to me absorbed, preoccupied. It wasn't the absorption of mere excitement or of plenitude. Nor that of anxiety or torment or unease, but that of someone struggling to understand or to decipher something.

And I did, in fact, spend time with my father and see my siblings and a few friends; I also visited Madrid's second-hand bookshops and generally mooched around. In one of those bookshops I bought a present for Sir Peter, a large book of propaganda posters from the Spanish Civil War, some of which, I noticed, bore the same 'careless talk' slogan as had appeared in his own country, with very similar warnings – I'd had a vague recollection of seeing something similar in Spain, although he never had – and he would be intrigued to see these Spanish precursors, as would Mrs Berry. I would go and see him as soon as I got back, without fail. And one morning, I returned to the area where Custardoy lived and, standing on the pavement opposite, looked at the street door leading to his apartment or studio in Calle Mayor. The door was still closed, so it may be that there was no doorman or only one who kept a very brief or idle or erratic timetable. In the end, however, I had decided that if I were ever to find him in, I would not approach the doorman; it was best that no one should see or identify me, still less associate me with Custardoy. If I were to go there in person to enquire after that copyist and forger, I might, depending on what happened later on between him and me, be putting myself in a vulnerable position, for you never know what might occur when two men come face to face and argue, or if one of them tries to get or demand something from the other, to force or convince or dissuade or repel. Standing on the same side of the street as the abominable cathedral, I looked up at the balconies, in the bizarre hope that I might have the great good luck that while I was there, Custardoy would appear on his – I would recognise him by his ponytail and from Cristina's grudging description – and I would know then, with no need for further effort or investigation, just where he worked or lived. There were balconies on all the floors until the fifth, where there were only the windows of what looked like an attic apartment. The balconies of the apartment immediately above the enormous door were made of stone and had little columns, while above that they were all fancy wrought iron, and every one had slatted shutters that stood open, an indication that each apartment was occupied and no one was away or travelling, and that Custardoy was in town. I studied each balcony and each window, trying to take in the fact – rather than imagine, which would have been a disagreeable and superfluous exercise – that behind one of them Luisa and Custardoy met and went to bed together, laughed and talked, discussed their day, that there they had perhaps argued and he had slapped her round the face with his open hand or punched her in the eye with his closed fist. He must be a very irascible fellow or perhaps not, perhaps he was utterly cold and had delivered both blows as a calculated warning, to remind her just what and how much he was capable of. And it might be that one night my wife would emerge from that ornate door opposite me, trembling with fear and excitement, simultaneously horrified and captivated. No, I didn't like that man or anything I knew or could imagine about him.

I also took to going to the Prado each morning, before I did anything else and as soon as I'd had breakfast, it was right across the street from my hotel. This wasn't just for my enjoyment and because I hadn't visited the place for ages. I also had in mind something my sister-in-law Cristina had said to me about Custardoy: '. . . sometimes he's commissioned to copy paintings from the Prado and he spends hours there studying and copying.' And so the first thing I did on the first day I went into the museum, and before looking at any pictures at all, was to search the place from top to bottom and from end to end, scrutinising the copyists who were working in the various rooms, in case one of them was a fifty-something man with his hair scraped back in a ponytail, a man prepared to spend hours and hours before some painting not of his choice, whether good, bad or indifferent. Needless to say I spotted none of these characteristics, indeed, most of the copyists were youngish women, although not all of them young enough to be art students. Perhaps it's another of those professions, like art restoration, that the female population has appropriated and which they do very well. I saw no one answering that description on the second day either. I carried out that same preliminary patrol, although I was filled this time with less hope or was it mere superstition: copying is such a slow task that it was likely that only those from the day before would be there again, or so it seemed; it would have been an extraordinary coincidence if Custardoy had started work on one of his copies or forgeries on the very day I happened to be there, on the alert. This, however, did not prevent me from repeating what I had done the previous morning and striding round all the galleries, studying the few people who were sitting or, in some cases, standing at their easels, intent on reproducing what was there before their eyes, something that already existed and which had, usually, been painted better several centuries before.

On the fifth day, I got up late, after a relatively wild night with some old friends, and only arrived at the Prado around one o'clock, about two hours later than usual. I wanted to visit some of the rooms containing works by Italian artists that I hadn't seen for years, and since those in charge of the museum have the ridiculous habit of moving everything around every so often – as if they were running a supermarket – and I suspected that it would take me a while to find the current location of those paintings, I dispensed with my preliminary patrol and inspection of the copyists. And it was there and then that I noticed in passing, in one of the long galleries on the ground floor, a man with a short piratical or matadorish pigtail who wasn't copying anything, but taking notes or doing pencil sketches of a painting in a fairly sizeable sketch pad, although not so large that he couldn't hold it in one hand. He was standing quite close to the picture in question and therefore with his back to me or to anyone else who was not right next to him or who had decided to block his view. I was perfectly within my rights to do either or both of those things, it is, after all, quite common nowadays for rude tourists – almost a tautology really – or indeed the rude natives of any city to impatiently, inconsiderately interpose themselves between painting and viewer and even elbow the latter none too subtly out of the way in order to occupy his or her more central position, the way of the world of which Tupra spoke has become ill-mannered, especially in Spain, although it's now a near-universal phenomenon. I kept a safe distance from him and not only so as not to appear rude. Initially, I observed him from behind, but just as there was no space to his right, only a rope barrier and the side wall, to the left of the painting there was a high door and to the left of that another painting (there were only two on that end wall), and so I moved cautiously in that direction to get as clear a view as possible of his profile, at the same time doing my best not to enter, or only minimally, his field of vision. I realised at once that I needn't worry about his seeing me, for he was totally absorbed in the painting and in his sketchbook, his eyes moving rapidly back and forth between the two, with no interest in anything else, he wasn't even distracted by the continuous ebb and flow of tourists, mostly Italians (come to admire their ancient compatriots), who, curiously enough, did not insist on crowding round him and bothering him by looking at what he was looking at, rather, on seeing him so absorbed in his work, they walked past without stopping, as if intimidated by that tense motionless figure and as if prepared, for the moment, to allow him exclusive usufruct and enjoyment of it. I noticed that he had a moustache and sideburns, which, although not long, were somewhat longer than is perhaps considered the norm nowadays, or perhaps they were merely striking because, while his hair was straight and rather fair and with no visible grey in it, his sideburns were curly and much darker, almost black, but streaked with white and grey, as if old age had decided to begin its work from the sides, leaving the pale dome for later. He was quite tall and thin, with perhaps some evidence around his belly of having drunk too much beer, but the general impression was of someone gaunt and bony, and what I could see of his cheek-bones and his broad forehead confirmed that impression, as did his swift active right hand, which had the long strong fingers of a professional pianist; alarming fingers, like piano keys.

Since I was unable to view him from the front, and so couldn't see his eyes or lips or teeth or facial expression (although I could see his nose in profile), it was impossible for me to interpret him, I mean, in the way I used to do at the building with no name when confronted by all those famous and unknown faces, whose voices I almost always heard as well, either in person or on video. From what I was able to make out (which was only his left side, whenever, that is, I pretended to be looking at the other painting separated from his by the high door and placed myself level with him, protected by the distance between us), everything seemed to agree with, or at least not contradict, Cristina's grudging but, as it turned out, accurate description of Custardoy. I had only asked her what he looked like at the end of our conversation, when she was already tired and eager to bring things to a close. 'Oh, I don't know,' she said, 'he's bony, sinewy, with a long nose like a flamenco singer, like the singer in Ketama, for example, you know the one I mean?' (I had an idea Ketama were some kind of semi-flamenco group.) 'And very strange dark eyes, I can't really describe them, but there's something strange, something peculiar about them that I don't like. Sometimes, he has a moustache and sometimes not, as if he kept shaving it off and then letting it grow again I suppose, because I've seen him with one and without.' 'What else? Tell me more,' I had urged her, just as Tupra or Mulryan or Rendel or Pérez Nuix used to urge me on, one more insistently than the others. 'That's all really. I can't think what else to say. Bear in mind that I only know him by sight. I've come across him over the years here and there, I know who he is and I've heard things about him as I have about a lot of other people (well, up until this business with Luisa, of course, since when I've heard rather more about him). But as far as I can remember, we've never been introduced, I've never been that close to him or exchanged a single word.' 'You must have noticed something more,' I had urged her again, knowing that if you press someone, there is always something more. 'Well, as I've said, he wears a tie on all occasions, as if he were trying to compensate for the slightly bohemian impression he makes with that ponytail and the half-grown moustache he sometimes sports: a contrast, a touch of originality. He dresses very correctly, very traditionally, he aspires to elegance I suppose, but doesn't quite make it. Perhaps because elegance is simply not compatible with the salacious look on his face, I don't quite know how to explain it, but he has one of those faces that oozes sexuality, absurd really, but maybe that in part explains his success with women, you can smell it on him. Even from a distance, you can tell what he's about. At least you can if you're a woman. He looks at you so brazenly, he sizes you up. He gives you the once-over, from head to toe, lingering shamelessly on your breasts and your arse, and, if you're sitting down, on your thighs. I used to see him do this, years ago, with loads of women at the Chicote and at the Cock, as soon as they walked in; and he's done it to me too, from a distance, because he doesn't care whether you're with someone or not. But he obviously didn't fancy me much or else could sense that he wasn't my type, because he never approached me. According to Ranz, he can tell immediately who is a willing prey, and he knows even more quickly whether he wants to sink his teeth in or leave well enough alone.' Given their present relationship, it had troubled me to think that he had spotted Luisa as a victim right from the start, as soon as he saw her. And I couldn't help but then go on to wonder if he would have seen the same thing in her had they met when she and I were together. The thought that followed was even worse: it wasn't impossible that they had met before I went off to London and before our official separation. That idea didn't bear thinking about, and so I did not pursue it.

In the man in the Prado I could see nothing of this, by which I mean his sexual voracity, although his gaze was intently fixed on a painting depicting a woman, a mother. Perhaps he had given her the once-over too, prior to any artistic, pictorial or even technical appraisal. Perhaps he had been put off by the fact that the woman appeared in the painting with her three small children; although not necessarily, if he was Custardoy, given that he was clearly attracted to Luisa and she, after all, was a mother of two. (True, the woman in the painting was a rather unattractive, matronly type, whereas Luisa kept herself very slim and, to my eyes, pretty and youthful, but I don't know how she appears to other eyes.) What I had noticed right from the very first instant was that he was wearing a jacket and tie and black lace-up shoes. They wouldn't have been made by Grenson or Edward Green, but they were plain and in good taste, with soles that were nei-ther thick nor made of rubber, I couldn't object to his choice of clothes, except to say that they were too conventional. Not the ponytail, of course, although in recent years, that's become fairly common among men of any age (age no longer acts as a brake on anything and has lost the battle against fashion and vanity). It gave him a roguish look, which was the adjective Cristina had so aptly used to describe him, if indeed it was him.

Once when I walked past, always keeping a prudent distance so that he wouldn't notice me, I managed to confirm my first impression: he was making sketches of the four heads in the painting and, at the same time, taking notes, both at great speed. If he was Custardoy, he might have been commissioned to make a copy and was carrying out a preliminary study. Or, if he really was as good as they said, perhaps he didn't need to stand in front of the picture itself with easel and brushes for long hours and even longer days, and it was enough for him to capture and memorise it (maybe he had a photographic memory) and then work from a good reproduction in his studio, the fact is I know nothing about the techniques used by copyists, let alone forgers (he wouldn't be creating a forgery on this occasion, no one would believe that the work in the Prado wasn't authentic, wasn't the original).

However, I didn't want to spend too much time in his vicinity: the longer I stayed there like his shadow, the greater the risk that he would turn round or glance to his left and see me there, although it was highly unlikely that he would know me or recognise me from photos Luisa might have shown him, though I doubted that she had, and the probability was that he had never seen me. Anyway, I moved away a little and looked briefly at another painting, 'Messer Marsilio Cassoti and His Wife' by Lorenzo Lotto, and then shifted closer again, I didn't want him to escape me now, to lose track of him; I ventured slightly further off and had a quick look at a 'Portrait of a Gentleman' by Volterra, but was drawn back at once to the man with the ponytail, I didn't dare take my eyes off him for more than a few seconds; I wandered away again and studied Yañez de la Almedina's 'St Catharine' – all in reds and blues, resting a long sword on the wheel of her martyrdom – and that figure distracted me, so much so that after only half a minute's contemplation, I started in alarm and almost ran back to the painting of the mother and her children. In between all these comings and goings and periods of waiting, I managed to get a good look at that painting: it was average size, about three feet something long by three feet wide I reckoned; and the painting was a family portrait, according to the label, 'Camilla Gonzaga, Countess of San Secondo, and her Sons' by Parmigianino, whose real name, I noticed, was Mazzola, like a famous soccer star from my early childhood who played against the Real Madrid of Di Stéfano and Gento, I seemed to recall he was a forward with Inter Milan. Against a dark almost black background stood the sturdy Countess, well dressed, discreetly bejewelled, holding in her right hand a golden, gem-encrusted

306

goblet which looked slightly out of place with so many children around her; or perhaps it wasn't a goblet, but the large tassel from her belt. She bordered on the plump, or maybe not (but she was certainly wide), her expression was rather absent and certainly not lively, although there was perhaps a remnant there of calm almost indifferent determination. She had slightly bovine, almost prominent eyes, very fine eyebrows, which looked as if they had been pencilled in, and rather thin and unalluring lips; her best feature was possibly her lustrous unlined rosy skin, so smooth and taut on her cheeks that it looked as if it might burst. More surprising was her lack of interest in her children, Troilo, Ippolito and Federico according to the label; she showed no signs at all that she was devoted to them, she wasn't looking at them or touching them, not even holding the hand of the child to her left, which was very close to her own inert left hand. The Countess was like an astonished statue surrounded by other smaller but similarly self-absorbed statues, because the odd thing was that the children weren't paying *her* any attention either, although two of them were distractedly clasping the braided belt of her dress. Each figure was gazing out of the picture in a different direction as if each and every one of them was far more interested in people or elements beyond the frame than in each other in the case of the boys, or in her sons, in the case of the mother, who was the central figure. The oldest child to her right was the least attractive and resembled a foundling or an orphan, partly because of his ugly and excessively severe haircut, and partly because of the sad expression on his face; the youngest didn't seem very happy or very affectionate either, just vulnerable, and about to tug at his mother's belt like someone performing a purely reflex or habitual action; the boy on her left, the prettiest of the children and the one with the most alert eyes, seemed completely oblivious to the rest of the group, as if he were anxious to escape both the others and the enforced patience of his extreme youth.

The only gaze that one could follow or imagine was that of the Countess, given that, to her right, beyond the high door, which kept them still further apart (a whim of that month's reorganisation), hung the portrait of her husband, at whom she was directing that distinctly chilly and possibly disappointed look, or perhaps it was a look that was wounded by the mere thought of him. 'They were painted separately,' I thought, 'husband and father on one side, wife and mother with the children on the other, two different portraits, in two distinct, isolated spaces rather than in one space common to them both: a bit like my now living alone in London, while Luisa stays here in Madrid with Guillermo and Marina, except that she's devoted to our children and they to her, at least that's how it has been up until now, it would be terrible if that Custardoy fellow were beginning to distance her from them, it happens with women sometimes, they suddenly have eyes and thoughts only for the new man they're chasing or for the old love they're losing – that's the only thing that can, very occasionally, create a rift and cause them temporarily to relegate their children to second place, just as the Countess perhaps has her gaze fixed on the distant soldier who is out of the picture and perhaps out of time, thus neglecting Troilo, Ippolito and Federico, who are accustomed now to the fact that their mother barely pays them any attention and lives obsessed with thoughts of her absent husband and perhaps sees them as a tie and an impediment and a hindrance, I don't think such a thing would ever happen with Luisa, although she does seem to have made frequent use of the Polish babysitter while I've been here, and there must be or could be a reason for that. And Luisa is clearly not obsessed with thoughts of me, however absent I might be. She, after all, was the one to expel me from her time and from the children's time, although I doubtless gave her some cause to do so.'

'Pedro Maria Rossi, Count of San Secondo. 1533–35', said the label and then went on to describe him: 'Pedro Maria Rossi (1504–1547) was a brilliant soldier who served under Francis I of France, Cosimo I de' Medici and Charles V' ('So he was a mercenary in other words,' I thought, 'as I am, too, in my own way'). 'The portrait was painted when he was fighting under the imperial flag, which explains the inclusion of the word "IMPERIO" and the many classical quotations.' The Count's blue-grey

gaze was even colder than that of his wife, almost scornful, almost steely and almost cruel, although it was harder to imagine that he was directing it at her than that she was directing hers at him. ('He could be Sir Cruelty,' I thought.) The long beard and moustache made him seem older (he would only have been about thirty when he posed for the portrait) and made it hard to know at first glance whether he was good-looking or merely elegant and severe, a second glance revealed that he certainly was (all three things, I mean). His noble nose was quite large, larger than mine but not as large as Custardoy's, which was, moreover, slightly hooked. Like St Catharine and Reresby, he had a sword, on his left side (which meant that he must be right-handed), but his sword was sheathed and you could only see the hilt and the guard, not the blade. He was wearing a fine costume trimmed with fur, and to his left was a statue of a helmeted youth also carrying a sword, presumably the god Mars. The Count had distinguished hands, with fingers that seemed too slender to be those of a warrior. But pretty much the most striking thing about him was the aggressive codpiece, seamed or stitched or whatever you call it (it must have been made of hard leather, not of reeds or wicker as they appear in most paintings), visibly and obscenely pointing upwards – a permanent reminder of his erection – far less discreet and modest, for example, than those worn by Emperor Charles V and Philip II in the full-length portraits, both by Titian, in the same museum. 'Perhaps this Count, this soldier, this husband, isn't like me at all,' I thought, 'the one who's leaving or has left, but like the one who is about to arrive or has arrived already and is a violent man who carries a sword, like that bastard Custardoy. Perhaps his wife's gaze then is one of devotion and fear, which is why she seems paralysed and will-less, for devotion and fear are such powerful dominant feelings, whether felt simultaneously or separately it doesn't matter, that they can momentarily cancel out all other feelings, even love for one's children. I hope Luisa doesn't look at Custardoy like that, I hope she isn't afraid of him, still less devoted. But precisely how she looks at him is something I will never know.'

I again looked away from the portrait and glanced over at Custardoy or at the man who might be Custardoy and I saw that he was also looking in my direction; I was convinced that, for a couple of seconds, our eyes met, but so briefly that it was likely that we had, in fact, each merely glanced simultaneously at the painting that more or less matched the picture we each had before us, I that of Pedro Maria Rossi and he that of Camilla Gonzaga with Troilo, Ippolito and Federico, their children; since I first spotted him, he must have spent at least seven minutes there jotting down words and scribbling lines but he'd doubtless been there longer than that too, and that's a long time to look at a single painting. In that couple of seconds, however, I was able to see his face full on for the first time, and it immediately impressed me as being crude, rough and cold, with its broad forehead or receding hairline, its sparse moustache (dark like his sideburns) and its nose which appeared, as is only logical, less hooked than it had in profile (yes, he did suddenly remind me of a long-haired singer I had seen on television, probably the singer with that group Ketama), and two enormous very dark eyes, rather wide-set and almost lashless, and both those factors, the lack of lashes and the wide-apartness, must have made his obscene gaze unbearable or possibly irresistible when turned on the women he seduced or bought and possibly also when turned on the men with whom he might be competing. They were eyes that grabbed, like hands, and one night or one day, they had alighted on the face and body of Luisa and made her his prey. ('And very strange dark eyes, I can't really describe them, but there's something strange, something peculiar about them that I don't like,' according to the description I had coaxed out of a reluctant Cristina.) And so, to give those eyes no time to fix on or grab me, I walked away from my portrait of the Count, retreated a few steps and went into the room next door, to the left and on a slightly higher level (a matter of going up three or four steps). From there I could peer in every thirty seconds or so to make sure Custardoy had not escaped without my realising, and, at the same time, I was much less likely to re-enter his field of vision. In that first lightning glimpse of his face full on he had reminded me of someone else, not the singer, but someone I knew personally, but it was too brief a glimpse for me to be able to remember who, or if my memory was right.

The next room was dominated largely by German art. It contained Dürer's famous self-portrait, as well as his 'Adam' and his 'Eve'. However, my eye was caught at once by a long narrow painting I had been familiar with since childhood, when, as was only normal, it had shocked and filled me with a degree of fear tinged with curiosity, 'The Three Ages and Death' by Hans Baldung Grien, which, like the two portraits, has its counterpart in another painting of the same format and dimensions next to it, 'Harmony, or The Three Graces'. In the former, Death, on the right, is grasping the arm of an old woman or has his arm linked through hers and is tugging at her gently, unhurriedly, and the old woman, in turn, has one arm round the shoulder of a young woman while with her left hand she's plucking at the younger woman's skimpy raiments, as if she, too, were drawing her softly away. Death is carrying an hourglass in his right hand ('An hourglass figure,' I thought) and in his left hand keeps a loose hold on a spear twice broken (it almost resembles a thunderless flash of lightning) on whose point falls or rests the hand of a sleeping child who is lying at the feet of that group of three, though it may be a long time until he joins them, and he is quite oblivious to their dealings. To his right, an owl; in the background, a solar landscape that looks instead lunar, grim and desolate, with a ruined tower in flames; the inevitable cross hangs in the sky. I had always wondered, ever since I was a child,

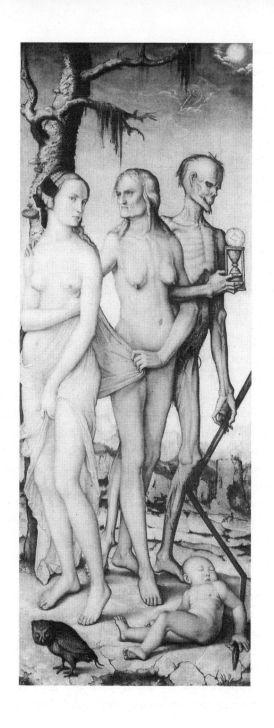

if the young woman and the old were the same person at very different ages or if they were two separate women, I mean, if the older woman had always been tugging at herself from youth onwards and into old age, when she finally allows herself to be carried off by Death, for if that were not the case, the subject would be graver and more troubling. However, the two women looked very alike to me: the blue eyes, the nose, the rather thin lips, the somewhat sharp chin, the long wavy hair, the stature, the smallish widely spaced breasts, the feet, the whole figure, there were even similarities in their facial expressions, or at least they were not entirely opposed. The young woman is frowning, either worried or annoyed, but not alarmed or frightened, as she probably would have been had the person drawing her away been a stranger, or just another person, or even her mother. She doesn't struggle or put up a fight or try to shrug off the hand on her shoulder, and at most, she tries to prevent her from removing all her garments. The old woman, for her part, focuses all her attention on the young woman and not on Death, and in her look there is a mixture of gravity, understanding, resolve and pity, but no ill will, as if she were saying to the young woman (or to herself when she was her age): 'I'm sorry, but there's nothing we can do' (or 'Come along, we have to go on; I know because I've already arrived'). As for Death, who has his arm linked through hers, she takes no notice of him, but neither does she resist or oppose him, she looks more towards the past than her future, perhaps because – despite the promises of the cross hanging in the air and the infernal tower in flames, with a large hole in the side as if made by a cannon ball – she knows that there is little or no future left.

'There's Sir Death,' I thought, 'as in the English and, generally speaking, the Germanic tradition: he's clearly male, *el Muerte* not *la Muerte*, because although he is cadaverous, a semi-skeleton with the skin clinging to bones it barely covers – like a disguise he's adopted to tread the earth, all the more so when you notice his eyes are more deeply sunken than the rest – you can see a few wisps of beard growing out of his chin, and other wisps, resembling tiny tentacles, more like the tentacles of a cuttlefish or a squid than an octopus, peeping out where his penis and his vanished testicles would have been, now there's only a hole where once a codpiece doubtless stood erect. He's certainly not like Sergeant Death in the Armagh ballad ("And when Sergeant Death's cold arms shall embrace me"), who is a man in his prime, a strong energetic warrior prepared to snatch lives away non-stop, an experienced professional with his cold disciplined arms always busy; this Death is the feeblest and most worn of the three figures, or of the four, with his meek broken spear, so meek that an unwary child can almost touch it. And yet there is determination and energy in the scrawny arm that grips, and he is, above all, the master of time, he holds the clock and knows the time and can see when it's running out, the sand or water, whichever it is that his hourglass contains and on which his red-veined eyes are firmly fixed, rather than on the old or the young woman, for time is his only guide, the only thing that counts for this Sir Death, as naked and decrepit as our Latin hag with her scythe, this Sir Death with neither helmet nor sword.' And I suddenly remembered 'the loud tick-tock' in that small sepulchral living room in the Lisbon cemetery of Os Prazeres, which, according to the traveller who 'with a degree of indiscretion' discovered and observed it, 'was to a normal tick-tock what a shout is to the spoken voice'; and I recalled the enigmatic words suggested by the sight of the alarm clock making the noise ('of the kind we used to see in our parents' kitchens, round in shape, with a bell like a spherical skullcap and with two small balls for feet'): 'It seems to me that time is the only dimension in which the living and the dead can talk to each other and communicate, the only dimension they have in common.' Perhaps when all the sand or all the water had trickled through, thus signalling the death of the old woman painted by Baldung Grien, and who was perhaps also the young woman, when he had finally sent them to join 'the more influential and more animated majority', he would still have to turn over the hourglass or clepsydra in order to begin the countdown again, about which my compatriot the traveller wondered: Was it the amount of time they had been dead or the time yet to elapse before the Last Judgement?

If it was measuring out the hours of solitude, was it counting those that had passed or those still to come?

I kept peering in at the larger Italian gallery, then turning back to spend a little more time with the German painting, which while it no longer frightened me, still intrigued me. From the threshold I saw, too, 'The Annunciation' by Fra Angelico, an excellent full-size copy of which had presided over my father's living room for as long as I could remember, he and my mother had commissioned it from a friend who was a copyist, a Custardoy of the 1930s and '40s, Daniel Canellada was his name I recall; seeing that painting was, for me, like being at home. On one of my brief forays into the German gallery, I lingered too long in front of the Baldung Grien and, when I returned to the Italian gallery, the man was no longer standing before the Parmigianino, I mean, before the Countess and her children. I bounded down the intervening steps, looking anxiously to right and left, but, fortunately, I spotted him at once, his now closed sketchbook under his arm, on his way to the stairs that led up to the first floor and then to the exit. That's when I started to follow him, or where I became more like his shadow, not in quite the same way as I had been with Tupra on the journeys we made together, but in both cases I relegated myself to the background. Once upstairs, he went to the cloakroom, and I waited with my back turned until he reappeared, looking round every three seconds so as not to lose him again, and when he emerged, I discovered with horror that what he had left there and retrieved was a hat, possibly a fedora ('A man wearing a ponytail and a hat,' I thought, 'possibly a fedora. Good lord!'). He had the good manners not to put it on while he was indoors, but only when he went out into the street, and then I saw – although it brought me little relief – that it was broader brimmed than the aforementioned fedora, more the kind of hat a painter or a conductor or an artist would wear, and black, of course. Duly behatted, he set off down the steps outside the museum, opposite the Hotel Ritz, and I followed after, always at a safe distance. He strode along the Paseo del Prado at a good pace, then stopped outside a brasserie, studied the menu, peered in through the window, shielding his eyes with his hand against the reflections on the glass (wasn't the brim of his presumptuous hat enough?), as if he were considering having lunch there — although it was early for Madrid unless you happened to be a foreigner; perhaps I was wrong, and he was a foreigner; but he didn't look like one to me, I could sense something unequivocally Spanish about his whole appearance, especially the way he walked, or perhaps it was the trousers — and so I took advantage of that pause to look in the window of a nearby shop selling artefacts from Toledo, including swords — obviously aimed at tourists, but nowadays they wouldn't be allowed to take such swords with them on a plane, they'd have to check them, and even then a sword wouldn't easily fit in a suitcase; it wouldn't be permitted on trains either, and I wondered who the devil would buy such swords now if they couldn't be transported anywhere, a collector of decorative knives and swords like Dick Dearlove would presumably have them sent to him some way or other. Most would be made of our famous Toledo steel, very Spanish and very medieval, but I noticed that among those on display there were also a few that were apparently Scottish and even bore the name 'McLeod' engraved on the guard, an ignoble concession to the movie-mad Anglo-Saxon masses. It occurred to me that I might buy one, not right then, of course, but later, for I had learned from Tupra a little of the effect that such an archaic weapon could produce. Almost all of them, however, were much longer and larger, doubtless far more difficult and far heavier to wield than the 'catgutter' or Landsknecht or *Katzbalger*, they had really huge blades. They would cut off a hand at a blow. They would slice through and dismember. 'No,' I thought, 'it would be best if it were a sword I didn't have to get rid of, one that I could return to its place, used or not, it wouldn't matter, one that I wouldn't have to throw away or deliberately abandon for someone else.'

The man who was now very probably Custardoy continued on along Carrera de San Jerónimo, past my hotel, where he peered in at the entrance and read the plaque there which states, incredibly, that the Palace Hotel was conceived, designed and built in the brief space of fifteen months spanning 1911 and

1912, by the Léon Monnoyer construction company, who were, I suppose, French or Belgian, I don't know how the builders of today – that plague, that horde – can hold up their heads for shame or indeed shamelessness; a little further on, more or less opposite the Parliament building, he paused momentarily by the statue of Cervantes – who also had his sword unsheathed – there were some police vans parked there, with five or six police-men armed with machine guns standing outside to protect the honourable members, even though there were none to be seen, they must all have been inside or off on a trip somewhere or in one of the bars. The man with the ponytail and moustache had clearly retrieved something else from the museum cloakroom, a briefcase with no handles, into which he must have put his sketchbook, and he was carrying said briefcase under his arm and walking quickly, confidently, head up, eyes front, looking frankly about him and at the people he passed, and I had quite a fright when, as he was passing Lhardy, he slowed his pace and turned his head to observe the legs of a girl with whom he had almost collided, possibly deliberately I thought. I was afraid he might see me and recognise me, I mean from before, from the Prado. His response to the young woman was very Spanish, one I often have myself, although whenever I turned round like that in London, I had the sense that I was the only man who did, less so in Madrid, although there are fewer and fewer men who dare to look at whatever we want to, especially when the person we're looking at can't see us and has her back to us, which means that we're not bothering or embarrassing anyone – in these in-creasingly repressive times the puritans are even trying to control what our eyes do, often quite involuntarily. His was a quick, appreciative, brazen glance, with those large dark marble-like eyes of his, intense and troubling, wide-set and lashless, which more or less coincided with what Cristina had told me about the way he visually grabbed at women; but perhaps that was an exaggeration, I myself sometimes look in a similar way at a pass-ing derrière or a pair of legs as they move off, perhaps with less penetrating appraising eyes, more ironic or more amused. His eyes looked as if they were salivating.

If when he arrived at the ruined Puerta del Sol, he continued straight on, if he didn't go down into the metro and didn't catch a bus or a taxi, we would be on the right track, that is, heading for Custardoy's house or workshop or studio, and then there'd be no further room for doubt that he was he. I feared for a moment that he was about to deviate from that route when, at the beginning of Calle Mayor, he crossed the street, but I was reassured at once to see that he was merely going into a rather fine-looking bookshop, Méndez by name. From the other side of the street, through the shop window, I saw him greet the owners or employees affectionately (patting them on the arm; and he was again polite enough to take off his hat, which was something), and he must have made some funny comment because they both laughed, a burst of generous spontaneous laughter. He left after a few minutes, carrying a bag from the bookshop, so he must have bought something, and I wondered what sort of thing he would read, then he crossed back onto my side of the road, and I retreated a few steps, until there was the same distance between us as there had been since we left the museum. However, I had to stop again almost at once and make a slow withdrawal from an ATM, in order to gain time and not overtake him, because he met a female acquaintance or friend – I caught a glimpse of blue eyes – a young woman in trousers, with short hair and a fringed suede jacket, à la Daniel Boone or Davy Crockett or General Custer when they skewered him. She smiled warmly at him and planted a kiss on each cheek, he must live in the area; they chatted animatedly for a few minutes, she obviously liked him (he didn't take off his hat this time, but at least he touched the brim with his fingers when he saw the young woman, the classic gesture of respect in the street), and she laughed loudly at something he said ('He's the sort of man who makes people laugh, like me when I want to,' I thought. 'That could explain why Luisa likes him. Bad luck. Bad news'). No one would ever suspect that he hit women, or one particular woman, the woman who still mattered most to me.

He said goodbye and continued on his way; he walked with great resolve, almost fiercely sometimes when he increased the pace, he would never be bothered by any of the pickpockets or muggers who abound in that touristy area and who, for preference, fleece the Japanese; perhaps beggars would leave him alone too, his walk was that of someone who, however pleasant, is not open to overtures of that kind; and the duty of beggars and thieves is to recognise this at once and to sense whom they're dealing with. He proceeded on past the San Miguel market on his left, where the road went slightly downhill. On the wall of a building I noticed a carved inscription which said soberly, gravely: 'Here lived and died Don Pedro Calderón de la Barca', the dramatist on whom Nietzsche, in his day, was so keen, as indeed was the whole of Germany; and a little further along, on the other side, a more modern plaque indicated: 'In this place stood the Church of San Salvador, in whose tower Luis Vélez de Guevara set the action of his novel *El diablo cojuelo* – *The Devil Upon Two Sticks* – 1641', a book it had never occurred to me to read, not even when I was at Oxford, but Wheeler, Cromer-Blake and Kavanagh would surely have known it. Custardoy went over for a moment to a statue immediately opposite, in Plaza de la Villa, how odd that a painter should be so attracted to the three-dimensional. 'To Don Álvaro de Bazán' was all it said underneath, the Admiral in command of the Spanish fleet at the battle of Lepanto, where Cervantes was wounded in 1571, losing the use of his left hand when he was only twenty-four, which meant that he could justifiably refer to himself as 'a complete man albeit missing a hand' in the same lines of farewell that I had quoted to Wheeler, even though he didn't want to hear them: farewell wit, farewell charm, farewell dear, delightful friends. There, too, was the Torre de los Luxanes, where it is said Francis I of France was held prisoner after being captured by the Spanish during the battle of Pavia in 1525; but since various other places in Spain also claim that he was held captive there, either a lot of people are lying or the Emperor Charles V trailed the French king round the country, exhibiting him like a monkey or a trophy.

Custardoy was still on the right track, the one that should lead him to his house, straight down Calle Mayor, and with me right behind, his rather distant or detached shadow. 'I've spent some time now being a shadow,' I thought, 'I have been and am a shadow at Tupra's side, accompanying him on his journeys and talking to him almost every day, always by his side like a subaltern, an interpreter, a support, an apprentice, an ally, occasionally a henchman ("No doubt, an easy tool, deferential, glad to be of use"). Now I'm playing shadow to this man who I'm not even sure is the man I'm looking for, but as regards him, I'm none of those other things; I'm a sinister, punitive, threatening shadow of which he as yet knows nothing, as is usually the case with those walking behind, who cannot be seen; it would be better for him if he did not continue along this route, or if his route turned out not to be the one I hope for and desire.' Just after thinking this, I thought he might escape me, because when he reached the Capitanía General or Consejo de Estado (where soldiers bearing machine guns stood outside the first door), he again crossed the street as if he were about to go into the Istituto Italiano di Cultura, which is immediately opposite. Except that he didn't, he went down a narrow street just beyond that, and I felt really alarmed: surely, at this late stage, he wasn't going to turn out not to be he and not approach that ornate door before which I had stood on two occasions now. At the end of that street, very short and for pedestrians only, I saw him disappear to the left and I quickened my pace slightly to not lose track of him, and to find out where he was going, and when I reached that same point, he very nearly did see me: there, in the corner, was an old bar, El Anciano Rey de los Vinos, where he took a seat outside, looking obliquely across towards the Palacio Real; in Madrid, what with global warming, it's almost like summer for nearly six months of the year, and so there are tables and chairs set outside cafés and bars long after and long before the appropriate seasons. I immediately turned round to hide my face from him and pretended to read, like a tourist, another metal plaque just above me (and, of course, I did read it): 'Near this place stood the houses of Ana de Mendoza y la Cerda, Princess of Éboli, and in one of them she was arrested by order of Philip II in 1579.' She was the one-eyed woman, an intriguer and possibly a spy, who had doubtless in her day spread outbreaks of cholera, malaria and plague, as Wheeler had done, or so he said, and doubtless Tupra too, or perhaps the latter had merely lit the fuses that provoked great fires. (No age is free of such contagions; in every age there are people bearing flaming torches and people who talk.) The lady was always shown wearing an eye-patch, over her right eye I seemed to recall from seeing some portrait of her, and I thought, too, that I had watched a movie about her, starring Olivia de Havilland.

Out of the corner of my eye I noticed Custardoy placing his order with the waiter, and I walked back down the street as far as Calle Mayor, pondering what to do next, apart, that is, from keeping well out of the way. There was a ridiculous statue there, which Custardoy, showing excellent taste, had not stopped to look at; it was one of the many 'anonymous' pieces that fill our cities (in the name of 'democratising' monuments, a contradiction in itself), but the fellow looked suspiciously like Hemingway, patron saint of tourists. And there was another plaque high up on the wall, that said: 'In this street, Juan Escobedo, secretary to John of Austria, was killed on 31 March 1578, on the night of Easter Monday.' Again this rang a bell with me, that murky murder; perhaps the Princess of Éboli had been involved, although it would have been very stupid of her to order an enemy to be killed right next to her house. (Later, I checked, and apparently it's still not known if the murder was carried out on orders from the Princess, from Philip II himself or from Antonio Pérez, his scheming secretary, who ended up being sent into exile; an as yet unsolved crime four and a bit centuries later, there in that narrow street which, at the time, was called Camarín de Nuestra Señora de Almudena. But why do I say 'still' or 'as yet', in some cases the passing of time serves no purpose, so much remains unknown, denied, hidden, even as regards ourselves and our own actions.) 'What a lot of one-eyed, one-handed, hobbling people there have been in these old streets,' I found myself thinking, 'what a lot of deaths. They won't notice one more, should it come to that.'

I decided to take a few short turns about the surrounding area, so that I could return every so often to a point from which

I could keep an eye on Custardoy and his movements from afar, I couldn't risk missing the moment when he paid his bill, got up and set off again, from El Anciano Rey de los Vinos to what I presumed was his house, just steps away; he would only have to cross two streets. And so I moved a little way off and stopped before another statue in Calle de Bailén, this time a rather rough bust of the admirable *madrileño* writer Larra, who committed suicide in 1837 by shooting himself in the head while standing in front of the mirror, before he was even twenty-eight (another member of the Kennedy–Mansfield fraternity, of which there are so many), perhaps over some unhappy love affair, but who knows; and then I stopped by yet another sculpture, slightly grotesque this time, of a certain Captain Melgar, all medals and curled moustaches – he reminded me somewhat of Tupra's improbable ancestor in the portrait by Kennington I had seen at his house – and who, according to the inscription, had died in the battle of Barranco del Lobo, in Melilla, during the African War, in 1909; it wasn't so much the actual bust of the Captain that was grotesque as a second disproportionately small figure – not so small as to be a Lilliputian or Tom Thumb, but certainly a midget – of a soldier dressed like Beau Geste and who was trying to climb up the pedestal or column with his rifle in his hand, whether to worship his Captain or to attack him and finish him off wasn't clear. And then I walked back the way I had come – although on the other side of the street this time, the same side as the Catholic monstrosity – and studied Custardoy where he sat outside the café. He had been served a beer, some anchovies and some *patatas bravas* ('So he treats himself to a proper aperitif, does he?' I thought. 'He obviously feels he's worked hard enough and he's in no hurry, he'll certainly be there for a while'), and had unfolded a newspaper, which he was sitting reading, legs crossed, now and then looking around with his huge eyes, which meant I had to be prudent, and so I again moved off, this time going as far as the Palacio Real, only to discover more hideous statues, a constant feature in Madrid: a whole line of Visigothic kings dressed like pseudo-Romans and each bearing a barely comprehensible inscription, especially for a foreigner, and I was feeling rather like a foreigner: 'Ataúlfo, Mu. A° de 415', said the first one, and the same enigmatic inscription (meaning presumably *Murió Año de* . . . He died in the year . . .) accompanied Eurico, 'de 484', Leovigildo, 'de 585', Suintala, 'de 633', Wamba, 'de 680' . . . Further on, stood a large monument, 'erected at the instigation of Spanish women to the glory of the soldier Luis Noval', who must have been a heroic soldier and obviously the darling of the ladies, for he, too, was dressed like Beau Geste or Beau Sabreur or Beau Ideal or all of them put together: '*Patria, no olvides nunca a los que por ti mueren, MCMXII*; My country, never forget those who died for you, MCMXII' (that word '*patria*' would have to be translated as 'country', the word used by Tupra on the night we first met and which had made me wonder if he might, in spirit, be a fascist in the analogical sense). But my country forgets everyone, both those who die for it and those who don't, including that fellow Noval – why, no one in Madrid will have the faintest idea who he was or how he distinguished himself or what he did. Every time I retraced my steps, and the café terrace once more came within my field of vision, the more settled the man with the ponytail seemed to be, and so I decided to set off in another direction and walk down Cuesta de la Vega, 'Near here stood the site of Puerta de la Vega, the main entrance into Muslim Madrid, from the ninth century onwards' and 'Image of María Santísima de la Almudena, hidden in this place in the year 712 and miraculously rediscovered in the year 1085' ('They hid it in the year following the Moorish invasion,' I thought, 'presumably so that it wouldn't be destroyed.' But that very white effigy of the Virgin and Child, placed in a niche, didn't look remotely like something made in the eighth century or even a replica of one, but was a shameless fake; Custardoy would have known), and even got as far as Parque de Atenas, where the inevitable bust, almost hidden this time because of the isolated position in which it had been placed, was of no less a person than the jubilant Boccherini, who lived for twenty or more years in Madrid and died here in penury, never having been honoured by this ungrateful city (it's not even known where his bones lie or if there was a grave to give them shelter); behind him was a stone plaque bearing the words of someone called Cartier which said: 'If God wanted to talk to mankind through music, He would use the works of Haydn; but if He Himself wanted to listen to music, he would choose Boccherini.' Yes, his music, like Mancini's, accompanied me wherever I went.

I had gone too far and hurried back up Cuesta de la Vega, fearing that I might be left not knowing what I needed to know, by a miscalculation or through carelessness. When I once again reached the point where Calle Mayor and Calle de Bailén meet – I glanced at the door to my right, but there was no sign of Custardoy going in – it occurred to me that the best place to keep watch over the café terrace, or part of it, without being seen, was from the top of the short double flight of steps that led directly to the statue of the Polish, *jota*-dancing Pope, and so up I went and stood leaning on the balcony, with my back turned on *totus tuus*, yes, his really was the ugliest of the statues, but not through incompetence on the part of the sculptor; people would assume I was another devotee, a few of whom were taking photographs of the figure and imitating his invitation-to-the-dance posture. I could see my man from there, he wouldn't escape me when he got up. I waited. And waited. He was still reading the newspaper, still wearing his hat (he was, after all, in the open air); he had placed his handleless briefcase on the chair beside him, and he seemed to possess special antennae for detecting any good-looking women, because whenever one passed or sat down, he would look up and check her out, perhaps he just had a very good nose. 'Luisa hasn't shown much judgement in that respect either,' I thought. 'He's probably the kind of man for whom one woman is never enough.' I wished I had some binoculars with me so that I could observe him more closely. Even at that distance, there was something about him that reminded me of someone else, an affinity or a resemblance, just as Incompara had immediately brought to mind my old classmate Comendador, now a respectable building contractor in New York or Miami or wherever it was he had gone. But I couldn't put my finger on it, I couldn't identify the model, I mean, the first individual of that sort whom I had, at some point, met.

Finally, I saw him hold up his arm and click his fingers twice, a disdainful and now antiquated way of summoning waiters. 'He can't be about to order another beer,' I thought, 'there are two empty glasses on the table already.' Fortunately, he was asking for the bill; he took some notes out of his trouser pocket (I carry them like that too, loose, rather than in a wallet) and put one down on the table, as we *madrileños* always used to do: money should never pass from hand to hand, but via a neutral place. He obviously knew the waiter, which made his previous very classist finger-clicks even ruder; as the waiter put the change down, likewise on the table, Custardoy patted him lightly on the arm, as he had with the booksellers, perhaps he took his pre-lunch drink in El Anciano Rey de los Vinos every day. He made some comment to the waiter as he left and the latter laughed out loud, as had the people in the bookshop and the young General Custer or Davy Crockett with her fringed jacket; he clearly had a sense of humour. Soon I would know whether he was he or someone else. He didn't leave that corner café by walking back down the narrow street of the unsolved murder, but via Calle de Bailén, which was a good sign. As he walked along, he looked into the windows of the shop selling musical instruments which occupies that whole corner, strode quickly across Calle Mayor and paused by the traffic lights in Bailén, which were red. At that point, I lost sight of him and hurriedly retreated until I found a position from which I could see him again, to the left of the shop belonging to that ghastly temple, which was to the left of *totus* (who on earth would want to buy anything there?). I could see the whole corner from there, from behind some railings, I was right in front of the door to his house – if it *was* his house – only on higher ground, where he wouldn't see me, because he was unlikely to look up, I felt like the Düsseldorf vampire lying in wait. Custardoy now only had to cross the street when the light turned green and go through the door towards which I was pushing him and which was, once again, closed. I could see him clearly now, he was unmistakable in his hat, I would see his footsteps too once he started walking. 'One, two, three, four, five . . .' I started counting in my head when the lights changed, he had small feet for a man his height, he followed the correct path, he wouldn't stop now, '. . . forty-five, forty-six, forty-seven, forty-eight, and forty-nine'. And he stopped outside the right door, his key ready in his hand. And then I thought with an ephemeral feeling of triumph: 'Got you, just where I want you.'

I waited for a few minutes more to see if a window opened, telling me what floor he lived on and confirming that he was home. There, however, I was out of luck. I walked down the steps, crossed the two streets that Luisa perhaps also often crossed, if, that is, she visited him much – she couldn't ever spend the night there – wondered briefly whether I should get a taxi back up to the Palace Hotel, but seeing none free, started to walk. When I reached Plaza de la Villa, I stopped to have a better look at the statue he had looked at, Don Álvaro de Bazán or Marqués de Santa Cruz, possibly the least ugly of the statues I had encountered. I walked round it and found an inscription at the back of the pedestal: 'I was the scourge of the Turk at Lepanto, the Frenchman at Terceira, the Englishman o'er all the seas. The King I served and the country I honoured know best who I am by the Cross in my name and the cross-hilt of my sword.' 'We Spaniards are always such braggarts,' I thought, still feeling distinctly foreign, 'I should learn from them and convince myself that my enemies will all flee before me, saying: "I go, victorious Spaniard of lightning and fire, I leave you. I leave you too, sweet lands, I leave Spain and tremble as I go . . ." Spaniards are always boasting like that, even when confronted by a compatriot who will not be so easily frightened off. And Custardoy and I are compatriots.' The Admiral had one arm raised and was holding something in his hand. I couldn't quite see what it was, it could have been a rolled-up map or, more likely, a General's baton. His other hand, the left one, was gripping the hilt of his sheathed sword, rather as the lone Count was in his portrait. 'What a lot of swords there are in these old streets too,' I thought.

VII

Farewell

Sometimes we know what we want to do or have to do or even what we're thinking of doing or are almost certain we will do, but we also need it to be spoken about or confirmed or discussed or approved, a manoeuvre which is, after a fashion, a way of shuffling off a little of the responsibility, of diffusing or sharing it, even if only fictitiously, because what we do we do alone, regardless of who convinces or persuades or encourages or gives us the green light, or even orders or commissions the deed. On occasion, we disguise this manoeuvre as doubt or perplexity, we go to someone and play a trick on them by asking their opinion or advice – by asking or requesting something of them – and thus, at the very least, we ensure that the next time we speak, that person will enquire about the matter, ask what happened, how it all turned out, what we finally decided to do, whether their advice had been of any help, whether we took notice of their words. That person is then involved, entangled, drawn in. We have forced them to become a participant, even if only as a listener, and to consider the situation and to ask how it ended; we have foisted our story on them and they will never be able to forget or erase it; we have also given them a certain right, or perhaps duty, to question us about it later: 'So what did you do in the end, how did you resolve the problem?' they will ask us next time we meet, and it would seem odd, would show a lack of interest or politeness, not to refer to the case we'd laid out before them and to which we've obliged them to contribute with words or, if they declined to offer a view or to say anything, to listen to our doubts. 'I have no idea, I can't and shouldn't give an opinion, in fact, I really don't want to know about it,' they might well say, and yet they have still said something; with that response they have told us that they find the whole thing distasteful, poisonous or murky, that they want no part in it, even as a passive witness, that they would prefer to remain in the dark, and that they like none of the possible options, that it would be best if we did nothing and simply let it go or removed ourselves from the situation; and that we should certainly spare them the details. Even if you say 'I don't know' or 'I don't want to hear about it', you've already said too much, and when you're asked that question, there's no easy way out, not even holding back or keeping silent is safe, because silence is in itself reproving or discouraging, and does not, as the saying goes, mean consent. Let us hope that no one ever asks us for anything, or even enquires, not for advice or a favour or a loan, not even for the loan of our attention. But that never happens, it's an entirely vain wish. There's always one almost final question, some laggardly request. Now it was my turn to do the asking, now I was going to make a request, one that would have proved compromising to anyone, except perhaps to the person who was about to hear it. I still had much to learn from him, a fact I found most troubling and that would perhaps bring me misfortune.

That evening, I phoned Tupra from my hotel room, for only he could advise me and, I hoped, give me instructions, make recommendations and serve as my guide, indeed, he was the ideal man to ask about matters in which talk was not enough; he was also the most suitable person, that is, the one I could rely on to confirm that I should do what I thought I should do or who would at least not dissuade me. I guessed that he would be at home at that hour, even though England was one hour behind, unless it was one of his convivial, festive days and he had recruited everyone, including Branshaw and Jane Treves, to go out together en masse. I dialled his home number and a woman answered, doubtless she of the attractive, old-fashioned silhouette (with her almost hourglass figure), whom I had seen at the end of that night of videos, outlined against the light of a corridor, at the door of his small study; if it was his wife or ex-wife, if it was Beryl, he would be able to understand my plight even better.

'How are you, Jack? How nice of you to call and keep me posted. Or were you calling to enquire about me and the others? That would be even nicer of you, especially in the middle of your holiday.'

There was a touch of irony in his voice, of course, but I noticed too a certain pleasure to hear from me, or was it amusement, for he still found me amusing. After the initial exchange of greetings, I preferred not to pretend or to deceive him.

'I have a matter to resolve here, Bertie. I'd like to know what you think or what, in your view, you think I should do.' I called him Bertie to please him, to put him in a good mood, even though he was sure to see through this, and then, without further ado, I summarised the situation: 'There's a guy here in Madrid,' I said. 'I think he's beating up my wife, or my ex-wife – or whatever – given that we're still not divorced – anyway, they've been going out for a while, I don't know how long, probably a few months. She denies it, but right now she has a black eye, and this isn't the first time she's accidentally – according to her, of course – banged into something. Her sister told me this, and she, quite independently, has reached the same conclusion. I really don't like the idea of my children running the slightest risk of losing their mother, because you never know how these things will end, so you have to nip them in the bud, don't you agree? Anyway, I haven't got many more days in which to sort it out. I'd like to have it all settled before I come back, anxiety is unbearable at a distance and very distracting if you're working. But neither would I want her to find out about my intervention, whatever form it takes. Mind you, she's bound to suspect something if – as I hope – the whole scene changes and that change coincides with my stay in Madrid. There would be no point in just talking to him about it, he would simply deny it. Besides, he doesn't seem the timid pusillanimous type, not at all; he's certainly no De la Garza. It would be equally pointless my trying to make her admit it, I know how stubborn she is. And even if I did get her to admit it, the situation wouldn't, in essence, be any different; after all, she's still with him despite what's happened.' I stopped. What I had to say next was more difficult: 'She must be really crazy about him, although they haven't been together long enough for that, I mean for her to be really crazy about the guy. That doesn't happen in a few months, feelings like that need time to take root. I suppose it's the novelty, the excitement of being with someone else, the first man she's been with since we split up, and the feeling won't last. But while it lasts it lasts, if you know what I mean. And it's lasting now.'

Tupra remained silent for a few seconds. Then he said, without irony this time, but not very seriously either, for he still spoke in a slightly frivolous tone of voice, as if my problem didn't seem that serious or as if he didn't see it as particularly hard to resolve.

'And you're asking me what you should do? Or what is it you're asking? What *I* would do in your place? Well, you know perfectly well by now, Jack, what I would do. I imagine the question is purely rhetorical and that you merely want me to reassure you. Fine, consider yourself reassured. If you want to get rid of the problem, do so.'

'I'm not sure I understand you, Bertie. I've already said that talking to him would get me nowhere – ' But he didn't let me finish my sentence. Perhaps he was in a hurry or irritated by my slowness (he could have said to me as he did once before: 'Don't linger or delay, just do it'). Perhaps I had caught him in bed with Beryl, or whoever the woman was by his side, which is why she had answered the phone, because she was nearer, above or below, on her front or her back, I had probably interrupted them while they were screwing, we never know what is going on at the other end, or rather, what was going on just before the phone rang. I wondered how many times when I'd called Luisa from London she would have just got back from seeing Custardoy in his studio or how many times he would have been there in her bedroom, in my home, watching as she sat, half-undressed, talking to me, waiting impatiently for us to finish our conversation. If, that is, he visited her. It might be that he didn't or only at night because of the children. I hadn't asked them, but neither

334

had they mentioned it spontaneously, in fact, they hadn't mentioned anyone new or anyone I didn't know.

'Look, Jack, just deal with him,' Tupra said. 'Just make sure he's out of the picture.' Those were his exact words in English, and I deeply regretted then that it wasn't my first language, because I don't know how they would strike a native English speaker, but to me they seemed too ambiguous, I couldn't grasp their meaning as clearly as I would have wanted; if he had said to me 'Just get rid of him' or 'Dispose of him', that would have been clearer although, again, not entirely; there are a lot of ways of getting rid of someone, not all of which involve killing; or perhaps it would have been clearer to me if he had said 'Just make sure you get him off her back' or 'off your backs', but I would still not have felt able to translate that expression into concrete unequivocal action, because there are also lots of ways of getting someone off your back. If only he had said 'Just scare him away, scare him to death', then I would have understood that he was telling me to do what he'd done with De la Garza, nothing more, and to transform myself into Sir Punishment and Sir Thrashing, but not into Sir Death or Sir Cruelty. However, the words that emerged from his lips were: 'Just deal with him. Just make sure he's out of the picture,' and that word 'picture' could mean many things: a painting or a portrait, a panorama or a scene or even a photo or a film, although it was the first meaning of painting that I opted for, I had to remove Custardoy from the picture, to erase or exclude him, just like the Count of San Secondo in the Prado, who was cut off from his family, isolated, and would never ever be close to his wife or his children again. If I had heard that advice as a brief bit of dialogue in an episode of *The Sopranos* or in *The Godfather*, I would have understood perfectly that he was urging me to bump him off. But perhaps the mafiosi use pre-established codes, just in case they're being bugged, allowing them to be very laconic in the orders they issue and yet still be sure that their orders will be interpreted correctly and at once. Besides, this wasn't a dialogue in a film and we weren't mafiosi, nor was I receiving an order, as I had on previous occasions from Tupra or Reresby or Ure or Dundas, I was merely being given

335

a little guidance, the advice I'd asked him for. Language, though, is difficult when you're uncertain as to what to do and need to know exactly what is meant, because language is almost always metaphorical or figurative. There can't be many people in the world who would say openly 'Kill him', or in Spanish '*Mátalo*'.

I decided to press him a little, even though this might annoy him. Or rather, I got my question in quickly before he could put the phone down, because those last two utterances of his had sounded distinctly conclusive, dismissive almost, as if, after that, he had nothing more to add. Or as if he were bored with my enquiry, my little story.

'Could you tell me how, Bertie?' I said. 'I'm not as used as you are to frightening people.'

First, I heard his paternalistic laughter, brief and slightly scornful, it wasn't the sort of laughter we could have shared, it wasn't the kind that creates a disinterested bond between men or between women or the kind that establishes a bond between women and men that can prove an even stronger, tighter link, a profounder, more complex, more dangerous and more lasting link, or one, at least, with more hope of enduring, perhaps Luisa and Custardoy were joined by the bond of spontaneous, unexpected, simultaneous laughter, given that he seemed to be able to make people laugh so easily. Tupra's laugh, as I myself had occasion to notice, always sounded slightly disappointed and impatient and revealed small bright teeth. Then he said:

'If you really don't know how, Jack, that means you can't do it. Best not to try and just let events take their course – leave it be, don't try to change things, let your wife sort things out, it's her business, after all. But I think you do know how. We all know, even if we're not used to the idea or can't imagine ourselves doing it. It's a question of imagination. But I have to leave you now. Good luck.' And with that he brought to a close a conversation that I had managed to prolong only very slightly.

I didn't dare phone him back, I would have to make do with what I had. 'Let your wife sort things out, it's her business, after all', those words had sounded like a reproach or a veiled criticism, as if what he'd really said was: 'You're going to abandon her to her fate, perhaps allow her to be killed one day and leave your children orphans.' Some other words of his had hit home too: 'It's a question of imagination.' What he probably meant by this was that the only way of imagining yourself doing something you have never imagined yourself doing is to do it, and then you have no trouble at all imagining it.

Next I called an old friend, well, a Madrid-style friend, namely, a fellow *madrileño* whom I had known superficially years ago and hadn't seen since: if there has been no friction or quarrel or dispute between you and such a friend, then, nominally, he can still be considered a friend, even though you might never have had a conversation alone with him, outside of the broad and ever -changing group of people that brought you together in that increasingly remote past. This friend was a bullfighter with a fanatical following, the sort of *torero* who retires, then returns to the ring every few years only to retire again – it wouldn't be long now before he would have to cut off his pigtail for good – and whom I had known slightly during one particular period of my life, with Comendador (who moved in all kinds of circles and had introduced me to him) and later on again, too, at the late-night card games that went on into the small hours and which the Maestro held at his house for members of his team, the odd colleague and all kinds of hangers-on like me; some bullfighters never spend a minute alone and will welcome anyone, as long as they come recommended by some trustworthy person, even at third hand: the friend of a friend of the person who really is a friend and not just a Madrid-style friend. He was a very amiable, affectionate fellow, and sentimental about anything to do with his past life, and when I asked if I could come and see him, he not only raised no objections or sounded remotely suspicious after that decade or more of silence between us, he even urged me to visit as soon as possible:

'Come today. There's a game tonight.'

'Would tomorrow morning suit you?' I asked. 'I'm only here for a few days. I live in London now, and I'd arranged to go and see my father today. He's getting on a bit and hasn't been too well.'

'Of course, say no more. Tomorrow it is then. But make it around one o'clock, for a drink before lunch. Tonight's game is sure to run late.'

'I want to ask you a favour,' I said, preferring to give him due warning. 'I need a loan, but not of money, don't worry. I have no problems in that department.'

'"Don't worry," he says,' he replied, laughing. 'You would never give me cause to worry, Jacobito.' He was one of the people who called me Jacobo, I can't remember why. 'Ask me for anything you like. As long as it's not my suit of lights.' I didn't really follow the bullfighting scene, certainly not from London, but I assumed from his comment that he was currently active. I had better find out before going to visit him, so as not to seem rude.

'You're getting warm,' I said. 'I'll explain tomorrow.'

'Just have a look around when you get here and take whatever you want.' These weren't mere empty words, he really was a very generous man. His name was Miguel Yanes Troyano, nicknamed 'Miquelín', and he was the son of a *banderillero*.

The following morning, up to date now on his latest triumphs, thanks to the Internet, and bearing a gift, I arrived at his vast apartment in the area which, in my childhood, was known as 'Costa Fleming', rather closer to Real Madrid's Chamartín stadium – which I prefer to call by its old name – than to Las Ventas, the bull ring through whose gates he had often been borne shoulder high. I would have preferred to speak to him alone, but that was impossible since he always had company. However, having been forewarned that I was going to ask him for a favour or a loan, he had been considerate enough not to embarrass me with too many witnesses, apart, that is, from his lifelong manager, who was always there, a discreet taciturn man of about the same age, and whom I scarcely knew at all even though I had known him since for ever.

'I hope Señor Cazorla won't find our conversation too boring, Maestro,' I said tentatively, just in case.

'Not at all,' replied Miquelín, making a gesture with his hand as if sweeping aside such an idea. He had greeted me with a warm embrace and a kiss on the cheek, as if I were his nephew. 'Eulogio never gets bored, but if he does, he simply thinks, isn't that so, Eulogio? You can say whatever you like in front of him, because he'll neither tell on you nor judge you. Anyway, how can I help?'

I found it hard to begin, because I felt slightly ashamed of what I was about to ask. However, the best way to overcome this was to say what I wanted and get it over with. Everything seems more embarrassing before than it does afterwards and even during.

'I wondered if you could lend me one of your swords. I'd only need it for a couple of days.'

I saw that my request took them both by surprise and that Cazorla started slightly and tugged at one sleeve. He was wearing a suit, complete with a waistcoat, in rather too pale a shade of grey; he had a handkerchief in his top jacket pocket and wore a flower in his buttonhole; he was, in short, old school. But he would not speak unless Miquelín invited him to do so, and Miquelín managed to conceal his surprise very well and replied at once:

'As many as you want, Jacobo. We'll go and have a look at them right now and you can choose the one you like best, although they're all pretty much the same. But forgive me, if you'd wanted to borrow some money, it would never even have occurred to me to ask what you wanted it for, but borrowing a sword is a bit more unusual. Is it for a fancy dress party?'

I could have lied to him, although a sword on its own wouldn't be much of a disguise. I could have invented some absurd excuse and said, for example, that I had been invited to a private bull-fight, but it didn't seem right to deceive such a kindly man, and I don't think I would have succeeded. I felt, too, that he would understand my reasons for borrowing it and wouldn't judge me either.

'No, Miquelín. I want to give someone a fright. It's to do with my wife, well, my ex-wife, we've been separated for a while now, although we're not yet divorced.' I always made a point of saying that, I realised, as if it were important. 'That's why I moved to London, so that I wouldn't be hanging around here while we

339

gradually drifted apart. Given what I've found out, though, I'm not sure it was a good idea. We have two kids, a boy and a girl, and I don't want them to come to any harm. The guy's no good for anyone, least of all her.'

Miquelín understood, I didn't need to say any more, I could see this from the way he listened to me, as if he were in agreement. He didn't ask any questions, friends were friends and you didn't poke your nose into their business. Then he gave an affectionate amused chuckle, he was a man much given to laughter, and age had not changed that or made his laughter less frequent.

'And what are *you* going to do with a sword?' he said. 'Did you hear what he wants it for, Eulogio? Are you actually going to use it, Jacobo? Are you going to stick the whole blade in or just the point? Or do you simply want to wave it around a bit and scare the living daylights out of him?'

'I was hoping not to have to use it,' I replied. I had no idea what I was going to do with it; having heard Tupra on the subject, I had thought only of the effect it would have when I produced the weapon.

'You have to bear in mind two things, my friend. First, the *estoque* only wounds with the point, by sticking it in, and that's why you need considerable momentum to drive it in really deep; the bullfighter's sword has almost no blade at all, so it won't be any use if you just want to cut someone up a bit. Secondly, if this sword can kill a bull weighing over 1,300 pounds when you stick it in up to the hilt – always assuming you don't hit a bone of course – just imagine what it could do to a man, one false move on your part and he'd be stone dead. Do you want to take that risk? No, Jacobo, the best way to frighten someone is to pull a gun on them. Preferably a clean one, because you never know.'

I hadn't made the connection until I heard Miquelín talking about what a sword could do to a man, but when I did, I felt a shudder of disgust run through me, although, oddly, strangely, not self-disgust; I must still have seen myself as quite separate from what I was planning to do, or felt that my plan was still empty of content, or was it just that one never experiences genuine

340

self-disgust, and it's that inability that makes us capable of doing almost anything as we grow accustomed to the ideas that rise up in us or take root, little by little, or as we come to terms with the fact that we're really going to do what we're going to do. 'I would be like that vicious *malagueño*, that nasty piece of work, that bastard,' I thought, 'the one who killed Emilio Marés on the outskirts of Ronda some seventy years ago, helped and urged on by his comrades, the one who went in for the kill and cut off Marés' ears and his tail, held them up in one hand and with the other doffed his red beret as if it were a bullfighter's hat, there in those sweet lands. The one who brutally murdered my father's old university friend, who, as my father told me, was rather vain, but in a funny self-consciously frivolous way, a really lovely man, always in a good mood, whom he had very much liked and who had refused to dig his own grave before being shot, thus allowing his executioners to bait him like a bull as well as to kill him. And then they had, literally, baited him with banderillas and pikes and swords. It's fortunate that Miquelín, all unknowing, has alerted me to that connection.'

'Clean?' I asked. I didn't understand the term.

'Yes, a gun that no one knows about, that hasn't been registered, and, above all, that hasn't been used in any crime. As I say, you never know.' Miquelín, like all bullfighters I suppose, was all too aware that one never could know what might happen.

'What do you mean "you never know", Miquelín?'

'What do you think I mean, child? Listen to him, Eulogio!' And he chuckled again, he must have considered me a complete novice, which I was in such matters. 'Because if you put a gun in your pocket, there's always a chance you might end up firing it. You just want to give someone a fright, fair enough, but you never know how the other fellow's going to react. He might *not* be frightened, and then what will you do?'

'Fine, but where am I going to get a gun like that?' I knew that the Maestro owned various weapons, which he used when he went hunting on his estate in Cáceres, where he'd spend longish periods of time. And perhaps other kinds of weapons too, the shorter variety that are of no use for hunting. However, it was likely that he had licences for them all, and therefore no entirely 'clean' ones.

'I'll lend you one, man, just as I would have lent you the sword or whatever else you might want. But where were you going to put a sword, my friend, I mean, really, what an idea! A gun, on the other hand, fits in your pocket.' This hadn't occurred to me either, that I didn't own an overcoat with a sheath in the lining at the back or even a raincoat. And it wasn't the weather for overcoats. Miquelín added: 'I'll get you one now. Eulogio, would you mind fetching me my father's Llama. And the other one as well, the revolver.'

'Where do you keep them now?' asked Cazorla.

'They're in the library, behind *The Thousand and One Nights* and a little to the left, behind several books with brown bindings. Go and get them for me, will you?'

The manager left the room (I wondered what kind of library the Maestro would have – I had certainly never seen it during those nights spent playing cards; but he was, like other bullfighters, quite well-read) and returned shortly afterwards carrying two boxes or packages wrapped in cloth which he placed before Miquelín on the coffee table.

'Would you be so kind as to bring some gloves for Jacobo, Eulogio?' he said. Then turning to me: 'If you're going to use one of them, it's best you don't touch them. Not being used to handling guns, you might forget to clean it afterwards.'

Cazorla was as helpful as ever, his admiration for the Maestro being infinite, bordering on devotion. He again left the room and came back with a pair of white gloves, like those a head-waiter might wear, or a magician. They were made of very fine cloth; I put them on, and then Miquelín unwrapped the boxes carefully, almost solemnly, less perhaps because they were guns than because they had belonged to his father. Many fathers who had lived through the Civil War still had a gun or two, standard-issue and otherwise, indeed my own father had a Star or an Astra, of the sort that used to be made in Éibar. I had never seen it myself, however, and I wasn't going to ask him about it now or start rummaging through his apartment. 'He must have taken a

342

risk after the War,' I thought, 'by keeping it and not surrendering it. Given that he was on the losing side and had been in prison.' Miquelín's father, who would, of course, have been older than mine, might well have been on the winning side, but we had never spoken about this, after all, it didn't matter any more. In fact, we had never talked about anything serious or personal. These Madrid-style friendships really are most unusual, often inexplicable.

'Is it all right to pick them up now?' I asked. They were very handsome objects, the revolver with its striated wooden grip, and the pistol forming almost a right angle.

'Wait just a moment,' he said. 'They both belonged to my father, and so those thieving bureaucrats have never got their paws on them. If they ever did, they'd probably sell them. The revolver dates from before the War, I think; it's English, an Enfield. It was a present from an English writer who was interested in bullfighting for a time, and my father persuaded one of the matadors in his group to let him travel around with them. He wanted first-hand experience for something he was going to write; his main character was called Biggles, a pilot I think, it was a series, and in one of the books the author thought he might send his hero off to have some adventures in Spain. My father was very proud of this, because apparently this Biggles fellow was very famous in his country.' There it was again, that word '*patria*'; perhaps it wasn't such a loaded word, Miquelín hadn't laid any special emphasis on it, maybe because he wasn't talking about his own *patria*, our country. 'The pistol dates from later on, a Llama, which is Spanish, an automatic. The revolver takes six bullets, the Llama ten. Not that this will matter to you if you don't foresee having to shoot. But if push comes to shove, you'll have more than enough with either gun: if not, it will be because you're dead. One magazine should be enough for the pistol. Here's your ammunition. Well-preserved and well-oiled, and all in working order, as my father taught me. The pistol can jam, of course, like all pistols. But on the other hand, look how big the revolver is, with the drum and the long barrel. I think you'd be better off with the Llama. Don't you agree, Eulogio, that a pistol is better for giving someone a fright?' Miquelín handled both weapons with ease.

'If you say so, Miguel. You know more about it than I do,' Cazorla replied with a shrug.

'Do you know how to use it?' Miquelín asked me. 'Do you know how it works? Have you ever held one before?'

'When I did my military service,' I said. 'But not since.' And I thought how odd that was, and how new, for there must have been many periods when it would have been unusual for a middle-class male not to have a weapon in his house, always close to hand.

'The first thing to remember, Jacobo, is never put your finger on the trigger until you know you're going to shoot. Always keep it resting on the guard, OK? Even if the pistol isn't cocked. Even if it's not loaded.'

He used what was to me an unfamiliar, seemingly old-fashioned word for 'guard', '*guardamonte*', but then Miquelín was himself in the process of becoming old-fashioned too, a relic, like his generosity. I didn't need to ask any questions, though, because he showed me what to do and I could see where he placed his forefinger. Then he handed the pistol to me, so that I could do the same, or copy him. I had forgotten what a heavy thing a pistol is; in the movies, they hold them as if they were as light as daggers. It takes an effort to lift one, and still more of an effort to hold it steady enough to aim.

And then the Maestro taught me how to use it.

I don't know, but I think perhaps by then I had absorbed Wheeler's dictum about how we all carry our probabilities in our veins and so on, and I was more or less convinced that I knew how to apply this to myself; I had, or so I thought, a pretty good idea of what my probabilities were, although not as clear an idea as Wheeler would have of his, given that he could draw on far greater experience: he'd had more time than me, more temptations and more varied circumstances in which to guide those probabilities to their fulfilment; he'd lived through and been involved in wars, and in wartime one can be more persuasive and make oneself more dangerous and more despicable even than one's enemies; one can take advantage of the majority of people, who were, according to Wheeler, silly and frivolous and credulous and on whom it was easy to strike a match and start a fire; one can more easily and with impunity cause others to fall into the most appalling and destructive misfortunes from which they will never emerge, and thereby transform those thus condemned into casualties, into non-persons, into felled trees from which the rotten wood can be chopped away; it's also the best time to spread outbreaks of cholera, malaria and plague and, often, to set in motion the process of total denial, of who you are and who you were, of what you do and what you did, of what you expect and what you expected, of your aims and your intentions, of your professions of faith, your ideas, your greatest loyalties, your motives . . .

No, you are never what you are — not entirely, not exactly — when you're alone and living abroad and ceaselessly speaking a language not your own or not your mother tongue; but nor are you what you are in your own country when there's a war on or when that country is dominated by rage or obstinacy or fear: to some degree you feel no responsibility for what you do or see, as if it all belonged to a provisional existence, parallel, alien, or borrowed, fictitious or almost dreamed – or, perhaps, merely theoretical, like my whole life, according to the anony-mous report about me that I'd found among some old files; as if everything could be relegated to the sphere of the purely imagi-nary or of what never happened, and, of course, to the sphere of the involuntary; everything tossed into the bag of imaginings and suspicions and hypotheses and, even, of mere foolish dreams, about which, when you awake, all you can say is: 'I didn't want that anomalous desire or that murderous hatred or that baseless resentment to surface, or that temptation or that sense of panic or that desire to punish, that unknown threat or that surprising curse, that aversion or that longing which now lie like lead upon my soul each night, or the feeling of disgust or embarrassment which I myself provoke, or those dead faces, for ever fixed, that made a pact with me that there would be no more tomorrows (yes, that is the pact we make with all those who fall silent and are expelled: that they neither do nor say anything more, that they disappear and cease changing) and which now come and whisper dreadful unexpected words to me, words that are per-haps unbecoming to them, or perhaps not, while I'm asleep and have dropped my guard: I have laid down my shield and my spear on the grass.' What's more you can repeat over and over Iago's disquieting words, not only after taking action, but dur-ing it too: 'I am not what I am.' A similar warning is issued by anyone asking another person to commit a crime or threatening to commit one himself, or confessing to vile deeds and thus ex-posing himself to blackmail, or buying something on the black market – keep your collar turned up, your face always in the shadows, never light a cigarette – telling the hired assassin or the person under threat or the potential blackmailer or one of many interchangeable women, once desired and already forgotten, but still a source of shame to us: 'You know the score, you've never

346

seen me, from now on you don't know me, I've never spoken to you or said anything, as far as you're concerned I have no face, no voice, no breath, no name, no back. This conversation and this meeting never took place, what's happening now before your eyes didn't happen, isn't happening, you haven't even heard these words because I didn't say them. And even though you can hear the words now, I'm not saying them'; just as you can tell yourself: 'I am not what I am nor what I can see myself doing. More than that, I'm not even doing it.'

What I had absorbed less well, or simply didn't know, was that what one does or does not do depends not just on time, temptation and circumstance, but on silly ridiculous things, on random superfluous thoughts, on doubt or caprice or some stupid fit of feeling, on untimely associations and on one-eyed oblivion or fickle memories, on the words that condemn you or the gesture that saves you.

And so there I was the following morning – the day was threatening rain – with my borrowed pistol in my raincoat pocket, ready to take some definitive action, but without really knowing what exactly, although I had a rough idea and knew what I was hoping to make clear: I had to get rid of Custardoy, get him off our backs, make sure he stayed out of the picture; not so much out of my picture, which was little more than a daub at the time or perhaps a mere doodle – 'You're very alone in London', as Wheeler used to tell me – but out of Luisa and the children's picture, into which that unwholesome individual was trying to worm his way and where he was perhaps about to take up long-term residence, or at least long-term enough to become an affliction and a danger. Indeed, he already was both those things, for he had already spent far too much time prowling round and circling the frame and making incursions into the picture or canvas, and he had already laid a hand on Luisa and given her a black eye and left her with a cut or a gash – I had been told about the second and had myself seen the first – and nothing would stop him closing his large hands around her throat – those pianist's fingers, or, rather, those fingers like piano keys – one rainy night, when they were stuck at home, when he judged he had subjugated and isolated her enough and little by little fed her his demands and prohibitions disguised as infatuation and weakness and jealousy and flattery and supplication, a poisonous, despotic, devious type of man. I was quite clear now that I didn't want to have the luck or the misfortune (luck as long as it remained in the imagination, misfortune were it to become reality) of Luisa dying or being killed, that I couldn't allow this to happen because once a real misfortune has occurred there's no going back and it cannot be undone, or, contrary to what most people believe, even compensated (and there is, of course, no way of compensating the person who has died or even the living left behind, and yet nowadays the living often do ask for money, thus putting a price on the people who have ceased to tread the earth or traverse the world).

As I walked along, I couldn't help touching and even grasping the pistol, as if I were drawn to it or needed to get used to its weight and to feel and hold it in my hand, sometimes lifting it up slightly, still inside my pocket, and whenever I did grip it properly, I always took great care to keep my finger resting on the guard and not on the trigger, as Miquelín had recommended me to do even when the pistol wasn't cocked. 'How easy it must be to use it,' I was thinking, 'once you've got one. Or, rather, how difficult not to use it, even if only to point it at someone and threaten them and just to be seen with it. Firing the thing would be harder, of course, but, on the other hand, it cries out to be brandished about and it would seem impossible not to satisfy that plea. Perhaps women would find it easier to resist, but for a man it's like having a tempting toy, guns should never be given to men, and yet most of those that are made or inherited or that exist will end up in our hands and not in the more cautious hands of women.' I also had a proud feeling of invulnerability, as if, as I walked past other people in the street, I were thinking: 'I'm more dangerous than they are right now and they don't know it, and if someone got cocky with me or tried to mug me he'd get a nasty fright; if I got out the pistol, he'd probably back off or throw down his knife or run away,' and I remembered the momentary feeling of pride that had assailed me on seeing the fear I unwittingly inspired in De la Garza when I went into his office ('You should feel very pleased with yourself: you had him scared shitless,' Professor Rico had said to me afterwards, neither mincing his words nor resorting to onomatopoeia). And I recalled, too, that immediately afterwards it had filled me with disgust that I could possibly feel flattered by such a thing, I had judged it unworthy of me, of the person I was or had been, of my face past and present, and which were both perhaps changing with the tomorrow that had now arrived. 'Presume not that I am the thing I was,' I quoted to myself as I walked. 'I have turn'd away my former self. When thou dost hear I am as I have been, approach me, and thou shalt be as thou wast. Till then, I banish thee, on pain of death, not to come near our person by ten mile . . .' These were the words of King Henry V immediately after being crowned and many years before the night when he disguised himself to go among his soldiers on the eve of the battle of Agincourt, with everything pitched against him and at great risk of being misjudged, or, as one of his soldiers says to him, not realising it's the King he's talking to, if the cause be not good, the King himself will have a heavy reckoning to make. Such words were unexpected coming from the man who, until only a short time before, had been Prince Hal, dissolute, reveller and bad son, especially when addressed to his still recent companion in revels, the now old Falstaff whom he was denying: 'I know thee not, old man,' for all it takes is a few words to abjure everything one has experienced, the excesses and the lack of scruples, the outrageous behaviour and the arguments, the whorehouses and the taverns and the inseparable friends, even if those same friends say pleadingly to you, 'My sweet boy,' as Falstaff does to his beloved Prince Hal when the latter has just abandoned that name to become for ever, with no possible way back, the rigid King Henry. Such words serve not only to mend one's ways and to leave behind the life of a debauchee or a *roué avant la lettre*, of a rake and an idler, but to announce that one is setting off along new paths, in new directions, or to announce a metamorphosis: I, too, could say mentally to Luisa and to Custardoy and to myself as I walked along: 'Presume not that I am

349

the thing I was. I have turn'd away my former self. I am carrying a pistol and I am dangerous, I am no longer the man who never knowingly frightened anyone; like Iago, I am not what I am, at least I am beginning not to be.'

And so I stationed myself exactly where I had waited two days before, at the top of the short double flight of steps leading up to the monstrous cathedral, behind the papal statue that seemed always about to join the dance, and once there I paced back and forth between that point and a point nearby, behind the railings and to the left of that shop incomprehensibly selling souvenirs of the monstrosity; it was only a few steps between those two points and from both I could see the four corners formed by Calle Mayor and Calle de Bailén, as well as the ornate wooden door that was immediately opposite the shop, albeit lower down, and so whichever direction he came from I would be sure to see Custardoy arrive, although I was convinced he would take the same route as when I had followed him, if, that is, he had gone back to the Prado, though it was quite possible that he hadn't yet finished his note-taking or his sketches of the four faces painted by Parmigianino, each of them looking in a different direction, or that, on another occasion, he would have to study the portrait of the husband and father, in which the Count stands alone and isolated, like me, or that he would have to study other paintings for some other commission or project. And if he hadn't gone out that morning, it was likely that, just before lunch, he would stroll over to El Anciano Rey de los Vinos to enjoy his usual couple of beers and some *patatas bravas* (it was hardly surprising that, despite being thin, he had a bit of a belly on him), so I would be able to observe him there too if he went and took his usual seat. I would, at any rate, see him enter or leave his house, whenever he did that, and I would have time to go down the steps, cross the road – there wasn't much traffic along that stretch – and meet him at the front door as he was opening it. At first, I was surprised to see that, for the first time, the door stood open, and I deduced that there must be a doorman, but that could present me with a problem, a witness. However, after a few minutes, I saw the man come out and shut the door (he obviously lunched early) and this reassured me, because the seconds it would take Custardoy to put his key in and turn it and push or pull the door open and then give it a shove from inside or a tug from outside could prove vital, my idea being that he would complete neither action. I was trusting that he would not arrive or leave with anyone else, certainly not with Luisa. 'You'll never see her again,' I thought, 'unless she happens to be with you today,' it's odd how we address our thoughts to anyone we have it in for or whom we're preparing to harm in some way, addressing them familiarly as '*tú*', as if what we were about to do to them were incompatible with any form of respect or as if any show of respect would, in view of our plans for them, seem utterly cynical.

I waited and waited and waited. I paced from one side to the other and back again, between steps and railings, looking down on each of the four corners and the eight stretches of pavement, Custardoy might come from the direction of the viaduct or pass beneath my eyes, staying close to the Cathedral or to the wall, or he might come from the direction of the Istituto Italiano or walk up Cuesta de la Vega from the Parque de Atenas; I kept a tight grip on the pistol hidden in my pocket and sometimes felt overwhelmed by nerves, I had a clear view of the whole scene, but there were too many fronts to keep watch over simultaneously and I constantly had to change my vantage point, I noticed that a few devotees were starting to eye me with interest – they didn't look Spanish, they were perhaps Lithuanians or possibly Poles, like their former boss – and, even worse, they were starting to copy me in my pacing back and forth as if they feared they might be missing out if they didn't do the same – people's tendency to imitate others' behaviour is becoming an international plague – I felt slightly beleaguered and longed to be able to leave. And that was when I saw him in the distance, the unmistakable figure of Custardoy walking along Calle Mayor, on the same side as the Capitanía General and the Consejo de Estado, that is, on the same side as his apartment or workshop or studio. I stayed where I was, I didn't move, I waited until he had reached the traffic lights, just in case he crossed over to take his usual seat outside the bar, but it was a cloudy day and not really warm enough for that. He was wearing a raincoat too, a good-quality one, black and very long, almost like a dustcoat, and that, together with the hat he had chosen to wear that day, a kind of Stetson, but broader brimmed and cream or white in colour like the hat Tom Mix used to wear in those ancient silent films (the man really was a fool), gave him the appearance of a character out of the Wild West; he and his friend, the female Daniel Boone or Jim Bowie, would have made a fine pair. Fortunately, though, he was alone, striding along, the tails of his coat, and doubtless his ponytail too, beating the air (he was still a follower of fashion even at his age, with enough energy to try and keep up), walking as resolutely as I had done a short while before, but then I'd had a pistol in my pocket. 'He won't be easy to bring to heel,' I thought, 'he won't be easy to intimidate or even kill. Besides, he has the kind of strength that comes from pure energy and impatience and a desire to be many, this man accustomed to spending hours alone with his brushes, focused and still, concentrating on tiny details and staring at one canvas in order to make an exact copy of it on another canvas, and when he stops and finally gets up and opens the door and goes out into the street, he'll be filled by a vast amount of accumulated tension and be ready to explode. No, he won't be the kind to beg, he'll put up a fight, he isn't timid or easily scared, so one thing is sure, I have to instil him with fear, more fear than he might try to instil in me, he's not going to freeze and draw in his neck and close his eyes as De la Garza did, nor am I Tupra, who seems to instil fear whenever he wants to, quite naturally, nor am I the two Kray brothers Tupra told me about and who taught him the value of the sword, and to whom a cellmate had, according to Reresby, given a very condensed lesson in how to get what you want: "Now these people, they don't like getting hurt. Not them or their property. Now these people out there who don't like to be hurt, pay other people not to hurt them. You know what I'm saying. Course you do. When you get out, you keep your eyes open. Watch out for the people who don't want to be hurt. Because you scare the shit out of me, boys. Wonderful," that's what Tupra had said,' I thought and remembered, 'in a fake accent which was perhaps his real accent, as he sat to the right of me in his swift silent car, in the lunar light of the streetlamps, with his hands still resting on the motionless steering wheel, squeezing or strangling it, he wasn't wearing gloves by then, but I've been wearing mine since I left the hotel and won't take them off until I return, having removed Custardoy from the picture, having done the deed.' 'That's the thing, Jack. Fear,' Tupra had added before urging me to go to his house to watch those videos that weren't just for anyone's eyes, and, after showing them to me, had asked again: 'Tell me now, why, according to you, one can't go around beating people up and killing them? You've seen how much of it goes on, everywhere, and sometimes with an utter lack of concern. So explain to me why one can't.' And it had taken me a long time to give him an answer, one that turned out to be no answer at all.

I hurried down the steps and very nearly collided with or, rather, almost flattened a devotee, Custardoy wasn't going to the bar, but to his studio, he had kept straight on and stopped at the traffic lights on Calle de Bailén, and I knew that when the lights turned green, it was only forty-nine steps from there to the door of his house, which was where we had to meet, not before he arrived and definitely not after, because afterwards the door would be closed again, with him inside and me outside. I decided to cross the road, taking advantage of the fact that the stop light was in my favour; now we were on the same side of the street, I saw him set off when the cars stopped, one, two, three, four, five, I lurked for a few seconds behind a tree, not a very wide tree, hoping that he wouldn't see me *before* putting his key in the door, a matter of only a few moments, it would be best if he didn't notice me *while* he was putting the key in the door either, it would be best if I remained behind him for as long as possible and for him to feel as frightened as possible because he wouldn't know who it was threatening him, because he wouldn't be able to see his assailant's face, my face, and would wonder whether this was going to be a quick doorstep mugging or a slow ransacking of his whole apartment or a swift and then eternal kidnapping Mexican-style, or whether I was alone or there were several of us, whether we were white, copper-coloured or black (although our blacks don't go in much for mugging), or an unexpected settling of accounts, a tardy act of revenge on behalf of someone he didn't even recall, which, in a way, was the case with me, he probably didn't even remember that Luisa had, or once had, a husband, forty-six, forty-seven, forty-eight and forty-nine, and just as he put the key in the lock and the door opened, I stuck the pistol in his back without taking it out of my pocket (that way he wouldn't know if it was cocked or not, even if he spun round, which he wouldn't, not that it was cocked of course, and my finger was resting on the guard, I was very careful about that), but pressing the barrel of the gun hard against his spine, so that he would haven't any doubt that it was a gun and would feel it.

'Get inside, and don't say a word,' I whispered into the back of his neck with its stupid affected ponytail hanging there and which, at such close quarters, I found quite disgusting.

The door was half-open and he went in, we both went in, our bodies glued together, I slammed it shut with my free hand. Now he knew that there was only one of me.

'What bullshit is this?' he asked. 'Is this some kind of joke?' He still wasn't frightened, perhaps he hadn't had time to feel frightened or perhaps it wasn't in his nature. He sounded slightly cocky or at most uppity, but certainly not alarmed. 'It's going to be difficult to make him take me seriously, he's not the sort to lose his cool,' I thought at once. 'A bad beginning.'

'No, it's no joke, so be quiet. Let's go up to your apartment. We'll take the stairs. If we meet one of your neighbours, we're together. Take off your hat and hold it with your two hands. And don't drop your keys, you've got hands enough for both.' He didn't have his briefcase with him that day, so perhaps he hadn't been to the Prado. I was still talking into the back of his neck, perhaps Luisa had kissed that neck, I could smell his hair, it smelled of something, but nothing bad, he obviously washed it every day. He obeyed and took off his ridiculous hat. He would know now that I was a local, and not from Eastern Europe or the Maghreb or from South America, that my accent wasn't Albanian or Ukrainian or Arab or Colombian or Ecuadorian, it hadn't even occurred to me to put on a different accent or to disguise my own and I had said enough to make it clear that I was unequivocally Spanish, so he would know, too, that I was white, things remain hidden for such a short time, nor had I thought of addressing him in English, for example, a language I was used to speaking. 'You don't want a bullet lodged in your spine, do you? Well, get moving then.' Now he would know that I was a reasonably educated person too, because 'lodged' wasn't a word that would spring to everyone's lips.

'Look, if it's cash you want, we can talk and come to some agreement. We don't have to go upstairs and you don't have to keep that gun stuck in my back all the time. And there's no need to take that tone with me.'

He sounded less uppity now, but not afraid. He was addressing me as '*usted*', not out of respect, but as a way of maintaining a distance. I was addressing him as '*tú*', and his not doing the same to me was an attempt to appear superior despite his evidently inferior position, I was holding the pistol, I was holding the hour-glass, like Death in the painting. I wasn't tugging at him, like the semi-skeleton of Sir Death, linking arms with the old woman, instead I was behind him and pushing him, which came to the same thing, I was the master of time and was propelling him up the stairs, he was trying to stop the flow of sand or water by talking, as have so many others, hoping to postpone events and save themselves, rather than remaining silent. He hadn't entirely lost his haughty manner, as indicated by the last words he spoke before I interrupted him. It was as if he had said to me: 'Don't you raise your voice to me,' except that wouldn't have made any sense because I was speaking in a whisper.

Then I took the gun out of my pocket for a moment and struck him hard on his right side with the barrel, as if I were slapping him except that I was striking him in the ribs and with the pistol, not across the face and with my hand, it made much less noise because he was, of course, wearing a raincoat. He staggered a little, but didn't fall. He didn't drop his hat either, but he did drop his keys.

'I've told you already, be quiet. Pick up your keys and get

going.' I said this in the same calm whisper, which was, I thought, more frightening than a shout. I was surprised how easy it had been for me to deal him that blow and that it hadn't worried me to do so with a loaded weapon; usually, people who aren't used to carrying a gun are always afraid it will go off, however careful they are. My main concern was to frighten him, I suppose, or perhaps his last words had bothered me, either that or his use of the word 'bullshit' before, or perhaps I had remembered Luisa's black eye with its thousand slowly changing colours, an image I summoned up every now and then because I needed to, it filled me with reason and cold fury and strengthened my resolve. It seemed quite right that Custardoy should experience pain, some pain, he instinctively raised his hand to his side and rubbed it, but I told him at once: 'Keep your hands on your hat.' I realised, too, that everyone likes to give orders that must be obeyed. One part of my mind didn't like the fact that I liked that, but I wasn't in the mood to listen to it then, the rest of my mind was fully occupied, I had more than enough to occupy me, it wasn't possible now to leave half-done what I had already started.

We set off briskly, one step at a time, with me right behind him, holding on to his ponytail at each turn in the stairs so that he wouldn't take advantage of the one second when I stopped pointing at him full on to run up the stairs and shut himself in his apartment if, that is, he was quick enough putting the key in the lock (there was no way he would manage that, but I preferred him not to try), it must have been humiliating for him to have me touch his hair, I abstained from giving it a good tug, although I could have. We were lucky, that is, I was and he wasn't, because we made it up to the third floor without meeting anyone; his was one of the apartments with a balcony looking onto the street.

'Here we are,' he said, standing outside his door. 'Now what?'

'Open the door.' He did so, a long key for the bolt and a smaller one for the lock. 'Let's go into the sitting room. You lead the way. But no funny business. I'm pointing at your spine, remember.' I could still feel the barrel of the gun against his bones, nice and central, if a bullet entered there it would take out his atlas vertebra.

We went down a short corridor and emerged into a spacious sitting room or studio with plenty of light despite the cloudy sky outside. ('Luisa has been here,' I thought at once, 'she'll know this room.') Then I saw the paintings lined up against the wall, in groups of three or four, their faces turned away, some might have been blank canvases, as yet untouched. Either he received a lot of commissions or he made numerous drafts before creating a final version; he was clearly in great demand and had no problem selling his work, for the room was comfortable, well-furnished and even luxurious, albeit slightly untidy; I particularly liked the fireplace. There were some paintings on the walls too, face out, of course, probably not his, although if he really was such a good copyist, who knows; I noticed a small Meissonier of a gentleman smoking a pipe and a larger portrait by Mané-Katz or someone like that, some Russian or Ukrainian who had spent time in Paris (if they were originals, they certainly wouldn't be cheap, although they weren't as expensive as the paintings I'd seen in Tupra's house). I noticed an easel, and the canvas resting on it was also face down, perhaps Custardoy always removed from his sight the thing he was working on as soon as he took a break, so as not to have to look at it while he was resting, perhaps it was the portrait of the Countess and her children on which he had already started work. Since I was the master of time and everything else, I could have looked at it. I didn't, though; I was otherwise occupied.

It was the moment for him to turn round and, therefore, to see my face. I didn't know whether he would recognise me from somewhere, from the Prado or from our shared walk or from photos that Luisa might have shown me; people are very keen on showing old photos, as if they wanted you to know them before the time when you actually met, it's something that happens especially between lovers, 'This is what I was like,' they seem to be saying to each other, 'would you have loved me then, as well? And if so, why weren't you there?' Before allowing him to turn round and before ordering him to sit down, I suffered a moment

of confusion: 'What am I doing here with a pistol in my hand?' I
thought or said to myself, and I immediately responded: 'There's
absolutely no reason to feel surprised. There is a good reason for
me to be here and even perhaps a real need: I'm going to rescue
Luisa from anxiety and menace and from an unhappy future
life, I'm going to ensure that she breathes easily again and can
sleep at night without fear, I'm going to make certain my children don't suffer and come to no harm and that no wounds are
inflicted on her, or, rather, no more harm, and that no one kills
her'; and as I gave myself this answer, another quote came into
my head, the words spoken by the ghost of a woman, Lady Anne,
who slept so uneasily between the sheets of her second husband's 'sorrow-haunted bed', cruel Richard III, who had stabbed
her first husband at Tewkesbury, 'in my angry mood', as he, the
murderer, once put it; and so she, after death, cursed him on Bos-
worth Field at dawn, when it was already far too late to flee the
battle, and in his dreams she whispered this: 'Richard, thy wife,
that wretched Anne thy wife, that never slept a quiet hour with
thee, now fills thy sleep with perturbations: Tomorrow in the
battle think on me, and fall thy edgeless sword: despair and die!'
I couldn't allow the same thing to happen to Luisa and for her
never to sleep a quiet hour with Custardoy if, one day, he occupied my pillow and my still-warm or already cold place in her
bed, I was the first husband, but no one in their angry mood was
going to stab me or dig my grave still deeper than the one I was
already buried in, my memory reduced to the first terror and the
first plea and the first order, all of me changed into a poisoned
shadow that little by little bids farewell while I languish and am
transformed in London, expelled from her time and from that of
my children (foolish me, insubstantial me, foolish and frivolous
and credulous). 'No, she is not yet a widow and I am not yet a
dead person who deserves to be mourned,' I thought, 'and since
I'm not, I cannot so easily be replaced, just as bloodstains will
not come out at the first attempt, you have to rub hard and diligently to remove them, and even then it seems as if the rim will
never go, that's the most difficult part to remove, the part that
resists – a whisper, a fever, a scratch. She probably has no wish

and no intention of doing so, but she will find herself obliged to say to this present or future lover, or to herself: "Not yet, my love, wait, wait, your hour has not yet come, don't spoil it for me, give me time and give him time too, the dead man whose time no longer advances, give him time to fade, let him change into a ghost before you take his place and dismiss his flesh, let him be changed into nothing, wait until there is no trace of his smell on the sheets or on my body, let it be as if what was never happened." But I'm still here, and so I must have been before, and no one can yet say of me: "No, this was never here, never, it neither strode the world nor trod the earth, it did not exist and never happened." Indeed, I am the person who could kill this second husband right now, with my gloves on and in my angry mood. I have a pistol in my hand and it's loaded, all I would have to do is cock it and squeeze the trigger, this man still has his back to me, he wouldn't even see my face, today or tomorrow or ever, not until the Last Judgement, if there is one.'

In fact, it didn't really matter whether he saw my face or not; after all, I was going to talk to him about Luisa and as soon as I did, he would know without a shadow of a doubt who I was, and she would probably have told him about my sudden return to the city after so many months away, indeed, it was highly likely that he had already guessed it was her wretched imbecile of a husband who was pointing the gun at him, what a pain, what a cretin, what a madman, why hadn't he just stayed put where he was? 'Unless I'm the one who would rather not see his face and his eyes, his gaze,' I thought, 'nor say any more to him than I said at the front door, those were mere indifferent words, impersonal orders, not an exchange between two individuals. It's always said that killers avoid looking their victim in the eye, that to do so would be the only thing that might sow a seed of doubt or stop them slitting their victim's throat or firing a bullet or at least delay them long enough for the victim to say something or to try and defend himself, that's the only thing that can sabotage their mission or make them miss their target, so perhaps it would be best to finish the thing here and now, in keeping with Tupra's motto not to linger or delay, without giving any explanations or showing any curiosity, just as Reresby gave no explanations and showed no curiosity about De la Garza – without Custardoy even turning around, a bullet in the back of the neck and that would be that, goodbye Custardoy, out of the picture, guaranteed, and as with any deed once done, no going back, but if I speak to him and look him in the face, I'll find it harder and I'll start to get to know him and he'll become "someone" for me just as he is for Luisa, because he's important to her, someone for whom she probably feels a mixture of fear and devotion, so perhaps I should see him and hear him in order to imagine that, which is all I can aspire to, because I never will know how she looks at him, that's my eternal curse . . .'

The truth is I didn't know what I should do to be certain, to 'just deal with him and make sure he was out of the picture' as a scornful Tupra had told me with a paternalistic laugh; if only he had been more explicit or if only I were bilingual and had understood him with total exactitude, or perhaps such insoluble ambiguities exist in all languages. 'If you really don't know how, Jack, that means you can't do it,' he had said. I didn't know how, but I was in too deep by then. I couldn't just shoot Custardoy in the back and leave him for dead, not without first getting into my angry mood, not without being absolutely certain: Luisa had denied to me and to her sister that he'd hurt her, and I hadn't seen the act only the results, which, in a trial, wouldn't have helped me prove anything against him. 'But this isn't a trial,' I thought, 'or anything like it, men like Tupra, like Incompara, like Manoia and so many others, like the people I saw in those videos, like the woman who appeared in one of them, with her skirt hitched up and wielding a hammer with which she was smashing a man's skull, and who knows, perhaps like Pérez Nuix and like Wheeler and Rylands, they don't hold trials or gather evidence, they simply solve problems or root them out or stop them ever happening or just deal with them, it's enough that they know what they know because they've seen it from the start thanks to their gift or their curse, they've had the courage to look hard and to translate and to keep thinking beyond the necessary ("What else? You haven't even started yet. Go on. Quickly, hurry, keep thinking," my father used to say to me and my siblings when we were children, when we were young), and to guess what will happen if they don't intervene; they don't hate knowledge as do most of the pusillanimous people in this modern age, they confront it and anticipate it and absorb it and are, therefore, the sort who issue no warning, at least not always, the sort who take remote decisions for reasons that are barely identifiable to the one who suffers the consequences or is a chance witness, or without waiting for a link of cause and effect to establish itself between actions and motives, still less for any proof that such actions have been committed. Such men and women need no proof, on those arbitrary or well-founded occasions when, without the slightest warning or indication, they lash out with a sabre; indeed, on such occasions, they don't even require the actions or events or deeds to have occurred. Perhaps for them it's enough that they know precisely what would happen in the world if no pressure or brake were imposed on what they perceive to be people's certain capabilities, and they know, too, that if they don't act with their full force, it's only because someone – me, for example – prevents or impedes them, rather than because they lacked the desire or the guts; they take all that for granted. Perhaps for them to adopt the punitive measures they deem to be necessary, they simply have to convince themselves of what would happen in each case if they or other sentinels – the authorities or the law, instinct, crime, the moon, fear, the invisible watchers – did not put a stop to it. They are the sort who know and adopt and make theirs – like a second skin – the unreflecting, resolute stance (or one based perhaps on a single thought, the first) that also forms part of the way of the world and which remains unchanged throughout time and regardless of space, and so there is no reason to question it, just as there is no need to question wakefulness and sleep, or hearing and sight, or breathing and speech, or any of the other things about which one knows: "that's how it is and always will be".'

It was assumed that I was like them, one of them, that I possessed the same capacity to penetrate and interpret people, to know what their face would be like tomorrow and to describe what had not yet occurred, and as far as Custardoy was concerned I knew him inside out, I had no proof of anything, but I knew I was right: he was the dangerous, seductive, all-enveloping, violent type, capable of making someone dependent on the horrors he perpetrated and on his lack of scruples, his despotism and his scorn, and I mustn't give him an opening, I mustn't give him an opportunity to explain himself, to deny or refute or argue or persuade, not even to talk to me. Tupra was right: 'I think you do know how,' he had said to me before hanging up. 'We all know, even if we're not used to the idea or can't imagine ourselves doing it. It's a question of imagination.' Perhaps it was just a question of me imagining myself as Sir Death for the first time, after all, I had the pistol in my hand and that was my hourglass or clepsydra, and I had my gloves on, and now all I needed was to cock the gun, move my forefinger from the guard to the trigger and then squeeze, it was all just a step away and there was so little physical difference between one thing and the other, between doing and not doing, so little spatial difference . . . I didn't need certainties or proofs if I could convince myself that I was entirely, at least for that day, a member of Tupra's school which was the way of many and perhaps of the world, because his attitude was not preventative, not exactly or exclusively, but, rather, and depending on the case and the person, punitive or compensatory, for Tupra saw and judged when dry, with no need to get himself wet – to use Don Quixote's words when he announced to Sancho Panza the mad feats he would perform for Dulcinea's sake even before being provoked into them by grief or jealousy, so just imagine what he would do if provoked. Or perhaps Tupra understood them – the various cases – even though they were pages as yet unwritten, and perhaps, for that very reason, for ever blank. 'But if I fire this pistol, my page will no longer be blank,' I thought, 'and if I don't, it won't be either, not entirely, after all the build-up and having thought about it and pointed the gun at him. We can never free ourselves from telling something, not even when we believe we have left our page blank. And even if there are things of which no one speaks, even if they do not in fact happen, they never stay still. It's terrible,' I said to myself. 'There's no escape. Even if no one speaks of them. And even if they never actually happen.' I studied the old Llama pistol at the end of my arm much as Death looked at his hourglass in that painting by Baldung Grien, the only thing by which he was guided, not by the living people beside him, after all, why would he be guided by them when he can already see their faces tomorrow? 'What does it matter then if things do happen? "You and I will be the kind who leave no mark," Tupra had said to me once, "so it won't matter what we've done, no one will bother to recount or even to investigate it." And besides,' I went on, still talking to myself, 'the day will come when everything is levelled out and life will be definitively untellable, and no one will care about anything.' But that day had not yet arrived, and I felt both curious and afraid – 'And in short, I was afraid' – and had, above all, time to wonder as those familiar lines assured me I would: 'And indeed there will be time to wonder, "Do I dare?" and, "Do I dare?" Time to turn back and descend the stair . . .' Even time to ask the whole question that comes later in the poem – 'Do I dare disturb the universe?' – the question no one asks before acting or even before speaking because everyone dares to do just that, to disturb the universe and to trouble it, with their small quick tongues and their ill-intentioned steps, 'So how should I presume?' And that's what kept my finger on the guard and my hand from cocking the gun, that is what happened, and besides I knew there would still be time to place my finger on the trigger and fire, having first cocked it with one simple gesture, as Miquelín had showed me.

'Turn round and sit down over there,' I said to Custardoy, pointing with my free hand at the sofa, a sofa on which he would probably often have sat or perhaps lain with Luisa. 'Put your hands on the table where I can see them.' In front of the sofa was a coffee table, as there is in most of the world's living rooms. 'Spread your fingers wide and don't move a muscle.'

Custardoy turned round as ordered and I finally saw his face full on and unimpeded, just as he did mine. He had a faint smile on his lips, which irritated me, and that long-toothed smile lit up his sharp-featured face and lent it a look almost of cordiality. He seemed quite calm, even amused in a way, despite that blow to his ribs, which must have hurt and frightened him. But, by then, he probably knew who I was, even if only by intuition or by a process of elimination, and relying perhaps on his own interpretative capacities, which were good enough for him to be sure that Luisa's husband wasn't going to shoot him, at least not yet, that is, without first speaking to him. (But then no one is ever totally convinced that someone is going to shoot him, not even with the gun barrel there before him.) His huge, dark, wide-set, almost lashless eyes really were most unpleasant and I immediately felt that grasping quality, how they quickly looked me over, with, how can I put it, a kind of intimidatory intent, which, in the circumstances, was both strange and inappropriate. His half-smile, on the other hand, was perfectly affable, as if he were able to be two people at once. I couldn't understand how Luisa could possibly like him, even if there was something cocky and common about him – crude and rough and cold – a quality which, as I've seen and know, a lot of women find attractive. Before sitting down, he stroked his moustache, repositioned his ponytail with a gesture that was unavoidably feminine, threw his hat down on the sofa and said:

'May I light a cigarette? If I'm smoking, you'll still be able to see my two hands.' And then he sat down, taking care not to crease the tails of his raincoat. He had begun addressing me as '*tú*' now, and that confirmed me in my suspicion that he had identified me.

'Have one of mine,' I replied, not wanting him to put his hand in his pocket. I offered him a Karelias and took another for myself. I lit both from the same flame and we inhaled the smoke at the same time, and for a moment we resembled old friends, taking that first puff in silence. We had both suffered a fright, and a cigarette was just what we needed. But the fright was not yet over, and his must have been far greater than mine, after all, I had merely frightened myself when I saw what I was doing, and that always supposes a lesser, more controlled fear, one you can bring to an end yourself. The conversation that followed moved very quickly.

'What the fuck's up with you?' said Custardoy. 'You're Jaime, aren't you?' The use of a swear-word denoted aplomb and a certain lack of respect, unless, of course, he always talked like that (after all, he had no reason to respect me and more than enough reason to be angry with me); regardless of whether such aplomb was feigned or real, it was clear, I thought, that I had not yet frightened him enough, and how was I to do that? I sat sideways on the arm of a chair, which meant that not only was I facing him, I was higher up as well.

'Who said you could talk? I didn't. I only said you could smoke. So smoke your cigarette and shut the fuck up.' I flung the swear-word back at him so as to place us on an equal footing and I waved the pistol about a bit. I hoped he wasn't used to handling firearms or wouldn't notice that I wasn't. It's not easy to frighten someone if you're not in the habit of doing so. I knew I could do it (I had done so before on occasion), just as I knew or imagined that I would be capable, or at least not incapable, of killing; but to do both those things, I would − perhaps − need to be completely crazy, agitated or furious or gripped by a long-lasting thirst for revenge, and at that moment, I wasn't, not sufficiently; perhaps I had relaxed once the first phase of my unplanned plan had passed without mishap, intercepting Custardoy, going to his apartment and shutting myself up with him there. I had too little hatred. I had too little knowledge. I was too lukewarm. I lacked the necessary heat. And, unlike Tupra, I wasn't cold enough either.

'OK, talk. I haven't got all fucking day to waste over this kind of crazy nonsense. Why are you pointing that gun at me? Just what are you up to, pal?' And he attempted another of those smiles that revealed long shiny teeth and which made him look almost pleasant and his profile less aggressive. He still reminded me of someone, but I didn't have time just then to think who it might be.

Custardoy was either brave or over-confident. Or perhaps he didn't want to appear daunted despite the weapon pointed at his chest by this madman, or maybe he was convinced I wouldn't use it. He had spoken scornfully, as if he wanted to diminish us, me and my gun. He had gone so far as to address me as 'pal' (and I hate people who use such terms), trying to belittle me and make me feel like some ridiculous child with my antiquated pistol in my hand. If he *was* over-confident, I wondered what more I would have to do to puncture his arrogance: I had already hit him and hurt him, and he must have registered that if I was capable of that, I was capable of worse things. If he continued in that vein, he ran the risk of getting me seriously riled or, as Custardoy might have put it, of getting on my tits. So it suited me that he should continue in that vein. Or perhaps not, he might just make me see myself in that situation as grotesque and puerile.

'Listen,' I said. 'From today on, you're going to stop seeing Luisa Juárez. It's over. No more beatings or cuts or black eyes. You never touch her again, right?'

I thought he would immediately deny ever laying a finger on her and declare: 'I don't know what you're talking about' or some such thing. But he didn't, that wasn't what upset him:

'Oh, really? What? On your say-so? He's got some nerve.' The way he said this irritated me, as if he were not addressing me, but some invisible third party, some imaginary witness with whom he felt at liberty to mock me. 'That's up to her and me, don't you think?'

Yes, that was precisely what I thought. I had no right to involve myself in her affairs, she was free, she was an adult, she might even be very happy with him, she hadn't asked me for my opinion or my protection, she hadn't even deigned to tell me about her day-to-day life, that life no longer concerned me; of course I agreed. None of that, though, was relevant now – I had decided to involve myself and to use force and fear, and at that point you have to leave aside all arguments and principles, all respect and moral reservations and scruples because you have decided to do what you want to do and to impose that decision on others, to achieve your ends without further delay, and then, as with any war once it has begun, being right or wrong should neither intervene nor count. Once that line has been crossed, right or wrong no longer matter, it's simply a matter of getting your own way, of winning and subjugating and prevailing. He had hit her and must be made to stop, that was all. 'Just make sure he's out of the picture,' I repeated to myself. I had to leave that apartment with Custardoy suppressed and erased like a bloodstain, that was all. And my determination grew.

'Yes,' I agreed, 'it should be up to the two of you to make that decision, but that isn't how it's going to be. You're going to decide on your own. You're going to give her up today. Which would you rather give up − her or the world. Be quite clear about one thing though: either way you're going to give her up.'

For the first time, I saw him hesitate, perhaps I even caught a glimmer of fear. I thought: 'He's realised that it's not at all difficult to shoot someone, it's just a question of not being yourself for two seconds or perhaps of being yourself − one moment you're not a murderer and then suddenly you are and will be for all eternity − that anyone with a weapon in his hand might suddenly up and shoot you, all it takes is for him to forget for an instant the magnitude of the gesture, of a single simple gesture, or rather two, cocking the gun and squeezing the trigger, which might be almost simultaneous as it is in Westerns, cocking the hammer and pulling the trigger, put this finger here and that finger there, first one and then the other, up and back and there you are, it can happen to anyone, a slip of the hand or the finger, the hand that, in just one movement, puts the bullet into the barrel or the chamber and then the forefinger drawing back − this is a heavy pistol, quite hard to hold, but hand and finger act on their own as if no one were moving them, no consciousness or will, they caress and stroke and glide almost, you don't even have to make the effort that a sword inevitably requires, with a sword you have to raise it up and then bring it down and both movements require the whole strength of one arm or even both, which is why neither children nor many women nor feeble old men can wield one, but on the other hand, the pistol can be used by the weakest, most fearful, most stupid and most worthless of people − the pistol democratises killing far more than the dishonourable crossbow − and anyone can cause irreparable damage with one, you just have to let things happen. And if I were to cock the pistol now, Custardoy would be terrified.'

And as soon as I thought this, and despite Miquelín's warning, I cocked the pistol. It was only a test and only for an instant, just to see a spark of panic in those strange dark eyes, it was only a spark, but I saw it. And then I immediately put my thumb on the hammer and lowered it and removed the projectile that had passed into the barrel or chamber or whatever it's called and put it away in my pocket; I uncocked the Llama. But he had seen how quick the pistol was to cock and how, once cocked, the bullets could fly out – a single gesture, then another and another – towards his head or his chest, towards an arm or a leg, towards his codpiece which would be reduced to a few fine hairs like the vanished codpiece of Death in the painting, or towards whatever part I chose to point it at. 'What a very odd feeling,' I thought, 'having a man at your mercy. Deciding if he should live or die, although it's not even really a matter of deciding.'

Custardoy, however, put on a brave face, or perhaps it was just that he wanted to be right, or, given that he had no weapon with which to defend himself, that he was trying to dissuade or ter- rify or destroy me, or to dig my grave still deeper with his ugly words and with his voice. His voice did not emerge cleanly, it was slightly hoarse, as if there were tiny pins in his throat similar to those on the revolving metallic disc or cylinder in a music box, which strike the tuned teeth of the comb and determine or mark the one repetitive melody. What he said emerged slowly, as if the spikes slowed down his speech. At any rate, he kept his hands on the table. He had finished his cigarette, but hadn't for- gotten my earlier order, which was a good sign.

'Look, Jaime.' And it bothered me unutterably that he should call me by my first name, the name that Luisa used and which he had doubtless heard her say (how embarrassing) when she spoke to him about me. 'This is all total bullshit, and in a while, when you've left here, you'll be the first to see that. What is it that bothers you so much? Is it the fact that I screw her now and then? It's a bit late for you to be complaining about that. You probably do the same in London with whoever takes your fancy, and you're going to have to get used to it, if you aren't already, for Chrissake, there was whatever there was between you two and now there isn't. It happens all the time. But *this* I really can't believe.' He stopped and gave a short laugh, the laughter that made him almost pleasant and more attractive, he was still not fully aware of the danger, of the danger I represented. 'I mean, it's funny really, this is the last thing I would have expected. It's like a scene straight out of an opera, dammit!' Again he said this as if he were talking to a third party, to a ghost present in the room and not to me, and that drove me wild. He was probably looking forward to telling the story later on to a friend ('You won't believe what happened to me today? Christ, it was weird') or perhaps to Luisa herself ('I bet you can't guess who came to see me today, and toting a gun as well. Fucking hell! You married a really nasty piece of work there, he's nothing like you said, he's a complete headcase'). But he wouldn't be seeing Luisa again, he didn't know that, but I did. I doubted that he would talk quite like that to her, although he did when she wasn't there, of course; foul language came naturally to him, much more than it does to me: I have no problem using swear-words when the situation calls for it, but I lacked his fluency in that particular register, with which I was as familiar as almost everyone else, but which I didn't often use.

'You know exactly what bothers me. You know precisely what I find unacceptable, you bastard. Like I said, from today on, you'll never touch her again.'

He was still unbowed. He was playing a dangerous game. As he must have noticed, he risked heating up my lukewarm blood and provoking hand and finger into action. Perhaps this was a useful stratagem: perhaps he was trying not only to show that he was right, but also to show me that I was not, to open my eyes, to rid himself of this stupid unexpected problem and get on with his life by making me give in.

'What? Oh. The bruises,' he said, and each rasping word was dragged out like the music from a music box, each one emerged slowly as if it kept snagging on something, there was also per- haps a little *madrileño* bravado in his way of speaking. Then he added a trite remark, which, nonetheless, wounded me when I realised what he was saying; it took me a few seconds because I found it hard to grasp or preferred not to grasp what he meant, or maybe it took me that amount of time to absorb the mean- ing. 'Look, pal,' again that hateful belittling term, 'everyone has their own sexuality, and with some partners it comes out natu- rally and with others it doesn't. Didn't the same thing happen when she was with you? I mean, what can I say, pal, I had no idea either. It just happened and you have to give people what they want. Or don't you think so? Look, I didn't do anything to her she didn't want me to. Is that clear? So don't damn well go blaming me for something I'm not guilty of, all right?'

Yes, it took me a few seconds. 'What *is* this guy saying?' I thought. 'He's telling me that Luisa enjoys being knocked about, he's telling *me* that? That's impossible. It's a lie,' I thought, 'I've known her intimately for years, although less so lately, and I've never seen the slightest suggestion of that, I'd have noticed it, however slight, a hint, a question mark, a glimpse, this guy's trying to slither out of it, trying to justify himself, to escape, he knows why I'm here and that my reason is a grave one and he's been thinking up this false explanation for a while now, he knows for certain that I'm not going to ask Luisa about it and he's taking advantage of that to tell me he only hurts women who want to be hurt, or something of the sort, but Cristina told me how frightened the women were who had slept with him, some at any rate, and their subsequent silence about or concealment of what went on, why wouldn't they speak, if he was a violent brute, they'd report him, they'd alert other women, they'd forewarn them, for example, those prostitutes he goes with, sometimes two at a time. No, it can't be true, it's not,' I thought, shrugging off the idea. It's dreadful to be told anything, anything at all, it's dreadful to have ideas put in your head, however unlikely or ridiculous and however unsustainable and improbable (but everything has its time to be believed), any scrap of information registered by the brain stays there until it achieves oblivion, that eternally one-eyed oblivion, any story or fact and even the remotest possibility is recorded, and however much you clean and scrub and erase, that rim is the kind that will never come out; it's understandable really that people should hate knowledge and deny what is there before their eyes and prefer to know nothing and to repudiate the facts, that they should avoid the inoculation and the poison and push it away as soon as they see or feel it near, it's best not to take risks; it's understandable, too, that we almost all ignore what we see and divine and anticipate and smell, and that we toss into

371

the bag of imaginings anything that we see clearly – for however short a time – before it can take root in our mind and leave it for ever troubled, and so it's hardly strange that we should be reluctant to know anyone's face, today, tomorrow or yesterday. 'What face am I wearing now?' I wondered. 'And what about Luisa's face, one I thought I had plumbed and deciphered and knew, to all intents and purposes, from top to bottom, from past to future and from tomorrow to yesterday, and then along comes this son-of-a-bitch talking about her sexuality and telling me she likes him to get rough with her in bed, it's a joke, I mustn't believe him or think about it, but people do change and, above all, make discoveries, the kind of wretched discovery that takes those people from us and carries them far away, as with young Pérez Nuix when I discovered the pleasure of pretending that I wasn't doing what I was doing or of making believe that what was happening wasn't happening, which is not, I think, quite the same thing, that had been political, a tacit game, but that's what this bastard would say, damn him, that it's all a game, an erotic game, anything is possible, but it can't be true. Luisa's black eye wasn't the result of some game, like hell it was, and yet Custardoy said: "What? Oh. The bruises," why did he use the plural when I've only seen one bruise, perhaps there are more underneath her clothes, on her body, I haven't seen Luisa naked on this visit nor will I, I'll probably never see her naked again, but this bastard will unless I stop him and make sure he's out of the picture now and for good, with no going back and no further delay, don't ever linger or delay, just cock the gun again and squeeze the trigger, it's a simple matter of running my hand over the slide to release it and moving a finger, this and then this, forward and back and a bullet in the head and that will be that, I am, after all, wearing gloves, he'll be out of the picture for ever and no more bruises, no more bed, no more wit or charm, it's in my hands to do all of that and I don't even have to listen to him or speak to him again.'

And so I did cock the pistol, and for the first time I moved my index finger from the guard to the trigger, remembering Miquelín's warning and believing that I was following his advice, 'Never put your finger on the trigger until you know you're going to shoot.' And for a few seconds – one, two, three, four, five; and six – I did know, but not afterwards. I have no idea what saved him that time, it wasn't his silence, perhaps there were several things – thoughts, memories, and a recognition – all crowded together into six or possibly seven seconds, or perhaps other things came to me later and so had more time to be thought or remembered once I was back in my hotel room. 'What face am I wearing now?' I thought again. 'It's the face of all those men and rather fewer women who have held someone else's life in their hands and it could, from one moment to the next, come to resemble the face of those who chose to take that life. Not Reresby's face, who did not, in the end, snatch away De la Garza's life, and who, if he has killed other people, did not do so in my presence, like Wheeler with his outbreaks of cholera and malaria and plague. But it would join the face of that vicious *malagueño* who baited and killed Marés, the face of that Madrid woman who boasted on the tram of having killed a child by smashing its head against a wall, of those militiamen who finished off my young Uncle Alfonso and left him dead in the gutter, even the faces of Orlov and Bielov and Carlos Contreras, who tortured Andreu Nin in Alcalá and possibly flayed him alive; of Vizconde de La Barthe, who ordered Torrijos and, according to the painting, seventeen of his followers to be shot on the beach as soon as they disembarked, but in reality and in history there may have been many more; the faces of the Czech resistance fighters or students who made an attempt on the life of the Nazi Protector Heydrich using bullets impregnated with botulin and the face of Spooner, the director of the Special Operations Executive, the SOE, who planned it all; the faces of the German occupiers who, in reprisal and with their hatred of place, destroyed the village of Lidice and killed either instantly or slowly one hundred and ninety-nine men and one hundred and eighty-four women on 10 June 1942; the faces of the thugs who machine-gunned those four unfortunates on another hidden beach, in Calabria this time, not far from Crotone, on the Golfo di Taranto, three men and a woman, a killing I myself watched; and the face of

the man who screamed at another man in a garage, his mouth so
close to the other's face that he sprayed him with saliva, and then
shot him at point-blank range beneath the ear lobe, as I could
do now to Custardoy with no one here to cry out "Don't!" as I
did to Reresby and probably stopped him, I could put the barrel
right there and that would be it, blood spurting out and tiny bits
of bone; the face of the woman in green, her skirt all rucked up
and wearing a sweater and a pearl necklace and high heels but
with no tights, who crushed the skull of a man with a hammer
and sat astride him to strike his forehead over and over; the face
of the European officer or mercenary who ordered the massacre
of twenty Africans who fell in swift succession, like dominoes;
the face of Manoia, yes him too, who scooped out the eyes of
his prisoner as if they were peach stones and then, according to
Tupra, slit his throat; and all those centuries before, the face of
Ingram Frizer, who stabbed to death the poet Marlowe in a tav-
ern in Deptford, even though his face is unknown and his name,
too, remains uncertain; and, of course, the face of King Richard,
who ordered his two little nephews in the Tower to be strangled,
and had many others killed too, whether in his angry mood or
not, including poor Clarence, drowned by two henchmen in a
butt of disgusting wine and held by the legs, which remained
outside the barrel and flailed ridiculously about in the air he
would never breathe again . . . My face will resemble and be
assimilated into that of all those men and rather fewer women
who were once masters of time and who held in their hand the
hourglass − in the form of a weapon, in the form of an order
− and decided suddenly, without lingering or delaying, to stop
time, thus obliging others no longer to desire their own desires
and to leave even their own first name behind. I don't like being
linked to those faces. On the other hand, I must remove Luisa
from all danger and suffering and torment, so that her ghost will
not one day say to this man what Lady Anne's ghost said to her
husband on the eve of battle, nor hurl at him the curse that I am
failing to carry out despite being in a position to do so: "Thy
wife, that wretched Luisa thy wife, that never slept a quiet hour
with thee . . . Let me sit heavy on thy soul, and may you feel the

pinprick in your breast: despair and die!" Yes, it would be best to kill him while I still have time,' I thought, 'I might not have another opportunity in the future, perhaps there is no other way of removing him from the picture for ever and this is the only way to make us safe.' That 'us' surprised me. And it gave me strength and encouragement to discover that I still thought of us as 'us'.

And although I was no longer at all sure that I would shoot him, I kept my finger on the trigger, and still more seconds passed. And as they passed and the risk remained that I might accidentally fire the gun, I was conscious that Custardoy was looking paler and less kempt, it was as if his immaculate appearance had somehow suffered a breakdown, his tie was crooked and he made the mechanical gesture of straightening it, reminding me of that other – unavoidably feminine – gesture he had made when repositioning his ponytail, then he obediently returned his hand to the table; his raincoat was creased now, the cloth seemed of poorer quality, and what I could see of his shirt looked grubby with sweat. As for his hair, it gave the impression of being plastered to his head and even his sideburns had lost their curl; he was trying hard to maintain his smile – obviously aware of its affable nature – but it no longer lit up his face; his nose had grown sharper, or perhaps it was simply that I had shifted position and the angle had changed; his eyes, I thought, were clouded and closer together, as if his whole being were striving to shrink and thus offer less of a target, a purely unconscious reaction, since, given the short distance separating us, it made no sense at all, for I certainly couldn't miss.

'Have you ever met my children?' I asked suddenly.

'No, I've never even seen them. I don't like getting kids involved.'

'How long have you been going out with her? How long have you known each other? And don't lie to me. I know her better than you do.'

The fact that I spoke to him and asked him civilised questions with no insults thrown in calmed him slightly, although he still kept glancing at the barrel of the primed pistol – 'primed', as I understand it, being another term for 'cocked' – with his large dark eyes, still cold and crude despite the fear in them, any roughness being attributable now only to his moustache and his nose.

'About six months.' And he allowed himself to add: 'Although longer isn't necessarily better. Look, why don't you just leave us alone? I've never liked a woman as much as I like her. You're out of the frame, we thought that was clear.' – 'Ah, so I'm the one who's out of the picture now,' I thought. 'He's right. But that's going to change. He talks about "us" as well, meaning Luisa and him.' – 'Anyway, that's clear to Luisa, and she assumed it was to you as well.'

'I don't know why you use the past tense. She's going to continue assuming that because you're not going to tell her anything about what's happened here.'

With a pistol in my hand, this sounded like a serious threat, although it wasn't, at least I didn't say it with that intention, but simply because I was sure they wouldn't be seeing each other again after that day. Custardoy was less mouthy now, I noticed, and was growing increasingly apprehensive. And then another thought or memory came into my mind, one that should have condemned him and yet, strangely, helped to save him: 'Good God, this man is my *ge-brȳd-guma*, Luisa has made of him and me unwitting co-fornicators or co-fuckers, just as Tupra and I probably are as well through the intermediary or link of Pérez Nuix, and as I, all unawares, must be of many other men through other women; we never think about that the first time we have sex with someone, about who we're bringing together and who we're joining forces with, and nowadays, these phantasmagorical relationships, undesired and unsought, would be a story without end. But according to that dead language, this man and I are related, indeed, according to any language, we have an affinity, and perhaps for that very reason I should not kill him, yes, for that reason too, because we have something very important in common, I've never liked another woman as much as I like Luisa either, so what it comes down to is that we love the same person, and I can't blame him for that, or perhaps he simply has sex with her, it's impossible to gauge what his feelings are.' I could have tried to find out and ask him if he loved her, but the question struck me as absurd, and besides, with a pistol cocked and pointing at him, I knew what he would answer but not if that answer would be true. At that moment, the truth would be the last thing he would tell me, if he really thought the truth might kill him.

'I don't want anyone to disappear,' was my next thought. 'I don't believe in the Last Judgement or in a great final dance of sorrow and contentment, nor in some kind of rowdy get-together at which the murdered will rise up before their murderers and present their accusations to a bored and horrified Judge. I don't believe in that because I don't belong to the age of steadfast faith, and because it's not necessary: that scene takes place here, on earth, in a fragmented individual form, at least it does when the dead person knows or sees who is killing him and can then say with his farewell glance: "You're taking my life more for reasons of jealousy than justice, I haven't killed anyone, not as far as you know, you're putting a bullet in my forehead or beneath my ear lobe not because you think I'm beating up the woman who is no longer your wife, as if I were some vulgar wife-beater, although you can't and don't want to avoid that suspicion and at least part-believe it for your own momentary justification which will be of no use to you tomorrow, but because you're afraid of me and are going to fight for what is yours, as do all those who commit crimes and have to convince themselves that their crimes were necessary: for your God, for your King, for your country, for your culture or your race; for your flag, your legend, your language, your class or your space; for your honour, your religion, for your family, for your strongbox, for your purse and your socks; or for your wife. And in short, you are afraid. I died in my apartment on a cloudy day, among my paintings and without even taking off my raincoat, when I least expected it and at the hands of a stranger who intercepted me at the front door and gave me a last cigarette which I did not enjoy. I will no longer go to the Prado to look at the paintings, I will no longer study them or copy them or even forge them, I will no longer walk through Madrid with my ponytail bobbing and my fine hat on or drink another beer or eat another portion of *patatas bravas*, I won't go into the bookshop or greet my female friends or stop to look at statues or the legs of some passing woman, nor will I ever make anyone laugh again. You're putting an end to all of that. It may not be much, but it's what I have, it's my life and it's unique, and no one else will ever have it again. Let me sit heavy on your soul each night and fill your sleep with perturbations, may you feel my knee upon your chest, while you sleep with one eye open, an eye you will never be able to close." No, I don't want anyone to disappear,' I thought again, 'not even this man. I do not dare, and there will still be time to turn back and descend the stair, I do not dare disturb the universe, still less destroy anything in it, in my angry mood. There will be room for Custardoy in these streets for a while yet, they are already awash with blood and no one should tremble as they leave them, and they are perhaps already too full of men brimming with rage and with thunderless lightning that strikes in silence, I should not be one more such man. "We are all witnesses to our own story, Jack. You to yours and I to mine," Tupra said to me once. My face would become one with that of Santa Olalla and, even worse, that of Del Real, two names that have always been for me the names of treachery; because when they betrayed my father at the end of the Civil War, what they wanted was his execution and his death, that was the usual fate of any detainee, for they were the masters of time, they held the hourglass in their hand and ordered it to stop, except that it didn't stop and didn't obey them and, thanks to that, I am here, and my father did not have to say as he died: "Strange to see meanings that clung together once floating away in every direction. And being dead is hard work . . ." No, I will not be the one to impose that task on this unpleasant man for whom I feel a strange blend of sympathy and loathing, he is part of this landscape and of the universe, he still treads the earth and traverses the world and it is not up to me to change that; at the end of time there are only vestiges or remnants or rims and in each can be traced, at most, the shadow of an incomplete story, full of lacunae, as ghostly, hieroglyphic, cadaverous or fragmentary as pieces of tombstones or the broken inscriptions on ruined tympana, "past matter, dumb matter", and then you might doubt that it ever existed at all. Why did she do that, they will say of you, why so much fuss and why the quickening pulse, why the trembling, why the somersaulting heart; and of me they will say: why did he speak or not speak, why did he wait so long and so faithfully, why that dizziness, those doubts, that torment, why did he take those particular steps and why so many? And of us both they will say: why all that conflict and struggle, why did they fight instead of just looking and staying still, why were they unable to meet or to go on seeing each other, and why so much sleep, so many dreams, and why that scratch, my pain, my word, your fever, and all those doubts, all that torment.'

I took out the second bullet and put it away, I uncocked the pistol, removed my finger from the trigger and rested it once more on the guard, as Miquelín had advised me to do unless I was sure I was going to fire. I saw on Custardoy's face a look of contained or repressed relief, he didn't dare feel entirely relieved, how could he, when he still had the barrel of a gun pointing at his face and when the man holding the gun was wearing gloves and had just done something very worrying: he had picked up the two ashtrays with the two cigarette butts in them and their corresponding ash, his own and Custardoy's, the ash from the burned-out Karelias cigarettes, and emptied them into his other raincoat pocket to keep them separate from the bullets, just as, in the toilet for the disabled, Tupra had put away his sodden gloves, wrung out and wrapped up in toilet paper, although he had done so only once his task was complete, while mine still lay before me. 'Now I do have his coldness, Reresby's coldness, that is, now that I've recognised my similarity or affinity with this man, which is why he's going to emerge from this alive,' I thought, 'and now that I've thoroughly frightened him, even though he has barely shown it and put on a brave face, anything else I do to him will seem all right and of no account, he'll think himself lucky and find it perfectly reasonable. I will not be Ser-geant Death or Sir Death or Sir Cruelty or even Sir Thrashing, I will be Sir Blow or Sir Wound or Sir Punishment, because something has to be done to keep him out of the picture, just as Tupra did with De la Garza.'

And while I was thinking (and much of this I thought later on), I realised who it was that Custardoy reminded me of; what, to use Wheeler's word, his affinity was; or his relationship, al-though in this case there was even a resemblance. And it was probably that very frivolous fact that saved him, truly and defini-tively, a nonsense, a mere nothing, a chance superfluous flash, an opportune association or a fickle memory that might or might not have surfaced; sometimes what we do or don't do depends on that, just as we decide to give alms to one beggar among many, whose appearance, for some reason, moves us: we suddenly see the person, see beyond his condition and function and needs, we individualise him, and he no longer seems to us indistinguishable or interchangeable as an object of compassion, of which there are hundreds; that's what happened to Luisa with the young Ro-manian or Hungarian or Bosnian woman and her sentinel son at the entrance to the supermarket, and about whom I had oc-casionally thought while I was far away in London, having first known of their existence through a story told to me. I associated Custardoy with my dancing neighbour opposite, with whom I had never exchanged a word, but who had so often cheered or soothed me with his improvised dances beyond the trees and the statue, on the other side of the square, alone or accompanied by his friends or *partenaires* or lovers. Yes, they had quite a lot in common: my dancer is a thin fellow with bony features – jaw and nose and forehead – but a strong athletic build, just as Custardoy is all sinew; he has a thick but well-groomed moustache, like that of a boxer from the early days, except that it's cut straight with no nineteenth-century curlicues, and he wears his hair combed back with a middle parting as if he had a ponytail, although I've never seen it, perhaps one day he'll reveal that he has one just like Custardoy, he also sometimes wears a tie as Custardoy al-ways does, even when he's running and leaping about his empty living room, the guy's mad, but so happy, so contented, so oblivious to everything that wears the rest of us down and consumes us, immersed in his dances danced for no one, it's fun and even rather cheering to watch, and mysterious too, I can't imagine who he is or what he does, he eludes – and this doesn't happen very often – my interpretative or deductive faculties, which may or may not be right, but which never hold back, springing immediately into action to compose a brief, improvised portrait, a stereotype, a flash, a plausible supposition, a sketch or snippet of life however imaginary and basic or arbitrary these might be, it's my alert, detective mind, the idiotic mind that Clare Bayes criticised and reproached me for years ago now, before I met Luisa, and which I had to suppress with Luisa so as not to irritate her or fill her with fear, the superstitious fear that always does the most damage and yet serves so little purpose, for there's nothing to be done to protect ourselves from what we already know and dread (perhaps because we are fatalistically drawn to it and seek it out so as to avoid disappointment), and we usually know how things will end, how they will evolve and what awaits us, where things are going and what their conclusion will be; everything is there on view, in fact, everything is visible very early on in a relationship just as it is in all honest straightforward stories, you only have to look to see it, one single moment encapsulates the germ of many years to come, of almost our whole history – one grave pregnant moment – and if we want to we can see it and, in broad terms, read it, there are not that many possible variations, the signs rarely deceive if we know how to decipher their meanings, if you are prepared to do so – but it's very difficult and can prove catastrophic . . .

I had interpreted or deduced Custardoy and even had proof, and both those things had been enough to condemn him. But what bad or good luck – how I regret it, how I celebrate it – that he should remind me of my contented dancer to whom I was grateful from afar, which was doubtless why I felt for Custardoy that inexplicable sympathy mingled with profound loathing. Perhaps they were alike in other ways too, perhaps there were other affinities apart from the pleasant smile and the superficial physical likeness: when Custardoy was sketching and taking notes as he stood before that painting by Parmigianino he was, perhaps, as focused on that as my neighbour was on his dancing, as happy and contented, and when he painted at home, when he made his copies or forgeries, he may have been even more abstracted and oblivious to all that wears us down and consumes us. And the dancer was often accompanied by two women, just as Custardoy sometimes took two women to bed with him in his need to be many or to live more than one life. And it was that, above all, that made me give up the idea of killing him: a nonsense, a mere nothing, a chance, superfluous flash of thought, a doubt or caprice or some stupid fit of feeling, an untimely association of fickle memories, or was it, rather, one-eyed oblivion.

Without saying anything, I went over to his enviable fireplace and thereafter I acted very swiftly, as if I were distracted or, rather, busy, yes, my attitude was as businesslike as Reresby's had been when he walked into that immaculate Disabled toilet. 'Now I have his coldness,' I thought again, 'now I know how to frighten Custardoy, now I can imagine myself, because it *is* just a question of imagining yourself and only then can you rid yourself of problems; now I can calculate how hard the blow should be, can bring down my sword without severing anything, lift it up and then bring it down again but still cut nothing and nevertheless give him the fright of his life that will ensure he never comes near us again, near me or, above all, Luisa.' I picked up the poker and without giving Custardoy time to prepare himself or even to foresee what I was about to do, I struck him as hard as I could on the left hand that he had placed, along with his right hand, on the table. I heard the crunch of broken bones, I heard it clearly despite the simultaneous howl he let out, his face, no longer rough or crude or cold, twisted in pain and he instinctively clasped his broken hand with his other hand.

'Fuck! You've broken my hand, you bastard!' It was a perfectly normal reaction, he didn't really know what he was saying, the pain had made him forget for a moment that I still had a gun aimed at him and that my last words to him had been: 'you're not going to tell her anything about what's happened here.'

I raised the poker again and this time, applying less pressure – yes, now I could calculate how hard the blow should be – I slashed his cheek, gave him *uno sfregio* or a cut much longer and much deeper than the one Flavia Manoia suffered, although it barely touched bone. He raised his good hand to his jaw, his cheek, it was the right one, and stared at me with a look of panic, of fear, which was not so much visceral as atavistic, the fear of someone who does not know whether more blows will follow nor how many because that is the nature of swords, that is the nature of weapons that are not loosed or thrown, those that kill at close quarters and when face to face with the person killed, without the murderer or the avenger or the avenged detaching or separating themselves from the sword while they wreak havoc and plunge the weapon in and cut and slice, all with the same blade which they never discard, but hold on to and grip even harder while they pierce, mutilate, skewer and even dismember. I did none of those things, it was hardly the appropriate weapon for that, indeed, it wasn't a weapon at all, but a tool.

'Keep your hands on the table, I said,' and again I cocked the pistol, but this time I didn't place my index finger on the trigger.

He looked at me with stupefaction and renewed alarm, or perhaps a different kind of alarm, his eyes, having grown momentarily closer together, were once more wide apart. I know what was going through his head at that moment, he must have been thinking: 'Oh, no. This madman's going to break my other hand too, the hand I paint with.'

'No,' he said. 'Why? No, don't do it.'

And so I had no option but to press the barrel of the gun to his forehead, so that he would take me seriously, to his broad forehead, where his hair was beginning to recede, although I knew now that I wouldn't shoot him. He, however, couldn't know that, he had no idea, and that was my great advantage, that he could not interpret me, no one can in such circumstances, not even the best of interpreters. Not even Wheeler or Pérez Nuix or Tupra would have been able to, as the report on me said: 'Sometimes he seems to me to be a complete enigma. And sometimes I think he's an enigma to himself. Then I go back to the idea that he doesn't know himself very well. And that he doesn't pay much attention to himself because he's given up understanding himself. He considers himself a lost cause upon whom it would be pointless squandering thought. He knows he doesn't understand himself and that he never will. And so he doesn't waste his time trying to do so. I don't think he's dangerous. But he is to be feared.' Custardoy didn't know at that point that I wasn't dangerous, but he knew I was to be feared.

'Put your hands on the table.' I said this calmly, it seemed to me unnecessary to raise my voice or to swear. 'Or would you prefer me to put a bullet in your head so that then there'll be nothing at all? It wouldn't be hard, it would only take a moment.' Yes, how strange that someone should obey our every order and be at our mercy and do whatever we want.

He squeezed his eyes tight shut when he felt the cold metal of the pistol on his skin, this skin of ours that resists nothing, which offers no protection and is so easily wounded that even a fingernail can scratch it, and a knife can cut it and a spear rip it open, and a sword can tear it even as it slices through the air, and a bullet destroy it. (Blood was seeping from the wound to his cheek, but it wasn't running down his cheek, it was just coagulating along the wound itself.) I saw the look on his face, the look of someone who thinks or knows he is dead; but since he was still alive, the image was one of infinite fear and struggle, mental struggle, of desire perhaps; his face turned deathly pale, just as if someone had given it a quick lick of grey or off-white or off-colour paint, or had thrown flour over him or perhaps talcum powder, it was rather like when swift clouds cast a shadow over the fields and a shudder runs through the flocks below, or like the hand that spreads the plague or closes the eyes of the deceased, because one is always instantly aware of any real danger of death and one believes in it and awaits the moment. Like De la Garza, he preferred to wait with eyes tight shut, they were trembling or pulsating – perhaps his pupils were racing about madly beneath the lids. And he put his hands on the table, you bet he did, the injured and the sound hand, the former he had difficulty placing flat. And again I acted quickly, I neither lingered nor delayed, I was sick of his company and wanted to get out of there fast; I was sick of his face too, despite its benign appearance, I used the poker to strike the same hand a second and a third time and just as hard, I think I broke the lower part of his fingers or some of them, between hand and knuckle, that's what it sounded like. He let out another two howls and clutched his left hand with his still intact right hand, he couldn't help but console the one with the other, his left was a terrible mess, but I tried not to look, I didn't want to see it or to contemplate my work as I had contemplated the broken hands of Pérez Nuix's father in that video as he tried in vain to protect himself as he lay sprawled on a billiards table, I didn't want to know exactly what damage I had done to him, if I didn't look, it would be easier for me to believe – later on, in years to come and, shortly too, when I went back to my hotel – that it had merely been one of those dreams one has abroad (I had a return ticket and abroad for me, at least in part, was Spain, and I was leaving). Despite the awful pain, Custardoy must have thought this nothing, a piece of good luck, when he had feared for his good hand and feared receiving a bullet in the brain at point-blank range. However, he still had sufficient courage to complain. Despite his panic, he remained unshaken, not at all like that dickhead De la Garza.

'What the fuck do you want,' he said, 'to cripple me?'

And then I told him what it was I wanted:

'I haven't touched your right hand, but I could give it the same treatment as your left hand or worse. And I can come looking for you whenever I want. I could hurt your right hand so badly that you'd never pick up a paintbrush again in your life.' And once more I couldn't help remembering Reresby again, when he gave me his instructions for De la Garza and I translated them to my compatriot where he lay on the floor. Tupra had issued a fluent list of orders as if he had thought it all out before, I must give the same impression of determination and wisdom and prescience, telling him what my pre-prepared plans for him were, telling him exactly what was going to happen and what he was going to do.

Custardoy had half-opened his eyes to gauge the damage done and I had not placed the barrel of the gun against his head again since dealing the second and third blow to his hand. His gaze was dull, stunned, almost oblique, but there was also a hint of vengefulness. Nevertheless, it seemed to me that any desire for revenge was muted and purely hypothetical, as if he understood that he would have to give it up however much he wanted it, or could see it only as a distant hope or postponed reward or deferred justice, rather as, during many centuries, people of steadfast faith would imagine and nurture the idea of the Last Judgement as something that would be given to them during their long death and which they could never have in life. I had removed the gun from his head when I struck him with the poker, and now it occurred to me that I didn't even need it, the threat of destroying his right hand had cowed him completely, overwhelmed him, especially as he didn't know if that was going to happen right there and then, and because he already had before him the vision of his left hand, and could feel it – the pain must have been terrible. In the state he was in, his ponytail looked even more ridiculous, as did his tie, his sparse moustache, his aspiration to elegance; at that moment he was an angry man, but fearful, too, almost imploring, his rage curbed indefinitely. However, I still didn't put the pistol away. And he did plead with me, although his tone of voice masked the fact. His words sounded more like a reproach than a plea, but they said what they said:

'For Christ's sake, don't do that. I earn my living with my right hand. Stop playing fucking games with me. What the fuck do you want?' Swear-words are good at masking feelings, of course, which is why almost everyone uses them in Spain – the most puerile, blustering country I know – in order to appear big and brave. But Custardoy had asked a favour of me ('Don't do that') and I did not, on that occasion, feel involved or enmeshed or entangled; on the contrary, I would happily have used a razor or a knife to cut the disagreeable bond joining us, him, Luisa and me, although she had created that bond of her own accord. All I had to say to the guy was: 'I want this in exchange.'

'I'm going to leave now and you're going to stay here quite still for thirty minutes from the time I leave, without moving and without phoning anyone, however much your hand hurts; you'll have to put up with it. Then call a doctor, go to a hospital, do what you like. It will take time for that hand to heal, if it ever does completely heal. Always remember that it could have been worse, and that we can always do the same to the other hand, or cut it off with a sword, I have a very clever friend in London who loves swords. While it's healing, leave Madrid, I know you've got enough money to be able to spend some time at a hotel, in a place that you like, somewhere with museums, and have a real rest. And if none of these ideas appeal, then do something else. I don't want Luisa to see you in this state; she must never ever associate what has happened to you with my stay in Madrid. You phone her and tell her that you've had to go away unexpectedly. Some important, urgent commission, copying or restoring some painting, or several, in Berlin, Bordeaux, Vienna or St Petersburg, I don't care. Or better still, Boston, Baltimore, or Malibu, with an ocean between you, after all, there are famous museums aplenty over there with no shortage of cash to pay you for your work; anyway, I'll leave you to invent something. Call her from a mobile phone or some number that can't be traced, just so that she can't find out where you really are. You can go and convalesce in Pamplona for all I care, but you must tell her that you're far away and very busy and that you'll phone her when you can, just in case, because if she thinks you're somewhere near, she might try and leave the kids with someone for a few days and come and join you.'

'She won't just let me go off like that without saying goodbye, especially if I'm going to be away for a while,' said Custardoy, interrupting me. I didn't mind because this meant he was accepting my plan and was prepared to obey it, and that I wouldn't have to damage his other hand or even consider doing so, because I would then have no other hold over him and would have to shoot him and that now seemed to me impossible. I had lost all my heat, what little I'd had. I had taken on Tupra's coldness only momentarily and half-heartedly. Perhaps not even Tupra was so very cold: after all, he hadn't, in the end, cut off De la Garza's head.

'Don't you understand? She won't be able to say goodbye to you, however much she wants to, because when you phone her, you'll already have left, you'll call her from somewhere else, do you see?'

'She'll think that very odd.'

'Try to make it seem perfectly normal. Emergencies do happen, as do unforeseen events. Besides, you don't see each other every day, do you? Or phone each other on a daily basis?' I wasn't expecting an answer, and I preferred him not to give one. 'While you're away, only phone her now and then, and make those calls less and less frequent, until, in two weeks or so, you'll have stopped phoning altogether. After two weeks, you give no sign of life at all, none, and if she does manage to locate you, be evasive with her, impatient. And when your hand has healed and you come back (if that wretched hand of yours ever does heal after what I've done to it), you won't call her then either. Sooner or later, she'll hear from someone that you're back, and if she's still interested, she'll be the one to seek you out or phone you or demand an explanation. And you can tell her then, bluntly and arrogantly, it should come easily enough to you, you've probably done it hundreds of times. As far as you're concerned, you'll say, she's history, you never even give her a thought. Tell her that on the beaches of Malibu you've met the new Bo Derek or a lady security guard or Getty's daughter or whoever. Or an heiress from Boston whom you're about to marry. You make it clear to her that it's all over, that she should leave you alone, that you don't want to see her. And you won't see her. As of today, you've said your farewells, do you understand? And if you utter one word to her about what has happened here, about this visit, if you lead her to suspect or, however remotely, imagine what went on, now or later, even if it's in ten years' time, you can say farewell to your right hand as well.' The words of the 'Streets of Laredo' came into my mind: 'But please not one word of all this shall you mention, when others should ask for my story to hear.'

Custardoy opened his coarse eyes a little wider, he looked suddenly older, as if the weariness that follows immediately on relief had put ten years on him. He was cautiously stroking his crippled hand, he must have been impatient for this to be over, to be rid of me once and for all, so that he could go to a doctor or a hospital, where they could do something to take away the pain.

'I'm not the marrying kind, I'm not like you,' he said with a tiny, barely perceptible remnant of scorn, which I nonetheless noticed. It didn't matter, it afforded him some small compensation. He didn't know that I *was* like him, even though I had got married, contrary to my father's expectations. 'Anything else?'

'Like I said, you stay here for half an hour without moving and without phoning anyone. You never lay a hand on her again. You never see her again. I'll know if you don't do as I say, and London is only two hours away. It would be easy enough for me to fly over and cut off your hand.'

I flung the poker into the fireplace, it had a little blood on it, but I'd leave him to clean it off. I removed the third unused bullet, put the pistol in my raincoat pocket and headed for the door without taking my eyes off him, until he disappeared from my field of vision. There he was sitting on his sofa, with his clothes all rumpled, his hand shattered and a mark on his face. He held my gaze, despite his sudden tiredness, his abrupt senescence. No one has ever looked at me with such hatred. Nevertheless, I wasn't afraid that he would try anything, that he would grab the poker and hit me on the back of the head. The terror and humiliation he had experienced might have made him risk doing something like that. His hatred, however, was impotent, frustrated and without consequences, it was tinged with fear and shock; or it was like the hatred of a child condemned to remain too long in the incongruous body of a boy, obliged to endure a fruitless wait that consumes him, but which he will no longer remember when he does finally grow up. He was looking at me in the knowledge that I was no longer within his grasp and would not be for a long time, possibly never: like a furious adolescent looking out at a world slipping by before his eyes and which he's not yet allowed to enter; or like a prisoner who knows that no one is waiting or refraining from doing anything just because he's not there, and that his own time is disappearing along with the world rushing by him, and that he can do nothing about it; it's a common experience among the dying too, only far more tragic.

When I left the living room, he disappeared from my view. His eyes, dark with hatred, had followed me right until then, and he may have kept his gaze fixed for a few seconds more on the door through which my gloved figure had departed. It would take him a while to get used to the idea of what he had to do. And then he would find it hard to believe that what had happened to him had really happened, but he had a useful reminder, or two; now he would feel on his hand and cheek what Luisa had felt with her black eye and its thousand colours and perhaps before that, according to her sister, the cut, also on her face. He would have many days ahead of him to observe the evolution of his scar, and to hope that the small bones in his hand were knitting together under the cast or whatever it is they use now, although an operation might also prove necessary. He would look at his good hand and think perhaps: 'I've been lucky. At least this hand is still intact.' And he would remember the metal barrel against his forehead and then he would think: 'I've been lucky. He could have shot me, I thought he was going to. But we would always prefer it to be the person beside us who dies, every man for himself. I was saved and here I am.'

I hurried down the stairs ('"Do I dare?" and, "Do I dare?" Time to turn back and descend the stair . . .'), anxious to leave the building and get away from there, to take a taxi and return Miquelín's old pistol to him as soon as possible, having first replaced the three bullets I had removed from the magazine, and to say to him: 'A thousand thanks, Maestro, I'll never forget this. Don't worry, here it is, there's not a bullet missing. It hasn't even got my fingerprints on it. It's as if you had never lent it to me, as if it had never left your apartment.'

None of the taxis passing by was free, the sky was still cloudy, full of thunderless lightning about to strike but never doing so, and so I set off, walking briskly, following the same straight route back, along Calle Mayor to my hotel, still with my gloves on, I wanted to get away from that place. I felt the lightness one feels on getting what one wants and a little of the conceit I had experienced when I discovered that Rafita was afraid of me, that, quite unwittingly, I filled him with fear. Seeing yourself as dangerous had its good side. It made you feel more confident, more optimistic, stronger. It made you feel important and – how can I put it – in charge. And, this time, that small rush of vanity did not immediately repel me. However, I also had a sudden feeling of heaviness, a feeling that can be triggered by various combinations: alarm and haste, the sense of tedium experienced at the prospect of having to carry out some cold-blooded act of reprisal, or the invincible meekness one feels in a threatening situation. I did feel something of that tedium, as well as haste, but my act of reprisal was over and done with. Only when I reached Plaza de la Villa and saw again the statue of the Marqués de Santa Cruz ('I was the scourge of the Turk at Lepanto, the Frenchman at Terceira, the Englishman o'er all the seas . . .' 'And in short, they were afraid') did I begin to think repeatedly, over and over: 'You can't go around beating people up, you can't go around killing them. Why can't you? You can't go around beating people up . . . Why can't one, according to you, go around beating people up and killing them? Why not? According to you.' And I remembered, too, what Tupra had said when we were at his house, after our session watching his store of videos: 'You've seen how much of it goes on, everywhere, and sometimes with an utter lack of concern. So explain to me why one can't.' And I gave myself the answer that I managed to give him just before we were interrupted by Beryl or whoever that woman was, the person at his side, his weak point just as Luisa was mine: 'Because then it would be impossible for anyone to live.' I had received no response to those words of mine, but by the time I reached Puerta del Sol, my thoughts had changed, and this was all they were repeating: 'What a lot of one-eyed, one-handed people there are in these old streets, but at least he's out of the picture. What a lot of cripples and what a lot of dead people there are in these old streets, but at least he's out of the picture. Yes, at least he's out of the picture and he'd better not try and climb back in.'

I didn't in fact think much about anything until I was in the plane on my way back to London, by which I mean that I postponed any form of ordered thought and, during the few days that remained of my stay in Madrid, restricted myself to feelings, sensations and intuitions. I devoted those days to the children and to taking them out and about (they were as insatiable as all children are nowadays, I suppose they've lost the habit of being at home, which feels to them like imprisonment, and require constant distractions in the exhausting outside world) and to visiting my father, who was getting very slowly, but perceptibly, worse.

The last time I went to see him, on the eve of my departure, he was, as he almost always was, sitting in his armchair, fingers interlaced, like someone who waits patiently without knowing what exactly it is he's waiting for – perhaps for night to fall and for day to come again – and now and then he would unconsciously raise his fingers to his eyebrows and smooth them, or use thumb and forefinger to rub or stroke the skin beneath his lower lip, a characteristic gesture of his, a meditative gesture. But I found it quite distressing to see him like that, in that strange waiting state, barely speaking to me, with me having to do all the talking and trying to draw from him the occasional word, racking my brain for questions and topics of conversation that might make him react and come to life – and without him putting into words or spontaneously offering me the results of his meditations, as he normally would; he had suddenly become as impenetrable as a baby, for babies must think about their surroundings, since they're equipped to do so, but it's utterly impossible to know what those thoughts are. At last, after various failed attempts to interest him in recent news and events, I asked:

'What are you thinking about?'

'About the cousins.'

'What cousins?'

'Whose do you think? Mine.'

'But you don't have any cousins, you never have,' I said, feeling slightly alarmed.

He looked somewhat taken aback, as if he were making a mental correction, then immediately adjusted his expression and did not insist, but answered again as if for the first time.

'About my Uncle Víctor,' he said. 'Ask him to please tell my father that I'm coming home.'

There had been an Uncle Víctor, but both he and my grandfather had been dead a long time, so long that I'd never even known them, either of them. This was the first time his mind had strayed like that, at least when I'd been with him. Although, perhaps that isn't the right way to put it – what had strayed was time itself, which, contrary to what we tend to believe, never entirely passes, just as we never entirely cease to be what we once were, and it's not that odd to slip back into the past so vividly that it becomes juxtaposed with the present, especially if it's the present of an old man, which offers him so little and is so unvaried, its days indistinguishable. Anyone who waits patiently or without knowing what exactly it is he's waiting for is perfectly justified in deciding to install himself in a more pleasing or more appropriate time; after all, if today chooses to ignore him, he's perfectly within his rights to ignore today – there's no room for complaint on either side.

'But your father's dead,' I said, correcting him again, 'he's been dead for years, as has your Uncle Víctor.'

Again he did not insist, but replied:

'I know they're dead. You're hardly telling me anything new, Jacobo.' And he gave an indulgent laugh as if I were the person whose mind was rambling.

Perhaps my father now came and went in time with great

facility and speed. Perhaps he was now the master of time and held in his hand the hourglass or clock, of himself or of his existence, and while he calmly watched time advance he was travelling wherever he pleased. Maybe that's the only thing left to the very old, especially if they're not astute old men, as Wheeler is, and no longer struggle to fill the vacancies, to seek out substitutes or replacements for the many people they have lost throughout their life; and are no longer part of the universal, continual, substitutional mechanism or movement – which, being everyone's lot, is also ours – and they stop accumulating and surrounding themselves with poor imitations, choosing instead to rediscover the originals in all their plenitude. They have no further need of flabby, pale, elusive life, only of thought, which becomes in them ever more potent and clear and all-embracing, since it only occasionally has to live alongside reality.

'You've got a pistol, haven't you?' it occurred to me to ask him then. It would turn up when he died, and I feared that his death would not be long in coming; and one of us, my brothers, my sister or myself, would inherit it as Miquelín had inherited from his father the Llama I had just held in my hands. Perhaps it would, in the future, be useful for me to know where to find another 'clean' pistol, without having to borrow it from someone.

A little surprised, he looked at me with those clear eyes of his that now saw only dimly.

'Yes. Why do you ask?' And this topic seemed to rouse him or return him to today.

'Where did it come from? Why have you got it?' I asked, not answering his question.

He raised one hand to his eyebrows, not this time in order to smooth them abstractedly, but in order to think or remember.

'Well, my father was very keen on guns. He wasn't just a hunter, he was a marksman. He loved that and was very good at it. He was a member of the National Shooting Club and owned a lot of weapons. A Mauser carbine; a Baker rifle; a very ornate Le Page target pistol; and even a Monkey Tail, although I can't recall now why they called it that; pistols and revolvers, some of them very old, from the Wild West era; there was an American

LeMat and an English Beaumont-Adams and a couple of Derringers, one of them with a double barrel, and pistols from the seventeenth or eighteenth century, and I can remember him having a heavily gilded blunderbuss, a Miquelet duelling pistol, and a silver-inlaid "Queen Anne", a really fine collection. And then there were knives and swords as well from exotic countries: gumias and yatagans, bolos from the Philippines, a Malay kris . . . As well as rapiers of course.' He paused and then remembered two more. 'Oh, and a Nepalese kukri and even an Indian bhuj, which was very rare, half-knife, half-axe, it was also known as an "elephant head", because it had a brass likeness of an elephant's head between blade and haft, which was long and narrow . . .' He was seeing it, I realised that he was actually seeing that bhuj from his childhood as well as all the other weapons, with that gaze so frequent in the old even when they're in company and talking animatedly, the eyes become dull, the iris dilated, staring far, far back into the past, as if their owners really could physically see with them, could see their memories I mean. It's not an absent look, but a focused one, focused on something a very long way away. And after a brief moment's absorption in thought, he went on: 'He passed on that enthusiasm to both my brother and me, but especially to me. He used to show them to us and explain all about them, and we got used to handling them with scrupulous care.'

'But what did he want with knives and swords? You can't shoot with them, can you? In the National Shooting Club, they don't let you fling a Malay kris at someone, do they?'

Now he was genuinely interested in the conversation, or at least in that remote reminiscence, and so he reacted quickly to my joke, amused but pretending not to be:

'Honestly, you are a silly lot, you never miss a chance to make some foolish remark.' He used the plural 'you' to encompass all four of his children, as he often did even when only one of us was present. 'Of course he couldn't use them to shoot with, he just liked them, I suppose. He was born in 1870, and people then had a liking for weapons in general. It was quite normal. And they were rarely put to criminal use as they are now.'

'Hm,' I said, 'although it doesn't seem very sensible to let children handle them. You and your brother could have blown each other's heads off or cut each other's throats. You say he owned rapiers as well. I know how sharp they can be. Nowadays, the authorities, no, what am I saying, the neighbours would have hit the roof over something like that. They'd have had your father banged up.'

The expression 'banged up' applied to his father must have annoyed him, even though I was the one using it and only jokingly.

'People do a lot of stupid things nowadays,' he replied reproachfully, as if I were one of those authorities or neighbours. 'Nowadays, everyone's afraid of everything, and people have very little freedom in their personal lives and less and less freedom in how they bring up their children. Before, we used to teach children all kinds of things as soon as they reached the age of reason, which is why it's called that, things that could be useful when they grew up, because in those days you never forgot that a child would one day be an adult. Not like now, it seems that adults are supposed to continue being children into old age, and idiotic cowardly children at that. That's why there's so much silliness everywhere.' He raised his fingers to his lips again and murmured: 'It's sad watching an era in decline, when one has known other far more intelligent eras. Where's it going to end? It will be one of the reasons I won't overly regret my departure, which, I believe, is quite close.'

'No, not that close, besides, who knows,' I answered, 'you'll probably outlive us all. No one knows who will die when, do they?' And when he didn't reply, I asked again: 'Do they?'

'No,' he agreed, 'but there is something called the calculation of probabilities, which works with some degree of accuracy. It would be an act of gratuitous cruelty if, at this point in my life, one of you were to die before me. It would be for all of you, but most of all for me. God forbid.' In his place, I would have touched wood. Not because I believe in wood, but simply as a gesture.

The conversation had taken a melancholy turn, which was

precisely what we tried to avoid with any topic or subject that might serve to distract him while he waited for the night and for the day, and for all the subsequent nights and days, until there were no more. This was my last visit before going back to London, and I would not be back in Madrid for a while. 'Perhaps I'll never see him again,' I thought with dismay. (And I realised as I did so, that I was *thinking* the Spanish word '*desmayo*', meaning 'fainting fit', but *meaning* the English word 'dismay'.) And so I placed one hand on his shoulder, a gesture he liked and that calmed him, but this time I did so to calm myself, to feel his bones and to accompany his breathing.

'Anyway, what were you saying?' I went back to what had roused and entertained him a little. 'That your pistol is from your father's collection?'

'No, of course not. The whole collection disappeared years ago, when the lean times came. My father would make a few big business deals and in the ensuing euphoria spend all the profits and, as you know, invest them in foolish things. Then, when common sense returned, he'd more or less recover those losses, but there came a point when recovery was impossible. The few remaining pieces were sold at the start of the Civil War, and his collection of clocks and watches suffered the same fate. Some may even have been confiscated.'

'So where does the pistol come from?'

'I've had it since the War, it's a 7.65 calibre Astra De Luxe. It's quite nice for a Spanish pistol, rather ornate, with the barrel etched in silver and a mother-of-pearl handle. Why do you ask?'

'Oh, nothing, just curious. May I see it? I've never seen you handling it. Where is it?'

'I don't know,' he said at once, and it didn't sound like an excuse not to have to show it to me. 'The last time I had it in my hands, years ago now, I decided to hide it away somewhere, so that the grandchildren wouldn't ever stumble across it when they come here and start rummaging around in everything. You had your mother to keep a check on you, but she's not here any more. And I must have hidden it so well that I now have no idea where I put it. I've forgotten. It was complete with bullets, well-preserved and well-oiled. What do you want it for?' It's odd, it was as if he knew that I wanted it for myself. This wasn't quite true, I had done what I had to do with another borrowed weapon, and so I no longer needed it, but carrying a gun in one's pocket certainly gave a sense of security.

'No, I don't want it,' I said. 'I was just curious. Why did you take the risk of keeping it after the Civil War? If they'd caught you with it during the Franco regime, if they'd searched the apartment, you'd have had it, especially with your record. Why did you keep it? Why do you still keep it, even though you can't remember where it is?'

My father remained silent for a moment, as if, perhaps, it was hard for him to give an answer or as if he needed to ponder his reply, I'm not sure. Then he said succinctly:

'You never know.'

'You never know what?'

'What you might need.'

He had always told me that, during the War, he'd been lucky – in one respect – to be able to stay in Madrid, consigned to administrative duties because of his short sight. And although he wore the uniform of the Republican Army, he had never been sent to the front and never fired a single shot. And he used to say how happy he was about that, because he could also be absolutely certain that he had never killed anyone, that he had never been in a position to kill anyone. I reminded him of this:

'You've always said how glad you were that you could be certain that, in the War, you'd never killed anyone, that you never had the chance. That doesn't quite tally with hanging on to a pistol afterwards, when things weren't so bad. I mean when life was less exposed and less chaotic, although during a dictatorship, of course, no one is safe. Why didn't you hand it in or get rid of it?'

'Because after you've lived through a war, you never know,' he said again. And then he fell silent, his hands resting on the arms of his chair, as if he were gathering the momentum to say something more, and so I waited. And he did say something more: 'Yes, I'm very glad that I never killed anyone. But that doesn't mean I wouldn't have if there'd been no other option. If any of you or your mother had been under threat of death and I could have prevented that, I'm sure I would have done so. When you were small, I mean, because now it's different, you can look after yourselves. I don't imagine I would kill for you now. Apart from the fact that I'm hardly in a position to do so – I mean, look at me – you're perfectly capable of doing whatever might be necessary. You don't need me for that any more. Besides, I wouldn't know if you deserved saving now, you lead your own lives and I don't know what you get up to. Before, it was different, I knew everything about you, when you were little and living at home. I had all the facts to hand, but not now. It's odd how your children become semi-strangers, there are lots of parents who won't accept that and stand staunchly by their children whatever the situation, even against all the evidence. I know the person you were and I think I can still recognise that person in you now. But I don't really know you as I knew that child, not at all; and it's the same with your brothers and your sister. Your mother, on the other hand, I knew until the end, and I would have killed for her until the end.' Now both mind and time were working perfectly, and after the briefest of pauses to mark the parenthesis, he returned to what we had been talking about before. 'You never know, never, and it may be that one day you might have to use a pistol. Look what happened in Europe during the Second World War. For a long time, we had no way of knowing if it would spread to Spain, despite Franco's promises, as if we could trust those, and the endless evasions and delaying tactics he used with Hitler. I don't know if you realise it, but during that War they had to use every resource they had, whatever it was, no one could keep back so much as a cartridge, whether legally or illegally acquired. It was much worse than our War in one sense. In another way, of course, it wasn't so bad. In a qualitative sense, the War here was worse.' Again he stopped and looked at me hard, although I had the feeling then that he wasn't seeing me at all, that he was looking as the blind do, without calculating distances. I noticed that he was excited by what he was about to say. 'But the thing I feel happiest about, Jacobo, is that no one ever died because of something I said or reported. Shooting someone, during a war or in self-defence, is bad, but at least you can go on living and not lose your decency or humanity, not necessarily. However, if someone dies because of something you said or, worse still, invented; if someone dies needlessly because of you; if you could have remained silent and allowed that person to go on living; if you spoke out when you should or could have said nothing and by doing so brought about a death, or several . . . I don't believe that's something you could live with, although many do, or seem to.' – 'That was perhaps how it was before,' I had time to think or thought later on when I was flying back to London and remembering our conversation, 'my father still imagines he's living in a world in which deeds left some trace and in which conscience had a voice – not always, of course, but for the majority of people. Now, on the other hand, it's the other way round: it's easy to silence or gag the majority, sometimes it's not even necessary: it's even easier to persuade them that there's no reason to speak out. The tendency nowadays is to believe that one is innocent, to find some immediate justification for everything, and not to feel one has to answer for one's actions or, as we say in Spanish, "*cargarse de razón*", I don't know how exactly one would say that in English, but it doesn't matter, I've lost the habit of speaking that other language all the time, although tomorrow I'll have to. Of course, people nowadays can live with that and with far worse things. People whose consciences torment them are the exception, as are old-fashioned people who think: "Spear, fever, my pain, words, sleep and dreams", and other similarly pointless thoughts.' – My father went on: 'And in our War there was so much of that, so much treachery and so much poison, so many slanderers, defamers and professional rabble-rousers, all tirelessly dedicated to sowing and fomenting hatred and viciousness, envy, and a desire to exterminate, on both sides, especially on the winning side, but on both sides . . . it wasn't easy to be entirely clean in that respect, perhaps in that respect least of all. And it was even more difficult for anyone who wrote for a newspaper or spoke on the radio, as I did during the War. You can't imagine the things that were read or heard, not just during those three years, but for many years afterwards. One sentence was all it took to send someone to the firing squad or the gutter. And yet I'm sure that I never said or wrote one word that could have proved seriously prejudicial to anyone. Nor later either, in the strictly personal sphere of my life after that. I never gave away a secret or a confidence, however small, I never told anyone about what I knew from having seen or heard something if that might do harm and if I didn't need to tell it in order to save or exonerate someone. And that, Jacobo, is what pleases me most.' My father was, I thought, drawing up a balance sheet of his life before he died. And for a second I wondered if it really was as he said or if he was deceiving himself like a man of my time rather than a man of his, and that he might perhaps have let something slip which, later, had terrible consequences. It was impossible to know. Even he couldn't know that, it's simply not possible to remember everything, as if you were the Judge of that old and steadfast faith. And sometimes we never find out about the consequences. I thought of those 'careless talk' cartoons that Wheeler had shown me: how could a sailor possibly imagine that something he had told his girlfriend could result in the sinking of a ship full of his compatriots? There's never any way of knowing this, that one is saying farewell with no weight on one's conscience. Then I remembered something else and it occurred to me that it was a memory that would help him to convince himself.

'You never wanted to tell me the name of that writer who took part in the baiting of your friend Marés, for example,' I said. 'And there was no reason why you shouldn't tell me or anyone.'

He looked slightly surprised, as if he had completely forgotten about that conversation we'd had a long time ago, when I was still living in Madrid. And from what he went on to say, it did seem that he'd forgotten I even knew about that episode.

'You know about that.' And this was a mixture of statement and question.

'Yes. You told me once.'

'And I didn't want to tell you, eh?' This was clearly a question. 'I didn't want to tell you the name, eh?'

'No. Because of his wife and his daughters. You said you didn't want to risk being the indirect cause of someone later dragging the whole business up and rubbing their noses in it. Even though, if I remember rightly, his wife is dead now too.'

'Yes, they're both dead. But that doesn't change anything.' And he said in a murmur intended more for him than for me: 'I didn't want to tell you, you say. Good, yes, very good . . .'

He sat there thinking, and his blue eyes took on the fixed intense gaze that did not, in a way, see me. And a few seconds later, I had the impression that the act of recalling those people had again transported him back to a distant time when my mother was alive, and the kindly cheerful wife of that infamous man was being so very very good to us and, in particular, to her. I let two or three minutes pass in silence. He was not speaking now and he looked tired. Perhaps I should leave, even if that might be the last time we would see each other.

'I'm going, Papa,' I said, and I got up and kissed him on the forehead.

'Where?' he asked in astonishment, as if he thought it utterly absurd that I or any of his children should go anywhere.

'To my hotel and then tomorrow I'll catch the plane back to London.'

'Oh, you're off on a trip. Well, have a good journey, son.'

'I live in London now, Papa. Have you forgotten?'

'Ah, so you live in exile,' he said, without giving that last word any solemnity at all. 'Like the Greek gods.'

'The Greek gods?' I didn't know what he was referring to or what that remark had to do with anything. But he never lost the thread, at least I never saw him do so. He might abstract himself from time and people and circumstances, but his mind and his memory were always working, albeit, at the end, very much after their own fashion. Then again, all minds and memories do that.

'Don't you remember that Heine poem?' he said, and immediately began to recite the lines in German, from memory. He had learned the language as a boy, at school, which was possible in the 1920s, but unimaginable now, and he had always prided himself on being able to recite whole poems, by Goethe, Novalis, Hölderlin, the giants of German literature.

'No, Papa,' I said, interrupting him, 'I can't possibly remember something I've never known, and, besides, I don't understand what you're saying. I never learned German, remember?'

'Honestly. You never learned German,' he replied with slight paternal scorn, as if not knowing German were an oddity, almost a defect. 'What kind of education did you have?' And he went on to explain, out of sympathy for my ignorance and out of enthusiasm for this poem from his youth: 'The poet sees a bank of white clouds in the middle of the night and these seem to him, as he puts it, like "colossal statues of the gods made out of luminous marble". Then he realises that they *are* the gods, Chronos, Zeus, Hera, Pallas Athene, Aphrodite, Ares, Hermes, Phoebus Apollo, Hephaestus and Hebe, grown old and at the mercy of the elements, cast down and numb with cold in their exile. "No," exclaims the poet, "these are no clouds!"' And my father began translating the poem for me, drawing it slowly out of his memory. 'They are the gods of Hellas, the very gods who once so blithely ruled the world, but who now, supplanted and deceased, ride like giant spectres the clouds of midnight . . .' But the words insisted on coming to him in the German of his childhood, or perhaps he found it wearisome having to translate, and so he lapsed back into German, and, at the time, I understood nothing more.

Later on, after his death, I tried to identify the words I had listened to without understanding them. I searched out a bilingual edition of 'The Greek Gods', in German and English (I couldn't find one in Spanish), and it was doubtless this verse that he had translated into my language in tentative extempore fashion: '*Nein, nimmermehr, das sind keine Wolken! Das sind sie selber, die Götter von Hellas, die einst so freudig die Welt beherrschten, doch jetzt, verdrängt und verstorben, als ungeheure Gespenster dahinziehn am mitternächtlichen Himmel . . .*' I assume he had a good accent. And I also noticed two other brief passages that he must have recited in German that day. In one, the poet addressed Zeus and said to him, more or less: 'Not even the gods rule eternally, the old gods are driven out and supplanted by the young, just as you yourself once deposed your grey-haired father . . .' The other was an image applied to that troop of disoriented deities adrift in the dark, whom he describes as: 'Dead shadows who wander the night, fragile as the mist that the wind drives away'. Those words must have come from his lips when I was there with him, even though, at the time, I couldn't understand them. And I wondered what he would have thought then, as he spoke them.

While he sat, absorbed in his own recitation, I bent down and kissed him again before leaving, this time on the cheek, as if we were bullfighters, and I placed my hand once more on his shoulder for a moment, like a silent farewell, while he was walking into the mist that the wind drives away, or into that exile in which one has to leave even one's own first name behind.

I had also managed not to think too much about Luisa until I was on the plane, in business class, an Iberia flight, which was, characteristically and infuriatingly, an hour late in leaving. My not thinking about Luisa had been helped by the fact that she didn't once suggest we have lunch or supper together, and I didn't insist or protest or express regret; after what I had done, I preferred to avoid such a meeting – I didn't feel I deserved it, and although I very much wanted to see her, I found it easy enough to resist and to pretend. And so we only met briefly and occasionally at the apartment when I went to pick up or return the children or stayed with them for a while until they went to bed. And once they were in bed, she never offered me a drink or invited me to sit down for a moment to chat. She didn't eject me with excuses or with words, but by her attitude: she was constantly doing things, going back and forth, cleaning, washing dishes and glasses, answering the phone, tidying, pick-ing up toys and clothes and notebooks and pencils – children always leave everything in a mess and never cease creating chaos – and it wasn't as it used to be when we lived together, when I would follow her from room to room, talking about something or other or telling or asking her something, as husbands often do trail through the house or apartment after their wives, who are more active physically and tend not to sit still in one place for very long, especially if they are mothers. I no longer felt I had that right, I mean, to go into just any room, not even into the kitchen, even accompanied by her or, rather, following in her footsteps. And so we would simply exchange a few words about the children or about my father's health, for she always asked after him, adding with feeling, 'I really must go and see him, I'll go this week without fail, be sure to give him my love,' and I would leave, having given her a discreetly affectionate, that is, almost friendly, kiss on each cheek, to which she responded passively and rather mechanically, hardly noticing.

Her mind was elsewhere and I knew where. She seemed rather subdued on the last few occasions I saw her. I thought: 'She's heard that she won't be seeing Custardoy for a while, a great disappointment that's caught her unawares and which she's still trying to absorb, so there's one less incentive now, probably the biggest incentive, the one that helped her to get through the day, to wake up filled with hope and go to bed contented, but that incentive will be missing from her life for good – that's something she doesn't yet know, nor that she will never see the man again or only if they happen to meet by chance; that knowledge will come later, gradually, whole weeks will pass, or possibly even more, before she fully understands that it's all over, that this isn't just an extended absence, but a final separation, like the one she has been inflicting on me for a long time now. And then she will look out of the window as I sometimes look out of mine at the lazy London night and across the square, its pale darkness barely lit by those white streetlamps that imitate the always thrifty light of the moon, and a little further off, at the lights of the elegant hotel and of the houses that shelter families or men and women on their own, each of them enclosed behind a protective yellow rectangle, as Luisa and I would seem to be to anyone watching us; and beyond the trees and the statue at my carefree, dancing neighbour, who, from now on, will always remind me of Custardoy, because these resemblances and affinities work reciprocally, and no one is immune to them: I will no longer like that happy dancing individual quite so much: he may unwittingly have saved a life, but, in doing so, has become contaminated by that same life. And neither Luisa nor I will dare to think, when alone: "I'll be more myself," not now that we've seen each other again and brought each other a new sadness, although she doesn't know that her current sadness comes from me.'

Strangely, given that I was the cause of the newly begun solitude that would gradually grow, I allowed myself to feel slightly sorry, seeing her like that, in such low spirits, lethargic, apathetic, possibly in the early stages of a lasting period of languor and decline, the loss of someone we love marks us very deeply, much more than that of someone who loved us, and I was sure now that for Luisa, Custardoy belonged in the first category. At least I was not so cynical as to tell myself it was for her own good, although it certainly would be in the long term: I knew now that it was, above all, for my good, for my relative tranquillity, my peace of mind while I was far away, so that I wouldn't have to worry too much about her or about my children, and so that I need not give up the fanciful hopes I still clung on to, despite all the time that had elapsed. And that was something I did think about in the plane with a clarity I had so far avoided: that I had been selfish and abusive and inconsiderate, that I had meddled in her life in the worst possible way, behind her back, without her knowledge, not just without consulting her on what could or should be done, but without her even having spoken to me about a problem that she didn't see as a problem, but possibly as a solution. I had acted like some nineteenth-century father with regard to his daughter, I had gone over her head as if she were a minor, not by approaching the lowlife in question and paying him to disappear, as had perhaps been the tradition of wealthy authoritarian fathers in that century, but by threatening him with death and by injuring him. I began to find the whole thing unbelievable, that I should have behaved like that, without a flicker of conscience, like a savage or as if I were a believer in the pragmatic idea that if something needs to be done then it's best just to do it, so that regardless of what happens next, the deed is done and there's no going back ('I have done the deed'). Officially, I knew nothing about Custardoy, at least not as far as Luisa knew, or indeed anyone else, apart from her sister Cristina, whom I would have to warn, by phone from London, as soon as she was back from her few days away – I couldn't remember if she'd said it would be a week or longer, I had already tried phoning each day during what remained of my stay in Madrid, just in case, but without success – I hadn't even been able to speak to her husband; and I kept calling during the first few days after my return, trying different times until I finally found her in.

'Cristina, it's Jacques, your brother-in-law, Jaime,' I said when she answered the phone, on my twentieth attempt. 'I'm back in London, but I wanted to bring you up to date on an important matter. Have you spoken to Luisa?'

'No, not yet, I've only just got home, my trip lasted longer than expected. Why? Has something happened?'

'Nothing bad, no. During my stay in Madrid I sorted out that business between Custardoy and her, at least I think I did, we'll probably have to wait a bit to be sure.'

'Really?' she replied, and there was curiosity and undoubted approval in her voice. 'How? What did you do? Did you speak to him? Or to her? Tell me.'

'That's what I wanted to say, that it's best if you don't know and absolutely essential that Luisa doesn't. I mean she must never even find out that I knew anything, or that you told me anything. That story's over now, or very nearly. What I absolutely don't want is for her ever to suspect that I had anything to do with it. As far as she's concerned I don't even know of Custardoy's existence, she never once mentioned him to me, and I want her to continue believing that. Now and always. If, one day, you were to mention our conversation, even if it's in ten years' time, she might still put two and two together and never speak to me again, despite the kids. She might never speak to you again either. I may have been the one who did the deed, but she would probably think that you were part of it too, that you had provoked or prompted me to act. You understand, don't you? If you betray me, I'd have no qualms about betraying you too.'

Cristina clearly did understand, but she was still curious.

'You *are* keeping your cards close to your chest. Whatever did you do to him? You needn't worry, if you've managed to get rid of him, I'll be the first to celebrate and safeguard your achievement. But surely if we're both going to keep quiet about it, it hardly matters if I know everything. What did you say to the guy? What did you do to him? Come on, tell me, given that it was all done at my instigation.'

'As I said, it's best not to talk about it. I prefer him to be the only one who knows, so that if by some stroke of bad luck they should meet later on and she should corner him, he'd be the only one who could tell Luisa what happened, not that I think he would, it wouldn't be worth his while and it would merely be his word against mine, with no way of corroborating the facts. It's not that I don't trust you, now, I mean. But you never know. One day, you might be angry with me for some reason and want to harm me. If something is best not known, then it's best that no one knows about it, not even your accomplice. Why else do you think criminals are always bumping people off?'

Cristina took this well, she laughed and didn't press me further. She said only:

'Don't worry, I won't say anything to Luisa. I hope you're right and that this story *is* over. I'll act surprised if she mentions it, the break-up I mean. She might be having a rough time and want to get it off her chest or just talk to someone. And if something has happened to Custardoy, I'll be bound to find out somehow, you know how people gossip.'

'No, I don't think you will find out. He's not in Madrid at the moment and he won't be around for several weeks at least. And when he does come back, he'll invent some tale, if, that is, he still bears the marks of our encounter. A garage door perhaps, or a bollard.' I realised that I had already said too much, it's so easy to let your tongue run away with you, especially when you're boasting, and I *was* boasting a little, even though several days had passed: I did feel slightly proud of my exploit, pistol in hand, and had no problem forgetting that the word 'exploit' is entirely misplaced when the other party was unarmed. I knew perfectly well that such private bragging was unforgivable, especially after what I discovered on my arrival in London, or just before. And yet that's how it was, and I couldn't help myself; I imagine it must happen to any otherwise non-violent person who, when forced to use violence, meets with success. And so I added: 'Not that I'm saying I did anything to him, or that anything happened

411

to him. Anything bad, I mean.' (In that brief conversation I had trotted out some of the classic lines recommending denial, ignorance and silence, appropriate to espionage and conspiracies and criminality, to the clandestine and the underhand: 'It's best if you know nothing; then, if they interrogate you, you'll be telling the truth when you say you know nothing, the truth is easy, it has more force, it's more believable, the truth persuades.' And: 'If you know only about your part of the job, even if they catch you or you fail, the plan can still go ahead.' Not to mention: 'Your ignorance will be your protection, so don't ask any more questions, don't ask, it will be your salvation and your guarantee of safety.' And even: 'You know the score, I've never spoken to you or said anything. This conversation and this phone call never took place, you haven't even heard these words because I didn't say them. And even though you can hear the words now, I'm not saying them.')

Cristina laughed again, perhaps because she was glad to think that her sister was now out of danger.

'You sound very mysterious and a touch threatening,' she said, half-serious and half-joking. 'This isn't the Jaime I know. It would seem that London and being alone there suits you. Just one thing, whatever you've done, I'm not your accomplice. So there's no need to bump me off.'

All this happened days later, when I was back in London again, and feeling more anxious and that the situation had changed for the worse. What I *was* thinking about on that return flight was that Luisa had still said nothing about herself right up until the last moment. On the final day, on the eve of my departure, I had gone to the hotel to change after visiting my father and then to Luisa's apartment to say goodbye to the children and, in passing, to her.

'So, when will you be back again?' Guillermo had demanded in accusing tones, even as Marina was insisting that I take her with me, up in the air.

'This time,' I had lied, unaware then that I wasn't lying, 'I'll be back soon, I promise.' And I had likewise promised Marina that, on my next trip, I would take her with me to that large island, knowing full well that small children barely remember what's said to them from one day to the next, one of their many privileges.

That was the sole occasion when Luisa seemed about to invite me to sit down in the living room for a while, as if she had suddenly realised that we wouldn't see each other again for some time and that we hadn't had a single proper conversation; that she hadn't asked me about my life in London or about my work, my habits, my prospects or my general state of mind or about my friendships or possible lovers (on that last point I could have declined to answer, just as she had done), not even about the slovenly, dirty, drunken or crazy – and definitely pantyless – women who had possibly dripped blood in my house or in Wheeler's house and who had caused her such amusement. Her lack of curiosity, her lack of interest in me, had been very marked during my brief stay, and were it not for what I had done behind her back, for my brutal interference in her life – in a way I had ruined or torn down the life she was trying to rebuild – and for my consequent feeling that I was in her debt, such indifference would have been more than enough reason for me to feel offended and to mutter darkly to myself about it. She, however, was so distracted and doubtless so immersed in her own story that she didn't even find it odd, my apparent resignation to the situation or my excessively discreet behaviour. She knew me well, probably better than anyone. She knew I was respectful and certainly not inclined to make a nuisance of myself, that I accepted what was given willingly and did not fight for what was denied to me, that my pride kept me from pestering anyone and that I acted in a roundabout way to achieve my ends, lingering and delaying for however long it took. Whichever way you looked at it, though, it was very strange that with time to spare I hadn't made more of an effort to see her alone, that I'd left all the initiative to her and taken a back seat, that I'd let the days pass without making myself a more obvious or visible presence and without demanding that we meet alone. All of these things should have made her suspicious, and yet they didn't. Her mind was otherwise occupied, doubtless with Custardoy, first with the incomprehensible excitement he aroused in her, and perhaps, too, with the tension she felt between desire and distrust – she must have seen that choosing a man like him would always, at least in part, be inadvisable – then with her disquiet at his abrupt and unexpected departure with barely a word of explanation, with her growing unease over his delay in phoning her, for he had perhaps not yet, as I had ordered, given any sign of life since his disappearance ('While you're away, only phone her now and then, and make those calls less and less frequent'), and when you wait in vain for something it does take on a degree of urgency and occupies all your time and fills up every space: you expect the doorbell to ring at any moment and each moment becomes intensely long and oppressive, like a knee digging into your chest, like lead upon the soul, until exhaustion overwhelms you and gives you a slight respite.

Perhaps it was precisely that kind of truce brought on by weariness that allowed her to look around for an instant and to see me, to remember who I was and to realise that I'd be gone the next day, and that she would have allowed me to pass through without – so to speak – making the most of me; that I was still there that night and could serve as a way of killing time and diverting her for a few minutes – with my stories about London, with comments or anecdotes about a world of which she knew nothing – from her obsessive thoughts that continued unabated. She would probably only have listened to me with half an ear, not even a whole one, like someone vaguely aware of the murmur of a steady comfortable rain, so strong and sustained that, when he does finally look up, it alone seems to light up the night with its continuous threads like flexible metal bars or endless spears; or like someone sleeping with one eye open who thinks he can hear and connect with the languid murmur of the river that speaks calmly or indifferently, or perhaps the indifference comes from his own weariness and his own sleeplessness and his dreams that are just beginning, even if he believes himself to be wide awake; or like someone who allows himself to be infected and drawn in by an insignificant humming that reaches him from afar, across a courtyard or a square, or when he happens to go into a public toilet and hears a happy man humming as he carefully parts his hair with a wet comb ('Nanna naranniaro nannara nanniaro', and then he can't help but add meaning and words to that catchy tune, if he knows it: 'For I'm a poor cowboy and I know I've done wrong').

That is how Luisa would have listened to me, inattentively, if we had ever had the brief conversation she was on the point of proposing. I had already said goodbye to the kids in their respective beds, and left them, not sleeping, but about to fall asleep. I had closed their bedroom doors and said to Luisa, who was waiting in the corridor:

'Right, I'm off. I'm leaving tomorrow.' Then I had gently touched her chin so as to study her profile and added: 'Your black eye's nearly gone. Be a bit more careful in future.' The bruise was barely visible now, apart from one small area that was still slightly yellow, but only someone who had seen how it looked before would have noticed it.

'Oh, of course, you're leaving.' And judging from the slightly wistful tone in which she said this, it seemed to me that she would probably miss me in a vague kind of way, now that she would be spending more time with the children and have fewer distractions. 'We haven't really seen much of each other, you've hardly told me anything about yourself – you caught me at a bad time, with a lot of previous commitments and a lot of work, things I couldn't cancel or change, if you'd given me a bit of advance warning that you were coming . . .'

It was an apology of sorts, she was the one feeling slightly in my debt, but only slightly, because one does usually try to accommodate someone who's only going to be around for a few days, and she hadn't. She seemed sad and distracted, as if filled with bad presentiments or, worse, a prescience of bad things to come. She was quite serene in her despondency, like someone who has thrown in the towel before receiving a single punch, like someone who knows what's about to happen. She must have been convinced that something strange was going on with Custardoy, whom she would probably call Esteban; true, he did occasionally travel and spend days or weeks observing and studying

415

paintings in various places, but such a sudden departure wasn't normal – without saying goodbye or seeing each other – nor was the ensuing long silence. I imagined with satisfaction that he must be following my instructions to the letter, or had perhaps gone even further: yes, it was quite possible that he hadn't phoned her again since that first time, after his supposed arrival in wherever it was he had told her he had gone. He might even have told her he was in Baltimore, when he hadn't, in fact, stirred from Madrid. I really didn't care, just as long as he did as he was told and disappeared for good.

'How are you?' I asked. 'You seem a bit down. Has something happened in the last few days?'

'No, nothing,' she replied, shaking her head slightly. 'A minor disappointment, nothing important. I'll get over it soon enough.'

'Can I do anything about it? Is it about anyone I know?'

'No, not at all. It's someone you don't know, someone new. And anyway, it's not his fault either, it was unavoidable.' She paused for a second, then added: 'It's odd; now there'll be more and more of my people whom you don't know, not even by name, and so there'll be no point in my telling you about them or mentioning them. The same thing will happen with your people. And that hasn't happened for years, or only rarely. It's strange, when you live with someone, you keep up to date without any difficulty at all, without making any special effort, and then suddenly, or, rather, gradually, you know nothing about the people who come after. I know nothing about your friends in London, for example, or about the colleagues you work with every day. You said it was quite a small group, didn't you? And that one of them was a young woman, half-Spanish, is that right? How do you get along with them? I'm not even entirely sure what it is you do.' And as she said this, she waved her arm in the direction of the living room, not in order to show me the door so that I could leave, but as if she were suggesting we go in there for a moment before I left so that I could tell her about my work, or maybe simply so that she could listen to me talking. Perhaps she had realised that I could help her get through a few minutes of her waiting or lift the lead that weighed cease-lessly upon her soul. I thought of asking about the young Gypsy mother and her children, who were, in a sense, her people and whom I knew about from when she and I were still living to-gether and sharing a daily life, and whom I'd thought about while in that other country.

We started walking in that direction, with her leading. We were about to sit down at home and talk, and, while it lasted, this would seem the most natural thing in the world, with none of the artificiality that would have surrounded an arrangement to meet at a restaurant or anywhere else. Then her mobile phone rang, the phone whose number other people knew and I did not, and she hurried on into the living room, almost ran, she had left it there, in her handbag, and I had left my raincoat and gloves in the room too, draped on the back of an armchair. I let her go ahead, of course, I didn't hurry, but since we had been walking along together, I didn't stop or hold back either, my discretion being limited to not actually going into the room, to lingering on the threshold, looking at the books on a shelf, my books, which I might, on one not too distant day, have to take away with me, although where I didn't yet know.

'Hello?' I heard her say, her spirits suddenly buoyant, as if the voice at the other end had managed to drive away her melan-choly (or was it sorrow?) with just a word or two. I was sure it was Custardoy, calling for the penultimate or antepenultimate time. 'Yes. Are you OK?' A pause. 'Yes, I understand. Although, to be honest, your leaving like that, so suddenly, did throw me a bit . . . And you've no idea how long you're going to be away? That's a bit odd, isn't it? Them not giving you a fixed deadline, I mean.' She instinctively moved away from me and lowered her voice, so that I would hear as little as possible. However, since she didn't want to be rude and close the door on me or go into another room, her murmured comments were still audible. I missed a few words, but not her tone of voice. She wasn't saying much, Custardoy was the one doing most of the talking, and the conversation was rather brief, as if he were in a hurry (he was obeying my instructions to be distant and

417

abrupt and concise). 'But that just leaves me completely in the dark. And what am I supposed to do if I can't even call you?' said Luisa almost pleadingly and raising her voice, only to lower it at once and add by way of explanation: 'Look, Jaime's here at the moment, he came to say goodbye, he's flying out tomorrow, he was just about to leave, why don't you call me back in five minutes?' Another longer pause. 'No, I don't understand. You mean you've got to go out right now, this very minute?' For a few moments I couldn't hear what she was saying, only intermittent words and odd phrases. 'No, I don't understand the situation; first of all, that rushed departure and now all these difficulties. I'm perfectly aware that we haven't known each other very long, and I don't presume to think that I know you inside out or anything, but I'm not used to this kind of behaviour from you, it's never happened before. And you sound strange, different.' She fell silent again, then spoke almost in a whisper, before raising her voice to say: 'Look, I don't know what's going on with you, it's as if I were talking to someone else entirely. It's as if you were suddenly afraid of me, and I'd hate to be any kind of burden to you.' – 'It isn't you he's afraid of, my love,' I thought. 'It's me.' – 'Fine. If that's how you feel. It's up to you. You're the only one who can know how you feel. I'm not a mind-reader.' And her last words, which followed immediately after, were spoken coldly. 'Fine. If that's what you want. Goodbye.'

In other circumstances I wouldn't have enjoyed hearing that conversation at all, hearing Luisa pleading with that other man, very nearly begging him, before reacting with wounded dignity to his evasiveness or indifference. But I had prepared that scene, almost set it up and dictated it, as if I were Wheeler, who doubtless devoted no small part of his time to the preparation or composition of prized moments, or, so to speak, to guiding his numerous empty or dead moments towards a few pre-planned and carefully considered dialogues in which he had, of course, memorised his own part. Except that I hadn't intervened in that conversation, or, rather, Custardoy had spoken for me, for he was, after all, not using his own words, but those which I, like an

Iago, had led him to say or obliged him to pronounce. Knowing that I was there, close by, must have increased his fear as well as his hatred of me. My presence had been a complete coincidence, but he would not have experienced it like that, he would have thought I was watching over the whole process, keeping an eye on things. So much the better for me.

Luisa came over to where I was standing, the mobile phone still in her hand, and the look on her face was a mixture of puzzlement, resignation and annoyance. 'You've still got a long way to go,' I thought, 'you'll know worse despair yet. And then you'll seek me out, because I'm the person you know best and the one who will always be here.'

'Right, I'd better be going,' I said, picking up my raincoat and gloves. She had initially asked the caller to phone back in five minutes, ready, at a moment's notice, to sacrifice our conversation, the one we had unexpectedly been about to have. Missing that conversation, having it or not, was only of secondary importance to her. And at that point, it was to me as well. My chance would not come on that trip, I would have to wait quite a while longer.

'I'm sorry,' she murmured. 'Problems at work. People behave in the strangest way. They say they'll do one thing, then forget all about it and disappear.' She didn't need to give me any false explanations. The conversation had clearly been of a personal nature, and nothing to do with work. I knew what was going on, and she as yet did not. I didn't mind being so far ahead of her, I didn't mind deceiving her. 'This isn't the Jaime I know,' Cristina would say to me later on, and I had already thought the same thing: 'No, I'm not. I am more myself.'

Luisa accompanied me to the door. We kissed each other on the cheek, but this time she embraced me too. I sensed that she did so more out of a feeling of vulnerability, or a sudden sense of abandonment and loss, than out of genuine affection. Nevertheless, I returned her embrace warmly and enthusiastically. I certainly didn't mind embracing her, I never had.

'Come, come back to me, I'll be patient, I'll wait; but don't delay very much longer,' I thought when I was on the plane, remembering that farewell. And then I quoted to myself a line from a recent poem in English that I'd read during one of my trips with Tupra, on a train: 'Why do I tell you these things? You are not even here.'

That was the last thing that happened before everything changed. I asked the stewardess for an English newspaper; I needed to get used to that other country again. I hadn't even looked at a Spanish newspaper that morning, I was still too involved in my own thoughts to bother with the outside world, although a copy of *El País* lay unopened on my lap. The stewardess offered me the *Guardian*, *The Independent* and *The Times*, and I chose the first two because I can't stand the dreadful decadence into which the third one has fallen under its present Antipodean regime. I glanced at the front page of the *Guardian*, and my gaze fixed instantly – familiar names always call to us, immediately attract our attention – on a report that must have made my eyes start from their sockets and which sent me straight to the front page of *The Independent* for reassurance and confirmation that this wasn't some absurd sick joke or a figment of someone's imagination. Both papers carried the story, so it must be true, and although it wasn't a headline or a long item, the report was given due prominence in both: 'Dick Dearlove Arrested Following Boy's Violent Death'. Obviously neither headline said 'Dick Dearlove'; Dearlove is just the name I have taken to calling him by.

I turned immediately to the relevant pages and read them fearfully, eagerly, then with a sense of horror and growing repugnance towards Tupra and myself – in fact, a feeling of self-disgust swept over me at once. The information was incomplete and the facts confused and did little to clarify the succinct, not to say hermetic, statements made by Dearlove's spokesman and his lawyers, who were the people who had reported the incident to

New Scotland Yard on the morning after the night of the murder, which made one think that they must have had a few hours to weigh up the situation and prepare and agree the best line of defence, about which, on the other hand, they gave little or no detail. In England, as I understand it, unlike in Spain, where there's an irresponsible clamour of voices right from the start, or even a verbal lynching, they take the confidentiality of legal proceedings very seriously indeed and never release any evidence or testimony that will form part of a trial, and no one who might be called on to testify is allowed to give his or her version of events to the press prior to that trial. Lawyers and journalists were thus limited to making veiled hints and prudent, rather discreet speculations as to what actually happened. They suggested a possible kidnapping attempt, a possible burglary, or even a settling of accounts between lovers. The victim was seventeen and apparently either Bulgarian or Russian (no one knew for sure, nor if he had a British passport, although this seemed unlikely) and he was referred to only by his initials, which, curiously enough, were the same as those of his killer, let's say R.D. Whatever the truth of the matter – and I saw at once what must have happened – one thing was sure: two nights ago the singer had stuck a spear, one of several he had hanging in a room next to the dining room, into the chest and throat of that very young young man. This doubtless meant that televisions around the world, especially those in Britain, but in my own country too, not to mention the millions of anonymous or pseudonymous voices on the Internet, would already have had a whole day to dissect the affair. But I had seen neither television nor Internet.

I briefly regretted that the plane had no low, sensationalist rag like *The Sun* on board, *The Sun* belonging, of course, to the same Antipodean empire as *The Times* and being therefore more given to scandal, moralising and rumour: such newspapers would be rubbing their hands with glee and prepared to risk breaking any law if it meant selling more copies. I had a glance at *El País*, just in case, but its treatment of the matter was sober and concise and revealed nothing more than its London colleagues claimed to know. My regret was short-lived or was, I should say, merely a moment of naïveté, because I didn't need to know the details or the circumstances or the background or the motives, or even the psychological explanations being pondered by journalists or whoever. It was clear to me that Tupra had projected onto that idol the maximum biographical horror, had plunged him into narrative disgust as if into a butt of disgusting wine, had lit a torch for him and inscribed him in letters of fire on the list of those afflicted by the K–M or Killing–Murdering or Kennedy–Mansfield curse, as it was known in our little group with no name and who knows, by a process of mimesis, in some other loftier place; that Reresby or Ure or Dundas had condemned Dearlove not just to a few years in prison, which, for someone as famous as Dearlove, with such a sordid crime behind him, would be a slow incessant hell – I mean slower and more incessant than for other people – unless, and this was the best-case scenario, those years were interrupted by a swift death at the hands of other prisoners; he had condemned him also to seeing his entire life story and achievements lost beneath a quick lick of grey or off-white or off-colour paint, its whole trajectory and construction plunged into immediate oblivion, condemned him to knowing that whenever anyone mentioned or read or heard his name, he or she would always instantly associate it with that final crime. Mothers would even use his name to warn their unwary offspring and, even worse, the message they gave would become distorted and exaggerated over time: 'Be careful who you mix with and who you go around with, you can't trust anyone. Remember what Dickie Dearlove did to that young Russian lad – he took him to his house and slit him open.' And I was as sure of this as I was that Tupra would already have in his possession a recording, a film of these events about which the press were now hypothesising and which were known to almost no one else; it would doubtless show the whole sequence, from the point where the young Bulgarian, R.D., arrived at Dearlove's house up to the furious, fearsome moment when the latter stuck a spear in him, causing his instant death, although it must have taken two blows – one in the throat and the other in the chest, or possibly the other way round – to silence him completely and put an end to him; and then, perhaps, still blinded by rage and gripped by a childish sense of triumph (a very short-lived emotion and one that he would deplore for the rest of his days), searching the young man's body for the mobile phone or tiny camera with which he would have taken his compromising photos and which Dearlove had failed to find when he playfully frisked him on arrival, perhaps because Tupra had told the boy he wouldn't need to carry a phone or camera because a camera would have been hidden somewhere in the house prior to that amorous or commercial assignation, like the gun that was famously waiting for Al Pacino in a restaurant restroom in the first episode of that great masterpiece in three parts, each part better than the last.

Tupra wouldn't need to make use of that tape or DVD (he hadn't, on that occasion, recorded and kept it for future use) in order to persuade Dearlove later on to do or not do something; the important thing had been to make Dearlove aware of just one of the deceptions of which he was the victim and of the irreparable act he had committed in response, so irreparable and unconcealable that his punishment would not be long in coming. Tupra would keep that video simply in order to have it and to watch it when he was alone or to revel in the perfect execution of his plan, the prize item in his collection. It wouldn't be of any further use to him, given that the main deed had been revealed as soon as it was done: Dearlove had done the deed, and the whole world knew about it. He had killed a young man with a spear.

In the final analysis, though, the person who had instigated that killing was me. Or perhaps not exactly: I had invented, conceived, described or dictated it, imagined the *mise-en-scène*. I had given Tupra the idea – no one is ever fully aware of how dangerous it is to give other people ideas, and it happens all the time, at all hours and in all places – and I couldn't help wondering how many more of my interpretations or translations might have had consequences of which I knew nothing, how many and which ones. I had spent a long time passing judgement on a daily basis and with ever greater ease and unconcern, listening to voices and looking at faces, in the flesh or hidden in the station-studio or on video, saying who could be trusted and who could not, who would kill and who would allow himself to be killed and why, who would betray and who would remain loyal, who would lie and who would meet with failure or with only average success in life, who irritated me and who aroused my pity, who was a poseur and whom I warmed to, and what probabilities each individual carried in his veins, just like a novelist who knows that whatever his characters say or tell, whatever is attributed to them or whatever they are made to do, will go no further than his novel and will harm no one, because, however real they may seem, they will continue to be a fiction and will never interfere with anyone real (with anyone in his right mind, that is). But that was not my case: I wasn't using pen and paper to write about those who have never existed or trod the earth or traversed the world, I was describing and deciphering flesh-and-blood people and pontificating and making predictions about them, and I saw now that regardless of whether I was right or wrong, what I said could have disastrous consequences and determine their fate if placed in the hands of someone like Tupra, who, on this occasion, had not restricted himself to being only Sir Punishment or Sir Thrashing, but Sir Death and Sir Cruelty and, possibly, Sir Vengeance. And I had not been his instrument, but something less common and perhaps worse, his inspiration, an innocent whisper in his ear, an imprudent and unwitting Iago. I didn't care nor was I particularly interested in what grudge he bore Dearlove or if he had laid that trap for him – my trap – on his own initiative or as part of some outlandish state mission or on the well-paid orders of some private private individual. That was the least of it. What troubled me most was the thought that he had put into practice my plan, which wasn't a plan at all, and that in order to ensure its success, he had shown no qualms about sacrificing the life of a young man: 'Strange to leave even one's own first name behind', indeed, and the victim didn't even have a name, only the initials R.D. Worryingly or improbably, I hadn't until then noticed the most serious implication of all and – as I realised at once, with the three newspapers unfolded on my lap in that plane – the one that would torment me for the rest of my life. And however tenuous I tried to make and succeeded in making that link later on, and however tenuous it did in fact become – for that is what would happen, it would seem to me remote and accidental, on my part at least, and my feelings of responsibility would diminish, and it would all seem like a dream, and with luck I would deceive myself entirely and make it disappear, especially when the last stubborn rim was finally erased and I was able to say to myself one day: 'But that was in another country' – that young Russian man who did not even know of my existence, just as I had known nothing of his while it lasted, had died because of my prediction or hypothesis or fantasy, because of what I had said and reported, and now, in my head, I would always have the words: 'For I am myself my own fever and pain.'

The first thing I did when I walked through the front door of the apartment, which, for a while, came to be my home, ingenuously furnished by an Englishwoman I never met, was to dial Tupra's home number. It was the weekend and no one would be at the building with no name, at least in theory, for I knew I wasn't the only one who went there out of office hours, to finish off some task or report or to rummage around or investigate. As had happened when I phoned him from Madrid, a woman's voice answered. I uttered the name I found repellent to use, Bertie, in order to show my familiarity with him – not that I needed to; my knowing his home number was indication enough.

'He's out of London at the moment,' the voice said. 'May I ask who's calling?' I didn't have his mobile phone number, which Tupra guarded jealously, and, besides, he was of the opinion that everything could wait 'as used to happen in the old days'.

'Jack Deza,' I said, and I unintentionally pronounced the 'z' as a Spaniard would, having got used to doing so again while in Spain, it would have sounded like 'Daetha' or 'Deatha' to an English ear. 'I work with him, and it's very important. Would you mind giving me his mobile phone number? I've just got back from Madrid and I have something urgent and of great interest to tell him.'

'No, I'm sorry, I don't think I can. He's the only one who

can do that,' replied the woman. And she added slightly imper-
tinently, which made me suspect that she was Beryl, although
I hadn't spoken to her for long enough at Wheeler's supper to
be able to recognise her voice, which wasn't particularly young,
although not old either: 'If you don't have it, it must be because
he didn't consider it necessary.'

'Are you Beryl?' I asked, at the risk of causing my boss some
domestic or conjugal upset if she wasn't. Not that I cared any
more; he would soon cease to be my boss – I had made my decision. Or almost, nothing is sure until it's over and done with.

'Why do you ask?' was her reply. And in a tone of voice that
seemed half-stern and half-mocking, she said: 'You don't need
to know who I am.'

'Perhaps Tupra has forbidden Beryl, if she is Beryl and she
must be,' I thought, 'from telling anyone that they're an item
again, still less that they're living together, or perhaps they prefer
to think of themselves like that, rather than as married, enjoying
the clandestine nature of their situation.' I remembered her long
legs and her unusual smell, pleasant and very sexual, which were
perhaps the things that drew Tupra back to her again and again;
sometimes our weaknesses are for the simplest of things, the
things we cannot give up. I was about to say: 'If you are Beryl,
we've met before. I'm a friend of Sir Peter Wheeler's. We were
introduced at his house some time ago now.' I resisted, however,
thinking that if I said any more, it would only make matters
worse.

'I apologise, I didn't mean to be impertinent,' I said. 'Could
you perhaps tell me when Bertie will be back?'

'I don't know exactly, but I imagine that if you work with
him, you'll see him in the office on Monday. I assume he'll be
there.'

This was a way of telling me not to phone him again at home
on a weekend. I thanked her and hung up; I would have to wait.
I opened the window to air the apartment after so many days
away, quickly unpacked my bag, did a little dusting, examined
the accumulated mail, and then, when evening was coming on
and I didn't really know what else to do – when you've just

427

arrived home, life lacks its normal rhythm – I went over to the window and saw my neighbour opposite dancing, beyond the trees whose tops filled the centre of that square: nothing had changed – why should it, time deceives us when we go off travelling, it always seems longer than it was. His usual two women friends were with him, the white woman and the black or mulatto woman, a well-matched trio, the women must be each other's *ġe-brȳd-guma*, with him as their link, another similarity with Custardoy, who enjoyed taking two women to bed with him at the same time, although not, I think, with Luisa – where would Custardoy have gone with his shattered hand, where would he really have gone, it was no affair of mine and I didn't care, just as long as he met my conditions and kept away from her and, most important of all, never told her of my intervention. The three dancers were performing some very fast steps, a kind of flamenco-style stamping or perhaps it was tap – I couldn't guess what loud music he would be playing in his living room on a Saturday – because they each had their right arm raised to hold something in place on their respective shoulders, some small and apparently living moving object, and this time I couldn't resist picking up my binoculars and when I managed to focus, I saw to my amazement that each of them did, in fact, have a very tiny dog draped around their shoulders, now I don't know anything about the different brands or, rather, breeds of dog, but the man's dog was snub-nosed and hairy, and the women's were more like rats, with pointed snouts, one of those scrawny dogs with a crest or bun or fringe or toupee on their heads, disgusting creatures whatever they were. The dogs certainly didn't look as if they belonged to them and I wondered where they would have got them from, perhaps they'd hired them especially in order to perform their eccentric dance, but whatever the truth of the matter, the poor creatures must have been feeling horribly dizzy, or indeed positively upset and desperate; the dancers' tapping would feel to them like a permanent earthquake or something similar. It was to be hoped that no member of an animal protection society, which are so fierce and so active in England, spotted what my neighbours were up to, because they'd doubtless be reported for the torture, harassment and bewilderment of small defenceless beasts. 'They must be mad,' I thought, 'they must think there's some special merit in being able to dance and, at the same time, balance a living being on their shoulders; one false move, and a dog could go flying off, hurled against a wall or a window.' I stood watching them for a few minutes until they all stopped abruptly amid urgent gestures of displeasure and alarm: the white woman's little dog had peed on her, spraying her face and hair, and because this had happened in the middle of some particularly frenetic stamping, it had sprayed the other two as well. Finding itself the object of such frenzied movements, the poor dog had doubtless judged that incontinence was its last line of defence. They released all three mutts – who tottered off – and began quickly and disgustedly taking off their soiled clothes, and just as the man was about to remove his elegant polo shirt, he looked straight across at my window and saw me. I immediately hid my binoculars and took two steps back, ashamed to be caught spying. However, they didn't seem angry at all, even though the two women had by then stripped down to their bras, a situation made worse – or better – by the fact that the mulatta wasn't wearing one. As on the previous occasion when they had spotted me, they waved cheerfully, beckoning me to come over. I had felt ashamed on that occasion too, but had managed to see an advantage in that reciprocal visual contact and thought that if one particular night or day proved truly desolate: I at least had the possibility of going in search of company and dancing on the other side of the square, in that happy carefree household whose occupant resisted all my deductions and conjectures, and inhibited or eluded my interpretative faculties, something that happened so infrequently that it bestowed on him a slight air of mystery. And the prospect of that hypothetical visit, that possible future contact, had made me feel lighter and less vulnerable, as if it provided a kind of safety net. That day could not have been more desolate, a whole empty Sunday stretched ahead of me until I could speak to Tupra, one of those desolate Sundays 'exiled from the infinite' or '*banni de l'infini*', as I believe Baudelaire once wrote and as English Sundays tend to

429

be; I knew them well from many years before, from the first time I had lived there, in Oxford, and I knew that Sundays in England aren't just ordinary dull Sundays, the same the world over, which demand that one simply tiptoe through without disturbing them or paying them the least attention, they are vaster and slower and more burdensome than anywhere else I know. So perhaps the moment had arrived to take advantage of the safety net offered by that jovial trio; what's more, the women had no compunction about showing themselves to me, especially the one I had always preferred and who had the most to show. I hesitated for a moment about whether to go downstairs, across the square and up to that other apartment, but instantly dismissed the idea. 'No, now it makes even less sense than ever,' I thought, 'in a few weeks or a month, at most two, I probably won't be living here or looking out on this square any more, and they will become merely a pleasant memory that will gradually fade. And now, alas, I can't help but interpret my dancer, because I can't help associating him with Custardoy and seeing an affinity between the two.' And so, smiling, I went back over to the window and wagged my forefinger at them to tell them 'No'. Then I opened my hand and raised it slightly in a friendly gesture, my way of saying 'Thank you' and perhaps also 'Goodbye'.

I shut the window and came back into the room. I decided to go out to a nearby grocery store and buy a few basic things to fill up the nearly empty fridge; the store also sold magazines and newspapers, but I no longer wanted to buy a copy of *The Sun* or any other paper of that ilk; and when I returned, I chose not to turn on the TV, sure that some programme, if not most, would be discussing the horrible crime of Dr Dearlove, former odontologist, now transformed into the new Hyde who could never go back to being plain Dr Jekyll: he would be a lascivious murderer from now until the Last Judgement, at which, in other times – the times of steadfast faith – people would have expected a Bulgarian or Russian boy called Danev or Deyanov, Dimitrov or Dondukov to confront him and accuse him with the bitter words of someone who died too young. Or perhaps he would address Tupra or even me. I preferred not to know too much, about him or about Dearlove, mainly because I didn't need to and because it would only increase my sense of sadness. I already knew enough, and the press would be full of ghoulish, misleading speculations. What no one would know was that there was someone behind it all, an expert on narrative disgust or horror and on the Kennedy–Mansfield complex and its all too effective curse, and that the murder had nothing to do with chance or a bad night or a moment of mental derangement. Danev or Dondukov could no longer tell who had hired him or how, nor what he had been hired to do, and I was in no position to prove anything. Nor, indeed, was I even considering the possibility.

I phoned young Pérez Nuix, who was at home, told her I had just got back and asked if we could meet that evening or the following day ('It's urgent, important; but it'll only take a moment,' I said, as she had once said to me, and on that occasion, 'it' had lasted until morning; an experience that had not been repeated). She said that would be fine, made no attempt to find out in advance what it was about and was happy to come over to my part of town ('It'll do me good to get a bit of fresh air, I've hardly been out all day, and besides I need to walk the dog'), we shared a kind of unconfessed loyalty. We arranged to meet in the bar of the luxury hotel I could see from my window ('Give me an hour and a half, no more, long enough for me to take the dog out and then come over'), and when she was installed there, with a drink before her, I told her about Dick Dearlove and the interpretations Tupra had elicited from me after the celebrity supper in London and, later, in Edinburgh. I laid out to her my arrogant reports, my hypotheses, my theories, my *mises-en-scènes*, and my predictions. As things had turned out, they appeared to indicate a high degree of prescience on my part.

'It's too much of a coincidence, don't you think?' I added, and I did not for a moment imagine she would contradict me.

I noticed that she seemed slightly uncomfortable, as if for some reason she felt impatient with or displeased by my anxieties, and she took a slow sip of her drink as you do when you need to think a little longer about what you're going to say. Finally, she said:

431

'Coincidences do happen, Jaime, as you well know. In fact, I think they're part of normal life. But not, I guess, where Bertie is concerned. Where Tupra is concerned,' she corrected herself, 'you're right, it's unlikely. With him almost nothing is coincidental.' She fell silent for a few seconds, giving me, I thought, almost a commiserative look, then she went on: 'But what is it that you find so troubling? Giving him the idea to lay a trap that you don't like? That someone else was harmed, rather than the person who should have been hurt by that trap? That someone, an instrumental victim, died? Yes, of course, what else do you want me to say, of course I understand your unease. But we've talked about this before,' she reminded me. And seeing my bewildered expression, she added: 'Yes, I told you that what Tupra did or decided was not our responsibility. Everyone, regardless of who they work for, occasionally provides their boss with the occasional idea, and if he thinks it's any good, that boss then takes up the idea and, a mere two minutes after hearing it, believes he was the one who thought of it in the first place. Sure it's irritating, they don't even give you a pat on the back, but it also means that we're absolved of all responsibility. At the time, I said that worrying about what happened with our reports was like a novelist worrying about what potential buyers and readers of his book would understand and take away from it.'

I remembered that, and I also remembered saying that I didn't think the comparison worked. She had made further comparisons, none of which had convinced me. Again, she seemed to me more experienced and, in a way, older than me. She was looking at me as if she were idly witnessing the end of time, something that she had already experienced and left behind. Perhaps that was the origin of her impatience, displeasure or discomfort: it's disheartening having to explain to someone else what it took blood, sweat and tears to learn and with no help from anyone. Or perhaps she had been able to count on Tupra's help, who was no mean arguer.

'I didn't think the comparison worked,' I said. 'Besides, a novelist *should* take care what he puts in his book, don't you think?'

'I doubt that any writers do,' she said firmly. 'If that were the case, no one would ever write anything. It's just not possible to live that cautiously, it's too paralysing. As you say in Spain, *son ganas de cogérsela con papel de fumar*. You just can't be that pernickety. And anyway, keep things in proportion. What do you expect, there are people in our field who do far worse things and get their hands dirty too. Or, depending how you look at it, perhaps they do better things because they're being of service to the country.' Since we were speaking in Spanish, I was grateful that she didn't use the word '*patria*' but '*país*', but it nonetheless sounded horribly like one of the first things Tupra had said to me at Wheeler's buffet supper. Perhaps those who stayed longest by his side, of whom I would not be one, ended up adopting his ideas. Pérez Nuix, however, said the phrase in such a neutral tone that I couldn't tell if she was serious or quoting our boss or being sarcastic.

'Don't tell me that arresting Dearlove, putting him inside for several years – if, that is, he doesn't get bumped off during his first few days there – has been of some service to this country. Or, for that matter, the death of that Russian boy; he'd probably only just arrived in England and was here illegally, thus ensuring that no one will dig too deep or kick up much of a fuss. What did you call him, "an instrumental victim"? I thought the usual term was "collateral victim", although in Spanish it should be "*lateral*" rather than "*colateral*".' I couldn't resist adding this pedantic clarification.

'They're different things, Jaime,' she pointed out. '*Víctimas colaterales* or *laterales* aren't usually instrumental, they occur more by chance or by mistake or by mere inevitability. Instrumental victims, on the other hand, always perform a function. They're necessary for something to succeed.' She paused again, took another sip of her drink, and remained silent. It occurred to me that perhaps she had often been through what I was going through now. When she did speak again, she did so hesitantly: 'Look, I don't know, I simply don't know; Tupra doesn't confide in me any more and hasn't for a long time now, and he didn't ever tell me much even when we were on better terms, I mean when he trusted me more or had more of a soft spot for me; he always keeps pretty much to himself. It seems unlikely that the state or the Crown or them,' and she pointed upwards, by which I assumed she meant the bigwigs in the SIS or Secret Intelligence Service, who, at least in the past, embraced both MI5 and MI6, 'would have ordered such a trap to be laid, such an operation, for a rock singer, a celebrity. But you never know: in America, declassification has uncovered the most ridiculous things – reports on people like Elvis Presley or John Lennon who were being kept under surveillance by the CIA or the FBI – so anything is possible. We don't know what Dearlove was doing, what he might have been getting up to, who he was involved with and who he might have blackmailed, who he could frighten with threats which, coming from him, would seem quite credible (insofar as someone like him can have any credibility, of course) or on whom he bestowed his favours. Insignificant, inoffensive and apparently purely ornamental people can prove to be full of surprises. Singers and actors often turn out to be real nutcases, they join weird sects or convert to Islam, which nowadays is no joke, as you know. One of the first lessons you learn in this job (although it's better still if you know it before you start) is that no one is insignificant, inoffensive and purely ornamental.'

'The time I talked to Dearlove longest was in Edinburgh,' I said, 'or, rather, I overheard him talking to an old friend of his, Genevieve Seabrook, which makes it more likely that he was telling the truth because, with her, there would be no reason for him to put on an act; anyway, it seemed to me that he wasn't involved with anyone, still less anyone desirable, that it wasn't even a possibility. He was complaining that in England he had no option now but to pay for sex. I doubt he could have been a serious threat to anyone, certainly not to anyone requiring the protection of the Secret Service. I had the impression that he was a man in decline, but eager to disguise that decline. In fact, he could already see himself disappearing, not so much from the world, but from people's memories. That worried him a lot, made him feel embittered and anxious.'

'As I said, it's highly unlikely that the state would have acted against him in this way. I'm more inclined to think it was a personal act of revenge by Tupra, some unfinished business – after all, they used to see each other socially quite a lot – unless Tupra did it as a favour to someone else. Or maybe it wasn't a favour at all, we shouldn't dismiss the idea of a contract.'

'You mean somebody paid to have it done?'

'Yes, why not, like I said before, this man Dearlove might to all intents and purposes be on the way out, but from what one hears, during his lifetime, he must have been with dozens of minors of both sexes, doubtless with some who were, in their day, desirable, to use your expression, either physically or socially or because of their family connections. Many of them will be adults now, some might be in possession of their own fortunes and would therefore have more than enough money to pay for such a contract killing. Then there are fathers and brothers too. I don't know, maybe Dick Dearlove ruined the life of Tupra's younger brother or sister. Perhaps he corrupted Tupra himself.' And she laughed at the idea.

'Is that possible, do you think? Tupra can't be many years his junior. And does Tupra have brothers and sisters?'

Young Pérez Nuix laughed again, this time at my naïveté or my literal-mindedness.

'No, of course not, I'm sure no one could ever have corrupted Bertie or done anything to him that he didn't want done. To be perfectly honest, I find it hard to believe that he was ever innocent and malleable. Besides, as I'm sure you realise, I was being ironic. I've no idea if Tupra has siblings or not, I've never heard him say a word about his family or his origins, I don't even know where his name comes from.' – 'Peter didn't know either,' I thought, 'although he made fun of it.' – 'No one knows much about him. It's as if he'd sprung into being by spontaneous generation.' Pérez Nuix had gone back to calling him Bertie and, in doing so, had adopted a slightly evocative tone, without realising, without intending to; I wondered just what had gone on between them. However, she immediately returned to the matter in hand. 'What I'm trying to say is that the possibilities are at once limitless and secondary, so there's no point delving into it.' Again I noticed that faintly commiserative look and again I felt that it perhaps saddened her to see me going through a process she had already been through herself. It might also be that the subject bored her, even annoyed her. 'Who cares anyway, Jaime. It's none of your business. Even what happened is none of your business, although at the moment you think it is. Well, it isn't. You've got to get used to that fact. It won't happen often, but I suppose it's the first time it has since you joined. It might never happen again. But you have to get used to it, just in case, simply because of those possible exceptions. If not, you won't be able to continue in the job.'

'I don't think I am going to continue,' I said.

Young Pérez Nuix looked surprised, but my feeling was that she was only pretending, as if she thought that not affecting surprise would be rude and show a certain disdain for me. According to Tupra, she was the best, she would know me well, perhaps better than I did, especially since I wasn't interested and had given up trying to understand myself – what was the point? ('No one can know you better than you do yourself, and yet no one can know himself so well that he can be sure how he will behave tomorrow', that, I thought or remembered, is what st. Augustine had said.) Yes, she was pretending, a little:

'Really? When did you decide that, while you were in Madrid or since you got back? Are you sure?'

'I'm almost sure,' I said. 'But I want to talk to Tupra first. He's not in London today.'

'And all because of this Dearlove business? And what are you going to say to Tupra? What are you going to ask him: why it happened? That's his affair or possibly someone else's, but he'll never tell you. Sometimes even he doesn't know why; he gets an order, carries it out unquestioningly and that's that.' She looked at her glass. I raised a cigarette to my lips in the hope that she would continue talking, I would pretend ignorance of the hotel's no-smoking rule until someone protested. 'It's your decision, Jaime, but it does seem a little over the top to me. As Bertie always says, it's the way of the world. Let things settle in your mind. Wait until it's sunk in that you have nothing to do with what happened to Dearlove and the Bulgarian boy. Ideas float, nothing is so easily transmitted. As soon as you put it into words, that idea was no longer yours, it was simply out there. And all ideas have the potential to infect others. Just wait a little, and one day you'll see I was right.'

'That isn't the only reason,' I told her. 'But it's definitely a contributing factor. I don't think I decided here or in Madrid, but in full flight, on the plane.'

'A man of firm principles, eh?' And her voice took on a slightly sarcastic edge, then immediately became more serious. 'They're not really so very firm, Jaime. No one who works in this field can afford to be that principled. You may be valiantly buckling on your principles now, but that's a different matter.' She sometimes used rather literary turns of phrase – '*con denuedo*', 'valiantly' – due to her inevitably bookish rather than real-life knowledge of Spanish. 'I'm not criticising you; it helps, it has its merits, we should all do it more often. But what you put on can always be taken off again.'

I remembered what Tupra had asked me the first time I was called on to interpret someone (the day when he had first urged me: 'Say anything, whatever comes into your head, go on'), when he asked me to stay behind in his office for a moment so that I could give him my opinion on General or Colonel or Corporal Bonanza or whatever he was, from Venezuela: 'Allow me to ask you a question: up to what point would you be capable of leaving aside your principles? I mean up to what point do you usually do so? That is, disregard it, theory I mean?' he had asked me. And he had added: 'It's something we all do now and then; we couldn't live otherwise, whether out of convenience, fear or need. Or out of a sense of sacrifice or generosity. Out of love, out of hate. To what extent do you?' And I had responded: 'It depends on the reason. I can leave them aside almost entirely if it's just in the interests of conversation, less if I'm called on to make a judgement. Still less if I'm judging friends, because then I'm partial. When it comes to taking action, hardly at all.' I had answered almost without thinking. When it came down to it, what did I know and what do I know? Perhaps Pérez Nuix was right in a way, and I *was* merely buckling on my principles or deciding not to set them to one side. However, she was not right about the last thing she had said: not everything that one puts on can be taken off.

'Not everything and not always either,' I said. 'You can't just take off a tattoo, for example. And there are some obligations that can't simply be unbuckled and discarded. That's why some are so difficult to buckle on in the first place and why others must be very firmly buckled on, so that there can be no turning back.'

There was not much more to say. I should have guessed that she would know nothing. Perhaps I had only phoned her as a way of stilling my impatience and sharing my astonishment with someone, giving vent to my feelings, possibly to convince myself, or at least to argue it through or to rehearse that argument. I stubbed out my barely smoked cigarette before anyone could call me to order. I paid for the drinks and we left. I offered to accompany her in a taxi to her house, but since we were just across the road from my apartment, she declined. And so I walked with her to Baker Street tube where we said goodbye. I thanked her and she said: 'Whatever for?'

'How's your father doing?' I asked. We hadn't mentioned him since that night in my apartment. She had told me nothing and I hadn't asked. I suppose I did so then because it felt to me as if we were saying farewell to each other. Even though we would see each other on Monday in the building with no name and perhaps on other days too.

'Not too bad. He doesn't gamble any more,' she said.

We exchanged kisses and I watched her disappear down into the underground, which is so very deep in London. Perhaps she envied my decision not to continue with the group, and that it was still possible for me to break away from it, having been part of it for far less time than her. There was, in principle, nothing preventing her from doing the same. But Tupra would certainly want to keep her at all costs, as he would the others, and me. He took whatever steps he deemed necessary and presumably hoped not to frighten us off in the process, and perhaps with that in mind he rationed and measured out the steps to be taken, gauging when we would be hardened enough to withstand certain major upsets. According to Wheeler, there were very few people with our curse or gift, and we were getting fewer and fewer, and he had lived long enough to notice this unequivocally. 'There are hardly any such people left, Jacobo,' he had told me. 'There were never many, very few in fact, which is why the group was always so small and so scattered. But nowadays there's a real dearth. The times have made people insipid, finicky, prudish. No one wants to see anything of what there is to see, they don't even dare to look, still less take the risk of making a wager; being forewarned, foreseeing, judging, or, heaven forbid, prejudging, that's a capital offence. No one dares any more to say or to acknowledge that they see what they see, what is quite simply there, perhaps unspoken or almost unsaid, but nevertheless there. No one wants to know; and the idea of knowing something beforehand, well, it simply fills people with horror, with a kind of biographical, moral horror.' And on another occasion, in another context, he had warned me: 'You have to bear in mind that most people are stupid. Stupid and frivolous and credulous, you have no idea just how stupid, frivolous and credulous they are, they're a permanently blank sheet without a mark on it, without the least resistance.'

No, Tupra would not be prepared to lose us so easily, the people who served him. I didn't consider that I as yet owed him any large debts or loyalties, nor had I established any very strong links, I had not become involved, enmeshed or entangled, I would not have to use a razor to cut one of those bonds when it ultimately grew too tight. I had tried to deceive him regarding Incompara, but now, with this Dearlove business, even if it wasn't quite the same thing, we were more or less quits. It was likely, on the other hand, that he had young Pérez Nuix caught from various angles, and that for her there could be no easy separation, no possibility of desertion. I remembered Reresby's comment when he froze the video image of her beaten father, the poor man lying motionless on the table, a swollen wounded heap, bleeding from his nose and eyebrows, possibly from his cheekbones and from other cuts, the broken hands with which he had tried in vain to protect himself – I, too, had broken a hand and slashed a cheekbone with apparent coldness or perhaps with genuine coldness, how could I have done that? Tupra had said: 'As I told you, nothing here gets thrown away or given to someone else or destroyed, and that beating is perfectly safe here, it's not to be shown to anyone. Well, who knows, it might be necessary to show it to Pat one day, to convince her of something, perhaps to stay and not to leave us, one never knows.' Perhaps he would show it to her, saying: 'You wouldn't want this to happen to your father again, would you?' 'How fortunate,' I thought, 'that my family is far away and that I'm all alone here in London.' But maybe he wouldn't need to go that far to convince Pat: after all, she may have been half-Spanish, but she was still serving her country. And I was not.

I slept badly that night, having resolved to get up early the next day. I had no intention of spending Sunday in London doing nothing but ruminate, with barely anything to occupy me (I'd dealt with any work pending before I left for Madrid), and with the television watching me while I waited for Monday to arrive so that I could talk to Tupra. I hadn't been to see Wheeler for a long time and, besides, there was the heavy present that I'd bought for him in a second-hand bookshop in Madrid and carted with me all the way to London: a boxed, two-volume set of propaganda posters printed during our Civil War, some of which – not only the Spanish ones and not all of them cartoons – used the same message as the 'careless talk' campaign or something very similar. And when you've taken the trouble to carry something with you, you feel impatient to hand it over, especially if you're sure the recipient of the gift will be pleased. It was a little late to phone him on Saturday night when I returned from Baker Street, and so I decided to go to Oxford in the morning and tell him of my arrival there and then; it wouldn't be a problem, he hardly ever went out and would be delighted to have me visit him in his house by the River Cherwell and stay to lunch and spend the whole day in his company.

And so I went to Paddington, a station from which I had so often set off in my distant Oxford days, and caught a train before eight o'clock, not noticing that it was one of the slowest, involving a change and a wait at Didcot. During what was still more or less my youth, I had, altogether, waited many minutes at that semi-derelict station, and I'd been convinced on one such

441

occasion that I'd lost something important because I'd failed – almost – to speak to a woman who was, like me, waiting for the delayed train that would take us to Oxford, and while we passed the time smoking, the hesitant pool of light surrounding us had illuminated only the butts of the cigarettes she threw on the ground alongside mine (those were more tolerant times), her English shoes, like those of an adolescent or an ingénue dancer, low-heeled with a buckle and rounded toes, and her ankles made perfect by the penumbra. Then, when we boarded the delayed train and I could see her face clearly, I knew and know now that during the whole of my youth she was the woman who made the greatest and most immediate impact on me, although I also know that, traditionally, in both literature and real life, such a remark can only be made of women whom young men never actually meet. I had not yet met Luisa then, and my lover at the time was Clare Bayes; I didn't even know my own face and yet nevertheless there I was interpreting that young woman on the platform of Didcot station.

The train stopped at the usual places, Slough and Reading, as well as Maidenhead and Twyford and Tilehurst and Pangbourne, and after more than an hour, I got off there, in Didcot, where I had to wait several minutes – on that so-familiar platform – for another weary and reluctant train to appear. And it was there, while I was vaguely recalling that young nocturnal woman whose face I soon forgot but not her colours (yellow, blue, pink, white, red; and around her neck a pearl necklace), that I understood what had made me get up so early in order to catch a train and visit Wheeler in Oxford without delay; it wasn't simply a desire to see him again nor mere impatience to watch his eyes when they alighted with surprise on those 'careless talk' posters from Spain, it was, secondarily, a need to tell him what had happened and to demand an explanation. I don't mean tell him about what had happened to me in Madrid, for which he wasn't remotely to blame (to be accurate, nothing had happened to me, *I* had done something to someone else), but about what had occurred with Dearlove; after all, Peter was the person who had got me into that group to which he had once belonged, the person who had recommended me; he had made use of my encounter with Tupra and submitted me to a small test that now seemed to me innocent and idiotic – and which in no way prepared me for the possible risks of joining the group – and then reported to them on the result. Perhaps he himself had written the report on me in those old files: 'It's as if he didn't know himself very well. He doesn't think much about himself, although he believes that he does (albeit without great conviction) . . .' He it was, in any case, who had revealed to me my supposed abilities and who had, to use the classic term, enlisted me.

Once in Oxford, I walked from the station to the Randolph Hotel and phoned him from there (now that I knew Luisa used a mobile phone, perhaps I ought to get one too, they may be instruments of surveillance but they have their uses). Mrs Berry answered and didn't even think it necessary to hand me over to Peter. She would ask him, she said, but she was sure my visit would make his day. A few seconds later, she was back: 'He says you should come at once, Jack, as soon as you like. Will you be staying for lunch? I'm sure the Professor won't let you leave before then.'

When I went into the living room, I experienced a moment of alarm – but not quite panic – because Peter's face had taken on the gaunt look of those whom death is pursuing although without as yet too much haste, not yet holding the hourglass in his hand, but keeping a close eye on it. That impression soon diminished, and I decided it must have been a false one, but it may also have been due to a rapid adjustment, as when we meet a friend who is much fatter or thinner or older than the last time we saw him and we are thus obliged to carry out a kind of rectification process, until our retina gets used to our friend's new size or new age and we can again fully recognise him. He was sitting in his armchair, like my father in his, with his feet on a pouffe and the Sunday papers scattered on a low table beside him. His stick was hooked over the back of his chair. He made as if to get up to greet me, but I stopped him. Judging from the way he was settled in his armchair, it seemed to me unlikely that he would find it as easy to sit down on the stairs as he had done very late on the night of his buffet supper. I placed one hand on his shoulder and squeezed it with gentle or restrained affection – that was the most I dared to do, for in England people rarely touch each other. He was impeccably dressed, with tie and lace-up shoes and a cardigan, as was, I believe, customary among men of his generation, at least I had noticed the same tendency in my father, who, when he was at home, always looked as if he were about to go out at any moment. Then, impatient to begin, I sat down on a nearby stool and the first thing I did, after exchanging a few words of welcome and greeting, was to remove from my bag the package containing *La Guerra Civil en dos mil carteles* – *The Civil War in Two Thousand Posters* – the next time I went to Madrid I would have to track down another copy for myself; it really was a marvellous book, and I was sure that Wheeler would appreciate and enjoy it greatly, as would Mrs Berry, whom I urged to stay and leaf through it with us. However, she preferred not to ('Thank you, Jack, I'll look at it properly when I have more time'). And she left us on the excuse that she had things to do, although throughout the morning, she came back into the room several times, came and went, always near, always on hand.

'Look, Peter,' I said, opening the first volume, 'the book also reproduces various foreign posters too, and I've stuck post-its on any pages that have posters connected to the "careless talk" campaign. It seems that, as a recommendation, it was pretty much a constant in all kinds of places. The British campaign was imitated by the Americans when they finally entered the War, but theirs sometimes verged on the kitsch and the melo-dramatic.' And I showed him a drawing depicting a dog grieving for its dead sailor master '. . . because somebody talked!' or as we would say in Spanish: '¡ . . . porque alguien se fue de la lengua!'; another in which appeared a large hairy hand wearing a Nazi ring and holding a Nazi medal and the words: 'Award for careless talk. Don't discuss troop movements • ship sailings • war equipment'; and a third more sombre one, in which a pair of intense narrow eyes peer out from beneath a German helmet: 'He's watching you.' 'And there are two English posters that I

...*because somebody talked!*

AWARD

FOR CARELESS TALK

DON'T DISCUSS TROOP MOVEMENTS · SHIP SAILINGS · WAR EQUIPMENT

HE'S WATCHING YOU

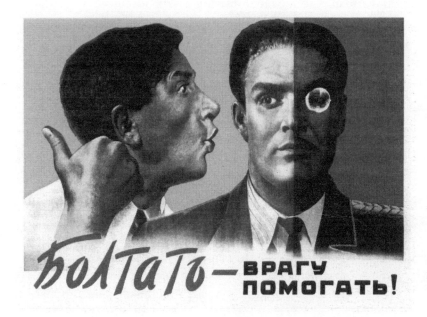

БОЛТАТЬ — ВРАГУ ПОМОГАТЬ!

Stärk fronten här hemma-

Bygg dammar för ryktena!

DESCUBRIDLO

Y DENUNCIADLO

DEPARTAMENTO de ORDEN PÚBLICO de ARAGÓN

don't think you showed me, but that you're bound to remember.'
And I turned to a page displaying a very succinct poster bearing only the words 'Talk kills', the lower half of which showed a sailor drowning as an indirect or possibly direct result of someone talking; and another signed by Bruce Bairnsfather, which revived his famous soldier from the First World War, 'Old Bill', alongside his son who has been called up for the Second. At the top are the words: 'Even the walls . . .' next to a swastika and above a huge ear; and underneath are written the young man's words: 'S'long Dad! We're shiftin' to . . . *Blimey. I nearly said it!*' And I pointed out to him a French poster, signed by Paul Colin: 'Silence. The enemy is listening in to your secrets' and a Finnish one, although the words were in Swedish, that showed a woman's full red lips sealed shut by an enormous padlock, and the text of which apparently said: 'Support our soldiers from the rearguard. Don't spread rumours!'; and a Russian poster in which one half of the listener's face and shoulders was much darker and had acquired a monocle, a moustache and a military epaulette (had taken on, in short, a very sinister appearance). 'And here are the Spanish posters,' I added, leafing through the second volume where most of them were to be found, although they were scattered throughout both. 'You see, these must have pre-dated the British ones and the others too.'

Wheeler studied them closely and with evident interest, even fascination, and after a moment's silence, said:

'They're different. There's more hate in them.'

'In the Spanish ones?'

'Yes, if you look at ours and even those from the other countries, they were warning people above all of the danger and urging them to keep silent, to maximise discretion and caution, but they didn't demonise the hidden enemy or stress the need to hunt him down, to pursue and destroy him. It's odd, they hardly condemn him at all. Perhaps because we were conscious that whenever possible, we were doing exactly the same thing, spying in Germany and in occupied Europe and were aware that in wartime, it's only to be expected (and so, propaganda apart, one can't really be too reproachful) that each side will do whatever

DESCUBRID Y APLASTAD SIN
PIEDAD A LA 5ª COLUMNA

la bestia
acecha

¡CUIDADO AL HABLAR!

CNT   FAI

cuidado con lo que haces

el enemigo te mira
un plano que traces,
un documento que
muestres,
puede ocasionar muchas muertes

EL ESPIA
VE

cuidado con lo que hablas

el enemigo te oye

EL ESPIA OYE

una palabra imprudente puede ocasionar muchos muertos

ayuda al gobierno a perseguir al espía

MUCHO OJO CAMARADA

Ayudas a la guerra si denuncias al espía. Aquí, escondido entre nosotros, trabaja para que maten a nuestros soldados en el frente. Es uno de los cómplices de los bombardeos.

MINISTERIO INSTRUCCION PUBLICA
DIRECCION Gral BELLAS ARTES

CONTRA EL ESPIONAJE

¡MILICIANOS!

No deis detalles sobre la situacion de los frentes

Ni a los camaradas
Ni a los hermanos
Ni a las novias

it can to win that war, with no limits, or only those demanded by public opinion, which doesn't, of course, mean that the limits we're told, officially, that governments won't cross are never crossed, only that they cross them furtively, in secret, without acknowledging the fact and even denying it, if that's what's required. But look at this: "Find him out and denounce him", and they depict the spy as a monster with elephantine powers of sight and hearing as well as smell, and they associate him with Italian fascism, and I'm not sure, but he may even be wearing a priest's biretta on his bald head, what do you think that is? Not to mention this other one: "Find and ruthlessly crush the Fifth Column" whose members are shown as a handful of plundering, bloodthirsty rats caught in the light of a torch, with the sole of a giant shoe about to flatten them and a spiked bludgeon about to batter them. The poster was obviously published by the Communist Party, which was dominated by Soviet Stalinists, and they called for both the enemy and the half-hearted to be mercilessly hunted down and unceremoniously killed, just as the Francoists on the other side did. And look at this next one: they refer to the eavesdropper as "The beast": "The beast is listening. Watch what you say!" and the beast is wearing a crown on his head and a cross dangling from a necklace, which makes him look rather effeminate, don't you think? It's describing the ambushee, it's saying who he is and what he's like, it's pointing him out. The other posters, though, the ones by the celebrated artist Renau with the eye and the ear and the one published by the Dirección General de Bellas Artes addressed to militiamen, are more like ours, less aggressive, more to do with defence and prevention, more neutral perhaps. They are simply a warning against spies. The text of the latter could easily have appeared on one of the later British posters: "Don't give away any details about the situation at the front. Not to your comrades. Not to your brothers or sisters. Not to your girlfriends." Those wretched girlfriends again. One tended to confide in them and they, in turn, confided in you, too much really, at a time when no one could trust anyone. It really is a most fascinating book, Jacobo, thank you so much for thinking of me and bringing it all the way from Spain, especially given that it weighs a ton.' He thought for a few seconds, then added: 'Yes, that hatred is very striking. Quite different. I'm not sure we experienced it in the same way here.'

'Perhaps in our War it was necessary to describe and characterise the spy like that,' I said, 'because they had fewer distinguishing marks and it was easier for them to pretend and to hide. Don't forget, for example, that we all spoke the same language, not like here, where you were fighting the Nazis.'

Wheeler shot me one of those occasional looks of fleeting annoyance and displeasure – those mineral eyes, like two marbles almost violet in colour, or like amethysts or chalcedony or, when narrowed, like the seeds of pomegranates – that made you feel you had said something stupid. That was when he most resembled Toby Rylands.

'I can assure you that most of those who spied here could speak English as well as you or I. In fact, probably better than you. They were Germans who had lived here since they were children, or who had an English father or mother. Some were renegade pure-bred Englishmen, and there was quite a large number of fanatical Irishmen too. It was the same with those who spied for us in Germany or Austria. They all spoke excellent German. My wife Valerie's German, for example, was impeccable, without a trace of accent. No, that wasn't the reason, Jacobo. I may have had only a very brief experience of your War, but I felt that hatred when I was in Spain. It was a kind of all-embracing hatred that surfaced at the slightest provocation and wasn't prepared to consider any mitigating factor or information or nuance. An enemy could be a perfectly decent person who had behaved generously towards his political opponents or shown pity, or perhaps even someone completely inoffensive, like all those schoolteachers who were shot by the beasts on one side and the many humble nuns killed by the beasts on the other. They didn't care. An enemy was simply that, an enemy; he or she couldn't be pardoned, no extenuating circumstances could be taken into consideration; it was as if they saw no difference between having killed or betrayed someone and holding certain beliefs or ideas or even preferences, do you see what I mean? Well, you'll know all this from your father. They tried to infect us foreigners with the same hatred, but, needless to say, it wasn't something that could be passed on, not to that degree. It was a strange thing your War, I don't think there's ever been another war like it, not even other civil wars in other places. People lived in such close proximity in Spain then, although it's not like that now.' – 'Yes, it is,' I thought, 'up to a point.' 'There were no really big cities and everyone was always out in the street, in the cafés or the bars. It was impossible to avoid, how can I put it, that epidermal closeness, which is what engenders affection but also anger and hatred. To our population, on the other hand, the Germans seemed distant, almost abstract beings.'

That mention of his wife, Val or Valerie, hadn't escaped me, but I was even more interested in the fact that, for the first time, he should refer openly to his presence in my country during the War; it wasn't that long since I had first found out about his participation, of which he had never spoken to me before. I looked at his suddenly gaunt face. 'Yes, his features have grown sharper and he has the same look in his eyes as my father,' I thought or regretfully acknowledged, 'that same unfathomable gaze'; and it occurred to me that he probably knew he did not have much more time, and when you know that, you have to make definitive decisions about the episodes or deeds which, if you tell no one, will never be known. ('It's not just that I will grow old and disappear,' poor, doomed Dearlove had said in Edinburgh, 'it's that everyone who might talk about me will gradually disappear too,' 'as if they were all under some kind of curse'; and who could say any different?) It is, inevitably, a delicate moment, in which you have to distinguish once and for all between what you want to remain for ever unknown – uncounted, undiscovered, erased, non-existent – and what you might like to be known and recovered, so that whatever once was will be able one day to whisper: 'I existed' and prevent others from saying 'No, this was never here, never, it neither strode the world nor trod the earth, it did not exist and never happened'. (Or not even that, because in order to deny something you have to have a witness.) If you say absolutely nothing, you will be impeding another's curiosity and, therefore, some remote possible future investigation. Wheeler must, after all, have remembered that on the night of his buffet supper I had asked him by what name he had been known in Spain, and that, had he told me, I would have immediately gone to look up that name in the indexes of all his books, in his War library, on his west shelves, and later on in other books as well. In fact, he was the one who had put the idea in my head, it hadn't even occurred to me until then: perhaps he had done so out of mere congenital pride and vanity, or perhaps, more deliberately, so that having once inoculated me with the thought, I would not be satisfied and would not let go of my prey, something which, as he knew perfectly well, I, like himself and Tupra, never did. Perhaps now he was ready to give me a few more facts and to feed my imagination before it was too late and before he would cease to be able to feed or direct or plot or manipulate or shape anything. Before he was left entirely at the mercy of the living, who are rarely kind to the recent dead. 'That's asking an awful lot, Jacobo,' he had said then in reply to my direct question. 'Tonight anyway. Perhaps another time.' Maybe that 'other time' had come.

'What did you do in Spain during the Civil War, Peter?' I asked straight out. 'How long were you there? Not long, I imagine. Before, you told me that you were just passing through. Who were you working with? Where were you?'

Wheeler gave an amused smile as he had on that earlier night, when he had played with my newly aroused curiosity and said things like: 'If you'd ever asked me about it . . . But you've never shown the slightest interest in the subject. You've shown no curiosity at all about my peninsular adventures. You should have made the most of past opportunities, you see. You have to plan ahead, to anticipate.' He raised his hand to the back of his armchair and felt around without success. He wanted his walking stick and couldn't find it without turning round. I stood up, grabbed the stick and handed it to him, thinking he was going to use it to help him get to his feet. Instead, he placed it across his lap or, rather, rested the ends on the arms of his chair and gripped the stick with both hands, as if it were a pole or a javelin.

'Well, I went twice, but on both occasions I was there only briefly,' he said, very slowly at first, as if he did not entirely want to release the information or the words; as if he were forcing his tongue to anticipate his actual decision, the not entirely definite decision to tell me all: he might want to tell me, but, as he had explained with some embarrassment, he might not yet be authorised to do so. 'The first time was in March of 1937, in the company of Dr Hewlett Johnson, whose name will mean nothing to you. However, you might be familiar with his nickname, "the Red Dean", by which he was known then and later.' We were speaking in English. Of course I knew the name, of course I had heard of it. In fact, I could scarcely believe it.

'*El bandido Deán de Canterbury!*' I exclaimed in Spanish. 'Don't tell me you knew him.'

'I beg your pardon!' he said, momentarily disconcerted by that sudden intrusion in Spanish and by that strange way of referring to the Dean as 'the bandit Dean of Canterbury'.

'As you may well remember from what I've told you before, my father was arrested shortly after the end of the Civil War. And several false accusations were made against him, one of them, as I've often heard him say, was that he had been "the willing companion in Spain of the bandit Dean of Canterbury". Imagine! That strange cleric was very nearly responsible – albeit indirectly, unwittingly and involuntarily – for my not being born, nor any of my siblings either. I mean that in the normal course of events my father would have been summarily condemned and shot; they came for him in May, 1939, only a month and a half after the Francoists entered Madrid, and in those days if you denounced someone, even if you did so as a mere private individual, you didn't have to prove their guilt, they had to prove their innocence, and how could my father possibly have proved that he had never in his life seen that Canterburian Dean' (I was speaking in English again and so didn't need to resort to the strange Spanish equivalent '*cantuariense*') 'or the falsity of the other charges, which were far graver. He was immensely lucky, and after a few months in prison was acquitted and released, although he suffered reprisals for many years afterwards. But imagine . . .'

'It's certainly a striking coincidence,' Wheeler said, interrupting me. 'Very striking. But let me continue my story, otherwise I'll lose the thread.' It was as if he thought the coincidence to be of no importance, as if he felt coincidences to be the most natural thing in the world, as did Pérez Nuix and I myself. Or perhaps, I thought, he had been planning his next encounter with me for a while, hoping that it would happen, and that I would deign to go and see him, and so knew exactly what he was going to tell me, what partial information he was going to give me, and did not want to be forced to depart from his script by impromptu remarks or distractions or interruptions (he never lost the thread). He may not have wanted any interruptions, but he would have to put up with at least one, when I told him what had happened to Dearlove and demanded, if not an explanation, at least some pronouncement on Tupra's behaviour. And so he set my father aside and continued, still slowly, rather like someone reciting something they have previously memorised. 'We were the first to break the naval blockade set up by the Nationalists (I always thought it scandalous that they should call themselves that) in the Bay of Biscay. We set sail from Bermeo, near Bilbao, in a French torpedo boat, and reached Saint-Jean-de-Luz without mishap, despite the widespread and widely believed rumours that the whole area had been mined. That was a Francoist lie, and a very effective one, because it kept boats away and stopped provisions reaching the Basque country. The Dean described the crossing in the *Manchester Guardian* and a few days later, a merchant vessel, the *Seven Seas Spray*, tried its luck in the other direction, leaving Saint-Jean-de-Luz after dark. And the following morning, when it sailed up the river to the dock in Bilbao, having encountered neither mines nor warships en route, the people of Bilbao massed on the quay and cheered the Captain, who was standing on the bridge with his daughter, and cried: "Long live the British sailors! Long live Liberty!" It was terribly moving apparently. And we paved the way. It's just a shame we were going in the other direction. The Captain was called Roberts.' Wheeler, eyes very wide, paused for a moment, deep in thought, as if he were reliving what he had not actually lived through, but of which he felt himself, in part, the artificer. Then he went on: 'Before that, we'd witnessed the bombing of Durango. We missed being caught in it ourselves by about ten minutes, it happened when we were approaching by road. We saw it from a hillside, in the distance. We saw the planes approaching, they were Junkers 52s, German. Then we heard a great roar and a vast black cloud rose up from the town. By the time we finally drove into the town after nightfall, the place had been almost completely destroyed. According to the first estimates, there had been some two hundred civilian deaths and about eight hundred wounded, among them two priests and thirteen nuns. That same night, Franco's general headquarters announced to the world by radio that the Reds had blown up churches and killed nuns in Durango, in the devoutly Catholic Basque country, as well as two priests while they were saying mass, one when he was giving communion to the faithful and the other while elevating the Host. All of this was true: the nuns had died in the chapel of Santa Susana, one priest in the Jesuit church and the other in the church of Santa María, but they had been bombed, as had the Convento de los Augustinos. I remember the names or those were the names I was given. It wasn't the Reds who had done it, though, it was those Junkers 52s. That was on 31 March' – He fell silent for a moment, a look of anger on his face, as if he were feeling the anger he had felt then, some seventy years before. 'That was what your War was like. One lie after another, every day and everywhere, like a great flood, something that devastates and drowns. You try to take one apart only to find there are ten new lies to deal with the next day. You can't cope. You let things go, give up. There are so many people devoted to creating those lies that they become a tremendous force impossible to stop. That was my first experience of war, I wasn't used to it, but all wars are full of lies, lying is a fundamental part of them, if not their principal ingredient. And the worst thing is that none are ever completely refuted. However many years pass, there are always people prepared to keep an old lie alive, and any lie will do, even the most improbable and most insane. No lie is ever entirely extinguished.'

'That's why one shouldn't really ever tell anyone anything, isn't that right, Peter?' I said, quoting his words. It was what he had said to me just before lunch, on the Sunday of that now far-off weekend, while Mrs Berry was waving to us from the window.

He didn't remember or didn't realise I was quoting him, or else he simply ignored it. He stroked the long deep scar on the left side of his chin, a gesture I had never seen him make before: he didn't usually touch or mention that scar, and so I had never asked him about it. If it did not exist as far as he was concerned, I had to respect that. I assumed it was from the war.

'Oh, I learned to lie as well, later on. Telling the truth isn't necessarily better, you know. The consequences are sometimes identical.' However, he didn't linger over that remark, but continued talking in this rather schematic manner, as if he had already drawn up a narrative plan for that day, that is, for the next time I went to see him. 'We were briefly in Madrid, Valencia and Barcelona, and then I came back to England. My second visit took place a year later, in the summer of 1938. On that occasion, my guide, or rather my driving force, was Alan Hillgarth, the head of our Naval Intelligence in Spain. Although he spent most of his time in Mallorca (in fact, his son Jocelyn, the historian, was born there, you've heard of him I expect), he gave me the task of watching and monitoring the movements of Francoist warships in the ports around the Bay of Biscay, on the assumption that I had acquired some knowledge of the area. Most, of course, were German and Italian ships, which had been harassing and attacking the British merchant fleet in 1936, both there in the Bay of Biscay and in the Mediterranean, and so the Admiralty was keen to gather as much information as possible about what kind of ships they were and their positions. I was travelling in the guise of a university researcher, on the pretext of delving into and rummaging around in Spain's old and highly disorganised archives, and I did exactly that – indeed some of the discoveries I made as a specialist in the history of Spain and Portugal date from that period: in fact it was in Portugal, when I was eventually deported there, that I started preparing my thesis on the sources used by Fernão Lopes, the great chronicler of the fourteenth century whom I'm sure you know.' The truth is I'd never heard of him. 'But that's by the by. I was arrested by the Guardia Civil when I was on the Islas Cíes, taking photographs of the cruiser *Canarias*, one of the few ships in the Spanish navy that had gone over to the rebels, as the Republicans called the Nationalists. They searched me, of course, and found compromising material, mainly photographs. Normally, as you can imagine, they would have executed me. We were, after all, in the middle of a war.' Wheeler paused. He may have been telling his story in that rather mechanical way, almost as if it had happened to someone else, but he nevertheless knew when to prolong the uncertainty.

'So how did you escape?' I asked, just to please him.

'I was lucky. Like your father. Like any survivor of any war. They took me in a launch to the Hotel Atlántico in the port of Vigo, and there I was interrogated by two SS officers.' – 'It's always hotels they choose to convert into police stations or prisons,' I thought, 'like the one in Alcalá de Henares where they tortured Nin and possibly flayed him alive.' – 'In 1935, I had spent part of the summer in Bavaria, at a Hitler Youth camp, for, shall we say, biographical reasons that are irrelevant here. When they found out and checked that I was telling the truth, they invited me out to supper with them. That saved my life. They consulted the Nationalist headquarters in Burgos and, as I understand it, Franco himself gave the order not to have me killed but simply to expel me. After a few minor hitches getting hold of an exit permit, I was taken to the international bridge at Tui where I crossed into Portugal. That was the slowest stretch of my journey, I mean the longest walk of my life, on foot and carrying a suitcase full of books. Two German machine-gunners had their guns trained on my back so that I didn't deviate from the path and ahead of me stood some armed Portuguese guards. And beneath me lay the River Miño. It seemed very wide, and perhaps it was. So, as you see, however disastrous Franco proved to be for the history of your country and for many, many people, he played a crucial role in my personal history. A paradox, eh?

And rather an unfortunate one for me, I must admit. Owing one's life to the clemency of someone who showed clemency to almost no one else is oddly unflattering. Being an ignorant provincial, he was, I suppose, impressed by educated foreigners like me.' He laughed briefly at his own mildly malicious remark, and I laughed too out of politeness. Then he went on. 'As I told you before, I merely passed through your War: I still use words precisely. I didn't stay there long on either occasion, and there would be no reason for either of my names to appear in the index of any of the books written about the conflict. What I did there is hardly worth telling and seems almost ridiculous now. As would my subsequent activities during our War, although some of the things I did were more spectacular or more damaging and, objectively speaking, more important. Toby was quite right when he told you years ago that in times of relative peace, wartime events seem puerile and, inevitably, resemble lies, conceits and fabulations. As I think I've mentioned before, even things I've experienced myself seem fictitious or almost fanciful. I find it hard to believe, for example, that I acted as custodian, companion, escort and even sword of Damocles to the Duke and Duchess of Windsor in the summer of 1940. That was one of my first "special employments" to adapt the term used in my *Who's Who* entry, if you remember. It seems like a dream now. And the fact that it happened abroad doubtless contributes to that feeling.'

I remembered the expression clearly, as I did every word I had read, urged on by Wheeler, in his entry in *Who's Who*. And I understood that dream-like feeling too: 'But that was in another country . . .'

'The Duke and Duchess of Windsor?' I asked. 'Do you mean the former King, Edward VIII, and the divorced woman he abdicated the throne for, that ugly American, Wallis Simpson?' Like almost everyone else, I had read about the couple who were, supposedly, deeply in love, and seen photos of both of them in magazines and books. She, if I remember rightly, was extremely thin, had a hairstyle like that of the housekeeper in Hitchcock's *Rebecca* and very thin red lips, like a scar. The exact opposite of Jayne Mansfield. 'And what do you mean: sword of Damocles?'

'Oh, she wasn't that ugly,' Wheeler said. 'Well, she was, but there was something troubling about her too.' He hesitated for an instant. 'I suppose I can tell you about it; it was a very harmless mission.' The word he used in English – 'harmless' – means literally '*sin perjuicio*' or '*sin daño*' 'without harm or hurt'. 'Although it, too, sounds like a lie. I was charged with escorting them from Madrid to Lisbon, and, once there, to make sure that they embarked for the Bahamas. You may remember that he spent the War years there, as Governor of those islands – it was a way of keeping them far from the conflict, as far away as decorum allowed. Both of them had been through an embarrassing, shall we say, Germanophile stage, and had, it was rumoured, visited Hitler incognito, before 1939 of course. There was no basis to the rumour, but the government feared like the plague the possibility that they might fall into the hands of the Nazis, that the Gestapo might kidnap them and take them to Germany, of course, but also that they might desert. That they might, in a word, go over to the other side. Churchill didn't trust them at all, and didn't dismiss the idea that if, one day, the Germans invaded us as they had the rest of Europe, the Germans would reinstate the former Edward VIII as a puppet king. Anyway, I and a naval officer from the NID (a very small escort, when I think about it, unimaginable now)' – I knew those initials, the Naval Intelligence Division – 'were given a pistol each and told, albeit not in so many words, that we should make use of them if there was the slightest risk of losing the Duke and Duchess in unfortunate circumstances, and regardless of the couple's own wishes.'

'Use them against the Duke and Duchess?' I asked, interrupting him. 'Against an ex-King? Or against the Gestapo?' The whole business really did sound like a lie, although it obviously wasn't.

'It went without saying that we should use them against the Gestapo, although I don't think we would have stood much of a chance. No, we understood that we should use those pistols against the Duke and Duchess. Better dead than in Hitler's hands.'

'We understood? Not in so many words?' I was surprised by such expressions. 'Do you mean that they didn't give you clear orders?'

'MI6 was obsessed with never saying quite what it meant. But you soon learned to decode their orders, especially if you'd been at Oxford. I don't know if they still keep up the custom now. What they said to us, more or less, was: "Under no circumstances must they fall into enemy hands. It would be preferable to have to mourn them."' The truth is that I would have interpreted this exactly as did he and the officer from the NID with whom he had shared responsibilities. And he went on to speak about the latter in an amused, almost jocular, gossipy tone: 'I bet you can't guess the name of the naval commander accompanying me.'

'No, I can't,' I said. 'How could I?'

'In fact, almost no one knows about this, not even his biographers.' Then he called out: 'Estelle!' And he automatically corrected himself: there was, after all, a witness present, even though I was a trusted friend and had occasionally heard him call her by her first name before. 'Mrs Berry!' Mrs Berry appeared at once, she was always close by, ready to be of service to him. 'Could you please bring me the Chocolate Sailor's passport? You know where I keep it. I want to show it to Jacobo.' That was what he said – 'Chocolate Sailor'. 'Now you'll see, it will amuse you no end.' And when, after a few minutes, Mrs Berry reappeared and handed him a document (I heard her go up the stairs to the top floor and then come back down again), he showed it to me with an almost childlike expression of shy pride on his face: 'Look.'

It was a safe-conduct pass or Courier's Passport as it said at the top, issued by the British ambassador in the city where I was born and valid only for a journey to Gibraltar and back, dated 16 February 1941, right in the middle of the Second World War, and then renewed ten days later and made valid for a journey to London via Lisbon. 'These are to request and require in the Name of His Majesty,' it read, 'all those whom it may concern to allow Mr Ian Lancaster Fleming *charged with Despatches* to pass freely without let or hindrance and to afford him every assistance and protection of which he may stand in need.'

Courier's Passport.

777

THIS PASSPORT IS ONLY
GOOD FOR THE JOURNEY
SPECIFIED AND MUST BE
GIVEN UP WITH THE
DESPATCHES.

Valid for a journey
to Gibraltar and
return to Madrid
16 February 1941.

Renewed and valid
for a journey to London
via Lisbon
26 February 1941.

Arthur Yencken.

By His Britannic Majesty's

Le Soussigné

Minister
at
Madrid.

Ministre de S.M.
Britannique à
Madrid

These are to request and
require, in the Name of His Majesty,
all those whom it may concern to allow

prie et requiert au nom de Sa Majesté
tous ceux à qui il appartiendra de laisser
passer librement

Mr. Ian Lancaster Fleming

charged with Despatches to pass freely
without let or hindrance and to afford
him every assistance and protection
of which he may stand in need.

chargé de Dépêches, et de lui accorder en
toute occasion l'aide et la protection dont
il pourra avoir besoin.

Given at Madrid the sixteenth day of February 1941.

Arthur Yencken.

'Oh, I see,' I said, unmoved. 'Ian Fleming.' Wheeler seemed a little disappointed by my lack of surprise. He didn't know that I had already stumbled on the dedications that the creator of James Bond had written in copies of his novels (*To Peter Wheeler, who may know better. Salud!*), which was why the fact that they were friends or acquaintances did not catch me entirely unawares. 'So they shared an adventure,' I thought, then said, in order to cheer him up: 'So the two of you shared an adventure in Spain, before he became a writer. How amazing.'

'This passport is from the following year. He gave it to me later on, when he was already famous, as a souvenir of our time in Portugal more than of our time in Spain. We were stuck there with that frivolous pair from June to August. Mrs Simpson, I mean the Duchess, was not prepared to go into exile, which is how they saw it, without her wardrobe, her table linen, her royal bedlinen, her silver and her porcelain dinner service, all of which was supposed to arrive from Paris, via Madrid, in eight Hispano-Suizas hired by the multimillionaire Calouste Gulben-kian, a risky journey in those days. (Oddly enough, that was the same year in which Gulbenkian, who was Armenian in origin, was declared "Enemy under the Act" and thus lost his British nationality and became Persian instead; so when he helped the Duke and Duchess, I don't know if he was still a friend or an enemy.) Anyway, we had to wait in Estoril and accompany them each night to the casino, either Ian Fleming or myself or, more often, to be on the safe side, both of us. It's hardly surprising that there are so many casinos in the Bond novels: since the 1920s he had been a frequent visitor to the casinos in Deauville, Le Touquet, and later Biarritz; he loved to play, especially baccarat, which was a real stroke of luck because it meant the Duchess was kept entertained when he was around. (He never won very much and even lost, he was a fairly conservative player, placing low bets, not like the fictional character he created.) As for the Duke, at least he was a reasonable conversationalist. We had a somewhat bland but cordial relationship: he had studied here, at Magdalen, and so when I couldn't think how else to entertain him, I could always resort to telling him the latest Oxford gossip. He would listen in amazement, and with a touch of possibly feigned innocence, especially to news of any sexual shenanigans. But he didn't know how to laugh. A dull man and possibly not very bright, but worldly in a pleasant way and, of course, with impeccable manners: after all, there's no denying that he came from a good family.' And Peter laughed again at his little joke. 'Finally, we managed to send the royal couple off safe and sound, along with all the silver and porcelain and bedlinen, in a British destroyer that had been anchored in the Tagus, and it was with great relief that we saw them head off across the Atlantic, bound for the Bahamas. We parted company then, Ian Fleming and I, and didn't meet again until some time later. He was a personal assistant to Rear Admiral Godfrey and had a lot of contact with Hillgarth and with Sefton Delmer, I think he and the latter had been together in Moscow and they collaborated on the PWE's black game . . .' – 'Black game,' he said. I had heard young Pérez Nuix use the term 'black gamblers' once, or was it 'wet gamblers'; it had made me think of cardsharps anyway. I didn't know what those initials, PWE, meant, but I didn't want to interrupt Wheeler. – 'We lost track of each other, well, that was normal during the War, we were sent here, there and everywhere, wherever they chose to post us, and you always said goodbye to someone knowing full well that you probably wouldn't see them again. Not because it simply wouldn't happen, but because they or you or both of you might easily die. It happened every time I had to leave and say goodbye to Valerie . . . Every time . . .' His voice had been growing fainter and fainter until, when he spoke those last words, his voice was barely a murmur; he had probably worn himself out with speaking. He did not go on. He placed his two arms on the stick that lay across the arms of the chair, as if he had just engaged in some physical exertion and needed to rest. He looked tired, I thought, and his gaze was slightly abstracted. 'Yes, Sefton Delmer's black propaganda, that's what it was,' he added thoughtfully, then fell silent again. Perhaps he had remembered too much, mechanically at first and with great animation subsequently, but all memories lead to more memories and there is always a moment, sooner or later, when one comes

465

upon a sad one, a loss, a nostalgia, an unhappiness that was not an invention. People then sit with eyes lowered or gaze abstracted and stop talking, fall silent.

'I don't know who Sefton Delmer was, Peter,' I said. 'Nor what PWE means.'

He raised his eyes and fixed them on me, wearily and with a certain bewilderment too. He said:

'Why are we talking about this? I don't know how it came up, I've forgotten.' The truth was I had forgotten too. 'Why don't *you* tell me something? You must have a reason for coming here today, without warning. I'm delighted to see you, but tell me, why *have* you come today?'

He was right. Wheeler still missed very little, even if his mind wasn't what it was and even though he now paid less attention to the outside world and was developing a form of loquacious introspection (or, I suppose, just introspection plain and simple when he was alone). Yes, I did have a reason for going to Oxford on that Sunday exiled from the infinite, to his house by the River Cherwell, whose quiet or languid murmur was just audible from where we were sitting, very faint, but still audible, and I recalled the words that my thoughts had attributed to it as they finally fell asleep, very late, on the night I had met Tupra there during a buffet supper: 'I am the river, I am the river and, therefore, a connecting thread between the living and the dead, just like the stories that speak to us in the night, I take on the likeness of past times and past events too, I am the river. But the river is just the river. Nothing more.' I had gone there to tell Wheeler what had happened to me or rather what I had done – after all, nothing had happened to me: other people had been the losers – and to ask him if he could have foreseen something like that happening when he first introduced me to the group to which he, too, had belonged; that is, in his role as intermediary, how far had he been aware of what he was getting me involved in and the risks he was laying me open to. He must have known about the possible consequences of our reports and about the uses to which they were sometimes put, to immediate and practical use or, in my case, to ruthless and criminal use. If, in times of relative peace, the result of one such report was a homicide and a scandalous arrest, the death of an innocent person and the ruin of another, tricked into being the guilty party, then, presumably, during the War, when the group had been created, and there would have been little margin for checking facts and when hasty decisions would sometimes have been made, the interpretation of people and the translation of lives or the anticipation of stories would inevitably have led to people being eliminated, to disasters and calamities. Although they would also have contributed to avoiding those things – I was sure of that. Wheeler would perhaps have found himself in a situation similar to mine now; he was not an un-scrupulous person, and even though he might, in his day, have spread outbreaks of cholera and malaria and plague, that wasn't the man I knew. Perhaps his words had killed not one man, but many, some perhaps who should not have died. However, had that happened, he would always have had the consolation, the justification, the excuse that a war was on. I did not.

'Yes, I do have a reason for coming here today, Peter,' I said. And I put him in the picture and explained what had happened, just as I had with Pérez Nuix the night before.

Wheeler heard me out in silence, without interrupting me once, with his walking stick upright now, the tip resting on the floor, and the palm of one hand cradling his cheek in the gesture of one listening attentively. I told him about that first encounter with Dearlove and about Edinburgh, thus affording his weary tongue a rest. I spoke to him of my suspicions – or, rather, cer-tainties – regarding the crime that had caused a frenzy of press speculation in the last few days and about which I assumed he would know.

'Yes, I read about it in the newspapers.' And he brushed the papers beside him with the tips of his fingers, as if he feared dirty-ing his hands. 'The contemptible Sunday papers are full of it, and Mrs Berry, who watches television more than I do, told me how shocked and horrified she was. And very disappointed too: ap-parently, she enjoys this Dearlove fellow's music. I'm clearly not au fait with all her interests.' He paused and added, as if issuing a statement: 'It would never have occurred to me that you and your colleagues had anything to do with it. It's surprising really that the group can still surprise me. Although, naturally, things must have changed beyond belief.' He thought a little more, then said: 'I don't know, Jacobo. I don't know what Tupra is up to, he rarely calls me and confides in me still less. The older one gets, the more distant people become, not that I'm reproaching any of you for that.' But there was reproach, towards me as well, in those words. 'And of course it's very much Tupra's style when he doesn't act impulsively and takes his time; insofar as I know him, that is, which isn't very well. Toby knew him better. At least he knew the Tupra who was his student, the person he used to be. I find it hard to imagine what possible danger that singer could represent, to necessitate laying a trap for him and getting rid of him. But one shouldn't discount anything; in time one learns that, in theory, as people in our line of work come to realise, anyone can be dangerous. And our line of work, don't forget, is about protecting other people. And about protecting ourselves, because if we don't safeguard ourselves, we won't be able to protect anyone. It would seem, though, that you're quite right, given that they've carried out your predictions to the letter. The man was clearly a real danger, a madman. A murderer. You mustn't torment yourself overmuch on his account.'

'You don't mind if I smoke, do you?' He shook his head. I offered him the pack of cigarettes, he shook his head again, and I lit a Karelias. 'I'm afraid that they fulfilled those predictions only because I made them, Peter,' I said. 'It's not that easy. The thing didn't just happen naturally and spontaneously. Calculation and artifice played their part, as did machination and scheming; there was the interested party to whom I gave the idea, as if I were an Iago. Without my prognostications nothing would have happened, I'm sure, and Dearlove would not be a murderer. And a young man who had nothing whatsoever to do with it wouldn't have died. He may not even have received his payment for the job. I doubt that Tupra would have paid him in advance. I don't know how I'm going to be able to live with that.' Wheeler said nothing. He sat looking at me, his hand on his chin, attentive, thoughtful, rather as if I were new to him, or as if he were wondering what to do with me in a situation that was not so much unforeseen as insoluble. He didn't even say 'Hm', but just sat there, looking at me. 'When I first got involved in this,' I went on, 'did you know that something like this might happen? That what you called my gift or my talent might be used for such things, with one person killed and another sent to prison? That it could lead to such drastic measures being taken, measures that could change lives so radically, and even put an end to one person's life? I don't think I can continue in this job. And I'd like you to know that before anyone else does, before Tupra knows. After all, you were the one who encouraged me, the one who first spoke to me about the group.'

Then I realised that he had got stuck again, that his voice or his words would not come out, that he had been assailed once more by that momentary aphasia, which, according to him was not physiological, but like a sudden withdrawal of his will: this was the third time I had witnessed this, so it obviously wasn't as infrequent as he had told me. As on the two previous occasions, it didn't happen in the middle of a sentence that I could then help him to conclude with conjectures, the way one does with people who stutter, but before he had actually spoken. This time, he was not pointing to anything that would help me orient myself (a cushion in the first instance, an Eric Fraser cartoon in the second, when the helicopter flew over). He merely made a gesture with one hand asking me to be patient, to wait, as if he knew that it would soon pass and that it was best to leave him be and not add any more questions to those I had already asked him, best not to pressure him. His lips were pressed tight shut, as if they had suddenly become glued together and he could not open them. His face, however, remained unchanged, it was still attentive and thoughtful, as if he were preparing himself to tell me whatever it was he was going to tell me as soon as he could, once he had recovered the power of speech or liberated the word that had got stuck. This finally happened after about two minutes. He made no reference to his difficulty and answered me as if that silent hiatus had not existed:

'The problem isn't the group, Jacobo,' he said. 'You'll find this out for yourself, but leaving it won't necessarily prevent what you feel has happened to you happening again. It hasn't, in fact, happened to *you*. It has simply happened, and that kind of thing can occur anywhere. You can't control what use other people might make of your ideas or words, nor entirely foresee the ultimate consequences of what you say. In life in general. Never. It doesn't make sense for you to ask me if I knew or didn't know: no one can ever know, in any circumstance, what they might be unleashing, and everything can be put to use, for one purpose or for its complete opposite. The risk that you might trigger misfortunes was no greater here than if you had never moved from your home, from Madrid, from Luisa's side.' I thought of Custardoy for a moment, of my hand holding the pistol and of his shattered hand. Wheeler, with his now recovered voice, was still looking at me hard, as if he were analysing me. I couldn't help but feel observed or more than that: spied on, decoded, laid bare. Then he added, as if, having examined me, he had decided to risk a diagnosis. 'Of course you can live with it. I can assure you that, unlike Valerie, you *can* live with what's happened to you or with what you think of as having happened to you. Strange though it may seem, in some respects I know you better than I knew her. We've studied you, but in her case, we were too late.'

I didn't know what to ask him about first, whether about the study that had been made of me or about Valerie, his wife, whom he had already mentioned; on that particular Sunday her name was haunting his tongue. I felt that if I showed too much curiosity about her fate, he might withdraw and say again: 'Ah . . . Do you mind if I tell you another day. If that's all right.' It was possible that there wouldn't be another day. It was best if that story arrived of its own accord, if it ever did.

'I know you've studied me,' I repeated. 'I've seen a report about me in some old files at the office. Who wrote that? Was it you?'

'Oh, no, it wasn't me, I've never written reports, I've only ever given them orally, you know, keeping to the bare essentials; writing reports would be too bureaucratic, too boring. No, that must have been Toby, during the time when you taught at Oxford. He was the one who discovered you, if I may use that expression. The first to speak of you to me and, I imagine, to the others.

The one who discovered your good gifts, as I think I told you, what, fifteen years ago? Twenty? No, it can't be that long.'

It didn't seem very likely to me. It was possible, but in that case, who were the 'you' and the 'her' alluded to in the report? '. . . *it's almost frightening to imagine what he must know, how much he sees and how much he knows*', it said. '*About me, about you, about her. He knows more about us than we ourselves do. About our characters I mean. Or, more than that, about what shaped us. With a knowledge to which we are not a party . . .*' Perhaps 'you' was Cromer-Blake, my other Oxford friend from that time and who was also a great friend of Rylands; and then 'her' had to be Clare Bayes, my former lover, from my youth, and whom I had never seen again. But that would mean that Cromer-Blake had belonged to the group as well, and that didn't fit at all; although, who knows, in Oxford everyone pretends all the time . . . I didn't believe Wheeler in that respect. I assumed that he didn't want to tell me who had written that report and it was easy to attribute it to someone who was dead. Or else he preferred not to confess it had been him, that was more likely. He was always reserved, except when he dropped his guard a little, as on that Sunday.

'What happened to your wife, what happened to Valerie?' And again I had that sense of abuse or sacrilege on my lips when I pronounced her name.

This time he raised his hand to his forehead, the same hand on which he had been resting his cheek and chin, while his other hand was holding, no, gripping his walking stick. He narrowed his eyes as we short-sighted people do in order to see into the distance and no longer directed them at me, but further off, at some point in the garden or the river, through the windows.

'We miscalculated, or, rather, it never even occurred to me that a calculation needed to be made. Had the group been formed earlier, if whoever had come up with the idea had done so a few months before (Vivian, Menzies, Cowgill or Crossman, or it might have been Delmer or even Churchill himself), she might not have been allowed to go so far. Or else I wouldn't have let her. *They* would of course: they would stop at nothing.' And here he used the Spanish expression *pararse en barras*. 'But I

472

wasn't around much during the War, I was away on those "special employments". I only came back occasionally and then only briefly, and so I probably wouldn't have been able to prevent it anyway.' He stopped. He must have been thinking that he had started, but that he could still stop. But I think he decided not to make a dilemma out of it and simply to carry on. 'Valerie, like almost everyone then, wanted to make an active contribution, to help in some way. As I said, she spoke excellent German, because she had spent many summers in her childhood and adolescence with an Austrian family who were old friends of her parents, and the couple's youngest daughter was about her age; there were three other children, the eldest of whom was ten years older than her. She used to spend the summers in Melk, on the banks of the Danube, in Lower Austria, near the famous Benedictine abbey, you know, the Baroque monastery.' He saw my blank look, and added, as a parenthesis: '(It doesn't matter, there's no reason why you should know it.) And the girl who was the same age as her used to spend Christmas with her here in England. When war broke out, Val thought of volunteering as an infiltrator and being sent to Germany. However, she knew she wasn't very brave and would easily have lost heart and been discovered at once. She was very willing and intelligent, but she just didn't have the right temperament for a job like that. She lacked the necessary aplomb and the ability to pretend or, indeed, to deceive. She would never have made a good spy. Contrary to popular belief, most people wouldn't or couldn't spy. Besides, she was very young, only nineteen when the War began; I was seven years older than her at the time, but now the gap in our ages is much greater, and I oughtn't to let that gap get any bigger.' As if to confirm this, he looked down resignedly at his own veined, wrinkled, freckled hand. 'She worked as a translator and interpreter for the Foreign Office until, in August 1941, all the propaganda, both black and white, was handed over to the PWE, and they recruited as many people with a good knowledge of German as they could. The Political Warfare Executive,' he explained at last, and I immediately tentatively translated this to myself: '"*El Ejecutivo de la Guerra Política*",' I thought; or '"*El*

Ejecutivo Político de la Guerra" or perhaps "*del Guerrear*" would be closer.' 'I thought this would suit her well. It was quite safe. I didn't want her running any risks, excessive risks, I mean, I didn't want her to be too exposed, because obviously everyone was running risks, as you know, at the front and in the rearguard. The PWE was a secret department and purely temporary, lasting only as long as the War, and began to be dismantled as soon as Germany signed the unconditional surrender on 7 May 1945. Its name or its acronym didn't become public knowledge until much later. A lot of the people who worked there didn't even know they were working for it and thought they were just part of the Foreign Office's PID, Political Intelligence Department, supposedly a small, non-secret section of the Ministry. The people who wrote the white propaganda (the BBC broadcasts intended for Germany and occupied Europe, for example, or the pamphlets that the RAF threw out of their planes on their raids, bearing the imprint of His Majesty's Government and all that) tended to know absolutely nothing about the existence of the black propaganda, or even the grey propaganda, which was being created by their colleagues, who were working in separate divisions and in utmost secrecy. The great advantage of the black propaganda was that no one ever acknowledged that it was British in origin, and we, of course, always denied authorship. As a consequence, the people involved had a completely free hand, with almost no restraints. Remember that officially we weren't doing certain things, even though we were doing them undercover. We never admitted it, because, among other reasons, hardly anyone knew that such things were being done. When Richard Crossman talked about the PWE in the 1970s, in a newspaper article about Watergate that had a lot of repercussions at the time (I remember that Lord Ritchie-Calder and others intervened), he admitted that during the War there had been what he called "an inner Government" with rules and codes of conduct that were completely at odds with those of the visible public Government, and he added that during total warfare, this was a necessary mechanism. Crossman was one of the key figures in the PWE, although not as important as Sefton

Delmer, who was the genius responsible for creating a whole new concept of psychological warfare as purely destructive. Crossman had been a member of Harold Wilson's Cabinet in the 1960s and so his views were respected and what he said couldn't easily be contradicted . . .'

Wheeler stopped. I thought he must have grown tired again or that his mouth was dry from so much talking. It was incredible how fluently he spoke when his words did not get stuck, even if he had perhaps lapsed again into that strangely introspective loquacity. I wondered when we would return to the young Valerie, for ever young and growing daily ever younger than him. I asked him if he would like something to drink, and he said, yes, a glass of water and told me to help myself to whatever I wanted, that I should ask Mrs Berry to bring it, and he apologised for not having offered me anything before. I replied that I would go to the kitchen myself, preferring not to bother her. I brought him his water and, after opening a cold beer for myself, took the opportunity to satisfy a minor curiosity:

'Was black propaganda also called "the black game"? Are they the same thing? You used that expression earlier.'

'Yes,' he said. 'Well, it doesn't only refer to propaganda, but to all black operations. It may have been Crossman and Delmer who invented the term, I'm not sure. According to them, the Americans – who, in part, copied us when it came to subversion techniques and who have revelled in using them ever since (rather clumsily, it must be said) – never learned to apply them as we did, to play it as a game despite the gravity of the situation. Far worse, they didn't give it up in peacetime. There was a book published about twenty or twenty-five years ago entitled *The Black Game*. I read it, it's written by someone called Howe.'

'Was it also known as "the wet game"?' I was almost certain now that 'wet gamblers' had been the term used by Pérez Nuix on the night she visited me unannounced.

'It's not a term I've heard very often, but possibly, yes. Perhaps because black operations often involved blood being spilled. White operations, on the other hand, rarely did; they were dry. But where were we?' he added, slightly irritated. 'Why am I telling you all this? Oh dear me, I've forgotten again.' The Spanish equivalent of 'Oh dear me' would be '*Ay Dios*', but in English there was no mention of God. Perhaps his memory could no longer stretch as far as it once could, from the beginning of a story to its end. Perhaps that was the one area in which his recent decline had become noticeable. He lost sight of the initial thread, although it took only the slightest of nudges for him to recover it.

'You were telling me about your wife,' I said to help him out. 'About what she did during the War.'

'Ah, yes, I was going to tell you how Valerie died, since you ask, and not for the first time either,' he replied. 'But it's important that you understand what the PWE was and how it worked, that you grasp precisely what she was involved in and what she became used to. In a sense, Sefton Delmer was the PWE's equivalent of Bomber Harris, except that he didn't have planes or troops at his command, just experts in deceit and forgery.' And when he saw that the name of Harris rang only a faint bell with me, he added: 'Arthur Harris, the Air Marshal, was the one who ordered the burning of fifty thousand Hamburg citizens and one hundred and fifty thousand Dresden citizens towards the end of the War on the cynical pretence that he was attacking military targets; he also flattened Cologne, Frankfurt, Düsseldorf and Mannheim; he was an implacable man with too much power, almost a psychopath really, willing to use any means at his disposal to crush the enemy and win.' Then I remembered him mentioning Harris before: 'A few months ago I read in a book by Knightley,' he had said, 'that the Commander-in-Chief of Bomber Command, Sir Arthur Harris, dubbed the members of the SOE amateurish, ignorant, irresponsible and mendacious', the same men who had been behind the assassination of Heydrich using bullets impregnated with botulin and behind many other acts of sabotage, destruction and terror. 'Harris and Delmer were, according to Crossman, possibly the only ones who were allowed, in their respective fields, to wage total war – the total war that Göring and Goebbels had threatened but never carried out. Indeed, Delmer was allowed to outdo the Nazis themselves (that is, he plumbed still lower depths than they did) in lies and calumnies, in the manipulation and invention of news and information and in deceiving the enemy population. Black propaganda, like strategic bombing, was nihilist in its aims and purely destructive in its effects, as Crossman himself acknowledged. And it turned out to be an enormously effective weapon, which is why everyone uses it now and with no qualms at all. Sefton Delmer was a real genius, as no one would deny. He was born in Berlin of an Australian father.' – 'Yet another bogus Englishman,' I thought, 'how many more?' – 'He had studied there and later here in Oxford; before the War, as the *Daily Express* correspondent in Berlin, he had met Ernst Röhm and, through him, Hitler, Göring, Goebbels and Himmler. He had a perfect understanding of the German character and psychology; in fact, his background meant that, when War first broke out, he was initially eyed with great suspicion here and wasn't allowed to occupy any responsible post until the security services had observed him and given him the green light – imagine that. From the people who worked with him he demanded absolute secrecy, discipline and determination, in other words, a complete lack of scruples. He gradually began recruiting Germans to his team: former members of the International Brigades, émigrés, refugees, then a few prisoners of war willing to collaborate, an important deserter who had escaped to London after the failed attempt on Hitler's life in July 1944, and even a former member of the SS. He said the same thing to all of them as soon as they arrived in Woburn, where the department was based: "We are waging against Hitler a kind of total war of wits. Anything goes, so long as it serves to bring nearer the end of the war and the complete defeat of the Reich. If you are at all squeamish about what you may be called upon to do against your own countrymen you must say so now. I'll understand that. However, you will be no good to us in that case, and no doubt some other job will be found for you. But if you feel like joining me, I must warn you that in my unit we are up to all the dirty tricks we can devise. The dirtier the better. No holds barred. Lies, phone-tapping, embezzlement, treachery, forgery, defamation, disinformation, spreading dissension, making false statements and accusations, you name it. Even, don't forget, sheer murder."' – 'Sheer murder' was the expression he used. – 'Valerie heard him say this more than once. She became quite close to him.'

Wheeler paused for thought, perhaps remembering Valerie being close to Sefton Delmer. Now he raised his hand to his lips and gently stroked them. Then he again ran his thumb down the scar on his chin, it was odd that I'd never seen him make that gesture until then. I wondered if he was inviting me to ask him about that too. However, as long as he did not mention it himself, I would abstain.

'And what were these dirty tricks? What exactly did the black game involve?' I asked.

'Well, most of their activities we only found out about after the War was over. Needless to say, they forged everything. That was one of the things we really excelled at: radio broadcasts, every kind of document, including orders from Reich bigwigs like General von Falkenhorst who was in command of the troops in Norway; soldiers' leave permits, entry passes into vital installations and buildings, circulars, satirical posters, postage stamps, rubber stamps, envelopes and letterheads, even packs of cigarettes, I remember seeing some called Efka – "Pyramiden", and everything had to be able to pass as genuinely German, or at least, when that proved impossible, as having been made in Germany or in Austria, which would create the uneasy sense that we had more infiltrators there than we really did, that we had far more people hidden in their territory, equipped with the infrastructure and the means and a tremendous operating capacity, which not only worried them, it made them waste a lot of time and effort pursuing and hunting down ghosts. We could reach everywhere with the radio, even submarines, whose crews had the demoralising feeling that they were being watched by us and could not conceal their positions from us. But the most important thing was to stir up enmity among the Germans themselves and to work to their detriment, both at the collective and the individual level, so as to foment distrust among them and make them fear each other. And of course, when feasible, to eliminate or bring about the downfall of high-ranking officials both civil and military. The black section of the PWE printed wanted posters of SS officers who were accused of being traitors, deserters, impostors or criminals wanted by the authorities: they urged people to shoot these men on sight and offered rewards of ten thousand marks or more, and assured them that even the Iron Crosses the officers might be wearing were mere forgeries. It was all very calculated. Some of those posters, supported by a radio campaign, showed the Reichkommissar Ley, a Nazi Party heavyweight with a somewhat dissolute lifestyle, and accused him of hoarding ration coupons, and Dr Ley was obliged to deny this indignantly: "I am a perfectly normal consumer!" he roared over the radio.' And Wheeler couldn't help chuckling, remembering something that Valerie herself might have laughingly told him, breaking the Official Secrets Act to which she would have been subject. 'They issued stamps bearing the image not of Hitler, but of that ambitious man Himmler, with the intention of setting them at each other's throats, giving more credence to the persistent rumours that the latter was hoping to replace the former as Führer and thus putting Himmler on the spot. But there were more serious things, too, much wetter things. A common practice of Delmer's was to have fake letters sent to the family members of German soldiers who had died of their wounds in military hospitals in Italy. They would intercept the uncoded cablegrams sent by the directors of those hospitals to the Party authorities in Germany and which contained all the information about the deceased and the address of his next of kin. The letters forged by Delmer's team, written in perfect German and on the hospital's headed paper, were supposedly penned by a distressed comrade or nurse who had remained by the dead man's side until the last, and what they usually said, in horrified tones, was that the soldier had, in fact, been killed by lethal injection on the orders of his superiors, when they were informed that he would no longer be available for active service. The Nazi doctors needed the beds for those soldiers who would soon be able to be returned to the front, and so they got rid of the badly injured men without compassion or gratitude, cruelly and expeditiously, as if they were so much detritus. Delmer and his unit were perfectly aware that they were the ones who were practising real and extreme cruelty by making a grief-stricken widow or someone's aged parents or orphaned children believe such a falsehood (which was, on the other hand, quite believable). However, if this served to feed discontent and rancour among the population, to lower the morale of the combatants, spread disunity among the troops and encourage desertions, that was what mattered. Don't forget, Jacobo, the Second World War felt like a battle for survival. And it was, it really was. And in wars like that the limits on what one can acceptably do are constantly broadening out, almost without one realising it. Times of peace judge times of war very harshly, and I'm not sure how far it's possible to make such a judgement. They are mutually exclusive: in time of war, for example, peace is inconceivable – and vice versa, a fact that tends to be overlooked. Nevertheless, there are still things that do seem reprehensible even while they're happening or being perpetrated in the most permissive of times, and you see, all those . . . yes, vile deeds, I suppose . . . were kept hidden at the time as well, when the War was being waged and no one knew how it would end. Sefton Delmer's unit didn't officially exist, and all its members were told to deny its existence (and, therefore, their own existence) both to the world as a whole and to other organisations that were almost (but not quite) as secret, like the SOE, or like us later on, silent and silenced for rather different reasons but mainly to do with secrecy and discretion. And do you know, after the War, not only was the PWE dissolved immediately, its black members were given more or less the following instructions: "For years we have abstained from talking about our work to anyone not in our unit, and therefore little is known about us or our techniques. People may have their suspicions, but they don't know anything for certain. And to keep it that way, we want you to continue as you have up until now. Don't allow anything or anyone to provoke you into boasting about the work we've done, about the tricks and traps we laid for the enemy. If we start to show off to people about the ingenious things we got up to, who knows where it will end. So, mum's the word.'" And I remembered having seen that last expression on one of the 'careless talk' posters. "'Propaganda should, by its nature, be a subject one doesn't talk about." This was doubtless out of prudence,' Wheeler went on, 'but also, I think, because the work was such that they couldn't feel entirely proud of it, and less so in the final stages of the War than at any other time. Valerie, *a fe mía*, certainly wasn't proud of it.' And he used that rather literary Spanish of his, *a fe mía*, the equivalent of the English 'forsooth'. 'When the German civilians were at their most desperate and confused, our phoney radio stations heaped still more confusion and desperation on them. We warned, for example, that an enormous number of counterfeit German marks were circulating in the country, which meant that people could trust neither their own money nor what other people gave them. The worst, however, came after the brutal bombings by Harris and the Americans, and again when troops were already invading Germany, ours from the west and the Russians from the east. During air raids, the German stations stopped transmitting so as not to serve as beacons for the RAF and USAF planes. But in a matter of seconds, don't ask me how, Delmer and his colleagues managed to take over their frequencies, pretending, in their immaculate German, that normal transmissions had been resumed, and sending out bewildering, disorienting, counterproductive or contradictory messages that wreaked the maximum amount of havoc and spread chaos. Initially, survivors in the devastated cities (Hamburg, Bremen, Cologne, Dresden, Leipzig and so many others) were advised not to move, not to leave their respective cities and to wait for help to arrive. Delmer, apparently at Churchill's behest, ordered them to do exactly the opposite, via a communiqué that he passed off, of course, as an official statement from the Reich. His team informed the people that seven bomb-free zones had been set up in the centre and south of Germany, to which refugees could go and where they would be safe from aerial attacks by the enemy. They were assured that neutral representatives of the Red Cross in Berlin had told the authorities of the Reich that Eisenhower himself was going to declare those seven areas to be safe, and that the banks were moving their securities there. This information was, of course, entirely false, but it had a tremendous effect. The roads were inundated with whole families fleeing towards those imaginary zones, with their ragged children, their wounded and their few household goods piled into carts, in dilapidated buses that ran out of petrol, even in hearses, in whatever they could find to carry them away from their infernos. It was total chaos. Many roads were blocked by such large numbers of people that it hampered the defensive work of the German army, who didn't know how to avoid these hordes, nor where to put them or how to get them out of the way, or what to do with them. And it's likely that still more bombs fell on many of those terrified displaced persons who set off en masse in search of those phantom safe zones, and who would perhaps have survived among the ruins of their cities, if they'd sat tight, because there were no safe zones anywhere in Germany, or only in those places that had already been destroyed.'

Wheeler stopped speaking and eagerly drank some water, finishing the whole glass in one gulp or, rather, in several slow prolonged gulps, the way children drink when they're very thirsty, but, who, unable to cope with too much liquid at once, have to pause now and then to recover their breath, although without for a moment removing their lips from the cup, as if they feared that someone might snatch the glass from them. Then he summoned Mrs Berry, asked her to bring him more water and a few olives as an accompaniment to my beer. 'That's how you still drink in Spain, isn't it, with something to nibble on so that the alcohol doesn't go to your head,' he said. 'I've got some Spanish ones, crushed olives with lemon, from Andalusia, I believe. They're very good. I understand you can buy them in Taylor's, almost opposite where you used to live.' I remembered that delicatessen well. It was a fairly expensive shop, but during my Oxford years, I had largely subsisted on its many frivolous products (I've never been much of a cook). I told Mrs Berry not to go to any trouble on my behalf, there was no need, but Wheeler had asked her for them and she wanted to please him. When she had left the room and I had my olives before me – although she never really left the room entirely, she continued to come and go, always silent and busy – I asked Wheeler:

'And is that what your wife became used to, Peter? To what you called "those vile deeds"? At the time, I suppose, they weren't seen like that. And it might be that they *are* vile deeds now, but that they weren't then. Just part of the struggle.' I paused, slightly perplexed because I wasn't sure that I myself quite understood what I had just said, which is why I added: 'If, that is, it's possible for something to be fine when you do it, or at least justifiable, but not when you've done it, since the two things are one and the same. I mean, I don't know if it's possible for the same thing to be different when it's present and when it's past, when it's an ongoing action and when it's just a memory. Oh, ignore me.'

Wheeler looked at me as if he really had become lost in my confused thoughts, and didn't answer me at once; indeed, he seemed to be taking me at my word and ignoring me.

'In one of his volumes of autobiography,' he said, 'I can't recall whether it was *Trail Sinister* or *Black Boomerang* (I read them when they were published in the '60s, partly to see if Valerie was mentioned or alluded to at any point; she wasn't, nor was the affair in which she played the largest part, the leading role), Sefton Delmer described travelling to Germany towards the end of March 1945 and seeing the spectacle with his own eyes, the same spectacle he had seen before in Spain during the final days of your War (he had been there too, as a correspondent) as well as in Poland and in France: people aimlessly fleeing, trudging through a series of ruined landscapes, dragging with them all that remained of their possessions or that they had been able to pile into their broken-down vehicles, or walking along roads and across fields with very young children on their backs, their eyes empty or terrified, sometimes with dead children whom they couldn't bring themselves to bury at the roadside or whom they didn't dare to abandon, but continued pointlessly to carry as if they were effigies . . . And Sefton Delmer said that he didn't stop to ask anyone if, by any chance, what had first impelled them to set off along the roads and begin their aimless wanderings had been the messages broadcast on Radio Cologne or Radio Frankfurt, whose frequencies he had taken over. I remember that he wrote: "I didn't want to know. I feared the answer might be 'yes'." So he did know. But he had done those things and would have done them again, just as almost everyone else was driven to do such things, just as almost everyone else does in time of war. During a war, very few ideas, even the most unlikely, fail to be put into practice. Almost anything that occurs to anyone as a way of harming the enemy finds an outlet, although it might not be publicly acknowledged afterwards. The trick we played with those radio broadcasts was so effective and had such grave consequences that the Nazi authorities were obliged to abandon the airwaves altogether as a way of issuing orders or instructions to the population. They had to fall back on the *Drahtfunk*, a wired diffusion network on which we could not intrude but which was much more problematic and restricted in scope. Yes, Delmer and his black game made a huge contribution. I don't know if he won the War for us, but he certainly contributed to our winning it more quickly.'

Wheeler really did seem weary now. At any moment, he might abandon his story, leave the rest for another day, fall silent or perhaps bring it to a definitive end. He might even regret having started, I didn't want to risk something, because I might never again find him in the same talkative mood, given that he normally kept himself to himself. 'Who knows, I might never find him again in any kind of mood,' I thought, 'if I'm going to leave here soon and go back to Spain. It's quite likely that I'll never see him again.' And so I decided to insist and even hurry him along.

'So what happened to Valerie?' I didn't mind pronouncing her name now. 'What was this affair in which she played the largest part? The leading role you said.'

Wheeler leaned forward slightly, rested both hands on the handle of his walking stick, which he had positioned upright between his legs, with his chin resting on his two hands, and I had the feeling that this was a way of gathering momentum or of preparing himself to make a major effort. His eyes shone and his voice sounded stronger, for it had grown weaker as he talked. It occurred to me that he might never have told, or only a long time ago and to very few people, what he was probably about to tell me. For I was still not certain that he would.

'Well,' he said, 'I'm not sure how familiar you are with the Nazi racial laws.'

'Not very,' I answered at once; I didn't want there to be any more pauses. 'Like everyone else, I have a vague general idea.'

'They were very precise, almost complex and, more than

485

that, from 1933 onwards, they kept changing. Their application also varied depending on the people and organisations who interpreted them. The Ministry of the Interior was less strict in applying them than Dr Adolf Wagner, the Nazi Party's chief authority on the subject, and he, in turn, was less rigorous than, for example, the SS. However, the relevant point here is this: you were considered to be a Jew if at least three of your grandparents were Jewish, regardless of any other factors; a person with two Jewish grandparents and who either belonged to the Jewish religion or was married to a Jew at the time the Race Laws came into effect was also legally Jewish (and, apart from a few very rare exceptions, "half-Jews" ended up being treated as Jews); then there were *Mischlinge* of the first degree, cross-breeds, who had two Jewish grandparents, but who neither professed the Jewish religion nor had a Jewish spouse; lastly, there were *Mischlinge* of the second degree who had only one "contaminating" Jewish grandparent and three grandparents who were "gentiles", that is, "Aryans" or what the Nazis termed "Germans". The difference was crucial, because, generally speaking, *Mischlinge* of the second degree were left in peace, and some were even able to obtain a German Blood Certificate, once the application had been studied by Hitler himself, who apparently judged the matter to be of sufficient importance to merit his spending time poring over each and every file and deciding whether or not the applicant should be "reclassified", as several thousand were. He did so at his own pace, of course, and I imagine that, unlike the applicants, he was in no particular hurry to make those judgements: some were "Jews" asking to be promoted to first-degree *Mischlinge*, or first-degree *Mischlinge* wanting to be recategorised as second-degree *Mischlinge*, with those in the second degree aspiring to "Aryanisation" and the Certificate. Not a few committed suicide when they were relegated to "Jewry". People deemed to be doubtful cases were so panic-stricken that they often attempted, sometimes successfully, to forge, substitute, conceal or destroy their grandparents' birth certificates, especially between 1933 and 1939, after which this became virtually impossible. Many officials in town halls and registry offices, or wherever the documents were kept, removed compromising documents in exchange for outrageous sums of money or even property, sometimes even making use of convenient fires that broke out in certain parts of their archives or of plagues of highly selective mice. Or, if the forgery brought to them was perfect, written on old paper and everything, they would agree to do a swap and convert a Jewish grandfather or grandmother into a Catholic or a Protestant, with a change of surname included. This was a frequent occurrence in smaller towns and cities, where it was much easier. Of course, these officials almost never actually destroyed the document that had been replaced or removed, unless the payer demanded that it be handed over so that he or she could take personal charge of its disappearance. This wasn't usually the case, Jews not being in a position to lay down many conditions, and so the official would then keep the document just in case things changed in the future. The evidence, then, only vanished temporarily. Pour me a glass of sherry, will you,' added Wheeler, as if telling me all this had cheered him up. Talking about history often does have a cheering effect on the old.

'Do you have any preference?' I asked, pointing to a high shelf to my right, full of bottles.

'Any of those will do,' he said. I got up, poured him a glass and handed it to him; he took two sips and continued (and now I had no fear that he might stop): 'When, in time, a "quarter-Jew" was revealed to be a "Jew" or a "half-Jew" in disguise or else a second-degree cross-breed, or when an "Aryan" was shown to be a first-degree *Mischling* in disguise, it mattered little what the laws said: their fate depended, above all, on who found them out and on what those people decided to do with the information and to whom they chose to give it. Taking the story to the local police or mayor wasn't at all the same thing as going to the SS or the Gestapo. It might be that nothing happened, the officials involved might turn a blind eye, or the guilty party, as punishment for his deceit, might be despatched to a concentration camp along with all his family. Apparently Göring or Goebbels – I can't remember which now – said: "I will decide who is a Jew." And when he said this, it wasn't in order to "judaise"

487

someone, but because, on that occasion, it suited him to declare a particular person to be a non-Jew. Contrary to popular belief, and contrary to Nazi propaganda, there were many *Mischlinge* and even "half-Jews" who served the Reich loyally, even in the army and in positions of responsibility, both administrative and within the Party. A few years ago, a book came out entitled *Hitler's Jewish Soldiers*, by someone called Bryan Rigg – have you read it? – which gave an account of some of the more remarkable cases. The photo of a blond, blue-eyed "half-Jew" called Goldberg was used in the propaganda press as an example of "The Ideal German Soldier". Can you imagine? There were colonels, generals and admirals who were "half-" or "quarter-Jews", although Hitler conveniently declared them to be "Aryans". However, a Major General, Ernst Bloch by name, like the philosopher, and a veteran of the First World War, had to be discharged after Himmler made a personal protest. I don't know or can't remember what happened to him after that: perhaps he went from commanding troops to wasting away in a concentration camp, perhaps he fell from grace entirely. Much depended on chance, or on having the friendship or favour of someone high up. Field Marshal Milch, for example, was a "half-Jew", and his friend Göring provided him with false (forged) evidence that he was not, in fact, the son of his official "fully Jewish" father, but of his mother's "Aryan" lover; nobody knows, of course, what his mother, if she was alive at the time, would have made of this extraordinary revelation, or if she actually had such a lover. Milch was reclassified as "Aryan" and awarded the Ritterkreuz for his actions during the campaign in Norway. As you see, in the Germany of the time, it was a blessing to be a bastard.' And Wheeler laughed again, in the mocking tone that always reminded me of his brother Toby's very characteristic laugh. 'But how did we get on to this, Jacobo? I'm sorry about these memory lapses, it only happens with the immediate present. What with them and my moments of aphasia, pretty soon, I won't be able to tell anyone anything.'

'He's not so bad yet that he doesn't realise it,' I thought, 'which is some consolation, but he wouldn't have suffered such blanks a year or even a few months ago. It's as if he and my father were marching to the same drummer, at the same speed, although Peter is in better shape. Despite being a year older, he'll probably last longer. How sad when neither of them is here any more. How sad.'

'You'll know better than I,' I said, 'but I think it had to do with your wife, with her death. At least I believe so.'

'Ah, yes,' he said, 'it has a great deal, indeed, everything to do with my wife. Yes, yes.' And as he repeated that word, he seemed once more to pick up the thread. 'As I said, in the black section of the PWE, there were people who didn't even know they were working for it, who didn't even know of its existence. Valerie, of course, had no idea. However, there was a fellow who probably knew very well just who and what he was working for; he only turned up at Woburn or Milton Bryan occasionally, with a whole battery of ideas and, it would seem, enjoyed complete autonomy, even from Delmer. His name was Jefferys, almost certainly an alias, and he had a truly diabolical mind, or so Valerie told me when I returned from Jamaica or the Gold Coast or from Ceylon or wherever I'd been posted, and we were able to spend a couple of weeks or a few days together. Jefferys' mission was to create disruption, to invent problems which, however secondary or outlandish, couldn't be ignored by the Germans, who would be obliged to try and find a remedy. And he got the staff all fired up too, something he excelled at apparently.'

'To spread outbreaks of cholera?' I couldn't help asking. But he didn't pick this up as an allusion to himself, perhaps because he no longer remembered saying it.

'Exactly. Or even chickenpox. We were all convinced, in all the divisions, sections, units and groups, in the SIS in general, in the SOE, in the PWE, in the OIC, as well as in the NID, the PWB and, of course, the SHAEF, that any setback that might distract the Germans from what was really important, anything that hampered their wartime activities or took them away from or made them neglect their tasks, that even minimally diminished their efficiency, would be hugely to our advantage, and would help us to gain time while we waited for the Americans to make up their minds to enter the War (how tedious and hesitant they were; and then they have the nerve to boast about their contribution). It was a matter of keeping the largest possible number of men occupied with bothersome or seemingly dangerous minutiae. Each time the Nazis had to send a soldier or a member of the Gestapo to tackle some unexpected task that had nothing to do with the War proper, it helped a little and gave us some advantage, or that was our feeling, which, up until December 1941, after more than two years of resisting on our own, was one of absolute desperation. Anyway, this Jefferys fellow would arrive – a whirlwind of energy – and stay for a week, issuing all kinds of instructions and urging the people there to come up with their own tricks and dodges, all intended to cause the maximum amount of damage. He was an enthusiastic, hyperactive, febrile, infectious kind of man, who raised spirits simply because he treated everything as if it were really important. According to him, the smallest obstacle could prove useful, anything to make them trip or stumble. A city in Germany or occupied Europe, for example, might be plagued with murders or burglaries, with fires in buildings and hotels, or else an epidemic, even if it was only flu, might be declared, or the supplies of electricity, gas, coal or water were cut off; there might be a shortage of medicines in hospitals or foodstuffs left to rot; all those things could help. The accumulation of problems and calamities and crimes breeds insecurity, distrust and anxiety, and having to worry about many things at once is what most exasperates and wears people down. The more off-balance the Nazis were, the more burdened with non-essential tasks, the more chance we had of landing them a blow in the solar plexus.'

'You're not telling me that ordinary murders were committed that weren't ordinary at all? You're not telling me that you and your group planned and committed random murders of civilians?'

Wheeler made an ambiguous gesture with his open hand at forehead height, as if he were raising the brim of an imaginary hat.

'No, I don't believe so. Sefton Delmer may have been a *bon vivant* and a pragmatist, with few scruples about the subversive techniques used to undermine and destroy the enemy, a man who, in the middle of all this, was seen blithely eating, drinking and laughing as if entirely unaffected, but he did have a remnant of conscience. According to Hemingway, who met up with him in Madrid during our War, when both men were correspondents, he looked like a "ruddy English bishop". Others thought they saw a resemblance to Henry VIII, because he was a big man verging on the obese, with rather bulging eyes and a florid complexion. And since razors were in short supply during the War, he had let his beard grow too. Jefferys, on the other hand, did advocate encouraging or even actually carrying out non-political murders: nowadays, this would be termed terrorism. I'm sure they took no notice of him in that respect, and besides, the SOE, with its local collaborators in every country, had quite enough objectives of its own, in particular, military ones. When it came to acts of sabotage and torpedo-ings, most of his exuberant ideas were well received. And Valerie gave him an idea of her own. Yes, Valerie had an idea.' And Wheeler's tone, as he spoke those last two sentences, grew suddenly much more sombre. He took another couple of sips of sherry, again rested his walking stick on the arms of his chair, gripped it with one hand, as if it were a bar to hold on to, and continued without further hesitation: he had decided to tell me this story and he was going to. 'Everyone wanted to help in those days, Jacobo. It was incredible how the whole country rallied round, first to endure, and then to destroy the Nazis. For those of us who lived through those times, what happened later on, in the Thatcher era, with the ridiculous Falklands War, when people got so fired up and cocky, was utterly shameful, a fake, a farce, a grotesque imitation of that other War. During the real War there was no cockiness and no vaudeville patriotism.' Wheeler pronounced 'vaudeville' with a French accent, as my father would have done. 'People simply resisted, but never bragged or boasted about anything. Everyone did what they could and, with a few rare exceptions, no one gave themselves a medal for it. They were real times, not phoney, not sham. Jefferys was a stimulus, a spur during the days he spent in Woburn, or, rather, Milton Bryan, and Valerie wanted to help as much as she could, to make a real contribution. She worked hard. Anyway, her Austrian friend's older sister, the one who was some ten years older, Ilse by name, had had a boyfriend in the days when Valerie still used to spend her holidays in Melk with the Mauthner family, and so she got to know him over several summers. The boyfriend was already a convinced Nazi by then – I'm talking about the period from 1929 or '30 to 1934 or '35, which was when Valerie stopped going to stay with them and her friend stopped visiting her at Christmas, when they were both fourteen or fifteen. The older sister and the boyfriend finally got married in 1932 or '33 and moved to Germany, and the younger sister, Maria, with whom Valerie corresponded during the rest of the year and up until shortly before the War, had told her how worried the family were about that entirely expected marriage. The Mauthners always hoped it would never happen, that Ilse would break up with her boyfriend, as often happens with couples who meet very young. The man, whose name was Rendl – '

Here I couldn't help but interrupt him.

'Rendel? R-e-n-d-e-l?' I immediately spelled it out for him.

'No. In Austria, it was written without the second "e",' he replied. 'But, yes, the Rendel you know and who works for Tupra is the grandson of that older sister and her husband. Not that I've ever met him and I only know his father slightly. I helped his father, Ilse's son, financially, so that he could come to England when he was still a child; afterwards, I preferred not to stay in touch. That's another story though. But let's not get ahead of ourselves. The husband, Rendl, and this was known by his in-laws, had a Jewish grandmother, who had died before he was born, and so he was a "quarter-Jew", a second-degree *Mischling*. As I said before, nothing tended to happen to such people because they were considered to be "German" and were assimilated, although they couldn't, in theory, aspire to holding any important post. However, that quarter of Jewishness worried the whole Mauthner family, the father, the mother and the other sisters. Not because they were Nazis – they were, it seems, apolitical, passive people, who did, later on, I imagine, become Nazified – what worried them was a fear of any "contamination", which was a very widespread fear at the time. Bear in mind that the Nuremberg Laws were passed in 1935, but in reality all they did was regulate many of the measures that had already been taken against the Jews unofficially (the whole business went back a long way) and to make official and legal an already existing situation, namely the intense social dislike of Jews and the discrimination against them. Now if Rendl hadn't been such a fervent Nazi, he could have lived a reasonably quiet life. However, he wanted to join the SS and achieved that ambition shortly after he got married. In order to do so, he first had to get rid of that Jewish grandmother, I assume by doing what so many others had done: offering a large bribe to the authorities in the place where she was born. And as a consequence of that concealment, that falsification, that imposture, the "stain" became a secret to be jealously guarded, and the Mauthner daughters were told as much as soon as the "cleansing" of the records had taken place. For one of them, however, it was too late.'

'She had told Valerie, I mean, your wife, Peter.' This time I corrected myself at once.

Wheeler noticed my uncertainty. Very few things escaped him even now.

'It's all right, you can call her Valerie. And she wasn't my wife at the time. She was called Valerie Harwood then and could have imagined very little of what was to come. She couldn't even have imagined me because we hadn't yet met. But, yes, Maria Mauthner had told a friend who, a few years later, would turn into an enemy. Not a personal enemy, of course, but . . . how could you best describe it? National, political, patriotic? I don't know what kind of enemy one becomes in time of war. You hate complete strangers and old friends, you hate all-embracingly, hate a whole country or even several. It's very odd when you think about it. It makes no sense at all, and it's such a waste. Maria had not only told her about it just once, she continued to mention it in the years that followed, by letter. They had been friends since childhood, they trusted each other, they talked openly, they gave each other their news. Valerie learned that Ilse had three children, a boy and two girls, she even met the oldest, when he was just a baby, during her last visit to Melk, in 1934 or '35. She also learned that Rendl, whom she had always considered an imbecile when she'd met him during her summer visits, a kind of pre-fanatic, was rising fast in the SS; and when the two friends stopped corresponding in 1939, she knew that he had reached the rank of Major, or perhaps Captain, in one of the Cavalry Divisions of the SS. One of those divisions, by the way, the 33rd, met a sad (for us joyous) fate when it was wiped out at the battle of Budapest in 1945, but I don't know if that was his division. Not that it matters, because, by then, Rendl wasn't in the Cavalry or in the SS, but, quite likely, in a concentration camp, in a mass grave or else incinerated.'

'What happened?' I asked so that he didn't get distracted recalling facts about the War.

Wheeler finished his sherry and hesitated as to whether or not he should have another. I encouraged him, got up to fill his glass, and he glanced across to where Mrs Berry had been coming and going, but then we heard her begin to play upstairs, in the empty room where there was nothing else to do but sit down before the piano: perhaps it was her practice time, before lunch, at least on those Sundays exiled from the infinite. Wheeler pointed with one finger up at the ceiling and then at the bottle.

'You know already, don't you, Jacobo? You can imagine what happened. Valerie told me that she had doubts about the plan and would have liked to ask me my opinion. But I was away most of the time, and communications were difficult and brief, there wasn't time to discuss problems. When she told Jefferys about it, she hadn't had any contact with Maria for three or four years, and didn't even know if she was still alive. Besides, everything in the past fades and seems less intense, and childhood friendships are the quickest to blur, mainly because children cease to be children and they change, they cast off and deny their childhood until it's far far away, and only then do they miss it. Jefferys appealed to the inventiveness and to the remote, oblique, improbable heroism of his black gamblers, both those who knew what they were involved in and those who thought they were white gamblers; he'd say to them: "Don't keep anything back, however trivial and silly it may seem to you, tell us about it: it could prove vital, could save English lives and win this War." He demanded incessant activity, initiatives, plots, schemes, and always more ideas, and Valerie gave him hers, or he created one out of what she told him: "Hartmut Rendl, SS officer, with the rank of Major or at least Captain – if he's been promoted in the last few years – is a *Mischling* on his Jewish grandmother's side, and has, moreover, destroyed or falsified documents in order to expunge that information and be admitted to the SS, the most racially pure institution in the Reich and the principal perpetrator of atrocities." Rendl was a member of the SS, a criminal and an imbecile, so why have any doubts or scruples? It isn't hard to imagine the excitement that such a case would arouse in Jefferys and in Delmer himself when he was told about it. They couldn't wait to get the machinery up and running: they not only ensured that the information about Rendl reached the ears of the SS high command, and, if possible, the ears of his boss, the irascible and purgative Himmler, they saw in this a new opportunity for black propaganda. They began forging birth certificates and pages from the register of births, marriages and deaths, which accused other army officers, high-up government officials and even members of the Nazi Party of being "Jews", "half-Jews" or "first-degree *Mischlinge*". Not many, of course, they didn't want to overdo this "plague", they spaced out those reports, issuing just a few at a time, those that seemed most believable and had most basis in fact. It was no easy job, but the PWE was brilliant at forgery: thanks to a collector, they had German types and moulds (or matrices or whatever they're called, I know nothing about printing) of what are called *Fraktur* or Gothic print, dating from the seventeenth century to the twentieth. And even if sooner or later those forgeries were discovered (although not all of them were), while the Nazis were carrying out their investigations and checking each of those suddenly suspect files . . . well, it was worth keeping them busy over nonsense like that

495

which had nothing to do with the War and making them waste time rummaging through the old archives of town halls and parishes (in the nineteenth century, many German and Austrian Jews had converted to Christianity, especially to Catholicism), and thus fomenting distrust towards their own kind, for as I mentioned before, one of Delmer's priorities was to bring the Germans into conflict with each other. And when the trick worked and brought with it the removal or fall from grace of a Colonel, a General, an Admiral, or a Party leader, that saved us a job and spread panic and lowered morale among the rank and file. It may seem idiotic to us now, but it was a real blow to them, the idea that there were infiltrators in their most select units, that the *Wehrmacht* was infested with "rats", and that no one, however loyal and whatever their merits, was safe from such "revisions". It was a pretty dirty trick. It was of course "black" in more than one sense, because what they did was to take advantage of the cruellest and most repellent aspect of the Reich and, by exploiting it, brought about the persecution of more Jews, whether real or imaginary. However, these "half-" or "quarter-Jews"were not your average Jew, they weren't poor innocents; they were, above all, convinced and active Nazis, who were either fighting us or hunting down "full Jews" or both, and so no one at Milton Bryan worried overmuch about the possible injustice of that tactic, based on false accusations or, worse still, on actual fact, as was the case with Rendl. No one lost much sleep over it. Nevertheless, Delmer, as I recall, chose not to mention it in his autobiography. I wouldn't have lost any sleep over it either, just as I lost no sleep over many of the other things I had to do and did. On the other hand, I did lose sleep over some of the things I *saw*, but that's different, it's easier to deal with what one has done oneself.' He paused briefly, as if he were starting a new paragraph or opening a long parenthesis, and he turned to look outside, at the river. 'I only disobeyed an order once, on a crossing from Colombo to Singapore. I was a Lieutenant Colonel at the time. I was accompanying an Indian agent who had first been recruited by the Japanese and who then, under threat of immediate execution, became a double agent for our side, a man whom I myself had interrogated and trained in Colombo. With the War nearing its end, I was told to dispose of him during the journey, since he was no longer of any use to us.' In that context, the words 'dispose of him' could, I understood, mean only one thing. 'It was suggested that I find him a watery grave.' And the expression 'watery grave' confirmed my first impression. 'His code name was "Carbuncle" and I'm sure that he, too, was expecting to meet his end on the crossing. Perhaps it was his conviction that he was going to die, and his apparent acceptance of the fact, that prevented me from finding the right moment. He had toyed with the Japanese and with us, as all double agents do, but then again, he had told a lie to the Japanese that had helped us intercept and sink the Japanese heavy cruiser *Haguro* off Penang, in May 1945. He had, after all, been instrumental in our laying that trap. I don't know why I did it, why I disobeyed. I didn't really see what reason there was to get rid of him, and, besides, the Secret Service was full of idiots. If he was no longer of any use to us, he would be of still less use to the Japanese: if he fell into their hands, they would soon find a grave for him, either watery or dry, or would leave him out in the elements to rot and be eaten by the pigs. I had seen what they had done in the Andaman Islands: part of the indigenous population piled into barges and shelled from the garrison, as target practice, when they were already far out in deep water; decapitations, terrible rapes, breasts not lopped off with a machete or a sword but crushed by repeated blows, a parade of soldiers in full array obeying the orders of a Commander whose years of atrocities, during the long Japanese occupation, I had to investigate when the Islands were liberated. I had had enough . . . Nowadays you hear or read that violence is addictive, or that once you've inflicted violence or seen it, it loses its impact, that you get used to it. In my experience this is totally false, a fools' tale told to fools. You can stand a certain amount, and possibly more than you imagined you could, but ultimately, it's not so much that you grow tired of it, more that it exhausts and destroys you. And it keeps coming back and you can't forget it . . . When we reached Singapore, I disembarked with "Carbuncle" still handcuffed to me, wrist to wrist, which is incredibly uncomfortable. Have you ever tried it? I shot a sideways glance at him from my great height, because he was much shorter than me. He seemed genuinely surprised to have reached his destination and to be on dry land again. Then I took out the key, unlocked the handcuffs while he stared at me in amazement, and then I said "Fuck off!" He took to his heels and I watched him disappear into the crowd filling the port. Yes, I'd had enough . . . But it wasn't over yet . . .'

He fell silent, looking out at the placid river that I had come to know years before in the house of his brother Toby Rylands, as if he could still see his prisoner 'Carbuncle' vanishing into the crowds filling that distant port. I had seen that look in my father's eyes more than once, and in Wheeler's eyes too when he had slowly followed Mrs Berry and me to the foot of the stairs and I had pointed out to them the place at the top of the first flight, where, during a feverish night spent at his house and after sitting up alone consulting books, I had found the bloodstain; it was a wide-eyed look that gave him a contradictory expression, almost like that of a child who discovers or sees something for the first time, something that does not frighten or repel or attract him, but which produces in him a sense of shock, or else some flash of intuitive knowledge, or even a kind of enchantment.

Wheeler took another long drink of water, almost unconsciously; it was hardly surprising that he was thirsty, he had been talking for a long time and, towards the end, had drifted into that strangely introspective loquacity of his. Apart from just one moment, I had been afraid all the time that he would decide to stop, because of fatigue or a more prolonged attack of aphasia or because he suddenly regretted telling me so much. He had never before spoken in such detail about his former life, or indeed about anything. 'Why is he doing this now?' I wondered. 'It's not as if I had insisted or even cajoled or flattered him into it, nor have I been trying to draw him out. I must ask him before I leave, if there's time.' I found everything he was telling me fascinating, but if I allowed him to wander off to the South-east

499

Asia of the special missions he had undertaken, there was a risk he wouldn't come back or only when it was too late, when Mrs Berry was already calling us in to lunch, as a mother calls her children. Not that I thought Wheeler would keep quiet in her presence or that he would have many secrets from her, certainly not regarding Valerie's death, which is what I most wanted to know about just then, perhaps because I had recently seen my own wife and had felt her to be in danger; but one has to be careful with stories, sometimes they don't allow witnesses, not even silent ones, and if there are any witnesses, they stop. I could still hear Mrs Berry at the piano, again she was playing some rather cheerful music – this time, I thought, pieces by the Italian Clementi, another exile, who had also lived in London for a long time, something from his popular piano exercises *Gradus ad Parnassum* or perhaps a sonata; he was another musician sidelined by Mozart (never, it seems, a good colleague), who had dismissed him as a mere *mechanicus* or automaton and with that remark had ruined him, perhaps because Clementi had dared to take part in a musical duel with him in Vienna before the Emperor, two virtuosi pitted against each other.

'What happened to Rendl?' I decided to get Peter back on track, but I didn't dare redirect him immediately to Valerie, although whatever I did, I might still end up losing her.

'Oh, yes, I'm sorry. That's why I don't like telling stories any more, especially in my current state. As you say in Spanish, I often go clambering about the branches – *voy por las ramas* – and I'm not sure how interesting those branches are. Ideally, they should be as relevant as the roots and the trunk, don't you think?'

'Oh, they're fascinating, Peter. The "Carbuncle" branch, for example, which, obviously, I've never heard before. It's just that I'm curious to know what happened to Rendl.'

'No one has heard this story before, not you or anyone. Until today,' he replied, and it seemed to me from the way he said this that he wanted to place due emphasis on the importance of this fact. 'Not even Mrs Berry, not even Toby. Not even Tupra, who is always rummaging around in people's past lives. As I believe I told you once before, in theory, I'm not yet authorised to say what my "special missions" were between 1936 and 1946, and the same applies to some I carried out afterwards, and I've kept my word. Until today. Of course for me to say "not yet" about anything is rather ironic and even in bad taste, since permission to speak will arrive too late. There's another reason to keep quiet about the "Carbuncle" affair: my superiors never found out that I'd let him go. Not that anything very bad would have happened to me just because I'd disobeyed an order: we weren't like the Germans or the Russians, and I didn't put anyone's life at risk by doing so. However, I preferred to tell them that, as recommended, I had found him a watery grave during the crossing. After all, the fellow was as untraceable and as unfindable as if he were lying at the bottom of the Strait of Malacca with a ridiculous golf bag tied around his neck, a bag I had, in fact, forced him to carry throughout the voyage, and which I allowed someone to steal from me in that same port. (Oh, yes, there were some real idiots in the Secret Service, like the ones who lumbered me with the golf clubs.) Having played that trick on the Japanese, it was in his best interests to be presumed dead, and there wasn't the slightest danger of him going and presenting himself to some other British person, *ni en pintura*.' And he used the Spanish expression – meaning literally 'not even in the form of a painting', but here meaning something like 'no chance' or 'no way' – perhaps because there is no exact equivalent in English, at least nothing quite as graphic. He'd had recourse to my language earlier when he'd referred to the expression '*me voy por las ramas*' and had then elaborated on the metaphor in English; such linguistic mixtures were commonplace between us, as they had been between Cromer-Blake and me in my Oxford phase. 'In Rendl's case, well, it wasn't just a matter of everything having its time to be believed, we were unfortunate in that the accusation wasn't false and that he wasn't in the regular German army, the *Wehrmacht*, let's say, where he might have received nothing more than a reprimand, a period of detention or a demotion, or all three. Even if he had been a Party leader, his deception, with luck – and depending on what friends he had and what influence – might well have been simply brushed under the carpet.'

I noticed his use of the first person plural, '*we* were unfortunate'. 'It was said that the SS, on the other hand, demanded that its members should be able to prove purity of blood as far back as 1750, at least in theory and in principle. Himmler must have realised that this was an impossibility for most applicants and that the number of men in his unit would rapidly diminish once they started to suffer any war losses. And so from 1940 on, the SS depended in large measure on volunteers from countries considered "Germanic", this being especially true of the Waffen-SS, the combat arm, which filled up with Dutchmen, Flemings, Norwegians and Danes. And later on still, towards the end, they also admitted "non-Germanic" volunteers, Frenchmen, Italians, Walloons, Ukrainians, Belorussians, Lithuanians, Estonians, as well as Hungarians, Croats, Serbs, Slovenes and Albanians. There was even an Indian Legion and Muslim divisions, I recall a Skanderbeg and a Kama division (and there was a third one, too, whose name I can't now recall); so much for Aryan purity. And there was even a tiny British Free Corps, which really only served for propaganda purposes. But the initial severity of the 1920s and '30s gives you an idea of how unacceptable it would have been for a veteran officer to have a not particularly remote Jewish ancestor, a grandmother to be precise, and for him to have lied about it and paid for incriminating documents to be removed in order to conceal the truth and so "contaminate" the corps. While the War was on, we didn't know exactly what had happened to Rendl after we'd unmasked him, although we did know that it must have worked, because his name disappeared from the lists of officers that periodically fell into the hands of MI6 or the PWE. Jefferys, or Delmer, or the East Germans, used to pass the accusations on to the Nazi authorities through our infiltrators, and the Nazis, I assume, then carried out their own investigations. It was relatively easy to pass such information on, especially in the occupied countries, where we could count on local collaborators. It wasn't quite so easy afterwards to find out what the results had been, to know which of our false reports had "taken" and what had been the fate of those affected, which forgeries had been accepted as authentic and which not, or only by checking which counterfeit "Jew" or "half-Jew" remained in his post, and was not removed or demoted or anything. At least we knew that Rendl, without having been declared or presumed dead, in action or in the rearguard, had ceased to be a Major or a Captain, or whatever he was at the time. He no longer appeared on the list.'

'And did that please Valerie? I mean, did it satisfy her?' I asked, spotting an opportunity to remind him of the person I was most interested in. This was pure naïveté on my part, however, because she was also the person Wheeler was most interested in and he hadn't forgotten her for a moment. He never, in my presence, entirely lost the thread.

He raised one arm to his forehead – or it may have been his wrist to his temple – as if he were in pain or checking to see if he had a fever, or perhaps it was a gesture of horror. Whatever its intention, it was the same gesture he had made when he finally opened his eyes and uncovered his ears after the capricious passes of the helicopter that made a sound like a giant rattle or like an old Sikorsky H-5, 'the noise alone used to be enough to provoke panic', on that other now distant Sunday in his garden by the river, as we sat on chairs with canvas covers the colour of pale gabardine, on those chairs disguised as mammoths or tethered ghosts, when I wasn't yet working for the group and he recruited me and suggested that I join and become part of it. He took a while to respond, and I feared that he might have got stuck on some word again. However, it wasn't that, but rather – I thought a little later – because he preferred not to let me see all of his face while he was telling me what he had not yet told me, or that he needed to keep his arm or wrist near his eyes, so as to be able to cover them at once, just as I had been tempted to do several times – and as I had done, I seemed to remember, on more than one occasion – when Tupra was showing me those videos in his house. As if he wanted to be ready to hide or to put his head under his wing.

'Yes, it did satisfy her,' he said. 'I suppose you could say that. It had been her idea, and it was her first personal, individual, distinctive contribution to the development of the War or to the search for victory. She was congratulated by Jefferys on one of his subsequent visits. As I said, he would come for a week, leave a trail of ideas and then vanish, and not reappear again for a month or more. I've never heard him mentioned since or seen his name in any book, which is why I'm sure it was an alias. Sefton Delmer doesn't mention him, so who knows who he really was. But it also left her feeling unsatisfied, uneasy. She wondered what had happened to Ilse, Rendl's wife, what Ilse's situation would have been after her husband's downfall. He was our enemy and not just any enemy, not some poor recruit, but a Nazi volunteer, determined to join the SS. More than that, he was a complete imbecile; but he was also the brother-in-law of her old friend, and the husband of the older sister who had always been so kind and patient with her. The War, though, allowed little time for doubts or regrets. For that reason, some people remember times of war as the most vital of their entire existence, the most euphoric, and in a way they even miss them afterwards. War is the most terrible thing, but when you live through a war, you live with extraordinary intensity; the good thing about them is that they stop people worrying about silly things or getting depressed or pestering those around them. There's no time for any of that, you move ceaselessly from one thing to another, from anxiety to fear, from terror to an explosion of joy, and every day is the last day, no, more than that, the only day. You walk, you *exist*, shoulder to shoulder, everyone is busy trying to survive, to defeat the beast, to save themselves and to save others, and as long as panic doesn't spread, there's great camaraderie. Panic didn't spread here. You'll have heard your father and others talk about this, and your War was the same.'

'Yes, I have heard people talk about it, not so much my father, but mainly people who were still children at the time, because my father, although very young, was already an adult when the War began. I imagine, though, that you can only miss such times when your side wins, don't you think, Peter? It can't be the same for my father as it was for you.'

'Yes, you're right. I can't conceive what it would have been like if we'd lost, but if we had, I would probably only remember

504

the horror, or have done everything I could to forget it, and perhaps, with great effort, would have succeeded. It's hard to imagine. I don't know, I can't know.' And Wheeler moved his arm away from his forehead and instead rested his cheek on his hand and sat pondering, as if the idea had never occurred to him.

'And what happened? What else?' That was what Tupra always used to say to me during our sessions together: 'What else, tell me more.' He would not do so again nor would there be any more sessions, that much was sure.

'The worst came after the end of the War, when the whole country raised its head to look around, and some, not many, started thinking about what had happened, what they had seen and how they had lived, and what they had been obliged to do. A few months after the surrender, Valerie received a letter from her friend Maria. They hadn't had any contact since 1939, since before war broke out. Maria didn't even know that Valerie was married and that her surname was now Wheeler. Val and I met in 1940 and got married in 1941, shortly before I turned twenty-eight and when she was twenty-one. The truth is that neither of them knew if the other was still alive. Maria sent the letter to Val's parents' address, and her mother forwarded it to Oxford, where we had moved after I'd been elected Fellow of The Queen's College in 1946. Val's father had died in one of the air raids on London. Valerie was overjoyed at first, but that feeling only lasted as long as it took her to open the envelope. That letter was our death sentence. Or rather, hers.' And when Peter added these words, some words Tupra had said came back to me, like a premonition, like an echo: 'While it isn't something any of us would wish for, we would nonetheless always prefer it to be the person beside us who dies, whether on a mission or in battle, in an air squadron or under bombardment or in the trenches when there were trenches, in a mugging or a raid on a shop or when a group of tourists is kidnapped, in an earthquake, an explosion, a terrorist attack, in a fire, it doesn't matter: even if it's our colleague, brother, father or even our child, however young. Or even the person we most love, yes, even them, anyone but us.' 'I wasn't there when she received and read it, but she showed it to me afterwards, or, rather, translated it for me: although Maria spoke English, Val's German was better, and that was the language in which they wrote to each other. It was a long letter, but not that long, I mean not enough for Maria to be able to explain all that had happened to her during the War years; she summarised the most important facts. She, too, had married and her name was now Hafenrichter; however, her husband had died at the Russian front, leaving her a widow. She was managing to scrape a living in the international zone of Vienna (as you know, Vienna, like Berlin, was divided into four occupation zones: American, British, Russian and French, and the centre was international, that is, it was controlled and patrolled by the four powers simultaneously). She spoke about her current hardships, the same dire situation as in German towns and cities, although Vienna had suffered less devastation, and she asked for help, although without specifying what form that help might take, money, medicine, clothes, provisions . . . Her parents, Mr and Mrs Mauthner, had died, as had one of the four sisters, the third, and it was presumed that the oldest, Ilse, was also dead, for she had vanished along with her two small daughters. The only surviving Rendl was the boy, whom she had taken in and whom she now wished to send to England, and she was asking Valerie's help in that regard too, if possible: the child had had a terrible time, and in Austria he faced a bleak, poverty-stricken future, and she could barely manage to support herself. But the worst thing was . . .' Wheeler's voice faltered and he hesitated for a moment, then recovered. 'The worst thing was that she explained to Val what had happened: "I don't know how," she said, and those were the words that tormented Valerie from the moment she read them until her death, the words that killed her: "I don't know how," she said, "but the SS had somehow found out that Rendl had a Jewish grandmother and had bribed officials to have her name removed from the records. The records in question, though, hadn't been destroyed, only moved elsewhere and replaced with false documents: the originals turned up and the accusation was found to be true. The SS were very strict on the matter of racial ancestry, Maria told Valerie (imagining that there would be no reason why Valerie would know about that), and it seems that the case reached the ears of Himmler himself, who was enraged by such deceit and determined to make an example of Rendl, mostly in order to wring confessions from any other SS officers who were in the same or a similar situation, promising them that if they did confess, he would treat them more leniently, or at least less severely, than their impostor colleague. The discovery, along with the rumours that followed Heydrich's death, that even he had been "half-Jewish"' – 'Heydrich,' I thought, 'who died slowly and in great pain, from those bullets impregnated with poison' – 'led him to believe, as I found out later, that his purer-than-pure body of men had, in fact, been transformed, since the enactment of the Nuremberg Laws, into a refuge for *Mischlinge* and even for "half-Jews", reasoning, as was proper to a mind as sick as his, that there could be no better disguise for the prey than to camouflage themselves as hunters. Well, perhaps his mind wasn't so very sick when you think of Delmer or, even more so, of Jefferys, who were both capable of dreaming up the most complicated plans and machinations. Or when you think of mine, perhaps, for we all had war minds, there are no healthy minds in wartime and some never recover. But returning to the letter: Maria had managed to learn what Rendl's exemplary punishment had been: to be sent to a concentration camp as a prisoner, even though he was only a "quarter-Jewish"; and not just that, but one day, the Gestapo turned up at his house in Munich, where he and his family were living at the time, and took the girls away. They didn't take the boy because he wasn't there when this happened, he was staying in Melk with his grandparents, and once the Gestapo had got over their initial rage, they didn't bother overmuch to seek him out. When Ilse, horrified, asked why they were doing this, all they would say was that the girls were Jewish, but that they had no proof against her; if she wanted to go with the girls, that was her business. Properly speaking, those girls were only one-eighth Jewish and would normally have been considered to be "German". But that was the reprisal, the punishment: making "full Jews" of the descendants of the man who had deceived and tricked them. After all, as Göring said, or Goebbels, or perhaps it was Himmler himself: "I decide who's Jewish." None of this became public, of course, it would have made a terrible impression; it was known only to the officers of the SS, as a warning to them to tread carefully, and that is why the PWE heard almost nothing about it. The SS were very keen on secrecy and childish rituals. According to neighbours who witnessed the scene, Ilse got into the car that was about to carry her girls away and no more was heard of any of them. It was supposed that, once in a concentration camp, all trace of them would have been lost and their "origin", which was the reason they were there, quite forgotten, and they would have become, in effect, Jews or, at best, "dissidents"; no, there was no "best" about it: their fate would have been the same. Maria didn't want to deceive herself with fantasies, she had no hope that they were alive. She assumed they were dead, with no room for speculation or doubt, especially once information was published about the gas chambers and the mass exterminations. So that was what the letter said, Jacobo. Maria ended by saying that she didn't know if Valerie was still alive or if she would ever read those lines, but she begged her, if she *was* alive, to send her news and help as well, especially for Ilse's son, young Rendl. He would have been about eleven or twelve at the time.' Wheeler paused, took a breath and added: 'If only those lines had never reached her eyes. If only no one had ever told her. I wouldn't have seen her kill herself. I wouldn't have been left alone and sad.'

Wheeler remained silent and thoughtful and again raised the back of his wrist to his brow, as if to wipe away some sudden beads of sweat or as if he were again taking his temperature. 'Give me your hand and let us walk,' I quoted to myself. 'Through the fields of this land of mine, edged with dusty olive groves, I walk alone, sad, tired, pensive and old.' I had known this poem since I was a child, they were the words addressed by Antonio Machado to his already dead child wife, Leonor, who died of tuberculosis at the age of eighteen. Valerie hadn't died, she had killed herself when she was only slightly older, looking at her own hourglass and holding it in her hand. But she, too, had left Peter alone, sad, tired, pensive and old. Regardless of all the things he went on to do afterwards.

I should have expected this revelation after what Wheeler had been telling me, but I was so taken aback that, for a moment, I didn't know what to say. And when he did not immediately go on, I gave voice to a thought that slipped unavoidably into my mind, even at the risk of diverting his thoughts elsewhere and missing the end of the story:

'That's what Toby said had happened to him. I told you, don't you remember?' And I recalled, too, the look of irritated surprise on Wheeler's face when he had heard the story. 'Is that what he said: "I watched the suicide . . ."' he had repeated, taken aback, without completing the sentence. 'That he had watched the suicide of the person he loved.'

Wheeler responded at once, but this time he was more sympathetic than annoyed:

'Yes. It disappointed and angered me a little when you told me that. After all, how were you to know? Nothing like that ever happened to him, but he enjoyed playing the man of mystery and hinting at a more turbulent or more tragic past than he actually had; not that his past didn't have its moments, but that's true of almost anyone who lives through a long war. He must have stolen my story when he told you that, to make his own more interesting. That's the trouble with telling anything – most people forget how or from whom they found out what they know, and there are people who even believe they lived or gave birth to it, whatever it is, a story, an idea, an opinion, an anecdote, a joke, an aphorism, a history, a style, sometimes even a whole text, which they proudly appropriate – or perhaps they know they're stealing, but push the thought to the back of their mind and thus hide it away. It's very much a phenomenon of the times we live in, which has no respect for priorities. Perhaps I shouldn't have got angry with poor Toby like that, retrospectively.' Wheeler stopped, took a couple of sips of sherry and then murmured almost reluctantly, almost with distaste: 'Fortunately for him, he didn't ever have to see that. It's not a scene that is easy to bear, I can assure you. It's best to avoid tragedies. Nothing can ever make up for them. Certainly not talking about them.'

'What happened?' And out of politeness I added as I had on another occasion, although this time I had to force myself to do what I had been taught as a child, never to put the screws on anyone. 'If you don't want to tell me, Peter, don't.'

I was afraid that, at any moment, Mrs Berry might close the piano and come downstairs and, so to speak, break the spell, although we could still hear her music; she seemed to have moved on to Scarlatti; she always played cheerful pieces, which that afternoon just happened to be by people who had changed countries, Scarlatti having spent half his life in Spain, although no one knows how or where he died or even if he had a grave, just like Boccherini: they probably both died in Madrid and both now lie in unmarked graves. A country indifferent to merit and to services rendered. A country indifferent to everything, especially to anything that no longer exists, or to matter in the past.

'It's not pleasant to remember, Jacobo, nor to hear either. But I think, nevertheless, that I can tell you. I suppose there comes a point when one has to tell things, after a lot of time has passed, so that it doesn't seem as if they simply never happened or were just a bad dream,' Peter answered. '"I don't know how," Maria had said in her letter, and Valerie, from the moment she read those words, kept repeating, even in German sometimes as if she were talking to Maria: "I know how, oh, I know how, I know very well, in fact, I was the one who told the SS." And she repeated over and over: "The children. How could I have forgotten about Ilse and the children? I should have thought of them, why didn't I? I didn't take them into account at all." She spent the last days of her life in torment, in hell, and at no point did she consider answering her friend's letter. "I'd rather she believed me dead," she said. "I couldn't possibly tell her what happened." "And what if you didn't tell her, but just helped her," I said, trying to convince her: "Perhaps we can do something for the boy, get him some kind of permit to enter the country and a scholarship, I don't know, I could talk to people about it and give him a hand financially." I've always had family money. My maternal grandfather, Thomas Wheeler, sold the newspaper companies he owned in New Zealand and Australia for a large profit, and Toby and I, when we were still very young, each received a large legacy when he died. I even suggested adopting young Rendl, even though I hated the idea myself. But Val was paralysed with horror and grief, she didn't want to hear any of those ideas, and she didn't respond. She lay awake at night, and even if, for a moment, she did drop off out of sheer exhaustion, she would soon start awake, crying and drenched in sweat, and would say to me in distraught tones: "Those girls. If I had just found out what happened on my own, I might have had some right, possibly, although I don't believe so. But I found out through Maria, and I betrayed her without a thought; how could I have done that, why didn't I realise? And those girls, who died because of me in a concentration camp, they wouldn't have understood anything, and their mother who got into the car with them, what else could the poor woman do, oh, dear God . . .'"

Wheeler stopped for a moment and bit his forefinger, thoughtful, tense. ('Let sorrow haunt thy bed,' I quoted to myself.) Then he said: 'Treachery just wasn't in her nature, still less betrayal. More than that, those were the very last things she would have been capable of in normal circumstances. She was a fine person, someone you could trust absolutely. She was the antithesis of bad faith, of deceit; she was, how can I put it, a clean person. But war turns everything upside down or creates irreconcilable loyalties. It wasn't in her nature either to spare any effort in helping her country when its very survival was at stake. She was still smarting because she had lacked the courage to infiltrate enemy territory, and so it would have been impossible for her to hold back that information about Hartmut Rendl once she was convinced that revealing it was important and could save English lives. Now, though, her perspective had changed, as always happens in peacetime, except for those of us who know that war is always on the prowl, always just around the corner, even though no one else believes it, and that what seems to us reprehensible, horrific and extreme in peacetime could happen again tomorrow with the consent of the entire nation. "War crimes" is the term they apply nowadays to almost anything, as if war did not consist precisely in the commission of crimes, which have, for the most part, received prior absolution. Now, though, Val couldn't see in what way the information she had given, the idea she had put forward, could possibly have contributed to victory. Or, rather, she was sure that if she had kept quiet the result would have been the same. And she was probably right in thinking that, as, with very few exceptions, would all the other Britons who had added their grain of sand. That's another thing that happens in time of war, Jacobo. You do everything that's necessary, and that includes the unnecessary. But who is capable of distinguishing one from the other? When it comes to destroying the enemy, or even merely vanquishing him, it's impossible to gauge what really is doing harm and what is merely a matter of shooting his horse from under him, or, as you say, lancing dead Moors or making firewood from a fallen tree.' And he said these last two expressions in my language: '*alancear moros muertos*' and '*hacer leña del árbol caído*'. 'I tried every means I could to make her see this: "Valerie," I would say, "it was wartime and in a war, soldiers sometimes even kill their comrades, you've heard of friendly fire, haven't you? Or those in command sacrifice their own troops, send them to be slaughtered, and that doesn't always serve any useful purpose either: think of Gallipoli, Chunuk Bair, Suvla, and you can be quite sure that in years to come we'll find out about similar and equally bloody cases in this recently won War of ours. In every war innocent people are killed, there are mistakes and frivolous, foolish acts, there are imbecilic or cynical politicians and military leaders. In every war there is waste. Do you imagine that I haven't committed repugnant acts, things which, if I think about them now or in the future, could perhaps have been avoided? I committed them in Kingston, and even more in Accra and in Colombo. They're repugnant to me now and will seem more so as time passes, the farther off they get, but they weren't then. And that's what you mustn't do, view these things out of context and coldly. You can't look back after a war, don't you see? Not if you want to go on living."'

Wheeler stopped again, this time, more than anything, in order to catch his breath. He clearly needed to. He had a slightly faraway gaze, which was directed at the stairs, although without actually seeing them. He seemed to me simultaneously very tired and very agitated, as if he had relived the words he had spoken to Valerie rather too intensely, words spoken perhaps in their haunted bed, perhaps when she woke him with her crying and with her nightmares that corresponded all too closely to reality, and those are the ones no one can bear, when reality only echoes the dream. 'Let us be lead within thy bosom, may you feel the pinprick in your chest. Despair and die.' I waited and waited and waited. Finally, I said:

'I assume it was no use.'

'No, it wasn't, and the worst thing is that, by then, I knew nothing would be of any use, that her life had been twisted out of shape for ever and could never be made straight again. I was already part of the group, which was created too late to save her life. Not that my gift, my capacity for interpretation was any less before I joined, of course, but you adapt your vision to the task in hand and you hone that vision; you grow used to deciphering and looking deeper into what tomorrow will bring. You must have noticed the same thing, that increase in perspicacity, since you've been with Tupra, or am I wrong?'

'No, you're right. I am more alert now. And I tend to interpret everything, even when I'm not working and no one wants me to report on what I've seen.' And I took the opportunity to ask him something that I couldn't quite understand, even at the risk of losing precious time and of Mrs Berry interrupting us: 'If I remember correctly, Peter, the first time you talked to me about the group, you told me that Valerie was already dead when the idea was first mooted by Menzies or Vivian or whoever. I don't understand, given that the group was formed during the War.'

Wheeler looked bemused, perplexed. He sat thinking for a few moments and then his face lit up like someone who has found the solution to a minor enigma (right to the end, he enjoyed linguistic curiosities) and he said in Spanish:

'Ah, I see. It's a problem of ambiguity, or a misunderstanding on your part, Jacobo. If I said it as you said it now, "she was already dead", that would translate in your language as "*estaba ya muerta*", but in the figurative sense, I meant that she was already doomed, not that she had literally died.' And he moved back into English again, because by then, it was clear that speaking a foreign language tired him more. 'What I probably meant was that by then it was too late, that she had already done the thing that would later lead her to kill herself, that her fate was sealed. And that was the thing, you see; if the group had been formed before, someone might have decided, doubtless I myself with my watchful, trained, alert eye, that just as Valerie wouldn't have got very far as a spy, as she herself knew, neither was she equipped for black propaganda, which was too dirty for her scruples and for her dislike of deceit. Still less was she equipped to put at risk or sacrifice the lives of innocent people, however German they might be. As you know, step by step, you start doing things for which you have no stomach or aren't suited, and war stretches people a lot, or they themselves, without noticing, stretch themselves beyond their capabilities and only snap when it's all over. If someone had spotted her limitations in time, they would perhaps have withdrawn her from Milton Bryan. She would have been sent back to the Foreign Office maybe, or been restricted to working on white propaganda.' Wheeler ran his hand over his forehead, almost squeezing it this time. 'Sometimes I tell myself that I should have known anyway. But it's easy to be wise after the event or *a toro pasado* as you say – once the bull has passed – when you know all the facts. I wasn't altogether sure what kind of work Valerie was doing in the PWE, and we were thousands of miles apart most of the time. And she never even mentioned the term "black propaganda", so she may well have been engaged in it without knowing of its existence, or, rather, without even knowing the concept. She may also have been following orders and divulging nothing, not even to me. I don't know. If Delmer was diabolical, then Jefferys was Lucifer in person.' He paused very briefly, then added: 'I'll never know who he was, who was hiding behind that name. I have very little time left, Jacobo. Almost none.'

The music stopped, and after a few seconds, I heard Mrs Berry coming down the stairs. 'That's it, it's over,' I thought. 'I'll never find out how Valerie killed herself and why Peter saw her do it, even though, in principle, I have more time than him, and not almost none. And why, if he saw her kill herself, he couldn't have stopped her.' And I added to myself: 'But I can't complain. I've found out a lot today, and that isn't even why I came.' However, Mrs Berry didn't come into the living room or call us in to lunch, but went straight to the kitchen, where I could hear her bustling about. Perhaps we would still have time if she was putting the finishing touches to lunch and if I hurried.

'How did Valerie kill herself, Peter?' I asked, this time with no show of tact. 'And how come you saw her do it?'

Wheeler shifted in his chair, trying to find a more comfortable position, and then he hooked one thumb under his armpit as if it were a tiny riding crop and he seemed to rest the whole weight of his chest on that thumb, at least that was my impression. It was as if he needed to lean on something, even something symbolic: a poor thumb, although he did have long fingers.

'We were living then in a house rather like this, but much smaller,' he said, 'with two or three floors, depending on how you looked at it, because the top floor was very small indeed, with only a *chambre de bonne* I suppose you'd call it, which we used now and then when we had visitors. It was and still is in Plantation Road, near where you lived. It cost a lot more than my salary could stretch to then, of course, but the money I had inherited allowed me such privileges, as it always has. Anyway, after four agitated nights during which she barely slept' – 'Yes,' I repeated to myself, 'sorrow did indeed haunt thy bed' – 'Valerie persuaded me to go and sleep in the little room on the top floor, so that I could get some rest until she calmed down; she hoped it wouldn't last very much longer, that vicious circle of nightmares and insomnia, of loathing herself when awake and being filled with panic whenever she fell asleep, of being unable to tolerate herself either awake or asleep. It worried me to leave her unaccompanied during those night hours, because they were doubtless the worst and the most difficult to get through, but I thought, too, that perhaps she needed to spend them alone in order to begin to recover, that it might be good for her not to have me by her side to talk to her and try to console her and ask her questions, to reason and argue with her, because this had served no useful purpose in the four days and nights she had spent awake, none at all. I don't know, when a situation doesn't change, you think all kinds of things. I remember feeling very uneasy as I got into bed, leaving the door open so that I could hear her if she called me, so that I could go to her at once – we were only separated by one floor, two brief flights of stairs. But such was my accumulated exhaustion that I soon fell asleep. Sleep must have proved utterly irresistible because I didn't even turn out the bedside light or close the little book I was reading and which lay on the counterpane. I only woke at dawn and I must have been lying very still because it was only then, and not before, that the book fell to the floor, with hardly any noise: it was *Little Gidding*, the last of the *Four Quartets*, the paperback edition published by Faber. I remember that clearly; it had only recently come out and I hadn't been able to read it during the War; books like that didn't reach Ceylon or the Gold Coast.' And he murmured what were doubtless lines or parts of lines: '"Ash on an old man's sleeve . . . This is the death of air . . . the constitution of silence . . . What we call the beginning is often the end . . ." etc.' Then he went on: 'So it wasn't the book falling that woke me. I don't know what it was. It took me a few seconds to realise that I was in the *chambre de bonne* alone and to remember why. I picked up the book and placed it on the bedside table, glanced at the clock – it was almost four – and automatically turned out the light, although not with the intention of going straight back to sleep, because that sense of unease had returned. I preferred or decided to look in at our room first, to see, without going in, if Valerie was sleeping or not, and, if she wasn't, to ask if she needed anything; or if she perhaps wanted me by her side. I put on my dressing gown and went very quietly down the stairs, so as not to wake her if she was asleep, and then I saw her sitting where she shouldn't have been sitting at all, at the top of the first flight of stairs, with her back to me.' Wheeler pointed upwards to his left, towards the top of the first flight of stairs in his current house beside the River Cherwell and not in Plantation Road. 'Just there, where you say you saw a drop of blood. It's odd, isn't it? She was still fully clothed, not in her nightdress or her dressing gown, as if she hadn't been to bed at all or was getting ready to go out, and that was what surprised me most of all, in the very brief instant during which I could feel surprise. But I didn't feel alarmed, the fact is that never, never, not during one of those fleeting moments or beforehand, did I ever suspect, did it even occur to me to fear that she was going to do what she did, not once. And there I failed. My gift or my faculty or my ability, whatever you want to call it, the gift that Tupra and you and that young half-Spanish woman have, the gift that Toby had and I have had regarding matters that were of no importance to me, failed me completely on that occasion. How could I not have guessed, how could I not have seen it, how is it that I had not the slightest glimmer? I've been asking myself that since 1946. How could I have been so stupidly optimistic, so trusting, so unaware, how is it that I saw no warning signs? That's a long time, isn't it? When it comes to the things that touch you most deeply, you never want to hear the warnings, but they're always there. In everything. One is never willing to think the worst.' Now Wheeler covered his eyes with one hand, placed it like a pulled-down visor, perhaps as I had done at some point while I was watching and not watching Tupra's horrific videos on that night when he was Reresby. 'I could understand her concern, her bad conscience, even her horror,' Wheeler continued to speak with his eyes covered, 'but I thought that sooner or later she would get over it or it would abate, just as almost everyone else got over what they had seen or done in the War, what they had lost or suffered. Up to a point, of course, enough to be able to live. It's one of the things that peacetime brings to people who are no longer at war, although it falls to some of us to continue and to watch. It brings forgetting, at least a superficial form of forgetting, or the sense that it was all a dream. Even if that dream is repeated every night and lies in wait during the day: just a bad dream. A terrible dream. But we had, after all, won the war. "Valerie," I said, and that was all I had time to say. She had her hair caught up. She didn't turn round, but I saw the back of her neck and her shoulders shudder and saw her fall violently backwards, and at the same time I heard the explosion. And only then, in the midst of my despair and my incredulity, I realised that she had been sitting there, for who knows how long, with the hunting rifle in her hands, pointing at her heart. Perhaps she had been hesitating or waiting until she felt brave enough, she who wasn't brave at all. I was probably the signal, my presence, my voice, hearing her own name.' – 'Strange to leave one's own first name behind. Strange to no longer desire one's desires. Strange to see meanings that clung together once, floating away in every direction. And being dead is hard work . . .' – 'She probably thought I would snatch the weapon from her and that there would be no more time later, I don't know.' – 'And indeed there won't be time to wonder, "Do I dare?" and "Do I dare?" Do I dare disturb the universe? Time to turn back and descend the stair . . . And in short, I am afraid . . .' And so it would be best not to wait. – 'She lay there.' And Wheeler again pointed up to the top of the first flight of stairs of his current house, where I had found the drop of blood and cleaned it up with such diligence and difficulty. 'It was very hard to get rid of that blood. It poured out, flowed out, even though I immediately stanched the wound with towels. I knew she was already dead, but nevertheless I covered the wound. She had got dressed and put on her make-up, she had put her hair up and put on lipstick to say goodbye to me, it was a matter of politeness, the age we lived in, her now very antiquated politeness, she never received a guest or went out into the street without her make-up . . . And even when there was no trace of blood, I could still see it.' – 'The last thing to go would be the rim,' I thought; 'although there would have been several, because there must have been more than one stain, and perhaps it made a trail.' – 'And then I moved house, I couldn't stay there.'

'But you didn't come to this house, did you, Peter?' I asked.

'No, I went to my rooms in college and lived there for three years, I preferred to have people around me. But you see, the one night, the one and only night, that I failed to watch over her sleep or non-sleep, Valerie went and killed herself. She couldn't live with what she had done. And I didn't foresee it. It never crossed my mind, not even when she sent me upstairs to the *chambre de bonne*. It was a perfectly reasonable excuse, and I wasn't prepared: it was the first time she had ever deceived me. You can't imagine the times I've wondered if I would have got there in time had I only been quicker to realise where she was when I woke up' – 'Don't linger or delay,' I thought – 'if I hadn't picked up the book or turned out the light or put on my dressing gown or if I'd gone down those two flights of stairs more quickly or gone down them just as quietly but without opening my mouth, without saying her name, without letting her know I was there. All nonsense of course. But you think those things over and over.' – 'Bloody and guilty, guiltily awake,' I remembered. – 'Some time afterwards, I wrote to Maria Mauthner and introduced myself, because she knew nothing about me. I told her that Valerie had died, but not how or why. The War, I said, and that was enough. I helped her nephew come to England, but I couldn't bring myself to have anything to do with him, it would have been like looking at Valerie's rifle. And I've helped his son, too, the Rendel that you know: apparently he's pretty good, but not as gifted as Tupra or you, he lacks vision. At least he has a good job, though. My vision, I can assure you, has improved greatly since then. I promised myself that such a thing would never happen to anyone again simply because I couldn't or didn't dare to see. Not that anyone was ever as important to me again, of course: most of the people I observed and interpreted subsequently, on whom I reported, of whom I said whether or not they might be useful and for what, haven't mattered to me one jot in comparison. But now at least I can say to you, with no fear that I might be wrong, that you *can* live with what has happened to you, with what you came here to talk to me about, because, unlike her, you find it hard to believe that you were responsible.' – 'Yes,' I thought, 'I will always be able to say to myself tomorrow: "Oh, I didn't intend to do it, I knew nothing about it, it happened against my will, in the tortuous smokescreens of fever and shadow and dreams, it was part of my theoretical, parenthetical life, of my vague parallel existence that doesn't really count, it only half-happened and without my full consent, in short, as it said in the report I found among those old files and which was headed '*Deza, Jacques*', I don't see myself or know myself, I don't delve into or investigate myself, I don't pay much attention to myself and I've given up trying to understand myself. And besides, that was in another country." And then the judge would say: "Overruled, case dismissed."' – 'And anyway, you're made of very different stuff and you belong to a different age, Jacobo, a much more frivolous age. No, don't worry, you're not like Valerie. In fact, no one ever has been, during all these years without her. Or only occasionally, in my dreams.' – 'Give me your hand and let us walk. Through the fields of this land of mine . . .' – Wheeler removed his hand from his eyes and looked at me with surprise, or fright, as if he had just emerged from a long dream. Or perhaps it was more that he opened his eyes very wide, as if seeing the world for the first time, with a gaze as inscrutable as that of a newborn child, born only weeks or days before, and who, I imagine, observes this new place into which he has been hurled and tries perhaps to decipher our customs and to work out which of those customs will be his. He looked very tired and very pale, and I suddenly feared for his health. I felt like putting my hand on his shoulder, as I had with my father a few days earlier. He noticed the olives, picked up two and ate them both. Then he drank a little more sherry, and the colour returned to his cheeks, maybe he had suffered a brief drop in blood pressure. When he spoke again and I heard a different tone in his voice, I felt completely reassured, realising that the evocation, the story, was at an end: 'Go and ask Mrs Berry if it's time for lunch yet,' he said. 'I don't know why she hasn't called us, she stopped playing a while ago now.'

I still live alone, not in another country, but back in Madrid. Or perhaps I live half-alone, if one can say such a thing. I think I've been back now for almost as much time as I spent in London, during my second English sojourn, which had been more be-wildering than the first but less transforming, because I was of an age when it's harder to change, when almost all you can do is ascertain and confirm just what it is you carry in your veins. Now I am a little older. Both my father and Sir Peter Wheeler have died, the former only a week after that last Sunday in Oxford, not so much in exile from the infinite as from the past. It was his death, in fact, that precipitated my return to my home city, to be with his grandchildren, my brothers and my sister, and to attend the funeral. There was a space for him in my mother's grave. No one else will fit in there now. It was my sister who told me, she phoned me in London and said: 'Papa has died. His heart stopped half an hour ago. We knew his heart was weak, but it was still very unexpected. I was talking to him only yesterday. He asked after you, as usual, although he was convinced that you were in Oxford, teaching. You'll come, won't you?' I said that I would, that I'd come immediately. And so I went, I consoled and was consoled, I only saw Luisa at the funeral and there she embraced me in order to console me too and then I returned to London, to sort out that ingenuously furnished apartment and leave every-thing in order before my definitive departure, which it would now be best to hasten; a great many things required my attention in Madrid: house, furniture, books, a few paintings – that copy of the 'Annunciation' – my own bereft children, a modest or

521

possibly not so modest inheritance; and the task of remembering. Both alone and in the company of the others.

There were no matters pending with Tupra, everything had been pretty much resolved and, indeed, settled the day after the Sunday I spent with Wheeler, in Tupra's office in the building with no name (and which, I assume, remains nameless). As predicted by Beryl or by the person who refused to tell me if she was Beryl or not, Tupra, having returned from his trip or weekend absence, was already in his office when I arrived on Monday. Our conversation was very brief, partly because it turned out to be a repetition, I mean that we'd had that identical conversation before, in the distant days when I still called him Mr Tupra. I went straight to his door as soon as I arrived, saying a quick good morning to Rendel and young Pérez Nuix as I passed; I didn't see Mulryan, perhaps he was with Tupra. I knocked.

'Yes, who is it?' asked Tupra from inside.

And I replied absurdly:

'It's me,' omitting to give him my name, as if I were one of those people who forget that 'me' is never anyone, who are quite sure of occupying a great deal or a fair part of the thoughts of the person they're looking for, who have no doubt that they will be recognised with no need to say more – who else would it be – from the first word and the first moment. I suppose I confused my point of view with his, for we sometimes erroneously believe our own sense of urgency to be universal: I had spent many hours impatient to see him, to demand an explanation and even to confront him. But Tupra wouldn't be the least impatient, I was probably just another matter or another person to deal with, a subordinate returning to work after two weeks' leave in his country of origin, I think he often forgot that I wasn't yet English. When I didn't receive an immediate response, and suddenly aware of my own naïveté or presumption, I added: 'It's me, Bertram. It's Jack.' I accepted calling myself by a name that wasn't mine right until the end; it was the least important of the compromises I made while I was earning my living listening and noticing and interpreting and telling. But at least I didn't call him Bertie on that occasion.

'Come in, Jack,' he said.

And so I opened the door and peered in. He was sitting behind his desk, making notes or writing something on some papers. He didn't actually look up when I went in.

'Bertram,' I said, but he interrupted me.

'One moment, Jack, let me finish this first.' I waited for a minute or perhaps two or three, enough, in any case, to foresee that what did happen would happen. I sat down in an armchair opposite him, took out a cigarette and then lit it. He automatically picked up his Rameses II cigarettes, which were in their lavish red pack on the desk. In theory, smoking was forbidden in any of the offices, but I couldn't imagine anyone stopping Tupra inhaling and exhaling smoke, nor complaining about it. There had to be some advantage in the fact that neither the building nor our group had a name, and that we barely existed at all, more or less like the black propaganda group run by the PWE and Delmer and Jefferys during the War. When he finished his note-making, he took out and lit one of those exquisite cigarettes. 'So, Jack, how did it go?' There was nothing unusual in the way he said this, it wasn't even a question, more as if he were taking a routine interest in a simple little errand he had sent me on the day before. 'They told me at home that you phoned on Saturday about an urgent matter. Problems with your problem in Madrid?'

But I didn't answer his question, I got straight down to my own business – without delay:

'What happened to Dearlove and that Russian boy? What have you done?' I said. 'You really dropped me in it, I mean, it was me who gave you the idea, *joder.*' That '*joder*' – that 'damn it' – came out in Spanish because it was what my anger required me to say, even if I was speaking in English.

He sat looking at me for a few seconds with his blue or grey eyes – they were grey in that light – through his long eyelashes, dense enough to be the envy of any woman and to be considered highly suspect by any man, with those pale eyes that had a mocking quality, even if this was not their intention, eyes that were, therefore, expressive even when – as then – no expression was required, warm or should I say appreciative eyes that were never indifferent to what was there before them. And he responded in the same tone of voice, identical, with which he had said: 'Yes, I have,' when I had asked him in that same office, on another morning many months before, if he had heard about the failed *coup d'état* in Venezuela, and it had occurred to me that perhaps it had fallen through because we hadn't seen – because I hadn't sensed – sufficient determination on the part of General or Corporal Bonanza, who was the first person for whom I acted as translator with Tupra and on whom I improvised a report and offered my interpretation.

'What happened is in all the papers.' Perhaps he took advantage of that extemporaneous Spanish expletive, incomprehensible to him, to pretend that he had only heard my first sentence and to ignore the rest. No, he wasn't pretending, it was a way of telling me that the rest of what I had said seemed to him inadmissible and that he wasn't going to tolerate it. 'You must have read about it. Even in the Spanish press, I expect, didn't you tell me once how famous he was there? Especially . . . where was it now? In the Basque country?' His memory never failed him. 'And you yourself warned me in Edinburgh that Dearlove was so concerned for his posterity that he might commit some barbarous act simply in order to be remembered. That having so little faith that his music would last, he might very well blot his own life and thus deliberately enter the ranks of the Kennedy–Mansfield clan, isn't that right? So you see, you were very sharp, it was clear he might come to a bad end. And on purpose too.' I had forgotten about that additional report of mine; he, on the other hand, had not and was now using it as an alibi. I realised that he was not willing to discuss the matter, that he wasn't even going to take part in the conversation, I was still just an employee who did my job and was paid well for it, but I had no right to ask about objectives or motivations, still less to demand explanations or make reproaches, at least that was how he saw it. Perhaps because he held me in a certain regard, because of his temporary fondness for me, he was putting me in my place only indirectly, almost tacitly, surreptitiously. And I understood this even more clearly when he added: 'Anything else, Jack?' It's what he had said on that other far-off occasion, after replying succinctly: 'Yes, I have.' No, he didn't usually comment on my successes and failures, or on his aims or motives, or on his pacts or transactions or commissions. He had said enough with the words 'you were very sharp'. In fact, I think that was the only time he complimented me.

'Yes, there is something else,' I said. 'I have to leave, I have to go back to Madrid. Things have got a little complicated there, I won't bore you with an explanation, it would take too long. But I can't stay here in London. I have no alternative but to resign. That's why I phoned you at home on Saturday, to let you know as soon as possible, in case you wanted to start looking for a replacement, although, obviously I can't help you with that.'

I played his same game, I resorted to an acceptable alibi, I preferred not to confront him, not to insist, after all, he would soon be merely the past for me, dumb matter, or perhaps a dream, as I would be for him. But I'm sure he understood the real reason for my leaving. It must have seemed ridiculous to him, but he didn't show it.

'As you wish,' he said coldly. 'It's your decision.'

'If you like, I can still come in occasionally, until I actually leave,' I added.

'Fine,' he said. 'That way some things won't be left half-finished. But it's not really necessary. You do as you like. Really.' There wasn't any spite in the tone in which he said this, but, rather, curtness or indifference, whether feigned or recently acquired, I don't know. It was, at any rate, new. He didn't care whether I came in or not.

'I'll see you around, then. If, that is, I do manage to come in on the odd day. Although I will have an awful lot of things to sort out.'

'Fine. Anything else, Jack?' he said again and picked up his pen as if intending to resume writing his notes as soon as I left his office.

And this time I gave the same answer as I had on that previous occasion:

'No, nothing else, Mr Tupra.' That is how I addressed him.

I got up and went over to the door, and just as I was about to open it, his voice stopped me:

'Just out of curiosity, Mr Deza.' When he addressed me in the same formal way, I realised that it amused him that I should have chosen such an odd moment to do so with him, just when we were saying goodbye. I turned round and thought I saw the tail end, just the shadow of a smile on that soft fleshy mouth, on those lips that were rather African or perhaps Hindu or Slavic, or even Sioux. 'Did you sort out that business in Madrid? Did you take care of that guy who's been bothering your wife? Did you make sure he's out of the picture?'

I stood still for an instant. I thought.

'Yes, I think so,' I replied.

And then he smiled broadly, waving his pen at me as if he were telling me off:

'Be careful, Jack. If you only think you did, that means you didn't.'

I didn't go back to the building, so that was the last time I saw him. But here in Madrid, I think of him more than I imagined I would. Despite that rather abrupt ending, despite the possible disappointment I must have caused him and the very real disappointment he caused me, I still feel that he is someone on whom I could always count. In a time of difficulty or confusion or trouble or even danger. Someone I could call one day and ask for advice or guidance, especially with the kind of situation I don't deal with very well. And now that Wheeler is dead, it's as if Tupra, strangely enough – possibly because of his link with Rylands, the brother whose student he was – were all that remained to me of him, even if only in my memory and imagination: his unexpected substitute or successor, his legacy almost, part of that permanent process of replacing the people we lose in our lives, of the shocking and persistent efforts we make to fill any vacancies, of our inability to resign ourselves to any reduction in the cast of characters without whom we can barely go on or survive, part of that continuous universal mechanism of substitution, which affects everyone and therefore us too, and so we accept our role as poor imitations and find ourselves surrounded by more and more of them.

Peter died six months after my father, although he was about eight months older than him. Mrs Berry phoned me in Madrid; she was very succinct, belonging, as she did, to the thrifty generation and doubtless mindful that she was phoning abroad. Or perhaps that was just her style, one of extreme discretion. 'Sir Peter passed away last night, Jack,' she said, employing the usual euphemism. That was all, or, rather, she added: 'I just wanted you to know. I didn't think it fair that you should carry on believing he's still alive when he's not.' And when I tried to find out what had happened and the cause, she merely said: 'Oh, it wasn't unexpected. I had been expecting it for weeks,' and informing me that she would write to me later on. I couldn't even ask her to whom it would have been 'unfair', to Peter or to me. (But presumably to both of us.) A few days later, I recalled that in England, in comparison with Spain, they take a long time to bury their dead and that I might still be in time to travel to Oxford and attend the funeral. So I phoned her several times and at different hours of the day, but no one answered. Perhaps Mrs Berry had gone to stay with a relative, had left the house as soon as her employer died, and I realised that there was almost no one I could ask now to find out more information. There was Tupra, but I didn't turn to him: it was hardly a moment of difficulty, confusion, trouble or danger, and he hadn't himself deigned to inform me of Peter's death. I was assailed by the feeling – or perhaps it was a superstition – that I didn't want to waste a cartridge unnecessarily, as if with him I only had a certain number that would last as long as our respective lives. Young Pérez Nuix didn't bother to tell me either: she may not have known Peter personally, but she would have heard. I could have phoned one of my former colleagues, Kavanagh or Dewar or Lord Rymer the Flask or even Clare Bayes – the very idea! – but I had long ago lost touch with them. I could have tried The Queen's or Exeter, the colleges with which Peter had been connected, but their bureaucracy would almost certainly have passed me fruitlessly from office to office. And the truth is I couldn't be bothered; memory and grief don't always chime with social duty. I was very busy in Madrid. I would have had to dust off my cap and gown. So I just let it go.

Mrs Berry's promised letter took more than two months to arrive. She apologised for the delay, but she'd had to take care of almost everything, even the recent memorial service, a ceremony which, in England, tends to take place some time after the death. She was kind enough to send me a copy of the order of service, listing the hymns and readings. Wheeler hadn't been a religious man, she explained, but she had preferred to fall back on the rites of the Anglican Church, because 'he always hated the improvised ceremonies people hold these days, the secular parodies that are so popular now'. The service had taken place in the University Church of St Mary the Virgin in Oxford, a church I remembered well; it was where Cardinal Newman had preached before his conversion. Bach had been played and Gilles, as well as Michel Corrette's gentle, ironic *Carillon des morts*; hymns had been sung; passages from Ecclesiasticus had been read ('. . . He will keep the sayings of the renowned men: and where subtil parables are, he will be there also. He will seek out the secrets of grave sentences . . . he will travel through strange countries; for he hath tried the good and the evil among men . . . Many shall commend his understanding; and so long as the world endureth, it shall not be blotted out; his memorial shall not depart away, and his name shall live from generation to generation . . . If he die, he shall leave a greater name than a thousand: and if he live, he shall increase it'), as well as the Prologue from *La Celestina* in James Mabbe's 1605 translation and an extract from a book by a contemporary novelist of whom he was particularly fond; and his praises had been sung by some of his former university colleagues, among them Dewar the Inquisitor or the Hammer or the Butcher, whose eulogy had been particularly acute and moving. And this had all been arranged according to the very precise written instructions left by Wheeler himself.

Mrs Berry also enclosed a colour photo of Peter taken some years before ('I thought you would like it as a keepsake,' she said). Now I have it framed in my study and I often look at it, so that the passing of time does not cause my memory of his face to grow dim and so that others might still see it. There he is, wearing the gown of a Doctor of Letters. 'It's made from scarlet cloth with grey silk edging or facing, and the same on the sleeves,' Mrs Berry explained. 'Sir Peter's gown had belonged to Dr Dacre Balsdon, and the grey had faded somewhat, so that it looked more like a dirty blue or a greyish pink: it had probably been left out in the rain. I took the photo in Radcliffe Square on the day he received that degree. It's a shame he took off his mortarboard to pose for the picture.' There is, of course, no word in Spanish for the untranslatable 'mortarboard'. Underneath his gown Peter is wearing a dark suit and a white bow tie, an outfit which is referred to as 'subfusc' and is compulsory at certain ceremonies. And there he is now in my study, fixed for ever on that far-off day, in a photo taken when I did not yet know him. The truth is that he changed very little from then until the end. I can recognise him perfectly when he looks at me with those slightly narrowed eyes, and you can clearly see the scar on the left-hand side of his chin. I never did ask how he got it. I remember that I hesitated over whether to ask him on that last Sunday, after lunch, when I was about to go to the station and get the train back to London and he accompanied me to the front door, leaning more heavily than ever on his stick. I noticed then that his legs were weaker than they had been on any other occasion, but they were doubtless capable of carrying him about the house and the garden and even up to his bedroom on the second floor. But he looked very tired, I thought, and I didn't want to make him talk much more, and so I chose to ask him something else, just one more thing before we said goodbye:

'Why did you tell me all this today, Peter? Believe me, I found it fascinating, and I'd love to know more, but I find it odd that, after years of knowing each other, you should tell me about all these things you've never said a word about before. And once you said to me: "One should never tell anyone anything," do you remember?'

Wheeler smiled at me with a mixture of slight, almost imperceptible melancholy and mischief. He placed both hands on his walking stick and said:

'It's true, Jacobo, you should never tell anyone anything . . . until you yourself are the past, until you reach the end. My end

is fast approaching and already knocking insistently at the door. You need to begin to come to terms with weakness because there will come a day when it will catch up with you. And when that moment arrives, you have to decide whether something should be erased for ever, as if it had never happened and never even had a place in the world, or whether you're going to give it a chance to . . .' He hesitated for a moment, looking for the right word and, not finding it, he made do with an approximation: '. . . to float. To allow someone else to investigate or recount or tell it. So that it won't necessarily be lost entirely. I'm not asking you to do anything, I assure you, to tell or not to tell. I'm not even sure I've done the right thing, that I've done what I wanted. At this late stage, I don't know what my desires are any more, or if I have any. It's odd, towards the end, one's will seems to become inhibited, to withdraw. As soon as you go through that door and walk away, I shall probably regret having told you. But I can be sure that Mrs Berry, who knows most of what happened, will never say a word to anyone when I'm gone. With you I'm not so sure, though, and so I leave that up to you. I might prefer it if you kept silent, but, at the same time, it consoles me to think that with you my story might even . . .' He again sought some better word, but again could not find it: '. . . yes, that it might still float. And that's really all it comes down to, Jacobo, to floating.'

And I thought and continued to think on the train back to Paddington: 'He's chosen me to be his rim, the part that resists being removed and erased, that resists disappearing, the part that clings to the porcelain or the floor and is the hardest bit to get rid of. He doesn't even know if he wants me to take charge of cleaning it up – "the constitution of silence" – or would rather I didn't rub too hard, but left a shadow of a trace, an echo of an echo, a fragment of a circumference, a tiny curve, a vestige, an ashy remnant that can say: "I was here," or "I'm still here, therefore I must have been here before: you saw me then and you can see me now", and that will prevent others from saying: "No, that never occurred, never happened, it neither strode the world nor trod the earth, it never existed, never was."'

Mrs Berry also spoke in her letter about the drop of blood on the stairs. She couldn't have helped hearing part of our conversation as she bustled around in the kitchen and came and went, on that last Sunday when I visited them (the verb she used was 'overhear', which implies that it was involuntary), and how Wheeler referred in passing to the stain as if it had been a figment of my imagination ('Just there, where you say you saw . . .'). She felt bad about having lied to me at the time, she said, to have pretended to know nothing, perhaps to have made me doubt what I had seen. She asked me to forgive her. 'Sir Peter died of lung cancer,' she wrote. 'He knew deep down that he had it, but he preferred not to. There was no way he would go to the doctor and so I brought one, a friend of mine, to the house when it was already too late, when there was nothing to be done, and that doctor kept the diagnosis from him – after all, what was the point in telling him then? – but he confirmed it to me. Fortunately, he died very suddenly, from a massive pulmonary embolism, according to what the doctor told me afterwards. He didn't have to endure a long illness and he enjoyed a reasonable life right up until the end.' And when I read this, I remembered that the first time Wheeler had suffered one of his aphasic attacks in my presence – when he had been unable to come out with the silly word 'cushion' – I had asked him then if he'd consulted a doctor and he'd replied casually: 'No, no, it's not a physiological thing, I know that. It only lasts a moment, it's like a sudden withdrawal of my will. It's like a warning, a kind of prescience . . .' And when he didn't finish the sentence and I asked him what kind of prescience, he had both told me and not told me: 'Don't ask a question to which you already know the answer, Jacobo, it's not your style.'

'In fact, the only symptom, during almost the whole time he was ill,' Mrs Berry went on, using a term doubtless learned from her medical friend, 'was the occasional haemoptoic expectoration, that is, coughing up blood.' – And I thought when I read that paragraph: 'So much of what affects and determines us is hidden.' – 'This used to be quite involuntary and only happened when he coughed particularly hard, and sometimes he didn't even realise; remember, although he may not have seemed it, Sir Peter was very old. So although it's impossible to be sure, that might be what you found that night at the top of the first flight of stairs and that you took such pains to clean up. I'm very grateful to you, because that, of course, was my job. On a normal day, it would have been most unusual for me to miss something like that, but I was so busy that Saturday getting ready for the buffet supper, with all those people, and, if I remember rightly, you pointed to the wood, not the carpet, where it would have been much more visible. Anyway, on your last visit, when I heard Sir Peter telling you about his wife's blood at the top of that first flight of stairs, sixty years before and in another house, well, I was afraid you might think you'd had a supernatural experience, a vision, and I had to let you know about this other real possibility. I do hope you'll forgive my pretence at incredulity, but I couldn't, at the time, mention something that Sir Peter preferred not to acknowledge. Well, the truth is he chose not to do so right up until the last. Indeed, he died without knowing he was dying, he died without believing that he was. Lucky him.' And then I recalled two things I had heard Wheeler say in different contexts and on different occasions: 'Everything can be distorted, twisted, destroyed, erased, if, whether you know it or not, you've been sentenced already, and if you don't know, then you're utterly defenceless, lost.' And he had also stated or asserted: 'And so now no one wants to think about what they see or what is going on or what, deep down, they know, about what they already sense to be unstable and mutable, what might even be nothing, or what, in a sense, will not have been at all. No one is prepared, therefore, to know anything with certainty, because certainties have been eradicated, as if they were infected with the plague. And so it goes, and so the world goes.'

Yes, now I'm living in Madrid again, and here, too, everything points towards that, or so I believe. I've gone back to working with a former colleague, the financier Estévez, with whom I worked for a few years after my Oxford days, when I married Luisa. He no longer refers to himself as 'a go-getter' as when we first met, he's grown too important for such nominal vanities, he doesn't need them. I contacted him from London, to sound him out regarding job opportunities, given my imminent return: I had saved quite a lot, but could foresee a lot of expenses on my return to Madrid. And when I told him briefly over the phone what I had been up to, I noticed that he was impressed when I said I'd worked for MI6, even though I'd been employed by a strange unknown group in a building with no name, which never gets a mention in any book – so ethereal and so ghostly that it didn't even require its members to have British nationality or to swear an oath – and even though I couldn't give him any proof, but only tell him what I knew. Not that I wanted to give him too many details, and those I did were invented. Anyway, he took me on at once to help with his various projects and he trusts my judgement, especially about people. And so I do still interpret people, just for him, now and then, and given my previous experience – given my record – he always listens to me as if I were the oracle. Thanks to him I earn enough money to be able to pay for Luisa to have some Botox treatment, if one day she should ever want to, or indeed anything else that might improve her appearance, if she ever starts to get obsessed, although I don't think she will, it's not in her nature. To me it looks as good as before I left, before I left my home for England, her appearance I mean. And what I didn't see for a long time – but which was seen by another in my absence – that, too, seems just as good. And when I say I don't live alone but half-alone, that's because I either take the children out or visit them almost daily, and on some afternoons Luisa comes to my apartment, leaving the kids with another babysitter, not the stern Polish Mercedes, who has married and set up on her own – she's apparently opened her own business.

This is how Luisa wants it, with each of us in our own apartment, which is perhaps why she has never said what I wanted her to say or write to me during my solitary and, subsequently, troubling time in London: 'Come, come, I was so wrong about you before. Sit down here beside me, here's your pillow which now bears not a trace, somehow I just couldn't see you clearly before. Come here. Come with me. There's no one else here, come back, my ghost has gone, you can take his place and dismiss his flesh. He has been changed into nothing and his time no longer advances. What was never happened. You can, I suppose, stay here for ever.' No, she hasn't said that or anything like it, but she does say other occasionally disconcerting things; during our best or most passionate or happiest moments, when she comes to see me at home as she must have gone to see Custardoy over a period of many months, she says: 'Promise me that we'll always be like this, the way we are now, that we'll never again live together.' Perhaps she's right, perhaps that's the only way we can remain properly attentive and not take each other or our presence in each other's lives for granted.

I haven't forgotten what Custardoy told me, not a single word; any information that the mind registers stays in it until oblivion catches up with it, and oblivion is always one-eyed; I haven't forgotten his insinuations or more than insinuations ('Everyone has their own sexuality,' he said with *madrileño* bravado, each rasping word dragged out like the music from a music box, 'with some people it's straightforward and with others it isn't. Didn't the same thing happen when she was with you? I mean, what can I say, pal, I had no idea either'), and on occasions I've been tempted to try hurting Luisa, just a little, as if unintentionally, distractedly, accidentally, to see how she would react, to see if she would accept it without protest, holding her breath, just to know how she would respond. But I've always stopped myself and always will, I'm sure, because that would be like accepting that Custardoy had been right and exposing myself to a new poison, and I'd had quite enough poison on that night with Tupra or, rather, Reresby. Also, it implied a danger, albeit remote: that of putting myself in the place of the man I had so feared, the devious fellow of my imagination, who might turn up one rainy night, when they're stuck at home, close his large hands around Luisa's throat – his fingers like piano keys – while the children – my children – watch from a corner, pressing themselves into the wall as if wishing the wall would give way and disappear and, with it, this awful sight, and the choked-back tears that long to burst forth, but cannot, the bad dream, and the strange, long-drawn-out noise their mother makes as she dies. ('While it isn't something any of us would wish for, we would nonetheless always prefer it to be the person beside us who dies,' Reresby had said that night. '. . . even the person we most love, yes, even them, anyone but us.') No, one mustn't slip or skate too close, one mustn't toy with the time, temptations and circumstances that might lead to the fulfilment of some probability carried in the veins, our veins, and my probability was that I could kill, I know that now, well, I knew it before, but I know it even better now. Best to shy away from it all and keep oneself at a distance, better to avoid it and not to touch it even in dreams ('Dream on, dream on, of bloody deeds and death'), so that not even in dreams could someone say: 'Your wife, that wretched Luisa your wife, Jacques or Jacobo or Jack, Iago or Jaime, that never slept a quiet hour with you because the names don't change who you are . . . Let me be lead within thy bosom and may you feel the pinprick in your breast: despair and die.' No, that won't happen, it doesn't happen. Best to keep away.

One day, I went over to his part of town, Custardoy's; normally I try to avoid it as much as I can, which isn't easy, given that it's so central. I don't avoid it for any real reason, it's just that places become marked by what you did in them, far more than by what they did to you, and then something happens that bears a very faint resemblance – a mere shadow, a poor imitation, nonsense, no comparison – to the grudge against a place, the spatial hatred, that the Nazis felt for the village of Lidice which they reduced to rubble, razed to the ground and wiped from the map, and for so many other towns in Europe, and the spatial hatred that Valerie Harwood felt perhaps for Milton Bryan and Woburn, and Peter Wheeler for Plantation Road, that pretty leafy street in Oxford, and I myself for the building with no name near Vauxhall Cross and the indiscreet headquarters of the Secret Intelligence Service by the Thames with its look of a lighthouse or a ziggurat, where I never venture if I go to London now, whether with Luisa or without her; I have a little money in bank accounts there – well, you never know when you might have to leave Spain in a hurry. But I did feel a kind of spatial hatred for Calle de Bailén and Calle Mayor, quite unconscious, because I like the area, despite the fact that various oafish mayors have done their best to ruin it. I was passing by the Palacio Real, where I sometimes go to see an exhibition, and, which is another building that can no longer be seen from any other angle but from the front – one of the many views that those same idiotic mayors and their town planners and venal architects have inconsiderately and idiotically stolen from both the inhabitants of Madrid and the people who visit it. I was returning from some errands on the other side of Plaza de España when I came across two policewomen on horseback – they regularly patrol there now that all the traffic has been sent underground in this, the capital of tunnels – one white horse and one black, and I passed so close to the white one that I almost touched him and felt his breath – you only realise how tall they are when you're next to them. I hadn't gone five steps beyond the crossroads when I noticed at my back the horse's agitation or anxiety: the dog belonging to a woman who happened to be passing had started barking at the horses and harassing them, and the white horse took fright, reared up and was about to bolt, and did indeed try to make a run for it, although it only got a few yards, while the dog – tis tis tis, aerial footsteps, it was a pointer like Pérez Nuix's, except that this one had a spotted coat and a brown head – got even more excited by all that reined-in skittering and the almost galloping clatter of hooves and barked more loudly. The policewoman regained control of the horse at once, although not without some alarm and some effort: she had to turn it in circles in order to rein it in and calm it down, and the owner of the dog finally dragged her pet off and put an end to its incursions – the tis tis tis sounded much sadder now – and stopped its barking. The other horse, the black one, wasn't in the least perturbed, either by the pointer's threats or by its companion's attempted escape, he was clearly less delicate. The sound of clattering hooves soon slowed, and when the momentary commotion had subsided, the policewoman and her horse stood quietly for a while, silhouetted against the royal façade, while she soothingly stroked his neck, under the gaze of two guards in nineteenth-century costume, inscrutable and motionless in their sentry boxes by the Palace gates. We weren't far from the monument to Captain Melgar, with its disproportionately small legionnaire, a kind of dwarf Beau Geste trying to scramble up to the Captain's beard or moustaches.

Then, from among the people who had stopped to watch this minor incident (of whom I was one), I noticed a man step forward, the kind of spectator who is prone to jump into the ring at bullfights, who always seems to be around eager to take centre stage, whenever there's an altercation, a spot of bother, and whose whole posture seems to be saying: 'I'll have this fixed in no time' or 'I'll knock some sense into these madmen and restore peace and amaze the onlookers'. His intervention was entirely unnecessary because the policewoman had by now managed to pacify her mount, yet the man strode over to them and, as if he were a wrangler or something, was patting the horse's neck and stroking its muzzle and whispering mysterious or trivial words. The first thing that alerted me was the glove, the black leather glove that stood out against the horse's white coat; it was a spring day, overcast but not cold, and covering your hands seemed odd, and even odder to have just one hand covered, because when he reached out his other hand and placed it on the horse's back, I saw that it, the right one, was bare, and that made me think: 'What a lot of one-handed people . . . Perhaps his left hand never healed properly and that's why he wears the glove, to hide a deformity or scars, who knows, perhaps he never shows it to anyone.' Then he turned to face me just as I was thinking this, it was simultaneous – he didn't turn to look at anyone else, but at me, as if he had seen me before the incident with the horse and knew where I was, or perhaps he'd been following me – and he gazed straight at me with those unmistakable eyes, crude and rough and cold, two enormous, very dark eyes, rather wide-set and lashless, and both those factors, the lack of lashes and the wide-apartness, that make his obscene gaze unbearable or possibly irresistible when turned on the women he seduces or buys and possibly also when turned on the men with whom he competes, and we were not just rivals, he hated me with the same fierce intensity as when we had seen each other for the last time on the sole occasion that I visited his apartment, with an old Llama pistol and a poker in my hand and wearing gloves like the ones Reresby had worn in the Disabled toilet and like the single glove he was wearing now. But it wasn't the same hatred, not identical: there, in front of the Palacio Real, it wasn't old or impotent, frustrated and without consequences, it wasn't tinged with fear and shock; nor was it like the hatred of a child imprisoned in a childish body, nor like a furious adolescent who watches whirling past him the world he is still not allowed to climb aboard; nor like the prisoner who knows that no one is waiting or abstaining from anything because he is not there; and his gaze was no longer murky, but unequivocal and clear.

It had taken me a few seconds to recognise him because Custardoy wasn't wearing a hat now or a ponytail or even a moustache, or only the merest shadow of one, as if he were starting to let it grow again after a period of shaving it off. He was stroking the horse with his gloved left hand and murmuring short sentences, but I didn't know now whether he was addressing these to the animal or to the policewoman – who happily let him carry on, perhaps she was already won over, with her high leather boots like those of a distant English gypsy girl in Oxford – or to me, knowing that I wouldn't be able to hear what he was saying. And when I saw the way he was looking at me, with utter loathing, I saw that there was insolence in that gaze too, and a threat, not one that was in any hurry to be carried out, but one that was prepared to linger and delay for as long as he chose or needed to; my expression must have changed and I thought: 'Damn. I didn't remove him from the picture, not entirely, I didn't make absolutely sure. This man might come after me one day or after us both, after me and Luisa, or all four of us, perhaps the children too. I humiliated him, I hurt him, and I took from him the person he loved. I should have removed or erased him from the picture for good, as if he were a drop of blood.' And suddenly an image flashed into my mind – like lightning in its brevity but not its brilliance, for it was terrifying, nauseating and sordid; or like thunderless lightning that strikes in silence – an image I had seen in one of Tupra's videos, a tethered horse, a defenceless woman, and I couldn't help but associate Custardoy with those well-dressed men sitting beneath white, red and green awnings, sporting thick moustaches and Texan hats most of them, although Custardoy no longer had a hat or much of a moustache, but I had seen them and the marks left by his abuse. That's the trouble once you've been inoculated with any kind of poison, whether through the eyes or the ears, there's no way of getting rid of it, it installs itself inside you and there's nothing to be done and it comes back to penetrate and contaminate any thing or person, saying each time, repeating, insisting: 'Let this sit heavy on your soul.'

I stood there for a few seconds, before turning and continuing on my way. I don't know if I looked at him with equal hatred, but I might have, it's very likely, more than anything because what I saw him do next troubled me greatly, I didn't like it at all: with his right hand, his bare uninjured hand, his painting hand, he took from his trouser pocket a watch and chain and checked the time with strange intensity. At first, I thought this was just some new eccentricity; having given up his ponytail, he had to find some other way to underline the fact that he was an arty type, as my sister had described him before I had even seen him; and from his stupidly archaic bohemian point of view, carrying such a watch in the twenty-first century was doubtless in keeping with that. Then I thought of another possibility: 'Perhaps he doesn't wear a wristwatch for the same reason that he wears a glove,' I thought, 'because he would have to lift up his hand whenever he wanted to know the time. Perhaps his hand really is irrecoverable, ruined, although there's no sign of the gash I made on his cheek. Whatever the truth of the matter, I don't like the image of him holding that old-fashioned watch in his hand and studying it; he may be measuring out my time.' I didn't want to look at him any longer, and when I was already a few paces away, I thought again, perhaps to exorcise him from my mind or perhaps to raise my spirits: 'But now I know that in my angry mood, I, too, am capable of measuring out his time; I counted it once and stopped the count, and he knows that; he was lucky, but I very nearly counted him out. That will dissuade him from coming near. And if he ever does, we'll see then who will be the first to leave his own first name behind.'

You can live with a threat hanging over you because there is always the possibility that it will never be carried out, and that's what you have to think. Sometimes we see what is approaching and nevertheless we pay no attention, and perhaps not only for the reason Wheeler gave: because we hate certainty, because no one dares any more to say or to acknowledge that they see what they see, what is quite simply there, perhaps unspoken or almost unsaid, but nevertheless there; and because no one wants to know, and the idea of knowing something beforehand, well, it simply fills people with horror, with a kind of biographical, moral horror; because we all prefer to be utter *necios* in the strict Latin sense of the word that still appears in our dictionaries: 'Ignorant and knowing neither what could nor should be known', that is, a person who deliberately and willingly chooses not to know, a person who shies away from finding things out and who abhors learning. '*Un satisfecho insipiente*, a nincompoop,' as Wheeler had said with a pedantry I now often miss. No, perhaps it's also because we fear wasting our life on our precautions and suspicions and our visions and alarms, and because it is clear to us that everything will have its end, and then, when we say goodbye, when we are already the past or our end is fast approaching and already knocking insistently at the door, it will all seem to us vain and naïve: why did she do that, they will say of you, why so much fuss and why the quickening pulse, why the trembling, why the somersaulting heart; and of me they will say: why did he speak or not speak, why did he wait so long and so faithfully, why that dizziness, those doubts, that torment, why did he take those particular steps and why so many? And of us both they will say: why all that conflict and struggle, why did they fight instead of just looking and staying still, why were they unable to meet or to go on seeing each other, and why so much sleep, so many dreams, and why that scratch, my pain, my word, your fever, our poison, the shadow, and all those doubts, all that torment?

I had arranged to see Luisa that afternoon: we see each other two or three times a week in this long truce we are enjoying. Indeed, she has the keys to my apartment and, on occasion, arrives before I do and then she waits for me, exactly as Tupra believed someone was waiting for me in London on that night of poison and dance, when no one was ever waiting for me, when there was no one to turn off any lights in my absence, the lights I left on all the time so as not to be entirely in the dark. No one had my keys and no one was ever waiting for me there. The doorman said: 'Your wife, I mean, your girlfriend has gone up already. I gave her a package that arrived for you earlier.' The man senses something marital about us, but is uncertain quite what our relationship is, and so hovers between wife and girlfriend. I've told him that Luisa is my wife, but he still doesn't quite believe it, or perhaps he doesn't understand why, in that case, she comes and goes.

Before opening the door, I could hear her humming to herself inside, she often does that now and she laughs a lot too, with me and without me, I suppose; she no longer rations out her laughter, and I trust this will remain so, if possible for ever, or so I think. Her return is nothing like Beryl's return to Tupra, according to my distant interpretations and always assuming they did, in fact, get back together, which was something I never found out: there's no self-interest, not a spurious self-interest, and there's nothing clandestine about it either. It's clear that Luisa benefits from and enjoys us seeing each other like this, just now and then, and not living together, although she might grow tired of that one day; she has already started leaving clothes here. And it suits me too. After all, in London, I got used to being very alone, as Wheeler paternally said to me early on, and sometimes I need to continue to be alone because I don't think I could bear someone's company all the time and never be able to look out at the world from my window on my own, the living world that knows where it's going and to which I imagine I still belong. I opened the door and saw on the coffee table in the living room the package that the porter had given to Luisa, who was in the kitchen, still humming and not aware that I had come in. I saw that it came from Berlin, shoes by von Truschinsky, from whom, since they have all my measurements, I still occasionally order a pair, even though they are very expensive. I always think of Tupra when I receive them, but then he's always vaguely in my thoughts, as if he were a friend on whom I continue to count – which is odd – and to whom I could turn for help. I haven't done so yet.

That afternoon, he was even more in my thoughts after my silent encounter with Custardoy, with two or three animals as indifferent witnesses. On the way home, something else had occurred to me, I had thought: 'I didn't want to frighten De la Garza when I went to see him at the embassy, and I was horrified to see the panic my mere presence instilled in him, but, on the other hand, I would have liked to see that same fear on Custardoy's face and in the way he behaved. He's completely recovered from his fright now or if a little remains – as it must – he doesn't show it. Nothing ever works out as we want or as we think, or perhaps I'm still too hesitant; such a thing would never have happened to Tupra, he would have removed him from the picture when he had him in the frame, and now I'll have to watch every corner, just in case he slips back in again, this time with sword or spear, although that might take some time, because once you've experienced fear, you never entirely lose it.' These thoughts continued to preoccupy me. Luisa noticed that I was quiet, and was perhaps even a little worried because I wasn't responding much to her jokes, for she's gone back to poking gentle fun at me.

'What's wrong?' she asked. 'Has something happened?'

543

'What do you mean?' I replied, half-suspicious, half-distracted. 'What sort of thing?'

'I mean, something bad.'

Yes, something bad had happened to me, and no, nothing bad had happened to me at all. Nothing out of the ordinary anyway. Someone hurts you and you become an enemy. Or you hurt someone and create an enemy. It's as easy as breathing, both things happen much more frequently than we imagine, often by chance and without our realising, it pays to stay alert and watch people's faces, but even then we don't always notice. I *had* noticed that afternoon, which is an advantage. But I couldn't say anything to Luisa, I couldn't talk to her about it, I couldn't tell her about that meeting. We have barely asked each other anything about our time of absolute separation, best not to. She has never spoken to me about Custardoy, nor have I to her, and I will never know how much she loved or feared him. That is perhaps the only thing about which I will never be able to say anything to her, not even when I am already the past or my end is fast approaching and already knocking insistently at the door, because I think I know her face and I stake everything on that, even the way she will remember me. Perhaps because of that, and also because I am usually perfectly content, I sometimes sing or hum to myself at times, as she does, and I have a tendency to sing or whistle that song of many titles, from Ireland or the Wild West ('Nanná naranniario nannara nanniaro', that's how the melody goes), 'The Bard of Armagh' who forecast: 'And when Sergeant Death's cold arms shall embrace me'; or 'Doc Holliday' who first justified himself by saying: 'But the men that I killed should have left me in peace' and then lamented: 'But here I am now alone and forsaken, with death in my lungs I am dying today'; or 'The Streets of Laredo', which is the version whose words I know best and which is therefore the one I sometimes sing out loud or to myself, perhaps, who knows, as a reminder, especially the last verse that ends by asking: 'But please not one word of all this shall you mention, when others should ask for my story to hear.'

'No,' I said, 'nothing bad.'

May 2007

Acknowlededgments

Throughout the writing of the three volumes of *Your Face Tomorrow*, various people have helped me at some point or other: with a fact, an image, a foreign word, some piece of historical or geographical information, a medical query, a bullfighting term, a few lines of poetry, some advice that contributed to clarifying the narrative, or by looking after my only two copies of the original (I still use a typewriter) until it was completed. They are as follows: Julia Altares, John Ashbery, Antony Beevor, Inés Blanca, Nick Clapton, Margaret Jull Costa, Agustín Díaz Yanes, Paul Ingendaay, Antonio Iriarte, Mercedes López-Ballesteros, Carme López Mercader, Ian Michael, César Pérez Gracia, Arturo Pérez-Reverte, Daniella Pittarello, Álvaro Pombo, Eric Southworth, Bruce Taylor and Dr José Manuel Vidal. To all of them, my heartfelt thanks.

Separate mention must be made of my father, Julián Marías, and Sir Peter Russell, who was born Peter Wheeler, without whose borrowed lives this book would not have existed. May they both rest now, in the fiction of these pages as well.

JAVIER MARÍAS

his expression one of scorn history contemptuous